WAR-TORN LOVERS

Finally Vanessa saw Eddie behind a tall marine. He was slender, bronzed from the sun, his face searching the crowd.

"Eddie!" Vanessa called out and waved. *He was all right.* He found her in the crowd and waved back while she pushed her way toward him. "Oh, Eddie!"

He dropped his knapsack to bring her into his arms. His mouth was warm and grateful and passionate.

"You look wonderful," he said huskily, holding her away from him. His eyes caressed every feature of her face.

"You're so tan," she marveled.

"Vanessa, let's go home." He swung his knapsack over one shoulder, dropped an arm about her waist. "Right now."

In the taxi he clung to her hand as though to reassure himself that she was beside him. The cab pulled to a stop before Vanessa's brownstone. Eddie paid the driver, and stood gazing up at the building.

"I'm here," he said softly. "Sometimes I was afraid I'd never make it."

Vanessa lifted her face to his, welcoming his mouth on hers. Her arms tightened about his shoulders and she forgot everything but the feel of his body against hers . . .

CATCH UP ON THE BEST IN CONTEMPORARY FICTION FROM ZEBRA BOOKS!

THE VELVET JUNGLE

Julie Ellis

ZEBRA BOOKS
KENSINGTON PUBLISHING CORP.

ZEBRA BOOKS

are published by

Kensington Publishing Corp.
475 Park Avenue South
New York, NY 10016

First Zebra Books printing: June, 1988

Printed in the United States of America

For Joan and Fred Paul — and Jimmy and Cathy and Andrea

ACKNOWLEDGMENTS

I would like to thank the staffs of the Genealogy Room of the New York Public Library, the Lincoln Center Library, the Mid-Manhattan Library, and the Donnell Library for their courteous assistance in my research. My gratitude, also, to the library staff of the Fashion Institute of Technology, the Museum of the City of New York, and the New York Historical Society.

My thanks, too, to the helpful staffs of the Union of American Hebrew Congregations; the Historical Society of Houston, Texas; the Italian Government Travel Office; and the Key West Chamber of Commerce.

Again, my thanks to my daughter, Susie, for her efficient copy editing and typing and to my son, Richie, for his research on my behalf at the various libraries at Columbia University.

One

In the small town of Pinewood in upstate New York in 1942, the war had wrought few changes other than a burst of American flags flying from front porches and gold stars on proud display in a sprinkling of windows.

The late June dusk air was sticky, pungent with the sweet scent of the honeysuckle that grew beneath the window of seventeen-year-old Vanessa Conrad's small bedroom. The rose-splashed wallpaper was stained and older than Vanessa, the ceiling paint cracked and peeling. Atop her much-scratched, pseudo-Victorian dresser sat a discolored oscillating fan, a relic from a shelf of her late father's modest grocery store. The drone of the fan blended with the sounds of the Arthur Godfrey radio show, and despite the fan's efforts, perspiration dampened the red-gold hair that framed Vanessa's delicate, lovely face.

Vanessa moved to the mirror to apply her makeup and wished with painful intensity that her father — dead of a heart attack almost ten months now — had lived to see her high school graduation tonight. He would be so pleased that she had been chosen class valedictorian. Daddy had always been proud of her standing in the class; her mother had always resented it. Even as a small child Vanessa had understood that her mother was different from the other mothers in Pinewood.

9

While she applied mascara with an inexperienced hand, Vanessa tried to accept the fact that her mother would not attend her graduation exercises tonight.

"This heat's too much for me. I couldn't bear sitting in that hot, crowded auditorium. I'd pass out for sure."

Daddy had always made excuses for Mother. Ever since she could remember, Vanessa had heard how Mother — born and raised in the Bronx — had given up the chance of a career as a singer to marry Daddy and move to Pinewood. She'd also heard the women in town gossiping about her mother.

"Della Conrad never wanted a child. She was shocked to death to discover she was pregnant when she was almost thirty-eight and married seventeen years."

The local ladies had much to say about her mother. None of it kind. Daddy had said people didn't always understand Mother. He said this town stifled her.

Vanessa had never known her maternal grandparents, and only faintly remembered her father's parents. They had moved to Pinewood from Austria right after their marriage in 1883. Then, as now, the Conrads — their name Americanized at Ellis Island — were the sole Jewish family in town.

Vanessa knew that, when they could afford it, her grandparents had traveled to an Albany synagogue to observe the High Holidays and had taken their only child with them. Her mother never concerned herself with religious observances other than lighting the Friday night candles, and Vanessa suspected even this was more habit than respected ritual. What Vanessa knew of her Jewish heritage she had learned from her father.

For Vanessa, to graduate high school meant she had to face the problem of her future. After her father's death, her mother had made it clear she had only enough funds to support them until the end of Vanessa's senior year. After that it would be up to Vanessa to take care of herself and her mother.

Vanessa had managed to save up enough money from her weekend job as a salesgirl at the bakery and from baby-sitting and occasional typing to pay for her school photograph and yearbook, her graduation dress, and the bouquet of flowers now being kept fresh in the icebox.

Usually the young people of Pinewood deserted the town at the first opportunity. A lucky few would go on to college. Two boys had dropped out to join the marines right after the attack on Pearl Harbor. One girl was boasting about joining the new Women's Army Auxiliary Corps as soon as it began to accept enlistments.

Her slender form encased in a white sateen slip, Vanessa concentrated on applying her makeup. She frowned at her destorted reflection in the cracked mirror, and mentally ran through the carefully memorized pages of her speech. Tonight Vanessa was thankful that she had belonged to the dramatic club for two years.

She paused at the sound of a car pulling up in the driveway. They had not owned a car since she was six. That would be Tina, coming to drive her to the high school.

Her eyes — blue-green and expressive — sought the noisily ticking clock on her dresser. Tina was early, and for her this was a miracle. She must really be excited about graduating.

Vanessa reached for her lipstick, the final act in her makeup ritual. Ever since their first year in high school, she and Tina had been best friends. She loved going over to Tina's house after school, playing the radio and the Victrola. Tina could coax her father into buying every new Andrews Sisters record that came out.

11

Vanessa's face tensed as she listened to the brief exchange between her mother and Tina. Mother was telling Tina she wasn't going tonight.

Tina lived in a big old colonial house at the edge of town with her father and her two single brothers, Gus and Nick. Her mother had died when Tina was twelve. Gus, the youngest Vigliano brother, was chewing his nails at the prospect of being drafted—he was even considering getting married in the hope of staying out of uniform. Nick had a game leg from a hunting accident, and was exempt from military service. Sal and Vinnie, the two older brothers, were married and living near Albany—both with pregnant wives. But Vanessa knew that all the Viglianos were upset by the thought that Italian-Americans might be fighting native Italians on the battlefield.

Tina stalked into Vanessa's bedroom in a full-skirted white crepe evening dress with a pink velvet rose at the neckline, a matching jacket trailing contemptuously from one scarlet-fingernailed hand. The girls in the senior class had voted on pastel shades for their dresses, but Tina knew she looked her best in white. Three inches taller than Vanessa, raven-haired and hazel-eyed, Tina was strikingly attractive. Her secret ambition—known only to Vanessa—was to become a movie star like Rita Hayworth.

"I can't stand this fucking dress." Tina grimaced at her reflection in the mirror that hung above the dresser.

Automatically Vanessa lifted a finger to her mouth in reproach. "Sshh." Mother would banish Tina from her life if she ever heard the foul language Tina had learned from her father and brothers.

"Your mother can't hear me," Tina giggled. "She's all wrapped up in seeing herself singing on Arthur Godfrey's program."

"That dress doesn't look like you," Vanessa said

sympathetically.

"I'd rather graduate in blue jeans. Tight, old, and faded." Tina described the teen-aged girl's favorite uniform. "And one of Pop's old shirts."

"This does have possibilities," Vanessa mused. "I saw a white crepe in the last issue of *Vogue* that was sensational. I think it was designed by Nettie Rosenstein," she added with infinite respect. Her one extravagance throughout high school—contrived by saving part of her baby-sitting money—had been to buy *Vogue* twice each month. She studied *Vogue* with the same intensity she devoted to her high school subjects, and regularly altered the latest shipment from Sears-Roebuck to look like the dresses she pored over in *Vogue*.

"Vanessa, I don't care who designed the damn dress," Tina sighed. "Can you make this thing look like it?" She glanced at the clock. "In twenty minutes."

"Do you trust me?" Vanessa asked.

"I trust you."

"It'll just be basted together," Vanessa warned, crossing the room to snatch up scissor, needle, and white thread. "You know I can't really sew."

"Do something, anything," Tina ordered. "I hate it." Her gaze settled on the sea green organdy that lay across the bed. "Now that dress is terrific."

"Thanks. It turned out okay. Now, that flower has to go." Vanessa reached for the neckline of Tina's dress and snipped the threads that held the flower in place. "Let's drape all the material in the skirt up this way—about the hips—and stitch it together at the waist. Have you got a scarf I can use as a sash to cover the stitches?" Vanessa was already tacking the graceful drapes into place.

"A red-and-white polka dot," Tina giggled.

"That's all right." Vanessa nodded her approval. "But first let me get this right."

13

"God, why didn't I bring it over to you before?"

"Because it didn't arrive from Sears-Roebuck until yesterday morning," Vanessa laughed.

"Pop and I had another one of our rotten battles," Tina reported while Vanessa continued sewing. Tina and her father fought every Sunday about her refusal to go to mass and take Communion. "He kept yelling at me to raise the straps of this dress. Why, when I'll have to wear the jacket anyway? They won't let me on the stage without it. You know, it's crazy. Here we are—the two best-looking girls in the while damn school—and we aren't going to the senior prom."

Though she was totally irreligious, Vanessa's mother became hysterical at the prospect of Vanessa going out with a boy who wasn't Jewish. And Tina's father distrusted every male over fourteen. Especially since the war began. "Today boys and girls got no morals. Just because we're at war, they think they can act like bums and tramps," was his constant refrain. The two girls went together to football games, basketball games, and spent Saturday nights over sodas at the Village Nook. They Lindyed with boys at occasional Saturday night dances in the high school gym—always chaperoned by teachers. And three weeks ago Mr. Vigliano had banned Tina from dating for three months after he pulled her out of a parked car in Lover's Lane. In truth, neither parent had to worry about their daughter being seriously pursued by local young men—prejudice against Italians and Jews ran too high for that.

"Tina, be quiet and let me figure out how to fix this," Vanessa commanded with an anxious glance at the clock. "We can't be late for our high school graduation."

Twenty minutes later they slid into the front seat of the 1934 DeSoto. While Vanessa clutched the two bouquets of pink roses—the choice of this year's graduating class—Tina drove them to the modern red-brick high school. The building was brilliantly illuminated tonight and the parking area was already filling up.

She ought to be excited about graduating, Vanessa reproached herself. It should be a very special night in her life. If only Daddy could be sitting out there in the audience, listening to her speech.

Vanessa and Tina made their way through the first-floor hallway, jammed tonight with relatives and friends of this year's graduating class. The air was scented with Lentheric's Tweed and Elizabeth Arden's Blue Grass, both applied overgenerously.

"Dottie and Fred want to marry right away, even if they are so young." The voice of Dottie Miller's mother soared above the animated buzzing. "If she's pregnant, Fred could be deferred."

"Wouldn't it be awful to be tied down to a baby when you're eighteen?" Tina whispered in distaste. "But that sounds like Dottie."

It seemed so silly to be making this big fuss over a high school graduation when just a few weeks ago Bataan and Corregidor had fallen to the Japanese, Vanessa thought. Even though the Americans were victorious at Midway, they'd lost three hundred men and two ships. How many boys in their class would die before the war was over?

"Girls in here." Tina interrupted Vanessa's introspection. "Boys in Miss Evans's room. Segregated again."

In the classroom small clusters of girls talked self-consciously about their plans for the future. By September at least three would be married. One girl talked importantly about taking a business course down at Albany and going to work as a "government girl" in Washington. Another would work in her father's real estate office. Others talked about possible jobs in town — rumors had it that the shirt factory, closed ever since Vanessa could remember, would open again soon.

At last the girls lined up for the processional into the packed auditorium. After tonight, Vanessa thought with a touch of panic, she wouldn't belong anywhere. Tina talked vaguely about going to the beauty school in Albany — if she could manage to get the gas to drive a hundred miles, back and forth, each day. But what would *she* do?

Now the boys were seated onstage. The girls followed, amid the loud buzzing of the audience. Careful not to trip on their long gowns, they took their places as rehearsed.

The next hour and a half passed in a haze for Vanessa. The speeches varied little from previous years, except that tonight Judge Fremont talked about "our boys on the fighting front." From somewhere in the audience came the sound of sobbing. One Pinewood boy had died at Pearl Harbor. Another had gone down with the *Lexington* in the battle of the Coral Sea.

One by one, the graduates left their seats to accept their diplomas and congratulations from the principal. The class sighed in collective relief when the exercises were at last over.

"Let's get out of here," Tina said, reaching for Vanessa's arm. "Did I tell you that Agnes Lowell is having a private champagne party at her house tonight? For a 'select group of graduates,' " she mocked. "Naturally we weren't invited. Any girl whose father is a butcher or who ran a grocery store isn't 'Pinewood society.' Especially if one's an Italian and the other's a Jew," she hissed.

"Agnes didn't invite everybody." Vanessa shrugged. Vanessa recognized the social distinctions drawn in the town. "And we were never real friends of Agnes."

"She was friend enough when she wanted to copy your English or math homework every other day," Tina was grim. "Someday I'll come back here and throw the

16

fanciest party this town has ever seen — and you know what? I know just who I won't invite!"

Tina pulled the car to a sharp stop in front of the Conrad house. Vanessa slowly got out, reluctant to call an end to this important night.

"I better get home. Pop will be yelling about me driving all over town and wasting gas." All four of Tina's brothers and her two sisters-in-law had been sitting in the front row of the auditorium. "I'm not supposed to know about the family party that's waiting for me at home, of course."

Tina drove off, and Vanessa walked up to the house. She had expected to find it dark, but one lamp in the living room was lit. She could hear the squeak of the ceiling fan. Her mother, prone to nine o'clock bedtimes, was waiting up. Involuntarily Vanessa tensed.

The back of her green organdy dress clung to her shoulder blades and in one perspiring hand she clutched her diploma. The other hand rested at the base of her bouquet, the carnations already wilting in the night's heat. From the house next door emerged a raucous rendition of the popular "Jingle Jangle Jingle." The little radio in the Conrad house was silent.

Climbing the steps to the paint-hungry front porch, Vanessa's face softened as she remembered how much her father had enjoyed listening to Jack Benny each week. Sometimes, after the program and long after Mother had gone to bed, he'd talked about the early days of his marriage. It was difficult to envision her mother gay and very pretty, sitting in a swing on the front porch and singing Daddy's favorite songs for him.

She never remembered her mother singing. The mother she knew was always angry and complaining. She didn't yell and carry on like Mrs. Reilly next door;

17

she nagged. A dozen times a day she would mutter about how she was going out of her mind because the icebox or the gas stove or the lock on the front door didn't work the way it should.

The screen door groaned as Vanessa pulled it wide. She closed it quickly, remembering her mother's repeated exhortation. "Don't let every fly in Pinewood in the house."

"Vanessa?" Her mother's voice had its usual coating of irritation.

"Yes, ma'am," Vanessa replied and walked down the hall to the living room.

A small, spare woman with short, graying, curly hair, Della Conrad sat on the wicker sofa that had been "porch furniture" in the days before her husband—unable to deny credit to impoverished customers during the Depression—lost his grocery store.

"It took you long enough to come home," her mother reproached.

"The exercises weren't over until almost ten o'clock." Vanessa looked down at the diploma in her hand and thought about her speech. Mrs. Reilly next door, whose niece had been among the graduates, had come over and kissed her and said it had been "just wonderful."

"Sit down, Vanessa." Mrs. Conrad's face was grim. "We have to talk."

"Yes, ma'am." Vanessa sat in the matching wicker chair. She knew that under the faded floral cushion was hidden her mother's current edition of *True Confessions*.

What was so important that Mother couldn't talk about it tomorrow? Had Mother talked somebody into giving her a job? They both worried about where she'd find a full-time job. It was clearly understood that her mother would never go out to earn a living. She hadn't worked since her marriage.

"I'm giving up this house the end of next month,"

Della Conrad announced, and Vanessa gasped in astonishment. "I've told Elvira Johnson I'll move into Mr. Simpson's vacated room on the first of August and board with her. Elvira expects me to pay her every Monday morning for that week's board and room."

"What about me?" Vanessa blurted out, stunned and bewildered by this unexpected news. "Where will I live?"

"I'll give you train fare to New York City. Girls find jobs there these days with no trouble at all. Businesses are just crying out for help. I'll give you enough money to get by for three or four weeks — if you budget the way you should," she emphasized. "When you start to work, you'll send me a set amount each week." Della Conrad's dark eyes dared Vanessa to contradict her.

"But I don't know anybody in New York," Vanessa cried.

"You don't have to know anybody. You go to employment agencies — you'll find a job. I saw you through high school because I promised your father I would. We took care of you for seventeen years. Now it's your turn to take care of me." Her mouth worked in familiar agitation. "I've spent thirty-four years of my life running a house. I raised a child." Her face set in its familiar look of anger. "Your father never should have saddled me with a child," she muttered.

Vanessa lay sleepless far into the night. She had kicked the top sheet to the foot of her bed in rebellion against the heat, and the bottom sheet was damp with perspiration. Moonlight spilled through the side of the ill-fitting window shades. A persistent mosquito buzzed menacingly outside one window.

She was seventeen years old, and she was going off alone to New York. *Where would she live?* She knew vaguely that there were YWCAs. In *Vogue* she had read about a girls' club called the Barbizon Hotel for Women — but she doubted she could afford that.

How would she find out about employment agencies? She had never been farther away from Pinewood than Albany. And her thoughts returned again and again to her mother's acknowledgement that she had been an unwanted child.

She'd leave right away, Vanessa vowed, excitement beginning to bubble up alongside the fear and doubt. Her whole life was about to change, just when she had been scared to death it never would. *Tina wouldn't believe it.*

The two girls sprawled across Tina's bed and sipped at the ice-islanded Cokes Tina had carried upstairs from the kitchen. Vanessa was reporting on the confrontation with her mother last night. Tina was mesmerized.

"When are you leaving?" she demanded.

"Monday," Vanessa said firmly, fighting down the recurrent panic. "I told my mother this morning. She said she'd give me the money tomorrow night." She ought to be thrilled, Vanessa rebuked herself. She was escaping from Pinewood at last.

"I'm going with you." Tina sat upright on the bed, her eyes triumphant. "I've got that money I've been saving to buy myself a mink-dyed muskrat coat this winter. It'll be enough."

"Can you?" Vanessa's eyes widened with anticipation at the prospect. "Will your father let you?"

"Who's asking him? When you go to Saratoga to take the train to New York," Tina said softly, "I'll be with you. I'll drive us there in the DeSoto." Her eyes lit with laughter. "I'll leave a note for Pop to come to the station to pick it up."

"Tina, you're sure you want to go?" Vanessa's heart pounded with hope.

"I am so tired of the way I live," Tina said. Ever since her mother's death, Tina had been taking care of the house and cooking the meals. She fought constantly with her womanizing father, who expected his only daughter to be as chaste as a nun. "I'm sick of this town. Look, to everybody in Pinewood I'm the dago and you're the kike. To them every Italian is a cousin of Al Capone, and every Jew killed Christ. I'm out of high school. What's there here for me except clerking in the five-and-dime?"

"But what about your father?" Vanessa pressed uneasily.

"He won't know where I am. I'll leave a note saying I'm heading for Hollywood," Tina decided. "He's not going to chase me out there. He couldn't even find me in New York. Vanessa, we ought to give your mother a present for kicking you out!"

The two girls settled down to formulate their plans. Tina's father and Nick left for the butcher shop every morning at seven. Gus left a few minutes later. Tina would wait until then to pack what she meant to take with her.

She recalled in soaring high spirits that Lois Bracken, who had been a senior when they were sophomores, was living in New York. "You remember Lois," Tina prodded. "Her family moved to Florida right after she graduated, and she went to New York to business school. She wrote me last Christmas—trying to find out if Ernie Hodges was still living in town. She used to be mad about him. I wrote her back and said he wasn't here. Anyhow, I have her address and phone number—in case Ernie returned." Tina giggled. "She'll help us get settled."

21

"Do you think we can find jobs in the city?" Vanessa's doubts threatened to erode her excitement.

"Everybody who leaves Pinewood finds a job. We're young and healthy, and there's a war on. Two years ago maybe I'd have worried. Not now. Baby, we're escaping this goddamn town! Down with Tina Vigliano. Up with Tina Gregory!"

Two

On Monday Vanessa awoke before six after a long night of troubled sleep. She lay still, her mind tuned to what lay ahead. *Never again would she wake up in this bed. Where would she wake up tomorrow morning?* But Tina would be with her. She wouldn't be alone.

Her eyes wandered over her room and focused on the vintage valise that she had packed last night. This was not a dream. Mother was moving to Mrs. Johnson's boardinghouse. In a few hours *she* would be on a train bound for New York City.

The air was hot and humid even at this early hour, the sky a murky gray. Vanessa got out of bed and crossed to the window. The iceman was delivering across the street. A lot of people in town had refrigerators — Tina's house had a big one, but Tina's father ran the busiest butcher shop in town. Mother never bought from him — said he was too fancy in his prices — she bought hamburger at the A&P, always on Tuesdays and Fridays. Mother did everything on a schedule.

Vanessa pulled up a chair beside the window and reached for the latest copy of *Vogue* from the pile on top of her dresser. She'd decided not to take them with her. She would reread *Vogue* until it was seven o'clock,

Vanessa told herself. Then she could shower without waking Mother. Mother got up at seven sharp every morning, put on her pot of tea, then sat on the porch to have tea and toast.

Vanessa flipped open *Vogue* with the delicious sense of touching an exotic world. She lingered wistfully over the School Directory at the beginning of the magazine. The New York schools fascinated Vanessa. Especially Parsons and Traphagen. But design schools were beyond her reach.

As soon as she heard the squeak of the screen door opening onto the porch, Vanessa went into the bathroom to shower. Climbing into the claw-footed tub, Vanessa remembered her mother's constant admonition: "Don't get water all over the floor." This would be the last shower she would ever take in this house.

While she stood under the erratic spray, Vanessa remembered when she was a little girl — no more than four — and they had moved into the old Canfield Hotel for two months because Mother had been tired of the responsibility of taking care of the house. But they had to move back home, Vanessa had realized later, because business was so bad at the grocery store that Daddy couldn't afford to keep them there. People in Pinewood still talked about "that Mrs. Conrad moving into a hotel like she was some rich lady at Saratoga Springs."

Mindful of the time — Tina would be outside with the car at seven-thirty — Vanessa climbed out of the shower, dried herself with one of the two thin, hard towels that hung on the hook behind the door, and dressed quickly. Back in her room, she put on makeup. Tina said every girl in New York wore makeup all the time. Tina was horrified by rumors that the government might pass a law banning the manufacture of cosmetics because of so many shortages; she said she'd die without lipstick and nail polish.

Vanessa geared herself to go out and fix her breakfast. Then she'd sit on the porch with her mother until Tina arrived. Mother didn't know Tina was going with her—Tina had made Vanessa promise not to tell her. After this morning she didn't know when she'd see Mother again. It seemed so strange that her mother would *let* her go off to New York alone.

She had never been away from home more than overnight—and then only at a slumber party. Twice, she remembered. She'd never been allowed to have anybody sleep over at her house, so the other girls had stopped inviting her. Nobody came here except Tina.

In the kitchen Vanessa reached for a glass, and frowned at the sight of a note lying on the counter.

"Be sure to watch the time so you don't miss your ride to the train. Tina might not be able to take you to Saratoga later. Mother."

All at once Vanessa's heart was pounding. Mother had gone off for one of her long walks—she didn't want to be here to say good-bye. Was it because she was upset that they were going to be so far apart? That was it, Vanessa convinced herself.

She slid two pieces of bread beneath the broiler and tried to cope with the idea of leaving without seeing her mother again. In a sudden panic she flipped over the bread beneath the broiler and ran back to her room to make sure the money her mother had given her yesterday was still there. Enough for the train fare and "to get by for three or four weeks—if you budget the way you should."

She returned to the kitchen with purse protectively in hand. The toast was burnt on one side. She scraped away the charcoal, buttered the toast, and sat down to eat. *Would* she find a job in three or four weeks? Suppose she didn't?

She finished her breakfast, washed her plate, knife,

and glass, dried them, and put them away. The morning quiet felt ominous. She started at the raucous intrusion of a car horn. Tina! She raced back to her bedroom for her valise and paused to stare about the room for one still moment. Then she hurried awkwardly to the front door.

Tina waved. Vanessa waved back. She reached into her purse for the house key. Lock the front door, slide the key under the mat. Mother would know to look for it there.

The street was empty except for a friendly collie out for a morning stroll. Vanessa walked to the DeSoto, hoisted her valise into the back seat and covered it with the car robe that also concealed Tina's luggage from prying eyes. Then, breathless from her effort, she joined Tina in the front seat.

"New York City, here we come," Tina chortled, reaching for the ignition. "Do you know how many fellows in uniform pass through that place? Young, able-bodied, and good-looking," she purred.

"First we have to find jobs," Vanessa reminded. "And a place to live. Then we worry about our social lives."

"I left a note for Pop," Tina said. "I said I was going out to Hollywood." She giggled. "He knows I'm mad about the movies. When he's had time to simmer down, I'll write and tell him where we are. Pop hates New York City. The only thing good about it according to him is that it keeps electing Fiorello La Guardia mayor."

"Do you suppose he'll talk to my mother?" Vanessa worried.

"Not a chance. He doesn't even know you're my best friend. All Pop knows is the butcher shop six days a week and whatever floozy he's screwing on Saturday nights. And his damn tomato plants every summer. You'd think he was growing orchids."

26

Vanessa was relieved that only a handful of passengers waited inside the high-ceilinged station. The train was not due to arrive for another twenty minutes, but the two girls went outside to wait by the tracks. New York City was just two hundred miles away, Vanessa mused; but it felt as though they were moving to another continent.

"Oh, God, do I have Lois's phone number?" Tina searched her purse as the train chugged into the station. "It's here," she sighed in relief.

"Tina, are you as scared as I am?" Vanessa whispered, her eyes glowing with excitement.

"Just remember, we're escaping from Pinewood." Tina's smile was triumphant. "You're going to be a famous clothes designer, and I'm going to be a movie star."

Vanessa and Tina sat in tense silence as the train pulled out of the Saratoga station. Instinctively they both knew they were leaving home behind them forever. Vanessa thought of her father. When she was younger — before the Depression, when they still had a car — Daddy loved to take a day off from the store during August to drive to Saratoga for the races. Not to gamble — just to mingle with the crowds and watch the horses run. Once he'd taken her with him. She must have been about six. She'd been mesmerized by the fashionable ladies in their beautiful dresses. But there would be no horse racing this summer, Vanessa remembered. Because of the war.

"We'll call Lois as soon as we arrive," Tina said, breaking the silence. "Maybe we can stay with her for a couple of days."

"She'll be at work," Vanessa pointed out. "We'll have to wait until she gets home." Lois lived somewhere in

27

Brooklyn.

Tina rummaged in her purse, brought out two Baby Ruths.

"I brought along something to keep us going till we get to New York," she said, and handed one to Vanessa. She grimaced. "The chocolate's melting already."

They sat and nibbled on the Baby Ruths, holding the candy carefully in their wrappings. Each was comforted by the presence of the other, both aware of the speed with which the train was taking them far from the only home they had ever known.

At Albany new arrivals flooded the aisle of the car. Did any of the other passengers guess that Tina and she were going to New York to *live?* Daddy would be pleased, Vanessa decided. He'd loved Pinewood, but had always said—sadly—that the town didn't have much to offer young people.

Tina jiggled one foot in impatience as the train sat in the Albany station. Young boys roamed through the car with sandwiches and soda pop, but Vanessa and Tina had agreed not to spend any more than was necessary. Anything you bought on the train always cost more than off. Maybe they'd go to lunch at the automat, Vanessa thought. Tina had been down to New York with her father three times. She'd been fascinated by the automat, the subways, and Coney Island. Tina had seen the Atlantic Ocean.

Because she had slept little the night before, Vanessa dozed off for much of the trip. She awoke with a start when Tina poked her in the side with excited small jabs.

"We're coming into Grand Central Station!"

Daylight was nowhere in evidence. The train was creeping through a dark tunnel, and Vanessa felt a tightness in her throat. It was frightening to be seventeen years old and adrift in a strange city. She'd feel lots

28

better, she thought suddenly, if she had ten times more money in her wallet. One day, she promised herself, she'd go back to Pinewood—just to visit—and she'd have so much money she could buy anything in the world she wanted.

In the awesome cavern that was Grand Central Station the two girls searched for a phone booth amid the sea of humanity. Struggling with their valises, they pushed their way through the hordes of arriving and departing people. A phalanx of young men in uniform marched through a gate to the train that would take them, Vanessa surmised, to an army base. She was touched by the sight of a very young marine and a solemn-faced girl who clung to his arm.

Tina found a nickel in her change purse, flipped open the notebook that held Lois's phone number, and dialed. Vanessa hovered at the open door of the booth and willed Lois to answer.

"She's not home yet," Tina conceded after endless rings. "Just as you said."

"Let's go find an automat and have a sandwich," Vanessa said with bravado. "We'll call her later."

"First we'll check our luggage," Tina said, and Vanessa stared at her uncertainly. "It's okay. We'll come back for it later. We can't walk around the city dragging these valises."

They walked out of the station onto bustling Forty-second Street. Vanessa had seen photographs of New York City, but wasn't prepared for the sight of buildings climbing into the sky. She stood still on the sidewalk and gaped at the structures towering around them.

"This is New York, baby," Tina flipped. "I'll bet there are more people in one square block of this town than in all of Pinewood."

They soon discovered an automat. Feeling incredibly

29

adventurous, they strolled into the clinically clean, marble-walled cafeteria with its highly polished slots that held sandwiches, cakes and pies, rolls, and tiny pots of baked beans.

They joined the line at the cashier's counter for change. Trying to appear nonchalant, they waited their turn — tray in hand — before the cubicles that contained sandwiches. With sandwiches and iced tea on their trays they settled themselves at the table. Vanessa ate without tasting. *What would they do if Lois wasn't home? Suppose she had moved? Where would they find a room for tonight?*

From the automat they strolled over to Fifth Avenue. Vanessa recognized the names of all the fine stores from her years of devouring *Vogue:* Lord & Taylor, B. Altman, and farther up the avenue, Saks Fifth Avenue, Best, Bonwit, and Bergdorf Goodman. But both girls were too awed to walk into these august stores.

Finally Tina decided it was time to try again to reach Lois. For an hour and a half she phoned at fifteen-minute intervals while Vanessa hung anxiously at the door of the phone booth. At last Tina's brilliant smile told Vanessa that Lois had answered the phone. But Tina's smile was short-lived. From Tina's responses it was clear that Lois was not extending hospitality.

"Sure, we'll be in touch," Tina said and slammed down the phone. "The little bitch! She's terribly busy on this important new government job," Tina drawled. "She said to sign up for a room at a 'Y,' read the *New York Times* classified to find a furnished apartment and a list of employment agencies. Oh, and she's sure we'll have no trouble landing jobs. Finding an apartment may be a headache."

By 8:00 P.M. They were settled in a room at the YWCA. They unpacked and went out in search for a place for dinner. Vanessa was shocked at the high prices on the menus pasted on the restaurant windows.

"Tonight we're celebrating," Tina declared. "My treat. If I'm giving up my mink-dyed muskrat, let's at least have a good spaghetti dinner."

Their small room at the YWCA was hot and stuffy, but both girls slept soundly — exhausted from their long traumatic day — until the sounds of the early morning city awakened them. Their first objective this morning was to find a place to live. Lois had advised them to look "somewhere in the West Seventies or Eighties because that's where there're cheap furnished apartments."

At yet another automat they sat over a roll and coffee and marked possible rentals listed in the morning's *Times*.

"Everything's so high," Vanessa lamented. "Ten dollars a week for a furnished studio and kitchenette! Mother pays fifteen a month for our house!"

"Jobs pay more here than in Pinewood." Tina refused to be pessimistic. "Lois says she's making thirty a week. Of course, she's been working for a year and a half."

"Let's start answering ads for apartments." Vanessa was mindful of what each night at the "Y" was costing them.

"Let me fix my lipstick first," Tina said, reaching for her wartime version of Tangee's "Dark Secret." She giggled reminiscently. "The first time I came downstairs with this on — it was almost two years ago — Pop yelled, 'What the hell have you got on your face?' and sent me upstairs to wash it off."

By noon they were hot, tired, and discouraged. They had checked out every furnished apartment, every furnished room advertised in the area. Either they were too late, the landladies would rent "only to businessmen," or the space was painfully inadequate for two.

"Maybe we should have taken that last room," Tina said, tugging at the neckline of her peasant blouse. "It was only five dollars a week."

"Tina, it had a single bed and a tiny dresser," Vanessa protested. "It was a walk-in closet."

They liked the neighborhood, Vanessa conceded: the four-story brown-stones and tall apartment houses, the grassed malls that divided Broadway, nearby Riverside Drive stretching for endless blocks, the Hudson River and Central Park.

"I'm dying of thirst." Tina paused before a candy store. "Let's go inside for a soda."

The man behind the counter served them without interrupting his conversation with an overweight, perspiring woman who was crammed into a pair of red slacks two sizes too small.

"They stuck me for two weeks' rent and on top of that ripped me off for the towels and sheets. Hereafter I get two weeks' rent in advance," she said firmly.

Vanessa and Tina exchanged an excited glance.

"Excuse me," Tina said with a diffidence normally foreign to her. "Do you have a furnished apartment for rent?"

The woman's eyes swept form Tina to Vanessa in practiced appraisal.

"Yeah. A studio and kitchenette. Got its own bathroom. Ten dollars a week, two weeks in advance," she stipulated.

"May we see it?" Vanessa asked.

"Why not?" the woman shrugged. She sucked noisily at the straw of her egg cream for a moment, relinquished the glass, and gestured to the girls to follow her.

The apartment was on the top floor of a brownstone that once must have been a beautiful private home but

32

was now shabby and run-down. It looked out over a small garden from which rose a gnarled old tree that, to Vanessa, provided majestic charm.

Vanessa and Tina exchanged delighted glances. The minuscule studio, furnished in typical furnished-apartment maple, was beautiful because it was their own. The gas stove and a tiny refrigerator that sat in a closet-sized alcove would let them cook their own meals.

Though ten dollars a week sounded frightfully expensive, Vanessa and Tina parted with twenty dollars in return for a receipt for two weeks' rent and a set of keys. Alone in the apartment they clutched each other in happy relief.

"It's great!" Tina chortled. "Though the refrigerator must be the first one GE ever made. But we have our own bathroom. Of course, if either of us gains five pounds we'll never get into the tub."

"It's ours." Vanessa gazed about in satisfaction. "Let's have another set of keys made up, then go to the 'Y' to check out. In the morning we start job hunting."

For job hunting Vanessa wore a cap-sleeved black cotton sheath that, shorn of its original red-and-white trim and glossy red belt, appeared young and cool and chic. At her throat, as approved in the pages of *Vogue,* she wore a strand of dime-store pearls. She prodded Tina into wearing a gray chambray rather than the green polka-dotted piqué scheduled for this morning. They both wore rayon-twisted-with-silk stockings rather than the increasingly popular leg makeup, and carried short white gloves.

"Once we have jobs we can wear leg makeup," Vanessa stipulated.

"So let's get jobs." Tina took a final glance at herself in the small mirror that hung over the chest of drawers.

"Did you dream a week ago that we'd be here in New York in our own apartment and going out to an employment agency?"

They steeled themselves for the morning rush hour of the subway station at Broadway and Seventy-second Street. Pedestrians walked swiftly toward their destinations—nobody dawdles, Vanessa thought, and was pleased. People in New York don't just exist, she told herself in heady comprehension, they *live*.

Both girls hid their anxiety beneath bright auras of confidence. Vanessa reminded herself with shaky bravado that the *New York Times* indicated an abundance of available jobs for receptionists, file clerks, and clerk-typists.

Still, they approached their first employment agency with trepidation. Every inch of space in the reception area seemed jammed with job seekers. But the job hunters exuded optimism. This was a seller's market. They had graduated high school at the right time.

In three days Vanessa and Tina filled out what seemed like an endless stack of applications and applied for a variety of jobs. Vanessa yearned to find a position in the fashion industry. Instead, she settled for the first definite offer: receptionist-typist at a law firm on West Forty-second Street. That same afternoon Tina was hired as a receptionist in the office of Friedlich Furs, wholesale furriers.

"All those gorgeous furs," Tina sighed while they lingered over cheese sandwiches and iced tea in a cafeteria on Broadway. "If I can save up enough money, I can buy a mink-dyed muskrat at the employees' price."

"I'll have to write my mother tonight." Vanessa was somber. "She's anxious to know how much money I'll be sending her each week." Mentally Vanessa grappled with how she would manage on half of her after-tax salary in the face of the high cost of living in New York. She'd have to stay out of cafeterias and eat at home.

"I think you're nuts," Tina said flatly. "Why can't the old bat go out and get a job herself? It would be easy for her to get a job in Pinewood."

"She won't ever work," Vanessa said with gentle reproach. "You know Mother."

"Maybe she'll decide to get married. If she'd smile once in a while, she'd be a good-looking woman."

"She won't do that either." Vanessa toyed with the straw in her iced tea. "It's okay. I'll manage."

Since neither of them would begin work until the following Monday, Vanessa and Tina embarked on a massive sightseeing tour. They took the ferry ride to Staten Island—twenty cents round trip. They traveled by the BMT to Coney Island, where Vanessa was awed by her first sight of the Atlantic. And they saw the Empire State Building—the world's tallest. They spent an evening zigzagging among the "Broadway theaters," marquees dimmed in deference to the war, that actually were located on streets criss-crossing the Great White Way.

Tina was intrigued by Radio City Music Hall, the Paramount, and the Capitol as well as the neighborhood movie palaces, though when they went to a movie on Saturday night it was at one of the cheap third-run houses on West Forty-second Street. Vanessa was enthralled by their visit to the Metropolitan Museum, where for the first time in its history the museum offered an exhibit of twenty-eight modern dresses. The exhibit included designs by Valentina, Germaine Monteil, Nettie Rosenstein, and Fira Benenson, and Vanessa was thrilled to see firsthand designs by some of the magical names of the fashion world.

Clutching at Tina, Vanessa walked past the Parsons School on East Fifty-seventy Street and then the

Traphagen School on Broadway at Fifty-second, with bittersweet delight. She relished her proximity to these temples of fashions, and was frustrated that she could not afford to attend classes — not even those given in the evening. Yet. Just ahead of them a girl was uninhibitedly singing "I Don't Want to Set the World on Fire," normally a song Vanessa loved. But today she balked at the sentiment. Oh, yes, she and Tina did want to set the world on fire!

On Monday morning Vanessa and Tina began their jobs. Vanessa worked for a law firm with six partners, whose cases largely involved estates and wills. She wished that Tina and she could switch bosses. Even the lowest of furriers was "Seventh Avenue" — magic words to Vanessa.

At lunchtime Vanessa accompanied another typist from the law office to a nearby drugstore lunch counter for a sandwich and soda. After today, she decided grimly, she would bring a sandwich from home and save on lunch money. The cost of living in the city was a shock each time out.

At Tina's insistence both girls opened checking accounts on their first payday. "It's so grown-up to have a checking account." Tina sighed blissfully. "Even though I'll have nothing left by the end of the week."

"It'll make it easier to send money home," Vanessa conceded. "I won't have to stand in line every Saturday morning at the post office to buy a money order." From Tina — whose father religiously reported each day's collection of butcher shop gossip over dinner — she knew that the check she sent home covered her mother's room and board at Mrs. Johnson's and allowed for a couple of twenty-five-cent movies each week.

Vanessa was disturbed that her mother had not answered the letter she had written the previous week. She debated phoning home, but at last rejected this, deciding that Mother would label it "an unnecessary extravagance."

By the end of their second week Tina was complaining of boredom with her job. Vanessa was simply grateful to know that money would be coming in regularly. She worried that she had still not heard from her mother, and in the middle of her third week in the city she decided to call home. With a handful of coins in her hand she went down to the pay phone on the first floor of their brownstone.

"I'm sorry. Your number has been disconnected," the long-distance operator replied after a moment.

"Thank you," Vanessa stammered. She hung up the receiver and slowly retrieved her coins.

It didn't really mean anything that the phone had been disconnected. Mother had always resented spending money on the phone, even on the party line. Mother had kept the phone for the baby-sitting calls and whatever else came along. But why didn't Mother write?

At the neighborhood newsstand Tina discovered a new theatrical newspaper called *Show Business,* catering to would-be actors and actresses. She searched its pages avidly for acting classes that met in the evenings and didn't charge much, and harbored secret notions of a Hollywood talent scout miraculously appearing at the class and declaring her a potential star.

Tina was jubilant when she returned from an interview for an acting class that met in a studio in Steinway Hall twice a week.

"Vanessa, I can afford it!" she bubbled. "As long as I stay out of the dress stores. And it's on West Fifty-seventh Street—I can walk there and back and save bus fare."

"I think you can afford the five-cent bus ride," Vanessa said with a laugh. The twenty-five a week that Tina earned wouldn't go far, she acknowledged; but it was all hers.

"Maybe there'll be some terrific boys in the class," Tina considered. "I wish you'd join, too."

"I can't spend that much," Vanessa reminded. "I went to the drama club at high school because it didn't cost anything—it was something to do after school."

But she'd sell her soul, Vanessa thought with a surge of frustration, if it would buy her admission to an evening class at Traphagen.

Three

Vanessa and Tina quickly fell into a pattern of life that was devoid of social activity other than Tina's attendance twice a week at her acting class. After a day at the office they hurried home to eat a quickly prepared dinner at the small table they kept by the window. After dinner they escaped to Riverside Drive to walk beside the river and find relief from the torpid New York summer.

On weekends they slept late and roamed about the free attractions the city provided. Once a week they went to a neighborhood movie. And on one Saturday afternoon they splurged and handed over seventy-seven cents each for admission to the very grand Radio City Music Hall. Occasionally they talked about home with fleeting nostalgia.

Vanessa was disturbed that her mother never wrote. Only the small, precise endorsement on the back of the checks she sent home told her that her mother had received and cashed them. Still, with each check she enclosed a brief letter.

Guilty that her father must be worrying about her, Tina wrote him without giving a return address.

"Even Pop won't be hot-headed enough to charge down here to look for me," Tina conceded.

"I saw a nice neighborhood bar on Broadway near Seventh-fifth," Tina mentioned while they tried to cool off on a bench on Riverside Drive on a hot early August night. "We could go in for a daiquiri or a rum Coke. My treat," she coaxed. Neither Vanessa nor she had ever tasted anything stronger than red wine.

"We can't pick up somebody in a bar." Vanessa was shocked.

"I'm not saying we should be 'Victory Girls,'" Tina mocked. They both knew about the fifteen- and sixteen-year-old girls who circulated around Times Square "doing their bit for the servicemen."

"No bars, Tina." Vanessa was firm, though she did share Tina's yearning for male companionship. They had both harbored colorful visions of an active social life in the city. *All* the boys were not in the service. "Tomorrow's Friday night. Why don't we just go downtown and look around?" Vanessa offered.

"Okay." Tina's smile was wry. "We'll walk past the Stork Club and Larue's and the Waldorf-Astoria. But when the hell will we find somebody to take us there?"

On Friday after work the two girls ate a hasty spaghetti dinner at home, spent elaborate care on their makeup and clothes—as though about to embark on a special date—and headed for mid-Manhattan.

"My boss says Friday and Saturday nights in New York in the summer used to be dead," Tina said while they waited in the dwindling daylight for a double-decker Fifth Avenue bus that included Riverside Drive on its itinerary. "Everybody used to run off to the country or the beach for the weekend. Now nobody has the gas for trips like that."

40

"Mmm," Vanessa replied, admiring the smart dresses of two girls who waited beside them for the bus. "Tina, you know that cocoa blazer you were talking about throwing out? Buy a pair of beige slacks and you'll have a great fall pantsuit." In the last year women had begun to wear pants wherever they liked.

"Vanessa, don't you ever think of anything but clothes?" Tina scolded as the bus approached their stop.

"I *was* scared when the government came out with that order about how clothes were to be made — Limitations Order L-85," Vanessa said and laughed at Tina's blank stare. "I know, you never read anything except *Show Business* and the *Daily News* columns. The government made laws about how much material can go into a shirt and the length of jackets and linings and all. But the American designers are coming up with some great clothes."

"Which we can't afford," Tina shot back.

"I know," Vanessa said ruefully. "At lunchtime yesterday I walked down to Lord and Taylor. They had gorgeous suits in the window, all of them with braid for trim. We'll add black braid to your red suit," she decided.

They rode on the upper deck of the bus, getting off at Fifth Avenue and Fifty-third Street. Friday night pedestrians seemed less rushed, Vanessa observed, following Tina's wistful glance at a pair of handsome young army lieutenants with pretty girls in evening dresses hanging on their arms. On weekends the city seemed full of soldiers and sailors on leave.

"Wanna bet they're headed for the Stork?" Tina whispered. "No cover charge, no minimum for men in uniform."

The two couples disappeared into the Stork Club entrance, and Tina smiled her approval. The two girls

41

headed toward Park and Fifty-first to stroll past the Waldorf-Astoria.

"Guy Lombardo and his orchestra are at the Starlight Room at the Waldorf," Tina told Vanessa. "We have to meet somebody who can take us to the Stork or the Starlight Room. Or to Larue's or the Commodore—that's where the young crowd hangs out."

"Let's find a Walgreen's and go in for a cold drink," Vanessa said comfortingly.

"Then to Forty-second Street for a movie," Tina decreed. "God, I thought when we were living in New York we'd be going crazy with things to do!"

By early fall Tina was bored with her acting classes. Her goal was Hollywood, not Broadway. She dropped out to look for a nonprofessional theater group casting for a production, and started saving money to pay for photographs, though she admitted she'd never have the nerve to "make rounds," as many young stage hopefuls did. But she wanted to have photographs ready in case she was cast in a play.

"Then I can write to the New York offices of the movie studios, tell them I'll be in a play, enclose a picture, and ask them to come down to see me," she said with a glibness acquired by reading *Show Business*. "You don't have to be a great actress to be a movie star. It's looks that count."

With a zeal that surprised Vanessa, Tina answered off-Broadway casting calls. Most evenings they left the apartment door ajar so they might hear the hall phone if it rang. There was no question of trying to put in a phone of their own—new phones were impossible to acquire in the middle of a war. Tina was restless, champing to see herself in a play.

"I need to be seen," she said plaintively, returning

from yet another futile interview. "I read for a part in *The Cherry Orchard*. A play by some Russian," she shrugged. "The director told me to get myself a bathing suit and go see Billy Rose."

The shrill ring of the hall phone downstairs prodded Tina into action. A middle-aged door-to-door salesman who lived on the ground floor picked up the receiver.

"Hello," he said briskly and Tina paused on the stairs while Vanessa hovered on the landing above. "You Tina Gregory?" the man asked and Tina charged down the stairs.

Vanessa waited with crossed fingers, listening to Tina's excited monosyllabic responses.

"Vanessa!" Tina yelled jubilantly as she put down the receiver. "I've got a part in a play! It's a crummy little group, but they've been doing plays in this church basement for two years now." Tina charged up the stairs. Her face was luminescent. "I'm going to play Alexandra in *The Little Foxes*. It was a big Broadway hit before it was a movie last year."

"I know!" Vanessa hugged Tina in her excitement. "Teresa Wright played Alexandra in the movie."

"We start rehearsals next week. We'll open early in December and play four performances," Tina reported. "Now I *will* have pictures taken!"

Three nights a week Tina went to rehearsals. On those nights Vanessa holed up in the Forty-second Street Library to read everything possible about the fashion world. She sketched endlessly, impatient that her skills were not as polished as she'd like.

Occasionally both Vanessa and Tina felt pangs of homesickness. Despite her defiance about being free of her brothers' highhanded treatment of her, Tina worried that her three able-bodied brothers — even though Sal and Vinnie were married — might be drafted. Finally, eager for news of home, Tina arranged to have

43

the *Pinewood Enquirer* shipped to her care of the furrier office.

"Nobody at the newspaper office will trace the subscription to me," Tina reassured Vanessa. "And it'll be kind of fun to read about what's happening back home."

When the first issue of the *Pinewood Enquirer* arrived, they learned that a member of their graduating class had died in North Africa. Mr. Leonard, their serious young history teacher, was missing in the Pacific. Shaken by the grim news—and worried that her brother Gus might already be in uniform—Tina wrote to her father and gave a return address.

A week after Tina mailed the letter to her father, Nick replied. He upbraided her for bringing grief to their father, for "shaming them before the whole town." Tina gritted her teeth and forced herself to respond without rancor. She wrote about her job, about her part in the play. And she asked Nick what he knew about Mrs. Conrad.

"Everybody in Pinewood knows everybody else's business," she pointed out to Vanessa. "He'll talk to the women in the butcher shop—somebody will tell him."

Two weeks later Tina heard again from Nick. The only message that came from her father, via Nick, was that living in a city like New York, she'd best go to confession regularly. Nick also reported that "Mrs. Conrad is living the life of Riley at Elvira Johnson's boardinghouse along with all the other old biddies."

"I think Pop's relieved that I'm living with you," Tina giggled. "He was scared I was living in sin with some guy."

Tina's theater company was having difficulties keeping a full cast. Just before Thanksgiving two male members were inducted into the army. The producer-director was optimistic about replacing them; the cast was less hopeful. Over a modest Thanksgiving dinner—a roast chicken and yams prepared in their tiny oven—Tina talked about saving up to tackle Hollywood.

"Give New York a year," Vanessa encouraged. It was frightening to contemplate living in the city alone. Tina had become her family. "Maybe some talent scout will come to the play—"

"If it ever gets on," Tina interrupted glumly. "Now we have to worry about another available two weekends at the church basement. Provided we get cast replacements."

Two replacements were found. Rehearsals continued. Then shortly before Christmas—with performances scheduled for early January—their leading lady defected to the night shift in a defense factory. Tina pretended that she was depressed this Christmas because of the uncertainty of performance dates. But Vanessa knew she missed the usual Christmas gathering at her family house.

"I thought Nick would write and say, 'Come home for Christmas, you little nut,'" Tina confessed. "But they act like I'm dead. Nick and Gus used to drive down to New York once or twice a year for the weekend," Tina remembered. "All right, I know they can't drive down when you only get three gallons of gas a week, but they could take the train or bus."

Vanessa didn't hear from her mother either.

By early January the theater group was disbanded, and Vanessa worried that Tina would decide to take off for Hollywood. When Tina read later that month about a newly opened rendezvous for show business hopefuls—euphemistically called the Genius Club— Vanessa readily agreed to drop in on Friday evening. She was eager to provide Tina with diversion from thoughts of her family and the defunct play.

On Friday, the temperature dropped to twenty-nine

degrees. "All day long I look at those gorgeous seals and Persian lambs," Tina said with a sigh. "And all I can afford is this piece of shit." She reached disdainfully for the mouton lamb she was buying "on time" from her boss. "One of these days, Vanessa, I'm going to buy myself the best-looking mink any furrier ever put together. After all, what's Rita Hayworth got that I haven't got?"

"Victor Mature," laughed Vanessa. "Come on, let's get out of here before I change my mind."

The Genius Club operated in a first-floor space at a West Forties hotel. For the price of a cup of coffee and a danish young theater hopefuls—short on money but rich in ambition—could sit and exchange gossip about "round making," classes, and agents. The room resounded with conviviality, high hopes for tomorrow, brash and extravagant claims. To Vanessa's astonishment Tina—always so ebullient—professed an air of detached amusement.

"You think anybody here will really make it big?" Tina whispered, surveying the clusters of people gathered at the small tables around them. "I'll bet most of them will go running home, tail between their legs, before they've been here six months." Her smile was triumphant: she and Vanessa had been here more than six months, and neither one of them was running home.

"Hi!" Vanessa and Tina glanced up to see a tall, blond young man smiling down at them. "Didn't I see you last week at the Pemberton office?" His question was directed at Tina.

"I wasn't at the Pemberton office," Tina conceded. "Sorry—"

"The Astor drugstore yesterday morning. I borrowed your *Show Business*," he said.

"No." Tina's eyes were carrying on another conversa-

46

tion with him. "But you can sit down while we pursue this."

"I'm Cliff Hopkins," he stated and dropped into one of the two empty chairs at the table. "From near Saint Louis."

"I'm Tina Gregory, this is Vanessa Conrad. We're from upstate New York." Tina inspected him speculatively. "You don't sound like you come from Saint Louis."

"Hey, I spent a year with a coach dumping the accent." His eyes were moving about the room. Suddenly he held up his hand and beckoned to someone to join them. "And here comes a guy who doesn't sound as though he was born and raised in Venice, Italy."

Vanessa followed Cliff's gaze to the slender, dark-haired, dark-eyed young man approaching their table. Vanessa was aware of finely chiseled features, a warm quick smile, an air of being eager to please. *He looks like Tyrone Power.* All at once her heart was pounding.

"This is Eddie Montino," Cliff said, introducing him, then waving him to the empty chair. "Eduardo," he said with a flourish, "this is Tina Gregory and Vanessa Conrad."

"Hi." He had a faint aura of shyness that appealed to Vanessa.

"Are you really from Venice?" Tina was intrigued. "My father was born near Florence. He came here when he was nine."

"I was born in Venice," Eddie confirmed. "I've been away for six years. My family sent me to live with my American grandmother and to go to school here when Mussolini started going after the Italian Jews." Vanessa was startled. Everybody knew about Hitler, but she hadn't realized that the Italian Jews, too, were in trouble. She was startled that she felt an instant kinship with Eddie because he was Jewish. She had never

47

known a Jewish boy. "Then Italy got into the war on Germany's side, and I knew I was here indefinitely." His face was somber.

"You two look like actors," Tina said, and Eddie laughed.

"Not me. I'm an engineering student at Columbia," he explained. "I graduate this term." His eyes were questioning as they rested on Vanessa.

"I'm not an actress," Vanessa quickly disclaimed. "I work in a law office as a receptionist-typist. Tina has been in rehearsal with a group downtown, but it just folded."

"I've done some magazine modeling," Cliff said. "You know the kind of stuff." He grimaced. "Shots for detective stories or confession magazine crap. And I did a play last spring that lasted about a week down in the Village. I was on 'Let's Pretend' twice. But for money I work part-time as a soda jerk. I just keep praying I make it on Broadway before my draft status changes from 4-F to 1-A. I'm blind as a bat without my glasses, but Selective Service is getting less fussy every day."

Vanessa felt a sudden chill. Sitting here the war seemed far away. But it wasn't. It was with them every day. She thought of Mr. Leonard, missing in action.

"The American army keeps putting me off," Eddie said humorously. He spoke English without a trace of an accent. "I can't even sneak into Italy to join the partisans. But I keep trying." He smiled, but his eyes were troubled. He was worried about his family, Vanessa decided. Her own concerns all at once seemed trivial.

"When they do pull me in, I could go for section eight or play queer," Cliff said. "I don't *have* to fight a war. I could be the Alfred Lunt of this generation."

"Do you like French films?" Eddie asked, his eyes clinging to Vanessa as though his life depended upon her reply.

"I've never seen one," Vanessa confessed and Tina nodded in agreement.

"They're rerunning *Le Carnet de Bal* with Louis Jourdan and Michèle Morgen down at the Apollo on Forty-second Street," Eddie said. "I've seen it three times. It's marvelous. I feel rich tonight—why don't I treat?"

They walked out of the Genius Club and into the sharp cold of the night. Vanessa reveled in the touch of Eddie's hand at her elbow.

For the first time since Tina and she arrived in New York, Vanessa felt truly a part of the city—no longer an onlooker, but a participant.

Four

Vanessa was startled when Tina invited Cliff and Eddie to come up to the apartment for coffee, though she was aware that, in the darkness of the Apollo, Tina and Cliff had been holding hands.

"It's Friday night," Tina effervesced as they strolled in the cold night air across Forty-second Street to Broadway. On weekend nights Times Square was jammed with men and women in service uniforms and their companions, all determined to eke out every ounce of enjoyment available from a weekend pass. "Nobody works, goes to school, or makes rounds tomorrow."

"Great," Cliff said at Tina's invitation, and Eddie, too, seemed pleased. "That's on our way home. We have a room with a hot plate and icicles up near Columbia."

"We have no icicles yet," Vanessa laughed, "but our landlady is working on it."

"You know the government regulation about keeping the thermostat no higher than sixty-five degrees?" Tina slid her arm through Cliff's. "She's super-patriotic about saving oil. She keeps it about forty-five."

Eddie's arm settled about Vanessa's waist as they strolled north on crowded, dimmed-out Broadway. Vanessa was content to listen while Eddie talked nostalgically about home. His family had lived in Venice since the early seventeenth century.

"Venice was kinder to the Jews than Rome," Eddie told her. "But even in Venice in the seventeenth and eighteenth centuries the ghetto was locked at night. Jews who traveled outside the ghetto — though it wasn't overcrowded and sordid like in Rome — had to wear an identifying badge. They needed special permits to travel out of town. The only profession they could enter was medicine." Unexpectedly he chuckled. "The papal physicians were Jews."

"My father said that my grandparents left Europe to escape the ghetto," Vanessa recalled.

"My father left Italy to escape the women," Tina contributed as she and Cliff fell into step beside Vanessa and Eddie. "Pop said that in the villages in Italy the men were nothing. The women were the bosses. Pop said his father wanted to come to America because here he could be a man." Tina giggled reminiscently. "And every Saturday night Pop makes sure to prove to himself he is a man. Even when Mom was alive. Mom just shrugged her shoulders and looked the other way."

"My mother would hit Dad over the head with a skillet." Cliff's eyes crinkled with laughter. "He's lucky to get away to his lodge meetings once a week."

"I wish my parents had come to America with me." Eddie's face reflected his pain. "I wish the whole family had come here. My parents, my older brother, and my two sisters. My mother was born here in New York, but she loves Venice. I haven't heard from them in three years — I don't know where they are."

"Everybody knows about Hitler," Vanessa said softly. "We just never think of Italy as being anti-Semitic."

"The Italian Jews tried to ignore what was happening, told themselves it was a passing phase. But Mussolini was following in Hitler's footsteps. In 1937 a man named Pietro Orano published a book called *Gli Ebri in*

51

Italia. It started a terrible anti-Jewish campaign in the Italian press. Then the next year a group of Italian scientists wrote a book supposedly edited by Mussolini. It talked about a pure Italian race of Aryan stock," Eddie said with contempt. "Two months later laws were passed forbidding Jews to study or teach in any school or institution of higher learning and ordering the deportation of all Jewish aliens who had arrived in Italy after 1919. That was just the beginning. Once Italy entered the war, the Fascists opened up concentration camps."

"Your family may be among the lucky ones," Tina said hopefully. "In Italy there are two kinds of families — rich and poor. My grandparents were peasants. Peasants couldn't send a son to America to go to school." Her eyes teased Eddie. "Money must buy a lot, even in Mussolini's Italy."

"My family was quite comfortable," Eddie conceded. His smile was wry. "My father was a hero in the last war. Because of this, my mother wrote me — when I could still receive letters — their property had not been confiscated. But I know my family. They must have fought against the Fascist regime." Apprehension crept into his voice.

"Pop says the Italians won't put up with Mussolini forever," Tina said. "They'll throw him out and get out of this crazy war," she predicted.

"Hey, let's stop in the automat on the next block and warm up with coffee," Cliff said. "For five cents a head we can gear ourselves for the hike uptown."

"Best cup of coffee in New York," Vanessa said lightly.

How awful for Eddie, not to know about his family. Yet she was envious of his obvious closeness to his parents. She was four hours away from her mother, a three-cent postage stamp away. But the only indication she had that her mother was alive was the regular endorsement on the checks she sent home.

Vanessa and Eddie and Tina and Cliff became inseparable. Tina, who had always been secretive about her movie ambitions except with Vanessa, was outspoken about everything with Cliff and Eddie. And Vanessa talked earnestly of her own ambitions. She was astonished when, shortly after their first meeting, Eddie confessed he had no wish to become an engineer.

"It's what my parents decided for me," he said. "It's that way in Europe." His face tensed. "But I've known since my first year at Columbia that what I want to do is design stage sets. I've managed to take design classes along with my normal studies. I *know* that's what I want to do. Not now," he acknowledged, "but when this rotten war is over. I'll make my family understand."

Occasionally Eddie took her to see a Broadway play whose set was of particular interest to him. Hand in hand they climbed "up to the sky" to the second-balcony seats that were no more expensive than a movie seat. Vanessa loved the excitement of the live performance, the give and take of the audience. Afterward Vanessa would listen as Eddie dissected the stage set.

Together they envisioned a future in which Eddie would design sets for Broadway plays and Vanessa would design the wardrobes. Vanessa could talk to Eddie knowing that he would understand: they shared a feeling for color, fabrics, lines.

For Vanessa and Tina the hours on their jobs were to be gotten through; the later hours, shared with Eddie and Cliff, were for living. Because none of them — especially Vanessa — had much money, they met like homing pigeons each workday evening at the girls' apartment for low-budget dinners of spaghetti, franks and beans, or hamburgers. "We don't have to worry about porterhouse or lamb chops," said Tina. "Who can afford them?"

On payday each week Tina—the most affluent since her recent raise—insisted on treating at one of the Chinese restaurants that dotted the side streets in the West Forties. And once, when Cliff received a birthday check from home, he took them to a foreign film at the Little Carnegie on West Fifty-seventh Street. They never missed any of FDR's radio speeches. Eddie idolized Roosevelt.

Each was quietly aware that the time they spent together was filled with urgency. Cliff lived with a draft call hanging over his head and Eddie hoped to be allowed to enlist at graduation despite his alien citizenship.

Soon Tina and Cliff were spending private hours together in the room Cliff shared with Eddie.

But on those occasions when they were alone, Vanessa and Eddie shared a tacit agreement to avoid the apartment. Eddie delighted in showing her New York. On a glorious April Sunday evening—with an exhilarating promise of spring in the air—he took her to an early dinner at the Café Royal on Second Avenue and Twelfth Street, the famous meeting place of Jewish actors, writers, intellectuals. He was amused at her lack of familiarity with such Jewish favorites as gefulte fish, potato kugel, and stuffed kishkes and took it upon himself to order for both of them.

"My mother hated to cook," Vanessa confessed. "And everything had to be cooked on top of the stove," she recalled ruefully. "To roast or bake meant the oven had to be cleaned. My father said that when my mother and he were first married she would bake wonderful cakes and cookies. But I guess the longer she stayed in Pinewood the more bitter and unhappy she became."

Vanessa felt a sudden need to defend her mother. "She gave up a singing career to marry."

"I think women have a right to have careers," Eddie said gently.

Vanessa warmed toward him. "Maybe if I had to live forever in Pinewood and forget about designing, I'd be like my mother, too." Eddie knew about the checks that went home to her mother every week, the letters that went unanswered.

"I don't think you could ever be anything but warm and sweet and beautiful," Eddie said, reaching across the table to hold her hand.

The waiter arrived with their dinner and Eddie hastily released her hand. Vanessa saw the approving twinkle in the waiter's eyes.

After dinner they walked in the crisp night air down Second Avenue — which Eddie explained was known as the Jewish Rialto — to Houston Street and then found their way east to Delancey Street, the major thoroughfare of the Lower East Side. Delancey Street was still vibrant with activity, even at this hour on a Sunday evening.

When they tired, Eddie insisted they stop at a cafeteria for tea and hamantaschen. He glanced anxiously at his watch as they dawdled over a second cup of tea.

"I suppose I ought to take you home. You have to go to work tomorrow."

"I suppose."

All at once they were both self-conscious. Usually they had a definite rendezvous point with Tina and Cliff, but tonight Tina and Cliff had wandered off with a vague statement about "meeting you later."

"Can we get a subway around here?" Vanessa was uncomfortable at the prospect of arriving at the apartment before Tina and Cliff.

"Sure." He pushed back his chair, rose to his feet, and reached out his hand to Vanessa.

On the subway they found a vacant seat for two that was located at one end of the car. They sat close together, Eddie's arm about her waist, her head on his shoulder. It seemed to Vanessa that Eddie had always been part of her life.

"We have to change at the next stop," Eddie said softly into the comfortable silence that engulfed them.

By the time they emerged from the West Seventy-second Street subway stop, the temperature had dropped. Eddie insisted that Vanessa wear his jacket. She welcomed the whisper of heat that met them at the door as Eddie prodded her inside the house.

"Tina and Cliff must be her by now," she said as they trudged up the darkened flights of stairs.

She was worried about being alone with Eddie. She didn't trust herself to say no to him, and his eyes, his hand at her waist, told her he desperately wanted to make love. *She wasn't ready for that yet.*

As they arrived at the top floor landing they heard Tina's Sears-Roebuck radio offering the haunting strains of "Embraceable You." Tina and Cliff were here.

Eddie suddenly pulled Vanessa into his arms in the shadowed hallway. "Vanessa, I love you," he whispered. "I think I've loved you since that first evening at the Genius Club."

His mouth was warm and tender, then suddenly urgent. They clung together with a passion that was new and disconcerting and exciting.

"Cliff, not here, silly," Tina's voice rebuked from behind the door to their apartment. "Besides, aren't you being greedy?"

"I'm twenty-three years old with one foot in an army uniform," he chuckled. "Why shouldn't I be greedy?"

"Tomorrow night," Tina promised while Vanessa and Eddie awkwardly separated. "Tell Eddie to take Vanessa to the Apollo. They're showing one of those French films he's so crazy about."

On the eve of his graduation from the Columbia School of Engineering Eddie gave Vanessa his class ring.

"Will you wear it while I'm away?" he asked quietly while they sat at a table at the West End bar.

"Yes," she whispered, dreading to think of the time when he might be fighting in the war. Though he rarely discussed his military status, she knew he had offered his services to his adopted country. "Every minute."

"We'll take it to a jeweler tomorrow to have it made smaller," he promised, laughing at the man-sized class ring on her slender finger.

"Eddie, how long before you have to leave?" she asked, fighting a sense of desolation.

"I haven't received my induction notice yet." All at once his eyes were somber. "I don't think my Italian citizenship will stand in the way, considering what's happening to Italian Jews. I can be useful, Vanessa. As an interpreter or in intelligence. I speak Italian, English, and French. I know my way around Italy."

"You don't have to go," she said. "You're not an American."

"I have to go," he chided and reached to bring her hand to his lips.

Five

Now each day was lived with a fresh sense of urgency. Eddie avoided reporting details, but Vanessa knew he was working hard at being accepted into the American army. She suspected, too, that this would be speedily accomplished.

All at once the city was enveloped in the first heat wave of the incipient summer. Heat seemed to ooze up from the sidewalks. The apartment was a steaming cauldron. On a Friday evening in late June Vanessa and Eddie and Tina and Cliff sought refuge from the soaring temperatures by heading down to the Staten Island Ferry via the Third Avenue el, the train windows wide open to tempt inside the cooling wind whipped up by the speeding train.

Each couple hand in hand, they hurried from the subway station into the ferry house. Their five-cent fare paid, they climbed onto the ferry's upper deck to watch the boat draw away from the Manhattan dim-out.

"Before the war," Eddie told Vanessa while a pair of sailors sang "I Left My Heart at the Stage Door Canteen," "there were Neapolitan musicians playing violins and accordions here. When I was homesick for Venice, I'd ride on the ferry." He dropped an arm about her shoulders. "Someday I'll show you Venice."

Before the half-hour trip was over, Vanessa was glad

she'd brought a sweater. So incredibly cool — so beautifully quiet — and only a five-cent ride from Manhattan. At St. George they left the boat to walk the streets for a while. They stopped for a soft drink, then — refreshed and exhilarated — returned to board the boat back to the city.

"Tomorrow's going to be another scorcher. Let's go to Coney Island," Cliff said. "Make sandwiches," he told Tina. "Plenty of them — we'll stay all day. I've got a thermos jug — we'll bring the lemonade."

"And bring your camera," Tina said. "Let's get some snaps." Saturday by 9:30 A.M., the day already blistering hot, they were already on the Sea Beach Express to Coney Island. Their bathing attire worn beneath their street clothes, Eddie and Cliff sported jeans and T-shirts, Vanessa and Tina colorful peasant skirts and white blouses. The trains were packed with humanity intent on escape from the overheated canyons of the city. The air stank of perspiration, garlic, and onion. Here and there an argumentative voice, the querulous crying of a baby, played against the generally convivial atmosphere.

Vanessa and Eddie clung to a pole, his arm about her waist. A shopping bag stuffed with towels and suntan lotion rested at their feet. Both were oblivious to the glances shot in their direction because they were young and beautiful and obviously in love. A few feet away Tina and Cliff swayed together in the protective covering of other passengers.

The train finally rose aboveground, and soon the faint breeze brought the scent of sea salt to their nostrils. To Vanessa this was a magic potion.

"This stop," Cliff called to them.

The car doors slid open and Vanessa and Eddie were propelled onto the platform by the push of the exuberant crowd. Tina and Cliff at their heels, they hurried down the stairs and crossed Surf Avenue to head for the boardwalk. The sky arched a brilliant blue, the sun shone dazzlingly, its heat mitigated by a salty breeze.

Vanessa smiled at two little girls making determined inroads on tall cones of pink cotton candy. Instinctively she glanced up at Eddie to share this moment with him, and was startled by the hunger she saw in his eyes as they rested on the children. Would there ever be children for them? Eddie never talked about marriage, but she understood. How could he think of himself when he didn't know what was happening to his family in Italy?

Vanessa stood on the boardwalk beside Eddie and stared at the ocean in awe.

"Stay right there," Tina ordered spiritedly. "Cliff, take a couple of snaps of them."

Eddie's arm slid about Vanessa's waist. Both smiled as Cliff worked at getting the best possible angle.

"Cliff, shoot before those smiles are set for life," Tina scolded. "You're not Edward Steichen."

"Okay, that's a wrap," Cliff decided. "Come on, Eddie, take a picture of the next Rita Hayworth and next Alfred Lunt."

The camera changed hands, and Eddie concentrated on catching Tina and Cliff clowning around. They were four young people intent on enjoying a day at the beach. Today they would forget about the war.

"Come on, let's go down to the beach," Cliff said when Eddie finally surrendered the camera.

Every square foot of sand appeared occupied. Hand in hand the two couples made their way past prone bodies, ball-playing teenagers, and tots engaged in the serious business of building sand castles.

"Just ahead," Tina cried out, pointing to a patch of unclaimed beach.

They spread their blanket out on the sand, un-self-consciously discarded outer attire, and collapsed in joyous abandon.

"Joey, you come back here this minute!" a young mother holding a bottle in the mouth of an infant called to her toddler son. "If Daddy sees you running loose that way, we'll go right back to the Bronx! You won't have no franks from Nathan's or no knishes."

"It's not exactly the Riviera," Cliff conceded complacently, rubbing suntan oil on Tina's bare back, "but for us New Yorkers it's the nearest thing."

"We'll have to cover up in a little while," Eddie warned and pointed to a lobster-red middle-aged couple taking refuge beneath an umbrella. His face softened. "My mother always used to remind us that sunburn is a real burn—it's an injury to the skin."

"You ever go to the Italian Riviera?" Tina asked Eddie.

"We didn't need it," Eddie said humorously. "In the summers we had a cabana at the Lido. It's the finest beach in Italy." His face grew somber. "I suspect my family won't be there this summer. Italian Jews aren't allowed to visit the holiday resorts. They can't own radios or enter public libraries or be partners in businesses with 'Aryan Italians.' It must have been a terrible shock—I know my parents never expected anti-Semitism in Italy to go so far."

"How do you know this?" Tina asked.

"The word came through." His voice was tense.

"I'm starving," Vanessa said in an effort to redirect the conversation. She jumped to her feet. "Who's ready for sandwiches?"

It was close to 10:00 P.M. when they gathered together the still damp towels and folded up the blanket Cliff had surreptitiously spirited from their furnished

61

room. The beach population had dwindled, but a stalwart few were clearly settling in for the night.

"God, I'm so sleepy," Tina yawned. "All that sun and sea air."

"You can sleep on my shoulder on the train," Cliff murmured, swaying with her. Just beyond them an amorous pair wriggled under a blanket.

They walked beneath the star-splashed sky, shoes in hand, to the steps that led up to the boardwalk, paused to put on their shoes, then crossed the boardwalk and headed for the train that would carry them back to Manhattan. As the train sped out of the station on the elevated tracks, Eddie pulled Vanessa toward an empty seat for two. Tina and Cliff were already settled between two young families juggling half a dozen youngsters in various stages of sleep.

"Vanessa, I have to report for induction into the army on Monday morning," Eddie said softly, his words muffled by the noise of the train.

"Oh, Eddie." Vanessa went cold with shock.

"I wasn't going to tell you until tomorrow night," he confessed. "But I couldn't be quiet any longer. When this rotten war is over, I'll come back for you."

"Eddie, it'll be awful with you away." *He said he'd come back for her.*

"We'll be married in Venice," he said. She hadn't dared to think that far into the future. "It won't be legal if my family isn't there," he teased. He knew the situation with her mother — her presence would not be a consideration.

"Will we live in Venice?" With Eddie she would be happy anywhere. How would she survive knowing he was fighting in the war?

"We'll live in New York," he said tenderly. "It's home to both of us. But we'll spend time in Venice with the family every year."

62

Vanessa knew how deeply he loved his father and mother, his sisters, Caterina and Annabella, and his older brother Victor. It was Victor who would one day carry on the family antiques firm that had been handed down through five generations. Though men of the Montino family had been bankers, printers, physicians to the popes and the royal families, it was tradition for the oldest son to head the Montino antiques firm, which for almost two centuries had been granted the privilege of furnishing ambassadorial apartments. One day, Vanessa thought tenderly, Eddie's family would be her family.

When they left the train at Times Square to change to the IRT Vanessa knew Cliff had told Tina that Eddie was being inducted on Monday. She saw it in the compassion that shone from Tina.

"Stay at the apartment with Eddie," Tina encouraged while the other two waited at the change booth. "I'll go on uptown with Cliff." She clucked at Vanessa's air of uncertainty. "Honey, there's a war on. Don't you want to be with him?"

"Yes." Vanessa's face flooded with color. Tina talked with candor about "going all the way" with Cliff. "Tina, I want to, but—" It was disconcerting to face up to emotions that had never surfaced before she'd met Eddie.

She'd worried all these weeks about Tina and Cliff. Scared that Tina would discover she was pregnant. Tina had laughed at her, Vanessa remembered: *"With all the drugstores in this city I'm going to get pregnant?"* But you couldn't be absolutely sure. Still, she wanted to be with Eddie tonight more than she had ever wanted anything in her life. He was going off to the war.

They hurried along the labyrinthine route from the BMT to the IRT, and boarded a crowded northbound express. Her hand in Eddie's, Vanessa was more conscious than usual of the military uniforms among the late Saturday evening crowd.

The train raced with the thunderous noise that in Vanessa evoked images of cannon fire, bypassed the local stops, and pulled into the West Seventy-second Street station with a swiftness that had once astonished her.

"Tina's going on uptown with Cliff," Vanessa whispered shakily and saw Eddie's eyes grow soft with comprehension and desire.

The crowds around them speeded their approach to the door and out onto the platform of the station. They walked swiftly up the stairs and out into the night, hand in hand, silent in their anticipation. Vanessa tried to forget that on Monday morning Eddie would be in military service. After this weekend when would she see him again?

Vanessa's hand was trembling as she reached for her keys.

"Let me," Eddie said and took the keys from her.

He unlocked the downstairs door and they moved into the night-darkened hallway. Halfway up the second flight Eddie paused to kiss her. Tonight his mouth was urgent, probing. One hand crept to her breasts.

"Hey, can't you wait till you get upstairs?" a male voice jibed, and they leapt apart to allow a heavy, middle-aged man—his drunken grin sympathetic—to pass them on the steps.

In the tiny, hot apartment Eddie threw open the two windows while Vanessa reached into the refrigerator for the pitcher of iced tea.

"Are you hungry?" Vanessa asked, pouring iced tea into glasses.

"Only for you," he murmured, but he accepted a glass of iced tea.

"Maybe you won't be sent overseas," she said tentatively.

"I hope I'll be shipped out right after basic training," he told her. "I hate Fascism, Vanessa. Italy won't be free until Mussolini's defeated. That might not be so far off—the war's not going well for him."

His eyes darkening in anticipation, he took the glass from Vanessa's hand and set it with his own on the table between the twin beds that masqueraded as studio couches.

"I never thought I could love anybody the way I love you," he whispered, pulling her into his arms.

She closed her eyes when his mouth found hers, her heart pounding. It wasn't wrong for them to make love, she told herself. Eddie was going off to fight in the war. They had no way of knowing when they would see each other after this weekend. Let Eddie go off to fight knowing she loved him. Let him know she would be waiting for him. When the ugliness was over, he'd come home to her. They'd be married.

They clung together in the soft lamplight. His mouth on hers, his tongue gently prodding past her lips into the soft warmth of her mouth. One hand tugged at her blouse, pulled it open, and moved beneath to the high, firm thrust of her breasts. Her slender hands tightened at his shoulders.

Eddie reached with one hand to push aside the coverlet of the bed, then with infinite tenderness slowly helped her out of her blouse. His mouth moved again to hers as he unhooked her bra. Vanessa felt a surge of exquisite pleasure as his hands fondled her breasts and then moved to unzip her skirt.

"I knew you'd be beautiful," he whispered when she stood before him in ivory nudity. Only then did he reach to switch off the lamp.

She sat at the edge of the bed, waiting for the touch of his hands, his mouth, while Eddie stripped in the darkness. He sat beside her and drew her close. Kissing her throat, the hollow between her breasts, his hands moved about her hips, her thighs. He lifted her onto the bed, lowered himself above her.

"I love you so much, Eddie." She felt such gladness as she welcomed him within her.

"Oh, God, Vanessa, how am I going to leave you?" he cried out as they clung together in satisfaction.

"Don't think about that now," she whispered. "Just hold me, Eddie. Hold me tight."

When Tina and Cliff did not appear at the apartment by noon the next day, Vanessa understood she and Eddie would have these last twenty-four hours before Eddie must report to his induction center for themselves. They dressed and went downstairs for breakfast at Walgreen's, then walked along the river hand in hand while Eddie talked about his family, their family when she and Eddie were married. He talked about the history of Italian Jewry.

"When the Jews were expelled from Spain in 1492, the Jews in Sicily and Sardinia were affected, too, because they were under Spanish rule. That's when my family left Sicily to move to Italy."

"When Americans think about ghettos and pogroms," Vanessa said softly, "we think about Russia and Poland and Germany."

"The Catholic church was nervous over the Reformation," Eddie explained while they lingered at the railing along the Hudson River. "Christianity was being divided into two camps—Catholic and Protestant. The Catholics wrongly blamed the Jews for the split. In 1555 Pope Paul IV moved the Jews into ghettos. They stayed there until the nineteenth century. But Italian Jews had been convinced—until Mussolini proved them wrong—that those days were gone forever."

"I suppose we have to fight this war," Vanessa said, her head at his shoulder. "But why do these things happen?"

They stood and watched the river in silence until Eddie burst out in a sudden flash of inspiration, "You know what we're going to do today? We're going to take a boat ride up to Bear Mountain."

"Where's Bear Mountain?" All Tina and she knew of New York was what was available by way of the subway system.

"Up the Hudson River. Let's go buy a *News* or *Mirror*—they'll have today's schedule." He dropped an arm around her waist and directed her toward a path that led away from the river. "The boat trip takes about three hours. It'll be cool on the river. We'll eat at Bear Mountain Inn. Not in the cafeteria," he said with a brilliant smile. "In the upstairs dining room."

Determined to make this last day memorable, they hurried to Broadway to buy a Sunday *News*, found the schedule for the Hudson River Day Line, and rushed to the pier at the foot of West Forty-second Street to make the next departure. Onboard the boat they stood at the railing, arm in arm, for the ride up the Hudson.

Eddie talked compulsively about his years in New York—his loneliness despite the efforts of his warm and affectionate grandmother, the horrendous final eight months of her life, when she fretted over the way her savings were being swallowed up by her hospitalization costs. Italy was at war, and there could be no money from home for his education.

"In all her pain she thought only about whether she would leave enough to see me through school," Eddie said tenderly. "It was tight, but I made it."

"The war won't last much longer," Vanessa declared with brave conviction. "We're pushing ahead in the

South Pacific. We've chased the Germans and Italians out of North Africa."

They enjoyed a very late lunch in the charming dining room at Bear Mountain Inn, and strolled along the paths through the park, pausing to embrace beside brooks and lakes. They were determined to wrest as much happiness as possible out of their last day together. It was a day that would have been blessedly tranquil but for the fact that every moment was weighted by thoughts of Eddie's destination early tomorrow morning.

On the return trip they discovered a quiet corner on deck where they could sit together in silence and watch the setting sun.

"We'll go up to Zabar's and shop for dinner," Eddie decided. And afterward they'd make love, his eyes told her.

Back at the apartment Vanessa brought out a bottle of red wine while Eddie got the plates and transferred food from paper containers. The room was quiet with the knowledge that once dinner was done they would lie in each other's arms for the rest of the night.

Vanessa awoke to the sound of the alarm with a startled sense of falling through space. Eddie's arm lay across her breasts, his leg thrown across her thigh.

"Eddie," she said softly and reached across him to silence the alarm. He was frowning, reluctant to abandon sleep. "Eddie." All at once her heart was pounding. In just a little while Eddie would walk out that door, and she didn't know when he'd come through it again.

"I'm awake." He opened his eyes and managed a weak smile. "Not happy about it, but awake."

"I'll get up and make breakfast."

"Not yet," he insisted and reached out to caress her

cheek.

They moved together with an urgency that was terrifying and exhilarating all at once, each caught up in the need to merge into one. They abandoned themselves totally to feeling. And suddenly it was over, and Eddie was pulling away to sit for an instant at the edge of the bed.

"Stay there," he said gently. "I want to go away with the memory of you like this. Radiant and sweet and beautiful."

Six

Evenings and weekends without Eddie were agonizingly empty for Vanessa. The war became an intensely personal affair. The air-raid fighting equipment — buckets of sand, shovels, and other paraphernalia — that adorned every New York apartment entrance was an ominous daily reminder that Eddie might soon be caught in air raids in England or Sicily or Italy. In August Sicily had been invaded and conquered — at the cost of twenty-five thousand Allied soldiers. On September 3 the Italian mainland was invaded by the Allies, but war correspondents spread the word that the Nazis would continue to fight Allied advances into Italy. Vanessa clung to the radio, praying for a report of some miraculous end to hostilities. *Let the war be over before Eddie is shipped overseas.*

Tina and Cliff tried to involve Vanessa in their activities, but she understood their need to be alone. Cliff's draft status had been changed to 1-A. Each day he woke with the conviction that this would be the day he would be called up for military duty. He made a lot of cracks about room and board, clothes, and "twenty-one bucks" a month — but he dreaded going into the service. Vanessa knew not to worry when Tina stayed away overnight. She was with Cliff.

Vanessa was grateful that her job took all her time.

Three girls in the office were leaving for defense jobs that paid higher salaries, and replacements were difficult to find under current conditions. Most days now she ate lunch at her desk, where a snapshot of Eddie sat in a Woolworth frame. Part of her lunch hour she devoted to writing to Eddie, and at night she reread his last two or three letters before going to bed. He was convinced he would be shipped out as soon as he was through basic training.

"The way the war is going, every man possible will be sent overseas. To my way of thinking, the sooner the better. Fighting in Europe I'll feel closer to coming home to you."

Like most people in America Vanessa became addicted to the radio, eager to hear the latest war bulletins. She and Tina went frequently to the movies, where the main attraction was the newsreel.

One Wednesday in mid-September, just as she was about to leave for the day, Vanessa was summoned into the office of one of the partners. She was delighted to hear that her salary was being increased by ten dollars a week. She had hoped for five.

En route to the apartment from the bus she detoured to the bakery to pick up chocolate eclairs to celebrate. Thirty-five dollars a week sounded like an enormous sum. Of course, she thought with wry humor, she was earning every cent of it. She paused at the mailbox. Nothing there. Tina was probably home already.

Halfway up the first flight of narrow, dark stairs Vanessa saw Mrs. Madigan, the middle-aged housewife who lived on their floor in the larger apartment at the front.

"Oh, you girls." Mrs. Madigan chuckled archly, waiting on the landing above. "Always rushing. The war hasn't put a crimp in your social lives."

"It has," Vanessa contradicted. She smiled but her eyes were grave.

"Oh, honey, I keep meaning to tell you." Mrs. Madigan lowered her voice to a semblance of confidentiality. "If you're having trouble with the damn rationing, Tim has this contact where we can get sugar and coffee and even stockings. Of course, it comes high — but at least we can get it." She patted Vanessa on the shoulder. "You need something, you just knock on our door."

"Thank you, Mrs. Madigan." Vanessa masked her anger, and slipped into her apartment, shutting the door firmly behind her.

Tina was properly impressed by Vanessa's raise, and snitched a bite of an eclair before she slid them into the refrigerator.

"If Cliff doesn't show, we'll split the third," Tina declared conspiratorially.

"Why won't he show?" Vanessa kicked off her shoes. It was routine for the three of them to have dinner together here in the apartment.

"He called this morning. He sounded kind of funny. We couldn't talk because it was busy at the office. You know how my boss has a fit about personal calls." Tina paused before the open refrigerator, pulled out a package of hamburger, and contemplated the other contents. "I'll make the salad. Don't you feel rich with that extra ten dollars a week?"

"Half will go to Mother," Vanessa reminded her. She felt guilty that she wished this could go instead into the bank toward tuition for design classes.

"Vanessa Conrad, you're nuts." Tina stared at her in frustration. "Your mother never answers your letters. She never even writes to thank you for the presents you send — which you can't afford." Tina's voice crackled with contempt. "Keep your raise."

"I can't." Vanessa sought for words to explain. How could she make Tina understand that she needed to feel that Mother was still part of her life? "I have to do it for

72

Daddy," she rationalized finally. But sometimes even Daddy had been impatient with Mother.

Both girls started at the sharp rap on the door. Cliff normally utilized what he called his "signature": two light taps, one brisk knock. Tina pulled the door open. Cliff stood there with an insouciant smile and a bunch of yellow chrysanthemums in one hand.

"Guess what?" he said. "I've been drafted."

Dusk was settling about Manhattan when Tina and Cliff left the Broadway bus to head for his room. They walked with his arm about her waist, hips brushing. Cliff's earlier ebullience had evaporated. The threat that had hung over his head for two years had become a reality. The need for men in the armed forces was desperate enough to overlook his nearsightedness and a trick knee acquired in college football.

"Maybe you'll land in a special services unit," Tina offered as they turned off Broadway onto 106th Street. "You could be acting in one of those companies playing for servicemen."

"I was keeping it as a surprise," Cliff said wryly, relinquishing her waist to reach for his keys. "I've had three readings for the new Jed Harris play. It's practically certain I'm set for a small part plus understudying the lead."

"Oh, Cliff." Tina's voice was rich with sympathy. "What bitchy timing." She managed a brilliant smile. "You see, your luck's finally turning. When the war's over, you'll come back and walk into something sensational."

"That's right." He unlocked the door, slapped her on the rump, and pushed her inside. "Nobody's going to stop the two of us. Isn't that what we always say? In five years I'll be the hottest star on Broadway, and you'll be wowing them in pictures. Hey, we've got what it takes to make it big."

Arm in arm they hurried up the dimly lighted stairs to Cliff's furnished room. Tina tried to analyze her feelings. She wasn't in love with Cliff, but he was fun to be with and in bed he was sensational. She'd miss him like hell.

Without Cliff around she'd be another of those hordes of girls who roamed about the city—in twos and threes or more—looking for whatever entertainment they could find. She thought of the lonely girls she saw in lines at the movie houses, lingering in the cafeterias and at the soda founts, strolling around the city. Trying to pretend this was a normal world—but all with that same lost look in their eyes because almost every man between eighteen and thirty-six was part of the armed services.

It was worse, Tina thought with sudden clarity, for those girls who didn't have a guy in uniform—either at some camp here at home or fighting in Europe. They looked at the casualty figures and were scared there would never be anyone for them. For her, Tina conceded in silent honesty, men came second. Making it big in pictures came first.

"Baby, you're quiet tonight," Cliff admonished while he opened the door to the small bedroom he used to share with Eddie. "Be festive. Enjoy tonight. I'm giving up the room tomorrow."

"You're being inducted tomorrow?" Tina was shaken.

"I'm going home tomorrow," he explained. "To spend a few days with the family before I report for induction."

"Then tonight has to be special." If she enlisted in the WACS or the WAVES, would Pop welcome her home to say good-bye? That would probably make him

74

happy. He could have another gold star in the window.

"Every night with you is special," Cliff drawled, turning on a lamp and closing the door behind him. "You're terrific."

Without preliminaries he began to peel away his clothes. Tina followed his lead, undressing with seductive slowness. She knew that the sight of her taking off her clothes excited him. Thank God, he never pulled any sentimental slush with her. They drove each other up the wall in bed, but neither made any pretense that this was anything deeper than great sex.

"I'll think about you when I'm in boot camp," he said, pulling her close. "I'll think about you over in North Africa or England or the Pacific or wherever they ship me." His hands were fondling her breasts while he thrust against her firm, flat belly. "And you'll remember tonight," he promised. He never stopped teasing her about the first guy she'd "gone all the way" with.

"Bragging again," she clucked, her hands at his shoulders while his mouth burrowed at her breast and his hand caressed her velvet thighs. Already she wanted him in her.

"Let's get this show on the road."

He straightened up and prodded her toward the bed, pausing to flip on the radio. Cliff had a thing about having music while they made love. That way, he said, people in the next room didn't hear them. He kidded her about being noisy in bed, but he liked it.

While the sounds of "That Old Black Magic" poured into the room, Cliff hovered over her. She lay expectant, eyes half closed, legs flexed.

"Maybe you'll join some USO company and we'll have a wild reunion," Cliff considered while his hands rippled over her.

"Not me," Tina said. "That's not the road to Hollywood."

She closed her eyes tightly, abandoning herself to feeling. The music, Cliff's hands, their shared passion — all built a driving impatience within her.

"Relax," Cliff ordered. "We've got the whole night ahead of us."

"I don't want to relax," she scolded.

"Easy, baby." He lowered his mouth to her navel, allowed his tongue to brush seductively while his hand teased between her thighs.

"Cliff, stop playing games." She reached out to find him, her blood racing.

"This is a game you'll love," he cajoled. "A variation of our usual theme."

All at once she capitulated. Let Cliff lead. This was their last night together — let him make it great.

His hand lingered between her thighs, insinuating and promising, while his mouth blazed a trail of moist kisses down her pelvis. And then his mouth found her. A soft sound of pleasure escaped her as his tongue probed. Her fingers twined themselves in his hair.

"Cliff," she whispered urgently. "Don't drive me out of my mind."

And then he was lifting himself above her. His mouth, pungent with the scent of her, closed in on hers. While his tongue filled the hot softness of her mouth, he moved between her thighs with an intensity she matched with each stroke. Their bodies moved together, fighting to meet. Wherever she could receive him, Cliff was there.

"Ssh!" Cliff cautioned when she cried out in ecstatic climax. But a moment later his own voice blended with her own.

They lay together limp and exhausted without moving. Her hair was damp at the temples, his breath hot on her neck.

"Oh, God, that was sensational." He brought a hand

to touch her breast. She knew that in a few moments he would begin to stir again within her.

"I'll call in sick tomorrow," she said, her hands tightening at his shoulders. "Tonight I'm doing my patriotic duty for a member of the armed forces."

On a wintry Saturday morning in November, several weeks after Cliff left for boot camp, Vanessa awoke to the sound of an impatient knock on the apartment door. Still groggy with sleep, she left the comfort of the blankets and groped for her robe. The knock was repeated.

"Coming!" In cold bare feet — tying the sash of her robe at her waist — she crossed to the door and pulled it open. She peered into the hall and her face was transformed, incandescent. "Eddie! Oh, Eddie!" She threw herself into his arms and lifted her mouth to his.

"You have a weekend pass?" Tina called from beneath a comforting mound of blankets while Eddie closed the door behind him.

"I have to be back at camp before reveille," he said, his eyes fastened to Vanessa. "I have to take a train from Penn Station at nine-forty tonight."

"I've never seen you in uniform," Vanessa said softly. "Except for those blurred snapshots you sent from camp." All at once her heart was pounding. "Eddie, why don't you have a weekend pass?"

"We're on alert. We'll be shipping out somewhere in the next three or four days," he explained, gripping her arms tightly. "There was talk about my going down to Fort Benning to OCS, but then they decided I can be useful in a special division shipping out now."

"I'll put up coffee and make one of my crazy omelets." Tina threw aside the blankets, shoulders tensed against the cold. "Keep your coat on, Eddie, until the oven

77

warms the place up a little."

Enveloped in a bulky flannel robe Tina busied herself at the gas stove, the oven lit and the door wide to emit heat into the dank chill of the room. Eddie cradled Vanessa in his arms. Though Eddie had been told nothing regarding his destination, Vanessa was sure he would be heading for Europe, to fight somewhere in Italy. On October 13 Italy had become a "co-belligerent" and had declared war on Germany. But the Allied drive—with most Italian soldiers disarmed by the Germans—was a painful, slow struggle. According to the news reports, the Allies were about seventy-five miles south of Rome, battling floods, mud, mountains, and winter cold as well as a German army of 400,000. Vanessa was afraid for Eddie.

After breakfast Tina made up her bed, returned it to its studio-couch dress, and disappeared into the bathroom to dress. Ten minutes later she emerged, extricated her mouton lamb—for which she still owed her boss twenty-eight dollars—from the overloaded closet, and crossed to kiss Eddie good-bye.

"Take care of yourself." She hugged him tenderly. "I look awful in black."

Vanessa and Eddie made slow, passionate love, drank coffee and talked, made love again. She had known that Eddie would be shipped out soon; but now that the time had arrived, she was terrified.

Her eyes kept seeking the clock on the end table. The hours were racing past. She didn't want to think of Eddie on a troopship on the blacked-out Atlantic. *Eddie fighting on the front lines.*

With WQXR playing the classical music Eddie loved, Vanessa lay in his arms and tried to gird herself for his departure.

"I'm going with you to the train," Vanessa decided when the clock warned her Eddie must leave shortly.

78

She moved to rise from the bed.

"You can't wander around New York alone at night," he reproached. His hand drew her back.

"Eddie, girls go about the city at all hours these days." She managed a shaky laugh. "So many of them work crazy shifts. I'll get dressed."

"In a few minutes," he promised, and drew her beneath the blankets again. "We'll take a taxi."

Seven

Four days after Vanessa said good-bye to Eddie at the gate in Penn Station, she received an official postcard with his APO address. Then for weeks there was nothing until she received a tiny folded-over scrap of paper — V-mail, the pipeline between American GI's and their loved ones. Though censorship demanded discretion, Eddie was able to convey via prearranged code that he was in Italy. Italy, a country cut in two, with southern Italy in the hands of the Allies and central and northern Italy — Venice, where his family lived — in the hands of the Germans.

In a surge of defiance Vanessa and Tina decided to go out to a restaurant for Thanksgiving dinner. Last year they had been alone. Since then Eddie and Cliff had come into their lives. Now they were alone again. The restaurant was lightly populated and exuded an air of desolation. Thanksgiving was not a time to eat in restaurants, Tina declared, angry, as she had been last year, that her father was too bullheaded to write and ask her to come home for Thanksgiving.

Vanessa and Tina sought to fill the void in their lives. Each night Vanessa wrote a letter to Eddie. Once a month, she promised herself, she would send him a package. Salami, cheese, Hershey bars — even if she had to go to every candy store in New York to find them.

Tina's letter writing was less dedicated, though she wrote fairly regularly. She conceded that while Cliff had been fun, neither of them had looked beyond the next day. Right now Cliff was at a camp in Texas.

Tina was restless without him. "With a million soldiers, sailors, and marines pouring in and out of the city each day," Tina mourned, "we ought to be having a ball."

Tina pushed Vanessa into frequent trips to the neighborhood movie houses. They avoided the stream of war movies coming out of Hollywood and saw *Best Foot Forward* with Lucille Ball, June Allyson, and Gloria DeHaven; *I Dood It* with Red Skelton; *Lassie, Come Home* with Elizabeth Taylor; and *Madame Curie* with Greer Garson and Walter Pidgeon. Musicians in particular were their great escape.

Vanessa coaxed Tina into "window-shopping" with her through the floors of B. Altman, Lord & Taylor, Saks Fifth Avenue, and the other Fifth Avenue department stores, though neither could afford to do more than look. Vanessa was intrigued by the clothes designed by Claire McCardell and impressed that they were featured in elegant Lord & Taylor as "Claire McCardell Clothes by Townley."

Vanessa had been enthralled by the establishment of the Coty American Fashion Critics Award, to be given each year to the designer who had contributed most to fashion during the preceding year. When a national jury of newspaper and magazine fashion editors chose to present the first award—in 1943—to Norman Norell, Vanessa pored over fashion magazines to study his clothes. Her driving ambition surfaced again. She needed to be completely absorbed in fashion to distract her from anxiety about Eddie.

Shortly after New Year's Vanessa arrived home to discover that the Madigans had moved out and that two girls were moving into the one-bedroom apartment Tina and she had coveted but could not afford. They were busy transporting a collection of Louis Vuitton luggage from the hall into the small living room. A sheared beaver coat was draped carelessly over one valise, a black Alaska seal over another. Both were tall, long-limbed, blond, and pretty. And expensively dressed, Vanessa noted with respect — low-key classic cashmere pullovers with simple skirts that had probably cost a small fortune at Saks or Bergdorf's. Vanessa recognized their shoes were by Ferragamo — the world's most famous shoemaker.

"Hi." One of the girls greeted Vanessa with an ebullient smile. "I'm Tracy Arnold. This is my roommate, Pat Owens." Her voice was velvet soft with a southern accent.

"I'm Vanessa Conrad," Vanessa said. "My roommate — Tina Gregory — and I live there." She pointed to the door of the studio at the rear.

"The phone company says we can't get a phone," Pat said. She seemed reserved, almost shy. "Did you have trouble getting one?"

"We don't have one." No need to say they couldn't afford this minor luxury. "Everybody says it's impossible because of the war."

"Honey, your mother will just have to call you on the phone down the hall," Tracy teased Pat. "We're not living in Houston now. We're in New York. And Jesse knows to come here instead of the club." She turned back to Vanessa. "Jesse Franklin is Pat's boyfriend. He's stationed out at Fort Dix. We couldn't bear living in that awful girls' residence hall another week. Most of the 'girls' have been living there fifty years."

"Only some of them," Pat rebuked. "They were sweet — they just lived in another century."

"Can you imagine a girls' club these days where you couldn't even bring a boyfriend up to your room?" Tracy shuddered. "You have to kiss a boy good night out on the sidewalk unless you want all those old bats glaring at you."

"Your mother won't be any happier about this than mine," Pat warned.

"They won't stop sending the checks," Tracy shrugged.

"Pat's studying drama and I'm going to modeling school," Tracy rattled on. "Why don't you and your roommate come in and have dinner with us? We'll bring up some stuff from the deli and have a picnic."

"I don't think Tina is home yet." No sounds emerged from the apartment.

"When she comes home," Tracy insisted. "We're giving a housewarming party," she bubbled, and Vanessa relaxed. She had been anxious about the cost of bringing up "some stuff from the deli." She knew that Tracy Arnold and Pat Owens would shop without looking at prices.

"It sounds like fun," said Vanessa. She was glad the two girls were moving into the house. Tina and she had few friends in New York. The girls at their offices were all much older than themselves and involved in their own lives. "Tina should be home sometime in the next ten or twenty minutes."

"Great. Pat, let's go shop. Knock when your friend gets home," Tracy called back. "If we're not back yet, try in another five minutes."

Why were two rich girls from Houston, Texas, moving into a cheap Upper West Side rooming house? Vanessa asked herself while she let herself into her apartment. Maybe they thought it would be fun to

83

"rough it," she decided with a touch of humor. Tina's eyes would pop when she saw that gorgeous sheared beaver and the Alaska seal.

Over a lush assortment of cold cuts washed down with white wine, Pat and Tracy—both nineteen— reported that they had been in New York since the end of August. Pat's father was a longtime congressman from Texas. Tracy's father was "in oil."

"Daddy made a lot of money because he was so stubborn he kept drilling all those wells Mother inherited, even though everybody said they were dry," Tracy confided with the air of having heard this repeated often. "Then one day, before I was born, those darn wells came in like Niagara Falls, and they haven't stopped yet."

Pat and Tracy had graduated from a posh boarding school the same year Vanessa and Tina had graduated high school. Vanessa and Tina told the other two girls about arriving from Pinewood and finding jobs in the city. Vanessa talked about plans to study clothes design in the future—but Tina was closed-mouthed about her own ambitions. Both Vanessa and Tina were slightly self-conscious in the presence of all this Texas affluence.

"We refused to go to college," Tracy giggled. "Our mothers hinted at Radcliffe or Vassar, but we'd had all we could take of girls' schools."

"Have you ever been to a parochial school?" Pat's smile was wry.

"Not me." Tina laughed and Vanessa shook her head.

"Those awful uniforms," Tracy moaned.

"Tracy, our dress regulations were the mildest ever," Pat reproached. "Of course, you were always in trouble with your crazy nail polish and the weird jewelry."

"You know, I was a junior before I realized ejaculation meant something besides 'Forgive me, for I have sinned,'" Tracy confided while Pat frowned in discomfort. "All the nuns taught us about sex was that our bodies were temples of the Holy Ghost."

"You'd have learned more in a coed high school," Tina assured her, her eyes alight with laughter.

"What was the point in trying for a coed college," Tracy shrugged, "when all the boys are gone from the campuses? Anyhow"—Tracy reached for another helping of potato salad—"I'm engaged to this boy from back home. He's out in the Pacific somewhere." She smiled dreamily. "I write Tommy every night. And then I go to bed and wish to hell he was under the covers with me. I mean, I get so *hot* sometimes."

"Tracy!" Pat was embarrassed.

"I know," Tracy mocked. "It's a sin if you just *think* about it." She turned back to Vanessa and Tina. "Then I came up with this idea about Pat and me studying drama in New York. I switched to modeling because Daddy thinks all actresses are immoral."

"Our folks were scared to death to let us come here unless we agreed to live at the residence club."

"What were they scared about?" Tina's eyebrows rose in astonishment.

"You know." Tracy gestured vaguely. "New York's a dangerous city. You're always reading about some girl being raped or murdered by some colored guy."

"Bullshit!" Tina said. "Girls in New York go anywhere they like, any time of night. And how many get raped or murdered? No more than in Texas or Georgia or California. And it could just as well be a white guy as a colored one who does the raping or killing." She laughed at their looks of consternation. "Stop believing those headlines in the *Mirror* and the *News*. You are not going to get raped or murdered."

"Have you seen that beautiful Negro boy who lives

85

two floors down?" Vanessa asked. "I think he's a dancer."

Tracy exchanged a long look with Pat.

"Mother would just die if she knew we lived in a house with coloreds."

"If it's going to bother her, don't tell her," Tina shrugged. "She'll find out soon enough that you've left that convent."

"We'll have to phone home," Pat said, nervous at the prospect. "Daddy's going to hit the roof. Actually my parents let me come here to study as a kind of consolation prize. For refusing to let me marry Jesse before he went into the army. They think Jesse broke up with me because I couldn't marry him." Her eyes — an astonishing electric blue — warmed with laughter. "They never guessed the big attraction in New York is that Fort Dix — where Jesse's stationed — is so close."

"Why did you let your folks keep you from marrying?" Tina asked.

"I didn't want to cut myself off from my family forever." It was a wistful admission. "Jesse and I figured we'd wait a while until they accept him. Once the war is over they'll get to know him."

"Darling little Pat won't do anything to make Mommy and Daddy unhappy," Tracy teased. "I'd have married Tommy before he shipped out, even though my mother would have had kittens; but we talked about it and decided it wasn't smart. I'll wait until Tommy comes home." For a moment her face lost its glow. "Tommy's folks are 'old Texas,' but they haven't got much money. Once we get married, Daddy can bring Tommy into the business and buy us a house and all."

"Jesse understands." Pat tried to smile. "We'll wait for each other."

"Jesse's a mechanic Pat met last spring when he fixed her Caddy," Tracy explained. "A few weeks after they met he was drafted." Vanessa understood; Pat's con-

86

gressman father would not welcome a mechanic for a son-in-law.

"He says Fort Dix looks like a permanent assignment." Pat crossed herself hopefully. "Most weekends he gets into New York on a twenty-four-hour pass."

"He couldn't stand that girls' club." Tracy's expression was eloquent. "That's how I persuaded Pat to move."

"Do you miss Texas?" Tina asked Pat. "Or do you live in Washington?" Vanessa knew Tina was awed by living across the hall from a congressman's daughter.

"Up until last year we circulated between the house in River Oaks — that's just outside Houston — and the plantation in Culpepper County, Virginia, about eighty or so miles from Washington," Pat explained. "Mother hates Washington, but of course Daddy has to be there. He keeps an apartment at the Shoreham Hotel, and he used to commute to the plantation for long weekends. But with the gas rationing he can't get down there often, so now Mother spends most of her time in Houston. My sister, Maureen — she's eleven years older than me — is Daddy's hostess in Washington." Pat reflected for a moment. "Sometimes I do miss Houston."

"I don't miss Texas," Tracy said flatly. "Mother bitching all the time about how hard it is to keep servants. Bitching about ration books and not being able to go to Paris to shop for clothes. Not that she's home that much. Houston is beastly hot and humid in the summer, so she's off to Bar Harbor for July and August. In January she heads for Palm Beach. In the spring she takes off for Hot Springs and the Homestead. It's a miracle Daddy and she got together often enough to have four daughters."

"She wasn't there last spring," Pat said. "Neither was my mother. The government took it over as an internment center for the Japanese diplomats."

"They both went in the summer," Tracy recalled, "when the Japanese were sent somewhere else. God, how did Mother survive without her Swedish massage machines and the hydrotherapy and the whirlpool baths?"

"Actually," Pat picked up with an apologetic smile, "Houston is a very special city. Especially now when it's booming the way it is. So many beautfiul estates are going up. And we have the Houston Symphony and the Houston Art Museum and the Houston Stock Show and—"

"And Sakowitz's," Tracy exclaimed. "The greatest women's shop anywhere in this country. Daddy says he might be better off if he just tried to buy it for us." Her face glowed with sudden nostalgia. "Okay, sometimes I miss Houston," she confessed.

"I don't miss Pinewood," Tina said. "I couldn't wait to get away."

The four girls spent many evenings together. Over the weekends they became a trio, with Pat off seeing Jesse.

"That Jesse is Texas's answer to Vic Mature," Tina drawled. "And boy, does he know it!"

"I don't like him," Vanessa confessed. How could somebody like Pat be so wild about him?

"He looks at every girl as though he can't wait to jump her," Tina said. "And I'll bet he'd think he was doing her a favor."

Vanessa was astonished when Pat and Tracy acquired a telephone.

"Vanessa, grow up," Tina clucked. "The congressman made a few calls, and the girls got their phone."

Tina was frankly fascinated with these two young Texas heiresses. That Pat was attending a prestigious drama school without any real aspirations to be an actress also intrigued her.

"Jesus Christ, Vanessa, they don't ever worry about paying the rent or having enough money at the end of the week for lunches and carfare. Buying a new coat or a pair of shoes isn't a crisis for either of them. With their kind of money I could take myself out to Hollywood and make a real splash." Tina's face was incandescent—for a moment. "You could go to Parsons or Traphagen or even to Paris to study. They're only living in a place like this because they think it's fun."

Vanessa adored shopping with Pat and Tracy in the fine Fifth Avenue department stores where they had charge accounts. It delighted her when Pat and Tracy consulted her before making choices. In a flurry of pleasure she would dart about in search of some especially smart dress or blouse or coat and bring it to their attention. Tina made a point of not accompanying them on these sprees.

"I know," Tina drawled while Vanessa rushed through breakfast on a brisk early April Saturday morning to accompany the two Texans on a trip to Saks. "You love looking at all those gorgeous clothes. But I turn green because I can't afford them."

"Someday you will," Vanessa said comfortingly. "We both will."

"I am so tired of not getting anywhere! I didn't think I'd be stuck in this silly job. Vanessa, in less than three months we'll have been in New York for two years!"

"These are crazy times," Vanessa reminded her. But she was also overwhelmed by frustration. She was no closer to becoming a designer than on the day they'd arrived.

"Maybe I ought to look for a part-time job and make the rounds the rest of the time," Tina considered. "But I'm not the Broadway type," she wailed before Vanessa could reply. "I don't want to be a stage actress. I want to be in pictures. All I need is that first little break."

Early in May Pat was devastated when Jesse's "permanent assignment" at Fort Dix came to an end. He was put on alert, bound for service overseas. He spent his final leave with Pat in her apartment while Tracy slept on an improvised bed of blankets in Vanessa and Tina's apartment. Shortly after Jesse's departure, Pat received the official postcard with his APO address. Jesse was somewhere in Europe.

With their school year drawing to an end, Pat and Tracy connived to persuade their parents to allow them to rent a cottage on Fire Island for July and August. Pat was restless, anxious about Jesse. Both girls had rejected spending the summer with their parents at Bar Harbor.

"We're too old for that!" Tracy declared. "And it's so gauche. We will have to go home for two weeks," Tracy told Vanessa and Tina with a touch of martyrdom. "You know, sort of touch base with our families. And promise we won't get so tan people won't know if we're white or colored," she drawled. "My mother never goes out in the sun without a hat and gloves. She means to protect her precious white skin until the day she dies."

"You think they'll really let us stay another year in New York?" Pat asked Tracy. Her face was troubled. She had vowed to stay in New York until Jesse returned from the war.

"We'll handle our folks." Tracy was optimistic. "After all, we've both been accepted at school for a second year."

"If your parents are willing to pay, the school's not going to say no," Tina said.

"You'll come out for weekends, of course," Tracy told Vanessa and Tina. "And for your vacation." Both Tina and Tina were scheduled for a one-week paid vacation.

90

Tracy giggled self-consciously. "Maybe we can invite Brian out for some weekends." Brian was the young Naval Intelligence ensign—soon to be lieutenant J.G.—whom Tracy had met recently. He was the brother of a former classmate and stationed in New York. "It's my patriotic duty to be nice to Brian," she explained. "It's not as though I'm sleeping with him. He just takes me out to the Stork Club or the Starlight Room or to the theater. We saw *Oklahoma* and *Something for the Boys* and *The Doughgirls* and *Kiss and Tell*. I still write to Tommy every week."

"Maybe some weekends we can go out to the cottage." Vanessa yearned to go, but trains to Bay Shore and ferries to Fire Island sounded like a lot of money. She just managed to survive from check to check.

"Every weekend," Pat coaxed and laughed. "The only decent meals we'll have is when Tina comes out. You know how Tracy and I cook. Besides, you'll have to bring out my letters from Jesse."

British and American troops had made landings, back in January, at Anzio and Nettuno in Italy. From Eddie's letters, carefully written to circumvent censorship, Vanessa knew that he was with the front-line American troops pushing toward Rome.

Early in the year the Russians had broken the siege of Leningrad. German troops had swept into Hungary. In the Pacific the Allies were making important advances, with all the Marshall Islands under Allied control. On April 22 Netherlands New Guinea had been invaded. And on June 6—D-Day—the Allies landed on the beach at Normandy.

In mid-June Pat and Tracy flew home to Houston for brief family reunions.

"Isn't it sensational that we can fly direct to Houston

in only eleven and a half hours?" Tracy bubbled to Vanessa as she and Pat prepared to leave for the airport. "We can spend a week at home and still get back in time to open the cottage on July first."

At Tracy's prodding Vanessa and Tina had arranged to take off the Monday prior to July Fourth. Vanessa had received another five-dollar-a-week raise because of the extra responsibilities she had taken on — and the extra hours she spent regularly at the office. And this time she heeded Tina's admonition not to share it with her mother. The extra money would make it possible for her to handle the transportation costs to and from Fire Island.

"Wow!" Tina gloated while she and Vanessa tried on bathing suits in the bedlam of the S. Klein dressing rooms the Thursday before their big weekend. "We'll have four whole days out at the beach!" She inspected herself in the dressing room mirror. "How does this suit look?"

"Sensational," Vanessa said.

"Try on bathing suits over your panties!" a loud feminine voice called out from the entrance as a would-be purchaser prepared to strip. "Can'tcha read the signs?"

"Linda, this suit don't do nothin' for me," a grossly overweight young girl across the aisle complained. "Let's go out and get some more."

"I wish I'd learned to swim," Vanessa whispered. Her mother had never allowed her to swim, skate, or ride a bike. She might get hurt, and that would be upsetting to her mother.

"I dog-paddle," Tina said with a shrug. During hot weather in Pinewood Tina and Vanessa had visited a local pond perhaps two or three times a summer. "How much swimming will we do out there? You lie on the beach and soak up the sun." Her face grew luminous.

"And maybe you meet somebody out there who'll look at me and say, 'Hey, you oughta be in pictures.' It sure won't ever happen out at Coney Island or Brighton Beach. At Ocean Beach it could happen. Pat says a lot of actors hang out there."

"Tina, don't tell yourself fairy tales," Vanessa scolded.

"But it'll be fun." They'd be moving into a different world, she thought with anticipation.

"You know, with your looks you ought to have a chance in pictures, too."

"Tina, sssh." Vanessa was embarrassed because the middle-aged woman struggling into a girdle in the next open-doored alcove was nodding vigorously. "Let's get dressed and into that line or we'll be here all night." Half the women of New York were at Klein's in pursuit of a bathing suit for the July Fourth weekend.

Friday night Pat and Tracy arrived at their apartment fresh from Houston, their suitcases bulging.

"First we shopped like mad at Sakowitz's. Then we went visiting cousins up in Dallas," Pat explained. "We both have family up there. I think Tracy arranged it so we could go berserk in Neiman-Marcus."

"Honey, they've got such gorgeous things. And Mother just adores shopping there. Even though she feels a little bit guilty because we do have Sakowitz in Houston, and everybody in the whole South knows it's a great store." Tracy turned back to Vanessa and Tina. "Come over and have dinner with us. We had the taxi driver take us up to Zabar's first." In New York the two Texan expatriates had become addicted to lox, sturgeon, whitefish, and bagels.

Over a festive meal that included a strawberry short-cake—acquired when Tracy ordered the taxi to stop at Tiptoe Inn—the four girls talked avidly about the cottage at Ocean Beach.

"You don't need to take enough clothes for a summer

in Europe," Tina reminded them. "You'll live in bathing suits."

"Would you believe that I picked up seven pounds while we were back home?" Tracy moaned. "And I bought all those shorts at Bonwit just before I left." She squinted appraisingly at Vanessa. "They'll fit you, Vanessa," she decided in triumph. "I'll go dig them out."

Vanessa battled with her pride. She shouldn't be embarrassed—Tracy wasn't treating her like a poor relation. She just had those gorgeous shorts, and she didn't want them to go to waste.

"I wish they'd fit me," Tina laughed. "Vanessa and you have disgustingly skinny hips."

"I *did*," Tracy corrected, digging into the armoire she and Pat had bought to handle the overflow from their wardrobes. "Lindy's cheesecake plus two weeks back home have ruined me for the next six months."

Vanessa sat with a half dozen pair of expensive shorts in her lap while they discussed their plans for the morning. Her fingers stroked the fine material of the shorts from Bonwit while her eyes admired the fine tailoring. Someday she would be out of that dull law office. Someday she would be designing exciting clothes for women who could afford the very best.

Eight

Vanessa was momentarily unnerved by the hordes surging about the Long Island Railroad Station even before 8:00 A.M. Groups of girls in a festive mood, families with small children, here and there pairs of young men, a few couples wrapped up in each other, a sprinkling of servicemen—all bustled in the early morning rush. All of New York seemed determined to escape the steamy city for this first long summer weekend.

The four girls huddled together, trying to figure out where they could buy their tickets. "This line!" Tina exclaimed and stared at her watch in comic alarm. "If we don't make this train, we'll have to wait for the ferry."

"I have a ferry schedule," Pat said reassuringly. "They run often on Saturdays."

Finally they pushed their way to the gate where the Bay Shore-bound train was arriving. Vanessa and Tina helped the other two with their piles of luggage. They moved with young energy and enthusiasm down the stairs and into the waiting train. They quickly found a pair of unoccupied seats across the aisle from each other and settled into them.

"We should have brought along bagels and coffee," Tracy sighed.

"We had breakfast," Pat reminded her. "You'll survive

till we get out to the house."

The train was filling up. All at once, Pat leaned forward to gaze in astonishment at two men who were seated a couple of rows ahead of them. She gestured to Vanessa and Tina.

"See that good-looking man two rows down?" She pointed to a tall, ruggedly handsome man with a golden tan. "The one in the aisle seat."

"He's old," Tracy shrugged. "Almost forty."

"That's Clint Ashley. A radio actor," Pat informed them. "He came to talk to a class at the school. He's been on 'Lux Radio Theater' and 'Inner Sanctum' and 'Ellery Queen.' And he has a running part on 'The Guiding Light.' "

Tina was fascinated. At the Genius Club they'd encountered actors and actresses who did bit parts on radio, walk-ons on Broadway. But Clint Ashley was an important radio actor.

"Mom listened to that program every day." Tina sat in awe for a moment. "Do you suppose he's headed for Fire Island?"

"We'll find out at the ferry," Tracy said, returning to *A Bell for Adano*, the new best seller by John Hersey.

At Bay Shore the Fire Island-bound passengers hurried from the train and out to the waiting taxis that would take them to the ferry. Boarding the ferry, Vanessa felt a pleasurable rush of anticipation, a sense of leaving the city behind her. Since Tina and she had arrived in New York two years ago, she had been no farther away than Bear Mountain.

"Hey, he's here!" Tina whispered to Vanessa.

"Who?"

"Clint Ashley." Tina cast a covert glance toward Ashley and the five younger men who constituted his entourage. "Do you suppose they're all actors?"

"A lot of show biz people come out here," Pat offered.

"But it's not built up—the beach is *never* crowded."

"At least, that's what everybody tells us," Tracy qualified.

Their luggage stashed away, the girls settled themselves at the rail of the deck for the fifty-minute crossing. Vanessa relished the scent of the sea and the soft caress of the breezes as the boat sped over the water. The sun rose high in the brilliant blue sky. Her mind darted back to the trip on the Hudson River Day Line to Bear Mountain with Eddie. He would love this, she thought, suddenly lonely. *How long before Eddie came home again?*

No cars except military vehicles were allowed on the island. Small boys with small, gaily painted wagons greeted the passengers at the ferry to carry luggage. Pat corraled a trio of them, and the four girls followed the chattering youngsters along casual paths between well-maintained cottages. The ocean sparkled all around them.

"This sure beats Coney Island!" Tina gazed about in ecstatic approval. "You can walk on the beach without stepping on bodies. And it's so quiet."

Their white, yellow-trimmed cottage faced the ocean. It was a low, sprawling four-bedroom house with a broad deck that provided beach chairs, chaises, and an umbrella table for al fresco dining.

"It's beautiful," Vanessa said, beaming her approval, when they'd gathered together in the living room. "If it's cool tonight we can make a fire." Neatly stacked piles of wood stood by in readiness.

"Let's go to the grocery store to shop." Pat rose to her feet. "If we want lunch, we'll have to cook it."

Vanessa went out to the kitchen to collect the wagon that was standard issue in every cottage, and they headed for the grocery store. The line-up of wagons out front told them the store would be crowded with shoppers.

Across the floor before a shelf of notions, Vanessa spied Clint Ashley. He'd changed into shorts and a flower-splashed sports shirt, and was surrounded by the group of similarly dressed younger men who had been with him on the ferry. Their high-spirited conversation carried across the aisle.

"All those queers coming out here now," a tall, white-haired woman in Saks Fifth Avenue slacks and blouse said loudly to her male companion, staring pointedly at Clint Ashley's crowd. Vanessa frowned. "Why can't they go to Cherry Grove or Saltaire?" the woman continued. "Anywhere but here."

Vanessa hesitated a moment, knowing the men across the floor had heard the ugly comment. Their only response was defiant gaiety. Deliberately Vanessa walked toward them, paused at the shelf of notions, and turned to the radio actor.

"I'm sorry." She smiled ingratiatingly at Clint Ashley. "Would you bring down a spool of white thread for me? I need another six inches to reach it."

"Sure thing." Ashley smiled in return. "They expect women around here to be Amazons."

"Thank you." Vanessa accepted the spool. She could always use white thread.

"Did you find what you wanted?" Tina stood beside her faintly breathless, eyeing the men.

"Got it."

"If you're not doing anything around five," Clint Ashley said to Vanessa and Tina, "why don't you drop by our place for a drink?"

"We're here with two other girls," Tina explained.

"Bring them along," Ashley said cheerfully. "We've got enough cocktail makings for an army."

Vanessa was aware of the curious glances of the other shoppers as Ashley gave them directions to his cottage and introduced himself and his friends. Probably they were thinking that she and Tina were on a manhunt and too dumb to understand these were not likely prospects, Vanessa thought in wry amusement.

Pat and Tracy had attended endless cocktail parties back in Houston, occasional parties in New York. Vanessa and Tina would have died before revealing this was their first. They closeted themselves in Vanessa's room to dress, the atmosphere electric with anticipation.

"Let's stick to one drink," Tina urged while they shared a makeup mirror. "It would be awful to fall on our faces."

"One drink," Vanessa agreed. Eddie, she remembered with nostalgia, had taught her to drink white wine. Was there a letter from Eddie waiting for her in the mailbox? For a moment she felt guilty that she was here at a house party while Eddie was fighting somewhere in Italy.

"What a waste for women that Clint's queer," Tina sighed. "He's so goodlooking."

"But you said he was old," Vanessa teased.

"No older than Cary Grant." Tina dismissed her earlier comment with a wave of her hand. She reached for her new lipstick. "Isn't it great that Dorothy Gray is putting lipstick in metal cases again?"

"I thought they couldn't use metal while the war is on."

"Dorothy Gray got an official release because this metal isn't suitable for war needs," Tina explained. "I'm wearing Evening in Paris. Why don't you wear my Mais Oui," she offered. She sighed. "One of these days I'll be able to afford perfume instead of cologne."

Shortly past five — informally attired because, as Pat

pointed out, nobody at the beach would bother dressing for cocktails — the four girls arrived at Clint Ashley's large, sprawling house. With charming deference Pat confided to Clint that she had heard him lecture at her school, and Clint nodded in pleasant recall. Tina told him of her mother's devotion to "The Guiding Light" during her last two painful years of life.

Gradually Vanessa and Tina relaxed. The men were bright and articulate, and the conversation sparkled. Four of the men were radio actors. Vanessa remembered Pat telling Tina that radio was supposed to be very cliquish — "It's so hard to break into." It seemed that the same group of actors were called in to fill every available job. The way Clint and his fellow actors tossed around the names of programs on which they'd appeared, Vanessa guessed this was true.

Phil and Robbie, who were not radio actors, talked with contagious enthusiasm about the interior decorating shop they were about to launch on Madison Avenue. Vanessa was enthralled. With them she could discuss fabrics and color and lines, the way she had with Eddie. What she missed most in her life, Vanessa realized suddenly, was the feeling of being inside the fashion world. She always felt on the outside looking in. It wasn't enough to keep filling up scrapbooks of designs. She needed to see those designs become clothes.

When the girls prepared to leave — at a discreet signal from Pat that it was time to call an end to the "cocktail hour" — they were invited to a barbecue the following afternoon.

"It'll really be a late brunch," Clint said engagingly. "Out here we sleep till two or three. Come at four," he ordered, "and prepare to admire my gourmet steaks."

"They'd better be good," his strikingly handsome young lover warned Clint fondly, "or you'll be sorry."

100

The weekend sped past, a heady experience for Vanessa and Tina. The Monday morning ferry arrived all too soon.

At the mainland they climbed into a group taxi headed for the train station. Vanessa struggled with a twinge of guilt over the expense of the weekend; but she promised herself firmly she'd watch every nickel during the week. No running into the candy store for an egg cream or a Pepsi on hot nights, no eating out once a week.

The sultry days at the office dragged. Tina was furious that Mr. Friedlich had decreed she could not take her week's vacation until mid-September, which ruled out the anticipated week on Fire Island. When Vanessa found out about Tina's situation she offered to work during her scheduled vacation in return for extra pay, for which the law firm was grateful.

Every week, each day at the offices brought them one step closer to the magical Saturday morning rush to the Long Island Railroad Station. They always carried with them the week's collection of mail for Pat and Tracy—which included almost daily communication from Brian—plus a bag of fresh-from-the-oven bagels. Devouring the latest V-mail from Jesse, Pat declared she could understand what mail call must mean to servicemen overseas.

After the first three weeks on the island Pat and Tracy adopted the habit of popping into the city for what Tracy called an "overnight." New York was sultry and uncomfortable, but Tracy was eager to sandwich in a few hours with Brian, who suspected he'd never acquire a free weekend while the war continued.

On the island it became a ritual for the four girls to go to Clint's cottage for a drink on Saturday afternoons

101

and to a "late brunch barbecue" on Sunday afternoons. They reveled in the breezy, colorful conversation, laced with inside stories about the fascinating men and women who made up the worlds of Broadway theater, radio, and the movies.

The men delighted in astonishing them with gossipy tidbits that never made their way into the fan magazines or the gossip columns. They were astonished to find that some of Hollywood and Broadway's most romantic male stars were homosexuals. In blunt detail Clint—who had spent some time doing radio on the West Coast—regaled them with stories about the heads of certain Hollywood studios.

"Wait'll you meet Del and Jim," Clint chuckled. "They both work for Imperial Films. They've got great stories about Nat Kelman." Kelman had brought Imperial up from a shoestring film company to a top position in the industry. "Nat expects every actress under contract to make herself available to him. The public sees Nat as a star maker, but most of them star in his bed first."

On Saturday nights they usually went to the tiny white clapboard movie house, where they sat among a sprinkling of stage and literary luminaries. Everyone casually ignored the presence of the celebrities.

Vanessa tried futilely to persuade Tina—normally so open and aggressive—to talk to Clint and the other three actors about her ambitions to become a movie actress. Tina had become obsessed with keeping her goals to herself—she hadn't even confided in Pat and Tracy.

"Honey, all these fellas know is radio," Tina pointed out." You need voice training and all for that. Besides, radio isn't what I want."

"They could be a contact, Tina." But Vanessa understood. Tina was counting on her sensational looks to carry her. In radio she'd be just a voice.

Phil and Robbie were running into delays opening their shop. Their investors were concerned they might be swept up into the army despite their homosexuality. Men who had been sure they would never serve on the fighting front were being called up. Tina's brother Gus had finally been drafted, despite his extreme myopia, and was in the Pacific already. The younger of her married brothers expected to be called up any day. But Phil and Robbie promised Vanessa that once their business was moving, they'd hire her as an assistant.

Already Vanessa dreaded the arrival of Labor Day, when the Fire Island weekends would cease. She loved her solitary walks along the beach on Sunday mornings while the others slept, the stretch of clean white sand deserted except for the seagulls.

She promised herself that one day she would show Eddie Fire Island. Together they would watch the sun rise over the Atlantic and stroll along the beach toward the orange-red splendor of summer sunsets. For Vanessa, these weekends were a brief escape from reality and the painful knowledge that there was no end to the war in sight and that each day Eddie's life was in danger.

In mid-August two of Clint's radio actor house-mates took off for summer stock jobs. At the usual Saturday afternoon get-together the girls were introduced to Del Miller and Jim Lanigan, their replacements for the balance of the summer.

"Jim does public relations for Imperial Films and Del's a talent scout in the New York office."

"Fun jobs," Tina commented in the low-key tone that had become her style. But inside, Tina's stomach was churning. *This was it*. From the glint of excitement in

Vanessa's eyes, she knew that Vanessa, too, was aware that this was the Big Opportunity. But Vanessa's eyes also pleaded for caution. *Don't rush. Wait for the right moment.*

Tina forced herself to be casual. She knew she would see Del at the barbecue tomorrow. She'd *die* if she screwed this up — she'd been waiting two years for this chance. She was impatient to be alone with Vanessa to talk about how best to approach Del.

On their way back to their own cottage Tina suddenly announced a detour to the grocery store.

"We don't have enough onions for the stew. The secret is to drown it in onions."

"I'll go with you," Vanessa offered. "I'll pick up a postcard to send my mother."

"So she'll think you're rolling in money? Spending weekends at Fire Island," Tina teased. "You're a masochist when it comes to your old lady." She was learning a whole new vocabulary — back in Pinewood she'd never heard the word masochist.

Once they were out of earshot of the other two girls, Tina and Vanessa erupted into avid conversation about Del and Jim.

"Imperial Films!" Tina crowed. "They're almost as important as MGM. Every time I pick up a movie magazine, Imperial's put somebody new under contract."

"Wear those white pants tomorrow." Vanessa squinted into the distance. "And tonight let me do something with your red blouse and that red-and-white polka-dot scarf. I'll have to cut it up," she warned.

"Cut it up," Tina urged, throwing her arms wide. "Vanessa, if I don't pull this one off, I'll kill myself."

"That would be a little extreme," Vanessa said. She was used to Tina's exaggerations.

Tina took a deep breath.

"I'll know when it's the right moment to talk to Del. I'll just know."

On Saturday evening the girls chattered about the summer and men while they got ready for the barbecue the next day.

"Tracy, may I borrow a little of your Tabu tomorrow afternoon?" Tina called out. Tracy had a bottle of the perfume, not just the cologne. "I forgot to bring along my Mais Oui."

"Sure thing." Tracy was adding a second coat of Chen Yu polish to her long, tapered nails.

"I know it's not as though we're having real dates." Tina mugged regret. "But the fellas like seeing us looking good. They notice."

Tracy put aside the nail polish.

"What do you suppose will happen if Brian gets a weekend pass and comes out to stay with us?" All at once Tracy seemed self-conscious.

"You won't be part of the partying at Clint's," Pat assumed. But her face betrayed her anxiety. She was thinking about Tommy, Vanessa surmised. Pat was the kind who always worried about "doing the right thing."

"It'll be awful not to see Brian all summer." Tracy was faintly defensive.

"You're getting serious about Brian?" Up till this moment Tina had figured Brian and Tracy were like Cliff and herself: together for laughs and bed. They all assumed Tommy and Tracy were the real picture. In the corner of her mind she was aware that it had been many weeks since one of Cliff's breezy letters had arrived. Every time she heard a news report about what was happening in the Pacific—Guam had just fallen to American troops after twenty days of bloody fighting—she went cold with fear. Both Cliff and Gus were out there. She shook off the chill resolutely: "And what about that splashy wedding your parents are giving you and Tommy back in Houston?"

Tracy toyed with Tommy's class ring on her finger. "I don't think I want it anymore," she confessed. The other girls stared at her in shock. "Look, I haven't seen Tommy since two weeks after Pearl Harbor, when he dropped out of Yale to enlist. Sometimes I'm not sure I even remember what he looks like." Her eyes pleaded for understanding. "Until we came out here, I was seeing Brian three or four times a week, even if I just ran downtown to meet him for lunch. It's been awful not seeing him. He feels the same way. It made us both realize we're crazy about each other."

"What about Tommy?" Pat asked quietly. "What are you going to do about him?"

"I guess I ought to write a 'Dear John' letter." Her eyes focused on the floor. "Wouldn't it be better to do that now than for him to find out when he comes home?"

"Tracy, he's fighting a war!" Pat protested.

"What good will it do for me to pretend I'm still in love with him?" Tracy was defiant. "We'd have an awful marriage—we'd end up hating each other. How do I know he's still in love with me? Brian's here, and I don't want to lose him."

"You've made up your mind to marry Brian," Tina said. Vanessa and Pat were visibly upset. They'd sit out the war till the bitter end waiting for their men to return home. But she could understand what Tracy was feeling. "Write Tommy and get it over with, Tracy," Tina said flatly.

"Tina, you sound so callous," Vanessa protested.

"Tracy's not the only one," Tina shrugged. "Girls here at home have a right to change their minds. And don't kid yourselves—plenty of the fellas have something else going on their girls never hear about."

"Suppose Brian is shipped out?" Pat challenged

Tracy. "Are you going to forget him, too?"

"When is this lousy war going to be over?" Tracy's voice was shrill. She slammed her hand on the bureau. "I want to marry Brian and go back home to Houston."

"I'd live anywhere with Eddie," Vanessa whispered, touched by Tracy's obvious anguish. "Just let him come home safely."

"Amen," Pat whispered.

Tina knew she looked good in the outfit Vanessa had spent most of the morning pulling together for her. It was funny the way Vanessa got so excited about clothes — but she really knew what would work. Rita Hayworth or Betty Grable or Lana Turner might have worn this in a movie, Tina thought to herself as she walked with the other three girls to their Sunday afternoon barbecue. She knew that the next two or three hours would be the most crucial of her life. Somehow, she must persuade Del Miller to help her land a contract with Imperial Films.

Clint, in the chef's hat he wore when barbecuing, was preparing the charcoal for the steaks. Appetizing aromas infiltrated the sea air.

Tina knew that Jim had left on a midday ferry because one of Imperial's "hot properties" was arriving from the Coast this afternoon. Del was stretched out on a chaise and sipping a Tom Collins. Tina headed directly for the vacant chair beside Del.

"Hi." With deliberate languor she lowered herself into the chair. So Del was "queer" — he'd recognize that she was sexy. That was a commercial commodity in Hollywood. Look what it did for Rita Hayworth and Lana Turner.

"You're looking sharp." His eyes trailed approvingly over the length of her.

"I like looking sharp," she conceded with a slow, detached smile. "Especially when I'm around you." He lifted an eyebrow in inquiry. "All through high school my big dream was to meet a movie talent scout and be sent out to Hollywood."

"And since high school?" His voice was casual, but Tina sensed fresh interest. She fought to stay cool, hide her excitement.

"I still dream about it, but I know the odds." She shrugged, her smile cynical.

"You've met me," Del pointed out. "I'm a talent scout for Imperial." He set down his glass, sat up straight on the chaise. Suddenly the atmosphere was charged with electricity. *It was Del's job to find future movie stars. If he didn't come up with prospects he'd be fired.* "How ambitious are you?"

"I'd do anything to be Rita Hayworth," she said. Her eyes convinced him of her sincerity. "I'd work my ass off."

"I can't promise anything," he cautioned, "but I'll send you to this photographer, Russ Bently. He'll take a stack of pictures of you and bill the studio. I'll see what we can do." He rose to his feet. "Let me go get a card from my wallet. I'll be right back."

Tina sat motionless, her heart pounding. She exchanged one eloquent glance with Vanessa, across the deck. She nodded in triumph, her smile brilliant. *God, it was really happening.* Lana Turner was picked up in that Hollywood drugstore—and Tina Gregory had met a talent scout on a deck at Fire Island.

Satiated with salad, steak, potatoes, and strawberry shortcake, the four girls returned to their cottage, dangling shoes from their hands as they strolled along the now deserted beach. With building excitement,

Tina recounted her exchange with Del Miller. Pat and Tracy were astonished that Tina hadn't told them about her ambitions, but they were impressed by her revelations.

"It's like something you'd read in a fan magazine!" Tracy said. "You could be headed for Hollywood!"

"If Del's bosses like the photos," Tina allowed. But in her mind she was already attending the premier of her first movie.

"You'll have to take the day off from work," Vanessa reminded, trying for a down-to-earth note. Tina sensed her ambivalence — she was scared to be too excited. They all knew this whole deal could fall flat on its face.

"I'll call in sick," Tina decided. "I'm never out — old man Friedlich can't bitch. What'll I wear?" she cried in alarm. *Everything was important.*

"Something simple," Pat suggested. "So you and not your outfit stand out in the photographs."

"That black cotton you found at Klein's after the July Fourth sale," Vanessa decided. "You brought it along this weekend."

"The neckline's too high," Tina objected. "I don't want them to think I'm the June Allyson type."

"I'll change it." Vanessa's face wore that incandescent glow that told Tina she was mentally redesigning. "I saw a sensational neckline on a dress in *Vogue* last month. It starts high at the right and then slashes down low at the left. If I take tiny stitches, it'll look fine."

"Wear my pearls," Pat offered. "I have them out here. I was afraid to leave them in the city."

Vanessa nodded enthusiastically. "Black cotton and pearls will be so smart and sophisticated."

"And you'll carry that Hermès purse Daddy bought me when he was in New York last month," Tracy ordered. "I'll bet those white anklet sandals I bought last week at Bergdorf's will fit you. They're so sexy,"

Tracy said, giggling.

The four girls lounged on their deck until dusk and hunger drove them inside. Vanessa accomplished a minor miracle with the black cotton from Klein's while they shared the barbecue's Hollywood gossip. Rita Hayworth — now married to Orson Welles — was pregnant. Joan Crawford was making a big comeback at Warners. Marlene Dietrich was wowing GI's on the fighting fronts. Tyrone Power — who Clint insisted "preferred boys to girls" even though he was married to Annabella — was in marine flight training. And Tracy was convinced that Tina would soon have her footsteps immortalized in cement at Grauman's Chinese.

"Boy, if they offer me a contract — I don't care if it pays twenty a week — I'm off and running!" Tina exulted. "I'll keep on paying my share of the apartment," she added quickly as Vanessa stared at her in openmouthed dismay. "I could be back in New York in six months."

"Let's try on the dress with the pearls." Vanessa was determined to appear cheerful. It wasn't just her half of the rent that bothered Vanessa, Tina knew. She was unnerved at the prospect of a three-thousand-mile separation.

"And then let's have dinner," Tracy bubbled. "I'm always hungry out here."

Well past midnight, when both girls should have been asleep after a day of sun and sea air, Tina left her bed and walked to the door of Vanessa's room, where moonlight spilled through the slightly parted drapes.

"You awake?" Tina whispered.

"Yeah." At dinner Vanessa had been yawning, but now she was wide awake. "I guess we're both too excited to sleep."

Drawing her robe about her Tina settled herself at the foot of the bed.

"Why am I suddenly scared out of my skin?" she said into the darkness.

"Because it's so important."

"I'm so fucking tired of being nobody," Tina said through clenched teeth. "Of having nothing. I want it all, Vanessa. A penthouse apartment on Park Avenue and a big house in the Hollywood hills. A chauffered Rolls and a dozen fur coats. And I want to drive back to Pinewood in that Rolls—with my gorgeous mink coat—and watch that whole goddamn town grovel because I'll be Tina Gregory, Hollywood star." Her face softened. "And you'll be Vanessa Conrad, designer to the stars. We're going to make it, Vanessa. Both of us."

"I know we will." Vanessa's voice was low and soft. They sat in the silence, staring at the moonbeam that lay across the floor.

"You don't think Del's just throwing me a line?"

"Why would he?" Vanessa countered. "He's a talent scout for Imperial Films. Finding talent is his job."

"Mind if I stay here with you tonight?" Tina asked sheepishly.

"Come to bed," Vanessa said warmly, her voice catching. She cleared her throat. "That alarm goes off in five hours."

Nine

As instructed by Del, Tina phoned the photographer on Monday afternoon. He scheduled a session for her the following afternoon. Del had not been handing her a line.

In the morning Vanessa phoned Tina's boss—with Tina hovering over her shoulder—to explain that Tina was sick but would be in the following morning. Tina grimaced while Vanessa accepted the polite expressions of sympathy from the other end.

"It's all right?" Tina asked anxiously when Vanessa replaced the receiver on the hook.

"Everything's fine," Vanessa soothed and rose to her feet. "Now I have to run. I'll be at least twenty minutes late getting in. Mr. Rappaport will have a fit."

"Let him worry," Tina giggled. "Where'll he find somebody as reliable as you?"

"Don't be late," Vanessa warned. Tina waged a running battle just to make it to her office on time each morning.

"Late for this? Are you kidding?" Tina hugged Vanessa in a surge of high spirits. "Go on to the salt mines. I have to wash my hair and set it. It had better dry before two."

"It's already seventy-six degrees," Vanessa reminded,

charging toward the door. "Just stick your head out the window, and your hair will dry."

"I'll be sweating like a pig," Tina moaned. "Thank goodness Tracy lent me her bottle of Ciro's Reflexion. I'll drown myself in it." The bottle of perfume cost more than she earned in a week.

Tina arrived—breathless and at the last minute—at Russ Bently's large, starkly modern studio to be ushered immediately into his private office. Russ squinted at her from several angles while they exchanged perfunctory small talk. Then he nodded thoughtfully and pressed a button on his desk. The makeup man appeared at once.

"Okay," Russ said briskly, "let's go to work."

Tina was impressed by the intense, serious attitude of the two men. The makeup man concentrated on stripping away the cosmetics she had applied with such dedication. Then he began to redo her face, all the while discussing her with Russ as though she wasn't there.

"Give her more eyebrows," Russ ordered. "She's tweezed them down like she was Garbo or Dietrich. She's too young for that. Play up the cheekbones."

"Don't rush me," the makeup man complained. "She's got sensational eyelashes. I'll use a hair-set lotion to turn 'em up, but it takes a while to do it right."

Never in her life had Tina felt so important. She tried hard to appear languid and amused. She'd never let them know she was so excited she felt sick.

When Russ at last approved her makeup, she was led into another room, where an assistant was setting up lights.

"Sit there," Russ ordered, pointing to a stool.

If this turned out to be a fizzle, it wasn't the end of the world, Tina told herself defiantly. Next time she'd go to somebody sensational to have her hair done.

She'd buy a great dress at Saks Fifth Avenue. She'd look cool and gorgeous instead of hot and jittery.

After a seemingly endless barrage of shots—during which she was convinced she did nothing right—Tina was summarily dismissed.

"The photos will go over to Del in the morning," Russ told her. "By hand."

"Great," Tina drawled and reached for her purse. "See you."

Dizzy from the trauma of the past three hours, Tina waited before the bank of elevators, her mind in a state of turmoil. What did they think? They wouldn't have spent all that time with her if they didn't think she had a chance of being sent out to Hollywood, would they?

Instead of taking the bus home, she wandered around Broadway, seeing her name up in lights on the marquee of the Paramount or the Capitol or Loew's State. She crossed over to Sixth Avenue to stand before Radio City Music Hall. She felt so close to realizing her dream.

At five-thirty she stood waiting in the lobby of Vanessa's office building. Please let this not be one of those nights when Vanessa worked late. She watched closely as the elevators began to disgorge their passengers.

"Vanessa!" she called out and waved in relief. "We'll go out for dinner," she announced when Vanessa reached her side, her eyes questioning. "My treat. Forget about the automat's beef pot pie for fifteen cents. We'll go to Schrafft's tonight!"

"Not Schrafft's," Vanessa rebuked. "Somebody told me they never hire Jews."

"Toffenetti's," Tina decided in triumph. "And not their fifty-cent plate of spaghetti with meat sauce. Lamb chops, dessert, and coffee, or maybe the roast chicken. Come on," she slid her arm through Vanessa's.

"To Toffenetti's!"

They headed west on Forty-second Street, jauntily pushing their way through the home-bound throngs, and turned north on Broadway to the huge modernistic restaurant already jammed with diners. As soon as they had settled at a table and ordered, Vanessa demanded a detailed account of the photographic session. Tina told it all in a rush and waited breathlessly for Vanessa's verdict.

"It went great," Vanessa decided in satisfaction.

"We'll see." Caution crept into her voice. "I gave Del my office number so he can call me. Screw old Friedlich and his craziness about personal calls."

The dawdled over dinner and ordered second cups of coffee. Toffenetti's was beyond their everyday budget, but this was an occasion and they meant to enjoy it.

"I can see my old man's face if I'm sent out to Hollywood," Tina said softly, toying with her coffee cup. "To him all movie stars are immoral because they kiss strange men in their pictures. I had to go to see *Gone with the Wind* on the sly because the Legion of Decency said it was 'morally objectionable.' To Pop that meant all Catholics should stay away. He nearly blew a gasket when he found out we saw *The Outlaw*. Didn't he know I could guess what Jane Russell's breasts looked like without seeing the picture?" Some of her exuberance evaporated. "He'll be sure I'll rot in hell forever if I'm an actress."

Tina's father still refused to write or to invite her to come home to visit for a few days.

"Tina, I'll bet your father hangs over Nick's shoulder every time a letter comes," Vanessa comforted. "You do hear regularly from Nick."

Tina shook off her depression. "I wonder how long I'll have to wait to hear from Del?" She reached to squeeze Vanessa's hand. "I'm so close, Vanessa!"

115

After dinner they walked across to Fifth avenue, caught a double-decker bus, and climbed to the upper deck.

"The city is so beautiful from up here," Vanessa commented as they traveled uptown past Saks Fifth Avenue and St. Patrick's Cathedral on the right, Rockefeller Center on the left.

"Any place is beautiful if you have enough money." Tina tapped restlessly with one sandaled foot.

"Your house in Pinewood is beautiful," Vanessa remembered. "I always thought you were so lucky to be living there."

Tina turned to stare at her in disbelief.

"That old barn?"

"The lines are so clean and elegant. I love those old trees out front and—"

"I want one of those gorgeous houses in Bel Air or on Bedford Drive, where Garbo and Marion Davies live," Tina interrupted. "The kind of houses we see in *Modern Screen* and *Photoplay*—with their own swimming pools and half a dozen servants to take care of them." Tina gripped the back of the empty seat ahead of them. "I don't care if I flunk out on this deal; I'll make it soon. You'll see."

"When my next raise comes through," Vanessa said softly, but with unexpected strength, "every cent of it goes into the bank. When I have enough put away, I'm signing up for evening classes at Parsons."

Tina didn't hear from Del until Wednesday afternoon.

"We'd like you to come in for an interview and a preliminary screen test tomorrow morning at ten." Del's voice was casual. They might have been discussing the weather. "Not at the offices. At the New York studio.

116

Can you make it?"

"Sure, Del." She pantomimed an apology as Mr. Friedlich waited, grim-faced, for her to finish. "Where?" She listened, not daring to write down the address. Tomorrow she'd have to call in sick again. Friedlich would be apoplectic.

At lunchtime she phoned Vanessa from a public phone in the downstairs drugstore.

"I don't know what Del means by a preliminary screen test," Tina admitted, "but it sounds good."

"It sounds wonderful!"

"What'll I wear?" Tina asked.

"We'll figure that out tonight," Vanessa soothed. "And start acting like you're not feeling well this afternoon."

"I'll ask for an aspirin. Maybe he'll figure I'm having a bad period."

The following morning at ten o'clock sharp Tina walked into the reception room at Imperial Films' West Side studio. After twenty minutes she was ushered into the lushly furnished office of Joel Crane. Del nodded to her as he spread photographs across Crane's oversize desk. She knew Crane was somebody important. Del had referred to him as "my boss, the big guy, head of talent." To hide her excitement she retreated into an air of cool detachment.

The small, compact man behind the desk inspected her with a matching coolness as Del introduced them.

"Why do you want to be a film actress?" he demanded tersely.

"I can't think of an easier way to make a lot of money," Tina drawled. "And it sounds like fun."

"Acting is hard work," he shot back. "Sometimes seventeen hours a day, seven days a week. You'll have to be at the studio at 6:00 A.M. for makeup. You'll work your ass off."

"Waitressing is long hours and hard work too," she

retaliated. "But what do I see at the end of the week?"

Unexpectedly he chuckled.

"Take her in to Morris. The usual deal." He was brusque in his dismissal, but his eyes glinted as he watched Tina sashay out of the room.

She listened to Morris Klein, the test director, explain the scene she was to do. A makeup man prepared her for camera. Del was standing by.

"If you blow a line, improvise," Klein ordered. "Joel doesn't like to waste time on these New York tests. I'll cue you off-camera."

"Sure thing." Tina smiled with a show of confidence. Inwardly she was terrified. *Please, God, don't let me freeze on camera.*

The next two hours were awful. Tina couldn't shake her nervousness. Morris kept having her redo the scene. He kept saying Joel Crane didn't like to waste time on New York tests. But she wasn't doing it right. The air felt leaden with their disappointment. Then Crane appeared. They couldn't keep rehearsing any longer; they had to shoot the test.

"Okay, that's a wrap," Morris said finally.

Joel Crane's face was an inscrutable mask when he spoke to Tina. "You can go take off the makeup now."

She sat before a mirror in the dressing room and tried to focus on removing the screen makeup and replacing it with her own. She had left the door cracked because she didn't want to feel any more shut off, any more alone.

She froze when she heard voices in the hall.

"Look, I'm only behind the camera," the cameraman said with exaggerated humility, "but I tell you, forget she can't act. That kid's got something special."

"She can't act worth a damn," Crane said flatly. "She can't even speak clearly."

"So they'll send her to a voice coach," Del tried.

"They do it all the time. The important thing is that she photographs gorgeous."

"She's the sexiest broad to come along since Hayworth," the cameraman insisted. "Every guy sitting in any movie house in America will want to lay her — and every woman will wish like hell that she looked like her."

"Joel, take a chance," Del pleaded. "Send the test to the Coast. Let them at least get a look at her. I'd take any odds she'll be top box office in five years."

"Okay, the test goes out," Crane capitulated. "But don't get your hopes too high on this one."

Tina stared at her reflection in the mirror. Her hands were shaking so hard she dropped the jar of cold cream on the counter with a thud. The voices moved down the hall.

Tina couldn't bring herself to go into the office on Friday. On Saturday morning she and Vanessa left for Fire Island.

"It's going to be weird seeing Del out there this weekend," Tina said tensely. "He went out on a limb for me, but Joel Crane wasn't happy about it."

"You had Del and the cameraman behind you," Vanessa reminded her. "That shows you have something special."

"Del says it'll probably be ten days to two weeks before the New York office has any word from the Coast." Tina sighed. "How am I going to live through all that time?"

"You'll survive," Vanessa said firmly.

Tina was relieved to learn that both Del and Jim had had to remain in New York on company business. Nobody on Fire Island knew about the screen test. She wouldn't have to talk about it.

Tracy was convinced that Tina was on her way to

stardom. Pat promised to pray for her. The girls' moods ranged from wild optimism to bottoms-out despondency. Tina insisted on recalling the negative attitudes of Joel Crane and Morris Klein, both of whom, Tina pointed out mournfully, outranked Del and the cameraman.

On Tuesday morning a secretary from Imperial Films phoned Tina at the office. She set up an appointment for 10:00 A.M. the following day with Joel Crane. Tina immediately phoned Vanessa.

"Would he want to see me if I flunked out?" Tina challenged, her voice shrill with anticipation. "Vanessa, I'll die waiting!"

At ten minutes before the scheduled hour—a small miracle for Tina—she sat in the reception room at Imperial Films and waited to see Joel Crane. And at exactly ten she was ushered into his office.

"Are you legally old enough to sign a contract?" he greeted her, and her heart began to pound.

"I was twenty-one last December," she lied.

"You're green as hell." Crane was brusque. "But the Coast is willing to gamble on you. We're signing you for seven years, with options for pick-up every six months. You'll be paid fifty dollars a week until such time as we feel you're worth more. Then the old contract will be ripped up, and you'll be given a new one."

"Great." Her mask of nonchalance was in jeopardy. "When do I sign?"

"You'll do that in the Legal Department at the West Coast studios," Crane told her, and touched the buzzer on his desk. "You'll leave Saturday morning on the Twentieth Century Limited. Larry Rogers from the Publicity Department will be your official escort." Only then did Crane relax into a grin that was surprisingly sympathetic. "We want to be sure you get on the right

120

train, make the right switch in Chicago, and arrive at the studio on schedule. Rosalind," he said to the woman who paused in the doorway of his office. "Take her over and explain our routine in sending out contract players." He reached out a hand to Tina. "Welcome to the family."

Ten

The sky was a depressing gray, hinting at an all-day
drizzle, and a damp chill hung in the air. Vanessa wore a
gray cardigan with her black-and-white polka-dot
blouse and black slacks while she restored the two beds
to their daytime dress. She wished that this Saturday
had been bathed in sunlight. As though the sunlight
might camouflage her towering sense of loss.

The covers smoothed into place over the two beds, she
paused before the one where Tina had slept for more
than two years. One hand trailed tenderly over the
much-worn coverlet. She shouldn't feel sad. *Tina was on
her way to Hollywood.*

"Vanessa, I should have given myself a Toni," Tina
wailed from the bathroom. "My hair's awful."

"Your hair is beautiful." Vanessa tossed the pillows
into place and crossed to the dresser to pull out the
going-away present she had bought for Tina. It seemed
to unreal that, after today, she'd be here alone.

"What'll I do for three days on the train?" Tina emerged from the bathroom. "I never did learn to play
solitaire."

"Pick up some magazines at Grand Central." Vanessa

122

handed her the festively wrapped small box. "To remember me by," she said lightly.

"Vanessa, you shouldn't have spent money on me." Tina carefully unwrapped her gift. Her face lit with laughter. "You were scared to death one alarm clock wouldn't get me up!" she accused.

"One by the bed and another on the dresser," Vanessa instructed. "You can't afford to be late at the studio." Tina was gorgeous, she thought affectionately. They'd love her in Hollywood.

"I may be back in six months," Tina warned. "It happens all the time out there."

"You won't be."

Vanessa wouldn't let herself dwell now on the problem of acquiring a new roommate if Tina's option was picked up. Maybe by then the war would be over, and she'd be married to Eddie. In every letter he wrote about how much he missed her. The Allies had pushed the Germans out of Rome already and he sounded optimistic about the way the war was going. The joke going around had it that the optimists in Germany were learning English; the pessimists, Russian.

"I have to meet Larry Rogers at Grand Central fifteen minutes before departure time." Tina's voice was high-pitched with excitement. "I thought this day would never come."

"Let's go." Vanessa was determinedly casual.

"I can't believe they're sending me out with an escort," Tina giggled as she picked up the Mark Cross valise Pat and Tracy had given her and headed for the door. Vanessa clutched the weekender she took regularly to Fire Island. As soon as Tina took off, she would take the next train to Bay Shore and head for Fire Island. It would be strange without Tina.

"Can you imagine how much that's costing them? go out alone, but the girls all get this fancy treatment."

Tina's eyes were speculative. "They wouldn't send me out on the Twentieth Century Limited, with my own compartment and a nursemaid, if they didn't expect me to go places."

"Don't let them know how excited you are about the contract," Vanessa urged with sudden intuition. "Probably every girl arriving out there is a nervous wreck. Be calm and collected the whole way."

"That's the way I'll play it, baby," Tina promised. "That'll keep me from being scared out of my pants." She frowned as Vanessa locked the door. "You think this Rogers character is going to try to get into my pants on the train? Three whole days and nights with nothing to do."

"That would be crazy," Vanessa admonished. "He's only an errand boy."

"You're right. I'll save it for somebody important," Tina teased. Her smile was brilliant. "Stop worrying about me, little mother."

In the taxi to Grand Central Tina confessed to misgivings about not having written her father and Nick about the trip west.

"I'll write as soon as I'm in California. I'm superstitious. If I tell Pop before I'm out there, I've got this crazy idea he'll try to stop me from going." She grew serious. "I haven't seen the old bastard in over two years. He hung up on me when I called him at Christmas." Vanessa's eyes widened in astonishment. "I know," Tina said shamefacedly, "I never told you. I guess it hurt too much to talk about."

"Call me as soon as you can," Vanessa pleaded. "Everything will be okay. I'll be dying to know what's happening."

In Grand Central a slender, nattily dressed young man charged toward them with an ebullient smile.

"Tina, we board in a couple of minutes!" Larry Rogers called out. "You play pinochle?"

"Teach me," Tina said. "I grew up playing poker with my brothers. I'll pick it up fast."

Vanessa stood beside Tina and managed a convivial smile while Larry Rogers and Tina bantered. It was wonderful that Tina had a movie contract. But she felt devastated. Eddie was gone, and in a few moments Tina would be walking down that ramp.

Vanessa fought against tears as she kissed Tina good-bye.

"Call me at the office," she ordered Tina. "I'll be there all day. And if it's in the evening, call me on Pat's phone. I'll leave our door cracked so I can hear the phone if it rings." It used to be their door. Now it was hers. "But give me time to get over there and pick up."

"I'll call you, baby." Tina hugged her exuberantly. "Take care of yourself. Don't pick up anybody I wouldn't approve of."

The tears she'd managed to hold back blurred in her eyes as Vanessa pushed her way through the Saturday crowds to wait for the next train to Bay Shore. Her thumb caressed the class ring Eddie had given to her. Several times she had been tempted to tell her mother about Eddie in one of the brief notes she sent with the weekly check. Each time she had brushed the thought aside. Her mother would only worry whether the checks would stop when she and Eddie were married. That wouldn't happen; Eddie understood.

At Fire Island Tracy talked enthusiastically about "Tina's terrific break." Pat cast compassionate glances at Vanessa, knowing how much she would miss Tina. And Tina's contract was a reminder that she had accomplished nothing in two years. She was no closer to being a designer than she had been when they stepped off that train from Pinewood.

When Tracy came back to the cottage with the Sun-

125

day *New York Times,* Vanessa grabbed for the Help Wanted section and perused the few ads for designer jobs. She had so little experience. And she couldn't gamble on quitting the job that provided the weekly check to her mother.

Tina listened avidly to everything Larry told her about Hollywood. He spent most of his time shuttling between New York and Hollywood as official escort to Imperial Films' latest young contract player. Tina was surprised that he made no effort to climb into her berth. She didn't think he was queer — not the way he ogled her sometimes. He must be under studio orders not to mess with the girls. They played a lot of pinochle. Tina thought about the stories Del and Jim had told about Nat Kelman. Was she going to have trouble with him — or was she too unimportant for him to notice? She'd worry about that when the time came.

In Chicago Tina and Larry left the train and the La Salle Street Station to race across town by taxi and board the Super Chief, which would carry them on to Los Angeles. Tina rarely bothered to glance out the window as the train raced across country. The only destination that interested her was Hollywood.

At last the Super Chief pulled to a stop at the modest Central Station in downtown Los Angeles. Tina abandoned her cultivated detachment to gape at the movie stars, producers, and directors she recognized from a long devotion to fan magazines. Each celebrity was accompanied by his own entourage, and a bevy of smiling porters carried their luggage to the waiting limousines.

Excitement charged through Tina. One day she would step down from the Super Chief and people would stare at her the way she was staring at Anne Sheridan right this minute.

The last three days she had lived in limbo, Tina told herself. Now her new life was about to begin. Larry had assured her that the studio would rent an apartment for her, something she could afford on her fifty dollars a week.

"This way, Tina."

In the taxi on the way to the studio, Tina remained silent. She noted the driver's speculative appraisal of her in the mirror above the dashboard. He figured she was "the new girl at the studio." His grin told her he approved. Would Nat Kelman approve? He had the final say on everything at Imperial Films. It would be awful to be sent back to New York at the end of six months.

Tina retreated into her air of practiced coolness, to mask a surge of insecurity. She wore the outfit Vanessa had specifically chosen for her arrival. She would look chic, Vanessa had insisted. But she felt as though everybody at the studio would take one look at her and know that her dress—though smartly altered by Vanessa—had been salvaged from the clearance rack at Klein's.

Why did she have to go to the studio *now?* After three days and nights cooped up in a train compartment she needed a hour-long shower and a good night's sleep.

Tina suspected that Larry's glossy picture of life at Imperial Films was false. But nothing would stop her. She'd be as big a star as Rita Hayworth or Anne Sheridan or Ava Gardner.

They drove through streets lined with cheap bars, sleazy shops, and drab apartment houses until they arrived at gates that announced that behind these portals lay the complex that comprised Imperial Films Limited. With an air of importance Larry pointed out the building that housed Nat Kelman's private offices, along with those of the studio's top directors.

Larry directed the cab to a stop and, valise in tow, prodded Tina into an office. There he introduced her to a tall, lean woman with iron-gray hair and an air of stern efficiency.

"Tina, do everything Bertha tells you," Larry ordered and kissed her on the cheek. "See you in about a week," he said blithely and took off.

"First we'll go over to Wardrobe," Bertha said briskly. "Find you a sexy evening gown, and then on to Makeup. Your test will go to the screening room before Mr. Kelman leaves for the night."

In a state of shock Tina allowed herself to be escorted to Wardrobe. She was to be tested again. *Before* signing the contract, she thought. The lousy bastards!

Vanessa awoke on Wednesday morning with the instant realization that Tina had arrived yesterday in Hollywood. *Today* she would phone. Not until afternoon, because of the time difference.

Though she knew Tina was probably fast asleep at this hour, Vanessa arrived at the office thirty minutes earlier than normal, just in case Tina hadn't yet adjusted to the change in time, was awake, and decided to call. Vanessa was anxious to hear Tina's voice. The apartment was desolate without her.

The weekend had been cold and rainy. At Clint's cottage she had learned that both Phil and Robbie had been reclassified as 1-A. Each had gone home for the weekend in anticipation of being called up at any moment. Clint was depressed. For the first time he admitted to being too old to fear the draft, but he worried about his friends.

Tracy had a bad weekend because Brian had expected to acquire a weekend pass for a brief forty-eight hours and come out to Fire Island. At the last minute he had to cancel his plans. Pat was convinced that Tracy would never marry Tommy and was prodding her to write to him.

"I know I'm chicken," Tracy admitted to Pat and Vanessa. "But I'll write Tommy soon. I promise."

Every time the phone rang, Vanessa tensed. Not until late in the afternoon did she pick up the phone and hear Tina on the other end of the line.

"Baby, I'm here!" Tina yelled into the receiver. "It's been wild!"

"Give me your address." Vanessa reached for a pen. "Do you have a phone yet?"

"I have!" Her voice deepened in triumph. "The studio arranged it so I'll always be reachable. They rented this dinky little apartment with a murphy bed for me off Sunset Boulevard. But guess what?" Her tone was cynical. "I had to take another test two hours after I arrived. I was furious—they were still thinking about shipping me back to New York! But an hour ago I signed the contract in the Legal Department. At least for the next six months I'm a contract player."

"Tina, that's wonderful!" Vanessa exclaimed happily. "Hey, this must be costing you a fortune."

"I'm calling on a studio phone," Tina laughed. "Anyhow, I'm making a big fifty dollars a week. I can afford a long-distance call every now and then. I'll even be able to save money," she replied recklessly.

"Are you going right into a movie?" Vanessa asked. She felt like she was living in a make-believe world— Tina was calling her from Imperial Films!

"I don't think so," Tina said. "First there's a kind of training period. I've been assigned a voice coach and a dramatic coach, and they're sending me to the dentist for some caps. I'm on my way now for an interview with the Publicity Department. They've got to work up a biography for me. At least they're letting me stay Tina Gregory. For about half an hour it looked like that was

129

going. But they finally decided it would look all right on screen credits and movie marquees."

"Tina, it's terrific." Vanessa's voice vibrated with enthusiasm. "I'll write you tonight. And write back and tell me *everything* that happens."

"Yeah, I know," Tina mocked. "I'd better get the hell off the line before one of those crazy lawyers starts complaining. Take care, baby."

Vanessa replaced the receiver slowly and sat immobile, gazing off into space. It was as though she had reached out and touched Tina these last minutes. Tina would be fine. She knew how to handle herself.

The apartment would be sticky and hot tonight, though the small fan they had chipped in to buy at the beginning of the summer offered some relief if she sat directly in front of it. She'd reread *Town & Country* while she ate dinner.

The days were still summer-long; it would be light when she finished dinner. Maybe she would go down to Riverside Drive for a walk. With Tina in Hollywood and Eddie off in Italy, she felt claustrophobic alone in the apartment.

At the mailboxes she paused to unlock her own and drew out several envelopes. A letter from Eddie! Her face was luminescent. Not one of the little V-mails, where Eddie and she struggled to use every bit of available writing space, but a regular letter—which meant two or three pages of onionskin paper covered on both sides with Eddie's neat, tiny scrawl.

Before collecting Pat and Tracy's mail, she inspected the other two letters. One was a charity appeal. She squinted at the other. It was addressed to Cliff. Had it been returned for postage? Suddenly she went cold with shock. Her eyes refocused on the rubber-stamped words at one side of the envelope. *"Killed in Action."*

Cliff Dead? Cliff who had been so lighthearted and so

sure he'd come home to light up the Broadway theater? *Cliff dead?* She stumbled into the hall and groped her way up the stairs.

She remembered the wry smile on Cliff's face when he had arrived at the apartment with that armful of yellow chrysanthemums to tell them he'd been drafted. She remembered his first V-mail to Tina, when he'd written with such confidence about his future in the theater.

Trembling and dizzy, she unlocked the apartment door. She dropped onto the edge of a chair, clutching the letters in one hand. From the moment Eddie had left her on his last night in New York, she had lived in fear for his safety. But now that fear threatened to suffocate her. *Cliff was dead.* For a little while he had been so much a part of their lives. Now they'd never see him again. Nothing remained of Cliff Hopkins except a dogtag to be sent home to his mother.

In a sudden frenzy to reassure herself that Eddie was all right, she opened his letter, only too conscious that the letter had been written ten days earlier. It took one minute for a bullet to kill. She wouldn't write Eddie about Cliff, she decided. Later she would tell him. But she'd have to write Tina.

Tina groaned as the alarm clock beside the bed in her closet-sized studio shrieked into the morning silence. Without opening her eyes she reached over to turn it off, knowing that in another five minutes the clock on the dresser would shriek with equal shrillness. Then she would force herself to face the new day.

She was still grieving over Cliff's death, though the letter from Vanessa had arrived three weeks ago. Ten days ago she'd received her first letter from Nick. The family was still obsessed by the conviction that every girl in Hollywood—except for Lassie and June Allyson—

was a whore.

And Gus was on his way home from the Pacific. "He's a hero," Nick emphasized. "He got a discharge because he was suffering from 'combat fatigue.' Pop says that's what they called 'shell shock' in the First World War."

Gus was coming home, but Vinnie was somewhere in France. They knew he had been part of the D-Day invasion. Nick wrote about the kids in her graduating class who wouldn't be coming home. What a goddamn rotten world!

The second alarm yelled out its message. Tina tossed aside the covers and crossed the room to silence it. She reached to switch on the radio. The haunting strains of "I'll Be Seeing You" floated into the room. She flinched and fumbled with the radio dial until "Mairzy Doats" with its wacky lyrics introduced a less painful mood.

She smothered a series of yawns as she walked into the minuscule kitchenette to put up coffee. God, she hated the studio's constant warning to "watch your weight." Once a week all the small-part actresses were weighed and measured to make sure they didn't add an ounce.

With the coffee up and two slices of bread in the toaster Tina went in to shower, a quick one because she had to be sitting in a chair in Makeup by 6:30 A.M. It was crazy the way all the would-be starlets had to go through the whole makeup deal every morning, then go on to the hairdresser for a setting. Just in case one of them was called for a walk-on or a bit part in some picture being shot at the studio.

In addition to the beautification program, Tina had voice lessons and dramatic coaching every morning. In the afternoon she had a dancing lesson and every day there were photography sessions. When she arrived at the studio and checked in with Bertha in the morning, she was told when to report the "shooting gallery." At first it had been fun to pose in all those silly shots — in as few clothes as the Hays office would allow. Now it was a pain in the ass. *Nothing was happening.*

She emerged from the shower, settled down to her toast and coffee. She'd have to write and tell Vanessa that she was to be publicized as "Miss Orange Grove" of some county or other. Vanessa would get a kick out of the bio the studio had dreamt up for her. She was supposed to be seventeen and fresh out of convent school. She'd been chosen as a model by John Powers; but before she could accept an assignment, Imperial Films had whisked her out to Hollywood. Wow, the crap they threw!

With one eye on the clock, Tina washed the few dishes. She hoped the secondhand Packard—probably tenth-hand, she thought with growing cynicism—would start up without trouble this morning. The studio had arranged for her to buy it; the payments would be deducted from her salary.

The Packard started without trouble. Tina was surprised that she still felt a tingle of anticipation when she drove though the studio gates each morning. Maybe this would be the day something special would happen. After all, she was an Imperial Films starlet. There would be pictures of her in the December issue of *Screenland.*

"Go straight to Makeup," Bertha said in greeting. "You're doing a walk-on. It's a beach scene. Wardrobe will have a bathing suit for you. When you're dressed, come back to see me. I'll take your over to the sound stage."

Tina smiled radiantly.

At Makeup she discovered the walk-on was in the new Gordon Faith film. Gordon was Imperial's top young male star. He was ingratiating, grossly overweight, and a highly talented comedian. According to studio gossip, Gordon was having a heated romance with his costar, the wide-eyed and beautiful Eileen Nolan, though Publicity was trying hard to keep this under wraps. Eileen had been billed as the untouchable young virgin who neither smoked nor drank. Eileen Nolan was the adorable "girl next door."

"Honey, that Eileen can cuss worse than you," the makeup man confided to Tina. He was one of her few friends at the studio. He relished her colorful swearing, laughed at her impatience, and confided that she was lucky that she wasn't Kelman's type. She was too much woman for Nat to handle; he preferred the starry-eyed little ingenues. "And don't smile too much at Gordon, or Eileen will scratch your eyes out."

At Wardrobe she acquired the briefest two-piece bathing suit allowed onscreen. The top offered a single strap fastened between her breasts and at one side of the back.

"With you in it that suit is sensational," Bertha said with approval when Tina arrived at her office. "Come on. I'll take you over to the set. They'll be shooting the beach scene in a little while."

Wearing the skimpy suit and the amused, slightly detached smile that was becoming her trademark, Tina stood at the sidelines and waited to be summoned for her walk-on. Behind her cool face her heart was pounding. It was exciting to be here on the set with Gordon Faith and Eileen Nolan. She'd seen them from afar, lunching at their special reserved tables in the commissary, each surrounded by high-level Imperial Films executives; but now they were here and she was working with them.

Even at this distance she could feel Gordon's magnetism, the draw that brought customers into the movie houses in staggering numbers. She couldn't imagine the ethereally lovely Eileen Nolan making love with him. He had the same beer belly as Pop and Vinnie.

She tensed as the take was finished and Gordon Faith turned to scan the room, looking for someone. Their eyes locked. He didn't look away. *He couldn't take his eyes off her.* Now he was walking toward her. She'd seen him smile like that a million times in movies.

"Bertha," he said jovially as he approached them, his eyes on Tina. "Who's this gorgeous thing you've brought us?"

even looked, the digits back away. We aren't even up to
it just Now, he says, waving at old ... She draws a line
smile like a million miles in the snow.

"Darling," he said, nuzzling as he straightened up. "Be
patient, Vina. We'll solve everything you've invested in."
real.

Eleven

Vanessa was relieved when Pat and Tracy closed up
the cottage on Fire Island soon after the Labor Day
weekend and returned to the apartment across the hall.
It was comforting to know they were there. She went
with them to help pick out their fall clothes, reveling in
the expeditions through Saks, Bonwit's, Bergdorf's, and
Altman's. She derived an earthy pleasure from the sight
and touch of the beautiful clothes—even though she
could not own them herself.

While Pat and Tracy registered for the term at their
respective schools—which guaranteed them another
nine months of living in New York—Vanessa triumphantly signed up for an evening class in fashion sketching along with her continuing night classes in Italian.
She was eager to be able to talk to Eddie's family when
they met.

Most evenings now Vanessa and Pat shared dinner
while Tracy chased off to meet Brian. The knowledge of
Eddie and Jesse somewhere in Italy was a strong bond
between them. Rome had been an "open city" since
June. Last month the Allies had captured Florence.

Ten days ago, Vanessa remembered as she climbed
the stoop of their brownstone, Tracy had written her
"Dear John" letter. That same night she and Brian had
decided they'd get married as soon as he could wangle a

few days' leave. Tracy hadn't told her parents yet. Nor did she plan on waiting for their approval before marrying Brian.

A lot of "Dear John" letters were being mailed, Vanessa thought unhappily while she unlocked her mailbox. How sad to be fighting in a strange country and to receive a letter like that. Her face lighted at the sight of three letters from Eddie. They had a way of arriving in bunches. The lilac envelope would be another of Tina's brief "keep in touch" notes. Standing in the vestibule, Vanessa ripped open the lilac envelope to read Tina's large scrawl. Upstairs, lingering over every word, she would read her three V-mails.

Except for the one walk-on, Tina reported, she was doing only "cheesecake" posing and was impatient for even a bit part. Gordon Faith was calling her regularly for dates, but she hadn't gone out with him. Somebody from Publicity had cornered her at the studio to warn her that Nat Kelman would be very unhappy if she went out with Imperial Films' prime star.

Upstairs in her apartment Vanessa read the cherished letters from Eddie. As always, he tried to assure her that he was in no danger; she believed not one word of this. He wrote how eager he was for his battalion to reach Venice. It had been years since he had heard from his family.

She reread each of Eddie's letters and felt for a moment as if she would reach out and touch him through the sheets of V-mail. It had been over ten months — *almost a year* — since she'd said good-bye to him at Penn Station. No matter how long it took, she vowed in anguish, she'd wait for Eddie.

She put the letters in the shoebox she kept for that purpose. This was the night she and Pat were having a spaghetti dinner here, she reminded herself, and crossed to the range to put up water to boil. She smiled at the sound of a light knock at the door. That would be Pat. She hurried to respond.

"Hi, Pat." Vanessa's smile froze. Pat had been crying. "Pat?" Her throat tightened in alarm.

"It's not Jesse," Pat said quickly. "I just had a call from Tracy's mother out in Houston. She was trying to reach Tracy. Tommy's parents just received word from the War Department. He was killed in action."

"Oh, Pat." A chill ran through Vanessa. "Do you suppose he'd received Tracy's letter?"

"We kept pushing her to write it," Pat tormented herself. "I wish we hadn't."

"Where's Tracy?" Vanessa asked.

"She was going straight downtown from school to meet Brian for dinner. He'll have to go back to the office afterward, but she figured they'd have an hour together," Pat shook her head slowly. "I can't believe Tommy's dead. Tracy and I have known him since we were little kids. It scares me—"

"I know." Vanessa's voice was a whisper. Cliff was gone, and now Tommy. "But nothing's going to happen to Jesse and Eddie," she said, her voice strong and sure. "They're going to come through this all right. I know they are."

"I wish Jesse and I had married out in Texas before he enlisted. I didn't have to tell my parents," Pat said with a passion that startled Vanessa. "I wish we'd married, and I'd gotten pregnant right away. At least I'd have his baby now."

"Pat, you'll marry Jesse when he comes home. And I'll marry Eddie." She struggled to sound confident. "And twenty years from now we'll look back and remember how awful the waiting was—but that they were worth it."

Too distraught to eat, Vanessa and Pat went to the other apartment to be there when Tracy came home. Pat remembered the first time she had realized that Tommy and Tracy were serious.

"All at once they were nutty about each other. Tracy's parents were pleased. Tommy's parents on both sides are 'old Texas.' Maybe they should have insisted on getting married before Tommy enlisted—" Pat's voice cracked. "Maybe then she wouldn't have met Brian."

Both girls tensed and turned to face the door at the sound of Tracy's voice in the hall. Tracy was singing, slightly off-key, her favorite of the year's hit tunes: "I'll Be Seeing You."

Pat was at the door before Tracy could knock. She pulled it wide. Tracy was startled. She gazed from Pat to Vanessa, and knew instantly that something awful had happened.

"What's wrong?" she asked.

"It's Tommy," Pat said softly. "Your mother called from Houston a little while ago. Tommy was killed in Guam."

"Oh, my God!" Tracy's voice rose in hysteria. "Do you think he got my letter? Do you think that made him careless? I killed him. I killed Tommy!"

"No," Pat shot back. "He died in the war. It had nothing to do with you. Tracy, stop it!" She grasped Tracy by the shoulders and shook her. "Tommy probably never received your letter." She released her hold as Tracy collapsed into sobs.

When would this awful war be over, Vanessa railed in silence while Pat rocked Tracy in her arms. In school they'd been taught that the First World War was *the* World War. How could they believe in anything when maniacs like Hitler and Mussolini and Hirohito could turn the whole world upside down?

Tina was unlocking her apartment door when the phone began to ring. She swore because her key was

139

sticking.

"Oh, hell!" She fumbled impatiently. It must be the studio with some crazy message about tomorrow. Nobody else ever called. Gordon Faith had given up weeks ago. She exhaled in relief when the key finally turned, and darted inside to pick up the phone. "Hello—"

"That is the sexiest hello I've heard in a long time." She recognized Gordon's voice. "Hope I'm not intruding at an inopportune moment," he drawled.

"I just came home from the studio." Tina kicked off her shoes and dropped into a chair. Gordon Faith wasn't the sexiest guy she'd ever met, but he was a full-fledged movie star. And nobody else was beating a path to her door. Still, she was mindful of the warning about Nat Kelman. Almost daily she read some item in Louella's or Hedda Hopper's column about Gordon and Eileen Nolan. Even stars as powerful as those two played along with Nat Kelman's wishes.

"Then you haven't had dinner yet," he pounced. "I'll pick you up in twenty minutes. We'll go to—"

"I can't," Tina interrupted. It was exciting to be pursued by Hollywood's biggest box-office star, even if she didn't feel like jumping into bed with him. Still, it would be fun to run around town with him.

"Why can't you?" he persisted.

Tina hesitated. They'd run these lines so many times before. All those other times she'd dreamt up a line of crazy excuses.

"I can't because Nat Kelman would kill me," she said in cool candor.

"Baby, you go out with me and everybody in Hollywood will start noticing you. You won't need Nat." He chuckled. "Fuck Nat Kelman. No," he corrected himself. "I'd rather fuck you."

"Good-bye," Tina said furiously and hung up.

The phone rang again. She didn't answer until the

140

twelfth ring. Then she picked up the phone, dropped it onto a chair, and covered it with a pillow. Everybody in Hollywood knew Gordon was a skirt chaser. And as soon as any girl let him into her bed, he moved on to the next.

An hour later, while Tina was finishing off a porterhouse — which cost her sixty-nine cents a pound and twelve points from her ration book — her doorbell buzzed. She stared grimly at the door. Gordon, she guessed, and walked to the door and called out in ice-cold tones. "What the hell are you doing here?"

"Flowers for Miss Gregory," a youthful male voice said timorously. *Not* Gordon Faith.

Tina pulled the door wide. Her apologetic smile was instantly transformed into a look of disbelief. Two delivery boys clutching half a dozen florist's boxes each stood before her. Gordon Faith couldn't believe somebody was turning him down.

"Where do you want them, Miss Gregory?" one of the delivery boys inquired.

"Put them on the sofa," Tina directed and went to take a dollar bill from her purse. She couldn't tip them less than that, could she?

As soon as she was alone again Tina opened the first box. A dozen exquisite long-stemmed red roses lay before her. The card said, "I'm sorry. Gordon." Each box contained a dozen red roses. Each box bore the same card. "I'm sorry. Gordon."

Tina put the roses in whatever containers she could dig out of her kitchen cabinet. A vase, a pitcher, a coffee percolator. She dumped out two inches of milk to use the bottle as a vase.

Tina made a point of going to bed by nine-thirty. Bertha kept warning all the contract players that if they didn't get enough sleep they'd look like hell before the cameras. She kept dangling before them that deal about

maybe tomorrow the bit part would come along to cata-
pult them to stardom.

Bertha kept telling them about how even a walk-on
could start letters pouring in from fans. Once the studio
bigwigs saw a starlet was drawing letters *("Who's the girl in
the beach scene with Gordon Faith?")*, they started to watch to
see how many came in. When the letters came by the
hundreds, the starlet was launched.

Tonight sleep eluded Tina. Her mind was running
through what would happen if she was seen around
Hollywood with Gordon Faith. Louella and Hedda
would run items. The fan magazines would show pictures of her and Gordon. Maybe Gordon *was* more
important to her career than Nat Kelman. Even the
great Nat Kelman wanted to keep his biggest star happy.

Before she fell asleep, Tina promised herself that the
next time Gordon phoned her—and he was not the kind
to take no for an answer—she'd go out with him. Let
Nat Kelman chew his fingernails up to his elbows. Nothing was happening to her career at Imperial Films anyway. She'd place her bets with Gordon.

Vanessa went to class four nights each week. Two
nights she attended her sketching class, which fired her
frustration even further. *She had so much to learn.* And yet
the encouragement of her instructor was heady. The
first time he said, "Vanessa, you have real talent," she
was dizzy with ecstasy.

Some Saturdays now she went into the office, grateful
for the overtime pay. She would be able to attend classes
for the second semester. She assuaged her guilt at spending money on classes by saving very diligently so she
would be able to send her mother an expensive purse as
a Hanukkah gift.

She told herself it was absurd to pretend that one day

the barrier her mother had erected between them would crumble. But her heart made inchoate excuses. Especially now, with Eddie and Tina so far away, she needed to believe that her mother was still part of her life.

On Columbus Day Pat and Tracy were off from classes. They tried to coax Vanessa to call in sick and go with them to the Paramount Theater to see Frank Sinatra in person. Tracy was running away from Tommy's death and punishing herself by seeing Brian only once a week now. She devoted every possible moment to listening to Sinatra on her new record player, on one of the many radio shows playing his latest Columbia record, or in person on "Your Hit Parade."

"But I have to go to work," Vanessa insisted when they tried again on Thursday morning as they prepared to leave for Times Square.

"You're too bloody conscientious," Tracy said with the almost hysterical gaiety she affected these days. "But come on, we'll take the bus downtown with you."

"You're going at this hour of the morning?" Vanessa reached for her purse. "On a day when you don't have classes?"

"The show will be mobbed," Pat explained. "And Tracy will die if we don't get in." She smiled indulgently at her roommate. "People must be in line already."

Vanessa understood: Pat was running downtown to the Paramount because this was an escape for Tracy. Like Pat she felt guilty that she had urged Tracy to write her "Dear John" letter. It had seemed so awful to let Tommy go on believing Tracy would marry him when he came home. But now Tracy couldn't bring herself to marry Brian, whom she loved in a way she'd never loved Tommy. Poor Brian was distraught.

She and Pat were lucky, Vanessa told herself while they walked through the crisp autumn air toward the downtown bus stop. They had uncomplicated love lives.

But this terrible waiting for the war to be over . . . . Every Sunday Pat went off to church to pray for Jesse and Eddie. And in her own private way, Vanessa prayed every night.

The three girls arrived at Times Square to find the area in a state of chaos. Already thousands of squealing teen-agers besieged the Paramount box office, clogged the streets, blocked traffic. Scores of policemen tried to cope with the hordes surging into the square from every side.

"Tracy, maybe we ought to go back home," Pat said uneasily as their bus stopped and started and stopped again every few feet.

"Are you kidding?" Tracy was exhilarated by the excitement. "We're going to see Frank Swoonatra in person."

Tracy and Pat left the bus. Vanessa's stop was at Forty-second Street and Fifth Avenue. She stared out at the mob scene before her.

"I'll bet there are ten thousand kids out there," one awed housewife said to Vanessa. "And look at those cops pouring in. Hundreds!"

"Maybe twenty thousand more before the day's over," a salesman predicted. "Those kids are nuts. Sinatra looks like a strong breeze would knock him flat on his face. With a million American boys in uniform, what do they see in him?"

"They go crazy over Sinatra," another male passenger suggested cynically, "because he's the only young man around."

"You're not going to the Paramount," the housewife said curiously to Vanessa. "You don't like his music?"

Vanessa smiled wryly.

"I have a job. I'm going to work."

Vanessa cast a backward glance over her shoulder as the bus made the turn east on Forty-second Street.

144

Those girls all seemed so young. *I'm nineteen, but I feel a dozen years older.*

In midafternoon Pat phoned her. "I couldn't wait until tonight to tell you," Pat said, her voice tender. "That letter Tracy sent to Tommy — he never received it. It was in the mailbox when we got home."

"Oh, Pat, thank God."

"Brian and she will get married secretly as soon as he can get a forty-eight-hour pass. We'll be their witnesses."

"How wonderful for them." Her pleasure was tinged with wistfulness. How long before Eddie and she could be married?

Tina was alternately defiant and defensive about going out with Gordon. Nothing was happening with her career. Her brief walk-on had gone unnoticed. She went through the usual makeup and hairdresser routine every morning, did endless "cheesecake" sessions. Not even a bit part surfaced. Yet now that Gordon Faith was chasing after her, she sensed a new respect among studio personnel.

She had been in Hollywood over two months. Although it was almost four months away, she was already mentally sweating out option time. How could she stand it if the studio dropped her? She'd have to leave Hollywood and go back to some crummy job in New York. To that shitty apartment.

On Sundays — with dreary hours ahead of her — she climbed into the Packard and drove through Bel Air and Beverly Hills. She admired the lush houses of the stars, producers, top directors and writers, eyed the sprawling estates with swimming pools and staffs of servants: *this was what she wanted.* Not that brownstone studio that cost them ten dollars a week.

So far she hadn't heard a word from Nat Kelman

about Gordon. One of the assistant directors had whispered that this was because he was having problems with Eileen Nolan and didn't have time to worry about anyone else. Eileen apparently had a passion for fourteen-year-old boys and was not always discreet. The mother of her current precocious lover was threatening to spill the story to the newspapers.

Tina sat soaking in a warm bubble bath before going out yet again with Gordon. She considered her situation. Gordon kept hammering at her about renting an apartment for her closer to the studio—though she had never let him cross the threshold of the one she had now. She had refused when he asked her to go to his house in Bel Air for a "nightcap." And every time he picked her up for a date they wrestled on the back seat of his white Rolls-Royce while his chauffeur drove them to Chasen's or the Mocambo or Romanoff's. He couldn't understand why she wouldn't let him go beyond a passionate kiss. He wasn't used to that. But she knew that the minute Gordon Faith made a conquest he moved on to somebody new. She also knew that if Gordon was really infatuated with her, he'd fight to keep her at the studio. Without him she might be dropped when option time arrived.

It irritated her that neither Louella nor Hedda said a word in their columns about her and Gordon. Nat Kelman's power to create an illusion—a romantic love affair between Gordon and Eileen—extended even to the gossip columns. Tina sighed and roused herself from her musings. She had to get ready for Gordon.

She was dressed and reading the *Hollywood Reporter* when Gordon's chauffeur came to the door.

"I'll be there in a couple of minutes, Ramon," Tina said casually.

She wouldn't let Gordon know she was sitting around waiting for him. What the hell was she going to do about him? If she slept with him, he'd be out of her life in three weeks. She relished her new position at the studio. She loved walking into movie-star-splashed nightclubs like the Mocambo or Ciro's or the Tracadero beside Gordon, table hopping with him, all eyes on them.

Gordon was important to her career. He said their picture was sure to be in the next issues of *Screenland* and *Photoplay*. If Imperial didn't pick up her option, maybe another company would sign her up. Being seen with Gordon Faith made her special.

Tina made one final inspection in a mirror and reached for her purse. She was so fucking bored with her life out here — except for the evenings with Gordon. She was developing a taste for Hollywood's night life. She remembered how Vanessa and she had clung to one drink at Clint Ashley's house on Fire Island. Now she handled champagne, gin, or tequila as though it was all one big cherry Coke.

She tugged at the chinchilla cape "borrowed" from Wardrobe as she stepped out into the cool night air. If Nat Kelman knew one of his fifty-dollar-a-week starlets was borrowing clothes from Wardrobe, he'd scream in outrage. But why shouldn't she, she asked herself defiantly. For fifty dollars a week — as long as they decided to keep her seven-year contract in force — she was a prisoner of Imperial Films. She couldn't leave Los Angeles without permission. She had that crazy morals clause in her contract.

"Baby, you look gorgeous." Gordon reached for her as the chauffeur helped her into the back seat. "Why don't we stop off at my place before we go to Chasen's?"

"Because I'm not climbing into your bed," she said in a mocking tone. "You know the rules."

"Damn it, Tina, is something wrong with me?" he

demanded, his face flushing.

"I think you're sensational," she purred in the fashion her dramatic coach encouraged. But she was scared by his unexpected anger. "Gordie, I'm small-town," she said, disarmingly ingenuous. "Small-town *Catholic*." She managed an apologetic smile. "I was brought up to believe I'll burn in hell if I sleep with a man before I'm married to him. It's all right to kiss and touch — I go to confession afterward and everything's all right." She hadn't been to confession since she'd left Pinewood. "I can't go 'all the way,' but I can go 'almost.'"

Gordon stared at her oddly.

"Holy Christ. You never slept with anybody?"

"No," she said with regret. "I couldn't confess that to the priest."

"It's not because you think I'm too fat?" He grinned self-consciously.

"Gordie, no." He seemed to like being called Gordie. She suspected that underneath his brash exterior was a shaky ego. He knew girls were eager to go out with him only because he was one of Hollywood's top box-office draws. "I think you're sexy. And you always make me laugh. It's fun going out with you." That much was true.

He was rich and famous and powerful. The studio — and Nat Kelman — would do anything to keep him happy and working. All at once Tina knew what she had to do to assure herself parts in important Imperial pictures. She had to marry Gordon Faith.

Twelve

Vanessa dreaded the approaching Thanksgiving holiday. Though Pat and Tracy had said nothing about going home, Vanessa assumed they would spend the long holiday weekend with their families. It was too far for the girls to go to Houston, but most likely Pat's family would have a reunion at their Virginia house. Tracy had talked about spending Thanksgiving with her family at the Homestead in Hot Springs, Virginia. Vanessa would be alone in the city.

She remembered her first Thanksgiving in New York. Tina and she had roasted a chicken and baked yams in their tiny oven. They'd bought a pumpkin pie at the bakery around the corner. And Tina had made nasty cracks about "my father, the pope" because he had not asked his "sinning daughter" to come home for the holidays. Up until the last minute she had thought he would. She'd insisted they'd go together to the Vigliano house for Thanksgiving dinner and return to New York the same night. But no invitation was offered.

Last Thanksgiving—their second in the city—had been desolate. Eddie had just been shipped out. Cliff was in boot camp. She and Tina had gone to a restaurant for Thanksgiving dinner. The room was almost empty, the waiters either stoic or resentful at having to work. Thanksgiving was a holiday that belonged in the home.

Mother would be having the traditional dinner at Mrs. Johnson's boardinghouse again. She'd find fault with everything, Vanessa surmised. She'd never liked Thanksgiving. When they had been home together, they'd had hamburger or spaghetti, something that could be made on top of the stove because cleaning the oven after a roast chicken was a repulsive task.

Vanessa assumed her mother still lived at the boardinghouse. She still looked for the familiar signature on the back of the checks that went to Mrs. Johnson's address each week. Her mother had never stopped mourning for the singing career she never had, Vanessa told herself with an effort at sympathy. She never got over being homesick for New York City and the life she'd known before she met Daddy.

Vanessa remembered in a rush of loneliness how her father had talked about his early years in Pinewood. Particularly the winters. Snow a foot or more deep, birch logs burning in the fireplace, the house filled with the warm aroma of fresh bread baking in the oven. Thanksgiving dinners where his grandparents had invited a dozen lonely souls to share their festive meal. Like his parents, her father had had great respect for the tradition of Thanksgiving.

Growing up in Pinewood, Vanessa had covertly longed to be part of the Christmas season, when most houses were decorated with the festive lights plus a colorfully decorated tree out on the front lawn. Not the religious Christmas. The happy "peace on earth, goodwill to men" Christmas.

Daddy always celebrated Hanukkah, in a quiet, almost secretive fashion. Mother refused to "go through the craziness of lighting candles every night for eight nights — worrying to death about a fire in the house." Daddy provided a Hanukkah present each year, which was usually displayed at school as "a Christmas present," because instinctively she knew not to call attention to her Jewishness. Once, in a rare moment of confidence, Daddy had admitted that at Christmas and Easter he felt like an outsider in Pinewood.

Eight days before Thanksgiving Pat reminded Vanessa that her boss owed her a day off for having worked late every night for the past week.

"Tell him you're taking it the Friday after Thanksgiving," Pat instructed. "We'll all go down to the Virginia house on Thursday morning and come back Sunday afternoon."

"Your parents won't mind?" Vanessa felt a surge of hope. She'd manage the train fare somehow, she decided. She'd never been to Virginia. She'd never been anywhere.

"They like a lot of people around the table on holidays." Pat's eyes were oddly cynical. "Anyhow, I promised to bring Tracy and you."

"It's too far to go to Texas, and it'll be fun roam around the plantation," Tracy drawled. "Brian will be working straight through on some secret project. After this, though he's sure to get a seventy-two-hour pass. You two stand by for a wedding early in December."

"Tracy, you didn't tell me!" Pat's face was radiant.

"I just found out. We'll be married at City Hall and spend our honeymoon at the Plaza," she said rapturously. "All we really want is a bed and room service."

Early Thursday morning Vanessa, Pat, and Tracy joined the last-minute throngs jamming Pennsylvania Station. The day was cold and crisp with faint gold sunlight bathing the city. Passengers juggled parcels and boxes along with their luggage, and here and there colorful chrysanthemums bloomed amid the coats and packages. The many servicemen and servicewomen were a grim reminder that the world was at war, yet today even this did little to dampen the feeling of fellowship that warmed the railroad terminal.

"We'll be lucky to find seats," Tracy warned, but she was philosophical about it: "Grab the first one you see."

Within a few minutes they were shuffling through the gate to the train that would take them down to Washington, D.C., where Pat's father would meet them for the long drive to the plantation. It sounded so grand, Vanessa mused while they joined the cluster of people waiting to board one of the middle cars. Plantations, in her mind, belonged to another century. It would be exciting to spend the long weekend in luxurious country surroundings.

As Tracy had predicted, the passengers scrambled madly for seats. Vanessa snared one directly behind Tracy and across the aisle from Pat. Tracy settled down to read her way to Washington. She'd bought the new novel by Kathleen Winsor, *Forever Amber,* which everybody said was the sexiest book on the bestseller list. Pat had a copy of *Town & Country* and Vanessa carried the current *Vogue.* Later they'd switch.

Vanessa fought against the waves of self-doubt that plagued her at the prospect of meeting Pat's mother and father, her sister, Maureen, and brother-in-law, Roger. Pat said her mother spent most of her time these days doing war work in Houston. And Mrs. Owens "adored clothes," Pat had reported, pleased that Vanessa and her mother would have this in common.

On occasion Vanessa had seen photographs of Madeline Owens in *Vogue* and *Town & Country* and *Harper's Bazaar.* She was an elegant blonde who was always exquisitely dressed, her jewelry fabulous without being ostentatious, her hair worn in a classic chignon that emphasized her fine features.

According to the newspaper and magazine articles Vanessa had read in preparation for her visit, Congressman Jim Owens liked to play at being "one of the people" despite the huge fortune he had amassed in cattle and cotton.

"At dinner parties," Pat had confided with a laugh, "Daddy loves to take off his jacket and sit around in shirt sleeves and suspenders. He says he got elected by the 'man in the street' because he's one of them."

Tracy had privately told Vanessa that the congressman had bought his seat in the House of Representatives eighteen years ago and held on to it in the same fashion. She suspected he harbored ambitions to sit one day in the White House. Right now he was a power in Congress, wheeling and dealing with the best of them.

As the train traveled south the sky turned gray with a hint of unleashed snow. Daddy used to love the snow, Vanessa remembered wistfully. Once, after an especially heavy snow, Daddy had taken her to the edge of town for "deer watching." She remembered the joy that lit his face as they watched a doe and three fawns cavort about a frozen brook. She wished with painful intensity that she had known her father better.

Her mother would be having Thanksgiving dinner around 2:00 P.M. at the boardinghouse. It wouldn't be fancy, Vanessa knew, because Mrs. Johnson's guests were always of limited means and the weekly charges small.

Vanessa had never looked forward to school holidays with the pleasure of her classmates. School had been a kind of refuge, she understood now. An escape from her mother's moods.

Why had her mother rejected her? Fresh frustration filled Vanessa. What had she ever done to make her mother push her out of her life? Her mother had always pushed her away. She'd tried to pretend her mother loved her, the way Daddy loved her. She'd always known that Daddy loved her.

Reluctantly her thoughts turned to the months—or was it years?—when she had awakened in the night with a chilling vision of being abandoned by her mother. Her mind catapulted back to the summer she was five. The summer before she started kindergarten . . .

Vanessa sat alone on the back seat of the ten-year-old Ford. Mama always said the child's place was in the back; the wife sat up front with her husband. It was fun to come all the way to Albany, Vanessa thought, bouncing a little on the seat while her father drove through the hilly streets of the city. Her wide eyes absorbed all the passing sights.

"I'll drop you and Vanessa off at John G. Meyers," her father said. "I'll do my buying and pick you up in about an hour." He was buying for the grocery store.

"I don't know why I let you persuade me to come along," her mother sighed. "What'll I do in the store for a whole hour?"

"Go up and look at the fur coats," Mr. Conrad teased. "You know you love that."

"Why?" The familiar martyred tone crept into his wife's voice. "It's not as though I'll ever be able to buy one. I'll be out in front of the store in exactly one hour. You be there. It's too hot to wait around."

Vanessa waited for her father to open the door for her. She knew she mustn't ever open the car door herself because something awful could happen.

"Be good, baby," her father said, lifting her from the car to the sidewalk. "And mind your mother."

Vanessa stayed close to her mother as they walked into the department store. Mama didn't like to hold her hand. She was too big for that now. But it was scary to wander around the store when so many people were here and not hold Mama's hand. They looked at the fur

154

coats, which was funny because it was hot enough to fry an egg, a man just said. They left the fur department to go to millinery, then dresses.

"Vanessa, you stay here," her mother said after a while. "Don't you move from this spot. I'll come back and get you."

"Mama, can't I go with you?" Fear crept into her voice.

"No, you can't. You stay here. I'll be right back."

Vanessa stood still. Not daring to move a foot away. She tried hard to pretend she wasn't scared. She watched for a few minutes while two ladies tried to decide which dress the younger one should buy. She wanted to tell her to take the yellow one — it was much prettier than the other. But then they went off to try on more dresses. *Where was Mama?*

The two ladies came out, and the younger bought the yellow dress. Vanessa tried not to cry. She tried hard.

"Mama?" She looked all around her. Everybody was so much bigger than she was. "Mama?"

A pretty saleslady came toward her, knelt in front of her.

"Darling, are you lost?"

"Mama's lost," Vanessa wailed. "She said she'd be right back."

"It's all right," the lady soothed. "We'll find her." She rose to her feet and took Vanessa's hand in hers.

"Mama!" Vanessa cried desolately. "I want my mama!"

"It's all right, we'll find her," the lady promised. "She's probably looking for you right this minute."

Together they walked through the whole floor, then went downstairs to the street floor. Vanessa sobbed softly, in the clutches of despair. Daddy would come back to the store, and he wouldn't know where to find Mama or her. Mama had been gone a long time.

"Tell us your name," a sympathetic bystander coaxed.

"Vanessa," she managed between sobs.

"Vanessa what?" somebody else prodded, but she was too scared to remember.

"I tell you, she must have just walked off with some-body—" Vanessa froze at the sound of her mother's voice. She couldn't see her because of all the people standing around her.

"Della, she has to be here!"

"Daddy!" Vanessa shrieked. "Daddy!"

Instantly she was swept up in her father's arms.

"Baby, you scared us half to death," he crooned.

Daddy was scared, but Mama *wanted* to lose her . . .

"Vanessa," Tracy's voice intruded from the seat in front of her, "start thinking about the kind of dress I should wear when Brian and I get married. Something that'll be all right at City Hall, but that I can wear when we all go to dinner at the Plaza."

"I'm thinking," Vanessa said gravely, thankful to have her mind off old memories. The faith that Tracy and Pat placed in her judgment was precious to her.

Vanessa wished they could linger in the capital, but they were expected at the plantation in time for a mid-afternoon dinner. Eddie would have enjoyed hearing about a day of sightseeing in Washington. One day, she promised herself, she and Eddie would visit Washington.

How strange to be on a train bound for a Thanksgiving weekend on a Virginia plantation! She mustn't let Pat's family know how awed she was. Tina would have loved being with them, but Tina was having Thanksgiving dinner with Gordon Faith and a bunch of his friends. When Tina had called last night, she'd admitted she was out to marry him. *"Honey, I was never the kind to look for a knight on a white charger. Just a guy behind the wheel of a bought-and-paid-for white Rolls."*

At last the train pulled into the huge, white Vermont granite Union Station. Congressman Owens, a tall, spare, prematurely white-haired man, was waiting for them. He exuded a charm and vitality that made most onlookers forget he was far from handsome. While he welcomed Vanessa in his liquid velvet southern accent, she could envision him hot on the political trail. His dark eyes were shrewd and crafty, weighing everyone and everything in view. He would be a dangerous enemy, she assessed, and was discomfited by this evaluation.

The chauffeur waited at the door of a pearl-gray Cadillac limousine. He greeted Pat and Tracy warmly and stood by at deferential attention while Pat introduced Vanessa. The three girls were seated in the rear of the limousine. Congressman Owens sat beside the chauffeur. He spent the two hours of the trip to the plantation reading through a sheaf of material he pulled from his briefcase.

"We're almost there," Pat said with a lilt in her voice.

After driving past a seemingly endless stretch of fieldstone fencing, the limousine turned into a long, poplar-lined roadway. The congressman stuffed his reading material back into the briefcase and turned around to talk.

"This is a working plantation, Vanessa," he explained. "We've got almost a thousand acres in tobacco. Of course," he chuckled, "you won't see the tobacco fields from the house. My wife wouldn't allow that."

An impressive red-brick Georgian mansion appeared at a turn in the roadway. The limousine pulled to a stop before the house as a pair of high-spirited Irish setters charged forward in welcome. A few moments later Madeline Owens appeared on the portico: a tall, slender woman of about fifty with a cold, brittle beauty. She wore a simple black crepe that Vanessa recognized as a

Schiaparelli design created in the workrooms of Bonwit Teller.

"You all must be exhausted." Mrs. Owens accepted a kiss from her daughter. "We'll have tea in the library. Dinner won't be for another hour yet."

Servants whisked the girls' luggage up to their bedrooms while Mrs. Owens led them into a high-ceilinged, wood-paneled, bookcase-lined room off the huge marble-floored entrance hall. Aubusson rugs covered the floor and at one side of the room a burgundy velvet loveseat and beige velvet Queen Anne side chairs flanked a Chippendale tea table. At the other side of the room stood an ornate writing table and chair, a Chinese lacquered screen, and an Oriental cabinet.

Mrs. Owens and the three girls settled themselves around the table, and almost immediately a maid appeared with a tea tray.

"I knew some Conrads in Boston years ago. Could they be your family?" Mrs. Owens asked Vanessa.

"No, we're from upstate New York," Vanessa said quickly. Their name courtesy of an immigration officer.

"Are you at Pat's school or Tracy's?" Mrs. Owens inquired.

"Vanessa's studying fashion design," Pat answered for her. Vanessa suspected Pat had told her mother earlier, but that Mrs. Owens had forgotten. Pat said nothing about Vanessa's job in the law office.

"How exciting," Mrs. Owens smiled. "I adore clothes. I so miss going to Paris to shop. Isn't it ironic that here in America we're terribly limited in our wardrobes because of this beastly war, but in Europe women are dressing as smartly as ever?"

"The top Paris fashion houses are still doing business despite the Germans." She was comfortable with Mrs. Owens in discussing fashion, Vanessa thought gratefully. "Alix, Paquin, Lanvin, Lelong, even Schiaparelli, though Madame Schiaparelli herself is here in this country."

"But only the European women can take advantage of Paris couture," Mrs. Owens mourned. "Here we're limited by the rationing to three pairs of shoes a year," she noted in disdain, though Vanessa would bet that Madeline Owens knew how to bypass the regulation. "In Lisbon for almost nothing you can have snakeskin and suede shoes made to order. And the women in Lisbon wear original French models. They're brought across the border regularly. In Rome, I hear, the shops are filled with exquisite clothes."

While the four sipped tea, Madeline Owens rattled on about clothes with an occasional contribution from Vanessa. Despite the war, Pat's mother lived in a rarefied world where servants still appeared on call, and idle women were chauffeured to social engagements and to their "war committees." Vanessa diplomatically refrained from pointing out that America fashions—which Mrs. Owens decried as tasteless and without style—were adapted to the needs of girls and women who worked in offices and factories, traveled on buses and subways.

During a pause in the conversation Mrs. Owens glanced at her diamond-studded Cartier watch.

"It's time you girls went upstairs to refresh yourselves," she told them. "We'll be sitting down to dinner in twenty minutes. Her face tightened. "I just hope Maureen and her husband can manage to arrive on time for once."

Upstairs Pat showed Tracy and Vanessa to their adjoining rooms.

"I'm sure you won't mind sharing a bath," she said with a glint of humor in her eyes. "Mother always apologizes because these two guest rooms don't have private bathrooms."

"Honey, your mother would apologize if she was entertaining at Versailles," Tracy laughed. "I'm starving. Let's rush through the washing up and get down to the table. Providing, of course, that her ladyship has arrived. That's Maureen," Tracy explained for Vanessa's benefit. "She even kept them waiting at her wedding."

Vanessa was entranced by the magnificent bedroom assigned to her. It was furnished in elegant antiques, the floor covered by an exquisite Oriental rug, the walls attractively papered. The bathroom she was to share with Tracy was a masterpiece of marble and glass.

"Don't bother changing clothes," Tracy said, opening the bathroom door from the other side. "And don't let Mrs. Owens intimidate you. She just *thinks* she's the royal princess of Houston, Texas. She's forever mad at Maureen for marrying Roger instead of some broken-down Italian prince she had picked out. She was dying to talk about 'my daughter, Princess Maureen,' " Tracy mimicked.

"Mrs. Owens said we should be downstairs in twenty minutes." Vanessa checked her watch.

"Vanessa, this is the South," Tracy giggled. "Nobody's ever on time."

But Vanessa and Tracy rounded up Pat — caught covertly writing a letter to Jesse in her bedroom — and the three girls headed down the wide, curving staircase. In the entrance hall Madeline Owens was welcoming her daughter and son-in-law.

"Darling, you're putting on weight," Mrs. Owens scolded. "Roger, tell her to behave herself or she'll have to go out to Maine Chance and take off those extra pounds."

"Mother, let the Duchess of Windsor starve herself to death," Maureen shrugged. "Roger likes a woman with a little meat on the bone."

"Maureen, must you always be vulgar?" Mrs. Owens turned her attention to Roger. "Are they working you to death up there in Washington?" she asked solicitously, though Pat had intimated on several occasions that her mother and brother-in-law maintained a semblance of friendly relations only because they were related.

"And this is Vanessa Conrad. Vanessa studies design up in New York," Mrs. Owens explained.

"Where's Daddy?" Maureen demanded when the amenities were over. "Filling himself with bourbon so he can endure another family dinner?"

Mrs. Owens frowned in silent reproach.

"He's probably at the table already. Hallie was ready to serve dinner fifteen minutes ago. Let's go to the dining room."

At dinner—which in addition to the traditional turkey, dressing, yams, and cranberry sauce, included Texas-style fried chicken and chili—Vanessa was increasingly conscious of the royal style in which the Owens family lived. Dinner was served by a white-jacketed houseman and a maid in a black uniform with stiffly starched white apron. Vanessa guessed that the exquisite china was Haviland, which Phil and Robbie had discussed in detail on Fire Island. The silverware was heavy, ornate sterling.

Vanessa remembered Thanksgiving dinners at home. Her mother bought china at the five-and-dime. Their silverware, a mixture of her parents' wedding gift silver plate and that inherited from the Conrad grandparents, was deposited in a glass or mug and placed in the center of the dining table—covered by an oilcloth rather than the fine Irish lace that graced the one at which she sat today. Oh, yes, Vanessa thought with heady delight, she would love to live in the style of the rich.

Yet as dinner progressed, Vanessa was aware of the veiled bickering between Madeline and Jim Owens. Bickering that, as the dinner progressed, grew less subtle.

161

"Vanessa, did Pat ever tell you about her her great-grandmother on her mother's side?" Jim Owens asked with a jovial smile that belied the malicious glint in his eyes.

"I don't believe so," Vanessa said politely, dreading what was coming.

"She was quite a gal. Born in Houston when it was little more than a cow pasture. When she was fifteen, she was a spy for the Confederacy. She was a terrific-looking broad, and I don't have to tell you that helped when she was after information from Yankee officers. Gossip was that she was might free with her favors — but then it was for a good cause." He winked at Vanessa. Mrs. Owens jabbed viciously at a slab of turkey breast. "After the war she married a riverboat gambler from Natchez, and the family was about to disown her. Then they realized she was using her husband's gambling table winnings — and he was on a winning streak for a long time — to buy up every small stretch of land that came up for sale. She made sure every scrap of land she bought bordered what she already owned. In less than ten years she had a spread of almost a hundred thousand acres. Land came cheap in those days. And she had half a dozen sons to grow up and run the ranch for her. The family may have come over on the *Mayflower*, but it was that little girl who married the gambler from Natchez who put them into the big money."

"Maureen, however are you managing with dinner parties in the face of all the rationing?" Madeline Owens inquired in a determined effort to rechannel the table talk. "Daddy told me he had the vice-president and half the cabinet to dinner last week."

Pat and Tracy initiated small talk at their end of the table, and Vanessa was relieved to be brought into this. With all that money and social position, Vanessa marveled, the Owens family was not a happy one. How had

Pat's mother and father come to marry each other? And then she remembered a bit of conversation with Tracy: *"It was all right for the daughter of one of Houston's First Families to marry a rich redneck, but they won't let their daughter marry a poor garage mechanic."*

Despite the tensions in the Owens household, Vanessa enjoyed the luxurious surroundings. It was like living in a page out of *Town & Country,* she marveled.

They saw Pat's family only at lunch and dinner. Breakfast was served buffet style, though trays going up the stairs indicated that Mrs. Owens and her older daughter preferred to breakfast in their bedrooms.

The congressman rose early. Lingering in bed each morning, Vanessa heard him in loud conversation with various servants as he helped himself to breakfast from the array of chafing dishes on the buffet. Once the congressman was gone from the dining room, Roger went downstairs to breakfast in solitary splendor. Then Pat would gaily summon Vanessa and Tracy to join her downstairs. After breakfast Pat and Tracy went riding, though Pat had offered to forgo this when she realized Vanessa didn't ride. Vanessa insisted she'd be happy roaming about the acreage in the company of the plantation's pair of Irish setters.

The three girls dawdled over lunch each day before an open fire in an octagonal sunlit room off the kitchen. In the afternoons Pat ignored the gas shortage and drove them about the beautiful countryside. And after dinner the birch logs crackled in the living room fireplace, lending charm to a room that might otherwise have been overwhelming in its richness.

After dinner one evening the congressman and Roger sat in chairs at one side of the room and argued about the progress of the war. Mrs. Owens and Maureen discussed recent Washington parties. The three girls were content to gaze into the fire and relax with small talk about what had happened during the day. Later the three of them would gather in the privacy of Pat's bedroom to talk about their men and Tracy's imminent — but secret — wedding.

They arrived back in new York in the midst of a light snowfall. Another year was almost gone, Vanessa thought as they settled into a taxi for the ride uptown. She was grateful that she was enrolled at design school, yet impatient that she was tied to a dull office job.

"I had an awful fight with Mother," Pat confided when they had settled down over coffee in her apartment. Earlier Vanessa and Pat had read their overseas mail, and Tracy had talked on the phone with Brian. "She knows we have the whole Christmas-to-New Year's period off from school, and she can't understand why I insisted I could only come down to the plantation for the long Christmas weekend."

"Ten days would be deadly," Tracy agreed. "And you'd die if you knew letters from Jesse were piling up here and you were down there."

"You still going to Palm Beach?" Pat asked.

"I have to." Tracy sighed. "It's a big family scene. My mother, my father, my grandmother, the four older sisters and their families."

"You'll come down to Virginia with me," Pat turned to Vanessa. "You made a big hit with Mother."

"Because I can talk about clothes with her," Vanessa said with a laugh. She was glad she wouldn't be alone in New York for Christmas. The city could be desolate for anyone alone over a holiday.

"This coming week we have to go shop for my dress," Tracy reminded her. "Brian and I have to get our marriage license. And I have to make a reservation for the dinner party at the Plaza."

"I'm giving the wedding dinner at the Plaza," Pat decided. Her smile was tender. "The bride shouldn't do that."

How long before the war was over and she would be preparing for her wedding to Eddie, Vanessa asked herself in a surge of loneliness. Why hadn't they married before he was shipped out? Just a private civil ceremony. Later they could be married by a rabbi in the presence of his family.

She remembered a scrap of poetry she'd learned in high school. Wordsworth, wasn't it?

> *We look before and after*
> *And pine for what is not —*

Thirteen

Tina pretended to ignore Gordon's sulking as they left Romanoff's and walked to the waiting Rolls. He was furious because once again she had refused to go back to his house. Ramon leapt from the car to open the door for them. Gordon climbed in first and huddled in a corner. Shrugging her shoulders, Tina joined him on the back seat. But she was upset. She needed Gordon's support. She was getting nowhere at the studio. It seemed unlikely that her option would be picked up.

"Gordie, don't sulk," she protested.

"Why can't you come back to the house with me like any normal girl?" he demanded. "Have I got B.O. or halitosis or something?"

"Honey, I told you," Tina apologized. "I was raised by strict parents. I just can't—"

"You never?" he asked again for the dozenth time.

"I never," she lied sweetly. "It's not that I don't want to." She made it a shy confession. "Sometimes, when I'm sitting with you like this, that wild side of me just drives me crazy." She leaned forward, knowing his eyes would be rivited to her cleavage. "Gordie, try to understand." She dropped one hand to his knee. "How could I go to confession on Sunday if I slept with you?"

"Baby, the Catholic priests in this town know more about who's sleeping with who than Louella and Hedda

166

put together." Gordon grinned. "So you sleep with me, you go to confession next morning, and zingo, no more sin."

"Gordie, you don't understand." She managed a little break in her voice.

"What I understand is that you make me hot as a pistol," he said grimly. "And I'm tired of the little games we play. I touch you there—" he mimicked, sliding a hand inside her dress. "And you touch me here—" He brought her hand to his crotch. "I want the whole scene, Tina, not playing like we're back in high school."

"Gordie, I do too," she whispered, and it wasn't entirely a lie. When he pinched her nipple that way, she went hot and cold at the same time. "But you can't understand because you weren't brought up like me." She felt him growing hard beneath her hand.

"We'll get married," he said amorously. "Then it'll be okay."

"After we're married, it'll be okay," she stipulated. Elation charged through her.

"I'll buy you an engagement ring tomorrow," he promised. "Let's go to the house now."

"After the priest marries us, we'll go to the house," she said softly. Nat Kelman might carry on like mad, but he couldn't stop Gordon Faith from marrying her. And Kelman wouldn't dare drop her option when she was Gordie's wife. "It'll be wonderful," she sighed.

Gordon pulled away. Tina stiffened in alarm. Was he changing his mind about getting married?

"Look, I've been married and divorced. It happened back when I was nineteen. How do I explain that to the priest?" All at once he grinned. "We don't have to tell the priest. We'll have a civil ceremony. I'll tell Nat tomorrow. The picture's in the can. We can take off a month for a honeymoon."

The next day at lunch break Tina met Gordon in his

dressing room. He made her close her eyes while he brought out the three-carat diamond he had bought earlier in the day on a surreptitious trip to Rodeo Drive.

"All right, you can look now," he said complacently.

Tina opened her eyes and gasped at the sight of the beautifully set diamond. Her smile was brilliant as she extended her left hand.

"Gordie, it's gorgeous." And it was hers. She was going to be Mrs. Gordon Faith.

"Don't run away at the end of the day," he admonished her. "We'll tell Nat we're getting married."

"You want me to go with you?" All at once she was uneasy.

"I need your moral support." He pulled her against him so tightly his belt buckle cut into her skin. "And don't wear that ring until after we've told Nat," he muttered through his kisses.

Tina went through the rest of the day with the three-carat diamond nestled between her breasts, the band pinned to her bra. She wished they could get married first and tell Nat Kelman afterward, but she understood. Nat's stars did nothing without telling the star maker.

By the time she and Gordon walked into the reception room of Nat Kelman's office, his secretarial staff had left for the day.

"Gordie, you'd better tell him alone," Tina said with a sudden flash of intuition. "I'll wait out here. Call me in later."

Gordon reflected for a moment. He was expecting trouble. But Nat couldn't stop them from getting married. Resolutely Gordon straightened his tie, winked at Tina, walked to the door, and knocked.

"Yeah—" Kelman's voice filtered through the door.

Gordon marched inside and closed the door behind him. Moments later Nat's outraged yell assaulted Tina's ears.

"What do ya mean, you wanna marry some two-bit contract player?" he yelled. "You can't find enough cunts at the studio to get into?"

"Nat, it's different with Tina. We're in love." Gordon's voice sounded strange, high-pitched.

"You stupid schmuck, she just knew how to get you so fuckin' hot you can't think straight. You're a big star. You'll marry somebody like Eileen Nolan. If you have to get married —"

"Eileen likes teenagers," Gordon snorted. "Nat, I'm in love with Tina," he pleaded.

"This week," Nat said. "Next week it'll be somebody else. You're too young for marriage."

"I'm thirty-four. Even if my studio bio says I'm twenty-four. I'm marrying Tina. There's nothing in my contract that says I can't."

Tina waited, her throat tight with fear. After what seemed an interminable silence, Nat spoke.

"All right, you dumb schmuck. But the studio plans the wedding. The quieter we keep it the better. You finish the picture, get married in a judge's chambers, and you can go off on your honeymoon and promote the new picture at the same time."

Outside in the reception area, Tina slowly smiled.

A light snow was falling in the Sunday twilight when Brian's naval lieutenant best man put Vanessa and Pat into a taxi in front of the Plaza. The occasion had been full of poignancy. Tracy had cried and said it was like a dress rehearsal for Vanessa's wedding, and Pat's. For months now Americans had been sure of victory in Europe and the Pacific — but *when?* Not by the end of the year, obviously, as so many had predicted. New Year's was less than three weeks away.

"Tracy looked beautiful," Pat said, awash in sentimentality. "Vanessa, you're so good about adding that special something to a dress or taking something away to make it just sensational. You ought to be working for Hattie Carnegie or Schiaparelli."

"In June, when I've finished my next evening course," Vanessa said, her face luminescent, "I'll take my sketchbook around Seventh Avenue and try for a job in fashion. Even if it's less money, I'll take it." Tina was on her way in Hollywood. It was time for *her* to move ahead. She'd still manage, somehow, to send a check to her mother every week.

She ached with frustration because, with Paris in German hands, Seventh Avenue had emerged as the world fashion leader — *and she was not part of it*. It wasn't enough to take an evening class, devour every issue of *Vogue* and *Harper's Bazaar* and *Town & Country*, make *Women's Wear Daily* her bible. She wanted to be working on Seventh Avenue, she wanted to know she was on the road to becoming a fashion designer.

Climbing the stairs to their floor, Vanessa and Pat heard the phone ringing in Pat's apartment. Pat charged ahead to open the door and pick up the phone before it stopped ringing. Vanessa arrived at her heels.

"Hello," Pat said breathlessly. Her face lit up. "Tina! Wait a sec — Vanessa's right here."

"Hi—" Vanessa dropped into a chair. Tina's calls, though infrequent in deference to her budget, were apt to be long.

"Vanessa, I'm married!" Tina yelled into the phone. "Just two hours ago. I didn't want to call until it happened. It'll be the lead item in Louella's column Monday morning!"

"Tina, are you in love with him?" Vanessa asked softly.

"What's love got to do with it?" Tina scoffed. Her

170

voice was low. "Sweetie, the studio is tearing up my old contract and giving me a new one. I'll have a speaking part in Gordie's next picture!"

They talked and laughed and cried until the impatient bridegroom pulled Tina away from the phone. They were heading for the first lap in their honeymoon — a week at Camelback Inn in Scottsdale, Arizona. From Camelback they would embark on a whirlwind tour of a dozen major cities to promote Gordon's new picture.

Vanessa was touched that Tina insisted on paying half the rent on the apartment for the next six months — "to make sure the sky doesn't fall on me and I'm back in New York again." She and Tina would be forever close. They'd shared too much for it to be otherwise. Yet Vanessa felt a nagging sadness because Tina had married without love.

The evening before she was to leave for Virginia for the long Christmas weekend — after much inner debate — Vanessa made up her mind to phone her mother. It had been two and a half years since she had left Pinewood. Pat diplomatically invented an excuse to go downstairs while Vanessa geared herself to make the call. It was going down to Virginia to a big family gathering that prompted her to do this, Vanessa thought while she waited for someone at Mrs. Johnson's boardinghouse to pick up the phone.

"Hello." A man answered.

"May I please speak to Mrs. Conrad?" Vanessa's throat was tight with anticipation. Her mother was her sole surviving relative.

"Just a minute." The voice at the other end seemed surprised. This was probably the first phone call her mother had ever received at the boardinghouse. She'd sent her mother a beautiful leather purse for Hanukkah. She'd mailed it early — it must have arrived by now.

"Hello," the voice came back on the line. "Mrs. Conrad don't accept phone calls."

"It's her daughter," Vanessa said quickly. "Vanessa."

"I'm sorry." A hint of compassion. "She said she don't accept phone calls from nobody."

Vanessa was trembling when she put down the phone. What had possessed her to think that her mother had changed? She had never wanted a child. She didn't want one now.

Don't think about Mother. Just send the check each week because that's a responsibility to Daddy. But forget you ever had a mother.

Vanessa went down to Virginia with Pat. The family tensions and quarrels were worse over the long weekend than on her previous visit. When she and Eddie were married and had children, Vanessa swore, their children would grow up in an atmosphere of love. Daddy had loved her, she repeated to herself; she clung to this sweet memory. She felt little genuine love in the super rich Owens household.

Vanessa and Pat spent New Year's Eve with Tracy in the small downtown apartment she shared with Brian.

"I know I have a nerve complaining because Brian is stuck with a double tour of duty, but wouldn't you think we could spend our first New Year's Eve as man and wife together?" Tracy mourned.

On New Year's afternoon Tina phoned from Chicago to wish them a happy 1945. Chicago was as far east as Gordon's tour was bringing them. Tina admitted she wished the tour was over and they were back on the Coast and settled in their new Bel Air house with four bedrooms and a swimming pool.

"Camelback was terrific," Tina reported. "We had our own adobe guest house with a balcony looking right out on Camelback Mountain. We also had Lester with us," she added drily. "Everywhere but in our bedroom. Les is the studio publicist who travels with us."

"Are you happy?" Vanessa asked uncertainly.

"I'll be happy when Gordon pushes the studio into a real buildup for me. And he will," she said with a surge of conviction. "Because I'm making him happy where it counts."

In January Franklin Roosevelt was inaugurated for an unprecedented fourth term. He was to leave in two days for Yalta for a top-level conference with Churchill and Stalin. Though the fighting continued on both fronts, victory was in the air. Eddie wrote that he was in Rome. Jesse was in Florence.

Early in February Vanessa began her second term of evening classes at design school. On her own — reading, studying clothes on display in the best stores — she was absorbing much about the world of fashion. She was elated when *Town & Country*, in its January '45 issue, devoted all its fashion pages to American *haute couture* — designs by Adrian, Mark Mooring, Fira Benenson, Hattie Carnegie, Arthur Falkenstein, Valentina.

She devoured *Women's Wear Daily*, spent hours every Sunday exploring the museums in search of ideas for dresses and coats, adapting these to Pat's and Tracy's wardrobes as well as her own far less extensive one. Pat and she were inseparable now, bound close by their mutual fears and hopes. Tracy was involved with Brian, who had been permanently assigned to Naval Intelligence in New York.

On April 12, President Roosevelt died in Warm Springs, Georgia, and the nation was thrown into mourning. For Vanessa's generation the only American president they could remember was gone. And for millions of Americans it was an intensely personal loss. But while Americans grieved for Roosevelt, they read ea-

173

gerly about the United Nations Conference opening in San Francisco on April 24, with delegates from fifty nations attending.

On Monday morning, May 7, radios blared out the unofficial news that Germany had surrendered. Torn paper and ticker tape streamed from office windows. Half a million people gathered in Times Square and milled about the streets until Mayor La Guardia's voice over a loudspeaker urged them to "go home or return to your jobs."

On the morning of May 8 Vanessa was at her desk by nine and typing up a brief—trying not to cling too hopefully to yesterday's reports about peace in Europe—when shouts outside her tiny office pulled her away from the typewriter.

"The war in Europe is over!" one of the law partners was shouting over and over. Vanessa knew he had a son somewhere in France. "It's true. Truman just went on the air to announce it!"

Shouts of jubilation rose from the street below. Joyous faces appeared in windows. Confetti and paper were fluttering down from offices. People poured out of buildings and into the streets and churches to celebrate victory in Europe. The workday was over.

Vanessa pushed her way through the raucous crowds surging toward Times Square. Her one thought was to get home and share with her joy with Pat on this most wonderful day in their lives. The whistles from the war-gray ships in the North River almost overpowered the other sounds of the city.

Vanessa abandoned any thought of taking a bus home today. She hurried down into the subway, pausing on the platform to try to call Pat, whose classes on Tuesday didn't begin until 10:30 A.M. Phone operators were also celebrating victory in Europe—there was no service.

Her train pulled into the station. She joined the festive crowds pushing inside the car. Her attention was suddenly held by a small, pretty young woman who was carrying a toddler. Her face was infinitely sad, in sharp relief to the laughing crowds around her. Vanessa's eyes filled with tears. For the young woman carrying the toddler this was not a joyous day. Had the soldier or sailor or marine who loved her ever seen his child?

At Seventy-second Street Vanessa left the subway and hurried through the streets to her apartment. Running up the stairs she heard a radio newscaster—his voice shrill with excitement—elaborating on the news of the unconditional German surrender.

"Pat!" She banged joyously on the door. "Pat!"

The door swung wide. Pat threw her arms about Vanessa.

"Oh, God, isn't it wonderful! Vanessa, they'll be coming home soon!"

Fourteen

Pat awoke to the insistent ringing of the phone beside her bed. Still bleary-eyed from sleep, she tried to focus on the clock on her night table as she picked up the phone. It was a few minutes before 6:00 A.M.

"Hello—" She struggled into a semi-sitting position.

"Pat, I'm back in the States!" Jesse's voice came to her, loud and clear. "I'm at Fort Dix."

"Oh, Jesse!" She sat upright, fully awake. Hearing Jesse's voice over the phone, she felt as though he had been away only weeks instead of almost fifteen months. "When will I see you?" *Jesse was home.*

"Start meeting the trains from Fort Dix around six o'clock," he said. "I'll be on the first one I can make." Pat heard a jumble of voices in the background. "I gotta get off the line," he sighed. "Half the army's waiting to use the phone. Meet me at Penn Station."

Pat sat immobile, clutching the phone, her eyes shining. She'd see Jesse today. *This* day. No more lonely nights, thinking of him wounded or dead somewhere in Italy. No more nights feeling empty inside. In a few months she'd be twenty-one—they could get married without anybody's consent. They wouldn't wait a few months, she decided in a dizzying revelation. They'd rent a car and drive down to that place in Maryland where a girl could get married at eighteen.

With a squeal of happiness she swung her legs to the floor, reached for the robe at the foot of her bed, and ran across the hall to knock on Vanessa's door.

"Coming—" Vanessa's sleep-drenched voice filtered through the door. A moment later the door opened.

"Jesse's at Fort Dix!" Pat bubbled. "I couldn't wait for you to wake up to tell you—"

"You heard from him?" Vanessa's face was radiant.

"He phoned. I'm meeting him at Penn Station at six o'clock. Or at least, I'm meeting every train from then on—he can't be sure when he'll be here. I'll be there at five," she decided. She threw her arms around Vanessa and hugged her tightly. "Oh, Vanessa, I can't believe it!"

Over coffee, Pat chattered to Vanessa about her plans. She wouldn't bother returning for the final three weeks of school. From now on her life belonged to Jesse.

"I'll run down to Altman's beauty salon and have my hair done. I know I don't have an appointment, but I'll beg for one. And then I'll shop for a gorgeous bridal nightie and negligee. After a year in the army Jesse will love to see me in something white and frilly."

"Pat, did he say if he was being discharged?" Vanessa's voice was faintly apologetic. Pat stared in shock. "You know what they said on the news about shipping men in the European theater to the Pacific."

"You mean Jesse may have to go back on duty?"

"He could be on furlough," Vanessa warned, but her face reflected her sympathy.

"Then we'll be married right away. I'm not letting Jessie go off to fight again without our being married." Fear battled with her exhilaration. *Would* Jesse have to go to fight in the Pacific? She wouldn't think about that now. Not when Jesse was only hours away. "One of these days, soon," she predicted, "my phone will ring, and it'll be Eddie asking for you. Oh, Vanessa, Jesse's home!"

When Vanessa left for the office, Pat went with her. It

was too early to get into the department stores, but she couldn't bear to stay inside the apartment alone. She dawdled over coffee and a danish in a nearby Schrafft's until B. Altman opened its doors.

She was ecstatic when she was given an immediate appointment in the beauty salon because of a last-minute cancellation — today was her day. With a candor born of the dramatic occasion, she confided to the hairdresser that she was soon to meet her returning soldier. The hairdresser was waiting impatiently for a reunion with her air force pilot husband. Her hair trimmed, shampooed, and set in a flattering pompadour, Pat rushed to phone Vanessa to meet her on her lunch hour. They'd have a fast luncheon in the Charleston Gardens and then look at the bridal sets in Altman's lingerie department.

Pat waited in the lobby of Vanessa's office building. When she appeared they headed south for Altman's, strode purposefully through the store, and took an elevator to the lingerie floor. Lunch would have to wait. From the activity in the department store it was obvious that other young women in the city harbored similar thoughts. Pat quickly chose a filmy white chiffon nightgown designed in the Grecian style with a matching negligee. Then they hurried upstairs to the Charleston Gardens.

"I have to buy a new dress," Pat said in a sudden panic while she and Vanessa waited to be served, and Vanessa laughed — because Pat's closet was packed with exquisite dresses. "I have to meet Jesse in something I've never worn before," she insisted. Her face was beaming. "Something chic and mature. I don't feel like I'm twenty. I feel like a woman."

"You'll find something that won't even need alterations," Vanessa surmised. "With me everything has to be shortened."

"Vanessa, what should I look for?" Pat pleaded for advice. "Where shall I shop?" Anxiety crept into her voice. "I don't have too much time. I want to be in Penn Station by five sharp. In case Jesse arrives early."

Their waitress brought their salads and iced coffee. The girls concentrated on what Pat should wear when she met Jesse at the train. It was the most important dress she would ever wear, Pat declared. More important than her wedding dress.

Before five Pat was standing before the escalator that delivered passengers from the Trenton trains to the waiting area. The palms of her hands were moist with perspiration as she watched the arrivals on the moving escalator. Returning GI's were much in evidence. Not this train, she decided at last. Jesse had said he wouldn't arrive before six at the earliest.

All at once her heart was pounding. Jesse! Still in his army uniform, a knapsack resting on the step ahead of him. He hadn't seen her yet—he was talking to the soldier behind him. How tanned he was! As though he was returning from some Adriatic resort instead of the Italian battlefield.

"Jesse!" she called out joyously.

He turned around, startled, grinning.

"Hi, baby!" He reached for his duffle bag and prepared to step off the escalator. But she had to wait yet one more moment while he exchanged some final word with the soldier behind him. Then he charged toward her, kissing her with a passion that elicited good-humored hoots of approval from other arriving soldiers. "Pat, you look gorgeous!"

"Jesse, I can't believe you're here!" Her eyes clung to his face. "Jesse," she admonished and glanced self-consciously about them when he reached to pinch her rump.

"Now you believe?" he chuckled. He seemed older.

179

More self-confident. And as always, he was devastatingly handsome. He looked like a movie star.

"Shall we go somewhere for dinner or straight up to the apartment?"

"I'm dying to soak in a tub," he admitted. And his eyes—his hand at her waist—told her he was impatient to make love. "But before anything else, I promised myself the best steak in town—across the table from you," he added amorously.

"We'll go to the Penguin," she said, wrapped in sentiment. "It's probably early for dinner, but we can have a drink first."

"Great," he said and smiled. The Penguin had been "their place" when he'd been stationed at Fort Dix. In deference to his army pay Pat had always picked up the tab. "They know just how to make a steak. And you like their wine," he recalled in triumph. "Let's go find us a cab."

In the taxi Jesse kissed her again. Pat felt weak with wanting him, looking at him. She reached out to touch his face. She would have been happy to forgo dinner, but she told herself this was one of those "coming home" fantasies that every GI must nurture.

"What was it like on the ship coming home?" she asked while the taxi driver weaved in and out of rush hour traffic.

"Christ, we were packed like sardines in a can." He clucked in distaste. "I slept on deck every night. Nothing to do but play poker or blackjack. I lost every bloody cent I had. I sold my watch this morning so I'd have train fare to New York."

"Why didn't you tell me?" she reproached, punching him playfully on the arm. "I could have sent you money by Western Union."

"At Fort Dix?" he laughed. "I probably wouldn't have had it till next week."

180

Pat sat with her arm through Jesse's, her head on his shoulder while he talked about the trip across the Atlantic. As they drove up before the restaurant, she hastily pulled several tens from her wallet and gave them to Jesse.

In the small, intimate restaurant — sparsely occupied this early in the evening — they were seated at a private corner table. Pat's face lit up when Jesse ordered the dry Alsatian wine that she particularly liked here. It seemed impossible that they had been apart for more than a year!

Over steaks, baked potatoes, and salad, and afterward a chocolate mousse and coffee, Pat listened — as girls and women all over America were listening — to Jesse's colorful store of army experiences.

"You're being discharged?" She finally asked the question that had been haunting her since Vanessa had brought up the possibility of his being shipped to the Pacific.

"Baby, no." His smile was rueful. "There's still a heavy shooting war going on in the Pacific. I'm on three weeks' leave. Then I'll be shipped out to Texas. For retraining for the Pacific," he shrugged.

Pat looked down at her plate. "Oh, Jesse—"

"Let's don't think about that tonight," he ordered.

But if Jesse was going to Texas and on to the Pacific, then they must be married sometime within the next three weeks, Pat calculated. Mother was talking about coming up to New York for graduation. By then she'd be Jesse's wife. Nobody would stand in the way.

Caught by a sudden need to be alone, they wasted little time over dessert and coffee. Taxis hadn't been allowed to cruise midtown since early 1942, so Jesse requested that one be called for them. They held hands and waited outside for the taxi to arrive.

"Here it is—" Jesse helped her into the waiting taxi.

He gave the driver the address in his broad Texan accent.

Tears welled in Pat's eyes as she remembered the beautiful and anguished night before Jesse had been shipped out, when Tracy slept across the hall. That was the first time she and Jesse had shared a whole night together.

"I've dreamed about tonight," Jesse murmured, pulling her into his arms. "Dinner at some great place, a hot tub, and making love to you."

"Jesse, the driver," Pat whispered in protest.

"Stop worrying —" His mouth came down on hers in the darkness of the taxi, and Pat forgot everything but her love for him.

At the apartment door Pat gave her keys to Jesse — his keys, too, until he had to report for reassignment to Texas. Maybe the war in the Pacific would be over before he had to leave, she dreamed recklessly. They'd go back to Houston to live. Mr. and Mrs. Jesse Franklin.

Together they hurried into the house and up the stairs to the apartment. Inside Jesse pulled her into his arms again. She felt his heart pounding, and the hardness of him against her. For one impassioned instant Pat was prepared to forget the bridal set she'd bought earlier in Altman's. She'd be out of it in minutes anyway. But Jesse was gently pulling away.

"Now about that hot tub," he drawled. "Do you have some crazy bath salts I can throw in it? I want to come out smelling like a whore in a Texas cathouse."

"Jesse, you're awful." Her laughter was husky. "I have lilac bath salts and honeysuckle." She ran to the bathroom.

"Start the bath running and dump in the honeysuckle," he ordered, sitting down to take off his shoes.

With the door half open between bath and bedroom — amid the sweet scent of honeysuckle on one side and Chanel No. 5 on the other — Pat changed into her white Grecian nightgown. She was suddenly shy when she caught her reflection in the mirror — her long, slender limbs, narrow hips, flat belly, small high breasts on provocative display — and she reached and pulled on the negligee.

Jesse abandonded his mock-bass rendition of "Bésame Mucho" for the tender "You'd Be So Nice to Come Home To." Pat stood still, fighting off tears of happiness. Jesse was so sweet. So handsome.

"Hey, I never saw you looking like that —" Jesse stood in the doorway, patting himself dry with one of the lush, thick towels her mother had ordered shipped from Saks several months ago. All of him was darkly tanned. His company, Pat thought — trembling with long-held passion — they must have sunbathed in their skins. Her heart began a slow thud.

"And I never saw you smelling like that." She tried to sound terribly sophisticated, like Ava Gardner in *Whistle Stop*.

"You can't see smell," he laughed and strode toward her.

"Oh, Jesse, I've missed you so much," she sighed. She closed her eyes as his mouth sought hers and his arms gathered her in against his still-damp body.

"Take off that thing," he said huskily and went to fumble in the jacket of his uniform. Jesse was always careful about not getting her pregnant. She loved him for it, but she wouldn't care now — they'd be married before he went to Texas.

Trembling, Pat dropped her negligee across the back of the slipper chair, hesitated only a moment, then pulled the nightgown over her head and let it fall to the floor. She felt drunk with her passion, impatient for the feel of Jesse's hands, his mouth on her. Legs, bodies entangled. A pulse low within her pounded harder.

She wished Jesse would turn off the lamps, though she knew he wouldn't. She relished the touching and moving together in total darkness, discovering and savoring again the emotions found only in such moments as these.

She closed her eyes, willing darkness. And she gave herself over to feeling. Jesse's mouth was at her breasts, his hand between her flexed thighs, demanding. In a surge of passion her own hand reached for him, and she heard him moan. She had always been passive, waiting to follow Jesse's lead. But the fifteen months of lying alone and empty had wrought a change in her.

"Jesse—" Now, oh, please, *now*.

"Easy, baby," he whispered.

Her hands caught at his shoulders as he moved within her. She heard the sounds emerging unbidden from her throat as they plunged together in exultant frenzy, and then the sounds of its own satisfaction. At last they lay limp and motionless, the weight of him heavy upon her.

"For a broad who's so proper in public," he kidded, "you're sure noisy in bed." He nuzzled her neck.

Only now did she allow her eyes to flutter open.

"You don't like that?"

"I love it," he admitted, his eyes dark. "And that crazy outfit you were wearing when I came out of the tub. Like something I saw Jean Harlow wear in a movie when I was back in eighth grade. I sat in the movie balcony with two buddies from school, and the three of us masturbated there in the dark like we'd die if we didn't."

"I'll buy a dozen of them for our honeymoon," she promised, her face luminous.

"But I'll only be here three weeks," he said with a startled air. He lifted himself from her and settled on his back.

"In City Hall it takes two minutes to get married," she teased. He was remembering how she used to talk about

184

a big church wedding.

"Pat," he said slowly. "I don't know about us getting married—"

She turned on her side to gaze blankly at him.

"Jesse, what are you talking about?" Then understanding swept over her, and she relaxed. "You mean you think we ought to wait until the war's over—"

"I'm not real sure about us, Pat." He avoided her eyes. "I mean, I've been away fifteen months."

"That didn't matter just now." *What did he mean?*

"Maybe it'll be right for us—I'm just not sure. I was away an awful long time." He cleared his throat self-consciously. "Pat, I can't lie to you. I think I'm in love with this girl I met in a little town near Firenze—that's Florence."

"I know," she whispered, trying to assimilate what he'd just said.

"It's crazy the way it happened. Three of my company were billeted in her family's house. I slept on a cot in the dining room. She made a habit of going through the dining room to the kitchen late at night." He paused. "I'd been away a long time, Pat—and there she was." He shrugged eloquently.

"You made love to her?" Pat asked, her voice low and still.

"You know how the girls over there are about GI's. They all want to marry an American soldier and live in the United States."

"Do you want to marry her?" Her voice was harsh with shock. "Do you?" Jesse was staring at her in a oddly appraising fashion.

"I told Antonia we'd get married after the war. I said I'l bring her over from Italy." He gazed straight ahead.

Fifteen months ago he'd said he wanted nothing in the world more than to marry *her*, a voice inside of Pat taunted. This wasn't real—it was a nightmare.

185

"A lot of American soldiers are marrying Italian girls," Jesse said defensively. "The government's bringing over a shipload of Italian war brides soon. I'm not saying for sure I'll marry her. After three weeks back here with you I might just change my mind." His eyes trailed over her speculatively. "I've been away fighting a war. You have to understand, Pat." He moved his hand to cup her breast. She flinched and pulled away.

"I understand completely, Jesse." He'd never been in love with her. She was just a girl to take to bed, a girl who always paid the checks. "Everything you ever said to me was a pack of lies!" Pat stumbled out of the bed and ran to the closet for her robe. She clutched the robe about her, trying to stop trembling. Her face was hot with shame. *What would she do with her life without Jesse?*

"Pat, baby," Jesse said cajoling from the bed. "Let's don't spoil these three weeks. We're here together again. Home with you I may forget all about Antonia." His smile was full of promises.

"Don't try," Pat spat out bitterly. He sat there naked on her bed, weighing that little Italian slut against the Owens millions. Mother and Daddy had been right — she'd never really seen Jesse for what he was. She'd been blind. "I'm going across the hall to spend the night with Vanessa." She reached for her purse, pulled a bill from her wallet. "This will take you back to Fort Dix. I want you out of this apartment by nine tomorrow morning. I want you out of my life."

Summer moonlight filtered through the drapes and laid a ribbon of gold across Tina's old bed. Pat lay still beneath the sheet, exhausted but too distraught for sleep. She was conscious of every small sound in the hallway. Jesse had not left her apartment.

"Pat?" Vanessa asked softly. "You still awake?"

"I can't sleep when I know Jesse's across the hall," Pat confessed. "Damn this war!"

"It's better to find out about him now than later," Vanessa said, searching for some comfort.

"He thought I'd spend his whole furlough with him — waiting for him to decide whether he wants to bring over his Italian girlfriend or marry me. How could he?" And yet — in a small corner of her mind — she asked herself if she should give Jesse this chance. "Tracy never liked Jesse," she said. "You and Tina didn't, either, did you?"

"We thought you deserved much better. You were caught up in the war fever and all — it seemed so romantic to be in love with somebody in uniform."

"I was so sure of him. We had our lives all planned. After the war he'd come back home and open a service station in Houston. I'd stay home and be a housewife. I figured, sooner or later, Mother and Daddy would stop being angry. Daddy's dying for grandchildren — and he'll never get them from Maureen and Roger. I thought they'd accept Jesse once we had children." Would she ever have children? Would she fall in love again and marry?

"I think Tracy was right to marry Brian," Pat mused. "Even if Tommy had survived this lousy war, she was right to marry Brian. It was what both she and Brian wanted more than anything else in the world. Like Eddie and you." Pat and Vanessa stared at the ceiling in the dark silence, each lost in her own thoughts.

Fifteen

Vanessa worried about Pat.

"I'm glad I didn't marry him before he went into service. My parents were right. I'm over him — and good riddance," Pat said. But Vanessa felt the hurt within her.

For the millions of American girls who had survived the war years without male companionship, the arrival of foreign war brides was a bitter postscript to the war, which — not yet over — had robbed them of hundreds of thousands of potential husbands.

But for many others this was a time of poignant reunion. Returning GI's were welcomed joyously by their loved ones. Many a returning GI held with wonder the small son or daughter he had never seen.

Vanessa waited impatiently for the sound of Eddie's voice on the telephone. One of the ships arriving from Europe would soon be bringing Eddie home to her. His letters revealed an impatience that matched her own. He was billeted in a town north of Bologna, hoping to receive a few days' leave so that he might go up to Venice and look for his family before his company was shipped back to America.

Pat decided to abandon her plans to graduate with her class. New York was tainted now by ugly memories — and she was ready to go home. She made it clear to her relieved parents that she had no interest in a stage career. At the end of June she would return to Houston with Tracy.

Tracy had decided it was time to tell her family and Texas friends that she was engaged to Brian. Nobody would know about their earlier wedding in New York. Optimistic about an early conclusion to the war in the Pacific—and with the promise of two weeks' leave if the war continued—Tracy and Brian planned a huge October wedding in Houston. Pat would be her maid of honor. Vanessa—and they hoped Tina—would be bridesmaids.

Late in the month, just as she was about to leave the office, Vanessa received a phone call from Tina.

"Vanessa, I've just been given a sensational part!" Tina reported exuberantly. She'd had two tiny speaking roles thus far. Neither had ignited fires in movie audiences, but Tina—with Gordon's prodding—had become an avid student of film acting. "It's a small part, but everybody in a movie theater will notice me. Gordie says it's sure to put me on the top. And baby," she paused dramatically, "they've torn up my contract and given me a new one. Three hundred dollars a week! My agent fought like mad for it." The agent had been acquired at Gordon's insistence.

"Tina, that's wonderful! And I thought you stood out in that last bit," she said with sincerity. "Pat and I saw the movie three times. Tracy and Brian saw it, too."

"It drew a handful of letters," Tina reported. "It takes hundreds to make a star. But this part is right for me. They're not trying to make me another June Allyson this time. It's something that Rita Hayworth or Ava Gardner might have played three years ago. Small but flashy."

"How's Gordon?" Vanessa asked. From Tina's frank letters she had gathered that theirs was not the perfect marriage.

"Gordie is a pain in the ass. Now that we're married, all he wants to do is sit at home and listen to baseball or run out for a few beers with the guys. Vanessa, I haven't been to a nightclub in months—and when we do go, Gordie's jealous as hell if I even look at another man."

"Concentrate on the acting," Vanessa encouraged. "Now's the time for you to push ahead."

"Hang on to the apartment," Tina said flippantly. "I may be back."

On June 21 the Japanese surrendered at Okinawa after two and a half months of fierce fighting. Almost 13,000 American lives were lost, and 40,000 American servicemen had been wounded. The Japanese losses were put at over a hundred thousand. On July 5 General MacArthur proclaimed the liberation of the Philippine Islands. The sweet smell of peace was in the air.

Vanessa waited anxiously for word from Eddie. She prayed the war in the Pacific would be over before he could be shipped there. The government was trying to expedite the return of American troops; but to the women who waited, the delays were agonizingly long. Vanessa continued to write each night.

The train moved in the late June heat from Bologna north to Venice, past modest towns that bore the deep scars of war, past sweeps of verdant landscapes, fields of reddish earth, parades of willows, sycamores, and acacias—and everywhere columns of tall Lombardy poplars. Soon, Eddie thought with a rush of nostalgia, the Alps would come into view, distant peaks against the sky.

He sat tense with anticipation and worry. He had fought hard for this brief furlough before rejoining his company to return to the States. His colonel had pulled it off by recommending him for a Distinguished Service

Cross.

God, it had been awful to be so close to Venice all these weeks but not able to go look for his family. He clung to the hope that they had not been swept into the extermination camps. From his connections in army intelligence he had learned that the Germans had arrested a thousand Jews on one day in Rome and sent them all to Auschwitz. He prayed that his father and mother, his brother and two sisters, had not been killed while working with anti-Fascist partisans.

He knew that Venice itself had suffered very little damage during the war, though the Germans had taken the city in 1943. Allied bombers had been careful to spare Venice in their raids, attacking instead the nearby port of Marghera.

Eddie was impatient for the train to arrive in Venice, yet he was fearful of what he might find. His heart began to pound when the train passed through the green flatlands of Mestre. Mestre was the last stop before his destination, no more than five miles from the Santa Lucia station in Venice. The train seemed to speed up, the sky became more brilliant as they approached the Adriatic. There were fewer trees now, and the field marshes changed to grey mudflats. Venice was a city built on 120 small islands in a sheltered lagoon — the one city in the world, perhaps, free of auto traffic, a city where walking was a necessity and a pleasure.

Eddie was on his feet the instant the train moved onto the causeway that joined Venice to the mainland. He had not been home since he was sixteen. His mind was assaulted by images of Venice in his boyhood.

He was aware of the familiar telegraph wires and cables that swung over the lagoons, of Torcello, Burano, and Murano in the dazzling distant haze. The domes of the towers shimmered against the sky. And the Campanile di San Marco rose above all, golden ochre, pink, and white blending with the black and ultramarine of the boats, their sails bright orange and red.

The train pulled into the small concrete terminus at the Piazzale Roma. Eddie felt a fresh surge of excitement. He bounded from the train to stand on one of the low-lying platforms. His eyes drank in the rows of potted flowers and palms in their earthenware tubs, the magazine stalls, the drinking fountain. In earlier years—and it would probably be so again shortly—white-suited men wearing hats that carried the name of their hotel embroidered in gold would be lined up on either side of the corridor to welcome and escort tourists to their various destinations.

Eddie headed for the landing quay where the gondolas and *vaporetti* (motor buses) and *motoscafi* (small, fast craft) waited.

From the quay he caught a glimpse of the Piazza San Marco, its rose-pink campanile and the blue-and-gold fronted clock tower. He hesitated only a moment, then rejected the public *vaporetti* and *motoscafi* for a more extravagant private gondola. The only way to see Venice was by gondola.

Aboard the gaudily painted gondola he took a seat on the prow and smiled at the architectural masterpieces lining the Grand Canal. Little had changed in this city of stone and flowers since the eighteenth century. Eddie was grateful that the Allied air forces had spared the most beautiful city in the world.

Would he find his family in the beautiful old palazzo where they had lived for five generations? He knew that in 1943 all Jews—without exception—had been ordered into concentration camps and all Jewish property had been confiscated. He knew, too, that long before his father and older brother had joined the partisans fighting the Fascists. How had his mother and sisters fared?

Mama, he thought tenderly. So elegant and serene

192

and beautiful. Mama was sure that the country she loved so deeply would survive even Mussolini. But in Venice, after the fall of Mussolini came the Nazis.

Eddie left the gondola to walk the narrow street that led to the Montino palazzo. His throat tightened at the sight of the still-regal Renaissance structure, shining orange-lilac in the brilliant summer sunlight. Suddenly he was running to the entrance.

He touched the bell and waited, hardly daring to breathe. *Let them be here.* Surely, with the war over property had been restored to its rightful owners.

The heavy oak door opened slowly. A small, fragile woman, elegant despite the faint shabbiness of her black crepe frock, stared inquiringly — almost warily — at the caller.

"Mama!" Eddie cried. Her once dark hair was now more gray than black, her face lined beyond its years. "Mama, you're here!" He reached out and enfolded her in his arms.

"Eduardo!" Her face was incandescent. "My baby. My baby."

They clung together at the entrance, caught in the joy of their reunion.

"Every day I thought of you," his mother said, leaning back to look at his face. "I prayed you were well." One hand rose to caress his lieutenant's bars. "I knew you would fight with the Americans. Your country, too."

"Papa?" Eddie asked. "The family?"

"Come inside," Sophia Montino said gently, her hand at his arm. "There's so much to tell. So much I want to hear."

In the entrance foyer Eddie noted that the palazzo had been shorn of many of its treasures. The exquisite antiques, the centuries-old foyer chandelier, were gone. The house had been returned to them, he realized, but the Montino fortune was a casualty of war.

"First the Fascists came and took away the paintings," his mother told him softly, leading him into what had once been the smaller drawing room. "Later—when we had fled—everything of value was taken." She spoke with a calm acceptance that unnerved him more than the stark near emptiness of the room.

"Papà?" he asked again uneasily.

"Papa is not well. He's sleeping now. In a little while I'll take you up to him." She paused, then roused herself. "Are you hungry? I'll go to the kitchen and prepare something for you . . . the servants . . ." Her voice trailed away. Eddie felt a coldness sweep through him.

"Later, Mama." He pulled her down beside him on the threadbare sofa. "I want to hear how you've survived these years."

"Your brother gave his life for the Italy he loved," his mother said softly and Eddie reached for her hand in his grief. "Like Caterina's husband."

"You don't know what you're capable of until the necessity arises," she said bitterly. "I, who could not bear to see a partridge shot down from the sky, have killed men. But we helped, Eduardo," she said with pride.

"Papa?" he asked again, fearing what she would say.

"Papa will not be with us for much longer." She lifted his hand to her cheek. "But he'll die happy because you've come home, my darling."

"Is there nothing that can be done?" Eddie fought against his mother's acceptance of death.

"We can only be with him. And love him."

Eddie listened to his mother's halting account of how his father, his brother, and she had contrived to escape when the Nazis ordered that all Jews be rounded up and sent off to concentration camps.

"Eddie, without the Castellos your father and I would be dead." The two families had known each other for years. "They hid us in their house when the S.S. troops came searching. When your father was wounded, and then I—" She smiled at his look of pain and squeezed his hand. "They took us in, nursed us, hid us until we could escape and rejoin the partisans. Many of the Italian people—non-Jews—helped hide Jewish families. And two thousand Jews fought with them. Some escaped to serve—like you, my darling—in the Allied armies. But without the Castellos your father and I would not be here. Even now they help us with money. For doctors and medication. The Nazis took everything of value," she reminded him softly. "The antiques business is ruined. We have only this house."

"Where are Caterina and Annabella?" he asked, reeling from all that his mother had told him.

"Your sisters have jobs in Switzerland. Annabella's husband is trying to find work there, also. There are few jobs in Italy."

"You'll come back to New York with me," he said resolutely. "We'll—"

"No. Italy is my home," she said. "And we have debts to pay. The Castellos have saved our lives, not once but many times. Now they need us."

"In what way?" Eddie was bewildered.

"They lost one son in the war. They have one daughter. Isa. Do you remember her?"

"Yes," Eddie said. "She was a little younger than I. We used to meet at birthday parties. She was very pretty."

"She's desperately ill. The doctors can promise no more than three or four years for her. Eddie, her parents want her to marry. Not to be a wife," she emphasized. "Her hold on life is too fragile. But to have a young man to be her companion when she's able to go to the Lido or to a dinner party or to the theater."

"Mama, I don't understand," he said tensely.

"Eddie, you can repay our debt to the Castellos," she answered. "And when Isa is gone, you'll be a very rich man. Her parents wish it to be this way."

"Mama, no—" Eddie went cold with shock. "There's someone in New York. I told her I'd bring her here so we could be married in the presence of my family. We—"

"Eddie, you're so young. Only twenty-four years old." Her dark eyes pleaded with him. "You can spare these few years for the family to whom we owe so much. Let your father leave this life with pride."

"Mama, you don't know what—"

"Sssh," she whispered compassionately. "Later we'll talk about this. Now we'll go up to Papa."

Sixteen

Tina and Gordon finished their act on the stage of the Hollywood Canteen. "Change and let's get the hell out of here," Gordon ordered as they left the stage. "I'll meet you at the back door."

Tina sighed. She would have enjoyed playing "straight woman" to Gordon's antics if he wasn't so wildly jealous. The applause was noisy and high-spirited, as much for her skimpy costume as for Gordon's one-liners. Gordon wanted to clout every man who looked at her.

Each time she was asked to serve at the Canteen—almost all Hollywood actresses did a turn—Gordon had found some excuse for her to refuse. It wasn't just that she'd be handing out coffee and doughnuts. She'd be jitterbugging with GI's. He was seething now because she'd insisted on appearing in the act with him when the star assigned opposite him had gotten ill.

Tina deliberately took her time changing into slacks and a light sweater. With her costume thrust into her weekender along with her makeup, Tina headed for the back door.

"Come on, let's go home," Gordon said tersely.

"I'm hungry," she demurred. "Let's go over to Romanoff's."

"Not with you in that tight sweater," he scoffed. "If

you're hungry, you can make sandwiches at home."

In silence they walked to Gordon's newly acquired white Cadillac convertible. The chauffeured Rolls was now used only for premiers and charity events. He pulled open the door of the car on the driver's side and slammed it behind him while Tina circled around and climbed in on the other side.

Gordon reached for the ignition key, his eyes focused straight ahead.

"You were throwing yourself at every guy out there in uniform," he accused. "You wanted to stretch out right there on the stage and take on every one of them."

"Even I wouldn't have the strength for that," Tina said dryly. Their first few weeks together in bed had been a ball. Gordie had opened charge accounts for her in all the shops on Rodeo Drive, and she'd bought the sexiest nighties she could find. But then something had happened. Now Gordie left her at the starting post, rolled over, and went to sleep.

"I'll drop you off at the house," Gordon decided. "I don't have to be at the studio tomorrow. I may as well go see if I can find a hot poker game."

Tina smoldered. She was so damn tired of Gordie's chasing after a poker game. She was tired of his filling the house with his buddies who talked about nothing except baseball and football. The only good thing in this marriage, she told herself, was that Gordie had hired her an agent. And Gordie had taught her tricks about screen acting the coaches overlooked.

She'd thought about divorce, but Pop would die if he read she was divorcing Gordie. If she was rich and important enough, she could probably get an annulment. Anyway, Pop had never recognized her marriage. She'd called home after the ceremony, but he wouldn't even get on the phone. She told Nick she was married.

Gordon drove through the gates to ultra-exclusive Bel

Air and down the road to their sprawling California ranch house.

"See you later," he said loftily, and drove off, leaving her standing in the driveway.

Inside the house Tina roamed restlessly. Today was the servants' day off, and she was alone. Defiantly she fixed herself a drink. Another trick Gordie had taught her, she acknowledged. She could handle her liquor drink for drink with anybody in Hollywood. After two martinis, she reached for the telephone and dialed Constance Marlow's number.

Constance was moving up fast at the studio. Faster than she was, Tina admitted without rancor. Nat was practically on his knees to keep Constance working — fan mail was piling up at the studio faster than they could give her parts. Connie could do whatever she wanted.

"Hello —" Connie's sexy little-girl voice came over the phone.

"Hi. I feel rotten," Tina complained. "Gordie dumped me at the house and took off for some card game. Why don't we go over to the Mocambo?" Tina's invitation was a challenge; they were probably the only two girls in Hollywood who would dare go to the Mocambo unescorted.

"Great idea," Connie approved without hesitation. "Wear something gorgeous and white," she ordered. "I'll wear black. Fuck men." Connie'd just broken off an affair with a billionaire industrialist because he'd told her she was a rotten actress. He'd wanted Connie to marry him and forget about pictures — when and if his wife agreed to a divorce.

"Not tonight," Connie corrected herself. "Tonight we hate men. I'll pick you up in forty minutes."

Tina thought about Connie while she dressed. Connie had been in Hollywood only a year longer than she had, and she'd already married and divorced a best-selling novelist and had affairs with the biggest names in Hollywood. That was something to remember—she didn't *have* to stay married to Gordie.

On a stuffy late July morning Vanessa was finishing up a call with a client when she noted a second call was on her line. She wound up the first with polite briskness and switched to the other.

"Good morning," she began.

"Vanessa—" The voice on the other end of the line was a joyous caress.

"Eddie!" She clutched at the phone as though it was a lifeline. "Where are you?"

"At Fort Dix. I'll be arriving at Penn Station by three or four—"

"I'll be meeting the trains," she interrupted breathlessly. "Oh, Eddie, I can't believe you're home. For how long?" she asked anxiously, suddenly remembering that men were still being shipped out to the Pacific.

"I'll be reassigned in six weeks," he said. "Meanwhile, I'm on furlough. Vanessa, every minute until I see you will seem like a year."

Something didn't sound right. "You're okay?" she pleaded for reassurance.

". . . I'm fine," he insisted.

"Your family?" she asked in a low voice. "Were you able to find them?"

"My father was badly wounded in an attack on a Fascist encampment." Eddie paused. "He's dying, Vanessa."

"Oh, Eddie . . ."

"We'll talk later. Vanessa, I love you."

"I love you, Eddie." Tears filled her eyes. Tears of joy that she would soon be back in Eddie's arms. Tears of sadness because she knew he grieved for his father.

As women were doing in thousands of offices across the country, Vanessa eagerly asked to have the remainder of the day off so that she could be at Penn Station when her returning serviceman arrived. She hurried home to change into the dress she'd been saving for this occasion. *Eddie was home.* Never had she felt such happiness.

New York had seemed a stark, deserted ghost town to Vanessa during the past few weeks. Pat and Tracy had left for Texas, and Tina had been in California for almost a year now. Suddenly the city was beautiful and exciting — because in a few hours she would be with Eddie.

Vanessa arrived in crowded Penn Station before 2:00 P.M. She hurried to the waiting area and stood by the escalator that disgorged passengers from Trenton. A special air of excitement among those waiting told Vanessa she was not alone in welcoming a returning soldier.

Eddie was not on this train. Though she knew it would be almost an hour before the next arrival from Trenton, Vanessa stayed where she was. She wanted to see Eddie the moment he arrived. She shifted from one foot to the other, her shoulders tense. The second train pulled in. She waited until it was obvious Eddie had not been on the train.

Eddie was all right, she repeated to herself. If he had been wounded, he would have told her. She brushed aside inchoate visions of Eddie appearing on crutches and minus a leg, or with the pinned-up sleeve that brought heartache to so many waiting at home. No matter what, she would love Eddie and be his wife.

She struggled with impatience. Eddie would be on the next train, she promised herself. Though there was another hour's wait she ignored her aching feet and the

201

pangs of hunger that reminded her she had skipped lunch.

Vanessa straightened her tired shoulders when the PA announced the arrival of another train from Trenton. She forgot her fatigue. The crowd pressed toward the stairs.

Soon the first passengers to disembark appeared on the escalator. A shout went up from the young woman beside Vanessa. A marine on the escalator waved in response, his face a blend of happiness and disbelief as the young woman held up a small boy about three years old for him to see.

"Wave to Daddy," the young mother ordered, half laughing, half crying. "Daddy's come home from the war!"

Then Vanessa saw Eddie behind the tall marine. He was slender, bronzed from the sun, his face searching the crowd.

"Eddie!" Vanessa called out and waved. *He was all right.* He found her in the crowd and waved back while she pushed her way toward him. "Oh, Eddie!"

He dropped his knapsack to bring her into his arms. His mouth was warm and grateful and passionate.

"You look wonderful," he said huskily, holding her away from him. His eyes caressed every feature of her face.

"You're so tan," she marveled.

"Vanessa, let's go home." He swung the knapsack over one shoulder, dropped an arm about her waist. "Right now."

In the taxi he clung to her hand as though to reassure himself that she was beside him. He talked about the difference between the journey across the Atlantic on a blacked-out troopship and the return voyage. He spoke of his three-day pass in Rome.

"I'd never seen Rome so calm and beautiful. There

weren't many buses running yet, just a few tramways. No private cars anywhere. The shops were filled with clothes. People seemed so well dressed. It was a shock after seeing the destruction in southern Italy. There every small village, every farmhouse, showed the devastation of the war."

"But Rome went through bombing, didn't it?" Vanessa remembered newsreels, newspaper photos.

"Oh, yes. The ruins about the city are witness to that. But somehow, I had the feeling that in Rome people had no real conception of the war. I went to call on a family who've known my parents for years. They insisted I stay for dinner. Their home was untouched. We dined in an unspoiled dining room with candlelight and fine china, and gleaming silver, and a pair of maids served us." He paused, his face compassionate. "Dinner was squares of bread with Spam, canned corned beef, and Vienna sausages. Dessert was a big blob of fluff the cook had managed to contrive from nothing. Food barely exists in Italy."

"And we complain about rationing," Vanessa said quietly.

"You don't know what it was like in Europe." Eddie's voice was uncharacteristically harsh. His grip on her hand was painful. "Thank God, you don't know."

The cab pulled to a stop before Vanessa's brownstone. Eddie paid the driver, and stood gazing up at the building.

"I'm here," he said softly. "Sometimes I was afraid I'd never make it."

"You're here," Vanessa said, her smile radiant. "And everybody says the war can't last much longer."

"Yes." He smiled, but his eyes were troubled.

In Vanessa's apartment Eddie gazed hungrily at the familiar surroundings, overcome by a warm sense of security. Vanessa brought out cold cuts and a pitcher of iced coffee, Eddie's favorite summertime drink.

"I wish it weren't so hot in here," she fretted. The small fan did little to alleviate the heat.

"It doesn't matter," he said gently and reached to take the pitcher from her. He placed it on the counter and slipped his arms around her waist. "It feels good to be home."

Vanessa lifted her face to his, welcoming his mouth on hers. Her arms tightened about his shoulders and she forgot everything but the feel of his body against hers. She was startled and disappointed when he released her.

"I'm sorry . . ." His eyes avoided her searching glance. He smiled in an effort to lighten the mood.

"We can't let that food go to waste. Not after two years of army chow."

She was disturbed by the undercurrent of seriousness in him as they ate, though Eddie talked only of how happy he was to be home with her again. Was he worried about reassignment? she speculated. Wasn't it enough that he had served in Italy for almost two years?

After dinner they carried their glasses of iced coffee to the couch nearest the window and settled into the cushions. Eddie's eyes told her how much he wanted to make love to her.

"Vanessa, something's happened," he said at last. "I don't know how to tell you—" His voice was anguished.

"Tell me," she said, all at once afraid of what he might say. But Eddie loved her. What could be so awful?

She listened as Eddie told her haltingly about his furlough in Venice. This is a dream, Vanessa told herself—a nightmare.

"I told my mother about us," Eddie said. "How we meant to come home to Venice to be married as soon as the war was over. But my family will be devastated—shamed—if I refuse to go along with this make-believe marriage. It's only for a little time, Vanessa. It's my responsibility to the family. Isa's parents hid my mother and father at the risk of being shot as traitors. It means financial security for my father and mother — and for my two sisters."

"How long?" Vanessa asked quietly.

"The doctors say no more than three or four years." His hand reached for hers. His eyes were pleading. "Vanessa, my father's dying. Let him die in peace."

"Then there's nothing for me to say." The world was suddenly a dark and lonely place.

"I want you in Venice with me," he said urgently. "Until we can be married."

Vanessa stared at him in shock.

"You'll have a wife," she protested.

"A mock marriage to provide whatever pleasure is possible for Isa," he reminded her. "I'll rent an apartment for you. I'll be able to be with you. We'll wait together in Venice until we can be married. We're young, Vanessa — we have our whole lives ahead of us. We can wait three or four years. But together," he stipulated.

"Eddie, I have responsibilities, too," she stammered. "My mother."

"You'll write and say you're accepting a job in Venice. You'll send money as always. I'll go into the business with Isa's father — he's a very successful lace manufacturer. I'll be paid well. It's not wrong for us to do this," he insisted. "You'll be my wife, Vanessa. No one else."

"Give me a little time," she pleaded. How could she let Eddie walk out of her life?

"I'll be here six weeks," he said gently. "With luck on our side the war could end tomorrow."

"Oh, Eddie, I'm so scared."

"I love you," he whispered. "You love me. We can't allow the craziness in the world to keep us apart."

"Please, Eddie," she asked again. "A little time?"

"You're my wife this minute," he said, his arms drawing her close. "This is our wedding night."

At Eddie's urging Vanessa asked for a week's vacation, to begin immediately. They rented a car and drove to a town far out on Long Island where, Eddie's colonel had told him, he'd find one of the most beautiful beaches in the world. Before they left New York, Eddie bought a gold wedding band and placed it on her finger. At the Bridgehampton boardinghouse where they would stay, they would be Lieutenant and Mrs. Eduardo Montino.

They spent lazy days walking along the pristine white beach, long nights making love in the large, square bedroom of the boardinghouse. They watched the sun rise over the ocean, enjoyed the splendor of late summer sunsets. And all the while they tried to forget what lay ahead in Venice.

Back in New York Vanessa returned to her job, to be met at the end of the working day by Eddie. On hot nights they walked along the Hudson River. When it rained, they went to a movie and held hands, shoulders touching.

On August 6 the atomic bomb was dropped on Hiroshima. Sixteen hours later President Truman addressed the nation: *"It's a harnessing of the basic power of the universe. The force from which the sun draws its power has been loosed against those who have brought war to the Far East."* On August 8 Radio Tokyo reported: *"The impact of the bomb was so terrific that practically all living things, human and animal, were literally seared to death by the tremendous heat and pressure engendered by the blast."*

Headlines of extras on the street read: "JAPS SURRENDER." The nation waited while wild rumors flew about the country, and the radio tried to keep up with the latest report. Though the world knew the Japs were defeated, it was not until Tuesday, August 14, that the official news came through, and President Truman announced the unconditional surrender of the Japanese.

For two days New York City celebrated the end of the war. In Times Square, Chinatown, and Little Italy crowds congregated in delirious performances. Throughout Manhattan's East Side jukeboxes were dragged out onto the sidewalks so that celebrants could jitterbug in the streets. Sunday was observed as a day of prayer in churches and synagogues throughout the city.

Vanessa rejoiced in the knowledge that Eddie would not be shipped to the Pacific. But now she knew she must answer the question in her heart and in Eddie's eyes. She battled with her conscience. How could she live with Eddie when he was married to someone else? But how could she bear waiting alone in New York until he was legally free to marry her?

For almost two years they'd been separated by the war. Enough, she told herself with fierce determination. When Eddie went to Venice, she would be with him.

Eddie was ecstatic. After much haggling and cutting of red tape he was able to book passage for Vanessa and himself. Early in September they left New York en route to Le Havre. From Le Havre they took the boat train to Paris, then on to Milan. Vanessa felt Eddie's excitement as they arrived in Milan to make their final change of trains.

"Normally," Eddie mused, "this would be the height of the tourist season in Venice. In September it always seems as though half the world has a rendezvous in Piazza San Marco. But since the war, of course . . ."

Vanessa's heart pounded as their train pulled slowly into the Santa Lucia station. She tried not to remember that there would be times when Eddie could not be beside her, times when she would be alone in this strange land.

She was quickly caught up in the drama of arriving in this exotic, magical city. Eddie rejected the public *vaporetti* and led her to a gondola, eager to show her the splendor of the city he had known as child.

"The only way to see Venice for the first time is by gondola," he declared grandly.

As the gondola proceeded along the Grand Canal, Eddie pointed out the colossal and forbidding Palazzo Labia, built in 1720, and the famous Fondaco dei Turchi — exotic and Oriental, with bizarre triangular battlements at its summit dating back to the middle of the thirteenth century. On either side of the Grand Canal was a parade of palazzi — gothic, renaissance, baroque, plus those of Oriental and Arabic influence — their loggias colorful with flowers, the decorative stakes of their landing places casting spirals of color upon the water.

Vanessa gazed enthralled at the procession of magnificent structures and listened to Eddie's descriptions of each. She was fascinated by the massive Venetian chimneys that looked like upturned cones.

"For a time Byron lived in a palazzo on the Canal. George Sand and Musset lived and loved here. And just ahead of us on the left bank — the palazzo with the fine stone lacework — is the Ca'd'Oro, where Wagner composed much of *Tristan und Isolde.*"

"Until we can find an apartment," Eddie explained, helping her from the gondola, "I'll settle you in a little hotel near the Piazza San Marco. It's right behind the square." He hesitated, his smile apologetic. "It's not one of Venice's luxury hotels. Hardly the Gritti Palace—"

"Eddie, we don't need that," she said quickly. He kept reassuring her that they could afford to live well in Venice, but she was uncomfortable knowing that their funds would come from Isa Castello's father.

The hotel had a small, attractive lobby, with a mirror

and several chairs. A flight of stairs led up to the office of the *padrone,* who sat at a desk littered with ledgers, police forms for tourists, and a telephone. He welcomed them warmly, nodding in agreement to Eddie's insistence that they have a room with a view of the Basilica of St. Mark. Vanessa sought to hide her confusion while Eddie politely explained that the room was for the *signorina.* She saw the *padrone's* puzzled glance at her wedding band.

"*Si,*" he nodded, and slapped a bell on his desk.

Almost instantaneously a small, round woman in a black uniform and starched white apron materialized to conduct them through labyrinthine corridors to a pleasant room hung with red damask wallpaper. The furniture in the room was ornate and massive.

The maid went to open the shutters and proudly announced; "*Ecco Venezia!*"

Vanessa ran over to admire the small balcony covered with climbing greenery. All of Venice lay before her.

Eddie closed the door behind the maid, locked it, and took Vanessa in his arms.

"Welcome to Venice, my darling." His mouth reached for hers.

"Eddie, the shutters," she warned.

"The shutters," he said with mock seriousness.

Vanessa waited for Eddie to close the shutters and return to her, needing his arms about her, wanting to be reassured of his love.

"Vanessa, you're my wife," he whispered while his hands fumbled with the buttons at the front of her blouse. "I'll never love anyone but you."

When her clothes lay in a heap on the floor, Eddie lifted her in his arms and carried her to the mahogany bed. Vanessa lay against a mound of goosedown pillows and watched impatiently while Eddie undressed. A faint beam of late afternoon sunlight trailed through a broken slat in the shutters and lay across the covers.

"Oh, Eddie," she whispered when he joined her on the bed and lowered his mouth to the white velvet valley between her breasts, "how could I have stayed in New York without you?"

Her hands caressed his back as he made his way between her soft thighs and found her. It hadn't been wrong to come here with Eddie. How could anything so beautiful be wrong?

Vanessa stood on the vine-draped balcony and watched Eddie's slender form disappear in the glittering twilight. She was oblivious of the view of the Basilica of San Marco. It was right, of course, that Eddie should go immediately to his family — and they'd agreed that she would not meet his family until he was free to marry her. But Vanessa felt shatteringly insecure. She was alone in a strange hotel in a strange country.

She fought a desire to run from the room, down the stairs, and out into the street in search of Eddie. He said he'd return to the hotel late this evening. *But suppose his parents persuaded him not to come back to her? What would she do?*

No, she rebuked herself. Eddie would not leave her alone in Venice. It was as though they were husband and wife already. Eddie would come back to her.

Seventeen

Pat stirred into uncomfortable wakefulness in her lace-draped, oak canopy bed in the northwest bedroom of the eighteen room antibellum mansion that was the Owen's ranch house. The drone of the ceiling fan reminded her that the air-conditioning was out of order again. Though it was only 9:00 A.M., the late September day was already hot and humid.

A smile lifted the corners of her mouth as she remembered the astonishment of the people in New York when she had mentioned missing her air-conditioned house in Houston. Even in New York air-conditioning seemed to exist only in offices, department stores, movie houses, and the better hotels.

The sounds of her mother's voice drifted up from the lower floor. She sounded fretful. Part of that was because Daddy had flown in from Washington yesterday without any word of warning. Mother loathed having her routine changed.

"Madeline, you don't have to plan any entertaining for me." Pat heard the irritation in her father's voice. "I'll be here for only a few days. Just long enough to get some new blood in my Houston office. Don't forget. I'm up for reelection next year."

"Jim, you're not worried about being reelected?" Madeline scoffed.

"We're in for a lot of changes in the next few years." The congressman's voice was grim. "We can't send our boys overseas to fight a war and not expect changes when they come home. Where's Pat?"

"Asleep, of course." Her mother's tone was disdainful.

"It seems to me she's just moping around. Maybe she ought to come up to Washington for a while. Meet some eligible young men."

"She's just twenty," Madeline reminded him.

"We were married when you were twenty," Jim pointed out. "I'd feel better if I knew she was settled down with the right kind of husband."

"Are you still upset about that ridiculous garage mechanic? She's forgotten all about him."

"Unless he comes tearing back into Houston like a conquering war hero," Jim warned. "She was living on her own up in New York for almost two years. She's not a little girl anymore."

"Perhaps Maureen can shepherd her around to some Washington parties," her mother acceded after a moment, and Pat flinched. She and Maureen had to fight just to be polite to each other. "After Tracy's wedding."

She had been so impatient to come back to Houston, Pat remembered. As though back home she could erase from her mind that horrible last night with Jesse. She'd told herself she never wanted to see him again—yet she kept driving around, secretly hoping she'd see him again. He'd said he wasn't *sure* he was bringing over that girl from Italy. He might still be in love with her.

Angry at her thoughts of Jesse, Pat thrust aside the top sheet and headed for the shower. *Forget about Jesse*. If she did—just accidentally—run into him, she'd smile politely and act as though she barely knew him.

Tracy was picking her up at ten-thirty. They were going over to Sakowitz's for a fitting of her dress for the wedding. She was disappointed that Vanessa couldn't be here. She felt so bad for Eddie and Vanessa. Only Vanessa would understand that Eddie had to marry that other girl first, she thought as she stepped into the shower.

When she came downstairs to the sunlit breakfast room, she found her mother having one of her endless cups of coffee.

"Pat, your father wants you to drop by his Houston office sometime this afternoon," Madeline Owens reported.

"Whatever for?" Pat stared at her mother in surprise.

"He's come up with the idea that it would be good if you were involved in his new campaign. You really must," she insisted. "He feels you'll be an asset in getting votes."

Mother refused to have any share in campaigning— she said she'd never be an Eleanor Roosevelt. But she would die of disappointment if Daddy didn't keep his seat in the House. She relished being the wife of an influential congressman.

"What can I do?"

"I haven't the foggiest notion," her mother conceded. "But be sure you stop by the office and talk to him."

Shortly before 10:30 A.M. Tracy arrived in her convertible to pick up Pat for the drive into town.

"It's so bloody hot," Tracy complained. "Why aren't we swimming or out on a boat?"

"Because we have to go to Sakowitz's for my fitting," Pat teased. "And how can you expect a city that's in the same latitude as the Sahara to be cool in summer?"

It shocked her to realize that Tracy didn't care that neither Vanessa nor Tina would be here for the wedding. It was as though she'd never lived in New York. Only Brian remained from the New York years as part of her life.

From Sakowitz's they drove to the country club for

lunch, dawdling in the comfortable air-conditioning. Pat strained to appear interested in Tracy's monologue on her wedding and honeymoon plans.

"Before Brian has to settle down to business, I'd love to spend two months in Europe, but Mother insists this is not the time to chase around London and Paris and Rome. And of course," she sighed. "Brian agrees with anything Mother and Daddy say."

Brian was respectful of the Arnold millions, Pat surmised. She took a final swig of her iced coffee and pushed back her chair.

"Drive me down to my father's office," Pat said. "I promised to stop by this afternoon."

The Congressman's office was already showing signs of becoming the 1946 campaign headquarters. Walking down the halls, Pat was greeted warmly by members of the regular staff.

"Your daddy's in his office talking with the new director of Houston operations," Mrs. Ryan — office manager for fourteen years and an asset in bringing out the Irish vote — told Pat. "I'll tell him you're here."

Pat and Tracy waited for a few minutes until Mrs. Ryan indicated Pat was to go into her father's office, decorated with antiques bought at enormous cost in the Irish countryside. Madeline Owens liked Texans to remember that, though her family had lived in Houston for five generations, they came originally from Irish gentry.

Pat left Tracy in the reception room and went into her father's office.

"Pat, honey, come sit down." He greeted her with a warm smile. "You're looking mighty pretty. As always."

She might have been a prospective voter, she thought wryly. "Thank you, Daddy." She sat in the classical Irish oak chair that flanked his carved mahogany writing table. Only after she was settled did she become aware of the tall, ruggedly handsome young man standing by the windows.

"Pat, let me introduce you to the new head of my Houston campaign operations," Mr. Owens said with the Old South charm that emerged on occasion. "Paul Roberts. My daughter, Pat."

"Mighty nice to meet you, ma'am," he said politely. His eyes said much more.

"Pat, I want you to become involved in the new campaign," Owens said briskly. "This one won't be the shoo-in that the others were. I'm going to be all tied up with meetings until I leave. Why don't you two have dinner one night this week so Paul can clue you in to what's expected of you?"

"Any night you like," Paul said. "Perhaps tomorrow evening?" he asked, and Pat was aware of her father's smile of approval.

"Tomorrow night will be fine," she accepted. So she'd campaign for Daddy.

"Around seven?" Paul suggested.

"I'll be ready at seven," she nodded.

Paul took his leave gracefully and left Pat and her father alone.

"I just wanted you to meet Paul and set your part in the campaign in motion. It won't be too demanding." Already he was inspecting the documents spread across his desk, returning to the important business of staying in power. "Paul's a hard-working young man. He went through Rice — played some great football there. Then he worked his way through law school. He was drafted a few weeks after graduation. He's damned ambitious — I like that."

Pat rose to her feet. Daddy was telling her that Paul came from a poor background — Rice was a tuition-free school — but that he had a successful future ahead of him. Why had he been so stubborn about her not marrying Jesse? Because Jesse hadn't gone to Rice and played "great football"?

Tracy jumped to her feet when Pat returned to the reception area.

"Pat, who was that gorgeous hunk of man who came out of your father's office just now?"

Tina knew she would arrive at the house well before Gordon. She had walked out of Nat Kelman's office — after a battle that ended in her suspension — and driven straight home. Probably by now the old bastard had sent for Gordie and told him she'd refused a part in his next picture. She wanted a better role in a stronger film. All this one had to offer was Gordon Faith. The script was a dog.

She went to the master bedroom and straight into the bathroom to soak in a perfumed tub. Gordie wouldn't blow up until after dinner. He had a thing about not fighting in front of the servants. But once dinner was served and they were gone, he would explode.

She filled the tub as high as possible. The mirrored wall and the mirror over the dressing table steamed over. The scent of roses permeated the air. She'd soak until she looked like a prune, she decided defiantly.

An hour later, while she lay back in the black marble tub, she heard Gordon's car in the driveway. She heard him slam into the house and head for the master bedroom. He stalked across the bedroom and flung open the bathroom door. So she was wrong — he wouldn't wait until after dinner.

"What the hell's the matter with you?" he yelled. "Nat's raving mad. It'd do you good to work with me. I bring people to the box office!"

216

"It's a shitty part, and the picture isn't all that great." He was too angry even to get excited at her lying this way before him, she thought calmly.

"I want you to get out of that fucking tub and call Nat. He's still at the studio. You tell him you're sorry for acting so crazy and you'd love to play that role."

"I won't call Nat," she said with deceptive sweetness. "I won't apologize. And I won't play that fucking role."

"You're a stupid little bitch," he spat at her. "I'm getting the hell out of this house. When you apologize to Nat, I'll come back."

Tina waited until she heard Gordon's car charge down the driveway. Then she left the tub, patted herself dry, pulled on a terry-cloth robe, and went out to dismiss the staff for the night. Dinner would go into the refrigerator.

Alone in the house she phoned Constance Marlow.

"I just had another brawl with Gordie," she reported. "You busy for dinner?"

"Andy's having a drink in the library," Connie reported. Andy was the multimillionaire sportsman with whom she was currently having an affair. "We're going to the Mocambo for dinner. We'll stop by and pick you up in half an hour."

Andy was pleased to pilot two young beauties to a choice table at the Mocambo. A stream of fawning table hoppers, paying tribute to Andy's millions as much as the spectacular good looks of his two companions, kept them entertained throughout dinner.

"There's Mannie Olson," Connie whispered and pointed to a middle-aged man with an aura of success about him. "Andy, bring him over here." She winked at Tina. Mannie Olson was head of a major studio.

In moments Mannie Olson was seated at their table and exchanging good-humored, ribald insults with Andy.

"Andy, don't put any more money into this rotten business," Mannie cautioned. "All you'll get for it is ulcers. Here we are in the first week of filming, and Beverly Lincoln walked out cold." Beverly Lincoln was the hottest young female star on the Hollywood scene. "She flew down to Mexico City with some refugee director who's teaching her to act. I just want her to wiggle her ass, wear gorgeous clothes, and bring them screaming to the box office."

"I'm between pictures," Tina said casually, her heart pounding. Any part handed to Beverly Lincoln had to be great. "I can wiggle my ass, wear gorgeous clothes, and — in the right part — sell a lot of movie tickets." She managed the slightly arrogant smile that carried such high-voltage sexual appeal. "Why don't you talk to Nat Kelman about a loan-out?"

Mannie Olson was taken aback by her blatant approach. "This isn't the kind of part you've been doing," he pointed out.

So he'd seen her pictures. That was something.

"It's the kind of part I should be doing." She leaned forward, allowing him a full view of inviting cleavage. "Oh, the studio's beginning to see the light," she shrugged. "They're not throwing me into the sweet young thing roles any more, but they don't see what I can do." Her eyes told him she expected him to recognize what she had to offer.

"Come to the studio tomorrow morning," he said with an air of indulgence. "Let's see how you fit into this role before I start tangling with Nat. But no promises."

"What time do you want me there?" Tina asked.

The long midday siesta was over. The warm late October sun painted a patina of gold on the Oriental domes and mosaics, the gothic pinnacles of St. Mark's Church,

218

and on the pink-and-white marble facade of the Doges' Palace. On the Piazzetta, a few yards beyond the Piazza San Marco, Vanessa strolled among the afternoon crowds wearing a small fixed smile. Normally San Marco was her favorite spot in all of Venice.

She paused to pretend to listen to an accordionist playing arias from *The Barber of Seville*. Her gaze swung compulsively to the top of the Clock Tower as a pair of huge bronze blackamoors struck the hour of 4:00 P.M. Her throat tightened in anguish. At this moment Eddie and Isa Castello were being married at the Castello palazzo. They were having a civil ceremony; Eddie had explained that the Castellos had too much respect for the Montinos to request a church marriage.

After the wedding ceremony Eddie and Isa, accompanied by Isa's nurse, were to leave for a brief honeymoon in Cannes. Isa's parents were determined that she experience — as near possible — a real marriage. Eddie was to play the devoted husband.

A slip of paper with the name, address, and phone number of the luxurious Cannes hotel where Eddie would be staying was tucked away in Vanessa's wallet. She was to call him in the event of any emergency.

Was the ceremony over already? Vanessa tormented herself. Eddie said it would be brief, with a small reception afterward. Then he and Isa and the nurse would travel by private railway car to Nice. This detail drove home for Vanessa the extent of the Castellos' wealth.

Vanessa withdrew from the cluster of people listening to the accordionist and walked across to the entrance to the Correr Museum, at the west end of the piazza. She could not yet bring herself to return to the russet-brown house that Eddie had rented for them. For the first night since Eddie returned from the war they would be apart.

* * *

Vanessa knew the days and nights would drag until Eddie returned to Venice. She spent hours each day studying the costumes in paintings on display in the Correr Museum and the Oriental Museum, where the top floor of the palace showed costumes collected in the ninteeth century by the Conte di Vardi. She focused on her sketching during the lonely evenings. Each day she wandered in and out of the shops under the arcades of San Marco and along the Rialto, stopping in the course of her excursions at a trattoria—a little open-air restaurant—where she sipped coffee or white wine while she watched the parade of passersby.

Vanessa approved of the Venetian habit of visiting a favorite *caffè*—for cappuccino or wine or an apertif—at least once a day. She understood, too, that Venice was the only city in all Italy where women frequented the *caffè*. But while Eddie was away, she avoided the celebrated Florian's—which boasted it had not been closed for the past three hundred years—because this was "their place," where they had sat for a while every evening that Eddie was free to be with her.

The afternoon before Eddie was to return to Venice, Vanessa went in search of a new dress in which to welcome him. He had given her a shocking amount of lire with instructions to buy herself some pretty clothes. A distraction, she thought, to lessen her loneliness.

In a little shop off the beaten track she paused before the window to inspect a moonlight-yellow silk frock on display in the window. It was one of those shops where the seamstress-owner made the dresses and altered each to fit the customer. The color was a perfect foil for her red-gold hair. She admired the drape of the sleeves and the skirt, frowned at the frilly neckline, the sedate narrow belt. Mentally she redesigned the dress as she hurried into the shop. Her Italian faltered as she excitedly tried to communicate with the warm, fashion-loving owner of the shop. The good-humored shopkeeper brought out a sheet of paper and a pencil, and Vanessa sketched the changes she had in mind.

Signora Torino nodded in avid approval and darted about the shop in search of a scarf in the shade of pink Vanessa described. Caught up in Vanessa's creative spree, Signora Torino brought out scissors, needle, and thread and happily assisted in the transformation.

"Any time the signora wishes to work in a shop, come to me," she said ebulliently and then paused, aghast at her temerity. *"Mi scusi —"*

"I'd love to work in your shop," Vanessa said impulsively. "But my Italian is not good."

"Is good enough," Signora Torino dismissed this, her round face alight with pleasure. "You design, I sew. The ladies in Venice will come to us. You will see," she predicted.

Vanessa lingered with Signora Torino, caught up in new plans for the small shop. She was thrilled by this chance to see her designs executed by a seamstress and pleased at the prospect of earning money on her own. She should earn enough to send to her mother, Vanessa told herself optimistically. Though Eddie had insisted he was happy to assume this responsibility, she wanted to handle it on her own.

She returned to their small house basking in a sense of achievement. In a little shop on a side street in Venice there was a shopkeeper who loved her designs. And the days would seem less lonely when she was designing.

Eddie would understand, she promised herself. He knew how much designing meant to her — as much as designing theater sets meant to him. The day would come when they'd return to New York and work at what was so close to their hearts.

* * *

Vanessa would not allow herself to leave their house on the day when Eddie was scheduled to return from Cannes. She planned a festive dinner, grateful that Tina had taught her to cook. As the day merged into dusk, she paced restlessly in front of a window that looked out onto the narrow flagstone street, waiting to spy Eddie's approaching figure.

At last she saw him coming toward the house, walking in that swift, impatient way that spoke of his eagerness to see her. Her face alight, she hurried to the door to greet him — first sneaking a reassuring glance at herself in the mirror. She hoped he would approve of the yellow silk dress.

"I've missed you so," Eddie murmured, holding her in his arms.

"I've missed you," she confessed. A hundred questions filled her mind.

"Isa was ill our last two days in Cannes." All at once his face was troubled. "I'll have to return to the palazzo tonight. Her parents will expect me to be there. But we'll have four hours together." His eyes pleaded for acceptance.

"We'll have dinner on the terrace," she said, fighting to mask her disappointment.

"We'll have dinner at the Danieli," he ordered with an air of mock conspiracy. The Danieli was the oldest and most famous of the palazzo hotels, dating back to the nineteenth century. "Where we'll mingle with the ghosts of George Sand, Alfred de Musset, Dickens, and Wagner. But we won't linger too long." His mouth brushed hers in promise.

They left the house to take a gondola to the Danieli, Eddie's arm about her as they watched the night magic of Venice. He dwelt briefly on the days in Cannes and listened with tender approval as she talked — haltingly at first — about her job with Signora Torino.

222

"Vanessa, you must submit some of your sketches to Paris, to the International Wool Secretariat," he decided. "Every year there is a design contest — anyone can enter. The winner's sketch is executed by a top couture house," he told her with a triumphant smile. "Let the world come to know Vanessa Conrad."

"Eddie, not yet," she retreated in alarm, but her face was luminous at the prospect of such recognition. "Next year," she hedged.

"Vanessa, you're good," he said softly. "I don't say that because I love you. I say it because of what I see in your work."

"A year with Signora Torino and I'll be ready," she whispered. "Eddie, this is a wonderful opportunity for me."

The hours sped by all too fast. As she watched Eddie dress in the moonlit room, Vanessa began to understand the depths of the loneliness that lay ahead of her. She saw long nights alone when Eddie must leave her for the bedside of his ailing wife. Nights when Isa was well enough to attend small diner parties or a concert, and Eddie must be with her.

She stood at their bedroom window and watched his departing figure. Knowing sleep would be long in overtaking her tonight, she sat down at the table in their bedroom to write to Tina.

Vanessa tried to concentrate on Tina's last letter: *"I've been out here over two years, baby, but I feel in my bones that this picture will make me a star."*

Sitting at the writing table in the stillness of the Venetian night, Vanessa thought about the summer at Fire Island. They had been so *young* then. She and Tina and Pat and Tracy had done so much growing up in the past fourteen months.

Tracy never bothered to write after she returned to Houston. It was as though she had never known them.

Vanessa had received two brief letters from Pat, who was seeing some young lawyer who worked for her father. She suspected Pat was still hurting from Jesse but was too proud to admit it. Pat said flatly she had no intention of rushing into marriage with anybody.

When will Eddie and I be married?

At terrifying moments she asked herself if she had made a disastrous mistake in coming to Venice. They had waited so long to be together.

Eighteen

Vanessa understood that Eddie had to be away from her and their small house at regular intervals, yet reasoning did little to alleviate her loneliness — her uncertainties — on those nights when she was alone. Eddie tried not to erect a wall between his life with Vanessa and that other life in the grandiose Castello palazzo. He told her about the dinners and concerts and art showings he attended when Isa's health permitted.

"It's so sad, Vanessa, to know that this lovely young girl has so little time ahead of her," he said compassionately. "It's devastating for her parents. They have only one other child, their son, Roberto, who lives with his wife in Milan. They're fine people," he reminded her. "I can never forget what they did for my family."

"I know you have to do this," Vanessa comforted him. Yet late at night, when she was alone, she asked herself if Eddie was falling in love with his wife. But when she lay in Eddie's arms she knew he loved only *her*.

On delicious, unexpected afternoons during the beautiful Venetian autumn Eddie would escape from his office an hour or two before sunset to arrive at the house with a bottle of chilled Prosecco and a bag of superb sandwiches acquired at Harry's Bar, that famous restaurant once frequented by Hemingway.

"We're having a picnic in a gondola on the Grand Canal," he would announce exuberantly. "Bring along a light coat — it'll be cool in the evening air."

The nights when Isa lay ill — and Vanessa knew that death hovered closely — Eddie would remain at his wife's bedside with her parents until the doctor dismissed them. On those nights he slept in his room at the Castello palazzo to be close at hand should the nurse summon him to Isa's side. For Isa, Vanessa came to understand, this make-believe marriage was precious. It was a poignant game to mask her painful reality.

When Vanessa sat alone at dinner, she focused her attention on the French textbook that Eddie had brought her. One day she would see Paris, and she vowed she would be able to speak the language. Her daytime hours were divided between Signora Torino's shop, the museums where she sought new ideas for dresses, and the elegant shops of the city, where she inspected the fashions on display.

Vanessa was frustrated when Signora Torino's patrons rejected the sketches she offered. Yet there was a small clique of ladies who understood that she was offering something special. Ironically, the ladies who admired Vanessa's designs were those who could not afford the fine fabrics with which she longed to work. Still, it was exciting to sit at an outdoor table at Florian's and see a woman dressed in one of her designs stroll past.

Vanessa was delighted when Eddie brought her an exquisite gold menorah at the approach of Hanukkah. On the day before the first evening of Hanukkah, he came to her in the early afternoon with the announcement that he would take her to visit the ancient Venetian ghetto.

"It's an important sight of the city," he told her while they walked from the house toward the Grand Canal.

The day was cold, the city enveloped in a shroud of mist. They took a *motoscafo* in order to save time because tonight Eddie must escort his wife to a dinner party at his parents' home. Vanessa knew that Eddie had made an effort to tell his mother of her presence in Venice. His mother had silenced him; it would have been disloyal to the Castellos for her to recognize Vanessa's presence.

At the once-walled ghetto, where fragments of the hinges of the gates could still be seen at the entrance, Eddie guided her past tall gray tenements. He explained that since the ghetto could not grow horizontally, it had been forced to grow vertically.

"The ghetto houses were the skyscrapers of Venice," Eddie mused. "By law they were allowed to be one-third higher than other buildings in the city. And within the ghetto not everyone was poor. A seventeenth-century writer tells in his records that there were ghetto ladies who were strikingly beautiful in sumptuous gowns and magnificent jewelry. Their trains were carried by servants as though they were royal princesses."

Eddie showed Vanessa the five surviving synagogues, the oldest continuously functioning synagogues in Europe. The Scuolo Tedesca, built by an Ashkenasi community around 1528, was the oldest, with the Scuola Spagnola—its elegant exterior resembling a miniature opera house—standing as largest and most famous.

"Only about twenty of the old families still live here," Eddie told her. "Christians live in most of the tenements. The Jewish families are scattered about the city, but they have a strong sense of community," he said with pride.

Mindful of the time, Vanessa and Eddie dallied briefly over cappuccino at a small *caffè* near the house. Eddie talked wistfully of the day they would return to New York and he could pursue his career as a stage designer.

"Vanessa, be patient," he said in a sudden burst of

anxiety. "I couldn't survive without you."

"I'll be here," she whispered.

Eddie took her home, then left to go to the Castello's palazzo to dress for the dinner party at his parents' home. As always, Vanessa stood at the window to watch Eddie's departing figure, fighting a desperate loneliness.

Houston was enjoying what Houstonians liked to call their Colorado weather. The air was cool and crisp, the sky a dazzling blue. Still, Pat dawdled in her bedroom in the River Oaks house before going downstairs to breakfast. She would shop this morning for the rest of her Christmas gifts at Sakowitz's, then meet Paul for lunch. She frowned, remembering Paul's clumsy efforts last night to make love to her.

She gazed at her reflection in the mirror. Why did she keep on seeing Paul? He'd drop her soon if she kept playing it so standoffish. She wanted him to make love to her, she taunted herself. She wanted *somebody* to make love to her.

It surprised her that her mother and father seemed eager for her to become seriously involved with Paul. Maybe because Daddy was so sure Paul had a great political career ahead of him. How could she marry Paul when she still turned hot and cold whenever she saw somebody who looked like Jesse?

Pat picked up her suit jacket and purse and headed downstairs. She ought to be at Sakowitz's when they opened. She still hadn't bought presents for Tracy and Maureen and Roger. Mother and she would be leaving in three days for Virginia, and all her Christmas shopping had to be finished before then.

She was relieved that her mother was not at the breakfast table. She could avoid more arguments about why she wasn't becoming involved in charity committees.

228

Paul kept telling her she *had* to be part of the political teas for Texan ladies. Wasn't that enough?

"Tracy's into everything," her mother complained regularly. "All you do is ride in the morning — if we're at the ranch, you spend a couple of hours a day working for Daddy, and the rest of the time you mope."

Tracy was into more than she should be, Pat thought grimly. She was supposed to be so crazy about Brian, but she was seeing somebody behind his back. She complained that Brian never got home from the office until eight or nine most nights. *"Pat, I'm bored out of my skull."*

If she had married Jesse, *she* wouldn't have been bored, Pat told herself while she ate her scrambled eggs with disinterest.

"The mail jes' came," Effie Mae announced good-humoredly, and deposited a sheaf of envelopes beside Pat's coffee cup.

"Thank you, Effie Mae." Pat smiled and flipped through the morning's letters. She recognized Tina's large, careless scrawl, and ripped open the envelope with anticipation.

Tina was elated over the sneak preview of her new film.

"My agent says this is the big one. The studio's looking for a major film for me now. At my home studio — no more loan-outs. I'm getting a fancy new dressing room — and that tells it all! Of course, Gordie has his nose out of joint. But nothing I do pleases my husband anymore. If this keeps up, he'll soon be my ex-husband."

Pat thought wistfully about Tina in Hollywood. Vanessa wasn't doing much with her designing, but she was living with Eddie in romantic Venice. It wasn't exactly the way Eddie and Vanessa had planned, she conceded compassionately, but one day everything would be right for them. That was one marriage that would last. And with Vanessa's talent she would break through as a designer one day. Pat wished fiercely that she possessed some special talent.

She drove into town, parked, and went into Sakowitz's. The aisles of the festively decorated main floor of the store were already crowded with shoppers. Only six more shopping days before Christmas! While she waited for an elevator, her eyes strayed about the floor.

At the same moment that the elevator door slid open Pat froze in shock. Jesse stood a dozen yards away. He hadn't seen her. He hovered above a small, busty blonde who was talking in a loud Texas voice. He slipped his arm around her waist. Pat darted into the elevator. The girl with Jesse was not his Italian war bride. Had he decided not to bring her over, or was the sexy little blonde a side issue?

Pat ordered herself to concentrate on her Christmas list. She wasn't in love with Jesse anymore — he disgusted her. Yet her body betrayed her mind. She wished for nothing more at this moment than for Jesse to make love to her.

She was at the restaurant waiting for Paul ten minutes early. At exactly 1:00 P.M. she looked up to see him being led to their table. He was never a minute late for anything. She watched the female heads turn as he walked toward her. He was good-looking in the same earthy way as Jesse. Only Paul was smarter, she assessed. He had learned how to dress and how to handle himself with people.

"Hi." Paul's smile told her that having lunch with her was a special event.

"Busy day?" Her own smile was warmer than usual. *Why did she have to run into Jesse?* Yet she remembered how she never passed a service station without subconsciously looking to see if Jesse was in sight.

"We're beginning to roll into high gear," he said. "Your father's brilliant about what's happening in the country.

He knows what the voters are thinking before they do."

Pat and Paul ordered, and when the waiter took their menus and retreated, Pat leaned forward slightly.

"What are you doing tonight?"

"I have a meeting with some people from the City Council." But his eyes were expectant.

"After that?" she pursued.

"Anything you'd like to do?" He was wary, afraid of misreading her signals.

"I thought it might be fun to drive out to the ranch, have coffee there, and then drive back. It's going to be a glorious night. Almost a full moon."

"Will ten o'clock be too late?" he asked casually, but Pat could sense his excitement.

"Ten o'clock will be great."

They'd drive out to the ranch, have coffee and cake before the fireplace, and Effie Mae or Carmen would fuss over them with a glint in their eyes. They'd start back to River Oaks, but Paul would detour to the lake — "to see the moon over the water." They'd neck, but he wouldn't try anything serious because of Daddy. And after tonight, he'd understand he was in the running for son-in-law of the congressman.

Once she was married, she wouldn't be "Daddy's little girl." She'd be free to do whatever she pleased. No more of those awful political teas, where she felt like an object on display. Two years at drama school had not made her any less self-conscious in those enforced public appearances.

They'd marry in church in June. A big, splashy wedding with Maureen as her matron of honor — because Mother would insist — and Tracy and Tina as bridesmaids. Maybe by then Vanessa would be back home and could come out, too, to be a bridesmaid. Somehow, it was important for Vanessa and Tina to be at her wedding. They knew about the ugliness with Jesse.

231

Mother and Daddy would throw a huge reception and dinner after the wedding. It would be a perfect opportunity for some politicking before Daddy hit the campaign trail.

She'd never known him to show such concern about an election. He kept saying the mood of the country was changing, that ex-GI's might not vote the way they had before the war.

The wedding would be reported on the front pages of the *Houston Post* and the *Chronicle* and the *Press*. Jesse would read all about it.

Early in March Eddie's father died. For eight days Vanessa saw nothing of him, heard nothing. She knew his grief and his involvement in the religious observance of *shivah,* the week of mourning for the dead. She thought of her own father's death, when her mother had dispensed with this tradition as "too much to endure."

On the ninth day, his eyes dark with sadness, Eddie came to her. Vanessa consoled him, reminding him that he had brought peace to his father by his presence in Venice and his marriage to Isa.

"He was happy," Eddie conceded, "but he was only fifty-six. Too young to die."

"Can you stay tonight?" Vanessa asked, longing to comfort him in her arms.

"I will stay," he said and pulled her close. Even death could not deny them love.

Vanessa was glad that the winter was past. For weeks the city had been enveloped in a raw dampness of teeming rain, or by a fog so dense it was impossible to see across the piazza. Now the swallows were arriving, the fog was gone, and the sun shone in the magnificent blue sky. The city was preparing for its first tourist season since the war. Vanessa was in love with the spring.

The only flaw in her happiness was Signora Torino's admission that she might soon sell the shop. The past winter had taken its toll on her health, and she hoped before the next winter to be able to join her widowed sister in Sorrento.

Vanessa worried that the new owner of the shop might not share Signora Torino's enthusiasm for her sketches. While they were beginning to attract a wealthier, more fashion-conscious clientele, Vanessa knew that because of her habit of choosing expensive fabrics for her designs, the profits were small. The shop was precious to her, her one tenuous grasp on the world of fashion.

Eddie had arranged a subscription for her to French *Vogue* and to *Paris-Match*, which helped in her continuing self-study of French. She was fascinated by what she read of Lucien Lelong, the doyen of Paris couturiers, and his two young designers, Pierre Balmain and Christian Dior. And a wealthy American tourist who came into the shop talked enthusiastically about a young man in Florence named Emilio Pucci, who she predicted would make a name for himself far beyond his native city.

"And do you know, he studied at the University of Georgia in Athens and got his master's in political science at Reed in Portland? He was a flier in the Italian air force during the war and smuggled Edda Ciano — that's Mussolini's daughter — into Switzerland. When he went back into Italy, he was captured by the Gestapo and tortured. Would you ever think that would be the background for a talented fashion designer?" The customer was too polite to pry, but Vanessa knew she was curious about why an American girl was working in a boutique in Venice.

"I don't think there's any one background that produces fashion designers," Vanessa said. "Mainbocher, who was born in Chicago, came to Paris to study voice, then became editor of French *Vogue.*"

"Ah, Paris," the tourist said sentimentally. "In Paris anything can happen."

In Paris French couture — aided by government subsidies — was bursting upon the postwar scene with fresh brilliance. Many of the great names once again catered to the world of fashion. In addition to Lelong, there was Piguet, Patou, Paquin, Mme. Grès, Jacques Fath, Lanvin, Balenciaga, and Nina Ricci. Vanessa longed to see Paris.

Late in May Vanessa was astonished to receive a letter from *Le Figaro,* together with a minuscule check in payment for four sketches. She stood with the letter and check in her hands for a bewildered moment before she understood. Eddie had submitted her fashion sketches to the newspaper without telling her. *Le Figaro* had paid money for them! *Now she was a professional designer.*

She waited impatiently for Eddie to come to the house. Her smile was radiant as she handed him the letter and check without a word.

"Now do you believe that you are very, very good?" he demanded. "All these doubts you have — they're absurd. Go change into something festive, and we'll have dinner at the Danieli to celebrate."

Pat was cold and trembling as she sat at her dressing table in a white satin slip while the makeup man — flown in from Hollywood — penciled her eyebrows. Tina stood nearby in her yellow bridesmaid gown and fussed with her hair. The ivory satin gown and old ivory lace veil that Pat would wear lay across her bed.

Her ultra-expensive trousseau, chosen under the sharp eye of her mother at Sakowitz's in Houston,

Neiman-Marcus in Dallas, and Bergdorf Goodman in New York, was packed away in Vuitton luggage stacked in a corner of the bedroom. Her wedding present from her mother and father—a diamond and ruby necklace with matching earrings from Cartier—lay in its elegant box on her dresser. She would wear it at the wedding reception.

"This all seems so ridiculous," Pat sighed, impatient with the lengthy efforts of the makeup artist. "I'm not a movie star."

"Today you're a star." The makeup man's smile was dazzling.

"You said it was important to look your very best," Tina pointed out calmly. "Henri will see to that." It was Tina who had arranged for Henri to be flown in from Hollywood—at an astronomical fee.

"Tina, I'm so glad you could come," Pat told her, then fell silent at Henri's admonition that she must be still. Mother and Daddy were pleased that an exciting new movie star was to be her maid of honor, even while they frowned upon the notoriety surrounding Tina's recent Reno divorce.

"I don't understand why Tracy couldn't be here for your wedding." Tina's eyes glittered with contempt. "She didn't *have* to go chasing off to Tangier to see the palace Barbara Hutton just bought. Does she expect 'Daddy darling' to buy her one, too?"

"Come in," Pat called out in response to a brusque knock and then gasped as the door swung wide. "Paul, you're not supposed to see the bride until the ceremony!" But she was conscious of an unexpected flutter of passion at the sight of him, bronzed and handsome in his formal wedding attire.

"Your father asked me to talk to you," Paul said tentatively, seeming uncomfortable in the presence of Tina and Henri.

"Go ahead," Pat said airily. "What's Daddy up to now?"

"He wants us to forget about the honeymoon in London and Paris. He—"

"But everything's arranged!" Pat stared at him in disbelief.

"Your father had a meeting this morning with his advisers. Everybody feels that with all the trouble between management and labor right now the family ought to appear more conservative financially. He's making arrangements for us to stay at a friend's villa in Acapulco."

"Paul, the honeymoon plans have circulated in all the newspapers," Pat protested. She'd looked forward secretly to a brief side trip to Venice to surprise Vanessa.

"There'll be retractions," Paul explained. "Your father's running a tight ship in this campaign. We have to respect his wishes."

"We'll go to Acapulco," Pat sighed. She wished Paul wouldn't give in to Daddy all the time. She was sure Paul's two sisters would have come down from Dallas with their husbands for the wedding if they'd been invited. Daddy was scared to death they'd embarrass him. Both were married to laborers in the oil fields. Today the groom's side of the church would be occupied by political associates. *Daddy's* political associates.

After the elaborate wedding dinner Pat and Paul and their rash of Vuitton luggage were flown in a chartered Boeing Stratoliner to Acapulco. On the flight Paul devoted himself to studying the lengthy report her father had handed him as they boarded the plane. It was just like Daddy, Pat thought in exasperation, to tell Paul in the midst of their wedding dinner that he meant for his son-in-law to run for the state legislature in the next election.

A custom-built white Rolls-Royce waited at the airport to whisk them to a marble-and-stone, multileveled villa that hung high over the Pacific among tall palms, giant philodendron, and bougainvillaea. They were ushered into a sweeping foyer with white Carrera marble parquet floors and led through high Spanish arches and up three pairs of low stairs to a guest bedroom suite. Three menservants carried their luggage while a maid led the way.

The marble-floored sitting room of the suite opened onto a broad terrace that looked down on the harbor.

"It's lovely," Pat said approvingly while the menservants deposited the luggage in the bedroom and departed. The maid remained to unpack.

"Your father's friend knows how to live." Paul was impressed.

The butler arrived with a serving cart bearing an array of finger sandwiches, two champagne glasses, and a bottle of Dom Perignon. He uncorked the champagne and departed. Pat lingered at the window wall.

"Isn't the view sensational?" She turned to Paul for corroboration and was all at once aware of her desire for him. This last week, with her father home from Washington, she had seen little of Paul. "Paul, come look —"

"In a minute." He was demolishing the sandwiches with relish.

She had allowed her mother to order exquisite nightgowns and negligees for her at Bergdorf's, but she meant to wear the black chiffon nightgown and negligee that Tina had smuggled in from a shop on Rodeo Drive. Tina said every man fantasized about a beautiful girl in a sheer black nightgown.

Sometimes it frightened her that she could be so passionate. It used to shock her when Tracy talked the way she did about making love — until she slept with Jesse.

237

She could not imagine her mother or Maureen ever feeling the way she had with Jesse.

She'd feel that way with Paul, she promised herself. Even though he'd never allowed himself to go beyond squeezing her breasts and French-kissing, she knew he could excite her. It was a small triumph over Jesse that she could feel this way with Paul.

"Your father's friend knows how to treat his guests," Paul approved again, inspecting the champagne bottle. "Think you can stay sober?" he teased.

"I'll try," she said. He grinned and poured the champagne.

She felt like a character in a Noel Coward play. Except that she was cool and sophisticated only on the outside. She reached for her glass as Paul approached. She didn't know one champagne from another, she thought with wry humor; but it was necessary to make some comment. Girls always did that in smart plays or movies.

"To us," Paul said with a jaunty smile as they clicked glasses.

"Isn't this a marvelous view?" She didn't feel like standing here talking with Paul. She wished they were lying together in bed.

"Sensational," he agreed with a casual glance at the splash of stars and the silver-washed Pacific below.

The room was dark and silent except for their breathing. "I'm glad we came here," she said into the darkness. If they hadn't, they'd still be on the plane to New York.

"What the hell is taking the maid so long?" he asked.

He disposed of his empty champagne glass and strode across to the bedroom door. "You can leave that now," he told the maid in brusque dismissal. "Finish unpacking in the morning."

The maid hurried out of the suite with a demure, sympathetic smile. Paul took the champagne glass from Pat and pulled her into his arms. His mouth was hard on

238

hers, his hands insistent on her body.

"Let's get this show on the road," he drawled.

Hand in hand they walked into the bedroom. Like the sitting room, it was furnished in a blend of modern and traditional, and a Chinese influence lent an exotic touch. The wide sweep of windows was blocked by handscreened white silk drapes.

Pat reached for the small weekender, not yet unpacked, and walked with it into the oversize, mirror-walled bathroom, its floor white Carrera marble. There was a marble dressing table and a sunken mosaic bathtub in white and gold, and a black marble-faced fireplace in one corner.

Pat's hands were unsteady as she brought the sensuously draped black chiffon nightgown and negligee from the weekender and pulled it over her head and about her slender frame. To the devil with the negligee, she decided, pleased by her reflection in the mirror. The spaghetti straps lay dark against her sun-kissed shoulders, her taut nipples pressed against the diaphanous bodice.

She touched her throat with Chanel No. 5, the inner creases of her elbows, and then — daringly — brushed her thighs. Then she left the bathroom to walk into the bedroom. Her eyes widened as she spied Paul, naked and ready, sprawled across the turned-down bed. She'd had a romantic vision of him in silk pajamas and robe. Like Cary Grant in a movie.

"You took long enough," he mocked, his eyes straying over the lissome length of her. "But it was worth it."

"Would you like some more champagne?" *Why do I suddenly feel self-conscious? Paul is my husband.*

"No." He flexed one leg and patted the empty side of the bed. "And take that thing off. You've made your entrance."

With what she hoped appeared to be an amused smile, she slid the spaghetti straps from her shoulders, and let the sheer blackness fall to the floor. Paul reached out his hand to draw her onto the bed. Her heart was pounding as he drew her down above him, imprisoning her between his thighs, thrusting insinuatingly against her firm, flat belly.

"Tell me what you want me to do," he whispered and she stiffened in dismay.

"No," she stammered.

"You're my wife now. We can do anything we like," he crooned. "Tell me what you want me to do." His eyes glittered with excitement.

"I can't," she whispered, her face hot. *Why didn't he turn off the lamps?*

"Do you want to touch me?" he challenged. "Here," he said, reaching for her hand and bringing it to him.

"Yes," she told him, her body making demands she could not voice.

"Sugar, it's okay," he encouraged. "Tell me. Say, 'Fuck me, Paul.' All you have to do is ask."

"I can't talk that way," she confessed. *Why must he play this crazy game?* "But yes, Paul. Please. Please!"

"Please what?" he taunted, one hand between her thighs, the other rough at her breast.

"Make love to me," she said. "We've waited so long."

"I knew you wouldn't be cold in bed." He swung her over on her back and lifted himself above her. "That ladylike coolness didn't fool me one bit."

She closed her eyes as he lowered himself between her thighs, his hands at her small, high breasts. It had been so long, she thought. Would it hurt just at first? But all at once he was driving into her with hungry fury and she was responding. The long drought was over. They moved together in a symphonic passion that seemed endless, and the sounds of their passion blended into one.

At last he lay spent upon her. She felt alive, relaxed,

enriched. And then he was drawing away from her. She opened her eyes in protest. He stood grimly beside the bed and glared down at her.

"You goddamn little slut," he said. "Now I know why your old man was so anxious to see you married! How many men did you sleep with before you hooked me?"

Before she could reply, he leaned over and slapped her hard across the mouth. She lay back, reeling from the blow. *She should have told him about Jesse.* She hadn't played the game, the way Tina had told her.

"A man doesn't have to know he isn't the first if the girl plays it smart."

She hadn't played it smart.

Nineteen

Vanessa loved the summer days she spent with Eddie at the Lido, where he had taken a cabana for them. From the moment they boarded the boat at the Riva degli Schiavoni for the trip to the Lido, she felt as though she and Eddie were alone in the world. In Venice Eddie was always on call for Isa and her family; but once they crossed the open sea to the gorgeous stretch of golden sand, Eddie belonged to her.

The Lido was a town of modern buildings and streets, and a striking contrast to Venice. It stayed deliciously comfortable when the city was oppressively hot. Its superb Gran Viale Santa Maria Elisabetta was lined with smart shops and elegant hotels.

Both Vanessa and Eddie found it exhilarating to listen to the roar of the Adriatic, to watch the waves driven into a fury by the winds coming across the sea. They walked along the beach hand in hand for hours. They spoke little because it was enough just to be together this way. At night they strolled along the main avenues and streets of the Lido, alive with music, brilliant with floodlights.

In mid-September Signora Torino began to negotiate to sell the shop. She hoped to head south for Sorrento in December. Vanessa concentrated on building up a portfolio of sketches to try to sell to *Le Figaro* or — with luck on her side — to some of the Paris couture houses.

Later in the month Vanessa heard from Tina. She wrote that the *Hollywood Reporter* had raved about her performances in the loan-out film. The studio had finally seen her potential and was giving her the kind of roles that suited her: the sensuous but coolly detached, elegant young beauty who lives a dissolute life. Tina mourned that she had emerged from her divorce with a settlement of only twenty thousand — and Vanessa worried that she was going through this settlement at record speed. Now a "hot property," Tina reveled in the role of Hollywood playgirl. Vanessa was awed by the stream of escorts she mentioned.

And Pat wrote that she was deliriously happy at being pregnant. She expected the baby late in February:

"I must have gotten pregnant on our honeymoon. Anyway, Paul is so handsome and so bright and so ambitious! And Daddy is bursting with pride at finally becoming a grandfather. He's gearing Paul up for the state legislature. You know Daddy — when he makes up his mind for something to happen, it does. He figures a few terms in the legislature, and Paul will be ready for Congress. I know Mother has always hated Washington, but I think it might be fun."

Occasionally, Vanessa was overcome by waves of homesickness. When Signora Torino sold the shop in early December, she felt something akin to panic. She feared the new owner would not be as experimental in the business as Signora Torino had been — and her fears were soon realized. The new shopkeeper was thoroughly conventional. Vanessa was told her services would no longer be required. She tried to sell more sketches, but not one was accepted.

This year the winter seemed drab and oppressive. She missed the hours at the shop, the fashion talk she had shared with Signora Torino. His father-in-law's business was requiring more of Eddie's time, and Isa's health continued its seesaw pattern. It upset Eddie when he had to phone her and say they could not go to the San Marco Cinema that evening — or to a long-planned concert or a dance festival or an art exhibit. He knew that, self-conscious about her situation, she'd made no friends in Venice.

Vanessa was fascinated by what she read in the Paris newspapers — and shortly afterward in *Vogue* — about the exciting new designer named Christian Dior, whose first collection was shown in February 1947. She remembered reading earlier that he, along with a young man named Pierre Balmain, had designed for Lucien Lelong. All Paris was talking about Dior's collection, dubbed the New Look by an American journalist. In the midst of the worst winter in Europe since 1870 — with Paris inundated by snow at a time when electricity was rationed and coal in short supply — a new designing star had bust upon the horizon.

Vanessa understood what Christian Dior was offering women. All through the war years American and British women had worn austere clothes whose outlines were dictated by the shortage of fabrics and labor. Now the war was over, and Dior was creating a fashion revolution. He was showing the kinds of clothes she created only in her sketchbooks. Skirts that required fifteen or even twenty yards of material, dropped past the knees to extend almost to the ankles. Dainty, feminine clothes whose time had come.

Christian Dior's towering success both stimulated and depressed Vanessa. She devoured every word written about him. If it happened to Christian Dior, it could happen — in time — to Vanessa Conrad.

She tried to conceal from Eddie her impatience. She was conscious of her isolation in Venice as New York became the fashion capital of the world. For most of the great Paris couturiers 1945, 1946, and 1947 had been difficult years. American ready-to-wear — Seventh Avenue — was enjoying fantastic success throughout the world. It was a no-holds-barred battle to conquer the female market.

American newspapers waged the battle for Seventh Avenue with headlines that attacked "the scandal of French luxury — an insult to American GI's." A Pentagon committee recommended "that newspapers, magazines, and agencies be prevented from publicizing French fashion." Seventh Avenue had never had it so good, Vanessa tormented herself — and she was thousands of miles away.

The arrival of spring freed Vanessa to walk endlessly about the city. Eddie talked of a trip to Paris in the fall. He would go on business and take her with him.

Vanessa clung to the vision of seeing Paris with Eddie. Though Paris was no longer the couture capital of the world, many women in Europe and America continued to pay homage to the great French designers. Vanessa yearned to see the couture houses of Lucien Lelong, the man who had personally contrived for Paris fashion to survive the German occupation. And Jacques Fath, who was awarded the Croix de Guerre and the Légion d'Honneur for his services to France. Piguet and Patou. And especially the House of Christian Dior at 30 Avenue Montaigne.

She fumed constantly at her lack of skills as a seamstress. She could design, but without a seamstress her designs could not become reality.

"Vanessa, millions of women can sew," Eddie scolded her while they sat at a table at Florian's on a hot June night. "Only a few can design as you do."

"I'm not selling any more sketches," she railed. "Not for months now." The money she received from *Le Figaro* and other newspapers for sketches was minuscule, but the selling had bolstered her ever shaky ego. And sketches in the newspapers could lead to interest in her

245

work from Paris couturiers. But even while she railed, she remembered that Eddie, too, was tied down to a selling job for the Castello lace mills when he longed to design stage sets. "Eddie, what am I doing wrong?" Her eyes searched his.

"You're designing ahead of your time," he said, squinting in thought. "The fashion world will catch up with you." He reached to cover her hand with his in a gesture of consolation.

"Dior came out with his New Look. It's revolutionary, but he's been an instant sensation!"

"It was Dior's time," he assessed. "And still, think of the hostility he's created along with his success. Even with *Paris-Match* and *Vogue* — most of the press — behind him, there are people who can't accept his designs. Vanessa, it's not your time yet. You're twenty-two. Dior is forty-seven. You can afford to wait." He glanced at his watch and frowned. In a few moments he had to leave to accompany Isa to a recital. "Be patient, my darling. One day the world will know Vanessa Conrad. You'll be as famous as Dior." His face was luminous in anticipation.

"And you'll design sets for the Broadway theater." Determinedly she picked up his mood. "I know I shouldn't complain," she apologized. "We're young — we have our whole lives ahead of us."

"Oh, I forgot to tell you," he reproached himself. "We'll be able to see *Lady of Mystery* in Venice next month!" *Lady of Mystery* was Tina's breakthrough film.

"Oh, Eddie, I can't wait to see it!"

Her happiness at Tina's success almost overcame her depression. She had said nothing to Eddie about Tina's advice to desert Venice for Hollywood.

"Baby, I can help you get a break designing for movies. If you need the fare, I'll send it to you."

Her day would come, and she would be a full-fledged designer. Not now. Now she had to be here with Eddie.

She would work on her portfolio; and when the right moment came to show her designs, she'd be ready. Still, deep within, she fretted at not being able to grasp the chance Tina could provide.

In mid-June Eddie told Vanessa that Isa's parents had bought a villa at the Lido because the doctors felt the cool breezes from the sea during the hot months would be beneficial. His father-in-law had decreed that he was to take a month's vacation from the business and spend it at the Lido villa.

"A whole month?" Vanessa's face betrayed her consternation.

"Isa must spend much of each day resting," Eddie said. "I'll be with you most of the time."

"But you'll be staying at the Lido—"

"As will you," he pointed out. "You'll be registered for a month at the Grand Hotel des Bains. I'll come to you every day. And some of the nights," he promised. "At the end of the month I'll come back to the palazzo and go to the villa perhaps three evenings a week."

"Eddie, the Hotel des Bains is so expensive," she interrupted, her eyes questioning. She knew of the elegant hotel; it faced directly onto the Adriatic and catered to the wealthiest of vacationers.

"We can afford it," he reassured her. "You'll love it." He smiled teasingly. "Much better than Coney Island."

"Much better than Fire Island," she laughed. She was still awed by the wealth with which Eddie lived. "But Eddie, is it all right?" she faltered.

"The villa is on the lagoon side of the Lido," he explained gently. "You'll never meet."

As Eddie had predicted, she adored the month at the elegant hotel, a playground of the internationally rich. The Hotel des Bains, set amid colorful flower beds, had its private beach with an underground passage from the hotel. When she was alone, she sat on the beach under a striped umbrella and read or sketched. When Eddie was with her, they walked for miles beside the Adriatic. Eddie told her how, over a century ago, Lord Byron had ridden horseback along this same stretch of beach. The Hotel des Bains maintained a restaurant and a bar on the beach so that it was possible to remain on the sands the entire day without returning to the hotel.

In the evening a wonderful quiet descended, the only sounds those of the Adriatic having a passionate affair with the beach. Under beautiful Venetian glass chandeliers, on those nights when his presence was not required at the long, white vine-covered villa that was reminiscent of those in Marrakech, Eddie and Vanessa waltzed to soft orchestral music. It was a magical interlude that Vanessa cherished.

After the month at the Lido Vanessa returned to the little house in Venice and Eddie resumed his residence at the Castello palazzo. Now he was able to spend the midweek nights with Vanessa, traveling to the Lido villa on Saturday afternoons and returning on Monday mornings.

Pat sent a batch of photographs of the baby, along with clippings from the Dallas newspapers reporting that Neiman-Marcus was awarding Christian Dior a Fashion "Oscar."

"Everyone in Texas is excited. Dior is coming to Dallas for the presentation. Mother says nothing will stop her from being there, though she warns there'll be some anti-Dior demonstrations. Can you imagine women getting so furious because Dior designs dresses with long skirts?"

Vanessa tried to involve herself in the museums and the art galleries, mingling with the tourists who once again gravitated toward Venice in the hot months. But she tired easily. She blamed this and her constant sleepiness on the torrid summer heat. Until suddenly reality broke into her dream world. She was pregnant.

Clutching her secret to her she walked among the Sunday crowds and struggled to cope. Eddie would come to the house for breakfast in the morning before going to the office. He would know what they must do, she told herself. Yet the prospect of having a doctor — no matter how skilled he might be — take away her baby was repugnant. *Eddie's baby and hers.* Under any other circumstances they'd both have been so happy.

She slept little that night. Eddie would be distraught when she told him she was pregnant, but she had to tell him. They'd been so careful. But she remembered one night when they'd allowed their love to make them careless. *Only one night.*

At dawn she was wide awake. She left her bed to look out upon the narrow, rose-washed street, empty and oddly threatening this morning. She sought to frame the words that would tell Eddie she was pregnant.

Her fault, she reproached herself. She should have pulled herself from Eddie's arms instead of lingering yet another hour that night. In a dark corner of her mind she must have known they were being careless.

Already she mourned for their unknown child. Their firstborn. Eddie adored children. He had so tenderly told her that their family would not interfere with her career.

She heard Eddie's key in the door before she expected it. Sometimes on summer Monday mornings she would wake to find him brewing coffee. After coffee they'd make love because for two nights Eddie had been away from her.

"Eddie?" Still in her little-girl nightgown she hurried into the hall, eager for the reassurance of his arms about her.

"I couldn't sleep last night," he told her, pulling her

249

close. "I missed you so much."

"Eddie, I have to talk to you—"

Faltering, her face against his, his arms holding her close to him, Vanessa told him. For a terrifying instant he was still and silent.

"Vanessa—" His voice broke. He took her face between his hands. "I don't think I've ever been so happy."

Did Eddie believe they could be married before the baby was born? They had never allowed themselves to consider how much longer he would be tied to Isa. But now she felt washed in guilt at such a thought.

"Eddie, how can I have this baby?"

"You'll have it," he said with glorious determination. "I'll find a little house for us near Mestre, in the suburbs. When we marry and return to New York, no one will know that we were not married when our daughter or son was born. I won't let anyone rob us of this baby, Vanessa. *Our child.*"

"Do we dare?" Her eyes pleaded for reassurance. *But there were times when Eddie could not be with her. Suppose she went into labor and she was alone?*

"We dare. I'll find us a little house with a garden. I'll hire a housekeeper who'll live in. You won't be alone for a moment." He saw into her heart and mind. "And whatever happens," he vowed, "I'll be with you when the baby's born. I swear, my love."

"Oh, Eddie, I want our baby." Tears filled her eyes and spilled over. "I couldn't bear to lose it."

"I've never loved you more than I do this minute," he whispered. "I've never felt so blessed."

Twenty

Eddie rented a charming little house for them about a mile from Mestre, just outside Venice. He bought a car to take him to and from the Piazzale Roma, where he could garage the car and proceed on his way by *motoscafo*. He found a local obstetrician to care for Vanessa during her pregnancy. The doctor was an unquestioning, middle-aged gentleman who gravely recorded her name as Mrs. Vanessa Conrad — and knew Eddie as Mr. Conrad.

Vanessa was delighted with the very young housekeeper — seventeen and fresh out of a convent orphanage — who took up residence in their tiny but comfortable attic bedroom. Small, dark-haired, and dark-eyed Maria was ecstatic at having employment and a room of her own. She was warm, resourceful, and amazingly competent.

Only in her darker moments did Vanessa dwell on the baby's illegtimacy. In time she and Eddie would be married; no one in America would ever know. She considered writing her mother about the baby, but discarded this thought. Her mother had not wanted a child. She would not want a grandchild. Vanessa was all the more saddened that Eddie's mother could not share their joy.

In early October Eddie went to Paris on business. Vanessa was ecstatic when he brought her a deliciously feminine tip-tilted hat by Maud et Dano—a replica of one worn at Dior's autumn collection

"The next time I go to Paris," he vowed, "you'll go with me."

Tina wrote that she was heading for the south of France to do a new film under the direction of Felix Koestler, the refugee director who was fast winning acclaim in the United States.

"When the picture's wrapped up, I'll come to Venice for a week or two. But this won't be a quickie. Felix is a perfectionist. Count on at least a four-month shooting schedule. I can't wait to see you again!"

Late in November Eddie's mother suffered a heart attack. She was clinging to life, but Eddie knew her time was short. Vanessa shared his grief. Eddie spent much of each evening at his mother's bedside, with his two sisters, who had come from Switzerland.

Vanessa yearned to be able to comfort Eddie. He felt guilty that he had been safe in America while his mother and father and older brother had given so much of themselves in the fight against Fascism.

On a raw, damp evening in early December Eddie arrived at the house earlier than usual. Hearing his key in the door, Maria picked up her sewing—all of which was planned for the coming baby—and hurried up the stairs to her own room.

"Maria just made a pot of fresh coffee." Vanessa lifted her face for his kiss. "You must be chilled to the bone."

"I want you to come with me to the hospital," he said gently and smiled at her astonishment. "I want Mama to see you. I want her to know she'll have a grandchild from her surviving son. That the family name will continue."

"You told her?" Color touched her high cheekbones. In the midst of her grief she felt a moment of happiness.

"It's the last gift I'll be able to give her, Vanessa. The doctors say she won't hold on for more than another forty-eight hours."

"Oh, Eddie—" A coldness invaded Vanessa.

"Tell Maria I'll drive you back by midnight." Since his sisters had arrived, Eddie had stayed at the family palazzo.

They drove through the night with her head on Eddie's shoulder. His sisters had gone home from the hospital, Eddie told her. They would be alone with his mother.

They left the car at the Piazzale Roma and went by *motoscafo* to the small private hospital where his mother was receiving care. At the nurse's station they spoke briefly with the nurse on duty, then Eddie led Vanessa to his mother's room. Here another nurse greeted them and at Eddie's request left them alone with her patient.

"Mama," Eddie said gently. "Mama?"

His prematurely white-haired mother—with a beautiful bone structure and an air of elegance even as death hovered over her—slowly opened her eyes. The corners of her mouth lifted in a smile. How like Eddie she was, Vanessa thought. She felt a sharp stab of regret that only now was she able to meet their child's grandmother.

"Eduardo, my darling." A blue-veined hand reached toward his.

"Mama, I've brought Vanessa to you," he murmured, and Vanessa moved forward.

His mother's eyes seemed to study her every feature as Vanessa stood beside the bed. It was as though she knew she would never see her again, Vanessa thought in anguish.

"He loves you very much," the older woman whisperd. Each word was an effort.

"I love him very much," Vanessa told her, sudden tears blurring her vision.

Eddie's mother withdrew her hand from his and tenderly laid her hand on Vanessa's belly, caressing the grandchild she would never see.

"*Mio nipote.*" Her smile was tremulous. "*Molto prezioso.*" My grandchild. Very precious.

Late the following evening Eddie phoned Vanessa with word that his mother had died. With his two sisters and brother-in-law he would sit *shivah* in the family palazzo for the next eight days. Vanessa assured him she would be all right.

"Maria is with me," she reminded him. "You're not to worry about me."

But the week was long and empty without Eddie. Vanessa sought comfort in filling a sketchbook with new designs that Maria, pausing in her household duties to inspect, declared suitable for the "the finest signoras." Each night she sat before the stove with Maria and talked nostalgically about New York. She knew how deeply Eddie grieved for his mother, and she was sad for him and for the child who would never know his grandparents.

When Eddie returned to their house, he was loving yet oddly withdrawn. Vanessa waited until at last he confided in her. He had hoped his sisters would welcome their baby. Instead they were outraged.

"They worry that the Castellos will learn about us, and that their brother may lose his pseudo-wife's inheritance," he said bitterly. "The war has done strange things to my sisters. But the baby will survive without their approval. My mother loved this grandchild even before its birth. She blessed the three of us."

Eddie told Vanessa how his sisters had been prepared to fight him for the Montino palazzo.

"My own sisters," he said in pain. "They said I was rich now. I had no right to share in what little remained of the family estate. I told them the palazzo — anything that remained — was theirs to sell as they wished. I signed the papers the lawyers drew up for them."

In every small way Vanessa tried to alleviate his grief. She was secure in his love, waiting for the arrival of their child in joyous anticipation. And with Isa's growing need to spend days in the privacy of her bedroom he was free to come to their house near Mestre more frequently.

And there was the comfort of Tina's letters, which arrived regularly from the south of France.

"Felix is terrific. He knows me better than I know myself. I'm sure the picture will be sensational. And baby, he's great in bed." Tina said nothing about marrying Felix. After Gordon, Vanessa guessed, she was wary of marriage.

Occasionally Vanessa heard from Pat. She wrote that she adored Cecile — now affectionately called CeeCee — and that Paul was on the road to a promising political career. They were building a gorgeous new house in River Oaks so they could entertain in the fashion her father considered essential for Paul's political future.

"You know I always hated meeting loads of strange people, but I'm getting over that now. We're living in an absolutely mad social whirl."

On a cold windy morning in early February — when the piazza was deserted, the restaurants devoid of patrons, and the Grand Canal choppy and dismal — Vanessa was startled by a sharp pain that hinted at the onset of labor. But the baby was not due for another five weeks.

She sat motionless in the comfortable chair before the warm fireplace and waited for a second contraction. She tried to remember all the doctor had told her and what Pat had written about her own delivery. It could be a false labor, she warned herself.

She remembered her mother complaining about her false labor. Her mother had loathed every moment of her pregnancy. Vanessa remembered. But for her — and for Eddie—it was the most beautiful time of their lives.

The pain caught at her. Instinct told her this was not false labor. She trembled with anticipation. Their baby was coming. The wait was almost over.

Was the baby all right? Again, fear infiltrated her excitement. Had something gone wrong? Please, God, let it be all right.

For almost an hour she sat before the fireplace without sharing her news. Maria sang in the kitchen as she prepared fresh bread for the oven. Eddie was a phone call away. But for this small parcel of time she focused on timing contractions, feeling an exquisite closeness to the baby inside her, intent on entering the world. Praying silently that all was well.

"Signora Vanessa?" Maria hung in the doorway, her face troubled. "Are you all right?"

"Yes." Vanessa's voice was exhilarated. "Maria, I'm in labor. But it's all right," she said reassuringly when she saw Maria's alarm. "It's too early to go to the hospital. I'll phone Eddie and tell him. I won't have to leave for hours—"

"Phone Signor Eddie this minute," Maria ordered. "Then I will pack for you."

Despite her insistence that there was no need to rush to the hospital yet, Eddie arrived within half an hour. He sought to ease her concern that the baby was arriving five weeks early, but Vanessa knew he shared her anxiety. He sat beside her and held her hand, flinching as each contraction silenced her. Early in the afternoon he took her to the hospital, and remained with her until the obstetrician insisted he leave.

"Go," the doctor ordered with wry humor. "The father doesn't need to be here to catch the child. That's the doctor's job."

"She'll be all right?" Eddie asked while Vanessa grappled with the final throes of labor.

"She'll be fine." The obstetrician waved him toward the door. "We don't need a claque here." He turned to issue instructions to the nurse.

Vanessa knew vaguely that Eddie was gone from the room. How could such a small baby cause such pain? *Five weeks early.* She worried about the baby even while she battled to give birth to the tiny form.

"Come, Vanessa," the doctor pleaded. "How much longer do you mean to keep your husband waiting?" Here in the small private hospital it was assumed that Eddie and she were husband and wife.

While the doctor and nurse hovered above her and murmured encouragement, Vanessa thrust her daughter into the world. She was to be named Janice Suzanne, in the Jewish tradition of using the initials of Vanessa's father and Eddie's mother. The baby weighed in at exactly six pounds, and had a mass of dark hair like her father's, with her mother's fine-boned features. Eddie declared her the most beautiful baby ever born.

Vanessa scolded Eddie and Maria tenderly, warning them that Suzy would grow up to be the most spoiled child in the world if all three of them hung on her every cry. Though the doctor assured them she was perfectly formed and well, Vanessa was eager to see Suzy gain weight. She obeyed the doctor's every instruction, and allowed Maria to coax her into eating even when she wasn't hungry, because it was important to keep up her supply of milk for her hungry little daughter.

Eddie rushed into the house each day and headed straight for the nursery. His delight in Suzy—his pleasure in watching her nurse—brought tears to Vanessa's eyes. No matter what the world might say about their union, Vanessa was happy that she had come to Italy with Eddie. She was happy that they were now a family.

On an early March morning while Suzy slept in the nursery and Maria was off to the butcher shop, Vanessa sat before the fireplace in the living room and dozed. Suzy's nursing schedule allowed no stretches of long, uninterrupted sleep. Slowly Vanessa became aware of an insistent ringing at the door.

It couldn't be Eddie, she thought as she struggled into wakefulness. He knew the door was unlocked during daylight hours. He would come right into the house.

"Un minuto." Vanessa called and hurried from the living room into the foyer. She pulled the door wide and cried out with delight. "Tina! Oh, Tina, how wonderful!"

"Show me my godchild," Tina ordered laughingly as they exchanged a joyous embrace. "I've been dying to see her."

"Tina, she's wonderful," Vanessa said softly, pulling Tina by the hand along the hall that led to the nursery.

"You didn't say much in your letter." All at once Tina was serious. "Did you have a rough time?"

"No more than others," Vanessa smiled. "Afterward you forget."

Tina lifted Suzy into her arms as though she were a fragile piece of porcelain.

"Am I holding her all right?" she asked, her eyes wide.

"Perfectly," Vanessa approved.

Within a few minutes Suzy announced she was hungry. Tina sat beside Vanessa while she nursed the baby. She was oddly silent.

"Didn't the picture go well?" Vanessa asked after a few minutes. "You seem upset."

"The picture is great. Felix is great." Tina took a deep labored breath. "And I'm about ten weeks pregnant."

"Oh, Tina—" Vanessa gazed at her in consternation. "Felix?"

"Who else?" Tina shrugged with a show of nonchalance, but Vanessa sensed her panic.

"Are you going to marry him?"

"No." Tina kicked off her shoes and rose to her feet. "He doesn't even know I'm pregnant." She crossed to look out into the garden. Her shoulders hunched with tension.

"Then tell him," Vanessa ordered softly.

"No point in that," Tina rejected. "Felix got out of Vienna just before the Nazis. His wife and daughter were not that lucky. The little girl died in a concentration camp. His wife sits in a dark room and stares into space. He has around-the-clock nurses to take care of her. He'll never get a divorce." She managed a wry grin. "Anyhow, he wouldn't want to marry me if he could. All he cares about is making great films. And screwing." She swerved away from the window. "Do you understand what this means, Vanessa? I'm finished in Hollywood. Nobody'll let me do a picture after this?"

"You mean because of the morals clause in your contract?" Vanessa was trying to understand.

"Because of the goddamn censorship," Tina shot back. "That and the morals clause." Her voice was shrill.

"You could arrange a marriage," Vanessa plotted. "For a price. Then divorce him afterward. What the Europeans call a 'marriage of convenience.' "

"Vanessa, I'm supposed to be a glamorous young movie star. A baby would destroy the image! Even if I were married, a baby would wreck my career. Everything I've busted my ass to build up! Because neither of us had the sense to make sure I didn't get pregnant," she added bitterly.

"What you're saying then," Vanessa tried to be rational, "is that you don't want to have the baby." It seemed obscene to be talking about abortion with Suzy nestled warm and small in her arms.

Tina dropped into a chair again.

"I can't do that, either," she confessed. "I don't know. Maybe it's all that Catholic upbringing. My mind tells me it's the only way out of this mess. But I can't do it." She flinched at the prospect. "I'm scared to death of an abortion. Oh, I know how many actresses go to some private clinic for abortions. Connie's had two already. But I'm chicken. Women die from abortions."

"Then have the baby—over here in Europe, where nobody'll ever know," Vanessa told her, searching for an escape route for Tina. "And then put it up for adoption." Suddenly she had an idea. "What about your brother Sal? You told me his wife couldn't have a baby, but Sal won't agree to adopting because they won't know what they'll be getting. Your baby will be his niece or nephew." She paused because Tina was staring at her as though she had just performed a miracle.

"That's it! Vanessa, I'll have the baby, and Sal and Eva will adopt it. I'll write the studio that I'm exhausted from this last film. That much is true." She laughed. "Felix is such a damn perfectionist he wore out the whole company. Nat can scream all he wants, but I'll insist I won't leave Europe until I'm completely rested up." Her face tightened in determination. "About seven months. By then the baby will be born. If Nat insists I return to Hollywood right away, then I'll go on suspension." She exhaled in relief. "Suspension I can handle."

"You'll stay here with me." Vanessa was firm. Eddie would understand.

"Nat will carry on about my being on suspension," Tina prophesied, "but he'll make it part of my 'tempestuous young star' image," she mocked. "Nat and I will have a grand reunion, and I'll go into a new major film."

"Write Sal and Eva right away," Vanessa urged. "They may be shocked and make nasty remarks, but they'll be grateful to have a baby that's a Vigliano."

"They won't say anything to Pop." Tina's smile was

bitter. "They won't want to burden him with another 'disgrace.' But they'll give this baby the best damn home a kid can have. It'll cost me seven months of my life, but it'll save my career."

"It'll be wonderful to have you here." Suzy was asleep at the nipple. Vanessa rose from the chair and took her to the crib.

"Eddie won't mind?"

"Eddie will be happy that I have you with me," Vanessa said tenderly.

"What about you?" Tina asked. "Are you happy living this way?"

"I have no other choice," Vanessa reminded her. "Eddie and I both know it's temporary."

"Of the three of us only Pat managed a normal marriage. I don't count Tracy as one of us anymore," she said with contempt. "Tracy's forgotten you and I even exist. But Pat, you, and I will forever be friends." She made it a benediction.

"Yes." Vanessa smiled in agreement. Suzy's two aunts.

"One normal marriage among the three of us isn't bad," Tina offered flippantly. "And in time—when Eddie and you get married—it'll be two out of three. Me, I'm married to my career," she said with soaring determination. "That I can handle."

Twenty-one

Pat stood before the closet wall of her Early American bedroom in their new River Oaks house and debated about what to wear to the afternoon's bridal shower. Daddy was forever impressing upon her the fact that Paul would run for the legislature in the fall and that his wife must fit the image of the handsome young legislator's wife.

In the early years Mother had played the role to perfection. Only when Daddy was well established in Washington did she begin to withdraw from the political scene. Was it because of the gossip about all his Washington "girl friends" that Mother drew away? Or did Daddy acquire that stream of younger women because Mother insisted on separate bedrooms?

How many people in Washington believe that Mother is in "delicate health"? Pat wondered. She's forever dashing about for fittings and charity committees. She gives some of the best dinner parties in Texas. If Daddy makes it into the White House—and everybody in Texas is sure he has a chance if he runs in the right year—will Mother go to Washington with him? Will Paul be in Congress in a dozen years, the way everybody says?

A glance at the clock broke Pat's reverie. She had just enough time to dress and drive to Marge's house for the shower. She chose a pencil-slim black wool from Christian Dior's spring collection. Mother adored Dior. Without Vanessa she tended to follow her mother's advice on fashion. She hoped to be able to fly to Venice to spend a day, at least, with Vanessa when they went to Paris in February for the spring collections.

She wouldn't be too warm in the black sheer wool, would she? This was the month when people in Houston said you ought to travel with both a fan and a winter coat—you never knew what to expect. Right now there was a sharp north wind sweeping down from the Rockies. But they'd swelter soon enough.

Pat dressed swiftly, touched her mouth with her new Elizabeth Arden lipstick, and reached for her black suede Koret purse and the gift-wrapped package from Sakowitz's. She started at a knock on the door.

"Come in."

The door opened. Babe—their big, warm, black nursemaid—walked in with CeeCee in her arms.

"I thought you might be wantin' to see the baby before I put her down for her afternoon nap, Miss Pat," white-uniformed Babe said in her soft Texas drawl. "She's mighty perky today."

"Thank you, Babe." A touch of color stained her cheekbones as she reached for her small, exquisite daughter. Had Babe heard that awful battle she and Paul had had last night? It was only because he'd been drinking, she thought quickly. He'd been to one of those political meetings where everybody drank too much.

"She's still fightin' me every time I put her down for a nap," Babe said indulgently. "That little girl sure got a mind of her own."

"Takes after her father," Pat laughed. "I have to run now, or I'll be late for the shower." She kissed CeeCee and handed her back to Babe. "You be good, CeeCee. You hear?" CeeCee had her father's charm, too, she thought. Daddy said Paul could charm the pants off even a Republican — if the pants were worn by a woman.

She left the house and slid behind the wheel of the white Cadillac. She enjoyed driving herself instead of being chauffeured everywhere. It was the one time she felt totally in charge of her life. She'd felt that way back in New York, she remembered. But New York was a lifetime away.

By the time she arrived at Marge's house the circular driveway was dotted with expensive cars. The prospective bride had already arrived — Pat could see Dottie's bright red Ferrari front and center. When the maid arrived to open the door, light feminine laughter and the sound of low-keyed piano music wafted down the hall. That would be Lisa Bradford, Pat thought wryly. Lisa was ever anxious to remind her circle of acquaintances that she had abandoned a music career to marry Jock.

"Darling, you look just gorgeous." Marge ran lightly into the black-and-white checkerboard foyer to greet her. "I'm not sure I ought to have invited you here to show us all up."

Pat was immediately swept into chatter about children, clothes, houses, and social and cultural events. Unwarily she remembered a remark of Jesse's about how Houston could always raise money for the Symphony but had trouble attracting funds for public hospitals. She couldn't remember when there had not been a Houston Symphony.

"Pat darling," Lisa called from the piano, "however do you manage to stay so slim when you have that sensational woman in your kitchen? You sure you haven't been running off to Maine Chance behind our backs?"

"Sugar, if you keep on giving those marvelous dinner parties," Marge reproached Pat, "we'll all go dashing off to Maine Chance to drop pounds." Marge lifted her eyebrows inquiringly as a maid appeared at the entrance to the living room.

"Phone call for Miss Dottie," the maid said.

"Call for the prettiest bride-elect in Texas," Marge drawled with her delicious southern sweetness. "Dottie, you can take it in the library across the hall."

"That's probably Mother," Dottie sighed but she darted across the room with commendable swiftness. "This wedding is becoming a bigger project than the opening of the Shamrock Hotel next spring."

"That hotel will just make this city," another guest said enthusiastically. "I hear it's costing Mr. McCarthy more than twenty-one million dollars."

"A little less than Dottie's mother is spending on the wedding," Marge giggled. "That woman is such a show-off. And wouldn't you think she'd have enough sense to tell Dottie she looks like a horse's ass in those New Look dresses they bought for her trousseau in Paris?"

Pat smiled and chatted with the dozen other socialites, but part of her mind wouldn't let go of the fight with Paul last night. Her shoulder still ached from where she'd hit the floor when Paul had pushed her. It wouldn't have happened if he hadn't been drinking — and she shouldn't have made that nasty crack about Anita Davis throwing herself at him every time they met. Women were just naturally attracted to Paul.

"Pat, you make sure that gorgeous man of yours is free for my fund raiser next month," Marge ordered. "I don't care how busy he is campaigning for the legislature, you tell him I expect him there."

"He wouldn't miss it for the world, Marge," Pat said

lightly. He couldn't afford to antagonize the wife of one of the heaviest contributors to his campaign fund.

"Does Paul expect there'll be trouble in the Democratic party with all this silly talk about a civil rights platform?" someone asked from across the room.

"Oh, honey, I don't know a thing about politics," Pat laughed. "You'll have to talk to Paul about that."

Every young matron here, Pat thought with bitter humor, was aware that her own man was rich and reaching for power. And the unmarried guests at the shower were searching for the same kind of man. They lived — all of them — in a rarefied world that sometimes seemed to suffocate her. The real world was those years in New York. Sometimes she wished they'd never ended.

Vanessa worried that Tina would soon be bored and restless in Venice. To forestall this Eddie bought a small second car in Vanessa's name. Vanessa — who had just learned to drive — relished the chance to improve her skills, and Tina was excited about their new mobility.

"I've worked my ass off in Hollywood," Tina said defiantly. "I deserve time out."

The studio had Vanessa's address as a point of contact, though Tina had intimated to Nat Kelman that she would stop in only to pick up messages. Vanessa was instructed to fabricate stories about her whereabouts each time Nat called from Hollywood. By early June — with Tina raging against her bulging figure — the studio wrote that Tina was on suspension.

"That's great," Tina approved. "The brat's due in September. I'll write Nat then that I've got my act together, and I'm ready to go back to work." As Tina had suspected, her brother Sal and his wife were euphoric at the prospect of adopting her baby. Presumably they were to adopt the child of a young unmarried Italian girl in New York.

Though Vanessa was grateful for Tina's companionship, Tina's presence was a constant reminder that she had accomplished little in the years since they had left Pinewood. She designed dresses for Tina to wear in her pregnancy. Dresses that were simple enough for Maria to cut and sew, though she was nervous at dealing with the exquisite fabrics Vanessa chose. For this special client Vanessa could be as extravagant as she liked.

In June, when Eddie took up residence at the villa on the Lido, Tina arranged a summer rental in a secluded villa a comfortable distance from the Castello villa. She was nervous about being recognized at the neo-Byzantine Hotel Excelsior or the Hotel des Bains, luxurious places where Hollywood stars might surface prior to the International Film Festival at the Lido in late August. Tina and Vanessa, along with Suzy and Maria, were installed in a lovely white villa facing the lagoon. Tina grew restless with the waiting, the awkwardness, and her swollen body. In the early months she had played the role of the beautiful young mother-to-be, adoring tiny Suzy, talking endlessly about the years in Hollywood, anticipating her return to the studio. Now she stalked about the house through much of each night, plagued by insomnia.

Ten days after Vanessa's small entourage returned to the house near Mestre early in September, Tina went into labor. Barefoot and wearing one of the loose caftan-style dresses Vanessa had designed for her, she walked from her bedroom into the nursery where Vanessa sat rocking Suzy.

"I just woke up in a small lake," she announced and suddenly hunched over in pain. "Oh, God, I'm having a contraction!"

"Maria!" Vanessa called out with unfamiliar sharpness. "Come get Suzy."

Vanessa was nervous. Tina insisted on having the baby at the house. She was paranoid about being recognized at the hospital.

"Aren't you going to call the doctor?" Tina demanded when the contraction had passed.

"Not yet," Vanessa said. "He'll have plenty of time to get here. Let's get you settled in bed." The doctor had assured Tina there was no reason she should not have an uncomplicated delivery. Still, Vanessa worried.

Sympathetic and anxious, Maria took Suzy in her arms and settled in the rocker. Vanessa went with Tina into her bedroom.

"I want to wear one of those gorgeous black things I bought in Paris," Tina pronounced. "In a few hours I'll be flat again!"

"We should start timing your contractions." Vanessa struggled to keep her voice even, cheerful. It seemed unreal to her that Tina would soon deliver a child into the world, and then turn that child over to others forever. Thank God Tina could be so realistic about it.

"Oh, shit!" Tina clutched at her swollen belly. "Another one."

"I'm calling the doctor," Vanessa said. "This baby is in a hurry."

With Tina swearing like a sailor—and Vanessa grateful that neither the doctor nor his nurse understood one word of English—they delivered an eight-pound boy. Tina lay back against the pillows, pale and exhausted.

"Honey, that's the last kid I ever have," she told Vanessa when they were finally alone in her bedroom. Tina's son, Federico Adam Vigliano, rested in Maria's tender care. "If that's the result of fucking, I'll be a nun from this day forward." She grinned at Vanessa's burst of laughter. "At least I'll be damned careful."

Her first morning aboard the *Queen Mary* Tina awoke to the sound of Adam crying in the adjoining suite. She brushed aside her guilt that at three weeks he was really too young to cope with an Atlantic crossing. He was her kid—he'd be tough. She lifted a hand to her breasts. His first meal had come from a bottle, despite the doctor's disapproval.

Nobody on board knew that the woman and baby in the adjoining suite were traveling with her. The three of them had flown from Venice to Paris, where she had filled a steamer trunk with dresses by Jacques Fath on Vanessa's recommendation. After three days in Paris they had dallied another three at Claridge's in London before heading for Southampton and the *Queen Mary*.

Only now, when they were en route to New York, did Tina realize how anxious she was to return to work. She'd been exercising since four days after Adam's birth. She'd snapped back fast. The costume department would never guess she'd had a baby. She'd blame the few extra pounds she still carried on rich European food.

Sal and Eva would come to the Hotel Pierre in New York and take Adam home with them. The nursemaid would head back for Venice. And she'd take the first flight out to Los Angeles. The studio would be ecstatic that she was back on the payroll. She'd warned Marty, the agent she'd acquired under Gordie's guidance, that she would be fussy about roles. He was sharp—he'd know not to show her shitty scripts.

How did Vanessa bear living the way she did? How could she bury her talent like that? Eddie was sweet, and Vanessa adored him. But she must be smoldering inside at all the delay, the waiting in Venice. Even women with children had careers these days. If she didn't escape from the hausfrau routine soon, Vanessa would explode from frustration.

On their second night at sea Tina abandoned her vow to travel in seclusion. In a sensuous Jacques Fath black velvet dinner dress, she made a dramatic entrance in the dining room. Three hours later she was sipping champagne in the lavish suite assigned to Hal Hogan, the eccentric and dynamic young billionaire.

Tina knew Hal as Connie Marlow's lover. Connie had been so eager to marry him she'd gone and ordered tons of linens embroidered "CH," Tina remembered; but Hal had preferred to free-lance. It amused her to follow in Connie's footsteps, though she harbored no yearnings to marry Hal Hogan. Or anybody.

"Everybody in Hollywood has been making wild guesses about why you're staying away," Hal murmured seductively, one hand reaching out to fondle her breasts. "You were having a mad, secret fling with Aly Khan. You were hidden away in a palace in Tangier with Howard Hughes—"

"I was bushed," she shrugged. "Felix Koestler does that to actresses."

"That's all he does?" Hal mocked, moving in closer.

"Everything he does, he does well," Tina said coolly. Her eyes told him she'd slept with Felix. God, she hadn't been with Felix — with anybody — for over seven months. She felt like a virgin again.

"Let's stop wasting time." He reached to take the half-filled glass of champagne from her hand and deposited it on the table. "There's a bed waiting for us in the next room."

"Are you good?" she challenged.

"The best," he boasted.

"Prove it." She lifted a hand to the zipper at the back of her dress.

"What about you?" His smile was quizzical.

"Honey, I'm so hot right now you'll be lucky if you can sit up tonight. Your thing may be in a sling."

Tina laughed when Hal refused to allow her to undress in the sitting room of the suite. He took her by the hand and led her into the bedroom.

"Now," he said, and hand already at his belt. "Do it slowly and gracefully. There, in front of the mirror."

Hal Hogan traveled with a six-foot-tall mirror in a rococo frame. Tina had forgotten Connie's amusement at this little eccentricity. He also traveled with an exercise machine and a Swedish masseur. He was a physical fitness nut. Tina remembered one of Connie's snide remarks, after their breakup: *That son-of-a-bitch probably lists fucking under 'penis muscle builder.'*"

She undressed carelessly, letting the Jacques Fath dress crumple at her feet, to be joined by the sheer black panties and bra, while Hal—already stripped to the skin—watched from the foot of the bed. He looked like an overheated sixteen-year-old in a luxurious French cathouse, Tina thought with a grin. But Hal was thirty-six and probably the richest man in America.

It was exciting to go to bed with power and money, with a man who controlled half a dozen international industries, a man who'd been the country's most eligible bachelor for a dozen years. He'd inherited a sizable chunk of money, but he had parlayed his inheritance into a fortune far beyond anything his grandfather had ever thought possible. That kind of power she respected, and found sexy.

"Not yet," he said brusquely when she reached for a garter. He rose, naked, to his feet. "Keep on the garter belt and stockings. Now walk over to me."

In her four-inch high heels—in them she was almost as tall as Hal—wearing her black garter belt and gossamer black nylons, she moved with sinuous grace to stand before him. Shoulders back, huge-nippled breasts thrust forward.

"You've got terrific control," she acknowledged. He was hard and ready, his face flushed, but he just stood still and inspected her inch by inch. For an instant she worried that some indication of her pregnancy would betray her.

"You'll have to take off ten pounds before you go in front of a camera again," he warned, and she remembered suddenly that he was said to be a major investor at two studios.

"Five," she guessed, and reached her hand between his thighs.

"You can't wait, can you?" he jeered.

"You want to play look and see, or do you want to fuck?" she said coldly.

"I want to fuck."

Hal grasped her by the wrist and pulled her down on the bed. She thought of the last time with Felix. She'd known she was pregnant; but, of course, he hadn't. Felix could be so rough and so tender at the same time. Damn, why did she have to think about him now?

"Everything you've ever done or ever thought about doing, he promised hovering above her, "we'll do tonight."

"First, let me get the hell out of these stockings and garter belt," she began.

"Let me do it," he said, his voice thickening in anticipation.

He reached to unstrap a garter, teased the stocking down her long thigh and leg, then repeated the process while Tina freed herself from the black lace garter belt. She lifted an eyebrow in inquiry as he straightened up and stretched himself beside her.

"You planning to take a nap?"

"Later," he grinned. "Right now just do what Daddy says."

She closed her eyes and sank back into the pillows, listening intently as Hal promised her in erotic detail a night she would not forget. The masculine scent of him was a powerful aphrodisiac as the faint stubble of his beard scratched her inner thigh, just before his mouth found its quarry.

"You had enough?" he taunted while she lay—at last—in the curve of his arm, his leg thrown across her own.

"For now," she yielded. This wasn't making love. This was a marathon challenge.

"Anybody ever go at you with leather?" he asked casually and she stiffened.

"No," she said tersely. "And nobody ever will."

"For a half-assed actress, you're not bad," he admitted.

"One, I'm not a half-assed actress," she shot back. "And two, I'm great."

"All right," he chuckled, "you're great. And just for that, you know what I'm going to do?"

"What are you going to do?" She stared back, wary and appraising.

"I'm going to buy Imperial Films. I'm going to make you the number-one box-office star of the whole damn film business."

"Can you do that?" she asked after a moment. Excitement and adrenalin rushed through her sated body.

"Can I buy Imperial Films?" he drawled. "Any time I want. And I can buy anybody it takes to make you number one. But don't expect me to marry you."

"I don't want to marry you," she replied, enjoying his start of astonishment. "I'll be your girl friend—or whatever—because you're terrific in bed. But I don't want any man running my life."

He stared at her, his expression unreadable. Then, "How would you like a massage?" he demanded abruptly and reached for the bedside phone without waiting for a reply. "I'll call Sven to come in and give us the good old Swedish massage deal. And after that," he smiled, "we'll settle down and talk about how we'll put the screws to Nat Kelman. If I'm going to buy Imperial Films, he's taking orders from me."

Just like this it could happen, Tina thought in dizzying exhilaration. Like Hal said, if he wanted it, she could be number one at the box office within a year.

She'd make sure he wanted it.

Twenty-two

Vanessa had known she would miss Tina. But she had not realized the extent of the void Tina's absence would create in her life. With Tina at her side she had been able to cope with those evenings when Isa—in agonizingly deteriorating health—needed Eddie at her side.

Vanessa adored her baby, loved Eddie, and was grateful for Maria's warm presence in the house. But more than ever she felt imprisoned in her exile. Tina and Pat were reminders of the ambitions she still harbored. Tina was reveling in the red-carpet treatment at Imperial, while Hal Hogan was secretly negotiating for a controlling interest in the studio. She was already at work on a new film.

"Marty made Nat tear up the old contract. I'm making $1,500 a week now! I'm starting a bank account for Adam, though nobody knows about it except my lawyer, who thinks Adam is my nephew. I can't wait till Hal takes over the studio. He says he'll make me bigger than Crawford, Garbo, and Davis together. And he's got the money and power to do it. Not bad for the dago kid from Pinewood."

Pat wrote that Paul was now a member of the state legislature, so she and CeeCee would be spending time each year in the state capital at Austin.

"Daddy says we shouldn't bother building a house in Aus-

tin. He figures in another six years Paul will be a congressman. It might be exciting to live in Washington as a congressional wife."

Ever sensitive to Vanessa's moods, Eddie decided she would be happier back in the center of things, in Venice. He found an apartment with a view of the Grand Canal and moved them into it. And he decided she must have a small shop of her own.

"Like those boutiques that sprang up on the rue de Faubourg St.-Honoré and the rue de Sèvres in Paris during the war," he said enthusiastically. "But you'll show more than just ready-to-wear copied from high fashion. You'll offer your own designs to be made on order by a seamstress working for the shop. The way Signora Torino presented your originals."

"Eddie, do we dare?" Her face was alight with anticipation. "It'll be so expensive."

"We can manage it," he insisted. She knew that his salary was rising at a startling rate. "Just a small shop," he pointed out. "Selling for the most part your own designs."

"But Suzy?" She hesitated, though she was already imagining a shop window that would attract the kind of women she yearned to dress. "I'd be away from the apartment all day." She wavered in maternal guilt.

"Maria will take care of Suzy," Eddie said, brushing aside her doubts. "You trust Maria as you trust yourself."

"Yes." Her smile was brilliant. "Oh, Eddie, I have so many ideas for the shop."

Vanessa searched until she found quarters that seemed right for her. Eddie supervised the alterations with the care he might have accorded a Broadway stage set. By mid-February, he promised, she would be able to open her shop.

Vanessa searched for a seamstress with the skills

necessary to handle the fine fabrics she meant to use in her designs. Eddie, with an eye for color and material that she respected, helped her select her fabrics. It was a euphoric period in her life.

Early in January, on the very day that Suzy took her first steps, Eddie came to the apartment to tell Vanessa that he would be traveling to Paris in February.

"Then Isa is better?" Vanessa asked. She recoiled from the realization that her own happiness revolved around Isa's death.

"No," Eddie said gently. "Roberto and his wife are coming to spend three weeks with her." His smile was wry. "They disapprove of Isa's marriage. Unlike his parents, Roberto and his wife are greedy to keep the family fortune intact. They resent my presence at the palazzo. This is a graceful way to handle the situation. I'm going to Paris for ten days," he said with a dazzling smile. "And Suzy and you will come with me," he announced, enjoying her astonishment. "And Maria, to take care of Suzy while I show you Paris. We'll celebrate Suzy's first birthday there."

Three days before Suzy's birthday, Eddie settled his small party in a pair of adjoining drawing rooms aboard the luxurious Simplon Orient Express. They were en route to Paris. While the train chugged out of the Santa Lucia Station, Eddie—in conspiratorial, triumphant silence—handed Vanessa a white invitation card that read, in French: *"Christian Dior requests the honor of Mr. and Mrs. Eduardo Montino's presence at the presentation of his spring collection at 10:30 a.m. Avenue Montaigne."*

Vanessa read this slowly, in awe and bewilderment. She raised her eyes to Eddie's.

"How did you get this?"

"Isa's mother arranged for it," he explained. "She

had hoped that Isa might be well enough for the trip. But Isa hardly leaves the palazzo anymore," he said compassionately. "Signor Castello told his wife to give the invitation to me in case I could arrange to be in Paris at that time. It would be well for me to talk about the Dior collection and how our lace could be adapted to the Dior designs."

"You're going?" Vanessa asked after a moment.

"We're going," he emphasized. "So that you may have a Dior original." He pulled her close. "You're my wife, Vanessa. In everything but name."

In Paris they stayed in a magnificent suite at the Ritz on the place Vêndome. Vanessa was enchanted by their rooms, rich with French *boiserie,* the walls upholstered in exquisite fabrics, and lush draperies at the tall French windows overlooking a serene rear garden.

"Coco Chanel lived at the Ritz for many years," Eddie told her, loving her reaction. "Straight through the war years, I've been told."

"Eddie, I can't believe I'm in Paris! At the Ritz!"

The following morning, beside guests draped in mink and sable and expensive English overcoats, Vanessa and Eddie presented themselves at the private town house that was now the House of Dior. Vanessa's eyes took in everything: the liveried doorman, the satin canopy, the vestibule hung with toile de Jouy, the lovely hostesses who sprayed them with Miss Dior perfume.

They sat in the flower-laden white-and-pearl-gray salon, with its dazzling crystal chandeliers, lush quintias palms, and soft gray carpeting. Both tried to appear sophisticated, to conceal their elation at being here for the spring collection as they eyed the illustrious company about them.

"Eddie, there's Carmel Snow!" Vanessa whispered,

gazing raptly at the exquisitely dressed editor of *Harper's Bazaar*. Her short, fluffy, blue-rinsed hair was topped by the Balenciago signature pillbox. "She's the most powerful American in French fashion."

"I'm glad we could come," Eddie whispered, looking about in avid delight. "This is like a magnificent stage set."

They were quickly swept up in the excitement of viewing the collection. Dior had titled it "Trompe l'oeil," and Vanessa remembered that he was the first couturier to name his collections.

She sat at the edge of her chair, caught up in memorizing every new line, every new detail introduced by Dior. She admired the flying panels or pleats on almost every skirt, which lent an air of slenderness to the figure until movement sent the material into fluttering gracefulness. She was intrigued by the bloused dresses and suits he had included in the collection, and in her mind she designed variations of her own.

She would open her shop two days after their return from Paris. It would be wonderful to say to prospective clients that she had just returned from Christian Dior's spring collection!

Their days in Paris — with Eddie's business appointments brief, successful intrusions — sped past in a haze of pleasure. They dined at Maxim's or at Left Bank cafés. They nibbled on *patisserie* at renowned Rumpelmayer's. Eddie showed Vanessa and Suzanne and Maria the sights of Paris he had known since childhood.

Vanessa and Eddie visited the dozens of new boutiques on the rue du Faubourg St.-Honoré and the rue de Sèvres. At the House of Dior Vanessa was fitted for a black wool suit that would be sent to her in Venice. It was the grand finale to a magical time in her life.

* * *

Vanessa was ecstatic when her shop began to attract a few of the elegant, wealthy ladies of Venice. She was continually astonished when they uttered no word of reproach at the extravagant prices Eddie had decreed she should ask. Her customers were difficult and demanding, but Vanessa relished the challenge. She tried to work with the limitations of Signora Rossi, the seamstress she had hired to sew for her on assignment. She realized the kind of talent she needed for cutting and fine tailoring was difficult to acquire. She was impatient that she herself did not possess these skills, and she sought to compensate by using exquisite materials, seeking a special rhythm in the details.

At her insistence Eddie handled all the business matters. Vanessa handed over the receipts at the end of each week, and he paid the bills through his personal checking account. He refused to allow her to worry that expenses were higher than income. Soon, he insisted, this would change.

"Your shop will be a huge success," he predicted with mock solemnity. "I see it in my crystal ball."

From Houston Pat wrote that she had bought some marvelous scarves with a Florentine art and architecture motif at Neiman-Marcus in Dallas.

"They're made in Florence by some young designer named Emilio Pucci. Vanessa, I hear that next year there'll be high fashion showings in Florence. If all goes well with the shop, perhaps you'll be showing your designs there."

When Eddie next went to Florence—where he would choose fabrics for Vanessa's shop as well as conduct business for the lace factory—he carried her portfolio with him. He looked into the plans for the international fashion showing the following year, plans that were meant to establish Florence as a fashion capital of the world. After much dickering—display-

ing her sketches and extolling her success in Venice —
he was able to arrange for Vanessa to show her designs.

"You'll probably be pushed off into a corner," he
warned. "But no matter. The American buyers will be
excited when they see your dresses. They'll buy," he
predicted. He hesitated. "Providing, of course, we're
still in Italy next year."

By mid-May the shop was showing a profit. In
addition to working on designs to offer to her small
clique of patrons, Vanessa was spending every available free moment on the designs to be shown in Florence. She was jubilant that Eddie had been able to
arrange for her to share in the project that was creating such excitement in the Italian fashion world. Eddie was convinced this was the breakthrough that
would establish her as a new young designer of merit.

Spring was the time of year in Venice that Vanessa
loved best. The city was sunlit and warm, and flowers
around the city burst into bloom. Vanessa felt reborn
after the raw, drab winter.

This morning, she remembered when she arrived at
the shop, she was to show designs to the Marchesa di
Ronzoli for a ball gown to wear at a masked ball at
the Palazzo Labia. The Marchesa, an elegant and
beautiful young socialite, could be most helpful to the
shop if she was happy with the gown. She had already
bought a sheer black wool for a dinner party, and had
been delighted by the compliments it received.

Reared to respect punctuality, Vanessa tried to sup-
press her irritation when the Marchesa had not appeared half an hour past the appointment time. In
Italy punctuality was hardly considered a virtue. She
focused instead on inspecting a dress the seamstress
was finishing up for another patron.

An hour later, she looked up to see the Marchesa

strolling into the shop in the company of an expensively dressed young woman who wore a supercilious smile.

"Vanessa, you must forgive me," the Marchesa apologized charmingly. "My friend arrived in town only this morning, and we lost track of the time."

Despite the arrogant attitude of the Marchesa's companion, Vanessa welcomed them both with ingratiating warmth. She brought out the sketches for the gown, and displayed the exquisite fabrics she meant to use.

"Really, Gina, the lines of that gown are most unflattering to you." Her friend winced in distaste. "Also, I saw the identical dress in the French *Vogue.*"

"Not this," Vanessa refuted, her color high. "It is my own design."

"Signora Castello is very knowledgeable about fashion," the Marchesa reproached. Vanessa froze. Castello was not a common name in Venice. This must be Roberto's wife. Isa's sister-in-law. "I'm afraid it would not be right for me."

"Gina, we will go to Milan to shop," Signora Castello shrugged. Her eyes inspected Vanessa with overt hostility for a moment. "Germana Marucelli is showing fantastic clothes."

Vanessa stood motionless as the two women left the shop. The Castello family knew who she was and why she was in Venice. It was no longer a secret. She was shaken by the realization.

When she arrived home from the shop, Eddie was in the apartment playing with Suzy.

"I can't stay more than half an hour," he apologized, his face serious. "Isa had a very bad night. Her mother sent for Roberto."

And while Roberto stayed at his sister's bedside, his wife socialized with the Marchesa di Ronzoli, Vanessa thought mutinously. But for now, she would not bother Eddie with what happened in the shop.

"It's time for Suzy's supper," Vanessa said when Maria appeared at the living room door.

"Go with Maria," Eddie told his daughter. "Be a good girl." He kissed her tenderly and chuckled as she ran with fifteen-month awkwardness toward Maria.

"You won't be home tonight," Vanessa surmised.

"No." He reached to pull her into his arms. "Not tonight, my love."

For three days Vanessa spoke with Eddie only on the phone. On the third evening he appeared at the house.

"Isa is out of immediate danger," he told her. "It would break your heart to see how she fights for life. But the doctors warn she'll never leave her bed again. We won't go to the villa at the Lido this summer."

"We'll be happy that you did as your parents asked," Vanessa said softly. Eddie and she had their lives ahead of them. They could give this little time to Isa.

"I'll drive out later in the week to see a little house I've heard is available for July and August. It's close enough to the city for me to be out often. I don't suppose you could go out with me?" His smile was a blend of wistfulness and understanding. He knew her dedication to the shop.

"Unless we could drive out on a Sunday," she mused, tempted by the thought of time spent with Eddie away from the city.

"I can only see it on a weekday," he explained. "On Sunday Isa's parents and her brother and sister-in-law will be at church services. I have to be with Isa then." He hesitated. "We've arranged for at least one member of the family to always be close at hand."

"It's bad," Vanessa interpreted.

"Very bad," he conceded. "Though she's out of im-

283

mediate danger, this could change in a matter of hours."

How awful, Vanessa tormented herself, that her happiness and Eddie's depended on Isa's death. But it was not in their hands. As Isa's mother said, it was God's will.

Tina frowned at the insistent sound of the doorbell. Belatedly she remembered that Joyce, her house-keeper, had left yesterday to attend a family funeral. She forced one eye open and peered at the ormolu clock on the night table. It was almost noon.

The persistent shriek of the doorbell forced Tina to toss aside the white satin sheet — one of a dozen given to her by Hal Hogan, who insisted she always sleep between satin sheets. With naked, feline grace she slid her feet into white satin mules and reached for the white velvet robe — dramatic against her Acapulco tan — that lay across the chaise longue.

"I'm coming!" she yelled, stalking from the master bedroom down the carpeted hall to the door.

Tying the sash of the robe about her waist, she thought of the trip back from Acapulco early this morning with Keith in a chartered plane. He'd waited until the last minute to return to Hollywood, to pack up and catch a morning flight to New York. He swore he'd never do another screenplay — even of one of his own best sellers — as long as he lived. Pity he had to rush back to huddle with his publishers. Acapulco with Keith Edwards had been mad and wonderful.

She wasn't sure she wanted to marry him. It was flattering as hell to be chased by a rich, best-selling novelist who was good-looking enough to be a Hollywood leading man. And he was sensational in bed. At first she'd thought Hal was sensational — until she realized that all he gave a shit about was satisfying himself. Keith wanted it to be great for her, too. Their second night in bed he'd asked her to marry him. And he hadn't stopped asking.

Tina scowled at the unceasing intrusion of the doorbell and pulled the door wide.

"What the hell's your fucking rush?" she demanded of Hal's bodyguard-chauffeur.

"Mr. Hogan sent me to bring you to the house," Buck said brusquely. His tone, always reflecting Hal's mood, told her his boss was pissed off.

"What for?" she demanded. "I thought he was tied up on business in New York." He'd left Hollywood almost two weeks ago. The day they'd finished with the retakes. And that night Keith had taken her to Ciro's. They'd closed up Ciro's and ended up at his place.

"We returned an hour ago," Buck informed her. "He said I was to bring you right back."

"You woke me up," she said coldly. She was fed up with Hal acting as if he was the Aga Khan. He whistled and she was supposed to jump. Well, not this girl.

"He said to bring you back," Buck repeated. "Go put some clothes on. I'll wait in the car."

Tina deliberated for an instant, shrugged, and slammed the door in Buck's face. She changed swiftly into jeans and a T-shirt. Hal hated seeing her wear jeans and T-shirts. He liked his women to look like Jean Harlow in her prime. She left the house and climbed defiantly into the back seat of the maroon Rolls that was Hal Hogan's trademark.

At the Elizabethan manor house built for Hal Hogan at a cost of $3 million—an exact replica, except for heating systems and plumbing, of a four-hundred-year-old house he'd owned earlier in northern England—Tina went directly upstairs to his baronial bedroom furnished with massive, magnificently carved eighteenth-century pieces. She opened the door without bothering to knock.

Hal looked up from the Italian writing table that flanked a window and swore under his breath.

"You look like a two-bit whore in those damn jeans," he complained.

"I'm comfortable." Her smile was nonchalant. Hal Hogan was one of the richest men in America. He owned the studio now. He owned this house. But he didn't own her.

"I don't like what I've been reading in the columns." He pushed back his chair and rose to his feet. "What's this crap about you and Keith Edwards?"

"He wrote the screenplay for my new picture." Her eyes met his with an air of amused tolerance. "We went out to dinner a few times. It's great in the columns."

"I don't want you in the columns with the likes of Keith Edwards." He moved forward menacingly. "He's a goddamn womanizer."

"Are you speaking as my producer or as my lover?" she drawled.

"Both." He reached out a hand and pulled her to him. "Have you been sleeping with that bastard?"

"You left me alone for almost two weeks," she taunted. "Who were you screwing in New York?"

"You went out with him to Ciro's the day I flew to New York," Hal said in a monotone, his eyes narrow slits. "Afterward you went to his house. You stayed there all night. Four days ago you flew with him to Acapulco."

"You had one of your goons watching me!" Tina pulled herself away from his grasp.

"You're a rotten little slut!" Hal yelled. "I don't like my women messing around!"

"I'm not one of your women," she slashed back. "I'm Tina Gregory!"

"Without me you'll be nothing!" He hit her so hard across the face that she fell to the floor.

Tina staggered to her feet and reached for a metal-based table lamp. "Touch me again and you'll get this over your head!"

"Get out!" Hal eyed her with startled wariness. "You're through in pictures!"

"I have a contract," she taunted. "But you can buy it back. At a price. Talk to Marty about it. I've had enough of this screwy business!"

Tina strode from the room, down the hall, and to the stairs. At the foot of the stairs she paused to consider how she could get back to the house on Mulholland Drive.

"Buck!" she called imperiously. "Drive me home," she ordered when he peered cautiously from a room off the foyer. "I never want to see that son-of-a-bitch again."

Keith was dying to marry her. They'd spend six months at his house on the French Riviera and the rest of the time between his New York town house and his place at Sag Harbor. Life would be one sensational party.

I don't need Hollywood!

Twenty-three

The early morning air was unseasonably chilly for mid-May, though the fire Maria had started in the kitchen stove before going for groceries lent a cozy warmth to the room. Clumps of dark clouds outside warned of imminent rain. Still in her nightgown and robe, Vanessa spooned cereal into Suzy's mouth. She made a ritual of feeding her small daughter each morning before going to the shop.

She started at the sound of a key in the door. Then her face lighted.

"Eddie?"

"No," he called back teasingly, "it's the ice-man."

Eddie sat in a chair at the table and encouraged Suzy to eat rather that abandon her meal to play with him.

"I have to drive to Padua on business," he explained. "If I make a small detour I can stop off and see the country house. I called last night to make an appointment."

"Eddie, it's such a dismal day for driving." She stared out the window at the menacing clouds.

"Spring rains never last." He brushed aside her worries. "I want to make arrangements for the rental, before somebody else grabs it. I shouldn't have waited even this long."

"You've had enough on your mind without worrying about a summer place for us," Vanessa commiserated.

"I'll stop by on my way back from Padua," he promised.

"Can you stay for dinner?" She had seen very little of Eddie these last weeks.

"No." He was apologetic. "Vanessa, it's rotten not to be able to spend the nights with you. You don't know how much I miss you and Suzy."

"I know." She reached for the latest stuffed animal Eddie had brought for Suzy and put it in her daughter's arms. "Eddie, I miss you, too."

They clung together for a few moments. His mouth was warm and hungry on hers.

"Where's Maria?" he asked when an imperious little voice interrupted their kisses with cries of "Mama."

"She'll be back soon." Vanessa's heart all at once was pounding. "Eddie, do you have to leave right away?"

"I can stay a little while." His eyes were hopeful. "And you, Signorina Suzy," he said with mock reproach, reaching for her. "Why aren't you sleeping late these mornings?"

"There's fresh coffee. I'll just warm it up." Vanessa crossed to the range. *Maria, hurry back. Let us have a little time together this morning.*

Eddie sipped at his coffee, enjoying these precious minutes with Vanessa and Suzy. Maria returned before he could finish his cup. With commendable swiftness she put away the groceries and whisked Suzy off to watch the morning activities on the narrow street below the apartment. A faint smile, a compassionate glint in her eyes, told Vanessa and Eddie that she and Suzy would be gone for quite some time.

In the chilly bedroom Eddie pulled Vanessa into his arms.

"You're cold," he whispered, though their voices could not carry beyond the heavy bedroom door.

"I won't be if you hold me tightly," she told him.

They made love with an urgency born of a stream of lonely nights. They clung together, reluctant to relinquish the sunlit morning, the ecstasy that charged through their bodies.

"Vanessa, I love you," Eddie whispered, his mouth at her ear. "Every night I stay away from you is anguish."

"Our time will come," she repeated the litany. "We can wait for our time together."

For a few minutes longer they lay motionless, caught up in their togetherness, willing time to stand still. "Honey, I have to leave." He paused for one final kiss before thrusting aside the comforter. "I'll stop by on my way back."

Late in the afternoon Vanessa phoned Maria from the shop with instructions to plan to serve Eddie his favorite cotolette alla milanese, just in case he had time for dinner on his way back from Padua.

"I'll stop at the butcher's on my way home from the shop," she told Maria. "With all the rain today nobody is coming in to buy. I'll close up early."

"I will make cannoli," Maria decided. "Signor Eddie likes this."

"I don't know if he can stay for dinner, Maria," Vanessa cautioned.

"I will make it anyway," Maria said. "You like it, too." She giggled. "And maybe a little piece for Suzy."

Vanessa closed up the shop earlier than usual and hurried through the narrow wet streets — some hardly wide enough for two to walk abreast — to the *macelleria* to buy the veal for the cotolette. The aroma of fresh-baked white Venetian bread blended in the damp air with those of cakes and vanilla and frying fish.

She frowned at the line waiting to be served. She was impatient to be in her cozy apartment. She looked forward to sitting in the small rocker in the corner of the kitchen, Suzy on her lap, a cup of espresso in her hand, while Maria reported on the day's activities.

"It was a terrible accident," one of the women waiting at the counter told another while Vanessa fretted at the butcher's slowness. "Why do they talk about bringing motor cars someday into the city? Always someone is killed. They are instruments of the devil."

Vanessa tensed. She knew it was ridiculous, but she always worried when Eddie drove in the rain.

"And such a young man," another woman continued as she handed the necessary lire to the butcher. "He belonged to a fine family."

"The road was wet," the butcher contributed. "The fog was heavy and he could not see the turn in the road. Pfft. It was over in a few seconds. Right over the cliff. It is in all the newspapers."

Vanessa's throat closed. She knew it was ridiculous to worry, but she had to see the afternoon newspaper and know that Eddie had not been involved in an accident.

She ran the few blocks to the nearest stall and bought a newspaper. In the pale sunlight of the late afternoon she held the paper in her trembling hands. Cold and disbelieving, she read the headlines. "EDUARDO MONTINO, SON OF WAR HERO, DEAD IN MOTOR CAR ACCIDENT."

It was a mistake, she told herself in defiant rejection. Only a few hours ago they had made love. *"I'll stop by on my way back."* They'd have dinner and—she forced herself to read the words. A few miles beyond

291

Mestre—on the road where he was to look at the summer house—the car had missed a turn and gone over a steep incline in the heavy morning fog. *Eddie was dead.* She clutched the newspaper in her hands. The rest of the page swam before her eyes.

She walked slowly toward the apartment in shock, struggling to understand. There was no one to whom she could turn, no one with answers or solace. She was a secret part of Eddie's life. Suddenly she knew that she must see this place where Eddie—so young and so in love with life—had plunged to his death.

She ran the remaining yards to the apartment. At the first sight of her white, stricken face Maria knew something terrible had happened.

"Signora Vanessa, what is it?" she asked fearfully.

"Stay with Suzy. There's somewhere I must go." She thrust the newspaper into Maria's hands and hurried to the bedroom she had shared with Eddie to dig her car keys from a dresser drawer. Oblivious to Maria's stunned, stumbling murmurs of shock and sympathy. "Stay with Suzy," she repeated, brushing past Maria.

Twenty-five minutes later she drove the small car Eddie had bought for her along the road he had traveled early this morning. The fog was gone now, and the early dusk was wrenchingly beautiful. Imprisoned in a shell of numb denial, she watched for the treacherous curve where Eddie's car had gone off the cliff.

On other fog-drenched mornings—according to the newspaper article that would forever be burned into her mind—other cars had taken the same tragic descent. *But Eddie would not have been there except that he sought a summer house for Suzy and her.* The relentless accusation ricocheted in her brain.

Here. Her heart pounded. Her hands were ice cold on the wheel. A sense of suffocation nearly overwhelmed her. She pulled off the road, left the car, and walked to the pieced-together guardrail that the police had set up temporarily as a warning to other drivers. She forced herself to look down into the abyss into which Eddie's car had plunged. The car was gone, but the flattened bushes showed her its path.

Eddie was dead. She would never see him again. She would never lie in his arms again. She couldn't even claim his body. *She was nothing.*

She hovered at the railing. She wanted only to follow that same path and join Eddie in death. Now, when their time to be together before the world had seemed so close, she had lost him. But she had to live. For Suzy's sake she had to go on with her life. Eddie would expect that of her.

She stayed at the railing, fighting for the strength to return to the apartment and pick up the torn threads of her life. She had a daughter. And there was her mother. Somehow, she must survive.

When she returned to the apartment, she found Suzy mercifully asleep. Maria's eyes were red and swollen from crying. She couldn't cry. She was numb.

"Vanessa—" The formal "Signora" was forgotten in grief as Maria held out her arms.

"If I had insisted he forget about the house, this wouldn't have happened." Vanessa's voice broke. "Maria. *Why?*"

They sat in the kitchen over the endless cups of coffee, the cannoli forgotten in the refrigerator. Maria pleaded with Vanessa to contact Eddie's sisters, but she remembered their outrage when they had learned of her pregnancy.

"They want no part of Suzy or me." She tried to focus on the empty years ahead, but it was too soon.

293

She could think only of Eddie, of his burial tomorrow in accordance with the dictates of the Jewish faith. He would be buried in the Jewish cemetery on the mainland, where only months ago his mother had been laid to rest.

"But they are Suzy's aunts," Maria protested.

"*You* are her aunt," Vanessa decreed.

"But you will go to the cemetery." Maria lifted her head in defiance. "They cannot prevent this."

"I'll be there tomorrow—" She could not bring herself to say the words: "when Eddie is buried."

She lay sleepless through the night. Her mind would not let her rest. She replayed all the precious moments in the brief years she had shared with Eddie's life. She relived each one, half expecting to hear the sound of his key in the door, half expecting to hear his voice: "*Vanessa, I'm home.*" When she heard Maria moving about in the kitchen, she left her bed to prepare for the painful day ahead. She would wear the simple black dress that was Eddie's favorite, with the pearls he had given her when Suzy was born. Last night Maria had gone out to buy the veil that she would wear over the Maud et Dano hat Eddie had brought back from Paris for her. She would go to the Piazzale Roma for the car and drive to the cemetery. She would stay at a distance; she could not join the family at the graveside. But she would be there when Eddie's body was lowered into its grave.

Maria came to bring her a cup of coffee and to embrace her in wordless consolation. Then Suzy's high, childish voice summoned them to the nursery. For a few moments Vanessa held Suzy close in her arms, grateful for this dear life.

"*Mangia,*" Suzy demanded in a burst of exuberance. "*Mangia.*"

"Eat," Vanessa said automatically. It was a house

rule that Suzy must hear as much English as Italian — and Maria, too, was eager to be fluent in English. "Eat."

"You eat so you grow big and strong," Maria crooned, reaching for Suzy. "We go to the kitchen."

Vanessa returned to the bedroom she had shared with Eddie. Last night she had instructed Maria to phone the Castello palazzo and politely inquire about the funeral arrangements. She concentrated on the morning schedule. After services at the undertaker's establishment, the funeral cortege — the black-draped water-borne hearse, rowed by two men in somber livery, and a train of gondolas carrying mourners — would travel down the Grand Canal to the Piazzale Roma where the cortege would become motor-borne for the journey to the cemetery on the mainland. She would follow the motor cortege to the cemetery. She did not dare appear for the services at the undertaker's premises. Even now she recoiled from the hostility that had radiated from Roberto Castello's wife in her shop. But at the cemetery, clothed in black and veiled, no one would know her real identity.

Pale and trembling, fighting for composure — a kerchief concealing her hair, dark glasses lending her anonymity — Vanessa left the apartment.

She remembered how many times she and Eddie had watched funeral processions moving along the Grand Canal. She could hear his voice, lilting and tender, as though he walked beside her.

"Vanessa, people come from all over the world so that they may die in Venice. Wagner, Browning, Diaghilev, Shelley's small daughter Clara all died here."

If they had stayed in New York after the war, Eddie would be alive. If he had not been so eager to find a place for her and Suzy for the summer, he would be alive.

At the garage in the Piazzale Roma Vanessa requested her car, and when the cortege — with almost two dozen limousines and cars following the hearse — appeared at the causeway, Vanessa joined it.

At the tree-bordered cemetery Vanessa parked and sat behind the wheel of the car while the other mourners drove inside. She was glad that her last sight of Eddie had been at the door of their apartment.

She clenched the wheel until her knuckles turned white, only vaguely aware of the sobs that racked her body. Then she thrust open the door of the car and ran stumbling into the cemetery. She stopped fifty feet short of the gathering of mourners.

Almost immediately she was able to identify Eddie's two sisters. The physical resemblance was strong. But there the resemblance ended. Eddie's sisters were bitter, angry women. Isa, of course, was not there. But Eddie's widow was here, Vanessa told herself. *She* was Eddie's widow.

She stood erect, both hands clutching the pearl necklace Eddie had given her. Her tears blurred the tableau before her. The rabbi's words were indistinct murmurings. Eddie would want her to be strong, she repeated again and again. She could not give way to grief. She had their child to raise.

The coffin was lifted into the freshly dug grave. She fought off an impulse to race to its side, to drop to her knees and reach out to touch the plain pine box that held all that remained on this earth of Eddie. The mourners moved forward to throw dirt on the coffin.

In desolation, alone, she whispered a soft farewell. "Good-bye Eddie. I love you. I'll always love you."

She turned away from the gravesite and walked blindly down the path that led from the cemetery. For a few moments she sat immobile behind the wheel of the car, gathering her strength, preparing herself for the drive back to the apartment, knowing she must pull together the strings of her life.

For three days and nights Vanessa sat in her darkened bedroom and relived her years with Eddie. She stored in a cavern of her mind the memory of a life that was forever gone. At intervals she slept from sheer exhaustion. She ate what Maria, solicitous and loving, brought her, because it was easier than arguing.

She knew she must plan for the future. Eddie had made no financial provisions for her and Suzy. How could he have known the future?

She would sell the shop, the furniture, her car. And Eddie had always kept a sizable amount of cash in the dresser drawer where she stored her jewelry — "for emergencies." If she was careful, she'd have enough money to take Suzy and go back to New York. She could find work there.

On the fourth morning Vanessa emerged from her bedroom, still shaky but determined to chart a course for the future. Only then did she realize that Maria had taken care of things while she grieved, that Maria had gone to Signora Rossi's house to explain that the shop was closed and she would be contacted shortly.

"Maria, I don't know how to tell you this —" Vanessa's voice broke. Maria was part of her small family. "I'll be going back home with Suzy. To New York. I'll miss you very much —"

"Take me with you!" A pulse pounded in Maria's forehead. "The money you have paid me I have saved. I can pay for the ship. I can sleep on the floor wherever you live. I will take care of Suzy while you go out to be a designer. How can you do this without Maria?" she chided, her dark eyes pleading.

"Maria, I don't know how we'll manage—" But there was truth in what Maria said. How could she work—and work she must—without someone to care for Suzy?

"We will manage." Maria beamed. "God will take care of us."

Vanessa and Maria sat over coffee in the kitchen and made plans while Suzy played on the floor. Someone at the door rang the bell.

"Signora Rossi," Vanessa surmised. Coming to offer her condolences.

Maria went off the admit their caller, clucking under her breath as the bell rang again. Vanessa picked up Suzy and walked down the hall. She mustn't cry, she reminded herself.

"Signora Vanessa—" Maria turned to her with a blend of apology and protectiveness. "Signor and Signora Castello are here to see you."

Vanessa went cold with shock. She managed a polite smile for the middle-aged, obviously wealthy couple who stood in the foyer of the apartment.

"Please come into the living room." She groped for the words. When she was nervous, her Italian was shaky. "Maria, take Suzy to the nursery, please."

In the living room the Castellos made it clear that this was no polite condolence call. They refused to sit.

"Signorina Conrad," Eddie's father-in-law said tersely. "we are acting on behalf of my daughter and of Eduardo's sisters. We have looked into his affairs. This apartment must be vacated by the end of the month." Vanessa gasped in shock. She had not yet brought herself to look this far ahead. "Proper disposition will be made of the furniture." He cleared his throat self-consciously and exchanged a glance with his wife. "May I have the keys to the shop Eduardo established?" *Her* shop. But she had insisted Eddie

298

handle everything through his personal account. There was no record of it as her shop. "The keys please," he repeated as the light sound of Suzy's laughter filtered down the hall.

"Tell her what we will arrange," his wife said. Like her husband she avoided meeting Vanessa's eyes.

"We will purchase passage for you to the States. You will be given this when the keys to the shop and to the apartment are in our hands."

Color flooded Vanessa's face. She remembered her mother giving her train fare to New York. And now the Castellos meant to send her back to New York.

"I must decline your offer," she said with intentional arrogance. Let them wonder if she planned to remain in Venice. "You may have the keys to the shop right now. I'll send you the keys to the apartment shortly. Will you please excuse me? I have much to do."

Twenty-four

Within a week Vanessa, Suzy, and Maria were aboard the *Île de France,* bound for New York in a tourist-class cabin that was little better than a wooden cattle stall. For Vanessa, the journey was colored by bittersweet memories of another trip—almost four years ago—from New York to Le Havre with Eddie.

Maria was enthralled by the prospect of living in America. Suzy caught her enthusiasm and babbled delightedly, *"Suzy go New York!"* Vanessa used the time she was alone in their cabin—while Maria roamed about the ship with Suzy—to sketch new designs.

She had sold to *Le Figaro* and to French *Vogue;* and she had run her own shop. Rich and fussy Venetian ladies had paid money for her designs. She would find a job on Seventh Avenue.

Though she was heading for the States, she felt very far away from both Tina and Pat. The day before they left Venice, she had received a hastily scribbled letter from Tina.

"I'm making him wait, but I'm pretty sure I'll marry Keith Edwards sometime in the next few months. He hates Hollywood even more than I do now. We're spending a few days at his house in Sag Harbor, a week in New York, and then we're flying to his place on the French Riviera for two or three months so he can plot his new book. I'll write as soon as we

settle on the Riviera. With any luck at all I'll be able to fly to Venice!"

Tina didn't know about Eddie. Vanessa's letter must have arrived in Hollywood after Tina had left. And Pat was on a six-week tour of South America with her mother. Vanessa was astonished that Pat had agreed to leave CeeCee in the care of her father and the live-in nursemaid for six weeks; but then, she reminded herself, Mrs. Owens could be terribly insistent.

Their final night aboard the ship, Vanessa plotted their goals for their first days in New York. They would go to an inexpensive hotel on the Upper West Side for the first day or two while they looked for a small furnished apartment. Then she would take her portfolio and tackle Seventh Avenue. She wasn't some kid just starting out — she would find a job in the fashion world.

Traveling in a taxi from the pier to the hotel, Vanessa felt a fresh surge of grief. This was where she had met Eddie, loved him, and waited for him to return from the war. She realized suddenly that for her New York would be full of ghosts.

During their first three days in New York — when she was not frantically searching for an apartment — Vanessa struggled to hide her anguish and show Suzy and Maria the city she had come to love. While she rushed about the familiar Upper West Side, she was secure in the knowledge that Maria was somewhere along the verdant stretches of Riverside Drive, watching Suzy play in the May sunlight with the other children.

Reading the *New York Times* and the *Daily News,* Vanessa was conscious of the changes that had taken place in New York even in the brief years she had been away. Apartments were even harder to find;

young people were once again pouring into the city in pursuit of their careers.

When she was nearing desperation, Vanessa discovered a vacant furnished apartment with the help of a sympathetic hotel desk clerk. He sent her downtown to the newspaper's headquarters on a Friday morning to pick up the classified pages of the Sunday *New York Times*. A brownstone apartment in the West Eighties was advertised. Vanessa shunned the bus or subway, hailed a cab, and hurried uptown.

The woman "super" showed her a shabby first-floor rear apartment with a closet kitchenette, a square, sunken living room whose windows overlooked a bedraggled garden, and a tiny bedroom that just managed to accommodate a double bed and a chest of drawers. Vanessa was baffled by the woman's stream of conversation. The rent was ninety dollars a month—low, the woman explained, because of the state rent controls.

"I got somebody who wants the place real bad," she said for the third time. "I ought to give it to them. But you look like such a nice young lady—" Her voice trailed off and her eyes glittered greedily. All at once Vanessa realized what she wanted: the woman was looking for "a little something under the table."

"I'm very anxious," Vanessa said softly and reached into her purse, grateful that she had cashed traveler's checks this morning. "Fifty dollars grateful—" She held up two twenties and a ten as an offering.

"A hundred," the woman replied at once, "and you can move in tomorrow. One month rent in advance and one month security."

Once they were settled in the furnished apartment, Vanessa girded herself to tackle Seventh Avenue. On a sunny early June morning she left her new home armed with portfolio, résumé, and the back issues of

Le Figaro and French *Vogue* that carried her sketches.

Walking through the streets that made up New York's fashion industry, Vanessa was caught up in the excitement that reverberated about Seventh Avenue. The streets were glutted with workers unloading double-parked trucks or guiding racks of clothing to their next destination, overflowing with voluble salesman, harried manufacturers, tense buyers, models carrying huge tote bags, designers clutching portfolios.

Her first calls on the more prestigious firms soon eroded her shaky self-confidence.

"You have too little working experience as a designer," one after another prospective employer told her. "And you don't know the American market."

Still, several conceded that her portfolio showed talent.

"Try for something lower on the scale," a sympathetic manufacturer suggested. "Start off as a cutting assistant or maybe assistant designer. Build up some experience in the business."

But for lesser jobs she would need skills she didn't have. She couldn't make a pattern. She couldn't drape. She couldn't even sew well. *She could design.*

There were top Paris couturiers who didn't have these skills, she told herself in defiance. Dior couldn't sew or cut. Jacques Fath couldn't sew or drape. Neither Chanel nor Schiaparelli could sew well. Somewhere on Seventh Avenue there must be a garment manufacturer who would see her as a designer.

After ten days of futile searching Vanessa forced herself to face reality. Her funds were limited. She had to find a job quickly. Tomorrow she must apply for a position at one of the less demanding manufacturers—those who produced the lowest-priced dresses.

She had learned by now that while the garment district sat within one block east or west of Seventh

Avenue, stretching from the low Thirties up to Forti-eth Street, the factories that made the low-priced merchandise were located at the lower end. That was where she would look for a job tomorrow. Though she yearned to design beautiful clothes made of exquisite fabrics, she must learn to use cheap fabrics and work with simple detail.

Day after day Vanessa followed up the job ads listed in the *New York Times* or applied at personnel offices. She was learning to exaggerate her experience, to lie about "studying at Traphagen." But nobody was willing to hire her as a designer.

By the end of three weeks she was desperate. She trudged home, footsore and exhausted in the late June heat, to collapse in a chair before their "non-working" fireplace. Maria brought her a tall glass of iced tea and reported that Suzy was taking a nap after playing for much of the afternoon on Riverside Drive.

"Nothing again, Maria," Vanessa reported in fresh frustration. "Everybody wants skills I don't have."

"You will find something soon," Maria soothed. "Every night I pray to Saint Jude."

"If I don't find something tomorrow," Vanessa said, her face set in determination, "then I'll sign up at one of the office temporary agencies. I'll go out as a typist."

It was frightening to see their funds dropping so fast. Maria was great at shaving their food costs, but money still had to be spent. The rent would be due in little over a week. And checks had to go to her mother.

Mother must have seen that the checks were being mailed from New York now. Didn't she wonder why? Again Vanessa reminded herself that her mother wished no part of daughter or granddaughter. But how deeply her father would have loved Suzy!

Late the following afternoon Vanessa sat in the grubby reception room of the New Amsterdam Dress Company, waiting to be interviewed for a designing job advertised in that morning's *Times*. Two girls had already been in and out of Mr. Goldwasser's private office. Another was in there now.

All three had worn copies of a dress popularized by Christian Dior a year earlier, one that had been poorly translated into a cheaper fabric. Vanessa was glad she had worn the black linen she'd designed after the Dior spring '49 Trompe l'oeil collection.

Suddenly the door to Mr. Goldwasser's office swung open, and a grim-faced girl stalked out. The girl's tense face made Vanessa nervous.

"Next," the receptionist called out without bothering to glance at Vanessa. She was absorbed in applying mascara to her eyelashes.

"Thank you." Her portfolio in tow, Vanessa stumbled to her feet and headed for the office. The receptionist looked like she was preparing to leave for the day. The interview would probably be brief.

A short, squat man with rolled-up shirtsleeves was talking on the telephone. He reached for a crumpled handkerchief to wipe the perspiration from his forehead.

"Sit down," he barked at Vanessa and continued his phone conversation.

All right, tomorrow morning she would sign up as a typist at a temporary agency. She might be rusty, but she ought to be able to pass a typing test. Clear this Mr. Goldwasser was not going to hire her.

"Show me your portfolio—" The man behind the desk startled her out of her introspection.

He looked at her sketches, listened to a recital of

her experience, grunted at intervals.

"We don't sell to Saks Fifth Avenue and Bergdorf's." He discarded the portfolio with an impatient frown. "We put our dresses on the racks at Klein's and the Lerner shops." He stared at her through narrowed eyes. "You able to make a first pattern?"

"No," she admitted. An assistant designer was usually responsible for making the first patterns.

"Can you supervise samplehands?" He rose from behind his desk and inspected her from head to toe.

"Yes," she said with fresh confidence. "I had my own shop in Venice. I supervised three seamstresses," she lied. Her mind quickly catalogued the other responsibilities of an assistant designer. "I chose fabrics and trim. I ordered these for my shop—"

"How good do you sew?"

"Not enough to make a finished garment," she conceded, "but—"

"You sketch?" he interrupted. "This is your own crap?" He pointed toward the portfolio.

"Of course," she shot back.

"Maybe I can work somethin' for you as an assistant designer." He rubbed a hand over the stubble on his jaw. "You and this other girl I seen this morning. You'll both be assistant designers," he decided. "Between the two of you you gotta be able to handle what I need. She makes the patterns. You go out into the stores to see what they're showin'. You got style," he approved, inspecting her smart linen dress. "In this business you oughta have an eye for what sells. You and this other broad—Tessie, I think her name is—will do the orderin', keep records. You type?"

"Yes. Sixty words a minute," Vanessa assured him.

"Okay. This'll work out. But nothin' goes through without my sayin' so," he cautioned. "We got one boss at New Amsterdam."

"I understand." Vanessa tried for a casual smile. Was she hired?

"You and Tessie work together to come up with the line for each season. She's got more experience; you got more class. It'll be okay. But I can't pay what the ad called for," he pointed out. "This is an assistant's job. When can you start?"

"Tomorrow." No matter what salary Mr. Goldwasser offered, she'd accept. It was a job!

The New Amsterdam Dress Company was beginning heavy fall production and at the same time starting up their special resort line. Mr. Goldwasser referred to this as a "new wrinkle." Vanessa sat with Tessie while Mr. Goldwasser outlined their duties between frantic interruptions and minor crises. The tension and pressure seemed to afflict not only Mr. Goldwasser but every one of his employees. This wasn't haute couture, she reminded herself. This was mass-market fashion, where one bad season could annihilate a small business like the New Amsterdam Dress Company.

"Tessie, you look through magazines for last year's resort styles," Goldwasser instructed. "We need a change here and there—what sold fine last year with some little gimmick to make it new. And remember, we sell cheap. Vanessa, you go downstairs to the cafeteria and have yourself coffee and a danish. Ask Flo for money from petty cash. You sit there and let your ears flap wide," he explained in response to her startled stare. "Listen to what they're talkin' about in the cafeteria. Who's got big orders for what—that kinda thing."

"You mean eavesdrop on the garment people who might be down there?" Vanessa stammered.

307

"Anybody there is garment people. Look, we ain't innovators up here. What's sellin' heavy for somebody else is what New Amsterdam puts out."

In blunt terms Goldwasser made it clear his line consisted mainly of "knocked off" designs. In the fashion industry in America—where, unlike France, the laws offered no protection against piracy—design piracy was considered a way of life.

"Okay," Goldwasser prepared to close their conference. "Tessie, you go to the library, then come back and start sketchin'. Vanessa, spend maybe an hour, an hour and a half, in the cafeteria. Then go uptown to Saks, Bonwit, Bergdorf, back down to Lord & Taylor and Altman's. Sometimes the classy stores start showin' their fall line real early. I wanna know what they're buying, what looks like it's gonna sell. Bring me back sketches."

Vanessa was determined to keep this job—at least until she had some experience behind her and felt secure in looking for a better one. The salary was small, the hours longer than she anticipated. Goldwasser made a nightly habit of corraling her and Tessie for conferences, to "pick your brains." She was assistant designer, typist, shopper, errand girl.

For Tessie—fortyish and dumpy—being "on Seventh Avenue" meant she was able to buy clothes for herself, her mother, and her four sisters at an admirable discount. Tessie could make patterns, but her idea of smartness was Klein's basement. She and Vanessa battled over designs for the resort line, which required Mr. Goldwasser's approval. It upset Vanessa that Tessie frequently won out, though Goldwasser had chosen several of her designs as "havin' class."

Vanessa was joyous when a letter arrived from Pat. Pat's letter was warm and sympathetic, and she offered to send Vanessa money to "see you through this terrible time." Vanessa immediately wrote back and told Pat about her job, avoiding the more unpleasant aspect of employment at the New Amsterdam Dress Company.

"I'm finally working in fashion in New York," Vanessa wrote, resolved to seem enthusiastic. She hated working with Goldwasser and Tessie; but it was a beginning. *"We have a cute little apartment in the West Eighties. Every time I walk past Zabar's, I remember our deli party the night we met."*

Ten days later Vanessa heard from Tina.

"Darling, I can't believe what's happened. I tried to reach you from Keith's villa near Menton—I thought I could drive to Venice and spend a week with you. Keith's so wrapped up in the new book he wouldn't even have known I was gone. When I couldn't get in touch with you, I phoned Pat down in Texas. She told me. I feel so awful that I wasn't there with you to help. Tell me if there's anything I can do. Anything. Do you need money? I can cable whatever you want—"

Tears welled in Vanessa's eyes. She and Tina would always be there for each other. And Pat. Sometimes, walking about the streets of the city, she felt as if she'd never been to Venice, that Tina and Pat were still here. She couldn't bring herself to take Maria and Suzy into an automat because she had eaten there so many times with Eddie. She couldn't take them out on a hot Sunday to Coney Island because she would see Eddie everywhere she turned.

In August Vanessa was assigned to be part of the showroom selling staff on the resort line, which she secretly considered unattractive and sleazy. She was shocked when Tessie warned her that Mr. Goldwasser would expect her to go out in the evening with certain buyers who came to the showroom.

"Don't do it." Tessie advised her. "If they want a good time, let the old man hire party girls to entertain them. That's not our job."

By the end of the first day of market week, Vanessa had politely rejected dinner invitations from two amorous out-of-town buyers. Mr. Goldwasser summoned her to his office.

"What's this crap I hear about you refusing to go out to dinner with Evans from Kansas and Abercrombie from Montgomery?" His face was flushed in anger as he leaned forward over his desk.

"Mr. Goldwasser, I'm in mourning for my husband," she said quietly. He knew about Eddie's death.

"It's gonna hurt him if you entertain some special customers? Evans and Abercrombie are heavy buyers. They're pissed off at me now! You know what that's costing me?"

"Mr. Goldwasser, I'm sure there are escort services who can help you," she said, recalling Tessie's words.

"Fuck the escort services!" he yelled. "My designers entertain, or they aren't my designers anymore."

"Then I'm not your designer anymore." She trembled in rage. "Because I'm not entertaining your grubby buyers!"

"Get out!" He rose menacingly from behind the desk. "I'll tell payroll to send you your final check. Get the hell outa here!"

Within two weeks Vanessa landed a second job. Her new boss, Hank Seidman, had nodded understandingly when she explained that "Mr. Goldwasser and I had a personal conflict."

"You mean the old bastard wanted you to entertain his buyers. Here we make other arrangements," he said delicately.

In her new job Vanessa was assistant to Ronnie Corelli, Seidman's designer for the past twelve years.

Corelli had a reputation as a foul-mouthed, arrogant woman who was feared and hated by all the sample-hands. Seidman warned Vanessa she might encounter some problems with Ronnie.

"Let her bitch and just carry on," he advised. "Remember, she may be the head designer, but I make the final decisions."

At a conference in Seidman's office, Vanessa watched Ronnie closely as Seidman explained to her that Clara—their most experienced samplehand—would create the first patterns rather than Vanessa.

"I want Vanessa to come up with a few designs that'll appeal to office girls, salesgirls, and young suburban wives—the ones who've got a yen to look like Saks Fifth Avenue or Bergdorf's but can't afford it. We'll squeeze the designs into the spring line."

For a moment Ronnie looked ready to explode. Then she smiled faintly and shrugged.

"If it makes you happy, Hank." She shot an insolent smile at Vanessa. "But don't count on heavy sales when the buyers come into town in November. All they want is some little changes from what they bought last year."

Vanessa was exhilarated. Hank Seidman, younger and more aggressive than Goldwasser, wanted to raise the image of his line, a line that already sold for slightly higher than New Amsterdam Dresses. And he knew Ronnie wasn't capable of turning out the smarter designs he was looking for.

Almost immediately Vanessa knew that Ronnie was suspicious of her role at Seidman Dresses. An operator whispered that assistant designers came and went with startling regularity. If she wanted to stay, she had to avoid any open confrontation with their head designer.

"Look, don't let Hank tell you he's the boss," Ronnie

311

said contemptuously when they ran into each other in the spartan women's washroom. "He's so heavy into the factors he can't take a shit without their okay. He can't cut one dress till they put up the cash. That's why he leans on me. He knows I'll design what'll sell." Unexpectedly she grinned. "Because I follow right on the tail of what's moving in the big stores. Don't believe that bull about Hank wanting to improve the image of Seidman Dresses. He plays that dumb game at least once a year."

Vanessa studied back issues of *Vogue* and *Harper's Bazaar* and combed her memory for details of the Dior spring collection she and Eddie had seen in Paris back in February. Haute couture was always a year ahead of mass-market. She was convinced that mass-market copies of Dior would be hitting American stores next spring. Nothing Ronnie was dredging up followed these lines.

Ronnie was a dangerous enemy, but it was important to convince Hank Seidman that *she* could design dresses that would ring up substantial sales in the retail stores. She wans't trying to push out Ronnie, she was just fighting to assure herself a job at Seidman's.

Ronnie was insidiously keeping her involved in supervising the samplehands and keeping records much of each day. She had to do most of her designing after hours. The line she was creating featured smart young dresses that were variations of Dior's Trompe l'oeil collection. This wasn't creative, she acknowledged, but it was a start. She was fighting on Seventh Avenue — the Velvet Jungle — where only sales figures made any real impression, where ripoffs were far more common than originals.

After she had a year or two as an assistant designer behind her, she could go after a job as a full-fledged designer—and she'd have a portfolio that would win respect in far better markets than New Amsterdam or Seidman. But without that background nobody would even talk to her.

As the time approached to make the final decisions on the spring line, the atmosphere in the Seidman factory became visibly tense. Vanessa was uncomfortably aware of Ronnie's hostility toward her when they sat down with Hank for the first decision-making conference. She struggled for poise as she pulled out her sketches. Attached to each sketch was a swatch of cloth suggesting the proper material.

Ronnie chain-smoked while Hank moved from one sketch to another in silence. Vanessa sat erect, her heart pounding, trying vainly to interpret Hank's inscrutable expression. The silence was unbearable.

Hank sat back in his chair and reshuffled the sketches. "Baby, these here are good," he said finally with a nod of approval. "We'll make samples."

"Our customers won't like them," Ronnie argued, her face flushed, eyes furious. "They'll die like dogs."

"We'll take a chance." Hank was unruffled. "They've got an air of class."

"We don't sell to classy broads," Ronnie shot back." And wait'll you see the costing," she added in triumph. "We'll never fit it into our price schedule."

"Give these five to Clara," Hank told Ronnie. "We'll take a gamble."

Twenty-five

Market week loomed ever closer, and the pace at the Seidman shop was frenetic. Vanessa was caught up in endless mundane assignments dumped on her by both Hank and Ronnie. Ronnie had contrived somehow to hold up the making of her five samples. As usual, the line consisted mainly of Ronnie's versions of last year's best sellers. Vanessa was furious.

She understood that some of the designs would be changed before they became part of the spring line. Some would be eliminated. She knew that Ronnie would do everything possible to make her designs appear too costly to be used.

Vanessa chased around the city in search of suitable fabrics and trim within the Seidman price range. Though this was not Paris and designers' names rarely appeared on the finished garments, she understood the value of being able to point to fast-selling merchandise that she had designed.

When at last the five samples of Vanessa's designs were made up, Ronnie fought to have them discarded.

"Hank, they're too fucking expensive!" she shrieked while Clara hovered nervously at her elbow, the dresses over one arm. "The factors will have a fit."

"That's not true," Vanessa shot back, her face flushed with anger. "We've worked out the costs.

314

They're—"

"Too fucking expensive." Ronnie repeated. "You haven't allowed for goof-ups." She turned triumphantly to Hank, daring him to contradict her. "They'll all need extra-careful cutting—God knows how many we'll lose. And look at all the material that goes into those goddamn panels!"

Hank chewed his cigar for a moment.

"Make 'em narrower. And cut down the width of the skirt," he told Clara while Vanessa gasped in dismay. "That'll bring the costs down."

When Vanessa saw the altered samples, she winched in despair. She knew—even before the arrival of buyers in the showroom—that her designs would never go into production. The "modifications" had obliterated their charm.

By the end of market week Vanessa was once again unemployed. She seethed with frustration. If the dresses had been presented as designed—and she was convinced they could have been produced at a profit—they would have sold well. It was little comfort that on Seventh Avenue this was a familiar cry.

Again she made the dreary rounds in search of a job. She haunted the cafeterias favored by the garment industry, drinking in the intense shop talk that percolated on every side of her.

"Now the bastard tells me to take a month off!" a smartly dressed woman in her late thirties complained to her companion. "The collection's finished. He doesn't want me around to scream when I see how my dresses are being modified," she said scathingly.

"It's the same every season," the other woman said with a shrug. "I break my back to come up with a line that's new and exciting, and then it's 'adapted' no matter how much I yell."

"Face it." Her companion sighed. "We've got no

clout. Without designers there's no collection, but if you or I balk they'll just hire somebody else."

"If we had our names on the labels instead of the names of the manufacturers, we'd build up clout. But only Claire McCardelle gets away with that."

Vanessa sat very still, her mind clicking into high gear. She needed a minor miracle to make Seventh Avenue aware of Vanessa Conrad. She needed her name on the label of a line of dresses in a Fifth Avenue store. It was completely crazy. But maybe, just maybe . . . Charged with optimism and energy, she left the cafeteria at a run and headed for the subway. She was impatient to sit down with a pencil, paper, and her checkbook.

Maria looked up from her mending in astonishment when Vanessa let herself into the apartment. Vanessa was never home at two in the afternoon.

"Suzy takes her nap," Maria said, rising to her feet. "I'll make lunch for you."

"Maria, I'm going into business." Vanessa's smile was dazzling. "I think — first I have to figure out costs. If I have enough left after putting aside money for rent and food for two months, I'm going to do it!"

"I still have a little money," Maria offered eagerly. "I give it to you now —"

"Wait till it's needed." Vanessa's face softened with affection.

"Where will you open the shop?" Maria asked.

"Not a shop exactly," Vanessa explained. "Not like in Venice. I'll design a line of six or eight dresses and show the samples to the department stores." Already her mind was creating designs that would be right for the moderate-priced departments of the Fifth Avenue specialty stores. Not the custom departments — like Sophie Gimbel at Saks — but ready-to-wear. The months at New Amsterdam and Seidman had taught her to be realistic. She couldn't afford to start off using the ultra-expensive fabrics she loved, nor to devote the time required for custom fittings. She would create young chic, she decided, at prices young career women could afford. "If just one buyer likes my dresses, Maria, I'm in business!" With orders on hand she could ask Pat and Tina to loan her operating money. Well, maybe not Pat, she thought. Pat had endless charge accounts but little cash. Tina would help. When the bills were paid, she'd return the loan and have capital to continue.

"But of course, this—this buyer," Maria stumbled over the unfamiliar word, "she will like your dresses. How could she not?"

"Tomorrow I must rent space to work in—small and cheap. I'll rent two sewing machines." She could buy more later. "I'll hire operators as soon as I have the material and trimmings on hand. Six dresses," she stipulated. Right now she would think only of the cost of manufacturing the samples. One step at a time. "I'll choose four from my portfolio, and I have ideas for the other two," she said exuberantly. "Maria, make another novena to Saint Jude," she laughed. "We'll need all the help we can get!"

It wasn't haute couture, Vanessa conceded; but it was a beginning. In the fashion world of Dior and Jacques Fath and Mainbocher Seventh Avenue still wasn't quite respectable. Not yet. But instinct told her that this would change, as so much in the postwar world was changing.

In the master bedroom of Keith's rented villa, high on the cliffs at Cap d'Antibes, Tina sat against a lush mound of silk-slipped cream pillows on the king-size bed and focused on applying nail polish to her toes.

Keith was on the phone, conducting an agitated conversation with his publisher in New York.

She admired the sprawling villa with its whitewashed walls and arches, its magnificent terraces, and the terrifying yet exhilarating slide from the swimming pool to the sea below. But she was irritated that she'd had to make heavy inroads on her bank accounts to put up the six months' rent for the villa.

"Come on, Seth," Keith was saying with that synthetic calm he used in moments of crisis, "you know goddamn well I'll do the book. I just need a substantial advance so I can keep on writing." He scowled as he paced about the thirty-five-foot bedroom, the telephone cord trailing behind him.

For a while, at the beginning, Keith had been so involved in his book he'd even talked about it while they were screwing. When she took off for Paris for three days, he'd hardly realized she'd been gone. Then, zingo, writer's block. And then the partying began. God, Keith threw money around like he was Aristotle Onassis! When his funds ran low, he started in on hers.

She'd never been truly comfortable with Keith's friends. In Hollywood the talk at parties revolved around movie gossip. But Keith's friends were mostly writers and musicians. They talked books and music and art. Hell, most of the time she didn't know what they were talking about!

"Seth, I took three years on the last book." Keith's voice was becoming strident. "You sold over a hundred thousand fucking copies! How do you expect me to go ahead with this one when I have to worry about where to get eating money?"

Seth Colby insisted that Keith air-mail him a chunk of the book before he sent money. Seth knew about Keith's drinking and partying. Tina flinched, remembering how much it had cost Seth—and her—to bail him out of that mess on the first villa. The Russian prince who'd rented it to them had been outraged by the damage incurred at their last party. Not only did he throw them out, he sued. Somehow they'd managed a settlement, but Keith was drained financially. *What had he done with all the money from the three best sellers?*

"No!" Keith yelled. "You can't see the book. Not until I see a check!" He slammed the phone down. He couldn't send a chunk of the book; all he had were boxes of notes and a rough outline. "That son-of-a-bitch. We owe bills all over town. Tina, you'll have to transfer funds to the bank here."

"I can't," she said sweetly. *Enough of this shit.* "Marty says I've got a tax problem. Practically everything left belongs to Uncle Sam."

"The IRS can wait," he said, brushing aside her news. "We haven't paid the servants for two weeks. The garage is screaming for money. The—"

"I'm getting out of here, Keith." This whole scene was crazy. She should have walked out on him months ago. "I can't afford to live with you."

"Baby, this is only temporary. You know what a bastard Seth is when it comes to money. I'll send him a hundred pages, and he'll start shipping money again. He knows I'm a gold mine." He squinted, lost in thought. "I suppose I could borrow on the Mercedes."

"You do whatever you like, Keith." She leaned forward to check her toenails. Dry. "I'm heading back for the States. Maybe I've still got a career in Hollywood."

"You hate Hollywood." He stared at her in rebuff.

"I hate being out of money." She moved toward the closet. "I'll call Marty from New York to see what he can cook up for me." She should have known Hal

319

wouldn't buy out her contract. That wasn't his style. Instead he'd offered her a tiny role in a B movie, knowing she'd turn it down. She was on suspension. Damn all paychecks that never came in.

"Okay, so you do a picture fast and come back here." He reached for her, but she brushed his arms aside. "By the time you're back," he said, his eyes holding amorous promises, "I'll have half the book done. The day I'm finished, we'll get married."

"Keith, we've scheduled a wedding a dozen times," she reminded him brutally. "You always find a reason to delay it. I don't think I want to marry you anymore."

"You're mad," he sighed. "I don't blame you. But you come back from whatever picture Marty sets up for you, and we won't even wait for me to finish the book. We'll be married as soon as we can get a license. Tina, it'll be hell without you."

"You'll survive." She shrugged. "We'll both survive." She'd had some sensational times with Keith. Almost as good as with Felix.

Tina decided to fly to New York. But all at once she longed to be back in Hollywood. Working. Could Marty swing something for her despite this mess with Hal? The studio had picked up her option again, even though she was on suspension. That was Hal's way of getting back at her. She couldn't work for any other studio as long as she was tied to Imperial Films.

Hiding behind dark glasses and a pre-New Look, mannish fedora, she left Idelwild by limousine for the Pierre. *"Darling, I'm here at the Pierre,"* she'd say and then they'd talk about a new picture for her. Let Marty fight for a great part in a major film. How long could Hal stay vindictive? She knew she was still hot at the box office. Wherever she went even in Europe, her fans recognized her and crowded around for autographs.

In the tiny cubicle that was Vanessa Conrad Dresses, Vanessa sat at her improvised desk and painstakingly double-checked the costing of the six samples to be cut and made by the three women she had hired earlier in the day. Thank God she'd had the experience of working at New Amsterdam and Seidman. She knew how to handle this operation.

Her only problem — an alarming one — was the lack of real working capital. But with an order from Best or Bergdorf or Saks in her hands she'd feel secure enough to borrow from Tina.

She pushed back her chair, closed the dime-store notebook she'd bought for record keeping, and rose to her feet to switch off the lightbulb that hung unshaded from the ceiling. Tomorrow morning her three hands would be here and working. When the six dresses were completed, she would show them herself at the Fifth Avenue stores.

Seventh Avenue was dark and empty when she left the building and headed for the subway. An hour earlier the district had been in a state of semibedlam. She relished the daytime excitement, the streets so full that just walking was difficult, the double-parked delivery trucks, the unceasing dissonance of horns — all the evidence on every side that this was the fashion center of the world. *Her* world.

She walked quickly, chilled by the sharp December night air and eager for the cherished presence of Suzy and the warmth of her apartment. Maria would be bustling about the closet kitchenette preparing a budget dinner that always managed, somehow, to be savory.

She arrived at the apartment and pushed the bell.

The door swung wide. Tina stood before her in one of her dramatic Paris dresses.

"Darling, how wonderful to see you!" Tina and her expensive French perfume enveloped Vanessa in an affectionate embrace.

Vanessa couldn't believe her eyes. "When did you arrive?" she demanded.

"Yesterday. I fell into my bed at the Pierre and just slept until two hours ago."

Over dinner Tina talked about living on the Riviera, the Hollywood movie stars and the famed novelists who had wandered in and out of Keith's villa. She reported in detail, knowing Vanessa would be fascinated, on her brief trips to Paris for clothes and a visit to the Italian salon of Sorelle Fontana to buy a costume for a masquerade ball.

"Fontana made that marvelous white satin bridal gown, appliquéd with old lace, seed pearls, and sequins, that Linda Christian wore last January when she married Tyrone Power."

Only when they were relaxing over Maria's fantastic cannoli did Tina talk about her problems with Keith and her career.

"The bastard was living like an Indian pasha and draining my bank account dry. I haven't earned a cent in almost seven months. I talked with Marty just before I left the hotel. He's miffed at me, but I'm money in the bank to him. He'll work something out. He says Hal is bored with the studio. Nat's back running things." Tina's face showed a simmering unease. "Nat can be damned nasty."

"Marty will be hungry for your kind of commissions," Vanessa encouraged. "And Nat Kelman knows you're a money-maker."

"There's trouble in Hollywood," Tina confided. "That's probably why Hal got bored so fast. Televi-

322

sion's killing off a lot of the movie audiences. Movie houses are closing all across the country." She grinned wryly. "Would you believe it? I read the *Hollywood Reporter, Variety,* and *Billboard* on the Riviera. Keith never missed an issue." She paused. "What about this business Maria tells me you're starting up?"

Slowly, still trying to absorb the knowledge that Tina's finances were in shambles, Vanessa reported on her operation.

"I'm working on a shoestring, but one decent order and I'll be in business." She tried to sound optimistic.

"What about filling the orders?" Tina asked with rare practicality.

"I'll have to find a way to borrow. Maybe from a factor. Half of Seventh Avenue stays in business because of factors."

"Factors—they're like legal loansharks?" Tina frowned, trying to understand as Vanessa nodded. "Honey, they won't loan a dime to a designer without a track record here in New York. I know you were doing great in Venice but—" She paused, squinting in thought. "Would a thousand or so help?"

"Yes . . ." Vanessa's face lighted.

"Okay. Tomorrow morning you and I pay a visit to the good old Provident Loan." Her lips parted in laughter. "I never did like that shitty diamond Gordie gave me when we got engaged. I insisted on keeping it as part of the divorce settlement just because it burned him up. It should be good for at least a thousand."

Tina's ring was worth fourteen hundred, enough to see Vanessa through an initial order or two. Only when Tina mentioned casually that Marty had wired her the money to pay her bill at the Pierre and buy a plane ticket to Los Angeles did Vanessa realize the seriousness of her financial situation.

"Thank God I've kept up the rent on the apartment in Hollywood," Tina said while her luggage was being piled into the taxi. "That's the kid from Pinewood wanting to make sure she has a roof over her head."

They exchanged a warm farewell, and Vanessa hurried downtown, determined to pay Tina back as soon as possible. She would ask her three operators to put in extra hours today and to come in on Saturday. They should be pleased at the prospect of overtime with Christmas almost here. It was an extravagant gesture in the face of her budget, but by Monday morning she wanted to approach her first dress buyer.

Right on schedule Vanessa's operators finished the samples. She spent Sunday meticulously pressing the half dozen samples and practicing her pitch to the buyers. *"I've sold sketches to le Figaro and French Vogue. In 1946 I began to design for a smart boutique in Venice, Italy. I opened my own shop there, catering to a fashionable clientele, in 1948. I sold the shop and came home a few months ago, after my husband was killed in an automobile accident."* She would not mention New Amsterdam or Seidman Dresses.

On Monday morning—a garment bag carefully draped over one arm—Vanessa set out to present her line to buyers in the Fifth Avenue department stores. The festive Christmas displays and the crowds of holiday shoppers attested to the rising incomes of the nation. Just in October President Truman had signed a minimum-wage bill that raised the minimum in some industries from forty to seventy-five cents an hour. The economists were all predicting a healthy buying season, despite the one and a half million unemployed.

Vanessa was turned away by the first four buyers

she tried to see. She told herself she was approaching them at a bad time. The fifth set up an appointment for early in January.

On the verge of admitting that she had taken on an impossible task, Vanessa pushed herself to make one final effort. She would call on the buyer at Best and Company, a professional noted in *Women's Wear Daily* as sympathetic to young designers. To her astonishment, she was ushered immediately into the buyer's office.

Cautious but friendly, the buyer listened to Vanessa's prepared sales pitch. Vanessa's hands shook a little as she began to display her samples, but her voice was even and sure. The buyer's face remained impassive until Vanessa showed her last two samples.

"Oh, I like these." The buyer nodded in approval and leaned forward to inspect them for workmanship.

Fifty minutes later, floating on a cloud of euphoria, Vanessa charged back to her tiny workroom. A label reading "VANESSA CONRAD" would appear on her dresses at Best and Company!

Now all she had to do was meet her promised late January 1950 delivery date. The sewing machine agency *had* to understand the urgency of her situation—she couldn't wait a week or two. She needed machines *now*. She found operators available for immediate work. She raced about town buying the necessary fabrics and trim. When the buttons she needed were no longer available from her first source, she traipsed miles about the city to find replacements.

With her workroom in motion again, Vanessa inspected every step of each garment to be sure the workmanship was just right. When one operator turned in slipshod work, Vanessa put her on warning. She pressed the finished dresses herself and hung them on the waiting racks until the order was ready to be shipped to the department store.

At six, when the operators were gone for the day, Vanessa rushed uptown to spend an hour with Suzy, and then rushed back to the shop to take care of myriad small details. And she was ever fearful that the buyer's excitement would dissipate before the dresses were delivered.

A few days before Christmas she received a card with a letter from Pat, who would be spending the holiday at the family house in Virginia. It seemed likely, Pat reported, that Paul would be running for Congress next November. A day later an exquisite Madame Alexander doll arrived for Suzy and a beautiful leather purse for Vanessa.

On Christmas Eve Maria went to mass, and Vanessa realized belatedly that Hanukkah had come and gone. Next year, she promised herself, they would observe Hanukkah. Suzy would be almost three. It would be time to start teaching her that she was Jewish.

Around ten o'clock, as Vanessa sat alone and relished the chance to catch up on the latest edition of *Vogue,* Tina phoned from California. The new contract was being ironed out. She expected to start work any day. And "the biggest teddy bear I could find on Rodeo Drive" was on its way to Suzy.

They talked nostalgically about their Christmases in Pinewood. Tina had never reconciled herself to her father's rejection. Vanessa claimed to be philosophical about her mother's silence.

"Anyhow," Tina drawled, "we've done a hell of a lot of living since Christmas 1941!"

On Christmas Day Maria prepared a festive dinner. After the early afternoon meal the three of them took a bus to midtown to look at the fanciful Christmas shop windows. It was a pleasant, leisurely day that

Vanessa cherished, but sleep that night was elusive. Why was it that on holidays she was always overcome by a sense of aching emptiness?

Two days before it was due, the first order from "Dresses by Vanessa Conrad" was being checked into the Best and Company stockroom. Three days later the triumphant buyer called Vanessa.

"Your dresses are selling like mad," she reported. "Drop by this afternoon and I'll write up another order."

Vanessa bought more fabrics and trim, rented additional machines, hired more operators. But by the time the second order was delivered, Vanessa discovered that her dresses had been pirated up and down Seventh Avenue in cheaper versions and were already appearing in other stores. Her anger, she knew, was futile: imitation was a way of life in the garment trade. It was, admittedly, heady flattery to have her designs "knocked off" this way; but it was a devastating blow financially.

She sat down alone in her shop and assessed the situation. She could expect no more orders from Best & Company for her current samples. Still, even after returning Tina's loan, she should have some operating capital left over. Could she create another best-selling dress before her money ran out?

She had to continue paying rent on the space. She had to keep the sewing machines — she might need them on a moment's notice. She'd already released the operators — she couldn't pay salaries without work on hand. So. She had to design another spectacular dress or two that would sell fast.

How could she cope with piracy on the next round? She recalled the Chambre Syndicale de la Couture Parisienne, formed in Paris to protect French designers. To the French the fashion industry was an economic force, protected not only by law but by tradition. Here in New York it was a matter of putting volume into the stores fast—before a top-selling design could be knocked off. That required more capital than she could raise, Vanessa conceded.

On a crisp, sunny April morning Vanessa went to the Metropolitan Museum of Art to peruse the historical costume books. She had decided in her first years in New York that all new fashions were adapted from older ones—that a successful designer was one who knew when the time was ripe to resurrect an older style, with revisions that made it appear new and intriguing.

After exhausting hours of studying various periods, she paused, entraced by the sketch on the page before her. In her mind she was already visualizing modern adaptations, debating practical fabrics. She sat on a bench in the cozy warmth of the museum and sketched page and page of possible designs.

Tired but excited by her new find, Vanessa clung to the strap in the subway and tried to be realistic about her next move. By serving as her own manufacturer—even on a very small scale—she ensured that her creations would not be watered down until they were unrecognizable, bastardized versions. And many manufacturers began on a shoestring. She would have to be sharp to survive—but it was possible.

As she emerged from the subway, a pang of hunger shot through her stomach. She'd been too engrossed with her sketching to stop for lunch, and now it was almost three o'clock. She'd stop for a coffee and danish before going up to the shop to work on the designs.

In the large, noisy, always busy cafeteria Vanessa struggled to juggle purse, portfolio, and tray. She sighed in exasperation when the portfolio slipped from her arm and fell to the floor — spilling out sketch pad, torn-out sheets, and drawing pencils.

"Let me help you." A young man with a sympathetic smile dropped to his haunches and collected the portfolio's contents.

"Thank you so much," she stammered gratefully.

"Ah, you're a designer," he guessed, shuffling through the sketches in her portfolio with interest. He surveyed her designs and then her, his hazel eyes disconcertingly probing. When he stood up again, she saw that he was perhaps five inches taller than she, yet he seemed to tower above her. "Let me carry these to a table for you." He wasn't asking permission; it was a decision. He glanced about the rapidly filling cafeteria. "There's one over there."

He settled her at a table for two, removed his topcoat and dropped it across the back of the other chair. Considering how few tables were unoccupied, Vanessa decided she couldn't reasonably object.

"It'll take me a couple of minutes to get coffee and one of those." He pointed to her danish. "I'd like to talk shop with you if I may." He was both ingratiating and wistful. He wasn't trying to pick her up, Vanessa reasoned. He was just someone like herself — fighting to make a dent in the garment industry.

"That would be fine." She was startled to realize how much she was looking forward to talking to this stranger.

In a few minutes he was back at the table with his tray.

"There's no time of day when this place isn't crowded," he complained good-humoredly. "For a lot of people in the business a table here is a private office."

"What part of the business are you in?" Vanessa asked curiously.

"I've been trying to set myself up as a tie manufacturer," he told her. "It's about the only creative area in menswear, and there's a lot of money to be made there. I roped in an investor who was dying to take the plunge, but my deal fell through."

"Why did he change his mind?" Vanessa asked.

"He's a sharp seventy-four-year-old businessman from Texas. He's a widower and bored with retirement, so he invests in things that he thinks will amuse him. He's backed plays, put up money for movies, invested in a new publishing house. I had him hot for this deal until my designer screwed it up. I knew Arnie when I was in the army during the war. Then I ran into him about seven months ago and we got excited about the possibility of bringing out a line of ties that would revolutionize the field. Arnie came up with sensational designs. I had a gut reaction that he was right for the time." He shook his head in bafflement. "I don't know what the hell got into him. He's loaded with talent but no brains. As soon as we sit down to seal the deal, Arnie goes temperamental. All of a sudden he thinks he's Picasso. Bill Bartlett wants no part of him."

"How awful for you." Vanessa was compassionate.

"I'm thirty years old. It's time I did something with my life."

Vanessa's mind raced: he had an investor. What about making dresses instead of ties?

She focused again on the conversation. "Basically I'm a promoter," he was saying, his eyes appraising her. "Before I went into the army, I was an actor in Hollywood." He chuckled. "I did extra work for a year and cat-sat for a couple of hot-shot stars. Then I figured on making a killing by freezing orange juice and marketing it in cans. I'd just optioned the crop of a big orange grove in Southern California. I had a money man ready to go. So what happened?" His smile was ironic. "I got drafted. After three years in the army — all the way from North Africa, Sicily, and Italy as far north as Milan, I —"

"I just came back home from Venice after almost four years," Vanessa broke in. All at once she felt close to this mesmerizing young man across the table.

"What the hell were you doing in Venice?"

Vanessa explained that "her husband" had been of Italian birth, and quickly sketched over his death and her return to New York with Suzy. He listened attentively while she told him about her fashion experience in Venice.

"My name's Frank Bernstein." They laughingly shook hands across their trays as Vanessa introduced herself. "Since the war I've been a press agent, a used-car salesman, a construction worker. For three months, when I was flat broke, I pushed a cart down Seventh Avenue for a men's suit manufacturer. That's when I got hooked on the garment business. It's the one field I know where a sharp operator can make a killing fast."

"It's not that easy," Vanessa said ruefully. "I've been trying."

"Tell me what you've been doing since you hit Seventh Avenue."

He listened intently, interrupting her to ask questions. This was not just casual shop talk, Vanessa realized. Frank Bernstein had an investor; he needed the right partner to set up a business, someone talented and cooperative. He was obviously smart about Seventh Avenue. She could be that partner.

"I need some education," he warned. "I don't know about Paris and haute couture. I don't even know about Hattie Carnegie or Schiaparelli or the other *mishegash*." He grinned. "That's Yiddish for —"

"I know." She chastised herself for interrupting him again. "It's one of the few words of Yiddish my father knew."

"So I'm talking to a smart little Jewish girl," he teased. "You'll understand when I say that the way for you to go is not trying to make clothes to fit a store's price range for a certain department. Make them ready-to-wear, but as expensive as hell. Women respect what costs a lot. If you design dresses that'll create demand, women will pay whatever the store asks. Maybe not every woman," he acknowledged, "but plenty of women will spend anything for something that really grabs them. Start at the top, baby. That's the way to go."

"That takes more capital that I can manage," she ventured, knowing this was the turning point in their conversation.

"Maybe my investor will see what your talent and my promotion can do." He radiated enthusiasm. "Vanessa, my instincts tell me that together we can set this industry on its ear. But before I talk to Bill Bartlett, you've got to give me ammunition. Can we talk tonight?"

"Come to my apartment for dinner," she said. "Maria's making spaghetti, and nobody makes spaghetti like Maria. I'll show you all my sketchbooks. I'll tell you about my shop in Venice. I'll explain the kind of dresses I really want to do," she bubbled, her excitement matching his own.

"I have the name for our company." He squinted into space. "Creations by Vanessa Conrad. We'll make old Bill come in with us."

Twenty-six

Frank arrived at Vanessa's apartment at exactly six o'clock. The living room was cozy with warmth and the smell of Maria's spaghetti, the radio offering the muted strains of the classical music Eddie had taught Vanessa to love. Maria had just finished feeding Suzy. After being introduced to Suzy and Maria, Frank dropped to his haunches to talk to Suzy at her level. He was warm and gentle, and Suzy was enthralled.

"All right, Suzy," Vanessa said with mock sternness after a few minutes. "Off to bed with you."

"No," Suzy objected, clinging hopefully to Frank's hand.

"Yes." Vanessa reached to scoop her reluctant daughter into her arms. "I won't be long," she apologized to Frank. "There are the sketchbooks." She nodded toward the coffee table. "We'll have dinner as soon as I bathe Suzy and put her to bed."

"Hey, don't I get a kiss?" Frank leaned forward to take Suzy's small face between his hands and kissed her on one cheek. Suzy exuberantly planted a moist kiss on his chin. "Sweet dreams, Suzy."

When Vanessa returned to the living room, Frank had shed his jacket and was thoroughly absorbed in her sketchpad.

"I like these," he said with satisfaction. "I don't know

much about women's clothes, but I know these are special."

Maria summoned them to the table and served heaping plates of spaghetti, salad, and Italian bread fresh from the oven. Vanessa had splurged on a bottle of inexpensive Chianti.

Over dinner, with Maria an avid listener, Vanessa and Frank discussed the women's wear industry. Frank was quick to pick up subtle angles, Vanessa noted. She argued against his insistence that they compete with the most expensive ready-to-wear lines. She tried to explain to Frank the costs involved in this kind of manufacturing.

"But your heart is in designing the best," he insisted. "And that's where the money is." Frank made no secret of his ambition: he wanted to be the richest man on Seventh Avenue. "Look, television is changing the whole fashion picture. Women don't depend anymore on what they see in the fashion magazines, clothes that have been photographed months earlier. On TV they're seeing Bess Myerson and Fay Emerson and what they're wearing that same afternoon or evening. People have money to spend, and more and more of it will be spent by women on clothes!"

Maria served them her superb zabaglione and coffee, and with a pleased smile retired to her bedroom.

Still not sure Frank's idea would work, Vanessa brought out paper and pencil and began to break down the cost of dresses that showed up in the most expensive departments of Saks Fifth Avenue, B. Altman, Bergdorf, Bonwit, Best. She knew they could not compete in the rarefied atmosphere of Saks Fifth Avenue's custom salon or the salons of Hattie Carnegie or Mainbocher, who had made the dress Wallis Simpson wore when she married the Duke of Windsor.

She presented her calculations to Frank.

"Okay, we'll tell Bill we need seventy-five thousand to get started," he decided. Vanessa gazed at him in astonishment. "Oh, he'll cut it down to fifty or fifty-five. He'll want to see us sweat a bit." Frank grinned. "Bill calls it 'creative management.' But we can manage on that if we watch what we lay out. I'll call him and set up a luncheon appointment for tomorrow." He glanced about the living room.

"We don't have a private phone, but there's one right outside in the hall," she explained.

"Stand by for lunch with Bill Bartlett. I don't want this thing to drag."

While Maria coaxed Suzy into her sunlight yellow jacket, Vanessa dressed for her luncheon with Frank and Bill Bartlett at the Colony. Most likely, Frank had told her, Bill would pick up the check. Vanessa hoped so.

She would wear the exquisite black suit Eddie had bought for her at Christian Dior. The weather was a bit chilly for the suit, but she would look right, she decided with satisfaction. In Venice she had discovered "her look." It gave her confidence.

She met Frank a block away from the Colony at a Madison Avenue art gallery so they could arrive at the restaurant together. Frank, too, was aware of the importance of appearances. He was wearing what he called "my dining-with-investors suit" and a tie he kept for special occasions.

Bill Bartlett was waiting for them in the red-and-crystal main dining room at the Colony. He was a tall, keen-eyed man who had given up the battle against excess weight. His white hair was striking against his perennial tan. He rose with southern courtliness as Vanessa and Frank were led to his table. Vanessa watched him scrutinize her Dior suit. While he might not recognize the designer, he knew it was expensive.

"You're a mighty pretty young lady," he said in his soft Texas drawl when Frank introduced them. "That's not a bad thing in business."

Bartlett insisted they have the Crepes Colony, stuffed with succulent seafood. He made it clear he was not yet ready to talk business. Instead, he spoke nostalgically of his ranch near Houston.

"One of my two closest friends lives in Houston," Vanessa told him delightedly. "Patricia Roberts. She was Patricia Owens before her marriage."

Bill Bartlett's eyes inspected her appraisingly.

"That wouldn't be Congressman Owen's daughter?"

"Yes," Vanessa said. She saw Frank's faint smile of approval. "Her husband is in the state legislature."

"And who's your other closest friend?" he joshed good-humoredly.

"Tina Gregory," Vanessa told him. Even Frank was surprised. "The three of us lived in the same house here in New York during the war. We shared a cottage one summer at Fire Island."

"Frank, I think your young lady is what we call well connected," Bartlett approved. "Now let's talk business."

Over Crepes Colony and boysenberry sorbet, they discussed Creations by Vanessa Conrad. Vanessa casually mentioned her success in Venice with such clients as the Marchesa di Ronzoli. As Frank had warned, Bartlett dropped the capitalization of the proposed new firm from seventy-five to fifty thousand.

"We mean to sell a line of dresses that a limited

number of women can afford to wear," Frank explained to Bartlett. "Others will buy, perhaps, one Vanessa Conrad a year, the jewel in an otherwise ordinary wardrobe. But there are enough of these women across the country to roll in gorgeous profits," Frank wound up. "And we can do it with a production situation that is too small to get out of hand. That's always a critical problem on Seventh Avenue."

"It's something to think about," Bartlett agreed cagily, but he was intrigued.

Frank talked knowledgeably about the value of publicity, with never a hint that only last night Vanessa had explained how Jacques Fath had manipulated the press—in stories frequently invented by reporters or himself—to build himself into a celebrity.

"With promotion, we can do in New York what Jacques Fath did in France," Frank said casually. "You say 'a dress by Jacques Fath,' and every woman's eyes light up. Not just the superrich who come every season to see his collection. *Every* woman who can read. The name of a designer who has been heavily publicized adds something special to his or her dresses. Here in this country manufacturers disregard the designer, but who cares about the name of the manufacturer? It's cold. Impersonal. By publicizing our designer—Vanessa—we'll add the same kind of cachet that Fath has brought to his business. That's money in the bank, Bill."

"Fath is doing two special collections a year now for Lord & Taylor—and they're being picked up across the country. Neiman-Marcus in Dallas, I. Magnin in Los Angeles—all the smart specialty shops. And it's the heavy promotion that's accomplished this," Vanessa emphasized.

"Vanessa is young and beautiful. Along with her fascinating designs, she's a natural for promotion,"

337

Frank assured their backer. "It'll be a breeze."

"My lawyer will draw up corporation papers." Bartlett turned from Frank to Vanessa with an elfin grin, knowing his sudden capitulation had startled them. "Start looking for premises." He lifted a hand to signal their waiter. "This calls for champagne."

When she and Frank had seen Bill Bartlett into a cab on Madison Avenue, Vanessa was light-headed— more from the triumphant outcome of their luncheon than from the Dom Perignon.

"Let's go downtown and start looking for space right now," Frank said. "By the time we find something and a lease can be drawn up, we'll have Bill's money in a checking account," he reasoned. "Vanessa, we've got a deal."

They spent the afternoon looking at rentals with no success. Either the areas were too small or too large or too expensive. Frank looked to Vanessa to make this decision. She knew what would be required for their operation. Shortly before five they admitted defeat on this first day and retired to a cafeteria for coffee and to talk about their first collection: a spring line, with a formal showroom opening the first week in November.

Vanessa and Frank agreed that Frank would handle all the promotion, negotiate the business deals, keep the books. Vanessa would design, buy fabrics and trim, work with a seasoned operator to prepare the samples. They would supervise the workroom together. They knew they must put in fourteen- and sixteen-hour days to survive in the Seventh Avenue jungle. In the beginning they'd be working seven days a week.

"I'll meet you here for coffee tomorrow at eight," Frank said when Vanessa suggested apologetically that they break for the day. She wanted to go home and spend time with Suzy. "A base for our operations is top priority."

For the next three weeks Vanessa and Frank searched for suitable quarters. Both were determined to find a place that was exactly right for their operation, and with room in which to grow.

Vanessa was grateful for the demands the new business made on her. With the arrival of May, she was all too conscious that one year ago Eddie had left her arms and gone to his tragic death.

Just when they were growing desperate, Frank discovered a place. At the same time they were summoned to the office of Bill Bartlett's attorney to sign the corporate agreement. Bill had set up the firm so that he owned 51 percent and Vanessa and Frank together owned the remaining 49 percent. Vanessa or Frank would sign checks.

"You don't need me for that." He brushed this aside as trivia. "I'm just interested in seeing results."

Every evening now, after Suzy was asleep, Vanessa worked on her designs. Their budget would not allow for an assistant designer or a sketching assistant. Vanessa would work directly with a seasoned samplehand, who would make revisions until Vanessa was satisfied with each sample. After much conferring on costs, Vanessa and Frank decided to keep their collection down to forty dresses. Small, but adequate for a beginning.

Vanessa confessed to Frank and Maria that she was exhilarated — and frightened — to be designing a whole collection. The responsibility was tremendous. Almost every waking moment was spent thinking fashion.

She began to keep a sketchpad in the bathroom, because while she was in the shower some interesting detail would dart across her mind that must be pinned down before it eluded her memory. She kept a sketchpad beside her bed because occasionally she awoke with a sudden solution to a problem. By flashlight, so she wouldn't wake Suzy, she would make swift notations.

Vanessa also had to choose fabrics and trim. She was ever on the prowl for something fresh. She studied the use of buttons by such masters of fashion as Dior and Balenciaga and Schiaparelli. She reveled in the luxury of a price structure that allowed her to use the expensive fabrics she loved.

Frank vowed to understand every aspect of the women's apparel field. At Vanessa's urging he spent long hours in the New York Public Library, devouring back issues of *Vogue, Harper's Bazaar, Town & Country,* and *Women's Wear Daily.* From these he compiled a list of fine stores across the country that carried dresses similar to those Creations by Vanessa Conrad would be offering. Soon the stores on his list would receive the first in a series of mailings extolling the new creations of Vanessa Conrad. Drawing on his brief experience as a press agent, he sent out press releases to trade publications such as *Women's Wear Daily.* He and Vanessa reluctantly decided against consumer magazine advertising, knowing it would make painful inroads in their bankroll.

"Let's face it," he said in a rare pessimistic mood, "we'll have to fight like crazy for *any* editorial mention if we don't advertise."

"You'll come up with a promotion," Vanessa offered. "We're not ready yet for advertising, anyway."

"We're ready." Frank startled her with this admission. "We show our line in November. Advertising is set up months in advance."

They both knew that Bill Bartlett was opposed to heavy advertising. It was unlikely he'd come across with more money. Frank prepared to dig for angles that would bring Creations by Vanessa Conrad into the public eye. Vanessa triggered the first such promotion when she announced one evening that Pat had phoned the office to invite her to lunch.

"Pat's in town with her mother to shop for summer clothes."

"Where are you having lunch?" Frank asked, a speculative glint lighting his eyes.

"At Le Pavillon. Mrs. Owens adores their arrangements of roses." Mrs. Owens favored restaurants where half the tables were permanently reserved for such patrons as the Duke and Duchess of Windsor, Cole Porter and his wife, and Mainbocher—the couturier whose clients included many society beauties. "Thank God I have my black linen suit from Venice."

"Talk to Pat and her mother about doing a special preview of our collection for charity down in Houston early in October." Frank's voice crackled with excitement. "I can nab some column breaks on the strength of that. Maybe even photographs in one of the slicks."

"Frank, the collection won't be important enough to merit a benefit." Vanessa was uncomfortable at the prospect of trying to pressure Pat and Mrs. Owens.

"It'll be important enough if Pat is one of the models and her mother introduces each dress," he pointed out. "The wife and daughter of an important congressman."

"I'll talk to them," Vanessa promised. But she was ambivalent. Still, Frank's frequent exhortation ticker-taped across her mind: *Vanessa, in business you have to use any ammunition you can get your hands on!*

The following day at luncheon—her black linen suit and pearls striking against the cerise damask upholstery of Le Pavillon's chairs—Vanessa broached the subject of a benefit fashion show in Houston, to be sponsored by Madeline Owens. The models would be young Texas socialites. And remembering Frank's coaching, she hinted at a spread in a prestigious national magazine.

"Mother, it would be exciting for you to introduce an important new designer." Pat swiftly took up Vanessa's cause. "In another year or two Vanessa will probably be walking off with a Coty Award."

"In early October?" Mrs. Owens repeated Vanessa's suggestion, weighing the advantages. Fashion was an obsession with her — she prided herself on being a trend-setter in Texas, and enjoyed the mention of her name in society columns, or being photographed at important charity events. "October can be beautiful in Houston. The hurricane season is over, and the skies are a marvelous blue. Yes," she decided, "I think October would be fine. Most important, the Houston ladies will be back from their summer houses."

"You could set it up as a benefit for your Children's Aid project," Pat said. "You always do something in the fall."

"On one condition," Mrs. Owens said with a dazzling smile. "Vanessa, you must come out with the collection. Let me introduce you to Texas society."

"And stay with me," Pat glowed. "It's been years since we've spent time together. Vanessa, it'll be such fun!"

Bill Bartlett prided himself on dropping in on their skeleton operation when he was least expected. They had few employees — Frank was determined not to spend an unnecessary cent on help. When they were prepared to move into production, he would hire, he explained to Bill. "Right now all we need is Vanessa's samplehand standing by."

"In business you watch every penny," their partner approved. He appeared startled when Vanessa admitted to the prices of fabrics she was using, but Frank always jumped in to explain that the final costing was well within limits.

Vanessa was concentrating on eliminating designs, making final selections of fabrics, and launching into the making of samples. Frank was always on hand to estimate costs and forecast profits. He prepared and sent out a steady stream of mailings to prospective retail outlets and the press. And he and Madeline Owens were already working on the benefit fashion show to be held at a Houston country club.

In mid-July, when Vanessa and Frank began to hire operators, Bill took off for the Balsams in New Hampshire. He'd had enough of the New York summer, he declared. He seemed pleased that Vanessa and Frank were industriously pushing ahead, and some of the tension that hung over them evaporated with Bill's departure.

Vanessa's sole anxiety aside from the business was her alarm — shared by parents across the nation — that the summer would again bring polio to the young. Maria allowed Suzy to play with only two other little girls — the three nursemaids had a pact to isolate their young charges from exposure. But Vanessa's terror returned each time new statistics appeared in the newspapers.

On a July Sunday, when Vanessa prepared to go to the factory to press the finished samples, Maria insisted on coming along to help.

"I can watch Suzy at the same time," she pointed out. "She'd enjoy the shop." Trips to the zoo or the beach were out of bounds during the polio season. "And Frank can play ball with her."

Frank won Maria's heart forever that afternoon when he took off and returned with a complete Italian dinner, brought up by cab from Little Italy. After this

Sunday, Vanessa decreed, Maria would take the day off.

On a sweltering August Sunday Frank borrowed a car and drove them, along with a hastily prepared picnic basket, over the winding hills of Westchester County, where the temperature was less torrid. It was almost as though they were a family, Vanessa thought unwarily. The summers at the Lido with Eddie, their summer at the country house seemed so long ago now. Would there ever be a time when she ceased to miss Eddie?

At the end of August—optimistic about the collection and determined to ship in volume before the designs could be knocked off by competition—Frank decreed they would go into immediate production on a dozen choice numbers. He was arranging a whirlwind tour of select stores in September to present these samples for early ordering.

"The most expensive lines always show first," he pointed out. "Even so, we'll jump the gun. The benefit in Houston will be our public preview. We'll show in New York two weeks after Houston. We'll be prepared to fill orders early."

They moved into what Frank labeled their lunatic period. He was working with mounting frustration to publicize Vanessa Conrad. One would-be promotion after another had failed. Only an occasional press release to a trade magazine made it into print. Frank was convinced that consumer promotion was what Creations by Vanessa Conrad required. The benefit show in Houston would help. But they needed more to bring the firm prominence.

"It's not enough that you've designed like an angel," Frank harangued, pacing about the small area they'd set aside as their office. "Women out there have to *know* that a dress by Vanessa Conrad is something

344

special!"

Tina slid behind the wheel of the Jaguar Imperial Films had presented to her as a homecoming present. She was exhausted from the long day's shooting, but pleased with the way the picture was going. Anderson was a sadist of a director. He wasn't happy unless everybody on the set knew he was boss, she thought, her anger rising—but he was damn good. When she sat in the projection room and watched the rushes, she knew that.

Marty was great the way he'd made Nat tear up the old contract—*again*—and come up with a new one. Nobody on the lot was making more money than she was. It killed Nat to pay it, but he knew she was worth every fucking dollar. The new picture was going great. She was making tons of money again. So why was she feeling so down?

Part of it, she realized, was because Sal and Eva were so bitchy every time she called to say she'd love to see Adam. She was willing to pay their way out here, put them up at a classy hotel for a few days. Sal kept making excuses.

She was beat, too. Three pictures in a row. Up before six, sitting under the dryer at the studio by seven-thirty. A stinking lunch of soup, salad, and black coffee because she'd put on a dozen pounds during the suspension and it had been tough to take it off—and she meant to keep it off. Watching the rushes after shooting was done for the day, then off with the makeup and home. Dinner and studying the next day's lines until she fell into bed at ten-thirty. Sundays she slept all day, worked in the evening with the coach Felix had found for her. No social life. No wonder she was depressed. She'd told Marty she had to have eight weeks off after this picture.

She was fighting off yawns by the time she pulled up in the driveway of her sprawling new contemporary in Bel Air. It had a staggering mortgage, but she'd pay it off eventually. Traveling with Keith had given her a taste for luxurious surroundings. Keith had been a liberal education in a lot of ways.

She'd have to put the car in the garage herself. This was Angela and Justin's midweek evening off. Dinner would be waiting for her in the oven. They'd left lights on in the house because she hated walking into dark rooms.

Tina frowned as she entered the house. They'd left on the radio or TV in the den. She froze. *Who the hell was in the house?*

"Angela?" she called out tentatively.

"It's Keith!" his exuberant voice filtered in from the den. "What the hell took you so long?"

He stood in the entrance to the den, as casual as though they'd seen each other this morning instead of over nine months ago. The Riviera tan against his sun-bleached hair made a dramatic picture. He'd slimmed down, too, since the last time she'd seen him.

"How did you get in?" she demanded. Damn it, now she knew why she'd been so depressed. She'd missed Keith in her bed.

"Angela and Justin read all the gossip columns," he drawled, coming toward her. "I told them I couldn't stand being apart from you — that I flew over for a reunion."

"Is that why you're here?" she asked, immobile while his hands moved about her back, fondled her behind.

"Life lost some of its luster without you," he whispered, kissing her ear. "The book's finished except for

346

the final draft. That's a snap — another week or so of work. There's a movie sale already on the strength of the outline and a hundred pages. It's being kept quiet."

"So that's why you're in California," she challenged. "To talk to the movie people." He was doing all those little things that made her want him so damn much. She'd sworn she'd never sleep with him again.

"I brought a little present for you," he said, suddenly releasing her. "Want to see it?"

"Hmmm—" All she wanted at this moment was to be in bed with him.

Keith crossed to the chair where his jacket lay. He reached into a pocket and pulled out a box from Cartier. "I stayed in New York just long enough to pick this up." He flipped open the box and with an insouciant grin held it before her. A broad band set with diamonds and sapphires. "It's a wedding ring," he said. "I've got one here for me, too, though nothing so fancy." He thrust the box into her hand and returned to his jacket for a plain, heavy gold band.

"That was a fat movie sale," she guessed, eyeing the diamonds.

"When will this picture be wrapped up?" he asked.

"In about ten days." She'd be crazy to marry Keith. He was forever running all over the world. She had a career to keep going. He was either a monk stuck at the typewriter or partying twenty hours a day. His friends bored the shit out of her. "Maybe less," she shrugged, playing the cool role Keith — and movie audiences — expected of her.

"I have to fly back to the villa day after tomorrow. I can't take any more time off from the final draft if we're to go to Istanbul for our honeymoon."

"Istanbul?"

"Fascinating city. And while we're there, I'll do

347

some research for the next book. Tina, you'll love Istanbul."

"I haven't said I'd marry you," she reminded him.

"You will," he said smugly. "We can't exist without each other." He took the two rings and dropped them on a table. "Let's go into your bedroom, and I'll prove it."

Vanessa returned to the factory, tired and triumphant from her search for a special kind of button, to learn that Tina had called twice from California.

"She sounded all revved up about something," Frank reported. "She said she'd be on the set most of the day but would try you again when she had a break."

Vanessa glanced at her watch.

"It's only just past noon out there." She started at the jangle of the phone on Frank's desk. "Tina," she guessed, her face alight with anticipation. "Hello—"

"Vanessa, I've been dying to talk to you," Tina shouted. "Darling, I'm getting married again!"

"Keith?" Vanessa asked uneasily.

"Who else?" Tina laughed. "I know. I said all those awful things about him. But he's got his act together. And you know me—I need a guy in my bed on a regular basis."

"Tina, are you sure it's going to work?"

"We're both determined to *make* it work," Tina said. "Maybe Keith and I will even have a baby. Not right away. I have to start another picture in eight weeks."

"Where will you be married?" Vanessa asked, trying to hide her anxiety.

All at once Frank was waving his hand to attract her attention. He reached forward to scribble on a piece of paper. She leaned over to read it.

"I'll be flying to the villa at Cap d'Antibes in a week," Tina said. "We'll be married there by some public official. Keith's got it all worked out. No Catholic service," she laughed. "I'm a divorced woman. *Nobody* knows yet that we're getting married. I wanted you to be the first to hear."

"Tina—" Vanessa finished reading Frank's hasty scrawl. He hung over her with an air of having won the Irish Sweepstake. "Frank has some crazy idea that he thinks would be great for the business—"

"We talked a bit when I called before. He sounds nice. What's the crazy idea?"

"He's working like mad on publicity for us. I wrote you about flying down to Houston for that benefit show. Pat's mother has set up. Now he thinks I should design your wedding dress. He's sure he could get some column breaks with that. Even if you don't wear it—"

"Not wear a dress *you* designed?" Tina chortled. "Would you have time to do it, Vanessa?"

"I'll make time!" Vanessa could visualize Tina in her wedding dress—and all the press coverage. "The studio must have your measurements on file—"

"I'll call you later and give them to you. Do whatever you like—and bill me for it," Tina ordered. "I can afford to pay. I'm working again."

"It'll be a civil ceremony, right? You won't wear anything dressy. What color—"

"Vanessa, I've always trusted you. Make up anything you like as long as it isn't bridal white," she giggled. "I'll stop off in New York for a day so you can do the final fitting. I'll make the marriage a scoop for Louella Parsons," she decided. "We'll talk about the wedding on the Riviera, and who'll make my dress. I'll tell her I discovered this *marvelous* young designer when I was in Venice, and that she's in New York and about to launch her own company." She laughed. "After that let Frank do whatever he likes. Maybe he can set up an interview while I'm in New York. Darling, I'm dying to help. After all you've done for me."

"Tina, this is a terrific break for us. We'll talk about how Frank wants to handle it when you call tonight."

"How're Suzy and Maria?" Tina asked.

For a few minutes longer they talked about Suzy and Maria and Pat and CeeCee. Tina admitted to being angry at Sal because he seemed to want to keep her at a distance from Adam.

"Damn it, in the eyes of the world I'm Adam's aunt. That's a close enough relationship for me to want to see him. Why does Sal act as though he was scared I'd take Adam back? I can't," she said with unexpected bitterness. "He's been legally adopted."

Vanessa threw herself into designing a spectacular dress for Tina. The dress had to be finished in record time. A couture dress could consume a hundred hours of workman time, Vanessa reminded herself. She must design a dress that would be dramatic, yet could be custom-fitted and finished by the time Tina arrived in New York.

Along with Louella Parson's effusive announcement of the wedding—"a carefully kept secret until Tina told me just last night"—was her report of Tina's discovery of "this divine young designer from Venice." *Women's Wear Daily* picked up the news that Tina's dress was being made by Vanessa Conrad. Frank arranged for Tina to be interviewed by *Life* and photographed in the dress she'd wear when she married "dashing best-selling novelist Keith Edwards."

Twenty-four hours after arriving in New York Tina was on a plane bound for Paris. She had been photographed in the exquisite, classically simple gray silk, pleated from shoulder to hem to emphasize Tina's curvaceous slenderness. In days, women all over America would be seeing the dress—designed by Vanessa Conrad—that famous movie star Tina Gregory wore at her wedding to Keith Edwards.

Despite the frenzied schedule, Vanessa insisted on going with Tina to Idlewild in her chauffeured limousine. On the return trip she leaned back and relaxed for a moment against the velvet upholstery. She and Frank were gambling everything on this first collection. They would have nothing left over to try again if this first line did not succeed.

Only now did she realize how exhausted and tense she had been in these last weeks. Guilty, too, that she could steal so little time to be with Suzy. Thank God for Maria.

By the time the night-lighted skyline of Manhattan came into view, she was focused again on business. Frank was leaving in a few days for a fast tour of the choice stores. "Twenty-five of the top stores will carry Creations by Vanessa Conrad," he'd decided. "No more than twenty-five. We're building an image." When Frank returned, she would fly out to Houston for three days for the benefit fashion show.

The limousine pulled up by the curb on the dark, drab block of Seventh Avenue that housed Creations by Vanessa Conrad. The night air was humid and oppressive. Vanessa left the limousine and headed into the near deserted building.

The sewing machines were quiet. Only Frank remained in the factory. He emerged from their office at the sound of her heels clicking in the night silence.

"Vanessa, I made an appointment for you with a photographer on Monday at four," he said, his everpresent coffee mug in hand. "I explained this was a rush deal—"

"Why am I going to a photographer?" Vanessa

stared at him in bewilderment.

"You'll need press pictures," he explained. "I have water boiling. You want coffee?"

Vanessa nodded.

"Why will I need press pictures?" she repeated, following him into their office.

"Honey, after that spread in *Life* I'll be able to set up a whale of a lot of promotion," he said exuberantly. "I talked to Madeline Owens out in Houston. She's giving a dinner for you. She asked for photos to give to the *Houston Post*, the *Chronicle*, and the *Press*. She figures she has a new celebrity on her hands."

"Is the publicity break with Tina that important?" She knew it was, but she wanted to hear Frank say it.

"Vanessa, that spread in *Life* will put Creations by Vanessa Conrad on the map. It's the magic that'll open doors to every buying office in the country."

"Provided nothing goes wrong—" Vanessa was quoting Frank on the vagaries of planned promotions. "We *know* they'll run the spread on Tina. She's a major movie star. But we *don't* know that they won't cut me out of the photos. We don't know if they'll even mention who designed Tina's dress. Tina and Keith are big names. I'm nobody."

"Yet. Louella Parsons mentioned you," Frank pointed out in triumph. "There's a good chance that *Life* will do the same." He paused, his smile wry. "A fair chance."

Twenty-seven

Vanessa and Frank scrutinized the New York dailies for news of Tina's wedding. They found it mentioned briefly in the *Times* and more fully in other dailies. They read and reread each newspaper item. *Nobody* mentioned the designer of the dress Tina wore at the brief civil ceremony. Frank was furious. Vanessa tried to be philosophical.

Two mornings later Vanessa awoke with a start, her heart pounding. Then she remembered that this was the day *Life* magazine would hit the newsstands. How absurd that the future of Creations by Vanessa Conrad could depend on a spread in a magazine! But Sally Kirkland, fashion editor of *Life,* could make Vanessa Conrad known to millions. Fashion was a business where success could arrive almost overnight — and disappear just as fast.

As usual Maria good-humoredly scolded Vanessa for having only toast and coffee for breakfast.

"I want to hurry downtown to see if Frank's picked up a copy of *Life,*" Vanessa explained, impatient to be out of the apartment. "Suzy's still sleeping," she sighed. "Tell her I'll try to be home early tonight." It was barely 7:00 A.M., but she was sure Frank would be at the shop.

At the West Seventy-second Street IRT station she

353

joined the morning subway crush on the express. She left the train at Times Square and hurried up the stairs into the early morning sunlight, too excited to think clearly or check the newsstands. She was confident that Frank would be at the office with the copy of *Life*.

In their building lobby she waited with growing irritation for the elevator. She was alone in the drab lobby. Finally the elevator arrived, and on the way up she exchanged industry gossip with the elevator operator.

The door to the shop was locked. Vanessa fumbled in her purse for her key. Normally Frank was the first to arrive. He must be chasing around the newsstands for a copy of *Life*. She went into the office she shared with Frank and put up the usual pot of water on the hot plate so they could make coffee.

She stood at the window and gazed down at the sparsely populated street that within an hour would be jammed with delivery trucks, pushcarts piled high with clothing, racks of suits and coats and dresses being wheeled to various destinations. Why was Frank so late? Maybe they hadn't been mentioned in the layout.

When the whistle of the teakettle interrupted her thoughts, Vanessa made herself a mug of coffee and sat at her worktable to sip the hot black liquid. She heard the entrance door click. She sat motionless, her heart pounding. Frank charged into the office.

"Baby, we did it!" His smile was triumphant as he dropped the copy of *Life* — opened to the spread on Tina's marriage to Keith — before Vanessa. He had circled in ink a photograph of Tina and Vanessa, along with her brief identification as designer of the dress Tina wore. "First Louella Parsons, now *Life*. We're in business!"

Frank rushed downstairs to buy a dozen more copies. As the operators arrived, he pressed copies into their hands. They were entranced by the spread, awed that Tina Gregory and Vanessa were "best friends." The woman they worked for had her picture in *Life!*

Frank couldn't wait for his selling tour to begin. Every buyer on the list would regard Creations by Vanessa Conrad with respect. They had cracked *Life!*

"I tell you, Vanessa," he said later in the day when they were alone in the shop, "the time will come when designers will be as important as movie stars. Clothes won't be just items brought into being by some manufacturer. They'll be special because somebody they *know* has designed them. There'll be a link between designer and wearer. It'll be a kind of magic." He grinned. "And the lucky ones, celebrities in their own right, will be so rich! God, I'm glad you're young and beautiful!"

For an electric instant their eyes met, and Vanessa was unnerved by what she read in Frank's eyes — by her own reaction. *No.* She was just excited about the spread in *Life.* They both were. They were business partners and close friends.

Vanessa forced herself to shake off this unexpected feeling of attraction.

"With you running the show how can we fail? Frank, you're really pulling it off."

"We're pulling it off," he said gently. "You design, I sell."

The night before Frank was to leave on his tour, Vanessa and two operators stayed late to press the samples that would accompany him. Like Frank, Vanessa was grateful they had gambled on moving ahead into production without waiting for buyer reaction—and had avoided the fear of the "late delivery" crisis that haunted every manufacturer.

Each night, exhausted from trying to keep production moving without Frank's catalytic presence, Vanessa rushed home to await his phone call. Tonight she sat down to dinner and listened to Suzy's lively chatter and Maria's comments, but part of her listened only for the ring of the phone in the hall.

"That's Frank!" she interrupted at its shrill noise. "I'll be right back."

Again Frank was enthusiastic, though he conceded that a few of the more conservative stores had a "wait and see" attitude; but he was writing orders in satisfying volume.

"And no sweat about late deliveries," Frank crowed. "Not when we're showing this early." Vanessa was touched when Suzy began to ask for "Uncle Frank." He was so warm and sweet with her. The absence of a solid family worried Vanessa.

Maria prepared a festive meal for Frank's return. Suzy was allowed to stay up two hours past her bedtime. Over dinner, they all talked about Vanessa's upcoming trip to Houston. Suzy was intrigued that her mother would be traveling by plane, and Vanessa tried to hide her fears about flying.

To Vanessa's astonishment she enjoyed the flight to Houston. Once the plane was airborne, all was quiet—no sewing machines whirring in her ears, no phones, no city noises. She sat back in her seat and washed business from her mind for an hour. Then she pulled out her sketchpad and returned to work.

The press had not yet seen the spring collection, but already she was busy with the summer line, which Frank would take on the road to sell in December—when she must begin planning the fall/winter line again. And most manufacturers, she remembered guiltily, also offered a resort line with formal openings in August!

Pat was at the airport with her new sky-blue Ferrari—a birthday gift from her parents—to meet Vanessa. On the drive to her house in suburban River Oaks, Pat talked about the new international airport that would soon be constructed.

"Houston's growing like mad," Pat said with pride. "Property on Main Street is just skyrocketing. Of course, you know what Glenn McCarthy's fabulous Shamrock Hotel hys done for Houston."

Pat's gaiety had a hasterical edge to it. "What about you?" Vanessa asked. "Are you happy?"

Pat seemed startled.

"You mean because Paul won't be running for Congress this year?" Her smile was uneasy. Vanessa hadn't realized his plans had changed. "He was disappointed. We were both disappointed," Pat emphasized. "But Daddy was right, as always. This isn't the year for Paul to try for national office. In '52 for sure, Daddy says."

Pat steered their conversation to Suzy and CeeCee, and spoke wistfully of bringing their little girls together someday.

"I'd adore for them to be close friends," she confided sentimentally. "The way we are."

Vanessa was impressed by the beautiful, sprawling ranch house with its vast expanses of glass and exquisitely landscaped grounds. About one hundred yards to the left and slightly to the rear sat a tiny version of the main house. Vanessa knew that this was the cottage shared by CeeCee and the governess, a situation she found disconcerting.

"Paul's talking about putting in a swimming pool in the spring," Pat told her while they settled down on the side patio for tall, frosted glasses of iced tea. "I've

357

been fighting it. It makes me nervous to have a pool when CeeCee's so little—I'm terrified she'll sneak out of the cottage and fall in. Paul promises we'll have a six-foot-high fence around the pool area."

"Pat, you're so slim," Vanessa protested gently. "Beautiful, but you look as though a strong breeze would blow you away."

"The better to model your dresses," Pat laughed. "Mother had quite a time ferreting out local ladies in the model sizes. But everybody's so excited, especially after you designed Tina's dress. Mother is giving a dinner for you tomorrow night, and of course there's the benefit luncheon and fashion show at our country club tomorrow. All the local newspapers will cover it. Mother's scheduled a run-through tonight, if that's all right with you."

"That's great," Vanessa approved.

"We'll have dinner here at the house and drive right over afterward. Paul's in Austin at a session of the legislature, but he'll be home for Mother's dinner tomorrow night."

"When do I see CeeCee?" Vanessa asked.

"Here she comes, with Miss Martin." Pat smiled, love lighting her face. "Mother and Daddy and Paul all spoil her to death." Vanessa was relieved when CeeCee was taken back to the cottage by Miss Martin. She felt no warmth toward Pat's daughter, a small replica of her mother but petulant, demanding, and arrogant. After CeeCee left, Pat led her into the house and to the guest suite.

"What should I wear tonight?" Vanessa asked, inspecting the bedroom with admiration.

"Slacks and a light sweater will be fine," Pat said, dropping herself across the foot of the wide bed with a familiar gesture that swept Vanessa back through the years. "The days are still hot, but the evenings cool down."

Pat sighed. "Tina and you. Both so talented. I'm the only one with no gift at all."

"Your gift is in caring for Paul and CeeCee," Vanessa said tenderly. "And giving of yourself to charity work."

"I adore them both, of course," Pat said, "but Paul is away so much, and Miss Martin is in charge of CeeCee most of the time. But that'll change when we move to Washington," she said with determined cheerfulness. "Everybody's sure Paul will be elected. In Washington we'll entertain a lot. Paul will be home most nights. And once CeeCee is in kindergarten I don't see that we'll need a governess."

The charity luncheon-fashion show was a glittering success. Vanessa felt herself playing a role, but it was one she felt comfortable with. She knew, too, that in Houston her dresses would sell at elegant Sakowitz's. From comments at the luncheon—and later, at the dinner in her honor—she felt confident that the local society women would rush to buy dresses by Vanessa Conrad as soon as they were delivered.

Back in New York again Vanessa threw herself into preparations for the November showing. November was a pivotal month in fashion. Impressed by the orders that were coming in, Bill Bartlett listened thoughtfully while Frank explained that they must make a splash in introducing Creations by Vanessa Conrad to the press and buyers.

"We need something with more pizzazz than the usual showroom presentations, where the manufacturer sets up a few fresh flowers and a big glass candy jar." Frank's own enthusiasm was contagious. "We've got something hot, Bill!"

"You think that item in *Life* and all that newspaper coverage in Houston is bringing in the orders?" Bill's gaze was quizzical.

"What do you think?" Frank challenged and opened the folder with the tear sheets from *Life* and the various clippings from the Houston newspapers. "This goes a hell of a lot further than advertising."

"How do you think we ought to introduce the company?" Bill asked, intrigued.

"With class," Vanessa said softly, just as Frank had coached her. "Perhaps a press luncheon at the Hampshire House." Vanessa waited, faintly breathless, for his reaction.

"That won't be cheap," Bill hedged.

"Neither is the line we're offering," Frank chuckled.

"We'll do it," Bill capitulated, his faded blue eyes glinting in anticipation. "It's about time something I put money into was successful. Every dime I threw into the theater and films in the past three years has gone down the drain. Not that you need to cry for me," he conceded in high good humor. "I'm still solvent."

In an era when the press considered a buffet of cold sandwiches and coffee a special effort on the part of manufacturers, the elegant Hampshire House luncheon created a small uproar on Seventh Avenue. No one objected to the show's running beyond the normal one-hour presentation. The atmosphere was electric. And everything depended on the reaction of the press.

The press wrote glowingly about the collection, but adopted a "wait-and-see" attitude. Vanessa understood—she'd received a lot of attention because she'd designed Tina's wedding dress. She'd appeared on the fashion horizon from out of nowhere. One critic blatantly pointed out that "while Conrad's designs are exciting, she could be a 'flash in the pan.'" Her next collection—the formal presentation scheduled for immediately after New Year's—would be observed closely.

Because the factory had gone into production without waiting for orders, Frank was able to begin shipping four weeks ahead of the customary period in January. They waited anxiously for the reorders that would indicate how long they could continue production on the spring line. And they both rejoiced when it became apparent that the reorders would come in steadily. They'd complete shipments by early April, a normal span for the garment industry.

While Frank supervised their production line and the modest shipping department, Vanessa worked on designs for the fall collection. Frank meant to present these in a formal opening in April—again, four weeks ahead of the general trade. Vanessa sketched feverishly, revising and rejecting before finally venturing out to select the fabrics for their samples. She was under a great deal of pressure to surpass her first collection.

By early February Vanessa had settled in to begin making the samples. She was too busy to take time out for lunch with Bill Bartlett.

"You and I will have lunch, Bill." Frank slapped him on the back. "We can't take Vanessa away from getting the samples ready. I'll be hitting the trail again next month." Without the push of a *Life* spread, Vanessa remembered uneasily. *Was she a flash in the pan?*

Three hours after Frank had gone off for luncheon at the Colony with Bill, Vanessa looked up from her desk at the sound of his whistling in the corridor. When Frank whistled, Vanessa knew he was in high spirits.

"You had a great lunch," she guessed as he strode

into view. "Bill wasn't angry because I couldn't go out with you two, was he? I was waiting for a call from the fabrics place about—"

"Bill understood," he brushed her worries aside. "He's a self-made millionaire, he enjoys seeing us break our butts." He slid behind his own desk opposite hers. "We had a long talk about money. I told him it was time we went on normal salaries. Retroactive to February first."

"Did he argue?" Vanessa sat at attention.

"He couldn't." Frank pounded on the desk happily. "I showed him the figures. We're doing fine. It's time you and I started living like human beings."

"What are normal salaries?" She knew they would be high if Frank looked so smug.

"As of February first we're on the books for a salary of four hundred a week. That's *salary*," he reminded. "It has nothing to do with our share of the annual profits."

"Frank, he agreed?" Vanessa was breathless with excitement. Four hundred a week was a fortune.

"He couldn't argue with the fact that we're making high profits. It's time we saw something for all our sweat." His eyes narrowed in speculation. "I don't know whether to buy one of those new hardtop Dodges or a Cadillac." He grinned. "Miss Conrad, would you and Suzy like to help me break in whichever I decide to buy on a Sunday drive up to Westchester or out to Long Island?"

"Frank, I'd love it," she declared, throwing the material from her lap. For so long all she had known were fourteen-hour days of work. "And Suzy would too."

Frank encouraged Vanessa to look for a larger,

more comfortable apartment for her small family. In early February, on Suzy's third birthday, she discovered an apartment on West End Avenue that enchanted her. The bedrooms were not large, but there were three of them, and there was an eat-in kitchen, a small dining room, and a square, sunny living room.

"I know it's too expensive," she confided to Frank, "but I told the rental agent to draw up a lease."

"It's not too expensive," he insisted. "You can afford it now."

"If the fall collection sells well," she stipulated.

On March 1, with Maria handling the move, Vanessa settled herself into the new apartment. She managed to shop for the furniture they absolutely had to have; later she would furnish it properly — providing the new collection went well and money continued to pour into Creations by Vanessa Conrad.

Suzy was enthralled and alarmed by the luxury of having her own bedroom. Frank bought her a huge teddy bear "to share the bedroom" with her, and once again Vanessa was grateful for his presence in their lives. He was Suzy's devoted "uncle."

Frank's swift tour of "their stores" was accomplished before the scheduled press preview in New York. Despite Vanessa's agonizing, the collection was well received by their buyers and again by the press. Frank was working to extend their elite list of stores to thirty. He decided this was still small enough a group to retain their image. And he talked about looking for larger quarters.

Frank was frustrated that he was too embroiled in the production line to develop important promotions.

"We're different from other manufacturers," he said. "We can push our designer instead of just the firm. We know you won't charge off to work for somebody else. And you're promotable! You're young, movie-star beautiful — you lend a personal touch that women like. That's the way of the future, Vanessa. I'm messing up on promotion."

"We're doing well." Vanessa refused to be upset. "We're selling regularly to thirty major outlets. We've almost doubled the line."

"It's important to business to build Vanessa Conrad into an important personality. I can see Creations by Vanessa Conrad showing a million a year in profits. What we're doing now is penny-ante stuff."

Word spread from the Paris winter collection that a new, young "discovery" named Hubert de Givenchy had just opened his own couture house after an apprenticeship with Schiaparelli. Vanessa read about him in the American fashion magazines as well as in *Paris-Match* and *Femina,* reminded that she was involved in ready-to-wear when she yearned for haute couture. But Seventh Avenue was the way of the future, she told herself. Frank kept saying that Paris couture belonged to the prewar world.

The months sped by as they moved from one collection to another, each receiving praise from the fashion press, each selling well to their cluster of elite stores. Vanessa scrounged for time to furnish the new apartment, a symbol of her success and a constant delight to both Maria and herself.

In June Vanessa tried to concentrate on designing their first resort collection. She was distracted by the terror of the polio epidemics that had affected over 60,000 children in the last two years.

Pat phoned from Texas to talk about how to safeguard their two little girls.

"You know how bad it was in Texas last year," Pat said, her voice unsteady. "There's no way to protect the children except to keep them in isolation. We'll stay at the ranch all summer. I told Paul not to expect me to campaign during the polio months. CeeCee will be terribly unhappy cooped up at the ranch, but she'll have TV, and the ranch is air-conditioned. I just feel so helpless."

"I'd thought about a cottage on Fire Island," Vanessa admitted. " I considered sending Suzy and Maria out there for the summer, and running out myself for the weekends. But you're right—the only way to handle the situation is to keep them isolated." Playgrounds, swimming pools, movie theaters would be near-deserted during the summer.

"Here in Houston the doctors have completed some major experiment. If it proves effective against the polio virus, then we won't face another summer like this. Vanessa, it's awful to think what could happen in the next ten weeks." Pat's voice dropped to a whisper. "I think of all those children in iron lungs. Wearing heavy braces. Or dying. Mother keeps reminding me that fifty out of every hundred children who catch polio recover completely and that only thirty have slight aftereffects. But I can't forget what happened here last summer. I spent time as a volunteer at the hospital, when the children were all out of the contagious stage. The children's game room crammed with iron lungs!"

"You'll be there on the ranch with CeeCee," Vanessa comforted. "She'll be away from contact with anybody. And we all might be scared for nothing. There may be only a few cases this summer."

"Vanessa, would you like to send Suzy and Maria out to the ranch for the summer?"

"It's a sweet thought, Pat; but I'd die if I was separated from Suzy for all that time," Vanessa confessed. "CeeCee and Suzy will be all right. They may be restless and bored and rebellious," she laughed, "but they'll be safe."

Vanessa had an air-conditioner installed in the living room and put huge window fans in all the other rooms of the apartment. Maria discovered that the roof could be a private playground for Suzy and the two little girls with whom she was allowed to play. On steamy Sundays Frank drove Vanessa and Suzy around Westchester County or on lightly traveled roads on Long Island to provide Suzy with some diversion.

Newspapers were filled with ugly statistics. Polio was spreading across the country again, and doctors were predicting the worst epidemic the country had ever seen. Vanessa was shaken when one of their operators, a woman in her thirties, was stricken by polio.

Frank made trips to FAO Schwartz each week to find some new toy that might appease Suzy in her near quarantine. Vanessa was having problems with the resort collection, which, though a July deadline had originally been set, would not be shown until August. Frank took an apartment two floors below theirs, and most nights he came upstairs to the apartment for dinner and to try and coax Suzy into a happier mood. On Monday nights Suzy was allowed to stay up and watch "I Love Lucy," the high point in her week.

After Suzy fell asleep, Frank usually insisted they go for a stroll along the Hudson, where many apartment dwellers sought relief from the summer heat. But on the night of July 11 they stayed glued to the TV set to watch the Republican National Convention nominate General Dwight D. Eisenhower for the presidency and Senator Richard M. Nixon for the vice-presidency. Like many Democrats, Frank was convinced no one could beat Ike in the coming election, even when, on July 26, the Democratic National Convention nominated the brilliant Governor Adlai Stevenson.

With the approach of the Labor Day weekend Vanessa felt a surge of relief. Soon the hot weather would let up, and the cases of polio would decrease. Over dinner Saturday night — while Suzy, who had been allowed to stay up late, showed only vague interest in her ice cream — Frank suggested they drive up through Westchester on Sunday for a picnic. While it might sound like a day of leisure, Vanessa knew that the conversation would inevitably become a working session. She and Frank both lived the business most of their waking hours.

"We'll leave early," he decided. "Make a whole day of it." He dropped to his haunches before Suzy. "You'd like that, wouldn't you, pussycat?"

"I want to go to sleep," Suzy said querulously. "Want Teddy?"

Maria lifted Suzy in her arms to carry her off to bed.

"A kiss for Mommy?" Vanessa held up her face and Suzy deposited a sticky, uninterested kiss. Vanessa frowned. "Maria, doesn't she feel a little warm to you?"

"Everybody in New York feels a little warm," Maria teased, but she reached to touch Suzy's forehead. "No temperature," she decided. "She may be coming down with a cold. Laurie didn't come over to play today. Pearl phoned to say she had a cold."

"Did Laurie's mother call the doctor?" Vanessa fought against her panic. Polio could start with a cold.

"Right away," Maria answered quickly. "Dr. Mixon said it was just a cold." Dr. Mixon was the woman pediatrician who cared for Suzy. "She said just to keep Laurie away from the other children until the cold was gone."

"I know we're all paranoid," Vanessa told Frank, trying to lighten the mood. "But let me take Suzy's temperature, anyway."

Suzy's temperature was normal, but Vanessa left her own bedroom to look in on her several times during the night. Suzy was restless; but that could be the cold, Vanessa told herself. When Vanessa hurried again into Suzy's bedroom at seven the next morning, Maria was hovering anxiously over the bed.

"She's running a fever." Maria tried not to show her alarm.

"How much?" Vanessa dropped a hand to Suzy's forehead.

"A hundred and two," Maria told her. "I'll wash her down with cold water."

"Stay with her." Suzy was moving restlessly about in her bed, one hand hitting at the guardrail. "I'm calling Dr. Mixon."

Within forty minutes Dr. Mixon was leaning over Suzy, her face impassive as she examined the tiny form.

"Now don't panic, Vanessa," Dr. Mixon said gently. "I don't know that it's anything more than a cold, but considering the symptoms we have to check her out. I can't do it here. I want her in the hospital."

"My God." Vanessa's face was ashen.

"Even if it is polio," Dr. Mixon continued, "it'll more than likely be a light case. In three or four days she should be fine."

Vanessa started at the sound of the doorbell.

"Maria, that's Frank—" She gestured for Maria to go to the door.

"Vanessa, you mustn't think the worst," Dr. Mixon chided. "Bring her into the hospital right away. We'll know within twenty-four hours."

"To what hospital do you want us to take Suzy?" Frank stood in the doorway of the bedroom. "My car's right downstairs."

Frank took charge, refusing to give in to any real alarm. He carried Suzy down to the car and deposited her in Vanessa's lap while Maria carried Suzy's teddy bear. At the hospital he arranged for Suzy's admission. Vanessa, white and shaken, clung to Maria.

The three were in and out of the hospital the entire Labor Day weekend. Late on Monday afternoon Dr. Mixon joined them in the waiting room to confirm Vanessa's worst fears: Suzy had polio.

"Her temperature's rising. But that's the course of the disease. Remember, Vanessa," she offered with assurance, "more than 80 percent of polio patients come out of it within three or four days."

"Vanessa, we have to sit this out," Frank said when Dr. Mixon left them alone. "She's going to be all right. I know she is."

"It's my fault!" Vanessa reproached herself. "I shouldn't have brought her to New York. This wouldn't have happened—"

"That's not true," Frank objected, his voice strong. "It is not your fault. It's not something you could have prevented."

"I'm going to church," Maria said softly. "I'll pray for our baby."

Twenty-eight

Vanessa refused to leave the hospital. She dozed sitting on the waiting room sofa, and each morning Maria brought her food from home, and a change of clothing. Frank ran between the shop and the hospital.

On Suzy's sixth day in the hospital Dr. Mixon told Vanessa and Frank that Suzy's temperature was back to normal. She showed no signs of paralysis.

"She'll be all right?" Vanessa stammered.

"She'll be fine. You can take her home tomorrow."

Trembling in relief, Vanessa cried in Frank's arms.

"Mommy, why are you crying?" Suzy asked curiously, when they went in to see her.

"Because I'm so happy, darling." She accepted the handkerchief Frank offered, brought it to her eyes. "You're coming home tomorrow."

"Can I have ice cream?" Suzy's face lighted.

"As soon as Dr. Mixon says it's okay," she promised. *Suzy was all right.*

Vanessa and Frank remained beside Suzy's bed until she fell asleep for the night. Then Frank insisted they go out for dinner to celebrate.

"I should go to the shop." She hadn't been there since Saturday. "Frank, I haven't even started the spring line."

"So you're starting at the same time as everybody else," he laughed. "Anyhow, you work faster than anybody in the business; you'll catch up. Let's go out for dinner."

"I look a mess."

"You look beautiful." For a moment his eyes were unguarded. Vanessa dropped her own in confusion. "We'll go to the Stage Delicatessen," he decided. "Great food and you don't have to look like a page out of *Vogue.*"

Over plates laden with succulent brisket of beef and vegetables they discussed the production schedule for the resort line. While they lingered over the flaky hot apple strudel, Frank talked about Vanessa's going out at the end of the month with a "trunk show"—a showing of the fall line by live models in specially selected stores.

"With the designer there the showing takes on special importance," Frank pointed out.

Vanessa nodded, but part of her was far away from the business. Frank had been wonderful these last few days. It was almost as though he was Suzy's father. The nurses at the hospital thought he was. From the first moment—when Dr. Mixon had said that Suzy had to be in the hospital—he'd been beside her.

"You're tired." He interrupted her thoughts. "I'll take you home. Get a good night's sleep. Tomorrow you'll go to the shop."

"Frank, thanks for being around when I needed you," she said softly.

"I'll always be around for you and Suzy," he promised, his eyes warm. He signaled for the waiter to bring their check.

In the taxi home Frank brought her up to date on industry gossip.

"You know that guy Galanos who was working in

371

California at some boutique?" Frank said as they pulled up before their apartment house. "He popped into New York with a collection of nine dresses, and the word is he walked off with a fortune in orders. Everything is madly expensive, I hear."

In the lobby of their building they reassured the elevator man, who was concerned about Suzy.

"Ah, I knew she'd be all right." His ruddy face beamed. "My wife and I were praying for her."

"Thank you, George."

"Have a glass of wine and go straight to bed," Frank told Vanessa when the elevator began its ascent. "That'll make you sleep."

"I'll settle for tea. Maria finished up the wine in the last batch of spaghetti sauce."

"No tea," Frank said firmly. "You don't need caffeine. Stop off at my apartment long enough for me to fix you a rum Collins—I've still got that bottle of rum Bill brought up from the Islands. That'll guarantee you a good night's sleep."

"I may fall asleep on the way up to my floor," Vanessa warned George when he pulled to a stop on Frank's floor. "If I do, be sure to wake me up."

"You can look at those figures from the West Coast stores while I fix your drink," Frank said, reaching for his apartment key. "I stuffed them into my jacket so I could look at them more carefully before I go to sleep."

She had been in Frank's apartment no more than three or four times, Vanessa thought, walking into the foyer. Usually he came up to her apartment. The living room was furnished with almost spartan simplicity, yet it seemed right for Frank. The shop claimed most of his waking hours.

"Take a look at these." He pulled out the sheaf of papers from his jacket pocket and handed them to her.

"Oh, you know those two dresses you liked so much in that back issue of *Vogue?* I found out who at Anna Miller designed them. A guy named Bill Blass. He comes from Fort Wayne, Indiana. Don't any American designers come from New York?"

"Hmmm." Vanessa pretended to concentrate while she settled herself on the brown tweed sofa. It startled her that she felt so happy when only a few hours ago she had been in such anguish. Suzy was all right. In the morning she would come home. "Claire McCardell comes from Maryland. Bonnie Cashin from California. Mainbocher from Chicago. Norell from Indiana. But somebody from New York is working on it, I'm sure."

She leaned back against the sofa and inspected the sales figures from their West Coast stores. She understood Frank's smugness about the state of the business. They were surpassing all their expectations for this year.

"This will cool you off and then put you to sleep," Frank promised, approaching the sofa with a tall, frosted glass. "Tomorrow you'll be back in the rat race."

"This week has been a nightmare." She sipped experimentally at the rum Collins.

"It's all over," Frank comforted her. "Suzy's fine."

"I haven't been to the shop in days." she apologized and smiled. "This is a great rum Collins."

"I'm a scotch-on-the-rocks person myself," he said, relaxing into the sofa. "But I like mixing these fancy drinks. You know, in case somebody from Seventh Avenue pops in for conversation."

Was that somebody a woman? Why should that disturb her? Frank was still a young man, and most women would consider him good-looking. He had a right to a life apart from the business. Though there wasn't much time for it.

Their talk was casual, yet Vanessa was conscious of Frank beside her on the couch. She saw the question in his eyes. He dropped his arm about her shoulders.

"You're still tense," he scolded, his strong fingers massaging her neck.

"It's been an awful week." Her voice was unsteady.

The atmosphere in the living room was suddenly heavy with emotion. Frank took the drink from her hand and set it down on the leather-tooled coffee table. His arms pulled her to him. His mouth sought hers. She had no will, she thought, and abandoned herself to the glorious, frightening excitement of his kiss.

She was disappointed, her eyes reproachful, when he drew his mouth from hers.

"Let's go into the bedroom," he said softly.

Feeling slightly unreal, Vanessa allowed Frank to lead her into the dark bedroom. Momentarily she considered running away, but then she was in his arms again, his mouth was on hers, and her body was responding to the hungry sweep of his hands. *She had been alone so long.*

She stood with her eyes closed, savoring every touch of his hands as he undressed her, his mouth at her throat, her breasts. Then he lifted her from her feet and deposited her on the bed. She waited with impatience until he lay on the bed beside her.

"I knew that first day, when you dropped your portfolio in the cafeteria, that you belonged forever in my life," he whispered, moving his leg across hers, his hand caressing her breasts.

"Frank, I never meant for this to happen," she confessed.

"It had to happen," he said and lifted himself above her.

Her hands gripped his strong back encouragingly as he lowered himself between her thighs. Slowly he teased her until she bit her lip to keep back the protest that welled in her throat.

"I love you, Vanessa," he whispered as he thrust himself within her.

From a far distance she heard the sounds that escaped her throat as they rocked together in passion. She heard Frank's grunt of satisfaction and her own cry. Afterward, they clung together, reluctant to let go of these moments. And soon he began to stir again within her.

Vanessa dozed in Frank's arms. She awoke with a start, guilty at the lateness of the hour.

"Frank," she said softly. "Frank —"

With a frown of protest he opened his eyes.

"I have to get up to the apartment," she said. "Maria will worry."

"Call and tell her you're staying here." He caressed her cheek.

"Not just like that," she protested, all at once self-conscious.

"Vanessa —" He reached for her hand. "Any time you're ready to take on a second husband, I'm first in line."

"I can't think about that." She must be honest with Frank. "Not yet." It seemed disloyal to Eddie's memory to feel this way about another man. But deep inside her she realized that she could love again.

"I'll be around." Frank's smile was reassuring. He understood that Eddie was still part of her life, but he didn't know that Eddie had never been her husband.

"We belong together, Vanessa."

"I'm confused," she confessed. "Give me time,

Frank."

"All the time in the world." He tossed aside the sheet. "Let's have coffee before you go upstairs."

They sat over mugs of Frank's strong black coffee and talked about the new spring line. Vanessa knew that he was deliberately stalling her return to her apartment.

"Seventh Avenue's changing fast," Frank said with a faraway glint in his eyes while he refilled her mug and his own. "It's earning a hell of a lot of respect in the eyes of the world. Look at how new Seventh Avenue designers are making themselves heard. Anne Fogarty, Donald Brooks, Ceil Chapman—and Vanessa Conrad," he concluded with a flourish.

"But it's time to work with more extravagant fabrics." Vanessa's eyes burned with zeal. "And to create independently of Paris."

"Do you want to go to Paris in November to see the collections?" Frank asked.

"Frank, how could I take the time?" she laughed. Some Seventh Avenue designers did make time for Paris. In addition to their own four collections a year they traveled twice a year to see the French collections. Some even made up an additional extra collection—using what they had seen in Paris—on their return.

"It's easy," Frank joshed. "You fly nonstop to Paris in a comfortable sleeper aboard a Constellation."

"No time." Vanessa was firm. "And I don't want to design carbon copies of Dior or—"

"Vanessa, do you realize that Dior started off just six years ago this month with three workrooms, and now he has five buildings with twenty-eight workrooms and over a thousand employees?"

"He's a marvelous designer," Vanessa said with respect.

"In five years," Frank predicted, bristling with enthusiasm, "we'll be one of the top names on Seventh Avenue. You'll be the darling of the fashion editors." Already she was winning praise from Eugenia Sheppard and Sally Kirkland and Diana Vreeland. "But we have to move faster. To the point where we don't die in one season if one collection doesn't make it big. Remember what you told me about Jacques Fath and how he used promotion?"

"Yes—"

"I'm too tied up with the business angles." Once samples were made and approved by Vanessa, he was responsible for seeing that the line was sold, manufactured, and shipped. He stressed the importance of leaving her free to create. "We need a public relations woman to work with us and keep your name before the public. Look what Eleanor Lambert is doing for her people!"

"Eleanor Lambert takes on only high-budget clients," Vanessa reminded him. They were making money, but they weren't up with Eleanor Lambert manufacturers. Their finances were still tight. And Frank was talking again about expanding their quarters. "I'd better run, Frank—" She rose to her feet. "Tomorrow I want to be at the shop early."

In the living room of CeeCee's cottage Pat sought futilely to soothe the outraged governess while CeeCee lay screaming on the white four-poster bed in her ultra-feminine bedroom. CeeCee was furious because her father had not appeared as promised to take her to the county fair. She was too young to understand, Pat told herself, that Paul was in the last three weeks of his campaign for Congress, and that this took precedence over everything.

377

"She bit me!" The governess's voice was shrill in repetition. "Not once but three times! Mrs. Roberts, that child is impossible!"

"I understand she's terribly spoiled," Pat said in apology. How many governesses had they lost in the last five and a half years? "But she'll change if you're firm with her. We'll work together," she coaxed. "And as of this week your salary will be increased by twenty-five dollars a week." She saw the instant respect this earned. "But she mustn't be spanked," Pat insisted. She recoiled from any violence. "Reason with her, and if that fails, punish her by denying her desserts for a week or not allowing her to go to a special birthday party or whatever."

"I'll try it for another six weeks," the governess said, capitulating. "But CeeCee is a handful."

Pat left the cottage, CeeCee's screams following her into the balmy mid-October afternoon. At least the hot weather was over, she consoled herself while she walked to the main house. No more worries about polio. She still grew cold at the memory of what Vanessa and Suzy had been through. Thank God it had been mild.

At the house she settled herself in the library to write several thank you notes to hostesses who had entertained her while she had been on the campaign trail this month. She loathed speaking at political teas, but both Paul and Daddy insisted they were important.

With the notes written, she watched television for a while. She'd have dinner on a tray in the master bedroom suite. Wistfully she remembered Dottie's dinner party tonight. She'd had to reject the invitation because Paul's schedule was unpredictable this close to the election. It wouldn't look right for her to show up at a dinner party alone.

She had dinner and settled down to read Steinbeck's new novel, *East of Eden*. Paul said he'd be home from Dallas tonight, but there was no telling when he'd show up. She hoped he'd stay in Dallas for the night. She wished she had the courage to divorce him. She could hear Daddy carrying on if she even mentioned it: *"My God, Pat, have you lost your mind? You can't disgrace the family like that. You can't ruin Paul's career. No divorced man will ever make it to the White House!"*

Was that one of the reasons Daddy had been so against Stevenson at the Democratic Convention? Because he was a divorced man? Or was he scared to death of Stevenson's liberal politics? Daddy surprised her sometimes with his predictions of things to come. He'd shocked Mother to death when he said the day wasn't too far off when Negroes would sit beside whites in schools and on trains and in restaurants. Even in the South. Well, why not? Pat thought.

She was in bed and engrossed in *East of Eden* when she heard Paul's voice in the hall.

"Zeke?" he called in irritation. "Zeke?"

Pat turned to look at the Cartier clock on the marble mantelpiece. It was past eleven—Paul knew Zeke would be asleep in the servants' cottage by now.

"The goddamn lazy bastards!" Paul strode across their private sitting room and into the bedroom. "We ought to fire the lot of them."

"Are you hungry?" Pat tried to be solicitous.

"Sure I'm hungry. I drove all the way down from Dallas without even stopping for dinner." He pulled off his jacket and threw it across a chair. "Couldn't Zeke keep his lazy hide vertical long enough to bring me dinner?"

"I'll get you a tray. Amelia put almost a whole roast beef in the refrigerator, and there's salad." She got out of the bed and reached for her blue satin robe. "How was the meeting in Dallas?"

"How do you think it was?" His face was flushed in anger. "We're still fighting for votes. Nothing's going right."

"Did you take Laura with you to the meeting?" she asked casually. Laura was Paul's "special assistant." But Pat suspected that Paul was sleeping with her.

Paul stared at her.

"What kind of question is that? Of course Laura went with me. She's terrific. She can wrap most of those old bastards around her little finger." Unexpectedly he grinned. "If she wasn't a woman, she'd be running for Congress."

"Would you like coffee with your dinner?"

"I'd like a drink," he told her. His tone was menacing—he knew she hated it when he drank.

"All right, I'll bring you a drink with your tray." She headed toward the door.

"Don't be such a fucking martyr!" he lashed out at her. "You think you're too damn good for me." His hand smashed against her face.

"Paul, no—" she sobbed, knowing what would follow.

"And what was that crack about Laura?" He clutched at her shoulders for a moment before he sent her crashing to the floor with a blow to her jaw. "You goddamn little whore. You were sleeping all over Texas before your father pushed you on me!"

"Paul, no," she whimpered and cried out in pain when he kicked her in the ribs. This was the last time, she vowed. Tomorrow she'd pack up and leave this house. She would divorce him. "Paul, no. Please, no."

It was over in a few moments. Paul hovered over her, pale and shaking.

"Pat, baby," he whispered. "I didn't mean it. You ask me such crazy questions." He reached to help her to her feet and pulled her close. "Baby, I didn't mean it," he murmured, rocking her in his arms. "You just get me going sometimes. But it'll be all right now. I'll make it up to you."

He lifted her in his arms and carried her to the bed. She forgot about the pain of the beating while Paul made passionate love to her. It was her fault that Paul hit her. She provoked him.

Vanessa was excited when the word came through that Paul had been elected to Congress. She phoned Pat to congratulate her.

"I'll be in Washington," Pat said with pleasure. "Daddy's already looking for a house for us. I'll be able to come up to New York often. We'll see a lot of each other."

They talked about Tina, who appeared to be commuting between Hollywood and the Riviera.

"How's this marriage?" Pat asked seriously.

"Not good. Tina says she's trying like mad to make this one work, but Keith and she have awful fights. He's trying to make her over into an intellectual," Vanessa said ruefully. "He's shoving Huxley and Fitzgerald and Shaw down her throat."

"I had a postcard from her months ago. She was in Florence for a few days and all excited about a new Italian designer who was working for Fabiano there. She thought Mother would want to see his clothes."

"She wrote me about him. Count Ferdinando Sarmi. He's in New York now and doing dresses for Elizabeth Arden. Virginia Pope raved about him in a review in the *New York Times*." Wistfulness crept into Vanessa's voice. "God, I'd love to do clothes that included custom fittings."

Vanessa was not surprised when Tina called her on

New Year's Eve, just as she and Frank were about to leave for a party given by Bill Bartlett at his Manhattan penthouse pied-à-terre, to say she was in Reno to divorce Keith.

"I'm through with marriage, Vanessa. All I give a damn about now is the career. And Adam," she added. "Even if Sal and Eva are such creeps about my seeing him. Four times a year, they've decided. Isn't that a bitch?"

Early in 1953 Vanessa and Frank agreed to gamble on hiring a publicist. While retail sales were high and the stores smug about the success of the line, Frank felt they were not moving ahead fast enough. He envisioned a fashion empire.

Vanessa interviewed half a dozen prospective publicists. Almost immediately she was convinced that Phyllis Hirsch—a slender, vivacious brunette in business for herself for only eight months—was right for Creations by Vanessa Conrad. Phyllis was young, aggressive, and innovative. She had gone straight into publicity from Hunter College three years earlier and had impressive contacts. Vanessa arranged for her to meet with Frank, who would make the final decision.

"I like that broad," Frank said when he had spent almost an hour with Phyllis. "She's bright, she's attractive, and she'll work cheap."

"Did you hire her?" Vanessa asked.

"We'll tell her over lunch tomorrow. She's taking us to the Stork."

Vanessa lifted an eyebrow.

"You said she works cheap?"

"It's part of her investment," Frank grinned. "She wants to show us she moves in the right circles."

"Is that a dress from your collection?" Phyllis asked

Vanessa in the Cub Room of the Stork.

"Yes," Vanessa told her with a slight smile.

"Good. I can't understand these Seventh Avenue designers who wear haute couture from Paris or something madly expensive from Hattie Carnegie. It's like saying their own dresses aren't smart enough."

"Except for a Dior suit that's over five years old, I always wear my own designs," Vanessa assured Phyllis.

They talked about other young designers on the Seventh Avenue scene, with Phyllis reporting that Bill Blass, who designed for Anna Miller, frequently showed up at the Stork, the Colony, and El Morocco.

"It's important for a designer bringing out an expensive line to be seen where the rich people dine," Phyllis summed up briskly. "I'll be able to get space in the society columns. You're a strikingly attractive couple," she approved, her eyes speculative. "I hope you don't mind if I hint at romance?"

"I don't mind at all." Frank's eyes settled on Vanessa, making no secret of his feelings for her. "Any time Vanessa gives the word, I'm running to Tiffany for wedding bands."

Vanessa looked down at the table. She had been alone for almost four years. What she had shared with Eddie seemed like a fairy tale now. She and Frank were reality.

"When would be a smart time for us to be married?" Vanessa asked Phyllis as she reached for Frank's hand. "What about just after the formal opening of our fall/winter collection in April?"

"Great!" Phyllis was radiant. "I'll leak your 'secret marriage plans' a few days before the opening. Then, when the fall/winter collection has been launched, you get married and dash off for your honeymoon. Somewhere exotic," she pleaded.

"We'll work on it," Frank promised. "As exotic as we can handle within two weeks." He brought Vanessa's hand to his lips.

"I think it's wonderful," Phyllis said, sighing with sentimentality. "Now the two of you look very romantic," she ordered, knowing that neither had heard a word she said. "I'm going to table hop across the room. Maybe I can stir up an item in Cholly Knickerbocker's column."

Twenty-nine

Suzy eagerly embraced Frank as her new "daddy." And Maria was ecstatic about the approaching marriage.

Vanessa geared herself to tell Frank that Eddie had never been her husband. She had to make him understand what had stood in their way.

She delayed for ten days, all the while terrified that Frank might decide against the marriage. She waited until they were alone in the shop late on a balmy evening to explain in a faltering voice the situation that had prevented her and Eddie from marrying.

"You poor little kid," Frank said and reached for her hand. Tears welled in her eyes. "What a rotten experience for you."

"I didn't worry so much for myself," she told him. "I worried for Suzy."

"As soon as we're married, I'd like to adopt her legally. She's like my own kid already," he said. "When she can't get her way with you, who does she turn to but me?"

"Oh, Frank, you're so good for me."

"Let's stop off at my place on the way home." His face betrayed his passion. "Thank God in a few weeks we won't have to play these games."

In addition to pushing ahead on the fall/winter collection — with sober awareness that Creations by Vanessa Conrad was only as good as its current collection — Vanessa and Frank were involved with wedding plans and honeymoon arrangements. Vanessa gave in to Frank's plea that they move into the nine-room apartment available in their building in October. Until they moved, they would keep Frank's apartment for what he referred to as their "more private hours."

He insisted it was time for them to entertain. Phyllis backed him up in this.

"Jacques Fath throws about twenty big cocktail parties a year, plus several smaller parties," Phyllis pointed out. "That gets him invited into the most fashionable homes in France. He's a terrific designer, of course — but his celebrity status has made him a household word not only in Europe but in America."

"Look how successful he's been with his special American collections because of that celebrity status," Frank added enthusiastically.

"We can do what Fath has done." Phyllis exuded confidence.

Frank's plans for their wedding in the Pennsylvania town where he had been born and raised were running into snags.

"What the hell's the matter with my sisters?" he raged. "Their only brother is finally getting married — and they've been on my tail about this for years — but they can't find a date that fits in with their schedules. The rabbi will juggle. My doting sisters won't," he jeered.

"Then we'll be married here in New York," Vanessa offered. Frank had been their "darling baby brother" only before their own lives were set. Nor were they particularly pleased, she suspected, that he was marrying a widow with a little girl.

"At City Hall," Frank decreed. "That'll piss them off."

Phyllis was upset that Vanessa and Frank's wedding announcement was lost in the flurry of fashion news about the fall/winter collections. Two other firms had latched on to Frank's idea of showing early. And as with every collection, Vanessa was fearful that this one would be a failure. But the critics loved it.

Vanessa and Frank were scheduled to be married at City Hall on Friday morning, with Tina and Pat as their witnesses. Also with them would be Suzy, Maria, and Phyllis. Tina would give a luncheon for the wedding party at Le Pavillon. Afterward, Vanessa and Frank would fly to Key West, where they would stay for five days, and then head for Nassau in the British West Indies for ten days. Phyllis had coaxed them to choose Nassau, vacation grounds for such couples as the Irving Berlins, the Leland Haywards, and the William Paleys, as well as such socialites as Prince and Princess Radziwill. It was the tail end of the season, but Important People would still be there.

Tina flew in from Hollywood the day before the ceremony so that Vanessa could see to the final fitting of the dress she'd designed especially for her to wear. The workers in the shop were wide-eyed with excitement at Tina's arrival. Pat, who planned to wear a Vanessa Conrad bought at Sakowitz's in Dallas, phoned the night before the wedding.

"Vanessa, I feel awful," Pat said. "I took a spill when I was riding this morning. I fractured my collarbone. I won't be able to make it."

387

Nervous that Tina would be late for the ceremony, Vanessa phoned her at the Pierre at 8:00 A.M.

"It's all right," Tina soothed. "Phyllis is picking me up with the limousine at nine. We'll come by for Frank and you. How's Suzy?" Tina's voice softened. "I'll bet she's adorable in that dress you designed for her."

"She's been awake since six," Vanessa laughed. "Dressed since seven. She looks so darling I feel like crying every time I look at her." Suzy would have a father she loved.

"We'll see you about nine-twenty," Tina said. "You picked a gorgeous day!"

With Suzy darting in and out of her room trying to help, Vanessa dressed for her wedding. Eddie would have wanted her to marry, she told herself. He would be grateful that Suzy had a father.

Today she was saying farewell to Eddie. Her eyes were wet with tears as she remembered the night he had come to her from camp, knowing he'd be on a troopship bound for Europe within forty-eight hours. She remembered the sweetness of their lovemaking. She remembered the late July morning eighteen months later when she picked up the office phone and heard Eddie's voice at the other end of the line. She remembered their glorious week at the boardinghouse at Bridgehampton, where they had registered as Lieutenant and Mrs. Eduardo Montino.

Vanessa was caught up in memories of her first sight of Venice, their visit to Paris, the little house near Mestre, the day Eddie took her to see his mother in the hospital. She blocked from her mind the horrible moment when a newspaper headline told her of his death.

"You should have flowers," Maria reproached from

388

the doorway. "It's not too late."

"No," Vanessa rejected gently. "No flowers, Maria. Just those I love most around me." She thought of her mother. It had been almost eleven years since she and Tina had left Pinewood. In all those years not one word from her mother.

Vanessa turned at the sound of the doorbell. That would be Frank and Tina. She pulled the door wide, Maria and Suzy at her heels. The chauffeur stood smiling at them.

"Miss Conrad, the car's downstairs. Mr. Bernstein and Miss Gregory are waiting."

Phyllis stood besiee the car smiling. Frank and Tina were inside. Phyllis prodded Maria and Suzy into the front with the chauffeur and joined the others in the back.

The wedding party emerged from the limousine at City Hall and headed toward the sweeping flight of stairs that led to the imposing porticoed entrance. They were instantly beseiged by a horde of reporters and photographers. Frank dropped a protective arm about Vanessa and Tina while Maria hurried ahead with Suzy. Vanessa was bewildered until a glance at Phyllis confirmed her suspicions. Phyllis had led the press to believe that Tina was being married this morning.

"No, no!" Tina shouted exuberantly to the questions hurled at her. "I'm not getting married. I'm here with my friends Vanessa Conrad and Frank Bernstein. *They're* getting married."

Tina obligingly posed for photographs with Vanessa and Frank and informed the reporters and photographers that her dress was a Vanessa Conrad. She parried all questions about any romantic interests and made several caustic remarks about her former husbands.

Vanessa tried not to be angry at the ploy the other three had used to gain publicity. *This was for the business.* Phyllis made no pretense about promoting the company name. Her job was to publicize Vanessa Conrad, designer.

"Sweetie, we'll be on the front pages of the *Mirror,* the *News,* and the *Post,*" Tina predicted. "This was a real brainstorm."

"We didn't tell you because we were afraid you'd be upset," Phyllis apologized anxiously. "Vanessa, it was too good an opportunity to let go."

"Vanessa understands." Frank hugged his bride. "She's as ambitious for the company as I am."

Vanessa was startled by the brevity of the marriage ceremony. It could hardly have been more than two minutes, she thought while they were swept from the judge's chambers to allow room for the next couple. When Suzy started kindergarten next September, Vanessa thought suddenly, she would be registered as Suzanne Bernstein. Her hand tightened on Suzy's tiny one. Her daughter had a father; she had a name.

Back at the shop the employees had prepared a spread of bagels, cream cheese, lox, and coffee. The stellar attraction was Tina, and for all her sophistication, Tina enjoyed the attention. Finally the wedding party left for the waiting limousine to drive to Le Pavillon for luncheon.

Amid the cerise damask upholstery and the exquisite banks of fresh roses of Le Pavillon Vanessa tried to brace herself for her separation from Suzy. They had never been apart for longer than the three days in Houston, she recalled with trepidation. She had explained to Suzy that she would be gone for a little while. Maria was like a second mother. Phyllis promised to drop by every day. Still, Vanessa struggled to rout out her apprehension.

For a moment—when she kissed Suzy good-bye at the apartment—Vanessa thought her small daughter was about to cry. Phyllis had arrived prepared for just such an emergency. A tiny stuffed puppy brought from the depths of her purse elicited an instant smile. At the same moment Tina produced a small gold bracelet.

Frank helped the chauffeur carry their luggage down to the limousine at the curb. After one last round of kisses, Vanessa left the apartment to join Frank for the drive to the airport. Soon they would be en route to Key West.

Vanessa was enchanted by Key West's nineteenth-century mansions and its vine-covered cottages, its bike-drawn rickshaws, lime-green fire trucks, lush tropical gardens. She loved their suite in the 1837 mansion that had been converted to a guest house. Each day she and Frank walked to the foot of Duval Street in Mallery Square to watch the magnificent sunset.

"I was talking to one of the shoeshine boys," Frank said as he stood beside Vanessa and watched the magic of the setting sun. Vanessa smiled. Frank had a way of making friends wherever they wandered. "He told me that in 1815 King Ferdinand of Spain gave Key West to a young soldier named Juan Pablo Salas and that seven years later Salas sold it for two thousand dollars to an American businessman from Mobile, Alabama."

"He did better than the Indians did with Manhattan," Vanessa laughed.

This would have been a euphoric period for Vanessa except for her first encounter with southern segregation. Vanessa remembered Tina's blunt declaration in the days before the two of them left Pinewood: *"Look, to everybody in Pinewood I'm the dago and you're the kike."* She remembered her shock when a drunken customer had referred to her father as "you damn Jew" and a giggling classmate had said with an air of superiority, "You're one of those Christ-killers."

Frank was more casual about such intolerance.

"It's happened through the years to every ethnic group," he said as they sat in the jasmine-fragrant dusk in a swing on the upstairs veranda of the guest house. "To the Jews, the Irish, the Italians, the Polish, the Chinese." He fondled Vanessa's shoulder in consolation. "It's part of living."

But it was wrong, she insisted rebelliously. In earlier centuries Jews had been forced to live in ghettos, as the colored people were segregated in the South. And no matter how Frank boasted about conditions being different in the North, there were still areas where blacks couldn't live. Clubs and hotels and apartment buildings where Jews were not allowed. And here in Key West they heard much talk about the revolutionary Fidel Castro, who was fighting to free Cuba from dictatorship.

When Vanessa and Frank left Key West, Vanessa carried with her the sketches that would be incorporated into their next collection. In Nassau, Frank ordered with mock sternness, she was to forget the business completely. Still, Vanessa remembered that they were visiting Nassau at Phyllis's instructions. They would make important contacts.

Frank was openly impressed by the display of wealth in Nassau. Vanessa enjoyed the leisurely way of life in the eighteenth-century colonial town, its appealing blend of the elegant and the simple. They stayed at the Fort Montague Beach Hotel, their room directly on the ocean. At unwary moments Vanessa gazed out at the magnificent blue of the water and remembered the Lido and Eddie. But that had been a fairy tale, she told herself again. This was reality.

Vanessa met a wealthy Houston widow whose daughter had modeled one of her dresses at Madeline Owens's charity event, and she and Frank were immediately swept up in the Nassau social scene. In the morning they swam at the Porcupine Club or at a private beach, then headed for Bay Street, parallel to the harbor, to shop. Usually by 2:00 P.M. they were having lunch at some exclusive private gathering. In the afternoon Frank played golf with their newfound friends while Vanessa talked about fashion with their wives. At dusk, when everyone else retired for naps before the late dinner hour, Vanessa and Frank made love.

Vanessa was delighted to see some of her own designs worn by the American women vacationing in Nassau. It was a source of wonder to her that she was regarded as a minor celebrity. Her dresses, while priced high, were not madly expensive like those of Galanos, who was attracting so much attention in the fashion world.

Vanessa was grateful that Phyllis had warned her that evening dresses, usually floor-length and strapless, would be worn at private dinners and at the Bahamian Club, where the gambling stakes were startlingly high. White seemed favored, in lace or embroidered organza or beaded piqué. But on movie nights the women wore cotton or surah late-day dresses. There were none of the crinolines here that still highlighted middle-priced ready-to-wear.

Each night before dinner Vanessa called home and listened with a twinge of homesickness as Suzy reported exuberantly on her day's activities. Maria reassured Vanessa that all was going well. Each morning Frank called Doris, their right-hand assistant, at the shop. She went over production figures with him, read him any mail that required immediate attention.

On Saturday Vanessa and Frank boarded a British Overseas Airways plane that would land at Idlewild in New York in four and a half hours. It seemed as though they had been away for months, not just fifteen days. But Vanessa knew that in the morning they would return to the shop and be caught up again in the familiar frenzy of shipping the fall/winter collection and preparing the resort line. At work she would still be Vanessa Conrad, but at home she was Vanessa Bernstein.

Early in July Pat appeared briefly in New York to accompany Paul to a political dinner. She met Vanessa for lunch at Le Pavillon, with Phyllis using the meeting of "the new darling of the fashion world" and "the most beautiful young congressional wife in Washington" as a press lead. Both Vanessa and Pat would have preferred a quiet corner table in some lesser-known restaurant, but both were aware of the value of publicity.

"I love the house in Georgetown," Pat reported. "It's a pre-Civil War red-brick Georgian that has been magnificently restored, and we've added a separate wing for CeeCee and the governess. Paul insists Cee-

Cee shouldn't be disturbed by all the entertaining. But tell me about you," Pat commanded. "I'm so proud of you, Vanessa."

Before they parted, Vanessa promised to come down to Georgetown with Frank for a weekend.

"Let's make it a real reunion," Pat said sentimentally. "I'll call Tina out in California and try to persuade her to come down for the weekend, too."

After much phone consultation, Pat set the reunion for the long Labor Day weekend. When Vanessa realized that CeeCee was out in Houston — "being spoiled by her grandmother and grandaddy" — she conceded that Suzy should remain in New York with Maria. She and Frank had worked madly all through the summer months except for three weekends when they had gone with Suzy and Maria to Southampton. Even these weekends, Frank pointed out, were actually "business weekends." Phyllis used their Southampton socializing for column breaks and editorial mention in the fashion magazines.

With her lustrous dark hair arranged in the new Italian cut, Tina arrived on Friday evening so that the three of them could drive to Washington together in Frank's new gray Cadillac convertible. She brought Suzy her own small television set on which to watch "Kukla, Fran and Ollie," "Lassie," and "Captain Midnight."

"Just like the one I sent Adam," she said, faintly defiant. "Sal and Eva were so annoyed."

After a hearty luncheon the Georgetown-bound trio took off. While Frank swore at the holiday traffic, Vanessa and Tina chattered in their customary rapid-fire pace.

"I had a black Cadillac with red leather upholstery delivered to Pop on his last birthday," Tina reported.

"Pop looks down on any car that isn't black. He didn't send it back, but he didn't say thank you either." Tina's smile was wry. "Nick says he had a fit when he found out I was divorcing Keith. He's sure I'll burn in hell."

"With all your friends," Frank laughed. "Better to burn with them than be bored to death."

"I didn't write my mother about marrying Frank," Vanessa said after a moment. "She doesn't even know about Suzy. That's the way she wants it."

"I asked Nick about her," Tina said softly. "She sits out there on Mrs. Johnson's porch and rocks away the day. Even when it's cold and nobody else wants to sit out, Mrs. Conrad's there."

In Georgetown, Vanessa read Pat's careful instructions while Frank, who admitted to having no sense of direction, tried to follow them. Because Georgetown was protected from modernization by an act of Congress, it wore an air of quiet affluence. It was now the "smart" area in which to live.

"There's the house." Vanessa recognized the entrance to the property from the snapshots Pat had sent.

"The congressman isn't paying for that on his salary," Tina commented. "Daddy must have come through again."

They drove through the arched entranceway that bore a plaque announcing it as Roberts Acres. The long driveway was edged with flowering shrubs and rose bushes. As they approached the imposing redbrick house, with its four Doric columns rising to the roof, they saw a slender figure rise from a chair on the veranda.

"There's Pat!" Vanessa leaned forward and waved.

In an exquisitely feminine flowered print from

Vanessa's latest collection—worn only a couple of inches below the knee because Dior had introduced the shorter length in his autumn collection—Pat greeted them warmly. How lucky for her, Vanessa thought, that her romance with Jesse had not worked out. She looked beautiful with her blond hair up in a classic Psyche knot. Pat had ignored the pageboy, the poodle, and now the shaggy Italian cut.

"Paul's playing golf. He'll be home any minute," Pat said while she settled them on the sprawling veranda, furnished with colorfully cushioned white wicker chairs and settees. "Caleb will bring us drinks in a few moments."

Frank gazed about in admiration.

"I expect Scarlet O'Hara to come sashaying through the front door any minute," he drawled. "And Rhett Butler to charge up the roadway."

"If he does," Tina laughed, "remember, I'm the only unattached female here."

Pat talked with quiet pride about Paul's activities in the House of Representatives.

"Paul's not one to sit back and be happy as the junior congressman," Pat chuckled. "He says his piece, whatever it is. And with Daddy there at his side, he's not getting much flak."

When Paul failed to arrive with the next hour, Pat took her three guests into the air-conditioned house for the grand tour before showing them to their rooms. The spacious center hall led to a double drawing room on the right, and to a large dining room on the left. Beyond the dining room were the library and a small sitting room—"where we watch TV when we have time." To the rear, Pat said with a wave of one hand, was the kitchen, a breakfast room, and the family dining room. The door at the end of the hall led to CeeCee's wing of the house.

The house was magnificent, Vanessa conceded, yet she wondered if she could ever relax in such elegant surroundings. Frank seemed fascinated, and asked endless questions. Once in their bedroom, amid the exquisite antiques, Frank threw himself across the canopied bed.

"I could get used to living on this scale," he said with relish. "And one of these days"—he opened his arms to her—"one of these days we will."

At dinner Paul went out of way to be charming to his guests. Vanessa watched him closely, deciding that Paul's efforts were for Tina's benefit. Vanessa was not entirely comfortable in his presence.

After dinner Paul took Frank off to the library to see his gun collection, and the three women retired to the sitting room.

"Paul and Frank will spend the next two hours rehashing World War II," Pat predicted. "Men talk about the war, and women talk about their deliveries."

Pat announced over breakfast the next morning that she was giving a dinner party for them.

"Just a dozen at the table," she said, almost apologetically. "After all," she said, "when I have such important house guests, how can I not show them off?"

After breakfast Tina and Frank went down to the pool—surrounded by a five-foot cedar fence designed to make it "child-proof"—for a swim. Vanessa was glad for some time alone with Pat. She wanted to talk to Pat, find out why she seemed so unhappy. Perhaps it was all the entertaining, which Pat had always loathed, Vanessa decided after futile efforts to pry past her protective facade.

The five of them gathered together for a leisurely luncheon on the wide patio off the family dining room. Frank and Paul seemed to get along, Vanessa observed. Why did she feel this odd wariness in his presence? She suspected that ever-present charm of his was part of the public Paul Roberts—but what was the real Paul Roberts like?

In the afternoon Pat drove Vanessa and Tina around Georgetown and the surrounding area. Paul and Frank elected to sit around the pool with cooling drinks at hand. Vanessa's mind catapulted back to the wartime visits to the Owens estate in Virginia, when Pat had driven them around the countryside. It seemed like another lifetime.

"Who's coming for dinner tonight?" Tina asked as they headed back to the house.

"Mostly political people," Pat said. "You know how it is here in Washington. Every party has an ulterior motive. And Paul asked me to invite Harvey Shiffman, the Texas industrialist, as the extra man. He's here in town to prod his lobbyists into action. Paul's already courting campaign funds."

"My dinner partner," Tina acknowledged with an amused glint. "He shows up in Hollywood every now and then. I believe he had something going with Connie several years ago."

"I've met him around town. He's about forty-five, divorced, has two sons," Pat recalled. "Most women find him terribly attractive."

"It's all that money and power," Vanessa said.

"Powerful men do exude sex appeal." Tina frowned. "They don't even have to be good-looking. But they expect their women to be gorgeous and young. Unfair," she mocked.

At the house Vanessa and Tina retired to their

rooms for a nap before dressing for dinner, while Pat went to confer with the household staff. Vanessa found Frank on their patio, dozing on a chaise. She dropped onto the chaise beside his own.

Vanessa knew she could not nap. What had Frank meant when he said it was time for Creations to move into mass-market? Was he just out to impress Tina and Pat? He was too conscious that despite their success they were hardly in the same financial league as Tina and Pat. If they expanded into mass-market, they'd lose their exclusive image. That was what Frank had insisted on from the very beginning. That was their *identity*.

Tense at the prospect of a confrontation with Frank, Vanessa decided to take the time for a leisurely bubble bath. Her frenzied New York schedule never allowed for such a luxury. But first she'd call home and talk to Suzy and Maria.

In white shorts that showed off her long, tanned legs, and a white halter top with red polka dots, Tina stalked restlessly about her bedroom. It was too early to dress. She was not the type to take a nap. What she needed was a drink.

Tina left her room and headed for the library bar, grinning as she remembered Vanessa's concern that she might be drinking too much. She could handle her liquor. There might be four million alcoholics in the country, as Marty kept yelling at his actors, but she wasn't one of them.

She paused at the entrance to the library. Paul was at the bar, his back to her. Was she being overly suspicious or had he made a subtle pass at her last night? No. She was at the point where she suspected every guy who looked at her was making a pass.

As though feeling the weight of her presence, Paul turned from the bar to face her.

"Hi." His eyes rested on the provocative thrust of her breasts beneath the halter top. "You're a kindred spirit. You felt the need of a drink."

"It's that time of day," she said with detached amusement and walked into the library.

"What would you like?" he asked, one eyebrow lifting suggestively. Tina knew she had not been wrong about last night. The bastard. Right in his own house. How did Pat fall for such creeps? First Jesse, now Paul.

"Whatever you're having," she shrugged and crossed to the tufted burgundy leather sofa that flanked the fireplace. She couldn't just turn around and walk out on Paul. That wasn't her style.

He fixed two Tom Collinses and brought them to the sofa. His eyes skimmed the length of her crossed legs, and he lifted his glass in appreciation. "To a great weekend."

"I'll drink to that." But her eyes told him her idea of a great weekend did not coincide with his.

"You get to New York often," he said. "Like me." The implication was unmistakable. One hand dropped to her bare thigh.

"No, I'm afraid I don't," she said bluntly and lifted his hand away.

"Let me show you the kid's wing." He rose to his feet. He smiled slowly. "It's completely private."

"No," she repeated with cold finality.

"Tina, we could have a marvelous time together." His voice deepened with passion. "Who's to know? A little aperitif before dinner," he drawled, hovering over her for a close view of her tantalizing cleavage.

"We're not playing house." Her smile was contemptuous. "And it's not just because Pat's my friend. I think that men who cheat on their wives are assholes."

His face flushed, he put down his glass and strode from the room. She hadn't liked Paul from the first time she met him, Tina thought, back at Pat's wedding in Houston. She'd known too many men like him.

Dinner in the formal dining room, with its massive crystal chandelier, the table laid with Meissen china and Waterford crystal, was a glittering affair. Vanessa was pleased that both Tina and Pat made a point of wearing a dress from Creations. Her own dinner dress was a white-and-black silk organza with on off-the-shoulder neckline similar to that of Dior's Cupola collection for autumn, though the dress had been designed before Dior's collection.

Vanessa realized why Pat was acquiring a reputation as a superb hostess. The guests each contributed to the sparkling conversation, and the menu was a gourmet delight. Iced brochette of shrimp, watercress vichyssoise, rare filet Stroganoff with individual artichoke soufflés and baked potatoes, and Belgian endive and grapefruit salad. For dessert there was a pomegranate sherbet and petits fours.

Vanessa knew why most women seemed to find Harvey Shiffman attractive. Though not handsome in a movie star fashion, he radiated strength and sensuality. Every woman at the table was conscious of his presence. He was candid in his pleasure at having Tina on his left, though he diplomatically shared his attentions with the wife of an important judge on his right.

While coffee was being served, Vanessa exchanged a long look with Tina. Tina winked. Her smile was dazzling. Vanessa understood. Tina meant to see more of Harvey Shiffman.

A few moments later, shamelessly eavesdropping, Vanessa overheard Harvey invite Tina to fly back to New York with him aboard his company plane. Tina accepted with alacrity.

Vanessa tried to hid her anxiety. Harvey Shiffman was a twice-divorced man with a nineteen-year-old and a twenty-two-year-old son. Tina was twenty-eight and headstrong. She was a nonpracticing Catholic. Harvey was Jewish. Anything other than a brief affair spelled trouble.

And perhaps that was all it would be—a tumultuous, fast affair. But as she watched Tina smile into Harvey's eyes, Vanessa's unease increased—this was something much, much more.

Thirty

Pat said a gracious farewell to the senator's wife who had chaired the charity luncheon at the Mayflower Hotel and hurried out to her waiting limousine. Paul made a point of having her accompany him to Union Station on those Thursdays when, like so many other congressmen, he boarded the 4:00 P.M. Congressional Limited bound for a long New York weekend of party conferences.

The early November afternoon was unseasonably raw, but Pat ignored the cold. She relaxed in the limousine and looked forward to a weekend alone in the house. No dinner parties. No social engagements with Paul out of town. Miss Leslie would be in charge of CeeCee. She would do nothing but lie in bed and read. She had the new Steinbeck and that Saul Bellow novel, *The Adventures of Augie March*, everybody was talking about.

Daddy wouldn't be popping in for dinner. He was driving down to Virginia to rest up after a grueling week in Congress. Thank God he realized he had to take things easier since his heart attack last summer. He was taking three-day weekends away from Washington except during crisis situations in the House. Still, he insisted he'd run for reelection next year.

She had expected Mother to spend more time in Virginia after Daddy's heart attack, but she still stayed in Houston. Pat wished her parents were closer, the way they'd been in the early years of their marriage. Her sister, Maureen, remembered those years; she didn't.

Walking into the house, Pat heard Paul talking on the phone in the library.

"Sign the letters for me, Roz, and make sure they go out. I won't have time to stop by on my way to the train."

"Paul, I have Jason standing by with the car," she called to him as she walked down the hall to the library. "You're running tight on time." Paul was forever late for appointments, but trains could not be expected to wait for him.

"I know," he shot back in irritation.

"Are you packed?" she asked routinely.

"Caleb's in my room now packing for me."

Since Labor Day weekend Paul had not shared the master bedroom with her. For almost a year before that he'd slept in a guest room on the frequent late nights when he was presumably tied up with congressional business.

Occasionally he exercised his marital privileges. Pat was always tense, fearful of provoking him into a new fit of rage, even while she welcomed his desire for her. So many nights she lay alone, wishing he was in her bed. She wasn't in love with Paul; he was an obsession.

"Do you want me to go with you to the station?" she asked while Paul threw papers into his attaché case.

"Goddamnit, you know I do."

They worked hard to build the image of the devoted young congressional couple. At their endless dinner parties he was attentive, almost fatuous. It gave her an odd satisfaction to know that Paul needed her — at least for his political career.

Saturday morning, awake at 7:00 A.M. after a night of restless sleep, Pat decided to have breakfast in the master suite. Last night she had muddled through yet another confrontation with Miss Leslie about CeeCee. In her ivory velvet robe and matching satin mules, she settled herself at the small table and looked out the window on the last of the late-blooming chrysanthemums.

Along with the breakfast tray, Delia brought her the New York newspapers. While she ate the fluffy herb omelet and sipped strong black coffee, she scanned the gossip columns in the tabloids. Tina and Harvey Shiffman were mentioned regularly now. Despite a business schedule that carried him around the world, Harvey managed to salvage weekends with Tina in Hollywood.

Pat's face lit up at an item about Harvey flying from Hong Kong to escort Tina to the premiere of her new movie. All the columnists were sure they'd marry. And their romance had started here at her Labor Day Sunday dinner party, she recalled sentimentally.

And then the fork in her hand froze midway between plate and mouth. Her face flushed hot as she reread the brief item that followed the one about Tina and Harvey. *"Who was the gorgeous dark-haired model-type seen with handsome Congressman Paul Roberts at El Morocco last night? They had eyes for no one else."*

Slowly Pat put down her fork. Until now she hadn't been sure. Oh, she had accused him several times. And she'd paid for her suspicions with a fractured wrist and three cracked ribs and endless bruises. But she had never been able to prove that Paul was having

406

affairs.

Half of Washington must have read the item about Paul and that girl. Tears of humiliation filled her eyes. She clutched one slender hand so tightly that her nails drew blood. *Had Paul seen it?* She hoped so. A man dreaming of living in the White House could hardly afford such sordid gossip.

With sudden determination she pushed back her chair and rose to her feet. She wouldn't stay here. She would take CeeCee and go home to Houston. CeeCee could go to school in Houston just as well as in Washington. She crossed to the telephone to make immediate flight reservations. She would pack a few clothes to take with her. Later she would arrange for Delia to pack the trunks and ship them to Houston.

Within three hours Pat, accompanied by CeeCee and Miss Leslie, was aboard the plane that would take them on the first lap of their flight to Houston. Mother and Daddy would understand that it was impossible for her to stay with Paul when everybody knew he was unfaithful to her. *How could he treat her this way?*

In Houston she went from the airport directly to the ranch without stopping to phone her mother. The servants greeted her warmly. Her mother, she was told, was at a committee meeting.

"She'll be home for dinner real soon, Miss Pat," Effie Mae said, stooping to hug CeeCee. "My, it's good to see y'all."

Pat went to her room. Exhausted, she settled herself against the mound of pillows on her bed and sipped the fragrant hot tea that Effie Mae brought her.

"Pat, what on earth are you doing in Houston?" Her mother walked in without knocking. "I thought we'd all be together at the plantation for Thanksgiv-

407

ing." Her eyes were cold with reproach. Madeline Owens loathed having her schedule disrupted.

"I've left Paul," Pat was faintly defensive. "I'm hoping for a Vatican annulment." She put her tea on the night table and swung her legs to the floor.

"After seven years of marriage and a child?" Mrs. Owens lashed back. "Who have you lost your head over this time?"

Color edged Pat's high cheekbones.

"I'm not leaving Paul for another man. I'm leaving him because he has no respect for his marriage vows." She was trembling. "He's hit the gossip columns—with some model. And I'm sure she isn't the first."

"Pat, grow up." Her mother frowned in irritation and closed the door behind her so the servants couldn't overhear. "You'll never get an annulment. You can't divorce Paul. You'll—"

"Mother, I won't live with him!" Pat rose to her feet. "Not when he's chasing after other women."

"He's a man." Her mother's smile was bitter. "Do you think your father was any different?"

"Is that why you stopped living in Washington?" she challenged.

"I stayed with him until he was well established in Congress and I was old enough to use the excuse of 'poor health' to spend most of my time elsewhere," she pointed out. "Remember, Pat, those women come and go; but you're still the congressman's wife. That's something nobody can take away from you. Before your father's heart attack I felt there was a good chance I might become First Lady. For that I would have gone back to Washington. But we both know that won't happen now. The doctors have warned your father he'll have to take things easier. The party knows this; he'd never be nominated. But in a dozen years

Paul might pull it off. Pat, *you* could be First Lady."

"I don't want it," Pat spat out.

"You owe it to this family," her mother shot back. "Your father will use all the power he's earned through the years to push Paul ahead. We will spend whatever it takes to put Paul and you in the White House. That's buying a place in history." Her face shone with ambition.

"I can't live with Paul," Pat whispered. "There's more —" She hesitated, gathering her courage to say what she had never told anyone. "Paul's a violent man. He —"

"I don't want to hear any more!" Madeline Owens turned away, but not before Pat saw one unguarded instant of comprehension. "You have obligations to your husband." Pat gaped in disbelief. "After one more term in the House, Paul will run for the Senate. Already your father in orchestrating Paul's path to the presidency. Don't deny us this, Pat." It was a command more than a plea.

"I don't want to go back to Paul," Pat stammered. "You don't understand." Her eyes met her mother's. "You don't want to understand."

"Your father will talk to Paul tomorrow night. He'll say that you've made an impetuous visit to Houston. We'll all meet at the plantation for the long Thanksgiving weekend." She paused. "Daddy will make Paul understand that he must be more discreet."

Paul stepped out of the shower and scowled at his reflection in the mirrored wall. The goddamn booze all went to his stomach. He pushed at the first signs of a paunch. He'd have to start working out at the gym.

He started at the sound of the phone he'd had

installed in the guest bedroom a few weeks ago, a private line known only to a few colleagues in the House. With a towel draped about his middle he stalked into the bedroom.

"Hello."

"You stupid prick," his father-in-law's voice came to him over the phone. "If you've got to screw around, don't you have enough sense to stay out of places like El Morocco?"

"What are you talking about?" Paul tried to sound amused.

"Paul, I know you fuck around," the older congressman said tersely. "Now Pat knows it, too. She's in Houston with her mother. All pissed off about it."

"Jim, I'm sorry as hell—" He hadn't wanted to go to El Morocco, but that little slut had insisted. If he hadn't been drinking so much, he wouldn't have gone. "I'll call Pat and—"

"You'll have to do more than that to keep her in line. I had my problems with Madeline back in the early years. She couldn't understand how a man gets all tensed up in politics, that he needs an outlet. She walked out on me when Maureen was ten years old. Swore she'd never come back. Oh, she wouldn't divorce me," he chuckled. "How could she go to the priest if she was divorced?"

"How did you handle it, Jim?" All of a sudden his mind was painfully clear. He *needed* Pat and her family. They had money and power.

"I groveled," Jim said. "I apologized and begged— and I got her pregnant as fast as I could. You get yourself back into Pat's bed, and you stay there until you've given her another kid."

"I—uh—I'll try, Jim." He sounded unfamiliarly humble.

"You'll do it." Owens bristled with confidence. "Oh, and a news bulletin, Paul. I'm acquiring a string of five radio stations. That'll buy you a lot of popular support. Think about that when you're screwing your wife."

On New Year's Day Tina called Vanessa, as she always had, to reminisce with unabashed sentimentality about the years of their friendship.

"Harvey and I are still in bed," Tina giggled. "He's out cold after all we drank. We're at this house in Acapulco. He said he just wanted to spend New Year's Eve alone with me. We're good for each other, Vanessa. He loves it when I cook for him. Remember all the spaghetti meals I made for us? He gave the servants three days off, and all we've been doing is eating spaghetti and screwing."

"Are you going to marry him?" Vanessa asked softly.

"As soon as he stops trying to convert me to Judaism," she said. "He want us to have a kid. I told him he can raise the kid Jewish, but I'm too old to switch." She paused. "Vanessa, I want to have a baby with Harvey. I never should have given Adam to Sal and Eva. I know he's being raised right, but he's *my kid*. I shouldn't have to fight to see him."

"What about the career?" Vanessa teased.

"Sweetie, times are changing in Hollywood. Liz Taylor got pregnant, and it didn't hurt her career. Maybe by spring or early summer we'll marry. Stand by to make another wedding dress!"

"Be sure before you do anything, Tina," Vanessa urged.

"I'm sure right now. Oh, God!" she laughed. "Har-

411

vey's awake. Harvey, wait," she scolded and Vanessa heard an amorous muttering not meant for the telephone wires. "Vanessa, talk to you soon," Tina said abruptly. "I don't want to get pregnant until after the wedding."

Vanessa rejoined Frank in the den. She was relieved that he was engrossed in the football game. Earlier he had been off on that same kick about moving the line into the mass-market field. Bill was goading him on. Business was going smoothly, so Bill was bored. She'd be glad when he went back to Palm Beach.

"Phyllis and Arnie are coming for dinner tonight, aren't they?" Frank asked during the commercial break.

"An early dinner," Vanessa reminded him. "So Suzy can eat with us." Suzy loved to have dinner guests.

"After dinner let's sit down and talk about how we'd handle the promotion if we went mass-market."

"Frank, we're doing well where we are," she protested gently.

"We're standing still," he corrected. "In business you either go up or you go down. You don't stand still."

In the afternoon Vanessa took Suzy for a walk along Riverside Drive, almost deserted today. She cherished these holiday periods alone with Suzy. Though she knew in her heart she wasn't depriving Suzy of anything by having a career, she still felt occasional twinges of guilt.

"Would you like to go over to Broadway and stop in somewhere for hot chocolate?" she asked when the chill of the afternoon became sharp.

"With whipped cream?" Suzy's delicately featured face was radiant. Both Vanessa and Maria rationed her sweets.

"With whipped cream," Vanessa promised and

reached for one mittened hand. How lucky she was to have Suzy! It filled her with pleasure when people admired Suzy's masses of lush dark hair, her quickness and prettiness. She was such a sweet child. She had Eddie's sweetness, Vanessa thought with a pang.

All through dinner Vanessa was tense. She hated fighting with Frank about anything, but she was convinced they'd sacrifice everything they'd worked for if they expanded into a mass-market operations. Much of the dinner conversation focused on the end of hostilities in Korea. And as often happened when Frank and Phyllis's husband were together, the talk turned to their experiences in World War II.

"I tell you, we had a great barter system out in the Pacific," Arnie reminisced. "I bartered a PT boat for a refrigerator. You know what that refrigerator meant to us!"

They moved to the spacious, comfortably furnished den for more coffee and talk. Vanessa's heart began to pound as Frank spoke enthusiastically about the potential for Creations if they moved into the mass-market field. Frank was so bright; couldn't he see mass-market was wrong for them?

"I've been checking around on sales figures. What we're doing is penny ante compared to what's out there for a smart operation," Frank wound up with a triumphant smile. "In a year our grosses will be in the millions!"

"I think you're off your rocker," Phyllis said with the candor the others had come to expect of her. "What Creations has going for it is that it's special. It's not available in mass-market. And Vanessa's designs won't translate well into cheap fabrics."

"She'll design to fit the market," Frank said, dismissing Phyllis' arguments. "You know Vanessa—she's

413

adaptable."

"Frank, be practical," Phyllis urged. "If you try to move into mass-market, you'll be up against fierce competition. Companies that have been there for a long time and are well entrenched. In your field you've climbed right to the top." For a fleeting instant her eyes held Vanessa's. Don't let him do this.

"This isn't the time, Frank," Vanessa said, deceptively calm. "Bill's called in all his loans to the company, which is fine if we don't do something crazy like overexpanding."

"Arnie, these two are running scared," Frank chuckled, but Vanessa knew he was irritated.

"It's a matter of timing," she cajoled. "We've done wonders in the short time we've been in business. But we can't throw away what we have. In time — not now, but in three or four or five years — why don't we try with a second line? Creations will lend cachet to a second, less expensive line. But now now," she said again. "The investment will be enormous."

"Frank, I've been thinking about our trunk shows," Phyllis said thoughtfully. "I think Vanessa should go out to tour the stores regularly. And maybe" — she turned to Vanessa with an apologetic smile — "the number of stores handling the line could be expanded to as many as fifty. You'll still be damned exclusive."

Vanessa was relieved when Frank focused on adding new stores to their list. She knew he was right — earnings in mass-market ready-to-wear could far surpass their already substantial profits — but she recoiled from the bank loans this would entail.

They must not abandon Creations as it was now set up, she thought with determination, not try to merge it with a mass-market line. One day Creations II would be mass-market ready-to-wear, and Creations by Vanessa Conrad would be their "couture line," lending a special mystique to Creations II. But not yet. They were not ready to tackle such a huge investment.

Early in March Pat came up to New York with Paul for a political dinner. Vanessa rearranged her hectic schedule so that she and Pat could have a leisurely lunch. Pat had seemed happy when they spoke occasionally on the telephone, Vanessa thought. She was wrong to have worried about Pat the weekend she and Frank had been down in Georgetown.

At a quiet corner at Le Pavillon—after they had exchanged warm greetings, updates on their respective families, and had ordered—Pat told Vanessa she was pregnant again.

"Just two months," she said, her smile radiant. "I'm not due until September. If it's not a boy," she laughed, "I'll have to leave town."

"I think it's wonderful." Vanessa reached a hand across the table to cover Pat's. "Boy or girl." Sometimes she felt guilty that she and Frank were avoiding having a child. It would be good for Suzy to have a little brother or sister. "Does CeeCee know yet?"

"We won't tell her for a while." Pat seemed troubled. "I hope she won't be upset. You know how spoiled she is—"

"Pat, she's only seven," Vanessa said gently. "She'll adjust."

As the months sped past, Vanessa sensed Frank's restlessness, despite his show of enthusiasm about almost doubling their outlets. Bill Bartlett, crotchety in his advancing years and smugly aware of the value of his share of Creations, was becoming a meddlesome nuisance. He tended to remind them frequently that he owned a controlling interest and sulked when his suggestions were rejected.

Both Vanessa and Frank were on edge about Bill's behavior. In the midst of a stormy late night discussion about how best to handle him, they were interrupted by a phone call from Pat.

"Vanessa, I did it," Pat said in exultation. "I gave Paul a son. He'll be baptized Paul Roberts, Jr., but already Daddy's nicknamed him Biff. He was born at four this morning, and he's beautiful."

They talked for a few tender minutes. Vanessa promised to run down to Washington over the weekend. It would be good for Frank to get away from the business. He was so upset about Bill's veiled reminders that *he* was majority stockholder. Vanessa wished Bill would leave New York for his annual stay in Palm Beach.

Shortly after Thanksgiving Bill swept Vanessa and Frank off for lunch at the Colony. He had a great new idea for the business, he told them. After they had settled at his favorite table, he announced that they should move into menswear.

"Bill, we're not equipped to handle menswear." Frank was shocked at the prospect. "Vanessa designs for women."

"We could hire somebody to design for men. It's a wide-open field. We could make millions."

"For somebody who's knowledgeable about the market," Vanessa said diplomatically. "We're not."

Bill's florid face flushed to an angry red.

"Maybe I'll sell out my share of the business," he said. His fading blue eyes moved from Frank to Vanessa with malicious pleasure. "I could sell out for half a million."

For the first time since they had begun to operate Creations, Vanessa and Frank feared for the future of their business. Frank was alternately furious and depressed when they returned to the office after lunch.

"Damn it, Vanessa, that old bastard could cut our throats!" he railed. "We've got to figure some way to buy him out."

"You think he'd sell?"

"He might. You know how he blows hot and cold." Frank stared into space. "We might talk to the bank about a loan."

Vanessa flinched.

"For half a million? They'd never go along with that."

"We have a lot on the books," Frank pointed out.

"Which we'll need for suppliers. We've just set up twenty more stores, Frank! We've almost doubled our purchases."

"Old Bill is not going to cut our throats," Frank said brusquely. "We'll figure a way out of this mess."

Tina came home from a shopping spree on Rodeo Drive in a jubilant mood. The new picture was in the can. In a week she was flying down to Rio to spend Christmas and New Year's with Harvey on his yacht. It had been crazy for them to fight the way they had before he flew down to Rio. Over *nothing*. She'd been tired and bitchy because the picture was running behind schedule. But they'd have one hell of a reunion on the yacht.

"Miss Tina," her housekeeper came down the hall, envelope in hand. "A telegram arrived about an hour ago."

"Thank you, Rita." She smiled and took the yellow

417

envelope. Probably from Marty, vacationing down in Mexico City.

She ripped open the envelope and pulled out the small sheet.

"Pop died in his sleep. Funeral Thursday. Love, Nick."

She went cold with disbelief. She hadn't exchanged a word with Pop in twelve and a half years. Now she would never talk to him again. He was gone, and he'd never forgiven her for leaving Pinewood.

Slowly she went into her room and stretched out across her bed. Her mind went back over childhood memories. Why did Pop have to keep her away like that? He hadn't even known that Adam was his grandchild.

She lay across the bed while darkness settled over the room. When Rita knocked to say that dinner was ready to be served, she asked for a tray to be brought to her room. She couldn't bring herself yet to tell Rita that her father was dead.

Much later—knowing she must make travel arrangements, must tell Harvey that she was flying home before meeting him in Rio—she phoned Vanessa. It was almost midnight in New York, but Vanessa would understand.

She waited impatiently for Vanessa to answer the private phone in her bedroom.

"Hello." Frank sounded irritated. Tina remembered this was a rush month for the business—but, then, every month was a rush month.

"Frank, it's Tina. I'm sorry to be calling so late. I forgot till just now the difference in time."

"That's all right. I'll put Vanessa on."

Fighting to keep her voice even, Tina told Vanessa about her father's death.

"Nick sends me a telegram." Tina's voice broke.

418

"Wouldn't you think the son-of-a-bitch could pick up a phone and call me?"

They talked in quiet tones for a few minutes, both of them thinking of Pinewood.

"Vanessa, I hate going back. Could you go with me to the funeral?" Tina asked—and then rushed on before Vanessa could reply. "No, it would be rotten for you with your mother living there."

"I'll meet you at the airport," Vanessa said. "What flight will you take?"

"Meet me with a limo," Tina said. "Hire it for four days. Tell them their man will drive me to Pinewood and stay there until I come back to New York. I'm flying down to Rio to be with Harvey over the holidays. Oh, Vanessa, why couldn't Pop talk to me?"

Though the limousine was comfortably warm, Tina drew her mink coat about her shoulders as they approached Pinewood in the early dusk. The last few miles the snow had been falling in dollar-size flakes. The houses on either side of the road were adorned with Christmas lights, and Christmas trees stood on the tiny patches of earth before the houses.

"Make a left at the traffic light," Tina leaned forward to instruct the chauffeur. "Stay on that road for about a mile."

Pinewood still had only one traffic light—at the intersection on Main Street. Christmas lights hung across Main Street, and the small shops were festively decorated. Tina tensed as they passed the darkened windows of the butcher shop, closed until after the funeral.

At least she'd see Adam, she told herself with satisfaction. Sal and Eva couldn't stop her from seeing her

419

baby. She'd never dreamt she could be so mad about a kid. Depsite her resolution not to cry, tears glistened in her eyes. Not because Pop was dead. Because he had been so stubborn about punishing her that he had never known Adam was his flesh-and-blood grandson.

When the car pulled up before the house, Tina sat still for a few moments. It seemed smaller than she remembered, and in need of a paint job. Pop was always too busy, always putting off a paint job until next year.

"Leave me here and go on to the motel," she instructed the driver. "Your reservations have been made. I'll phone when I need you."

In fragile, high-heeled suede pumps and clutching her Vuitton valise in one hand, Tina walked over the snow to the steps that led up to the rambling porch. She heard Eva's strident voice issuing from inside, in conversation with another of her sisters-in-law. Straightening her shoulders, Tina rang the doorbell. A pale and distraught Nick opened the door. How old he looked, she thought as they exchanged a warm embrace. The air was heavy with the scent of flowers and the aroma of coffee.

"Thank God you're here," Nick whispered. "Already the women are fighting over who gets what."

Hand in hand Nick and Tina entered the room her father had always persisted in calling the parlor. The other three brothers and their wives greeted Tina with a show of grief that she immediately distrusted.

"How sad," Gus's wife said with forced compassion, "that Pop and you were estranged so many years."

"Where's Adam?" Tina asked Eva.

"At home with my sister," she said, avoiding Tina's eyes. "He has a cold. I didn't want to drag him out in this weather."

"I want to see him while I'm here," Tina said quietly, fighting to control her anger. "I have a car with a chauffeur. We'll drive over before I leave for New York."

Tina excused herself to go up to her old room. Nick had taken for granted that she would stay here, and her old room had been prepared for her.

"The others are at a motel near Saratoga," he told her while they walked to the dark stairs leading to the second floor. "I'm glad. The women can't wait for Pop to be buried so we can hear the lawyer read the will." Bitterness tinged his grief. "The three vultures."

Tina's throat tightened as she walked into her room. The years raced backward. Why had Pop been so stubborn? He'd always expected the worst of her. But she had left this town a nobody, and now she was somebody. Tina Gregory, movie star.

She pretended to be asleep when Nick came up to say it was time to go to the funeral parlor. She didn't want to see her father dead; she wanted to remember him alive. She brushed aside Nick's efforts to awaken her with an incoherent rejection.

Tina felt like a stranger in Pinewood. Her brothers—except for Nick—and her three sisters-in-law were cold and disapproving. They couldn't accept her life or her two divorces. Wait till they find out I'm going to marry a multimillionaire Jew, she thought with bitter amusement.

Of her nieces and nephews, only Vinnie's eight-year-old daughter—shy but awed by the presence of her movie star aunt—appeared at the funeral services. Every pew in the church was occupied. Not out of respect for her father. Most of them were here for a look at the real-life movie star who had once lived in Pinewood. The dago. The wop kid.

The day after the funeral the family gathered in the office of the local attorney who had served the Viglianos since Tina's father had bought the house forty-one years ago. Pop always said the butcher shop would go to Nick, who had worked behind the counter since he was fifteen. Nobody was prepared for the disposition of the house.

"To my daughter, Tina, I leave my house so that she may know she will always have a roof over her head," the attorney read solemnly.

Tina leaned toward Nick, sitting in a chair beside her own.

"Your house, Nick. You've earned it," she whispered, but her eyes filled with tears. Pop was mad at her all these years, but he worried about her future.

Back at the house for the family dinner, the sisters-in-law were already squabbling over how to divide the furniture.

"You get the house, Tina," Vinnie's wife pointed out defiantly. "The will didn't say nothing about the furniture. Pop always said he'd leave me the dining room set."

"Nick gets the shop and you get the house," Vinnie picked up, exchanging a wary glance with his wife. "It ain't no more than fair that the rest of us get the furniture and the car."

"Take the furniture," Tina said with malicious pleasure. "And the car. Nick, I want you to drive over to Albany and pick out whatever furniture you like. Charge it to me. And after that I'm buying you a gorgeous red Ferrari. You're the only one who stayed here with Pop all these years—you deserve it."

Pleading concern about more snow and bad roads, Sal and Eva prepared to leave immediately after dinner. Vinnie and Gus and their wives joined in the early exodus.

"I'm driving over to see Adam in the morning," Tina told Sal and Eva, daring them to deny her this. "Tell him his aunt is coming over to deliver her Christmas presents in person." The ones mailed from Hollywood would arrive any day. But she wanted to see the look on his face when she walked in with the fanciest two-wheeler she could find in Albany.

Later, while she and Nick sat in the kitchen over cups of freshly made espresso, she inspected the scrapbooks Nick had brought downstairs from their father's bedroom.

"He wouldn't let me say one word to you," Nick said softly, "but he was as proud as hell of Tina Gregory. The drugstore saved a copy of every movie magazine every month. He'd sit here in the kitchen drinking coffee looking for pictures of you, stories about you. It's all here."

"Nicky, why? Why did he have to cheat us both out of twelve years of our lives?" Tears spilled over unheeded. "Why did he have to be such a stubborn old man?"

Sitting in the kitchen, slowly going through the four scrapbooks her father had so painstakingly kept, Tina told herself that the Hollywood part of her life was over. She would fly down to Rio and be with Harvey. After a respectable period of mourning for Pop, they'd marry. They'd waited so long, they could wait a few more months. She didn't need the damn career any more. She'd be Harvey's full-time wife. She'd have his baby. They'd be a family.

Thirty-one

Shortly after New Year's Vanessa and Frank sat with Bill Bartlett over luncheon at the Colony and listened in disbelief to his ultimatum.

"Look, I know you kids have worked hard," Bill said expansively, "but it's time I moved on to something new. I'm not asking for an immediate decision. I've been offered half a million for my share of Creations. Either you buy—and I'm willing to spread the payments over a period of one year—or I'm selling."

"I'll call you Friday morning," Frank said. "Vanessa and I have to work this out."

He spoke with a calm that, Vanessa knew, masked his inner rage. They were heavy into the selling of the summer collection. She was about to leave for a fast tour of the fabric houses in Switzerland, France, and Italy to buy for their fall/winter collection, already on the drawing board. This was not the time to cope with such a monumental task.

In the taxi traveling south to the shop Frank cursed Bill. Vanessa shared his frustration. If somebody else moved in with Bill's 51 percent, they would lose control of the business.

"We can't let him sell to somebody else," Frank repeated. "We have to switch over into mass-market and fast. We have no choice, Vanessa."

"We'll talk about it tonight." Vanessa tried to forestall further discussion. Did Frank mean they should drop their expensive line after this collection? The prospect was shattering.

"That's where the real money is!" A vein pounded in Frank's forehead. "Bill won't squeeze us. He said he'd give us a year."

"But Frank, half a million dollars!" Could they pull that much out of the business in one year, even in mass-market? If they began to manufacture for mass-market, they'd face a heavy investment in equipment, a tremendous increase in rent and labor. They'd need extensive bank loans just to start operating.

"We're not going to do it with our exclusive line," he said flatly. "Maybe if we'd pushed our way up to three or four hundred stores, but it's too late for that."

"Frank, we'll talk about it tonight." The daytime hours belonged to getting orders out, working on new designs. In the evenings, after dinner and time spent with Suzy, they sat down to grapple with crisis problems. "I'll ask Phyllis if she and Arnie can come over for dinner. We'll thrash this out afterward."

"Don't we have some dinner party?"

"Not tonight. That's tomorrow." About three evenings a week they were caught up in socializing. Seventh Avenue was gaining steadily in respectability. With Mollie Parnis in and out of the White House as Mamie's favorite designer, Seventh Avenue was even acquiring a certain glamor.

Vanessa was irritated when her mind refused to focus on her sketching that afternoon. She was too upset by Bill's threat to sell out to a stranger. They should have seen it coming, she chastised herself. He'd dropped enough hints.

Vanessa left with Phyllis at the normal quitting

time. As usual, Frank remained behind. He'd been paranoid about each new line being knocked off ever since a break-in some weeks earlier. Now he remained in the office each day until their night watchman arrived. *"I'd like us to get at least one full season out of a dress before it becomes a Ford."* A "Ford" was any design that showed up in the stores at a dozen different prices at the same time.

In addition to sharing breakfast each morning with Suzy, Vanessa made an extra effort to be with her small daughter each night when she had her dinner and reported on the activities at her kindergarten. Tonight, despite her show of interest, Vanessa's mind was on their business emergency. How would they manage the operating capital for a mass-market line? Both she and Frank were against using factors, though it was a common situation on Seventh Avenue.

This was an insane time to move into mass-market. Right now there was a growing demand for expensive clothes, "dress-up" clothes. Women were willing to pay for the exclusiveness they found in her dresses. They couldn't get this from Ceil Chapman or Harvey Berin. Look how well James Galanos was doing with his wild prices. And that Italian designer at Elizabeth Arden's—Count Sarmi.

Vanessa saw huge profits in elegant ready-to-wear for special occasions. Clothes that were close to Paris haute couture. But she didn't see profits to pay off half a million dollars in the next twelve months. Frank was right. They needed a great year in mass-market ready-to-wear if they were to buy out Bill Bartlett.

After dinner Frank and Arnie retired to the den

while the two women lingered over second helpings of Maria's superb chocolate mousse. Nostalgically they rehashed the fashion happenings of the past year: Schiaparelli closing her house because it was so heavily in debt, the tragic death of Jacques Fath, Coco Chanel's comeback collection the past August.

"I love what *Life* said about Chanel," Vanessa recalled softly. " 'She's influenced all today's collections. At seventy-one, she brings us more than a style—she has caused a veritable tempest. She had decided to return and to conquer her old position—the first.' "

As they deserted the dining room and walked down the hall to the den, Vanessa heard the two men in heated conversation about Bill's ultimatum. Arnie was wary about expansion, Frank quick to gamble. Yet Vanessa knew they had little choice.

"Arnie, look at what's happening," Frank said impatiently. "Cheap Paris copies have never sold so well. With plane travel what it is these days, Paris is practically in our backyard. Look what Ohrbach's is doing with their Oval Room! I know," Frank acknowledged quickly, "the Oval Room copies are not cheap. But the Paris copies filter down to the Lerner Shops and S. Klein."

It was a paradox, Vanessa mused, that cheap Paris copies and ultra-expensive clothes were booming at the same time. But when was fashion ever logical? The problem, she knew, was to find a way to move into mass-market without drowning in the overhead.

"I've already talked with a building a couple of blocks down from us about taking on more floors," Frank pursued. Arnie exchanged an anxious glance with Vanessa. He knew that Frank would be grandiose in his plans. "I'll see what kind of a deal we can work out for machines and —"

"Frank, wait," Vanessa interrupted. As always, she felt uncomfortable opposing him. Frank was the sharp business mind. She was the designer. But she had learned a lot about the business over the years. She knew the pitfalls. Their future depended on how they handled themselves in the next twelve months. And she was determined not to abandon her cherished "couture"—couture in the American fashion, expensive but not custom-made. "We can offer two lines. Our expensive collection going to our fifty stores, plus Vanessa II, to sell mass-market. We can do this in a way that won't entail heavy investment," she said, shaping the new venture in her mind. "We can contract for the cutting and sewing. That way we won't have too—"

"No," Frank rejected. "No contracting. That's too dangerous; we won't have control. We could miss our delivery deadlines. You know what happens, Vanessa!"

"It won't happen with us." Vanessa leaned forward confidently. "We're powerful enough to have contractors cater to us. We won't have to buy equipment. We won't need more space—or very little. And we won't have to worry about carrying employees during the slow periods in production."

"She's right," Arnie said, a glint of respect in his eyes. "Frank, that's the only way to go!"

"I don't like it," Frank stalled. "Our stores have never had to wait for deliveries. They know that when I give them a date, their dresses will be there."

"You'll stay on the contractors' backs," Vanessa said. "You won't *let* them miss a deadline."

"Vanessa II can ride in on the coattails of the regular line," Phyllis agreed. "Not as expensive, but from the same designer. Women will love it."

"Vanessa, how the hell will you handle two collections?" Frank challenged.

"I'll handle it," Vanessa promised. "If I have to work twenty-four hours a day."

For a moment a heavy silence hung over them while the other three waited for Frank's reaction.

"We'll set up a special design studio," Frank capitulated. The room was charged with excitement. "Nobody will be allowed to bother you, Vanessa. You'll concentrate on designing with none of the old crazy interruptions. And if any bastard of a contractor doesn't deliver on time, I'll cut off his balls."

Vanessa vowed to come up with her first Vanessa II fall/winter collection for formal showing in late May, just five weeks after what was now labeled their couture collection. She flew to Europe as scheduled but cut the trip to five days.

She arrived in Paris shortly after the Dior collection was shown. His H line had been adapted into the A line, and French women were fascinated. Undoubtedly, American manufacturers would flood the market with copies. They always followed in the footsteps of Dior, whose clothes could be copied easily, whereas Chanel and Balenciaga were difficult to present in ready-to-wear because their success depended on superb cut and imaginative and expensive detail.

In Florence, where she ordered exquisite fabrics for six special evening dresses, she noted the excitement surrounding Emilio Pucci. She remembered Pat's letter from Houston raving about his marvelous scarves.

Along with column breaks about Vanessa's "whirlwind trip to the fashion centers of Europe," Phyllis was winning editorial space with the news that Tina

Gregory would personally present the new couture collection in Hollywood, and Pat Roberts — the beautiful wife of the young congressman from Texas — would present it in Washington, D.C.

Vanessa worked with the knowledge that control of her company hinged on the success of the Vanessa II collection. She and Frank had one argument after another about expenses. While he was eager to spend heavily on entertainment and advertising — at a time when the *New York Times* was beginning to focus on daily fashion news — he was tight with their salespeople, screaming over expense account sheets, convinced that the sales force was stealing from them. He complained that Vanessa was extravagant with materials for the couture line.

In late April the couture line was presented to high praise from all the fashion critics. A month later — with Vanessa exhausted and nervous — the first Vanessa II line appeared. Again, Vanessa's designs were applauded on every side. Sales soared.

On summer weekends they escaped to a rented house in Southampton, where Suzy and Maria were in full-time residence. As in the New York apartment, Vanessa kept a sketchpad by the bed, another suspended on the bathroom door, a third in the kitchen for those occasions when Maria was off and she prepared dinner.

In July Vanessa flew to California with Pat for Tina's wedding to Harvey. Harvey's family was not present. His mother refused to acknowledge either of his divorces, and his two sisters and brother disapproved of his life-style.

Tina's wedding dress was again designed by Vanessa. Reporters had a field day with the glamorous trio of movie star, designer, and congressman's

wife. Of the three of them, Vanessa thought affectionately, it was Pat who was living the storybook life; the
sheltered young wife and mother, unaware of the outside jungles — velvet though they might be — in which
she and Tina lived.

They all flew back to New York the day after the
wedding. Harvey pointedly spent most of the flight in
the pilot's cabin, leaving the friends time for cherished
private conversation.

Pat was obviously proud of Paul's rising political
influence. "He's outraged over all this talk about civil
rights," she admitted, her smile apologetic. "Washington isn't much different from Texas. Though it's 50
percent black, the 'coloreds' lead segregated lives. But
what truly astonishes me is that Daddy — whom I've
always considered dyed-in-the-wool Old South — sees
this as a movement whose time has come."

Congressman Owens probably saw it as a political
necessity, Vanessa thought. He was considered one of
the sharpest men in Congress. Even though he might
not agree on a personal level, he knew what the polls
said.

Back in New York Vanessa sequestered herself each
day in her new design studio. Except for her assistant,
Doris, she saw no one. The task of designing two lines
was awesome, but she was determined to bring it off.
She refused to accept the possibility of losing control
of Creations.

In addition to Doris, who worked with her on both
couture and ready-to-wear, she hired a sketching assistant, Linda Odell, to do technical sketches of the
couture for their files, work up sketches and artwork
for their presentations, and follow through on the
clerical work. But only Vanessa was allowed to buy
fabrics and trim.

At home Frank was increasingly short-tempered. Vanessa knew he was plagued by the need to meet their payments to Bill. Arnie had handled the deal well: Bill's stock was in escrow until he was paid off. Arnie had worked out a contract that gave them until March 31, 1956, to pay off. They controlled 100 percent of Creations stock.

They had delivered the first payment of $100,000 in July. It seemed reasonable, looking at the sales, that they would duplicate this in September. But both Frank and Vanessa knew that if the mass-market collection failed, it would mean disaster.

The months flew by. Doris was heavily involved with the ready-to-wear. She had even taken over the preliminary research on fabrics and trim for the line. And Linda was eager to accept new responsibilities. She was creating first patterns, draping, reporting on trends in the stores.

Vanessa moved without a break from one collection to the next. The profits were piling up. Creations by Vanessa Conrad was taking Seventh Avenue by storm. Frank stayed on the backs of the contractors—screaming and cursing—to make sure deliveries were on schedule. He was earning a reputation as a miracle man.

On March 30, 1956, Vanessa and Frank made their final payment to Bill Bartlett. They owned the business free and clear. Frank swept Vanessa, Phyllis, and Arnie off to lunch at Lindy's to celebrate.

"You know, Vanessa"—he dropped an arm around her shoulder and winked at Arnie—"it's time we talked about buying a house up in Westchester."

"Frank, we'd only be able to sleep there," she protested. "With our schedule, a suburban house would be ridiculous."

"You could design gorgeously at the house, with all the comforts of home," he cajoled. "And it would be great for Suzy."

"Suzy's doing fine in New York. And I would die being so isolated all day in Westchester." Vanessa refused to take him seriously.

"You're isolated in your studio on Seventh Avenue," he reminded.

"When I want to be," she declared. "I need the stimulation of New York. I need to be around people and know what's in the air. It's all part of creating clothes, Frank."

"You'd have a hell of a time trying to persuade people to drive up to Westchester for a dinner party," Phyllis pointed out. "And that's part of the business."

Their waiter arrived, and they concentrated on ordering lunch. But Vanessa's unease over Frank's suggestion wouldn't go away.

"What about a country house, Frank?" Vanessa offered. "It would be wonderful to escape from the city on the weekends."

"We couldn't go too far," he said thoughtfully.

"Maybe around Croton-on-Hudson," Arnie suggested. "You can drive up in an hour, Phyllis and I have seen some great houses up there."

Vanessa and Frank began to take weekend trips in search of just the right house. They looked throughout the spring and summer and into autumn. Frank was more grandiose in his demands than Vanessa, but she conceded he could afford to be. Their profits from the mass-market line were impressing the entire industry. Still, Frank wasn't satisfied. He was obsessed by the potential of their mass-market line, and was determined to increase their profits still more. If they could just get away for the weekends, Vanessa told herself, Frank would relax.

Vanessa was worried. Frank had become so ambitious for power on Seventh Avenue that their marriage was suffering. Of late their lovemaking was mechanical, rote. Frank was brusque at home, even yelling at Suzy. He'd always been so sweet and understanding with her. A weekend house would be good for Frank, Vanessa told herself. If they could just find a house that pleased him.

"Betsy, make me some coffee," Frank yelled to his secretary from his cluttered office.

"Okay, okay," Betsy said, lifting her eyebrows at his sharp tone.

If she didn't like it, she could quit, Frank thought. He went back inside and closed the door. On top of everything else he had to worry about hiring a showroom model. He'd scheduled interviews for after five, when the madness outside settled down a bit. With their spring couture opening just two weeks away and the mass-market following in three weeks, everything had to move exactly on schedule. And he still didn't trust the contractors.

Maybe they'd run up on Sunday for another look at that house near Croton. Vanessa had had a fit when the broker told them the price, but it was a showplace. Fourteen rooms and a guest house on seventeen hilltop acres. His sisters would shit in their pants when they saw it. To see his country house they'd come to New York for a few days. They still hadn't met Vanessa.

Betsy came in with his mug of coffee and darted back to her typewriter. Frank swigged down the coffee while he checked over the costs of the couture fabrics

Vanessa had ordered. Phyllis was working her ass off on the couture showing, using the mystery touch. Everybody on the Avenue was dying to know just what Vanessa was coming up with for the spring collection. Security had never been so tight on their designs. Though he would never admit it to Vanessa, he knew their couture was responsible for the high sales on their ready-to-wear.

He frowned as one of his three phones rang. He forced himself to be polite when he recognized the voice of a major department store manager in the Midwest, but irritation welled up in him as he listened.

"No!" he barked to a complaint that Creations wouldn't share losses on markdowns—a common arrangement. "Look, you know how I work. If you overbuy, it's your problem. Buy less next season. Keep pestering me, and I'll take away the line. Women want our dresses—they'll go where they're sold." He nodded in amusement as the customer backed off at the other end of the line. You had to be tough with these bastards.

He hung up the phone and went into his private bathroom. Maybe he ought to shave before the girls came in for the interviews. He paused in front of the one-way mirror he'd had secretly installed. The mirror gave him a good view of the couture shipping area.

What was the matter with those two packers? Shooting the breeze like they were on their lunch break. He went back into his office to call the foreman and tell him to chew out the two idlers. He glanced at his watch. In twenty minutes the help not scheduled for overtime would be leaving for the day. He was sure half of them were already heading for the wash-

435

rooms.

He left his office and headed for the elevators. Once a week he made a routine late afternoon trip down to the lobby. If anybody saw him, he was buying a magazine. But he was checking covertly to see if any employees were walking out early. He ducked behind a post when he saw Linda emerge from the elevator and cross to a man waiting at the entrance. Linda slipped him a large manila envelope, and the man rushed through the revolving door to the street.

Frank waited until Linda had returned to the elevator before leaving his hiding place. That little bitch! She was handing over their designs to somebody else!

Trembling with rage, Vanessa confronted Linda in the designing studio.

"Linda, don't lie," she warned. "Frank saw you. You're stealing our designs."

"You can't prove anything," Linda shot back definately, smoothing the hips of the black capris that, along with a turtleneck, had become her uniform. "What are you going to do? Call the cops? They'll just laugh."

"I thought we had a fine working relationship. You said you liked being part of our team." Just a few weeks ago she had pushed Frank into giving Linda a substantial raise.

"Vanessa, knock it off." Linda's smile was arrogant. "Where can I go from here? *You're* the designer. You'll never let anybody else work on the collections. I'm ambitious. I have to take care of myself. And Frank deserves it," she said with contempt. "Every worker in the shop hates his guts. He's Seventh Avenue's Simon Legree."

Vanessa stared at her in shock. Linda was lying,

trying to justify her actions.

"I'm sure this has been going on for weeks," she said, her mind fighting off the panic. *The little bitch had pirated the whole collection.* "You're selling us out to the competition."

"I was going to give notice in two weeks." Linda backed away. "I've got a new job where I'll have a chance to design."

"Get out," Vanessa ordered through clenched teeth. "Right now. I don't ever want to see your face again."

Vanessa sat motionless at her desk, listening to the sound of Linda's stiletto heels clicking down the hall. By the time their buyers saw the new collection, knock-offs at lower prices would be hanging in other showrooms. The spring couture collection would be a disaster.

She waited until she knew most of the employees had left for the day. Then she took the stairs down one flight to their quarters. At the door to the business offices she paused for a moment, remembering that Frank was interviewing showroom models.

She sat at the edge of Betsy's desk, impatient to talk to Frank. A tall, slim girl emerged from his office. She was radiant.

"Okay, doll, see you in the morning. Remember, you're on probation."

The new showroom model smiled sweetly at Vanessa, a glint of recognition in her eyes. It always astonished Vanessa when strangers recognized her.

"Come on in, Vanessa." Frank gestured with one hand.

"You found somebody," Vanessa said.

"She'll do," he shrugged. "The usual. No ass, no tits — she'll wear clothes great. You talked to Linda?"

"I threw her out," Vanessa said calmly. Frank yelled

and screamed—she always made a point of appearing unruffled. "Frank, she's fed the whole collection to whoever she's working for. We have to scrap the whole line."

Frank gaped in disbelief.

"Are you crazy, Vanessa? You can't do another line in two weeks!"

"I'll have to do it." Her face wore an incandescence born of commitment. They had to save the company from bad reviews and a brutal drop in sales. A poorly received couture collection would have a drastic effect on their ready-to-wear as well. "I'll design a spring collection totally different from anything I've ever done. Frank, we've got to make fashion news. We won't let Linda Odell and her people cut our throats."

"Even if you could do a new collection that fast, Vanessa," Frank said slowly, "how the hell do we get our samples out that fast?"

"We'll do it, Frank. If Doris and I have to sleep in the shop for the next two weeks. Keep our best operators on as much overtime as they can handle without falling in their tracks. We open on schedule—and with a totally new line."

Thirty-two

Vanessa's life became a frenzy of design, fabric, and work. She focused on the fabrics already purchased and on hand, and tried to create an opulent, romantic collection that would guarantee a whole season without imitations. The collection had to be too expensive and too intricate to copy. Designs, she conceded only to herself and Doris, that belonged in a custom salon.

She knew their race against time would prevent Frank from working out the exact costing of each garment. Though she was using the same fabrics, she was quite aware that the longer skirts, the new expensive trim, the intricate detail, would send the costing skyrocketing. Frank would scream if he realized what she was doing, but this was their only way to save the season — perhaps their entire future on Seventh Avenue.

She discarded all thought of raising their prices to the stores; the price tags would be out of line. They would work an entire season without a profit. Let them charge it off to promotion. But they'd make fashion headlines. Creations by Vanessa Conrad was offering exciting, revolutionary fashions, clothes totally different from anything any other company was showing. Women would love them.

Vanessa dashed about town in her newly acquired Cadillac limousine with chauffeur. She was exhilarated as each new design became a sample. She and Doris were working as one to meet the deadline.

Vanessa was exasperated by the American devotion to Paris. Ohrbach's and Macy's chased to France, and even Saks Fifth Avenue, which had been promoting their own Sophie couture clothes, was into the Paris-copy act.

Vanessa designed this collection with reckless disregard for Paris trends.

As Vanessa feared, Frank was apoplectic when he realized the cost of manufacturing the spring couture line.

"Damn it, Vanessa, have you lost your mind? We'll be lucky to break even! A whole season lost!"

"Frank, it's our only salvation." She managed a confident smile. "This is the most exciting line I've ever done. Phyllis is out of her mind over it, and the publicity will be sensational. No knock-offs. Even if they try, they won't sell. You can't fake what I've done with these dresses."

"This kind of publicity we can't afford." Frank was grim. "Do you know how much money we're losing?"

"We couldn't show what we'd planned," Vanessa protested. "Not when Linda's group will come out with identical styles. Our *identity* is our exclusiveness."

"Thank God we have Vanessa II, or we'd be in deep financial trouble."

"We'll lost Vanessa II if the couture falls on its face," Vanessa pointed out. "But it's going to work, Frank. We'll break even on the season. We can afford not to show a profit on the spring couture."

Phyllis arranged an elaborate formal opening. Vanessa's new collection sparked great excitement in

440

the fashion world. Creations dominated coveted editorial space in the fashion magazines, in *Women's Wear Daily,* and in daily newspapers. Frank took advantage of the furor to add another thirty stores to their list. Vanessa was uneasy; the couture line must not be manufactured by contractors. She was afraid of losing quality control. With the extra stores they would have to lease additional space, buy more equipment, hire more people.

And Frank was insisting they buy the house in Croton.

"We need it for our sanity. Ten weekends a year at Southampton are not enough. We need a year-round escape hatch. Write it off as a business expense," he said persuasively, calling on his favorite exhortation. "I know you don't have time for buying furniture and decorating. Hire an interior decorator to handle it."

Vanessa thought about the pressure-cooker pace of their lives, and went along with Frank's decision. Arnie dealt with the real estate broker, pushed through the closing in record time. With bitter sweet pleasure Vanessa hired Phil and Robbie, friends from the early summers on Fire Island, and turned the house over to them. They had become prominent decorators—how far we've all come, thought Vanessa, and remembered the painful war years, when she had waited so anxiously for letters from Eddie.

With Frank setting up their enlarged operation, Vanessa envisioned yet another venture: a custom salon on Madison Avenue to cater to private customers. Like Hattie Carnegie, Mainbocher, the custom salon at Bergdorf, or I. Magnin's custom salon in California. Galanos had private customers. This was the kind of prestige she longed for. But Vanessa didn't discuss the idea with Frank until spring. She knew

Frank would rebel. He was concerned with profits, and the custom salon could not compete with their American version of couture nor with Vanessa II.

"You're out of your mind, Vanessa!" Frank yelled. "How many dresses can you design in one year?"

"I can do it, Frank. And think of the prestige a custom salon would bring."

"A custom salon is a plaything," Frank said dismissively. "Even Paris is beginning to understand that the money is tight in haute couture. Dior's profits come from his ready-to-wear. Chanel No. 5 has made a mint. It's the licensing that brings in their fortunes, not their couture houses."

Exactly, Vanessa agreed in frustrated silence. Because of their reputation in haute couture. With a custom salon she could build up that kind of name. "You have to save your time for what's important," he interrupted her thoughts. "Our couture and Vanessa II. Maybe in a few years, but not at this point. We're on top, baby," he said with a sudden grin. "We're not doing anything to jeopardize that."

"No," Vanessa conceded.

Her every waking moment was spent in the business. The only exception was the time she spent each day with Suzy. The custom salon would have to wait. But in one small part of her mind she hoarded this precious dream. Its time would come.

In May Tina flew to New York from Hong Kong to stay at Harvey's triplex penthouse on Fifth Avenue until the summer. Pat came up from Washington and they had a weekend reunion at the house in Croton. Frank apologized over Saturday dinner that the two-bedroom guest cottage was not yet ready.

"Frank, when the three of us get together, we'd be happy in sleeping bags in the den," Tina laughed.

"And I can't get over Phil and Robbie doing the house!"

"That was a good summer," Pat recalled nostalgically. "God, we were so young."

"And how are your two young ones?" Frank asked Pat.

"Oh, they're fine. They're down in Virginia with Mother and Daddy for the weekend." Pat's eyes grew serious. "The doctor insists that Daddy retire after this term. He's had two minor heart attacks."

"I was going to wait until after dinner to tell you my news. But I can't," Tina said and paused dramatically. "I think I'm pregnant."

"Tina! How wonderful!" Vanessa leaned forward to grasp Tina's hand in hers.

"I flew back home to check with the doctor," Tina said. "I haven't told Harvey yet. I wanted to be sure." She radiated maternal tenderness. "He'll be so pleased — and proud. He'll be fifty next month. I can just hear him bragging to his friends!"

On a mid-July Saturday afternoon Tina stood before the mirrored wall in the black-and-white marble bathroom of the beachfront house Harvey had bought for their summer use. They'd chosen Southampton not only because Harvey had business associates who came out every summer, but because Vanessa and Frank had rented a house close by.

"I look so fat already," Tina mourned to Harvey as he stepped from the stall shower. "Look!" She tugged the loose printed silk top she wore over shocking pink pants snugly across her stomach. "I've just started my fourth month."

"I can't wait till you're sticking out to here." He

gestured broadly. "My kid."

"Mine, too." She reached to pull him close. "Ours." Adam's half-brother. She'd make sure they were close, no matter how much Sal and Eva carried on. Harvey knew about Adam.

"I guess you had something to do with it," he conceded good-humoredly. "I can't wait to see Mama's face when I tell her I have another child. For that she'll forgive me the two divorces."

"Haven't you told her I'm pregnant?" Tina pretended to pout.

"I never tell Mama anything ahead of time. I give her surprises. The gray Rolls-Royce, the penthouse on Central Park South, the two minks—one for everyday and one for special occasions," he chuckled. "Mama loves surprises."

"Do you have to fly out to Phoenix?" She hated every minute they were apart. "Two days after our second anniversary? I thought we'd celebrate for a week." For their anniversary Harvey had given her a Harry Winston custom-designed masterpiece of diamonds, emeralds, and platinum.

"A major deal in the works," he apologized, nuzzling against her. "I've been telling you for weeks."

"I could go along," she tried again.

"Not with that little one you're carrying." He treated her as though she were a porcelain figurine, and she loved it. "After the baby is born we'll go on a trip around the world. He'll be a veteran traveler before he's a year old."

"When do you have to leave?"

"In about forty minutes."

"That's long enough for a quickie," she drawled. "So I won't forget you while you're gone. And relax," she ordered, because Harvey always seemed scared when they made love now. "You're not going to disturb him."

Tina settled herself on a chaise on the deck to gaze lazily at the sea. Vanessa, with Suzy, Frank and Maria in tow, would be popping in any minute now, she judged with a confirming glance at her watch.

She had never felt so relaxed. Nobody was making demands on her. All she had to do for the next five months was loll in idleness and watch her tummy pop out. No worries. It was a whole different ball game from when she was carrying Adam.

She had not made a picture in almost a year. Harvey had agreed that she had to finish off her last contract. He was proud of her success. It wasn't a threat to him. But she had meant it when she said she was through with Hollywood.

She heard the sound of a car rolling over the pebbled driveway, and with a smile she left the deck and went inside.

"Don't bother with the door, Cynthia," she called out to the maid as she hurried across the sprawling living room and into the entrance foyer.

Tina welcomed the arrivals with exuberant kisses and led them into the living room. This was her real family. She fussed over Suzy, who was old enough at nine to be proud that her Aunt Tina was a famous movie star, admired Maria's new Audrey Hepburn haircut, twitted Frank about wearing a fashionable pink shirt.

"Remember when any man wearing anything pink was definitely queer? But I suppose we ought to be glad he doesn't have a ducktail haircut," she chuckled. "When I talked to Adam a couple of weeks ago, he told me nobody in his school was allowed to wear a ducktail." Her voice was jestingly solemn.

Tina presented Suzy with the latest in what was becoming a collection of Madame Alexander dolls and was hugged in ecstatic gratitude. Then Maria and Suzy left for their Southampton rental. Frank lingered with Tina and Vanessa over a cocktail while they marveled over the transcontinental speed record set by Major John Glenn. Then he phoned the house with instructions to have the chauffeur pick him up and take him to an appointment at the golf course.

"How do you feel?" Vanessa asked Tina solicitously when they were alone.

"Like the luckiest woman alive. Would you believe it, that's only the second drink I've had since the doctor told me I was definitely pregnant? The first was when I told Harvey. I'm taking such marvelous care of myself. It stuns me that I can feel so maternal."

A phone rang in the house, and Tina was suddenly alert.

"That's my private line." The ringing stopped. One of the servants had answered.

"How long will Harvey be away?" Vanessa asked.

"Just a few days," she began and looked up inquiringly as Cynthia appeared at the door.

"It's for you, Miss Tina," Cynthia told her.

"Thank you, Cynthia." She rose to her feet. "Come on with me to the bedroom, Vanessa. It's probably Harvey calling from the airport. They may have had some delay in takeoff."

Hand in hand, enjoying each other's company, they walked down the hall that led to the master bedroom. In the dramatically modern black-and-white bedroom Tina picked up the phone from the night table while

Vanessa stood at the expanse of glass that offered a view of the summer-blue Atlantic.

"Hi." Tina's greeting was effervescent.

"Hello, Tina—"

"Oh, William. I was expecting Harvey."

"Tina, I think you'd better drive to New York," William Shiffman said solemnly.

"What's wrong? Has something happened to your mother?" Tina asked in alarm.

"Mama's fine." William cleared his throat. "There's been an accident."

"Harvey?" Her voice was shrill with shock. "William, where is he? I have to go to him! What hospital is he in?"

"I don't think that would be wise," he began.

"What do you mean, it wouldn't be wise? He's my husband!"

"Tina, are you alone?" William asked nervously.

"No." She tapped one foot nervously. Vanessa watched, her face anxious. "I want to be with Harvey! Tell me this minute where he is! William, how badly is he hurt?"

"He was badly injured in the crash. He—Tina, he's dead."

"No! It's not true!" Tina screamed. "Vanessa, talk to him—" She held the phone out to Vanessa. "He's trying to tell me that Harvey's dead!"

"Sit down, Tina," Vanessa ordered gently, her own face pale. She reached for the phone. "This is Vanessa Conrad. Tell me what's happened."

Tina listened—dazed and sick—to the brisk questions Vanessa shot into the phone. *It wasn't true.*

"Why would they call William and not me?" Tina demanded, searching for something to focus on. "I'm his wife."

"Cynthia, call my house," Vanessa instructed the maid. "Tell my husband to come immediately."

"Vanessa, you didn't answer me." Tina was ashen. "If something had happened to Harvey, wouldn't they call me and not his brother?"

"Darling, you have to think of the baby now," Vanessa said gently. "The police called William because Harvey kept his name in his wallet for contact in emergencies. He didn't want either you or his mother to be told of — of a bad accident by a stranger."

"I want to see him!" Two hours ago they'd been making love.

"We'll drive into New York," Vanessa soothed. "William is arranging for the funeral on Monday morning. In the Jewish faith the burial must be quick."

"I don't believe it!" Tina screamed. "It's a lie! It's a goddamn lie!"

"Tina, it's terrible," Vanessa said, her voice anguished. "But you have to remember you're carrying Harvey's baby. You mustn't allow yourself to be torn apart this way."

"Vanessa, why?" Tina collapsed sobbing into her arms. "Why did this have to happen when we were both so happy?"

Worried by Tina's distraught condition, Vanessa called her obstetrician, who prescribed a mild sedative. Under this medication, Tina sat between Vanessa and Frank on the drive to New York while Vanessa and Frank murmured futile consolations.

At William's instructions they went to the home of Harvey's mother, where Tina met her husband's family for the first time. His mother had been sedated and put to bed. Now his brother and sisters planned his funeral. His sons had not yet been reached. Harvey's first wife was cold and vindictive toward Tina. The family made it clear that they regarded this first wife as the real widow.

Vanessa insisted that Tina stay at their apartment rather than at the penthouse she had shared with Harvey. For Vanessa, Tina's grief was a painful reminder of the tragic accident that had claimed Eddie's life. A small, aching part of her relived that nightmare with Tina. She ordered all newspapers to be kept from Tina, the TV and radio kept silent lest newscasts invade the apartment with reports of Harvey's death.

Pat phoned from Washington immediately when she heard the news. She wouldn't be able to come up for the funeral. CeeCee was ill with chicken pox and hysterical about being scarred.

"Tina will understand," Vanessa comforted her.

Sunday evening Tina, Vanessa, and Frank went together to view Harvey's body at the funeral home. Tina collapsed over the coffin. When she was sufficiently composed to leave, they encountered a barrage of photographers on the sidewalk, all eager for pictures of the grieving widow.

Determinedly Vanessa remained at Tina's side, knowing her agony, frustrated by her inability to assuage her grief. She held Tina's hand through the services at the funeral home, through the emotion-laden Orthodox Jewish funeral. Harvey's first wife fainted at the gravesite, and Tina was blatantly ignored by all the relatives. The elder son crossed to tell Tina that she would not be welcome when they sat *shivah*.

"The bastards are worried that Tina's gong to inherit Harvey's estate," Frank whispered as he helped

Vanessa into the waiting limousine after the burial in Westchester County.

Vanessa insisted Tina return to the apartment with her and Frank. Tina was in no condition to be alone. Maria had prepared a sumptuous luncheon, but Tina wanted only to cling to Vanessa and talk about Harvey.

"Vanessa, how did you survive when Eddie was killed?" she demanded. "Where did you find the strength?"

"I had to, Tina. For Suzy. The way you have to survive for Harvey's child."

Late that afternoon Tina cried out suddenly in pain.

"Vanessa, I have an awful stomachache." Her eyes were wide with terror.

"Nerves," Vanessa said. "But I'll call the doctor, just to be sure."

She rose to her feet, trying to conceal her own alarm. Again Tina cried out, clutched at her stomach.

"Vanessa, it hurts. It hurts almost like labor."

Vanessa darted out into the hall.

"Frank! Call an ambulance!"

Four days later, still pale and shaken but no longer pregnant, Tina listened to the reading of Harvey's will. He had provided for each member of his family, including small bequests to his two ex-wives. The remainder of the estate he left to Tina.

Alone with the two lawyers, Tina listened to their uneasy elaboration on the extent of the estate, an inheritance rumored to be worth at least twenty million.

"Harvey was in the middle of some intricate speculations," the older attorney explained. "Only if he had lived could they have been carried out. His taste was expensive—there are a lot of creditors. After the creditors and the other bequests are paid, the estate will be surprisingly small."

"How much?" Tina was jarred back into reality.

"Perhaps sixty or seventy thousand," the other attorney said.

Tina stared in shock.

"What about the property?" she asked. "The Manhattan apartment, the house in Southampton, the house in Acapulco—"

"All mortgaged to the hilt," the older lawyer explained. "Harvey was gambling everything on a huge international syndicate he was putting together."

The syndicate he meant to be a gift to their child, Tina thought in fresh pain. He'd talked about it, but business bored her. She'd just smiled and pretended to be interested.

"What do I do about the property?" For a while she wouldn't have to worry about money. For a while.

"Sell it and pay off all the mortgages. You might realize another forty or fifty thousand from that."

"Could you handle that for me?" She gazed from one lawyer to the other. "I just want to settle this thing as fast as possible."

Briefly Tina considered returning to Hollywood. But in Hollywood she had been happy with Harvey. It would be full of ghosts. She'd go to London for a few months, she decided. Harvey had always liked London. No problems with a strange language. What he had called a civilized culture. Maybe in London she'd figure out how to put her life together.

Thirty-three

Vanessa threw herself into the feverish race against collection deadlines. But she still found time to worry about Tina. She received letters from London — where Tina had discovered an exciting boutique called Bazaar on King's Road, which offered clothes designed by a young Welsh girl named Mary Quant — and from St. Tropez. In September the letters arrived postmarked Paris. Knowing her reverence for Christian Dior, Tina phoned Vanessa in late October with the sad news of his sudden death.

"All Paris is in mourning. The day of the funeral the Boulevard was crowded with people — everyone from textile workers to the Duchess of Windsor."

When Paris became too depressing in the winter, Tina flew to St. Moritz. She was part of the new international set. She wrote of parties given by Elsa Maxwell, Aristotle Onassis, Countess Lilli Volpi, and Barbara Hutton. But back in New York, Vanessa worried about Tina's determined extravagance. She knew Tina's funds would not let her play this scene forever.

When twenty-one-year-old Yves Saint Laurent, whom Dior himself had decreed was to succeed him, introduced his first collection on January 30, Tina was among the international celebrities applauding.

She wrote Vanessa about the demonstration in the streets after the showing, with Parisians chanting Saint Laurent's name and declaring he had saved France. Vanessa understood this; Dior had been responsible for almost 50 percent of French fashion exports. The continued success of the House of Dior was essential to the French economy.

Early in spring Frank began to talk about moving to the more fashionable East Side. And he was again nursing thoughts about adding to their list of stores. *"I know we can sell to another fifty without diluting our exclusivity, Vanessa."* When both the fall/winter couture and Vanessa II collections had been presented to the press and buyers and received warmly, Vanessa acquiesced to the move. It would be a diversion for Frank, Vanessa thought; he'd forget about the store expansion for a while.

With Frank guiding the accelerated fall productions, Vanessa made a sudden decision to fly to France and Italy to buy fabrics. She promised herself that, while she might fly to Europe to search for exciting new fabrics, she would never join the semiannual dash to Paris—and more recently to Florence and Madrid as well—to see the fashion collections. She was determined not to be influenced by European design.

"Why do you have to run to Europe?" Frank joshed in high spirits. They had just signed the lease on a luxurious fourteen-room Park Avenue apartment and hired Phil and Robbie as their interior decorators. "Are you worried about Tina?"

"I want our fabrics to be spectacular in the coming collections. Frank, I have a strong feeling that fashion is in for drastic changes. I can't put my finger on it, but there's a new energy, a burst of young people in the industry." They were coming to New York from all over the country, lured by the new glamor that radiated from Seventh Avenue. "I feel a . . . freshness," she summed up with conviction, "that'll bring about vital changes."

"Because Yves Saint Laurent is still wet behind the ears?" Frank chuckled and then grew serious. "Do you think his trapeze look will sell in America?"

"It'll sell." Vanessa was confident. "American women don't like the sacks. That'll be dead before the end of the year. But the trapeze can be flattering—it plays up the bosom and plays down hips and thighs, which a lot of women are happy to hide. But all this copying of Paris is beginning to backfire. Seventh Avenue is going to have to stop copying and become more innovative."

"You could be right." He respected her fashion judgment. "Not only about the trapeze, but about something young in the air. A restlessness. Not just the beats. The young are fighting to be heard." He paused. "You're not exactly an old lady," he said flirtatiously. "You just hit thirty-three." His eyes narrowed, and Vanessa knew he was worrying about turning forty.

"It'll be a quick trip," Vanessa promised. "With maybe a day of talking to the textile people in Zurich. A week altogether," she planned. "And I'll take Suzy and Maria with me."

"Why? I thought this was business."

"It'll be a wonderful experience for Suzy," Vanessa said softly. "I'll call it a late tenth birthday present."

"You're taking her out of school?" he said reproachfully.

"School will be over," she pointed out. Suzy's school closed earlier than the public school system. "We'll be

454

just ahead of the mad tourist rush."

As Vanessa had suspected, Suzy was ecstatic when she heard about the trip to Europe. They flew first to London, where Tina was staying at the elegant Hotel Claridges. While Maria settled Suzy in bed in their suite, Vanessa and Tina relaxed in Tina's sitting room over breakfast.

"You look well," Vanessa decided, smiling in pleasure.

"I feel like such a heel." Tina's smile was rueful. "I've been seeing a man for the past three weeks. That's why I'm in London."

"It's been almost a year," Vanessa said gently, her eyes questioning.

"We've made a point of seeing each other in public only when other people are around. Nobody knows he's in the suite next door."

"An Englishman?"

Tina laughed. "Honey, it's Clark Fitzgerald."

Vanessa's mouth opened in astonishment. Clark Fitzgerald had stayed on top of the Hollywood movie heap for almost ten years, despite a mercurial temperament that kept him in a constant battle with his studio. He was considered one of Hollywood's most active playboys. And he was married. Tina had always avoided entanglements with married men.

"I thought he was married," Vanessa said with forced casualness.

"He's been married for twenty-two years," Tina admitted. "Since he was twenty. It hasn't been a working marriage for the last ten years. His wife's Catholic — so's he. She won't give him a divorce. But that doesn't bother me. I couldn't marry again after Harvey. With Clark it's just fun and games."

"Tina, you could get hurt," Vanessa warned gently.

"I've been hurt," Tina replied bitterly. She looked away, and when she faced Vanessa again, she wore a bright smile. "Now tell me what's happening back home. As soon as Clark sits out his feud with his studio, we'll both head for Hollywood."

"You're going back to work?" Vanessa was relieved.

"What else is there?" Tina shrugged. "Marty's already into negotiations."

Back in New York, Vanessa told herself that Frank was short-tempered because his fortieth birthday was breathing down his neck. Phyllis said that was like a man's version of menopause — and Vanessa tried to make him understand he was still attractive and desirable.

Vanessa was happy — so many nights now Frank reached for her the moment they were settled in bed. It was like the first year of their marriage. For a while she had feared his obsession with the business might ruin their personal lives.

Early in September Vanessa suspected she was pregnant. They'd been so careful, except for a couple of times out at the Southampton house. She had pushed from her mind all thoughts of another child because Frank had persuaded her that they must put careers ahead of everything else. They had Suzy — they were a family.

Walking on the beach of Southampton on a glorious Sunday morning — the sun high, the sky a cloudless blue, the waves lapping leisurely against the shore — Vanessa told Frank her news. He stopped dead to search her face in shock.

"You're sure, Vanessa? Maybe you're just late."

"I'm sure, Frank." Her heart was pounding.

"I never thought I could have a kid." The admission was self-conscious. "Back in the army, in Tunisia, I picked up something. The docs cured it fast, but I thought I was sterile."

"You're definitely not sterile," Vanessa laughed. "Unless this is another immaculate conception." *Was he upset about the baby?*

"You're happy about this?" he probed.

"Frank, yes. Oh, yes."

"Then so am I." His grin was irresistible. "But we have to do a lot of figuring with the business."

"Frank, nothing will change," she said swiftly. "I'll work right up to the last minute. I'll be back at the drawing board a week after the baby's born."

Their world became the business and the new baby. Both Vanessa and Frank spent a lot of time with Suzy, making sure she understood that the new baby was not competition, but someone who would enrich their lives. Before the news of her mother's pregnancy, Suzy had been madly in love with rock 'n' roll and Elvis Presley. Her prize possession was an Elvis Presley T-shirt. Now she was madly in love with the idea of a baby brother or sister.

Vanessa delayed telling Tina, worried that it would only remind her of her miscarriage. She was happy when Tina wrote that she was "back on the old treadmill again"—Tina needed to work. But the gossip columns reported on her continuing affair with Clark Fitzgerald with increasingly unsavory undertones.

At Christmas Vanessa, Frank, Suzy, and Maria drove down to Georgetown to spend three days with Pat and her family. Pat was delighted to see CeeCee and Suzy together.

Vanessa told herself she was ridiculous to suspect that Pat was unhappy with Paul. He seemed devoted to her and the children. Still, she could never forget that he had made a pass at Tina that Labor Day weekend.

Early in April, while in the midst of plotting the next trunk show with Phyllis, Vanessa felt her first labor pains.

"Don't say a word to Frank yet—you know how nervous he is," she cautioned with a conspiratorial grin, "but he could be a father by morning."

"You're in labor?" Phyllis didn't know whether to be happy or concerned. Her face glowed with a blend of anticipation and anxiety.

"Let's finish up these plans," Vanessa said calmly. "Then I'll call Maria and have her meet us at the hospital with my valise. You can phone Frank a little later."

By the time Vanessa arrived at the hospital, the labor pains were close together. A nurse ordered a wheelchair and took her up to the maternity floor, where they found Maria and Suzy.

"Suzy insisted on coming with me," Maria apologized.

"Mommy, does it hurt?" Suzy's eyes were wide with concern.

"It's worth it, darling," Vanessa insisted, but she was grateful when she was whisked off to her room.

Four hours later Vanessa held her second daughter, Wendy Elizabeth Bernstein, in her arms. Already she had a fan club of four: her father, her sister, Maria, and Phyllis.

"She looks just like you," Frank decided in approval and reached with determination to take his new daughter into his arms. "Wait'll my sisters hear about this! They didn't even know she was on the way."

* * *

Vanessa's life was perfect except that she had to be away from Wendy hours each day. In addition to a daily houseworker, the domestic staff now included a full-time cook so that Maria was free to devote all of her attention to the new baby. Still, when she was away from the house, Vanessa called in for reports.

Frank was eager to move into the Croton house full-time, keeping the New York apartment for those nights when they might be tied up late in the city.

"Vanessa, it'll be great for the kids," he urged. "Suzy already loves it up there."

"She loves it for weekends," Vanessa conceded. "All her friends are here. And her school. Frank, I would hate driving back and forth between the city and Croton every day. We're not suburban people."

This summer, Frank decreed, they would commute to Croton instead of renting a house at Southampton, where the most they could manage were weekends. Why should they spend sweltering summer nights in the city when they had the house up there? Vanessa refrained from reminding him that their fourteen-room apartment on Park Avenue was fully air-conditioned. She would miss Southampton.

In the summer Suzy was enrolled in day camp in Westchester. Each morning the camp bus arrived to pick her up at the door. Wendy was thriving. Vanessa and Frank were driven into the city in the limousine and used the traveling time for business discussion.

Frank insisted they continue the "summer commuting" until school opened and Suzy had to be back in the city. Vanessa was happy to abandon the long drives back and forth on the highways five days a week. But Frank became reproachful and sullen when she again refused to move up to the Croton house on a full-time basis. This was a side of Frank that was new to her.

As a conciliatory gesture, Vanessa suggested they spend the four-day Thanksgiving weekend up at the Croton house.

"We could drive up Wednesday night in your car," she coaxed. "I'll send the children up with Maria in the morning in the limo. And I'll ask Phyllis and Arnie to come up on Thursday for Thanksgiving dinner."

"Maybe they can stay for the weekend." Frank enjoyed playing host. "Arnie gets tired of the city rat race," he said pointedly, and walked away, leaving her sitting alone in his office.

Frank was tired, Vanessa told herself. *She* was tired, or she'd brush aside Frank's moodiness. They had not had a real vacation since their honeymoon six and a half years ago.

Vanessa left his office to return to the design studio and paused in the women's washroom. She was startled by the new sign tacked to the wall above the washbasins. "This is a washroom — not a recreation room. NO LOITERING."

She frowned. She had heard Frank complaining that some of the women spent more time in the washroom than at their machines, but a public sign was too harsh. He should talk to the guilty ones individually.

She became aware of labored sobbing in one of the stalls.

"Are you all right?" she asked solicitously. "This is Vanessa. Is there something I can do?"

Slowly the door was pushed open. A middle-aged seamstress who had been with them for over four years stood there, red-eyed and accusing.

"Mr. Bernstein fired me. I was ten minutes late coming back from lunch. My two daughters came to take me out for my birthday. With Christmas no more than six weeks away he fired me." Her voice broke.

"Molly, was there something else?" she forced herself to ask. Could Frank have been so capricious? But involuntarily she remembered Linda Odell's accusations: *"Every worker in the shop hates his guts. He's Seventh Avenue's Simon Legree."* "Molly, I have to know."

"Nothing else!" Molly's eyes flashed. "It wasn't right to fire me for nothing."

"Molly, I need another hand up in the design studio," she improvised. "You'll work for me. I'll make the arrangements with the office. Tomorrow morning report to the design studio."

Vanessa left the washroom and headed back to Frank's office. She had to give him a chance to explain.

Frank was on the phone, and she sat down to wait. She was too isolated in the design studio, she reproached herself. It was her job to know what was happening in every phase of the business.

"Frank, I just met Molly in the washroom," she began when he put down the phone.

"Molly?" He looked up with an air of inquiry, and Vanessa saw a glint of wariness in his eyes.

"Molly," she repeated, impatient with his game playing. "Molly Ryan, who's been with us for over four years. She's a hard worker, and she's reliable."

"She went bawling to you," he said contemptuously. "She was ten minutes late coming back from lunch. And it isn't the first time. I have to set an example around here—they'll all be goofing off if I let Molly get away with it."

"I've arranged for her to start working for me up in

the design studio as of tomorrow." Vanessa was trembling but determined. She struggled to push back the recriminations, the resentment. This was not the time for a confrontation with Frank.

"Why take on somebody I've fired? How does that look to the others?" He stared at her as though she had dealt a mortal wound.

"Frank, it was Molly's birthday — her daughters took her out to lunch. It was —"

"Bullshit! This isn't a nursery. It's a treacherous business. I have to be a tough, smart operator, or we'll be out on our asses." Then with chameleonlike swiftness his voice softened. He leaned back in his chair with an air of indulgence. "Baby, will you stick to your designing and let me run the business? We can't let the workers walk all over us. What are we doing tonight?" He dismissed the subject. "Isn't there some debutante shindig?"

The alarm jarred raucously into the early morning stillness. Tina cursed and reached over to shut it off. It was obscene to get up before six in the morning. Once the picture was in the can she could sleep every day until noon. Maybe Clark and she would take a run down to Mexico City.

She pulled herself up against the headboard and contemplated her schedule. It didn't get easier through the years. Last month — December — she had turned thirty-five. Every shadow, every imagined line in her face had to be erased before she faced the cameras. God, in five years she'd be forty. For a movie star that was over the hill.

"Tina, it's the middle of the night," Clark complained, turning on his side to throw one leg across her thighs.

"I have to get up." For a moment she considered calling the studio and saying she was sick. They had only a day or two of retakes left. She and Clark had made love until past one. He'd been drinking too much, and it had taken him a while to get going. That always made her absolutely wild. It had been sensational. "Clark, go back to sleep," she ordered. She was never late on the set; it was an obsession with her.

"With this?" he clucked and tossed aside the comforter to lie naked and erect before her.

"Sweetie, go to the bathroom and pee," she laughed. "Then go back to sleep."

In the shower Tina considered her situation with Clark. She wasn't breaking up his marriage. He hadn't been in his wife's bed for a lot of years. The only reason his wife wouldn't divorce him was because of her religion, though Clark kept insisting she would let him off the hook eventually. *"She says it kills her to have the whole world know I'm screwing a gorgeous actress a dozen years younger than she is. If she's mad enough, she'll let go."*

Clark could afford to give his wife a great divorce settlement, though right now his career seemed to be at a standstill. The studio was having fits about the affair. They kept trying to make sure she was never alone with him in public. Clark was nervous about the way the Hollywood scene was changing — TV was killing the studios. So many movie palaces were becoming supermarkets it was scary.

Other than this house and her Jaguar, she didn't have much to show for the fancy salaries. Vanessa was right — she should hire a business manager. Right now she was still at her peak earnings, but how long would

463

that last? She should stash it away while it was coming in.

While Clark snored on in bed, she pulled on jeans and sweater and hurried out to the garage. The couple who took care of the house wouldn't arrive until eight. She allowed herself a giggle; her servants were still asleep, but she was racing to work.

When she returned from the studio at the end of the day, she found a note from Clark on the bedside table. He'd taken the first flight to New York. His daughter — playing at becoming a Broadway actress — had just undergone an emergency appendectomy. He'd be in New York for a week or ten days. Though he saw little of his kids, Clark turned to mush when anything happened to either of them.

Tina ordered her dinner served on a tray in the den and settled down to watch TV. Mindless entertainment, she told herself with amusement. That's what she needed tonight. Thank God she had no lines to learn.

Her housekeeper came in to say good night, and minutes later she heard her car pulling out of the driveway. It was nice to be alone in the house. Clark was so frenetic. And he was drinking too much. At least he had enough sense to stay away from drugs.

Stifling a yawn, she flipped off the television set and headed for the master bedroom. As she reached the door, the phone rang. Probably Clark. She hurried to pick up the phone and sat down on the edge of the bed.

"Hello," she said in a sultry drawl that was her trademark.

"Hi, Tina!" Vanessa said warmly.

"Darling, how are you?"

"On the same mad schedule. I've decided to fly to

464

San Francisco for three or four days to get the feel of the beat scene." Vanessa's voice crackled with animation. "I figure I can squeeze in one day in Los Angeles."

"When do you plan on flying out?"

"Day after tomorrow," Vanessa told her.

"I'll meet you in San Francisco," Tina decided on impulse. "Don't bother with reservations. I'll arrange for a suite at the Mark Hopkins, and meet you there day after tomorrow."

"Tina, that'll be such fun. The two of us alone in a strange city. Suddenly I feel so sentimental." She burst into laughter.

Vanessa arrived at San Francisco International at 12:20 P.M. and quickly found a taxi to take her to the Mark Hopkins. She felt an unfamiliar sense of adventure. This wasn't trunk show travel, where a limousine met her at the airport and was at her disposal. She was not here to sell; she was here to learn.

It was a time for a drastic change in their couture line, she thought again in the taxi to the hotel. A season later the change would trickle down to their mass-market. This was the start of a new decade. The mood was *young*. And the young that were making themselves heard were the beat generation, coming of age in the late fifties and capturing the imagination of the American public.

Tina was waiting for her in their elegant suite at the Mark Hopkins.

"Darling, I arrived last night and went berserk at Gump's this morning," Tina confessed. "Harvey taught me to love jade, and nobody has finer jade."

"Your business manager allows this?" Vanessa

465

asked, pretending shock.

"I'll figure a way out," Tina laughed. "God, it's great to see you. Shall I call room service and order lunch sent up, or do we go out?"

"Tina, I'm here on research," Vanessa reminded her. "We go out."

In casual pantsuits, sweaters, and concealing sunglasses, Vanessa and Tina walked about the city, seeking out the haunts of the beats. Vanessa took it all in: the girls in their black leotards, no lipstick, and outrageous eyeshadow; the short-haired, bearded men in khaki pants, sweaters, sandals; the scent of marijuana everywhere.

"You know, even a soap—'Helen Trent,' I think—added a beat character to the cast," Vanessa remarked when they stopped for coffee.

"Hollywood's done some awful so-called exposés," Tina recalled.

"They're today's bohemians, and we should listen to what they say," Vanessa whispered with such intensity that Tina laughed.

"I can't say their clothes excite me," Tina admitted.

"Not what you're seeing here," Vanessa agreed, her face radiant, "but what they could be." She reached into her purse to pull out her notebook, made several swift sketches. "Let's go back down Columbus Avenue to the City Lights Bookshop. I haven't read Kerouac's *On the Road*. I think I should."

The City Lights Bookshop, run by poet Lawrence Ferlinghetti, fascinated Vanessa. It was the literary headquarters of the beat movement. Ferlinghetti published not only his own poetry, but the work of Allan Ginsberg—the "minstrel of the beats"—and the poetry of Gregory Corso, the *enfant terrible* of the movement.

After each day spent wandering about the part of

the city staked out by the beatniks — sitting around over cups of coffee in the favored coffeehouses and eavesdropping on conversation about Zen, Miles Davis, and Thelonious Monk, the urgent need for "bread" or a "pad," sources for the best reefer — Vanessa produced a stream of rough sketches. Then she and Tina changed into smart dinner dresses and made their nighttime tour of the fine restaurants of San Francisco. On their fourth and final day they returned to the Mark Hopkins before dusk to witness the sunset from the glass-enclosed Top of the Mark, surely the world's most romantic bar.

The next morning Vanessa headed back to New York, knowing she would spend the hours in flight adding to the sketches already packed away in her luggage. She was fascinated by the prospects of her "Beat Collection," impatient to see her designs take shape.

Phyllis and Frank were excited about the newness of the collection, and their excitement increased when Yves Saint Laurent's spring collection — shown in Paris in late January — was praised for its youthfulness and hailed by the critics as the finest the house had ever offered.

Only Doris expressed doubts. "The women who buy Vanessa Conrad are going to think you're off your rocker," she protested glumly over a meeting in February to cement final plans for the collection. "Can you see Eugenia Sheppard or Sally Kirkland liking these? So much black!" she grimaced. "And all these turtleneck collars."

"We'll have to set up just the right background when we show them," Phyllis said with enthusiasm. "It's revolutionary. You're bringing the beat mood into fashion."

"I know exactly how it should be presented," Vanessa broke in. She had talked about it with Tina back in San Francisco. "I want a reproduction of the City Lights Bookstore, with the runway emerging from the center of the store. The music should be jazz," she pursued, caught up in the image. "Thelonious Monk."

"God, no, Vanessa!" Frank was shocked. "We're not selling to a bunch of badly dressed beatniks. You can borrow from the mood, but it has to be presented with class. It has to look expensive."

"Frank, it'll look lost against one of our elegant backgrounds," Vanessa protested, and Phyllis nodded in agreement.

"Look, we're sticking our necks out with this collection," Frank said tersely. "We have to—"

"I thought you loved it." Vanessa said uneasily. She always looked to Frank for moral support.

"Part of me loves it," Frank hedged. "The other part understands what Doris is saying." He hesitated. "It could be a disaster."

"Are you saying we should scrap it?" Vanessa's heart was pounding. They'd gone through that rat race once. She'd sworn never to go through it again.

"We've got too much invested," Frank dismissed this. "But we have to present it in the fashion buyers and reviewers expect from us. Lush and expensive."

Vanessa tried not to let Frank's apprehensions affect her thinking. She was still committed to the collection, but she worried about its reception. She relaxed a little when Tina called to say she'd be in New York to publicize the opening of her new picture the week of the collection.

"Tina, narrate for us again," Vanessa coaxed. "I'm scared to death. Frank thinks I may be way off base."

468

"I'll narrate it and wear one of the outfits," Tina said immediately.

"How are you and Clark?" Vanessa asked.

"He's become a habit," Tina said flippantly. "Actually," she said more seriously, "he's fighting like mad to persuade his wife to give him a divorce. Their lawyers are finally talking about it. And he's working up a nightclub act for Vegas—to do before the summer circuit."

"Oh, Tina, I hope it works out." She paused. "Frank's not happy about this collection." Vanessa was somber. "He's afraid it's too far out."

"Do you like it?" Tina demanded.

"I love it," she confessed. "And Suzy loves it. I promised her she could come to the formal opening."

"It'll be great," Tina predicted. "You couldn't do anything that wasn't great."

Vanessa was a nervous wreck as they prepared to show the collection. They had spent lavishly on the showing, but Vanessa felt the clothes were out of tune with the lush background Frank had insisted on. Tina looked marvelous, Vanessa comforted herself, in black pants, a black knit sweater with exaggerated turtleneck and a bomber jacket of alligator and mink over one arm. But Vanessa knew that the collection should have been shown against a City Lights Bookshop background.

Ten minutes after the first model strode down the runway, Vanessa knew the critics were repelled by the designs. She didn't have to wait to read the reviews. She knew they would be bad.

After the showing Vanessa took Suzy down to the waiting limousine so that she could return to school.

"Mommy, it was wonderful," Suzy squeezed Vanessa in delight. "I wish I was old enough to wear the clothes!"

Maybe the collection would have been better received if it had been properly presented, Vanessa considered. Maybe not. Frank would be in a foul mood. This would be their first collection to receive bad notices. But they could afford a bad season, she told herself defensively. They were a major company on Seventh Avenue.

Thirty-four

Most of the reviews of the fall couture collection were bad. Tina predicted there would be some among the fashionably young who would adopt Vanessa's designs as de rigueur, but Vanessa realized her timing was off—and the setting had been utterly wrong. The mass-market line was more conventional, she consoled herself, while she settled in to design the resort collection. Sales would be good. Not as good as they would have been if the couture had won great reviews, but good enough to carry them along comfortably.

Summer arrived. Again, though he knew how she loved the beach, Frank decided against renting a house at Southampton. Vanessa harbored a disconcerting conviction that Frank was punishing her for the failure of the fall couture collection. And she knew he was irritated each time she left her design studio to come down to the shop floors.

Vanessa forced herself to be honest. Frank *wanted* her up in what he called her "ivory tower." Downstairs, he was in total control—when she wasn't there. In an industry where tough bosses were the norm, Frank was considered an ogre. She worried about this, not knowing how to handle it.

Even in their personal lives—in bed—she felt hostility radiating from him. She was bewildered. Where was the Frank she knew—or thought she knew? How could a man change the way Frank seemed to be changing?

When she had first met Frank he'd been vocal about his admiration for President Truman and Truman's fight for a civil rights program. He had been concerned about peace in the world. And when they were in Key West on their honeymoon, he'd been full of sympathy for Cuba's fight against Batista.

But lately he was prone to snide remarks about blacks and Hispanics—even though, as a Jew, he himself was a victim of prejudice. He had derided Arnie and Phyllis's excitement when, last February, four young blacks had made a stand against segregation in a Woolworth store in Greensboro, North Carolina. He tore into her defense of the four hundred college students from Harvard, Boston University, MIT, and Brandeis who had picketed a dozen Woolworth stores in greater Boston in March, three days after three hundred Yale divinity students had marched in New Haven in support of the protests.

Early in July, with Suzy away at camp for the first time and ecstatic about the experience, Vanessa accepted Pat's invitation to spend a weekend at the Georgetown house. It would be a welcome relief before the madness of the resort line showing at the end of the month. They were in Washington, Pat explained, because Paul was campaigning on the East Coast and he wanted the house open.

"Paul's insisting I build up a dramatic fall wardrobe," she confided. Vanessa knew Pat's style leaned toward understated, simple lines. "While he's rooting for Lyndon Johnson to win the Democratic nomination, he's sure Johnson doesn't have a chance against the Kennedy machine. Jack Kennedy's been campaigning for four years."

"What's your wardrobe got to do with Jack Kennedy winning the presidency?" Vanessa laughed.

"Jackie Kennedy is a clothes horse," Pat reminded her. "Paul doesn't want anyone, even the First Lady, to outshine his wife. I might lose some of the exposure I'm getting now." Cynicism crept into her voice.

"We'll plan your fall/winter wardrobe while I'm down there," Vanessa promised. "But not dramatic. Classic elegance is your style."

Vanessa was faintly uncomfortable at taking off alone for the weekend, but Frank was embroiled in the mass-market production, and Maria would be at the Croton house with Wendy. She needed this weekend away from everything, Vanessa told herself. She hadn't had time to recover from the bad reviews.

Pat met her at the airport in her new white Ferrari. Vanessa felt her anxieties roll away as they drove toward the Georgetown house and talked avidly about the children.

"Biff's an angel," Pat said softly. "Little as he is, he has this marvelous zest for living. And he thinks his big sister is just wonderful. He'll do anything for Cee-Cee."

"Most people will," Vanessa said indulgently. "She's such a lovely little girl." Willful, devious, but unquestionably charming, Vanessa conceded. But like herself, Suzy disliked CeeCee. She doubted that Suzy and CeeCee would ever be close friends.

"Suzy's happy at camp?" Pat asked.

"She's having a great time. I'm the one who worries," Vanessa confessed. "You know me. Next weekend Frank and I are going to drive up to see her. She phones home once a week—so I won't worry *too* much."

On Saturday morning, each wearing California capris and flat Capezio thong sandals, Vanessa and Pat lingered over coffee in the breakfast room to plan Pat's fall/winter wardrobe. Running through Pat's social calendar, Vanessa made rough sketches of dresses and suits to be made up especially for her.

"Vanessa, will you have time for this?" Pat asked eagerly. "I hadn't expected a custom wardrobe. I thought you'd choose for me from your couture."

"My flop collection?" Vanessa mocked herself.

"Tina told me she's wearing several things and loves them," Pat said softly.

"Thank God for you and Tina," Vanessa laughed. "And Phyllis. She's mad about my bomber jacket. But I want special clothes for you, Pat. You and Tina are my two private customers."

"When are you going to open your custom salon?" Pat asked in soft reproach.

"Not for a while," Vanessa hedged. "But I will one day."

When Vanessa closed her sketchbook at last, Pat confided that she wished she and Paul and the children could live in Houston. She hated the politics of being a Washington wife.

"But the children like living here," she acknowledged. "And of course Paul's whole world revolves around politics. He's not worried a bit about the election in November — he's sure to be reelected." For a moment her eyes were opaque. "Daddy will see to that."

"When can I see the children?" Vanessa asked, feeling uncomfortable at the look in Pat's eyes.

"Miss Donnelly will bring them up to the house any time now. For what she calls their 'morning spoiling,' " Pat said. "When the children arrive, let's change into swimsuits and go down to the pool. CeeCee won't go in—she's terrified of the water—but Biff swims like a fish."

"I hate you! I hate you!" CeeCee screeched, her angelic face contorted in rage as she tried to hit Biff with her small flailing fists. "You're a mean little bastard!"

"CeeCee, you're not to use such language," Miss Donnelly scolded, lifting Biff into her arms. "Your mother would be upset if she heard you."

"Daddy says it!" CeeCee retaliated shrilly. "I hear him!"

"Stop trying to hurt Biff," Miss Donnelly ordered. "He's your little brother, and you—"

"He made my dress all sticky with his lollipop," CeeCee wailed, pointing to the skirt of her favorite "St. Tropez" pink gingham, a miniature copy of Brigitte Bardot's wedding dress. Mother said it was too old for her, but Grandma had bought it for her from Sakowitz's. "Biff can get away with anything!"

"You know you're not to give Biff lollipops," Miss Donnelly said. "Your mother doesn't want either of you to eat sweets except on special occasions. It does awful things to your teeth."

"Biff stole it," CeeCee lied. "From my room," she improvised quickly. Miss Donnelly wouldn't believe her, even if it was true. Nobody would. They only believed what Biff said.

"I didn't steal it," Biff said defiantly from the haven of Miss Donnelly's arms. "You gave it to me 'cause I drank your orange juice for you when Miss Donnelly went to bring in our eggs."

"I did not!" CeeCee's voice rose again.

"CeeCee, be quiet," Miss Donnelly said with the icy

475

calm that meant she was furious. "Now if your dress is sticky, go change it."

"I don't want to," CeeCee sulked. Just wait till Grandma came next week. She'd tell her how awful Miss Donnelly was to her.

"All right." Miss Donnelly set Biff down on his feet. "We're going up to the house now to see your mother and her guest—" She frowned at the sound of the phone ringing in the kitchen. "Just let me answer the phone."

Biff stood regarding CeeCee warily for a moment, then crossed to the coffee table to retrieve the small boat he'd abandoned when his sister had started to hit him.

A faint smile lighted CeeCee's face.

"Biff, I'm sorry I was mean to you," she apologized sweetly, persuasively. "Why don't we go down to the pool and sail your boat?"

"Mommy says we can't go to the pool without Miss Donnelly or her," Biff wavered.

"Biff, I'm thirteen," CeeCee said. "That's old enough to go to the pool with you. A girl in my class even baby-sits for money." She reached for his hand. "Come on, let's go sail your boat." Miss Donnelly was talking to her sister. They'd talk forever.

Her small brother's hand in hers, CeeCee led him from the house into the morning sunlight and down the path that led to the fenced in pool. Biff clutched lovingly at his new sailboat.

"Won't your sailboat look pretty on the water?" Cee-Cee purred, her throat constricted with excitement. "There's enough wind this morning to make it sail—"

"Paul has been talking about sending CeeCee to

476

boarding school next year, but Mother and I are both against it," Pat told Vanessa, and Vanessa remembered that CeeCee had already changed schools half a dozen times. At least twice, she knew, the change had been at the request of the school.

"I couldn't imagine sending Suzy to boarding school," Vanessa admitted.

"Miss Donnelly! Miss Donnelly!" The serenity of the breakfast room was destroyed by CeeCee's hysterical shrieks. "Come quick! Biff fell in the pool!"

"Oh, my God!" Pat raced from the room and down the hall toward the entrance. "What was he doing near the pool?"

"You said he swims like a fish," Vanessa comforted her breathlessly, running beside Pat.

"Miss Donnelly, Biff ran away from me!" They heard CeeCee cry out as the governess charged into view. "He took his sailboat and went to the pool. Somebody left the gate open! Somebody go in after him!"

"Biff?" Pat screamed, hovering at the open gate. "Biff?"

Vanessa kicked off her sandals and jumped into the pool, her eyes searching for Biff.

"Where is he? Vanessa, where is he?" Pat's voice soared in a high, thin wail while Miss Donnelly struggled to deal with CeeCee.

"Somebody left the gate open!" CeeCee repeated between strangled sobs. "I couldn't catch up with him. He leaned over with the sailboat. And then he fell in—"

Her throat burning from her efforts, fear turning her to ice, Vanessa emerged from the pool with the small body in her arms.

"Biff! Oh, my baby, my baby!" Pat reached in anguish to take her son from Vanessa.

"Miss Donnelly, call for the rescue squad," Vanessa ordered sharply. But she knew it was too late.

Pat was kept heavily sedated until the funeral. She clung to Vanessa. She wanted no one else. Her mother drove up from Virginia, and Paul and her father rushed to Georgetown. Her sister, Maureen, and brother-in-law, Roger, flew in from their home in California. Tina was unreachable, on a yacht somewhere off the south of France.

Paul threatened to fire every member of the domestic staff.

"What stupid bastard left that gate unlocked? It was put there to protect Biff!" he raged.

"You'll fire nobody," Pat objected, seeming to fight her way out of drug-induced sedation. Vanessa understood; Pat knew that CeeCee had pushed Biff into the pool; only the suddenness of his fall had caused him to drown. *"Biff swims like a fish,"* Pat had said. "It was a terrible accident," Pat forced herself to finish.

Biff was to be buried the day before the Democratic Convention. Vanessa helped Pat dress for the funeral.

"Vanessa, why?" she asked again. "Why do these terrible things happen to us? Eddie, Harvey, and now Biff. Why?"

"We can't ask questions, Pat," Vanessa said, momentarily lost in her own pain. "We have to learn to live with our grief."

Paul frowned when the two women joined him in the living room.

"Pat, not that dress. Something much smarter. A dozen congressmen, two cabinet members, a Supreme Court judge, and possibly the vice-president will be there."

"Pat," Vanessa said softly, masking her shock, "the black silk you bought from Givenchy last year."

Vanessa sat with Pat and Paul in their limousine, Pat clinging tightly to her hand. Neither she nor Pat had said a word about CeeCee's part in Biff's drowning.

At the cemetery Pat fought back her tears knowing that Paul expected her to be strong for the press. Her eyes on the tiny white casket, Vanessa longed to be back home in New York, to hold her own two precious children in her arms.

During the graveside services, she watched CeeCee and was repelled by the girl's show of sadness. She didn't cry. In her dainty white linen dress, she clung to her father's hand and exuded a lost-little-girl grief.

When the wives of two senior congressmen came to offer their condolences to Pat, Vanessa overheard one of the husbands: "That son-of-a-bitch even uses his son's death to build up his popularity. I hear he tried to have him buried in Arlington."

The night of the funeral Vanessa gathered with the family in the library of the Georgetown house. Cee-Cee had been taken to her room by Miss Donnelly. With precarious composure, Pat announced that she and Paul must arrange for psychiatric care for Cee-Cee. The library richocheted with shock. Suddenly everyone — everyone but Pat and Vanessa — was talking at once.

"Quiet!" Congressman Owens thundered. His face was flushed. "Pat, if the word leaks out — and it will, like everything does in this town — then it'll look as though CeeCee had opened the gate for Biff. You know how people talk. I don't like it."

"It's for CeeCee's own good," Pat said. "This has

479

been a terrible shock for her."

"Absurd," Paul said dismissively. He thought for a moment, then said, "We'll send her to a fine boarding school. She'll be better in a different environment for a year or two."

"You're right, Paul. A boarding school would be fine," Madeline Owens approved. "Poor baby, she's so distraught. I know a lovely school in Virginia. She could spend weekends with me at the ranch."

"Then it's settled," Paul said, and Vanessa watched compassionately as Pat's face set in cold, white lines. Didn't the others understand that CeeCee needed help?

"Pat, we'll go down together to the school in Virginia," her mother said. "You and CeeCee will spend the rest of the summer with me at the plantation."

And tomorrow, Vanessa realized with distaste, Paul and Pat's father would fly to Los Angeles for the Democratic Convention.

On her return to New York Vanessa was touched by Frank's sympathy.

"An awful thing to happen," he repeated for the dozenth time as they prepared for bed, and she knew he was thinking about Wendy. "I would fire everybody who works at the house."

"Paul wanted to," Vanessa conceded, "but Pat wouldn't let him." Frank gazed at her in astonishment. "It would be wrong to punish the whole staff for one person's carelessness," she fabricated. Not even to Frank would she confide her suspicions about Cee-Cee.

"It must have been an awful experience." He reached for her with a compassion he had not shown for a long time.

"That poor little baby." Her voice broke. "I knew he was dead when I brought him out of the pool."

"It'll never happen to us," he comforted. "Suzy's too big, and Maria watches over Wendy like a hawk."

In the weeks that followed, Vanessa tried to push the horror of Biff's death into the dark place of her mind that also kept Eddie's and Harvey's deaths. She emerged from the tragic July weekend with a sharp awareness of the value of each day. And she remembered her dream of opening a custom salon on Madison Avenue. Nothing could provide her with as much satisfaction.

She found some comfort when the House of Dior presented Yves Saint Laurent's fall collection in Paris in July. Saint Laurent, too, had adopted the beat mood. And he, too, was criticized by much of the press.

In October, while they were preparing for the opening of the spring couture, Frank came charging into the design studio with a look of complete triumph.

"Let's get out of here, go to the cafeteria," he said exuberantly. This close to a formal opening they didn't have time for the opulent lunches at the Colony or Le Pavillon that Frank enjoyed. "I've got news for you."

Down in the cafeteria where they had first met, Frank told her they had an offer to use her name for a children's line.

"It'll be all gravy, Vanessa," he chortled. "No expenses—nothing—they use your name and pay us a royalty for every garment sold."

"No," Vanessa rejected firmly.

Frank glared at her. "What do you mean, no?" We're talking about the wave of the future."

481

"Bill Blass tried a licensing deal in the children's field a year or two ago," Vanessa reminded him. "It was a disaster."

"For Blass it was a disaster, but it won't be for us. And Blass is doing great now with licensing in bathing suits. This children's firm is prepared to pay us a royalty of—"

"Frank, I don't want to do it," she said. "We don't know the children's field. I don't want my name used on a line I haven't designed—"

"Goddamn it, Vanessa, you always think small," Frank said loudly. People turned to stare.

"Frank, you're always talking about image," she reminded him, deliberately keeping her voice low. "Lending my name to somebody else's line could kill our image. We'll have no control."

"I can make approval of every garment part of the deal," he tried again.

"No. If we're going to take on something new, then it should be a custom salon."

"There's no money in it!" Frank shouted. "Even in Paris they know that now. Last year," Frank said, his voice tight and furious, "Cardin started showing his ready-to-wear in Paris because he knows the financial limitations of haute couture. I'm talking about big bucks. We ought to be drawing a million a year after taxes. You're still penny ante, Vanessa." He reached for the check and rose to his feet. "They'll think I'm a real schmuck to throw away such a terrific offer."

Vanessa reached for her coat and followed Frank to the cashier's counter. Would they ever be earning enough to please Frank? Would he ever be satisfied?

Vanessa had to face up to the deterioration of her

marriage. Frank rarely made love to her. When he did, it was as though she wasn't here. Afterward she'd lie awake, unsatisfied and strangely shamed. She felt as if was living with a stranger. Making love to a business partner.

She was astonished when Frank announced over dinner on a snowy night in March that he'd talked to a broker about buying a house in Southampton.

"Southampton," Frank repeated with a new air of anticipation.

Maybe a little beach house would bring Frank back to normal, Vanessa thought. They both worked so hard. He needed something to break up the daily tensions.

"It'll be great for summer socializing," Frank continued. "It's more classy to entertain at our own estate. It's a business expense," he said with relish. "Get those two boyfriends of yours to decorate the place for us. Make it plush. Let the crowd out there understand we're making a hell of a lot of money."

"I'll call Phil and Robbie as soon as we have a house," she said quietly, but her mind was racing.

If they could spend money on a beach house—and it was clear Frank was looking for a showplace—then she would have her custom salon. She didn't have to ask for permission.

She would search for the right place, and then she would tell Frank she was opening a custom salon. She didn't care if they made money in the salon. She would be satisfied to break even. But there she could achieve perfection. Dresses and suits that were works of art. The ultimate design creation. A fulfillment that would make her life complete. Her personal, private dream.

Thirty-five

Tina sat watching the rushes on the final day of shooting without seeing anything on the screen. She'd just finished a screaming match with Nat. He was livid because the goddamn gossip columnists had turned on her for supposedly wrecking Clark's marriage. He was furious, too—like Marty—because she refused to sign a new contract right away. She needed to feel free for a while. To figure out where the hell she was going with Clark.

Three weeks ago Clark's wife had entered a suit for separate maintenance, and the columnists had declared open season on *her*. Hell, the whole world knew he hadn't slept with his wife in years. He'd gone through a dozen affairs, including a wild one with Connie, before they had started seeing each other.

She was upset by the hate mail that was pouring in to the studio, reviling her for destroying Clark's marriage. That was the joke of the year! And she was sick of the way Clark kept dragging his entire clique around with them wherever they went in Hollywood. He didn't care about appearances in Europe or Mexico, but his wife and kids lived here and he didn't want to be seen alone with her. If he was so worried about his wife, let him go back to her!

Tina exchanged a few words with the director,

promising she'd hang around for the next week for any retakes he decided to do. Then she went out to her car and prepared to drive home. She would have it out with Clark once and for all. Either he got a divorce from his wife and they got married, or she was finished with him. The hate mail was the last straw.

She was damn tired of Clark's constant jealousy. He had a fit if she even smiled at another guy. And that hot Irish temper of his. He shouldn't have thrown that plate of spaghetti in the photographer's face last night.

At the house she had dinner on a tray in the den, where she could watch television. Clark wouldn't be here till late — this was his first day on a new picture. They'd stay home so he could learn his lines for tomorrow's shooting.

"You want anything else, Miss Tina?" the housekeeper hovered at the entrance to the den.

"No." She stifled a yawn. "I'm bushed. I'll be asleep by nine."

Tina walked to the master bedroom and stripped to the skin, letting her clothes lie where they fell. She dumped quantities of honeysuckle bath salts into the black marble tub and ran her bath.

The stillness of the house was stifling. She went back into the bedroom and turned on the radio. Bobby Darin's "Mack the Knife" poured into the room.

Tina returned to her bath and lay back in the scented water, abandoning herself to the music and the sultry fragrance.

"Hey, just what the tired actor needs," Clark drawled from the doorway. She hadn't heard him drive up to the house, come inside. "Don't move a muscle. I'm joining you."

His eyes strayed over her as he rushed to undress. This was why she stayed with Clark, Tina told herself. He could walk in and make her feel passionate in seconds. For a little while she could forget that Harvey was dead, that their baby was gone. This was the real world.

"The next house I buy will have a tub for two," Clark said, edging himself into the water beside her, his hand caressing one sun-kissed breast, the other fondling her thighs. "Or maybe three."

"But think how cozy this is," she drawled. Had he meant it — the last time they had made love in the tub — when he said they ought to call Connie to come over and join them? She just didn't dig sex *à trois*. Maybe part of her was still a dumb little hick from Pinewood.

"I'll let the water out and we'll shower," he said, his voice thickening in excitement. "I've had enough of honeysuckle. I want the scent of you."

"We could go into the bedroom. . . ."

The water streamed over her shoulders and breasts. Clark was on his knees before her, his mouth trailing down her pelvis, his hands cupping her rump. "Clark —"

"In time, baby," he promised.

She closed her eyes. Her mouth parted in anticipation. This was why she stayed with Clark.

Tina was sunning herself beside the pool when Della came out to say Felix Koestler was on the phone.

"I'll be right there," she called back. She ought to have the phone reinstalled out here. After Biff's death, she had had the pool drained and had ignored it for months. But life went on.

"Tina, let's have dinner tonight," Felix said briskly after the usual preliminaries. "I want to talk business. Word's around town that you're stalling on re-signing with Imperial."

"For the moment."

"I'm doing a film in Rome. There's a sensational part in it for you. A real acting role, Tina," he emphasized. Last time they'd met she'd talked about maybe going to New York to study at the Actors' Studio.

"I don't see myself chasing off to Rome," she demurred.

"Let's get together for dinner, anyway," he coaxed. "I'll pick you up at eight. We'll go to Chasen's."

"Okay," Tina acceded. She found a strange pleasure in sitting across the table from Felix and knowing she was with Adam's father. Felix didn't know it. Nobody knew except herself and Vanessa. "But don't count on Rome."

When Felix called for her the next evening, she was wearing the classically simple lemon chiffon Vanessa had last designed for her. She left a note for Clark on the foyer table.

She and Felix were at his favorite table and halfway through their steaks when Clark stalked into Chasen's. He was alone. Now that his wife was suing he didn't have to pretend.

"Clark, what the hell's the matter with you?" Tina demanded when he reached menacingly for Felix.

"I know all about you, buster!" He swung at Felix's jaw. "You think you can screw every actress in Hollywood!"

Several waiters rushed forward. Clark was dragged away from the table, out of the restaurant, and into the street. The maître d' helped Tina get Felix from the dining room and out to his car. She drove him to the hospital and waited anxiously in the emergency room. When at last she was allowed into his room, she learned that his jaw was fractured.

"I'll do the picture with you in Rome, Felix," she promised. "I never want to see that son-of-a-bitch again."

Tina sprawled across the sofa of her rented flat in the Belgravia section of London.

"Darling, you *have* to see King's Road," she said into the phone. "All the new boutiques springing up. I know Frank keeps saying you're off base in thinking 'young' for the collections, but the action is here! You're on target, baby."

"I am intrigued by Mary Quant," Vanessa confessed. "Suzy's only thirteen, but she adores the clothes. I had a Mary Quant jumper copied for her, and she practically lives in it."

"Vanessa, there is definitely a fashion upheaval and you have to come to Chelsea to see it."

"I'm in my own mad upheaval here," Vanessa laughed, but she hungered to see what was happening in London.

"You're always in a mad upheaval," Tina chided. "I've got this great flat rented for the next three months—until Felix settles everything in Rome. Fly over, stay three days, fly home," she coaxed.

"I'm coming," Vanessa decided. "Right after we show the collection early next week—no, I'll wait till the end of the month so I can bring Suzy with me."

Late in May, with the collections shown to fine reviews and the orders pouring in, Vanessa and Suzy boarded a 707 for the flight to London. Suzy felt very grown up traveling alone with her mother and staying at Tina's flat in Belgravia. After the London trip she would go off on a cross-country bus tour with a group of children her own age.

Tina met them at Heathrow with a chauffeured Mercedes.

"I wouldn't dare drive in this town," she laughed, bubbling with pleasure at seeing Vanessa and Suzy. "I'd kill somebody for sure."

Tina talked animatedly about the new film to be shot in Rome. Clark had called several times to plead with her to return to Hollywood. He was tied down to a movie that seemed destined to run overtime and overbudget, and from there he had to go on tour with a summer theater package.

"He vows he'll get a divorce, but I'll believe that when I see the papers," Tina shrugged. "Meanwhile I love London. It makes me feel so young."

At Tina's flat, Vanessa and Suzy were given the grand tour of the strikingly modern rooms: the two guest bedrooms with walls and beds covered in matching fabrics, the master bedroom with a dais for the huge bed and a freestanding sculptural receptacle for the TV set, the living room done in African safari, and the dining room all glass and chrome.

Eyelids drooping despite her determination to beat jet lag, Suzy was shipped off to nap until dinner, but within a few hours she was awake and determined to see London. Tina took them off to Chelsea, to take in the sights and sounds of King's Road. They saw laughing young girls in tight, short skirts and black stockings or tall black boots, and bearded young men—with hair so long Suzy was wide-eyed in disbelief—in leather jackets, leather ties, skinny pants.

"It's not San Francisco," Vanessa said, caught up in

the excitement that radiated from these Londoners, "but the mood is close. Frank will probably be furious with me, but I have to absorb this look into the collections. Tina, we're moving into a fashion revolution," she said with zest. "What we're seeing here on the streets has got to filter up into haute couture." The leadership in fashion was definitely shifting.

The three of them roamed up and down King's Road, in and out of the boutiques. Under pressure Vanessa bought Suzy a red leather skirt that barely reached to her knees.

"Maria will kill us both," she laughingly warned Suzy. "It's so short!"

Despite Tina's pleas that they stay longer, Vanessa and Suzy boarded their return flight on schedule. The Seventh Avenue rat race would allow no further dalliance. Vanessa's mind was already racing ahead to spring 1962; she visualized a short coat that owed its line to the army surplus duffle coats the girls were wearing along King's Road.

Back in New York she worked to make Frank understand that what she had seen in London was sure to be part of tomorrow's fashions.

"I was ahead of my time with the beat collection," she admitted. "But the London scene is breathing down our necks. Mary Quant is preparing to go wholesale."

Vanessa's convictions were reinforced by the reports on the clothes by André Courrèges, who had worked for Balenciaga for ten years before opening his own small salon in Paris. Again, the word was "short skirts." His designs were young and startling.

While Vanessa was absorbed in the violent shifts on the fashion scene, she managed to find time to search for the custom salon she had promised herself. Early in September she located the perfect spot. She called Arnie immediately and asked him to arrange for a short-term lease. The following morning over breakfast she told Frank.

"What's this fixation you have about a custom salon?" he yelled. "Every six months you bring up the same shit again."

"Frank, please." She glanced uneasily toward the entrance to the breakfast room. Suzy was just out of bed. Wendy usually slept until almost eight. Frank used to be more careful about his language around the children.

"On the one hand you're crying about how everything's changing in fashion, how tough it is to guess what'll sell the next season — and then you talk about a custom salon. We've got a business to run — no time for playing, Vanessa." He dared her to defy him.

Vanessa paused. Her instinct told her that if she gave in this time, she would never open her custom salon. And a custom salon would be great for their other lines.

"I called Arnie last night and told him to arrange a lease," she said quietly. "I know I can fit it in."

"You think you can do any goddamn thing you want." He glared at her in fury. "Miracle woman," he mocked, and pushed back his chair. "Excuse me. I've got to get downtown and run a business."

Frank left the apartment and took the elevator down to the basement, seething with rage. Vanessa was turning into a real prick. All that publicity Phyllis was always building up about her had gone straight to her head. But *he* had made her.

All she cared about was the designing. Screw him.

Screw the kids. She had to play with her design salon. Everybody on Seventh Avenue knew he was the heart of Creations by Vanessa Conrad. Without him there would be nothing. If he walked out today, she'd push the business into the ground in a year.

The way they were set up now he needed her. He would exploit the business until some conglomerate walked in and offered them seventy or eighty million. Even Vanessa wouldn't fight him on that. It was only a matter of time. Once that happened, she could go her way, and he'd go his.

Vanessa would drop Suzy off at school and then arrive at the shop at around nine or nine-ten, Frank contemplated. It was barely seven-twenty now. A faint smile lifted the corners of his mouth. That new showroom model Edie Russell had made it clear she was dying to play house with him.

Sitting behind the wheel of his new white Cadillac convertible, Frank fished in his wallet. She had slipped him her address and phone number several days ago. Typical showroom model—no ass, no tits—but this one was as sexy as hell. Edie looked like a young Lauren Bacall.

Frank was whistling when he drove out of the garage and onto the street. A quick call on the garage phone had confirmed that, yes, Edie would love to have him drive her downtown this morning. She was just about to go into the shower, but she'd be out by the time he cut across to her West Seventies studio.

In her studio apartment Edie went into the bathroom, threw off her pajamas, and fiddled with the faucets in the shower. Under the hot spray she contemplated with pleasure this new development in her life.

She'd be twenty-two next month, and so far the

guys that had tried to throw her into bed drove trucks or worked on the docks or tended bar like Pop. To them a house in Levittown was a step up in the world. But she was after the high life she'd glimpsed in the gossip columns. From Fort Hamilton High to a Sutton Place penthouse—that was Edie Russell's destination.

Her family had flipped out when she had announced she was leaving home for Manhattan. Only Mom had understood. Mom told her she was meant for better things. *"Don't get stuck like me, baby. With your looks you'll find a rich guy. To marry you or keep you in style. Maybe some Jewish guy. They treat their women like queens— and they're great in bed."* All she had going for her was her looks. That had to be enough.

Pop told her she was crazy when she quit her job selling cosmetics at an Eighth Avenue drugstore. She wasn't meeting any guys there. She wasn't the type to have many girl friends. Then Mom started cutting out ads in the "Help Wanted" for showroom models. In her highest heels she just made the height requirements.

The first job Edie applied for was at Creations by Vanessa Conrad, and Frank Bernstein had hired her right off. At first she thought he was hot for her, but he was so damn tied up with the business that all he did was an occasional eye-rape job. She did go out with the buyers several times. But all that netted her was some fancy dinners and nights in hotels. Anyway, the buyers were always married. She was after bigger game.

Frank was loaded, she thought complacently while she dried herself with one of the lush dusty pink towels Mom had given her for her birthday. For an older guy he was good-looking. And sexy.

Frank cursed in irritation until he found a parking place a half a block from Edie's building. But he was whistling by the time he strode down the block and up the brownstone stoop where she lived. He rang the doorbell, and she buzzed him in right away.

Heading up the dark, narrow stairs to her apartment, he thought about the hungry male glances that often followed Edie about the showroom. She had something something going for her. That "I'm hot as a pistol" look in her eyes, that faint, inviting smile. He knew she wasn't on to him because he looked like Rock Hudson or Gregory Peck. He didn't. It was because she knew he was rich and powerful. *That* was sexy.

As he rounded the top of the stairs he saw Edie before him, posed in the doorway in a see-through negligee with feathers all around the neckline, like something from a Marilyn Monroe movie.

"Hi," she drawled, allowing the negligee to fall open. "What took you so long?"

Thirty-six

Tina liked the apartment Felix rented for her in Rome. Part of a tall seventeenth-century building at the top of the romantic Spanish Steps, its huge windows looked out on a panorama of modern and ancient Rome. Felix had hired a married couple — a maid-cook and chauffeur-butler — to care for her needs. With the apartment came a white Rolls.

She stood in the dramatic drawing room talking to Felix on the phone. Her first two weeks in Rome, it had been amusing to sit at a table on the Via Veneto to people-watch or just read the *Rome Daily American*. She'd enjoyed the good jazz at Le Grotte del Piccione. And twice she had persuaded Felix to go to the Rugantino in Trastevere, where she could chacha with one of the handsome young Italians or waltz with Felix.

He'd been amused by the young people from good families who congregated at the clubs. It was an indication of the change in times, he'd told her: "Twenty-five years ago these kids wouldn't have been allowed out of their houses at this time of night."

But now she was bored, and impatient with the delays in their shooting schedule.

"Tina, it's only a matter of another week or two," Felix cajoled. "In Rome nobody hurries. Two weeks at the most," he promised, "and we start to work."

"Thank God," Tina said with an exaggerated sigh. "I can't stand one more Rome nightclub."

Two of her films were currently showing in Rome, and the Italians had welcomed her as one of their own. She couldn't walk out of the apartment without attracting admiring crowds.

She crossed to one of the tall drawing room windows and gazed out into the mid-September twilight. She tried to visualize Adam in her Hollywood swimming pool. Of course, by now he and Sal and Eva were back in upstate New York. She hoped Sal had taken lots of snaps of Adam during the three weeks they had stayed at the house.

It was almost as though they were doing her a favor by vacationing there, she thought. Sal had nearly had a heart attack when she phone from London to see how they were doing. All he could stammer was, "God, Tina, how much is this costing you?" She'd wanted to talk to her son for a few minutes.

Sometimes she hated herself for letting Sal and Eva adopt Adam. Why hadn't she had enough sense to pretend to adopt him herself? Sure, there would have been a lot of flak from the studio, but they expected her to pull off crazy stunts. She could have raised Adam herself.

But each time these thoughts intruded, she forced herself to be realistic. Adam was growing up a normal child, with a father and a mother who loved him—no matter how much they resented her. That was the finest present she could give Adam.

The phone rang in the library. Tina arched an eyebrow in surprise when the maid announced that "Signor Roberts" was on the phone. The only "Signor

Roberts" she knew was Paul. She hadn't seen him since that crazy weekend in Georgetown. How long had it been? Eight years ago. She saw Pat maybe once or twice a year. In New York or Paris or London, when they happened to be at the same place at the same time. She felt a twinge of pain. The last time she'd seen Paul she'd met Harvey.

"I'll take it in my bedroom," she told the maid in broken Italian. Paul knew enough not to make another pass, didn't he? She sat at the edge of the fifteenth-century Spanish bed and picked up the phone. "Hello."

"Hi, Tina," Paul's voice came to her with calculated charm. "Pat told me to be sure and look you up while I'm here."

"What are you doing in Rome?"

"Official business. Nothing terribly important. A diplomatic gesture. I'm only here for forty-eight hours. At the Excelsior." He paused. "Could we have dinner tonight?"

"Provided you have pictures of CeeCee with you," she said lightly. He was too wary to make a pass again. Rejection damaged his ego. He was one of the youngest and most handsome congressmen in Washington — he probably wasn't rejected often. Did Pat suspect? She was too much the lady to say anything even if she did. "Pat tells me CeeCee's absolutely gorgeous."

"I've got a rash of snapshots. And yes, she's gorgeous," Paul said with pride.

Tina was unexpectedly cheered by the prospect of an evening with a new face. Felix was so intense, all business. And nobody else in the company interested her. She distrusted the handsome young Italians who

497

shot hot glances at every foreign woman, believing they were all rich. And she had not seen Clark since the big blowup in late May. Nobody who knew her would believe she hadn't slept with anybody since Clark.

"Pick me up around eight," she told Paul. "I'll have the chauffeur waiting at the curb with the Rolls. Anywhere special you'd like to go?"

"I'm a tourist," he said. "Your choice."

"All right. We'll start off with a drink at Doney's on the Via Veneto, the 'mad, mad mile,'" Tina plotted. "It's like the Brown Derby or Chasen's in Hollywood—except you pay in lire, drink negronis instead of martinis, and cluck about the awful black stockings all the Italian starlets wear. Everybody in the Italian film business stops by at least once a day to exchange gossip."

"Sounds very Italian."

"It's old European," she confirmed. "And from Doney's we'll go to dinner at Angelino's. No," she amended, "let's go to Meo Patacca. It's the in place right now. After dinner—" She paused. "Are you involved in late night conferences?"

"I'm clear until nine tomorrow morning," he said in high good humor. "Plan away."

"You'll want to see Bricktop's and maybe stop in at Jerry Chierchio's bar for a nightcap." He'd be too tired after all that to make any passes even if the thought crossed his mind. "Pick me up at eight," she repeated. "And bring the photos of CeeCee!"

Paul arrived fifteen minutes late and abjectly apologetic. "That damn italian traffic," he reminded her. His eyes skimmed her very short, sleeveless black shift. Not the Audrey Hepburn–Jackie Kennedy uncluttered look but the audacious young look she had found in a boutique on King's Road in London. "How do you stay so young?" he reproached. "If I didn't know better, I'd guess nineteen. Maybe twenty."

"Thanks for those tender words," Tina chuckled and reached for her alligator-and-mink jacket from Vanessa's beat collection. The last couple of nights had been unseasonably cool. "With thirty-seven staring me in the face I'm grateful."

They went first to Doney's for a drink. Paul clearly enjoyed being seen with an American movie star; he beamed every time a film celebrity—Italian or otherwise—stopped at their table to exchange greetings. While they sipped their drinks they pored over his endless array of snapshots of CeeCee.

"She looks so damned grownup." Tina stared in astonishment at the perfection of Pat's face duplicated in her daughter. Yet CeeCee seemed so unlike Pat. It was the eyes, she decided. That wide-eyed innocence that still managed to be sexy as hell. It looked oddly obscene in a little girl. She remembered Nabokov's novel that caused so much talk three years ago—*Lolita*. "How old is CeeCee?" she demanded. She must be a handful to raise.

"She'll be fifteen in February." Paul seemed faintly self-conscious. While he clearly adored CeeCee, he wasn't comfortable at being the father of a teen-ager. He cleared his throat. "I'm getting hungry. Do you suppose we can find a decent steak at this restaurant you're taking me to?"

"Without a doubt," she promised. "It'll come from Florence, where the finest cattle are raised. Veal from Lombardy, chicken from Tuscany. Italians like to eat well."

They left Doney's for dinner at Meo Patacca. And from there they went to the small, intimate Bricktop's, on the Via Veneto between the Excelsior and the Flora Hotel. Now sixty-six and well padded, the freckle-faced black entertainer—who hailed from Alderson, West Virginia, and had been the toast of Paris before World War II—entertained from a tiny, rectangular stage, alternately puffing on a cigar and sipping bourbon and ginger ale between songs and chatter.

"The blacks get everywhere these days," Paul said sardonically, and Tina frowned.

"Bricktop's known everybody in her time," Tina replied. "Royalty, politicians, writers, artists, actors. Back in the twenties she taught the Price of Wales to do the Black Bottom."

Paul soon suggested they move on. Tina suspected that he was a closet bigot. While in Congress he might be forced to subscribe to the clamor for civil rights, but in his heart he was still the Texas boy outraged by school integration. They left Bricktop's to stop at Jerry Chierchio's. Paul seemed cheered by hearing that Chierchio came from Louisiana.

"I haven't had so much to drink since California," Tina confessed when they left for her flat. "I feel very mellow."

"So do I." Paul dropped his arm around her shoulders in the darkness of the car.

"I'll have Carlo drop me off at the flat and then take you on to the Excelsior," she said, all at once aware of his warm breath against her throat.

"Later," Paul urged, running his tongue along the rim of her ear.

"Paul, this is crazy," she objected. *What the hell was the matter with her? This was Pat's husband.*

500

"We'll both be crazy if you send me straight back to the hotel," he warned huskily. "Let me come up for one drink. We can't say good night properly in the back seat of a car."

"I'll tell Carlo to wait at the curb," she said after a moment. "One drink." She paused. "I'll send Carlo to the garage."

Tina fumbled with her key at the door. She shouldn't have had that last brandy, she rebuked herself.

"Let me." Paul took the key from her. "No need to wake up the servants."

"They're off for the night," Tina said, surrendering the key. Why had she told Paul that, she asked herself in a vague haze.

Paul unlocked the door and flung it wide.

"I'll fix you a drink." She dropped the alligator-and-mink jacket on the floor of the night-lit foyer, kicked off her black pumps, and sauntered into the library-study.

"I don't need a drink, baby." His voice whirled her about to face him. He was beside her, his arms around her. "I need you. You need me."

"Cocky bastard, aren't you?" She tried her "amused detachment" smile, so successful onscreen.

"You want me as much as I want you." He pulled her to him, his thighs against hers, his passion telegraphing a heated message. "Do we have to waste time with silly word games?"

She knew she would go out of her mind if she threw him out now. It wouldn't mean anything to either of them after tonight. So why not? If not her, he'd climb between the sheets with some Italian girl in a short, tight skirt. He was right. She wanted it as much as he

501

did.

"Come with me, Mr. Hot-and-Bothered," she drawled. "Let's see how good you are."

In her dramatic, linen-walled bedroom, they stripped in the faint illumination of the smoldering logs in the fireplace and inspected each other like a pair of gladiators poised for action in the arena. Tina saw the hint of a paunch that was the result of too many three-martini luncheons, too many after-dinner brandies.

"You've got great tits," he approved and moved in to imprison both nipples between his fingers. "I knew that when I first saw you in a bathing suit."

"That was eight years ago," she reminded him, inspecting him through narrowed eyes. "You've held up well," she acknowledged.

"I'll show you just how well," he boasted and brought his mouth to hers, his tongue meeting hers as his hands left her nipples to close in on her hard, lean rear.

"That's not bad for a start," she conceded when they parted. *Lord, she needed this.*

"Let's try the bed," he said heatedly. "I believe in comfort." Together they walked to the bed. "What's your favorite sexual fantasy?" he drawled.

"To be filled everywhere I can be filled," she taunted. "To go out of my mind with touching." Her hazel eyes were black in anticipation. "There's a bottle of Dom Perignon chilling in the refrigerator," she said, stretching out luxuriously on the sheets. "Go get it."

"Now?" he said, irritated at this delay.

"I have another fantasy. To sip Dom Perignon with you in me," she murmured.

"Christ, Tina!" His hands tightened at her shoul-

502

ders.

"Go," she ordered. "The kitchen's down the hall to the left. Two glasses and the champagne. You won't forget tonight."

Paul strode from the room, and Tina crossed into the bedroom to spray herself with Chanel No. 5. She felt totally in control. Later they'd lie in the oversize Roman tub that dominated the bathroom. Paul was free until nine tomorrow morning.

She smiled at the sound of the cork popping in the kitchen. When Paul returned with the bottle of Dom Perignon and a pair of champagne glasses, Tina had settled herself against a mound of pillows, a bedside lamp spilling light on her nakedness. She saw him swallow hard as his gaze focused on her long thighs. She wasn't bad for a broad facing forty in three years.

"Pour me a drink."

"What about that sexual fantasy?" he argued. "Aren't we missing the major event?"

"Pour the drinks and put them here." She pointed to the night table. "So they'll be there at the right moment."

Paul poured champagne into the two glasses, deposited them on the table, and sat at the edge of the bed. His hands moved up the sensuous length of her legs; his mouth, hot and moist, trailed his hands. She reached to cradle his head while his tongue moved to fill the hot, dark warmth between her thighs.

"Mmm, that's good," she approved.

He lifted himself above her.

"You have a fantasy," he reminded her. "Let's not waste time."

He probed, entered her, and thrust with sudden urgency. She closed her eyes and moved with him.

503

She felt his breath at her throat and then his tongue wet in one ear.

Don't let it be over yet. Not until she was ready.

She felt his hand beneath her rump, a finger searching for entry. And then his mouth was hard on hers. Their tongues entwined while their bodies fought in frenzy for climax. Her nails dug into his shoulders.

"Don't leave me," she commanded when his mouth released hers and she felt him limp within her. "Stay."

"What else?" he clucked. "You said you wanted to sip champagne with me in you. I'm a man who aims to please."

Awkwardly he reached for the glass of champagne from the night table while she propped pillows behind her head with a provocative smile.

"For you," he grinned, handing her the glass and reaching for the other. He drank briefly and returned his glass to the table.

She watched the excitement on his face, as she sipped the Dom Perignon and his hands fondled her breasts. Already he was beginning to stir in her. Not bad, she congratulated herself, for a couple past their prime. He began to move within her, and soon he was driving with heat. She grunted in approval.

"Fantasy fulfilled?" he challenged, panting.

"You're on the way," she conceded, impatient to be free of the champagne glass. Her hands caught at his shoulders while the glass shattered on the floor. "You're great, baby. Don't stop. Don't ever stop!"

Tina lay in the curve of Paul's arm while they shared his glass of champagne. Tonight made up for the boredom of these past few days. She felt mellow and relaxed.

"You grew up, baby," he said smugly.

"What do you mean?" She tilted her head in curiosity.

"The last time I made a pass at you, you said—and I quote—'I think men who cheat on their wives are assholes,'" he recalled with relish.

Tina sat up and put the champagne glass on the night table. "I feel like coffee." She rose to her feet, suddenly uneasy. If it hadn't been her, Paul would have been in bed with somebody else. "Do you want some?"

"Come back to bed," he coaxed. "The sun isn't up yet."

"Paul, why do you mess around with other women when you have somebody like Pat at home?"

"What the hell's the matter with you?" He sat upright, his face flushed with color. "You didn't ask questions when I was screwing you!"

"Just curious." She shrugged. "I can't figure out men like you. A beautiful, bright, sympathetic wife." She refrained from adding "rich." "And it's still not enough?"

"Knock it off, you goddamn whore!" He leapt to his feet and smacked her across the face.

"Nobody hits me!" Tina yelled, hitting back.

"You deserve it!" Paul punched her in the jaw and she staggered. "Rotten little whore!" He lifted his hand to hit again, but she ducked and reached for the andiron beside the fireplace.

"Come one step closer and you get this over the head!" she blazed. "Now put on your fucking clothes and get the hell out of here. I mean it," she said when he hesitated. "Get out before I call the cops."

"You don't have the nerve," he jeered.

"Don't try me, Paul. The only reason I'm not doing it this minute is because of Pat. Next to Vanessa she's the closest friend I have in this world. I don't want to hurt her."

"You're no different from any slut I can pick up in a massage parlor back in Washington," he said contemptuously, but he was putting on his clothes. "Except that you give it away."

"Out!" Tina screeched. "Get out!"

Thirty-seven

Vanessa knew it would be a tight squeeze, but she was determined to present her first showing at the custom salon in late July—the same time European designers would be showing their fall collections. Shortly past New Year's, 1962, the renovations were completed. Phil and Robbie chased around town in search of just the right furniture. And Vanessa began to interview for the salon staff.

Doris would be in charge of the custom salon. She needed Doris there, and the friction between Frank and her cherished assistant had grown, even though Doris now spent most of her time in the design studio. Frank was respected, Vanessa knew, but he wasn't liked. It disturbed her that he didn't care. Only to Phyllis did she confess her anxieties.

"Frank's got an ego problem." Phyllis was characteristically blunt. "He's got an ego bigger than the Mississippi River after a spring thaw."

Frank ignored her preparations for the design studio. He had not been consulted, therefore it did not exist. He was on another spending rampage; but in the face of her expenses for the design studio, Vanessa refrained from saying anything. Anyway, she reasoned, the money was available.

Each year Frank turned in his Cadillac for a new model. This year he had bought a grey Ferrari. He brought in Phil and Robbie—"Vanessa's fag club"—to redo the showroom. When he visited stores, he flew on chartered flights. He talked about buying a race horse.

Vanessa tried to tell herself this was just a phase, that their marriage was not falling apart. Frank was hitting what Phyllis called male menopause. It happened to a lot of men. They turned forty and went into shock. Their youth was behind them, at fifty they were afraid of losing their sexual prowess, of being tossed into a job market where fifty was a dirty word. At sixty they fell apart when they realized they hadn't achieved what they'd expected, and death seemed shockingly close.

"My father is sixty," Phyllis said with baffled affection over lunch at a small restaurant near the Madison Avenue salon. "And he drives my mother nuts. He reads the obits every day. He's sure he's got cancer or a heart condition or whatever the newspapers are spouting statistics on that week. But he won't go for a checkup—he just fumes and worries."

"I thought Wendy would make Frank feel young forever," Vanessa confessed. "But he has no patience with her anymore." Lately he often lost his temper with Wendy, for no reason that Vanessa could see. "Remember how he used to spoil her?"

"The novelty of being a father is over," Phyllis said dryly. "And it's safe to yell at Wendy. She can't fight back—she's only three. Suzy will, you know." Suzy was high-spirited and fiercely independent. At fourteen she was as tall as her mother, reed slim and proud and embarrassed by her developing figure.

508

Vanessa was frustrated by the amount of time their social lives usurped, even as she realized the importance of this in their business. The press was elevating Seventh Avenue to the New York socialite world. Wealthy women dropped the names of their favorite designers, and reporters eagerly spread the word. John Fairchild's *Women's Wear Daily* was becoming a star-maker.

Women's Wear Daily mentioned Vanessa's attendance at dinners, parties, theater openings. Her photograph appeared at various festivities featured in *Vogue*, *Harper's Bazaar*, and *Town & Country*. And Frank and Phyllis always said that this was the most valuable kind of advertising.

After a hiatus of seven weeks, Tina wrote from Paris. The film was finished. Clark had arrived in Rome during the final three weeks with a dramatic diamond-and-emerald necklace from Van Cleef and Arpels in Paris as a peace offering.

"Vanessa, Clark's Reno divorce came through. Maybe I'll be a three-time loser, but by the time you receive this we'll be married. Never mind the studio publicity that says we won't marry until spring. I'm thirty-seven years old. I want to have a baby with Clark while I can. We both have to be back in Hollywood in March for pictures, but until then we'll be holed up in this darling little house about forty minutes outside of Paris. Of course, if I'm pregnant they'll have to postpone the picture."

Vanessa worried about Tina marrying Clark. She suspected that Tina's decision revolved around her longing for a second child. At the same time Tina's happiness made her painfully aware of the state of her own marriage. Frank had moved into one of the guest rooms on the pretext that he often disturbed her by his sleeping habits—"Hell, I rarely settle in before close to 3:00 A.M. and I'm always up before seven. I know I wake you up when I come to bed, and a lot of mornings now you sleep close to eight."

She and Tina were both driven by their careers, Vanessa reminded herself. Did a successful career rule out a successful marriage? No, Vanessa rejected this. Phyllis had a career. She loved to watch Phyllis and Arnie together, so solicitous of each other, so genuinely happy in being together. A rare marriage? Perhaps. She thought about Pat. Did Paul wander regularly, or had his pass at Tina been a one-time thing? Pat was a full-time wife; Paul had no reason to wander. As close as she and Pat were, Pat never discussed her marriage.

Despite her declaration about being "holed up" in a Paris suburb with Clark, Tina wrote to say that she had attended the January 29 showing of Yves Saint Laurent's first collection under his own name—the first since his nervous collapse shortly after being drafted into the French army and the opening of his own couture house—and that it was superb. She wrote, too, about the clothes by Courrèges, shown in his small white salon to a background of sultry Spanish guitar music. *Darling, his skirts are going so high nothing will be a secret!*

Vanessa kept abreast of the London fashion scene, convinced that new designers like Mary Quant—and Courrèges in Paris—were changing the face of haute couture forever. She filed a copy of a February London *Sunday Times* that featured a Quant dress worn by an exciting new model named Jean Shrimpton.

Vanessa was drained by her efforts to design for her custom salon in addition to her already frenetic schedule, but she vowed she would open as planned. Frank was irritated when he found out that Phyllis was circulating stories about the Madison Avenue salon.

On a cold, blustery mid-February Friday night she and Frank fought about this on the way home from a charity ball.

"It's like you're looking down your nose at our regular lines," he complained.

"Frank, it'll add cachet," she repeated. "And aren't you pleased about that interview Phyllis set up for you?" At her insistence, Phyllis had initiated interest in a national weekly article about Frank as the "financial wizard behind Creations by Vanessa Conrad."

Frank grinned. "I handled that bastard just fine. They're giving me three times the space originally planned."

"Marvelous, Frank!" When he was in the mood, Frank could be a charmer.

In the night-darkened apartment Vanessa went to look in on the children. Suzy was sleeping soundly in her room. She went to Wendy's bedroom, and was startled to discover the bed was empty. Probably Wendy had had a nightmare and Maria had taken her into her own bed. She walked across the hall to Maria's room and opened the door carefully so she wouldn't disturb Wendy and Maria.

She stood in the doorway and stared into the room in disbelief. *Where was Wendy?*

"Maria—" Her voice was shrill with terror. "Maria!"

"What—what is it?" Maria struggled awake. "What's happened?" She sat upright in alarm.

"Wendy isn't in her bed. I thought she'd be here with you—"

"Maybe she went out to the kitchen." Maria reached for her robe at the foot of the bed, fumbled for her slippers on the floor. "She's discovered there's still ice cream from Suzy's birthday dinner in the freezer."

The two women raced to the kitchen. The room was deserted.

"She's not here!" Terrifying thoughts chased across Vanessa's mind.

"I put her to bed at seven-thirty," Maria said. "I went in to make sure she was covered before I went to sleep at eleven." She was white and trembling.

"Frank!" Vanessa ran down the length of the hall to Frank's room. "Frank, Wendy's disappeared!"

"What do you mean?" He emerged from the bedroom in bare feet and trousers. "Where could she have gone?"

"She's not in her bed." Vanessa was fighting for control. "I thought she might be with Maria. She wasn't. Frank, where could she be?"

"Mommy?" Suzy appeared at her doorway. "I heard you talking. What's the matter?"

"Go back to sleep, darling," Vanessa ordered with a show of calm. "Everything's fine."

"It's not fine," Suzy objected, her face registering alarm at the sight of the white, stricken faces before her. "Has something happened to Wendy?"

"We—we can't find her." Maria broke into tears. "She was in her bed when I looked in on her. Sleeping like an angel."

"I'm calling the police," Frank said and turned back into the bedroom.

"Wait!" Vanessa ordered. "The phone's ringing in the den."

Frank sprinted to answer it and Maria and Suzy followed in his trail. Vanessa ran to pick up the extension in the kitchen.

"Hello," Frank said tersely.

"Call the cops and the kid's dead," an arrogant male

voice warned. Vanessa clutched at the countertop in anguish. "Do like we say, and you'll have her back in twenty-four hours."

"What do you want?" Frank demanded.

"One hundred thousand dollars in twenties and fifties," the caller told him. "Put the money in an overnight bag and bring it to—"

"It's going to take time for us to raise that," Frank interrupted.

"The bank opens at nine," the kidnapper shot back. "I'll call at noon. Make sure you have it. Twenties and fifties. I'll tell you where."

"Don't hurt her," Vanessa pleaded. "Please, don't hurt her."

"That's up to you, lady. Do like we say—don't call the cops—hand over the money. You'll have your pretty little girl back tomorrow night."

"I'll go to the bank," Frank said. "We won't notify the police. We want Wendy back."

"Let me talk to her," Vanessa said. Suzy stood beside her, pale and trembling.

"When we get the money, you can talk to her." The phone slammed down at the other end.

"Frank, he didn't tell us where to take the money!" Vanessa cried. "Oh, God, what are they doing to Wendy?"

"They'll call back at noon. I'll have the money," Frank soothed. "We'll get her back."

"She must be so scared," Vanessa sobbed. "My poor little baby. And she's just in her pajamas! On a cold night like this—"

"Vanessa, I think we ought to call the police," Frank said.

"We can't do that!" Vanessa gasped in shock. "You heard what he said!"

"They may take the money and" — Frank hesitated, then pushed himself to continue — "and we may never see Wendy again. We have to bring in the police. We can't trust these creeps."

"But the police have to agree that we pay the ransom," Vanessa stipulated. "And it's all got to be kept out of the papers. We can't let them know we've gone to the police." The kidnapper's words burnt into her brain. *"Call the cops and the kid's dead."* "I don't care how much it costs — I want my baby back." She closed her eyes, fighting off the image of Wendy in the hands of the kidnappers.

"We'll give them the ransom," Frank promised, a bead of sweat trickling down his brow. "I'll make the police understand that we're taking no chances. We want Wendy back. After that, I hope the police electrocute the bastards."

In ten minutes they were sitting in the den with detectives. Vanessa rejected all proposals delaying the payment.

"They have my little girl! We'll do anything they say," she insisted. "We don't care how much it costs."

The detectives established that there had been no forced entry. There were no fire escapes. The service entrance was locked. Frank railed about the careless doorman, allowing a stranger into the building. Both Vanessa and Frank refused to believe one of the servants was involved.

Shortly before nine o'clock Frank left for the bank with a weekender dug from a closet. He was back at the apartment within an hour. Vanessa's throat tightened as she watched him carefully recount the money.

All three phones in the apartment were bugged, though the detectives warned it was unlikely the kidnappers would remain on the phone long enough to trace the call. At noon the kidnappers made contact. They gave directions to a dropoff point on the West Side Highway. Frank was to come alone at 7:00 P.M., and again they warned about the consequences if the police intervened.

Frank went to the garage to pick up his car. Vanessa paced about the apartment and tried to console Suzy.

"Wendy's going to be all right, darling," she said, trying hard to believe it. But what kind of monsters would kidnap a little girl? Don't let them hurt her.

"What's taking Daddy so long?" Suzy asked, giving voice to Vanessa's own apprehensions.

"It's only a little past eight," Maria scolded. "He probably ran into heavy traffic." But they all knew it was no more than a fifteen-minute drive at this hour of the night. Maybe the police had been careless. Maybe the kidnappers had been frightened away.

"There he is now!" Vanessa's face was incandescent as she raced into the hall. Frank stood in the entrance foyer. Alone. "Frank?" Vanessa was ice-cold.

"They didn't show," he said, his face sagging in defeat. "I was there with the money. Where the hell were they? I waited forty minutes."

The ringing of the phone was a jarring intrusion.

"Let me take it!" Frank ran to the den. At the same moment the doorbell rang. Maria went to respond. Vanessa and Suzy followed Frank.

"Hello—" Frank gripped the phone with such intensity his knuckles turned white. "I was there like you said!" He frowned as someone spoke at the other end. "No, no cops—nobody was there," he protested. He gestured to Vanessa to hand him pencil and paper. "I got it. I'll be there in twenty minutes. And have my kid with you."

Two detectives hovered in the doorway.

"They gave you a new destination?"

"Right. I'm heading there now." He handed over the sheet of paper with the address.

"We'll call ahead and set up surveillance."

Again, Maria and Vanessa gathered in the kitchen for coffee. Suzy stood at the window and gazed out at the snow, the silver-dollar-size flakes beginning to stick to the ground. The roads would be treacherous. Let everything be all right, Vanessa prayed.

Frank turned onto the West Side Highway at Seventy-ninth Street. Alarm and rage and frustration churned within him. He'd like to castrate the fucking bastards. Vanessa should have listened to him when he said they should move full-time to Croton. The city was a rotten place to raise kids.

The snow was coming down heavily now. Frank flipped on the windshield wipers, then the heater. He crouched over the wheel, squinting at the road ahead. His eyes sought the weekender beside him. If they'd laid a hand on Wendy, he'd kill them.

He watched the exits, his mouth dry as he thought of the encounter ahead of him. If they didn't have Wendy with them, he wouldn't hand over the money. This was an exchange. If they wanted the money, they had to give him his kid.

The next exit. Then drive fifty feet. Look for a black van on the right side of the road. Swing over into the exit lane. Pray nobody else was getting off.

The car skidded; Frank swore, managed to straighten it out and make the exit. His eyes settled on a black van at the side of the road, and adrenaline raced through his body. He moved ahead of the van and parked. He reached for the weekender. What would he do if they tried to grab the money and run? He had to take the chance that they'd hand over Wendy.

He thrust open the door on the passenger side, as instructed, and stepped out of the car into the eerie darkness of the night. Both hands held high, the weekender dangling awkwardly.

"Where's my kid?" he demanded when a man emerged from the van and beamed a flashlight in his direction.

"Let's see what you got to trade," the man said, his voice muffled by the ski mask he wore. "Put your hands down slow and open the case."

Frank obeyed, opening the weekender to show the neat piles of twenties and fifties.

"Close it and throw it over here," the man ordered.

"Where's my kid?" Frank's voice was strident with anxiety.

"Shut up!" the man at the wheel hissed. "You want her, throw the case."

"When I see her," Frank stalled. They could kill him and run, but he'd take that chance. "This is a trade."

"Bring out the kid," the man behind the wheel muttered to someone in the rear.

Frank waited, clenching his teeth. He saw a small bundle lifted from the car and thrown into the bushes. Was it a trick?

"Now throw the case or we'll kill you both!" the man in the ski mask ordered, his voice rising to drown out the sound of a faint cry that came from the side of the road.

Frank tossed the case at him and dove into the bushes. He groped in the darkness and found the small, squirming, warm body entangled in a blanket.

He heard the van racing away.

"It's all right, baby." Frank lifted his small, frightened daughter into his arms. "It's all right. I'll take you home to Mommy now."

Thirty-eight

Once Wendy was safely home again, Vanessa tried to settle down to a normal routine, but she was sleeping badly. Even though the kidnappers—a disgruntled former employee and her husband—were behind bars, she woke up two or three times each night to rush to Wendy's room to make sure she was there. She knew it was illogical to blame Frank's tough attitude toward their employees for what had happened, but the thought nagged at her.

Frank blamed Wendy's kidnapping on living in the city. He insisted they move up to the Croton house full-time.

"We'll talk about it after the salon opening," Vanessa hedged over a Sunday morning breakfast in Croton in early April. The crocuses were blooming on the front lawn and the forsythia bushes were bursting in golden splendor, and Vanessa wanted only to enjoy a quiet morning.

"And meanwhile," Frank taunted, "we have to worry every minute Wendy and Suzy are out of our sight."

"I don't want to live up here," Suzy said suddenly. "Not all the time."

"But you love this place," Frank reminded her.

"I love it for weekends and Thanksgiving and Christmas and Easter," Suzy rattled off. "Not all the time."

"We'll move up in September," Frank decreed. "After Labor Day weekend and the summer at Southampton. In time for you to start school up here."

"I don't want to leave the city!" Suzy blazed. "I like my school. All my friends are there."

"They've got great schools up here. And what about your friends Lorna and Marcy?" Frank challenged.

"They're weekend friends. If we move up here, I'll run away." Suzy's eyes blazed in defiance. "I'll go to live with Marcy's sister on East Seventh Street. Her sister has an apartment there, and kids are always coming in to stay for a while. Last week she had four kids sleeping on the floor."

"To hell with Marcy's sister!" Frank turned grimly to Vanessa. "Where does she meet these creeps?"

"Marcy's sister is in an off-Broadway play," Vanessa explained, striving to appear calm. "Down in the East Village. It's becoming kind of an attraction for teenagers."

"If you try to make me live up here, I'll run away," Suzy said again. "I could get a job as a waitress or —"

"You're fourteen years old!" Frank yelled. "You're going to school! You're —"

"Suzy, didn't you tell me you were supposed to go riding this morning with Lorna and Marcy?" Vanessa interrupted with a warning glance at Frank.

"Oh, wow, I've gotta run. Will you excuse me, please?" she asked politely, already on her feet.

Vanessa waited until Suzy had left the room.

"Frank, let's stop this talk about moving up here. It's not for us. We both hate running up and down the highway twice a day in all kinds of weather. It was bad enough the summer that we did it. And Suzy's too old to transplant to suburbia."

"You always have an answer for everything." He glared at her with hostility and pushed back his chair. "I won't be home for dinner."

Tina and Clark announced their marriage in the spring. The studio downplayed the union because of the unfavorable publicity surrounding Clarke's divorce. Tina wrote Vanessa that Clark was going to Tangier in mid-July for another film. She wasn't making any commitments so that she could join him two weeks later, once her own film was finished.

Vanessa worried that Tina was not happy in this third marriage. But Tina was planning to stop off in New York for the salon opening before flying on to Tangier — they'd have time to talk then. Tina and Pat were to be surprise celebrity models in the grand finale.

Vanessa was spending formidable hours preparing for the opening. She was grateful for Phyllis and Arnie's moral support. Suzy, too, was intrigued by her mother's latest venture.

Already Phyllis was arranging the invitation list for the salon opening. No buyers were to be invited to this made-to-order show — only potential private customers and the media. At Phyllis's urging, Vanessa decided to dispense with a commentator. Nothing must distract from the clothes.

The audience would be coming from Bar Harbor, Newport, Southampton, and even St. Tropez. The ladies of the jet set were eager to be identified with a celebrity designer — and to have their photographs appear in the fashion magazines.

This summer Suzy would be staying with Wendy and Maria at the Southampton house. Vanessa would come out on Friday afternoons and drive back on Monday mornings. Frank planned to arrive on Saturdays in time for lunch and return with Vanessa.

They opened the Southampton house early in June. Almost immediately Frank's attitude toward Vanessa's custom salon changed. He was impressed by the interest of the New York socialites they met at weekend dinner parties. Frank assumed the role of indulgent husband, allowing his wife this new toy.

Pat was scheduled to come up from the Virginia plantation the morning of the fashion show, after fittings earlier in the month. Once again Paul was on the campaign trail. Occasionally Pat made brief appearances at his side. In 1964, Pat confided over the phone ten days before the show, Paul would run for the Senate. Her father was carefully guiding Paul's rise. Owens had decided that 1964 would be the ideal year.

"CeeCee's at camp in Switzerland," Pat told Vanessa. "She would be bored to death at the plantation all summer." Vanessa knew Pat was uncomfortable around CeeCee. She loved CeeCee, longed to protect her — and was afraid of her.

"Will Tina be in town for the show?" Tina's movie was running behind schedule.

"She'll be here," Vanessa said. "Just for a couple of days. Then she's heading for Tangier to meet Clark. He's doing a picture on location there."

"How's this marriage working out?" Pat asked, her voice serious. "Is Tina pregnant yet?" They both knew Tina's obsession to have a baby with Clark.

"They're fighting a lot," Vanessa admitted. "And Tina isn't pregnant."

"She'll be thirty-eight in December." Pat's voice was edged with sympathy. "She's running short on child-bearing years."

"Stay with us at Southampton for the long weekend after the opening," Vanessa urged. "Frank's giving a dinner party afterward at the Pierre. Then we'll drive out to Southampton."

"I need that," Pat confessed. "Campaign years are so tense at the Georgetown house and the plantation. Daddy hates not being in the House anymore. It makes him impossible. And Paul's always tense, only more so when he's running for reelection."

"Frank will be going to Saratoga for the opening of the racing season, so he won't be out at the house that weekend, but Phyl and Arnie are coming out on Saturday." She was so pleased that they had finally been able to persuade Arnie to abandon his law practice and come into the business. Arnie knew a lot about the way things worked because Phyllis brought Seventh Avenue home with her. "They're both very much involved in the civil rights movement, but I persuaded them to take off one weekend."

"I'm looking forward to it," Pat said affectionately.

Vanessa was a mass of nerves as the opening approached. She was consumed by worry and a sudden lack of confidence. Frank had not seen any of the designs; he had shown no interest in the collection. For so many years she had depended on his support. Now she relied on Phyllis, Doris, and Suzy. They were rapturous about every piece.

Arnie had come in after long hours at the shop to work out the costing of each garment, since Frank professed to be too busy. Vanessa respected Arnie's knowledge and was grateful for his time. But she was a perfectionist, never entirely satisfied. It was an effort not to scream at her workers when she discovered some minor imperfection. She was firm but polite, determined not to emulate Frank's tyranny.

Sometimes, late at night when everything looked impossible, she prayed for some catastrophe that would prevent the showing of her first made-to-order collection. It wasn't right. She would be ridiculed. Because of the painful lack of time the run-through took place the morning of the opening; she had hoped for a careful rehearsal three days earlier. Here was the culmination of her most cherished dream—and she felt painfully inadequate. She had chosen her fabrics with the utmost care, knowing the perfect fabric could assure a marvelous look even if the cut proved disappointing.

At Phyllis's prodding she conceded that she was pleased with the run-through, though she cautioned that this was no guarantee of success. Not until the collection was shown to prospective customers and to the press would she know whether or not this was a successful collection.

After a frenetic last-minute meeting with the staff, Vanessa left the salon for the drive to the airport to meet Tina's flight. She was edgy at the delays in traffic as the chauffeur maneuvered his way through the parade of cars and trucks heading out of the city. She was impatient to be at the airport. Not only to welcome her dear, dear friend, but to gain newspaper publicity for tomorrow's showing. Phyllis had arranged for the press to be at the airport. Tina and Vanessa would be photographed arm in arm. Tina would explain that she was in the city especially for the opening of Vanessa Conrad's custom salon.

Vanessa left the limousine and raced into the airline terminal. Tina's flight had just arrived. And there was Tina, surrounded by photographers and reporters. A studio representative hovered solicitously.

"Tina!" Vanessa called out joyously, a surge of love bringing tears to her eyes. "Tina!"

"Darling!" Tina gestured to the cluster about her to clear a path. "Oh, it's so wonderful to see you!"

They hugged and posed for photographs, talked about the custom salon. Tina fielded questions about the state of her marriage to Clark and her new film. She brushed aside rumors about feuding between herself and her costar. Finally, Vanessa guided her through the terminal to the waiting limousine.

"Thank God that's over." Tina leaned back in the limousine with an air of satisfaction. "I don't know why I play this stupid game." She uttered a mocking sigh. "But how else can I make tons of money so fast? Of course, the good scripts are not coming in the way they used to." Her smile was rueful. "All the good ones seem to be written for actresses under thirty. I used to tell myself the only thing in life I could depend upon — besides my few real friends — was my career. Now it's money. The career can go. At least, an actress's career can go. But as long as I pile up the money I know I can survive this crazy rat race. Even Pop knew that," she laughed. "He left me his house so I'd always have a place to stay."

"How's the marriage?" Vanessa asked.

"Shitty. Clark's being so rotten about having a baby. He says he's too old to go through that again. Hell, all he has to do is knock me up," she laughed. "He won't have to worry about changing diapers or burping the little brat." She paused. "His kids are so rotten. Clark and I took them out to dinner — finally, after three refusals — and they acted as though I'd broken up their happy home. God, they know better."

"How's Adam?"

"Bright," she said with pride. "He gets that from his father. Not from my side. Sal's got some weird notion about Adam coming into his auto repair shop when he finishes high school. But Adam's going to the best college he can get into," she said with conviction. "He'll have every chance to make his way right up to the top. Now tell me about Suzy and Wendy," she commanded.

The showing was scheduled to begin at 7:00 P.M. sharp. Vanessa had chosen this hour as the most tranquil in a July day. Phil and Robbie had created a masterpiece, she told herself as she walked about the wild-orchid-laden salon with Phyllis half an hour before the first guests would arrive.

The lighting man was making last-minute adjustments, and the disk jockey was running a final check of his records. The models had miraculously all arrived on time. The dressers and makeup man were gearing themselves up for the show. In a charming, brief, Liberty-sprigged print from Mary Quant, Suzy sat on a bottle-green velvet sofa in the area reserved for the most important guests and devoured *Silent Spring*, the new book by Rachel Carson that Phyllis had given her a few minutes earlier.

"You don't think Phil and Robie went overboard on the mirrors?" Vanessa asked Phyllis anxiously as she scanned the sixteen-foot mirrored doors, the mirrored panels about the salon.

"They're marvelous," Phyllis soothed. "Relax, Vanessa, everything is just right. Just the tone of elegance your clothes deserve. Go back and hold Doris's hand," she coaxed. "She's almost as nervous as you are."

"She's still fussing with the dresses Tina and Pat are modeling," Vanessa managed a shaky laugh. Frank hadn't arrived yet, she noted.

At exactly seven o'clock, with every seat in the salon occupied and press photographers grappling with cameras and lighting equipment, the music began. The first model moved regally onto the runway. Vanessa hovered in the crowded backstage area with Phyllis and Doris, engrossed in making sure each model would emerge with the proper accessories. As in all fashion shows, the first clothes were casual.

"They like the casual wear!" Vanessa's voice was electric with pleasure at the sound of the applause. "But will they like the 'after five'?"

The audience adored the casual clothes; they were ecstatic about the 'after five' and 'big evening' dresses. And when Tina and Pat, wearing glittering beaded gowns, appeared together on the runway, the applause threatened to drown out the music. A famous movie star and the most publicized political wife in Washington — after Jackie Kennedy — appearing on the runway! In the excitement of Tina and Pat's surprise appearance, the traditional walk of a model in an extravagant wedding gown, indicating the conclusion of the show, was almost lost.

Radiant and beautiful in yellow chiffon, Vanessa appeared from behind the scenes to a burst of bravos. Women eager to be private customers rushed forward to congratulate her. Suzy hovered at her mother's side with endearing pride. Frank remained engrossed in conversation with a pair of ladies noted for their fine racing stables.

Waiters circulated with platters of Scotch smoked salmon, caviar, sturgeon, English biscuits, and trays of Dom Perignon in Waterford crystal. Vanessa searched the faces of the press people anxiously.

At the dinner party at the Pierre Frank played the proud, adoring husband. After the party Vanessa, Suzy, Tina, and Pat headed for the waiting limousine for a brief return to the apartment before heading out to Southampton. They lingered at the curb with Frank, exchanging farewells. He was charmingly apologetic to Tina and Pat, explaining he was on his way to Saratoga for a yearling sale and the opening of the racing season.

Frank was two people, Vanessa thought as she joined the others in the limousine. The second, darker side had surfaced with success and pushed the Frank she loved into the shadows. But that other Frank had existed. She had not imagined him. She felt as though she had been widowed a second time.

Edie was waiting in the vestibule of her brownstone when Frank doubled-parked on the narrow street.

"Hi, honey!" She emerged, weekender in tow, when he left the car with a wary glance at the others that trailed behind the Ferrari.

"Hurry up, Edie," he gestured from the curb. "Before some bastard clips the car."

It had become a ritual for him to pick up Edie on Friday evenings. They'd go out to dinner, head for a motel on the Island for the night, and in the morning he'd put her on a train for New York and then drive to Southampton. Twice a week they had dinner somewhere in the Village — in a restaurant where he would not encounter anyone he knew — and then went back

528

to her apartment. Occasionally he slept over. Edie had gone to Brooks Brothers and bought him slippers, pajamas, and robe for those occasions.

"How was the dinner party?" Edie asked, snuggling against him on the seat as he reached for the ignition.

For a moment Frank tensed, smoldering with rekindled rage. That fucking photographer, calling him *Mr.* Conrad. Everybody on Seventh Avenue knew he was Frank Bernstein.

"*WWD* will carry the story," he surmised. "Cost me a bundle, but it was worth it." He took one hand from the wheel to rest it for a moment on her thigh.

"Are we going to stop for dinner anyway?" she asked with a hint of reproach in her sultry voice.

"I'll eat again," he chuckled. "But let's wait until we move up the West Side Highway a piece." Edie never said anything, but he knew she resented eating in out-of-the-way places. She fancied herself at the Pierre, or Le Pavillon or El Morocco. But she was smart enough to keep her mouth shut, he thought complacently. Nobody knew he was having a fling with one of his showroom models.

Edie turned on the radio, fiddled with the dial until Neil Sedaka's voice filtered into the air-conditioned interior of the car. She was satisfied to hum along with Sedaka. Thank God he'd made her understand right off he hated women who talked incessantly.

After tonight Vanessa would be impossible. Right away he had known the rich broads Vanessa ran with were mad about the collection. Ditto the reviewers. Even so she'd be lucky if the salon broke even. Why the hell should she waste time on that stupid ego-builder? So she was acquiring some fancy status—that wouldn't pay for the town house in the East Sixties the broker had called this morning to say was for sale. It had everything he wanted. And it was the business *he* had built up that would pay for it.

They found an all-night diner an hour up the highway and stopped to eat. Edie was all excited about going to Saratoga. They'd stay at a motel somewhere between Albany and Saratoga, he plotted. And he'd keep a wary eye out for the social crowd at the racetrack. Nobody had to know he was up there with Edie.

"Frank" — Edie leaned toward him when the waitress had served their dessert and coffee — "do we have to drive all the way up beyond Albany? Why don't we stay at that motel across the way tonight and drive up early tomorrow morning?"

Frank cleared his throat, looking down Edie's blouse and thinking of her in bed.

"Okay, baby. We'll drive across the road." Edie was almost half his age, but he could make her climb the walls. She was uncomplicated and available. She thought he was hot shit. What more could any man ask?

By the time he had locked the door of their motel unit and pulled the drapes shut, Edie was out of her clothes and in bed. When they got back to New York, he'd send her over to the furrier to be fitted for a mink coat. That should make her happy for a long time.

"Frankie, I'm so hot," she pretended to sulk as he undressed leisurely. "Why do you keep me waiting this way?"

"I'm ready." He grinned in satisfaction and walked to the bed. With Edie he was always ready.

"That was so good, Frankie," Edie murmured when he rested, tired and sated, beside her. "Was it good for you?"

"Great baby," he approved. "But you're fired."

530

"What do you mean?" Her voice was shrill with shock.

"I mean you're not working for Creations any more," he mocked, lifting himself to smile down at her. His hand closed around one adolescent breast. "I'm setting you up in an apartment. Your only job, Edie, is to make me happy."

"On Sutton Place," she stipulated, her smile electric. "I've always wanted to live on Sutton Place."

531

Thirty-nine

Vanessa was upset when Frank announced, early in August, that they were buying an East Sixties town house. She loved their sprawling Park Avenue apartment. But she knew the expensive, six-story town house was his price for forgetting suburbia. All right, she told herself: she had her custom salon; Frank would have his town house.

Not until five days before the closing did Vanessa find time in her schedule to go with Frank to see their new home. She emerged from Frank's gray Ferrari to stand before the imposing limestone town house with four columns, a Palladian arch, and a pair of bay windows.

"It's a beauty," Frank said complacently as he joined her at the curb. "Come on, let me show it to you."

Opening the door into the marble-floored entrance foyer, Frank explained that the house was air-conditioned, with four fireplaces, five bedrooms with private foyers and baths, plus a huge master bedroom and bath. The living room, dining room, and library had unusually high ceilings, and the kitchen and breakfast room were large and bright.

"I'll have the master bedroom floor made over into an apartment for myself," Frank said casually as they ascended in the small elevator. "That way you and the girls won't be disturbed by my crazy hours."

Vanessa struggled to conceal her shock. It was clear that Frank would never share her bed again. When was the last time they had made love? Months ago. It hadn't been right for years. Their marriage had been long in dying; now it was officially dead.

While she accompanied Frank on a tour of the house, she tried to cope with the knowledge that Frank was putting an end to their marital life. She knew there were other wives who would be relieved to be free of their conjugal obligations. There were occasions when Frank went crazy at not being able to perform. She had always been sympathetic; she had never reproached him. What had she done wrong?

"Get Phil and Robbie on the job right away," Frank intruded on her stunned introspection. "They'll tell you this house is a gem."

Phil and Robbie were ecstatic about decorating the new house. Frank told them to spare no expense—he wanted a masterpiece. With their annual gross, and an operating cost that was the envy of Seventh Avenue, they could afford to be extravagant.

Mindful of Wendy's kidnapping, Frank arranged for an intricate security system. Phil and Robbie were in touch with Paris contacts for antiques that would be right for the house. After careful estimations, the decorators concluded it would be possible for the family to take up residence in time to host a lavish reception on New Years' Day, 1963. Just as Phyllis prepared to send out invitations, Frank decided the dining room had to be enlarged to accommodate thirty at dinner.

Late in January Vanessa left for a brief trip to Europe. She would buy fabrics, meet up briefly with Robbie in Paris to consider several expensive antiques, and spend two days with Tina in Rome.

Clark's film, on location in Tangier, had wrapped weeks ago. He had returned to Hollywood, while Tina had gone on to Rome, declaring she would remain there indefinitely. She was delighted to be able to lease the same apartment at the top of the Spanish Steps where she had stayed while doing the film for Felix.

Tina explained that whenever Clark could fit it into his schedule, he would sue for divorce. *Darling, I was out of my mind to marry that son-of-a-bitch. He drives me crazy.*

Vanessa enjoyed her search in Ireland and Belgium for rare and exciting fabrics. The forty-eight hours in Paris with Robbie were fast and pleasant, yet even now Paris—like Venice, which she still avoided—was a bittersweet experience. Memories of Eddie haunted her.

In Rome, Tina met her at the airport with the white Rolls-Royce. The years seemed to roll backward as they caught up on news during the drive into town. Tina plied her with questions about Suzy and Wendy, about Pat and CeeCee. She was irritated, as always, by Sal's efforts to keep her away from Adam.

"I phoned him just last week. Sal tells me Adam's at basketball practice," Tina jeered, "when I can hear the Beatles singing away in the background. Now you know Sal and Eva were not listening to the Beatles!"

Over dinner at the Cabala, with its pleated silk ceiling, Tina talked about the breakup with Clark.

"I think I married him because I felt I had to after all the shit from the press about breaking up his marriage. And I wanted another baby. God, I've always felt so cheated because I'm not bringing up Adam myself."

"He's still your son," Vanessa comforted her. "And

to Adam you're his very special aunt."

"Harvey was the only man in my life who meant anything real," Tina said softly. "I'll never marry again. I'll play," she said with candor, "because I'm a woman who needs a man in her bed. But no permanent man in my life — except Adam."

"Do another picture, Tina," Vanessa encouraged. "You're always happiest when you're working."

"It's not that easy." Tina's smile was defiant. "Marty sends me one lousy script after another. I can't afford to make a rotten picture. I need something sensational. I could wait five years for that." Her eyes held Vanessa's. "Tell me the truth, baby. Don't I look rotten?"

"You look as though you've been drinking too much." Vanessa was serious.

"I drink to make myself sleep. It's better than pills. I drink because I'm bored. I've got everything in the world I ever wanted — and it's not enough." Tina shrugged. "Maybe I'll check into one of those fancy spas in Switzerland for a few weeks. Drop a few pounds, stay off the booze. But the day my divorce comes through, I'm drowning in Dom Perignon."

On a blustery Friday evening early in March Vanessa was summoned to the telephone from dinner with Suzy.

"It's Mrs. Roberts in Washington," the maid said. "She says it's urgent."

"Thank you, Dorothy." Vanessa left the table and hurried across the hall to the library of their new town house. She was aware of Suzy's anxiety. Ever since Biff's drowning Suzy had felt a special tenderness towards Pat. "Hello, Pat?" She tried to mask her own

535

concern.

"Vanessa, I'm out of my mind." Pat's voice rose hysterically. "CeeCee's school called about an hour ago. She's run away. Her roommate finally admitted she's gone off to New York."

"Oh, God!" The idea of CeeCee on her own in New York was terrifying.

"She left all her clothes behind except for a few things she stuffed into a knapsack. She's sixteen, Vanessa. I'm scared to death."

"Did you notify the police?"

"Paul didn't want to at first. You know what the tabloids will make of it, and he's already into the Senate race for next year. He was furious with me—I pulled him out of an important House committee meeting. But he did check with the police. They weren't very hopeful. They said hundreds of kids Cee-Cee's age run away every day. All of them heading for New York. They suggested a private investigator."

"Would you like me to hire somebody right away?" Vanessa's mind snapped into action. "Arnie has contacts. I'll ask him to help. I have snapshots of CeeCee we can give to the investigator."

"Please, Vanessa." Relief crept into her voice. "I'm leaving for New York as soon as I get off the phone. I'll have Jackson drive me and then take the car back to Georgetown."

"Have Jackson bring you here," Vanessa ordered. "You'll stay with us." Pat should not be alone.

"Vanessa, I'm so scared." Pat's voice was an exhausted whisper.

"She'll be all right," Vanessa comforted. "And we'll have a private investigator on her trail immediately. Pack a bag and come on up. We'll be waiting for you."

"What's happened to CeeCee?" Suzy asked and

Vanessa swung about to face her worried daughter.

"She's run away from school. Her roommate says she's coming to New York."

"She'll go to the East Village," Suzy said with a matter-of-factness that startled Vanessa. "That's where all the runaways land."

"How do you know that?" Vanessa was astonished.

"On Saturday nights we go down to the coffee-houses," Suzy explained, and Vanessa was suddenly awash with guilt. She had thought Suzy and her friends circulated among one another's houses or apartments, went to the movies or out for dinner. There always seemed to be a birthday party. But Suzy never failed to be home by her established curfew. "Sometimes we go to the East Village to see an off-Broadway play," Suzy continued. "The *school* took us down to a Saturday matinee," Suzy emphasized to stress the East Village's apparent respectability. "We see the kids floating around. Somebody always has space for them to sleep. What they call 'crash pads.' "

"I'm calling Arnie."

Within an hour Arnie and Phyllis were at the house, and Arnie had a call in to a top-notch private investigator. Vanessa brought out a cluster of photographs.

"Maybe you and Phyllis should go over to Penn Station to watch the trains come in," Arnie said. "Suzy can come with me to the bus terminal. She'd recognize CeeCee right off."

"What about the man you called?" Vanessa hesitated.

"Have Maria tell him the situation. We'll watch the trains and the buses till midnight," Arnie stipulated. "A hundred to one she's already here in New York if she cut afternoon classes like you said. But let's give it

537

a try."

With Don—the chauffeur—parked outside Penn Station in the limousine Vanessa and Phyllis hurried inside the cavernous terminal. They met an endless parade of trains, their eyes searching for a small, slender blonde with the face of an angel. But CeeCee was nowhere in sight.

"Poor Pat," Vanessa said, her face lined with anguish, when they at last abandoned the search and headed for the limo. "I could kill CeeCee for doing this to her."

They arrived at the town house minutes before Arnie and Suzy returned. The private investigator was waiting in the library. As they started to explain, Pat arrived.

"I brought along more photographs," Pat said, handing them to the investigator.

"I don't mean to be discouraging," he said sympathetically, "but this won't be fast. These kids have a way of covering for one another. There's a steady stream of them coming in all the time."

"I could go down and look," Suzy said warily, waiting for objections. "I'm one of the kids."

"Suzy, no!" Vanessa said in alarm.

"Mother, it's safe in the East Village," Suzy cajoled. She hesitated. "The kids that come down there, they're just ordinary kids. They're rebelling."

"Against what?" Pat demanded in exasperation. "If they're ordinary kids, they have homes and families. Why are they rebelling?"

"Maybe they think their families don't understand what's happening in the world." Suzy was self-conscious. "I mean, it's awful the way blacks are treated in so many places. And there are so many hungry people. Kids worry about another war."

538

"And for that they have to run away from their comfortable homes?" The investigator shook his head.

"They get together with other kids and pretend there's no greed or bigotry or war. Just love," Suzy said softly.

"She may be right, though," the investigator brought the others up sharply. "She'll probably have a better chance of finding this little girl than I will. I'll be on the case, but let her circulate. Nothing's going to happen to her down there in broad daylight."

Suzy sat at breakfast with her mother and Pat while the sunlight streamed into the breakfast room. She looked out at the garden, which boasted early crocuses and the first daffodil shoots breaking through the winter earth. She was troubled. Suppose she found CeeCee? How would she convince her to come home? She couldn't just phone the private investigator and tell him to drag CeeCee off bodily.

"Suzy, are you sure you want to do this?" her mother asked.

"Oh, yeah," Suzy said with an apologetic smile. Pat looked desperate. "I was trying to figure out what to say to make her come home with me." It was weird to think of CeeCee down in the East Village. CeeCee was such a spoiled little brat. That wasn't her scene at all. "It's not enough just to find her —"

"If we bring her back forcibly," Pat acknowledged, "she'll run away the next chance she gets. We can't keep her under lock and key." She paused in thought. "She's been nursing some idea about becoming a model. Photography, not fashion," she added quickly. CeeCee wasn't tall enough to be a fashion model. "Vanessa, do you suppose she could get work as a model during school vacation? She photographs beautifully—"

"Pat, that's it." Vanessa turned to Suzy. "You tell CeeCee if she goes back to school, she can come stay with us during the summer and I'll help her find modeling jobs. I'm sure I can work out something," she said with a surge of confidence. "Not necessarily the cover of *Vogue*, but assignments that would help her learn the ropes."

"Suzy, find her," Pat pleaded, her face pale and drawn from lack of sleep. "Before something terrible happens to her."

Wearing her beloved blue jeans and sneakers, a bulky gray cashmere sweater under her bright red car coat, Suzy left the house. She had persuaded her mother that it wouldn't be right for her to arrive in the East Village in the family's chauffeur-driven limousine. She walked briskly in the morning cold across to Second Avenue and boarded a south-bound bus.

Suzy didn't actually care if CeeCee stayed forever in the East Village. She didn't even like CeeCee. But Pat was upset, and her mother was upset. It gave her a good feeling to know she might be able to do something to help. Maybe she would find CeeCee. CeeCee would probably jump at Mother's offer to help her become a model.

Suzy left the bus at Tenth Street and headed down to St. Mark's. Her hand closed around the snapshops in her pocket. She ought to top and ask people if they had seen CeeCee.

At St. Mark's Place she forced herself to show the snapshots of CeeCee to the shopkeepers.

"She's a friend of mine from back home," Suzy explained with an ingratiating smile. "I'm trying to find her."

540

After an hour of futile wandering, she walked south on Second Avenue. At a laundromat she saw a trio of teen-age girls throwing clothes into a machine. She went inside, showed them the snapshot, and asked if they had seen CeeCee.

"No," they chorused, and one of the girls inspected Suzy curiously. "You need a place to stay?"

"No, I've got friends near Tompkins Square," Suzy lied. "But thanks."

Suzy walked south to Houston, then began to weave in and out of the side streets above Houston, veering from Avenue D to the Bowery. She asked about CeeCee in all the neighborhood stores. She asked other young people she passed on the street. She wondered how the private investigator was making out. So far their paths had not crossed. At Fourth Street and First Avenue she realized she was tired and hungry. She had been wandering around for almost four hours.

At the corner of Second and Fourth she looked for a place to have a sandwich. She spied a bakery on the west side of the street, and hurried over. Tempting aromas drifted from the door.

Inside she ordered a grilled cheese sandwich and a glass of milk, gazed interestedly at a half dozen young people sitting at the table ahead of her. From their conversation she deduced they were part of a theater company in rehearsal nearby.

A lanky, bearded young man in paint-spattered jeans and an army jacket was buying bagels at the counter. Instinctively she knew he must be one of the "flower children," who walked out on conventional middle-class homes and schools. She felt a little guilty that she had no urge to run away from her own comfortable life. She knew about all the injustice in the

541

world, but she was fifteen years old. Like Mother said, she had to go to school and learn before she could contribute.

All at once her heart was pounding. Was that Cee-Cee coming into the bakery? She squinted nearsightedly at the superthin young blonde in black tights and a black-and-white checked dress that stopped at midthigh. Her army-surplus jacket swung loose, and her hair was cut in a short, blunt style, different from the slightly bouffant look—*à la* Jackie Kennedy—that CeeCee had affected when Suzy had last seen her. Pale pink lipstick, dramatic dark eye makeup.

"CeeCee?" Suzy called out tensely when the blonde paused to inspect the danish on display. She was encouraged by the swift, stiffening reaction. "CeeCee," she said with confidence.

"What are you doing here?" CeeCee hissed in recognition and walked to the table. "Are you going to snitch on me? I'm supposed to be at boarding school."

"Your parents know you ran away," Suzy said calmly. "You didn't think the school wouldn't tell them. Your mother's in New York right now."

"Did she send you down here to look for me?" Cee-Cee sat down across from Suzy, her expression accusing. "Are you going to snitch on me?"

"Your mother hired a detective to look for you," Suzy reported defensively. "CeeCee, she's scared to death something awful will happen to you. You're only sixteen."

"I'm a year older than you," she shot back.

"We're in the same grade," Suzy reminded.

"So you got pushed ahead a year," CeeCee shrugged. "In the real world that doesn't mean anything. Are you going to call Mother and tell her you saw me? I can disappear in five minutes," she said

542

triumphantly. "She'll never find me."

"I came down her to look for you," Suzy admitted, "to make a trade."

"What kind of trade?" CeeCee was skeptical.

"Your mother said you'd like to model," Suzy began.

"Sure." CeeCee smiled with a show of exaggerated bliss. "I'd love to be photographed by Richard Avedon in the nude. Like that girl in the ad in *Harper's Bazaar*. The one that caused all that uproar."

"Your mother talked to my mother. They decided that if you go back to school and finish out the term, you can spend vacation with us at our house here in New York. My mother will help you get some modeling jobs."

CeeCee's mouth dropped wide.

"Can your mother do that?"

"She's a famous designer. Of course she can," Suzy said matter-of-factly.

"How do I know you're not lying?" CeeCee challenged suspiciously.

"Because I don't lie." Suzy's blue-green eyes defied contradiction.

"Okay," CeeCee agreed after a probing assessment of Suzy. "Let's go talk to Mother. But first I want one of those." She pointed to the danish as the waitress hovered at their table. "And black coffee."

"I ought to phone and let them know." Suzy looked about for a phone booth.

"They can wait," CeeCee shrugged. "I'll have my danish and coffee, and then we'll find a cab to take us uptown."

"Where did you stay last night?" Suzy asked curiously.

"I had the key to my roommate's apartment on

543

Fifth and Sixty-fourth. Her parents are down in the Bahamas for six weeks." She giggled. "I had a little trouble getting past the doorman."

"Why did you run away?" CeeCee had not come to the East Village in search of a crash pad and rebellion.

"I couldn't take another minute of that Seminary for Young Virgins," she drawled. "The headmistress is a frustrated old bitch. She's living in the nineteenth century. Last week she expelled a student because the maid found a diaphragm on the floor."

Suzy's eyes widened in shock. Faint color touched her cheeks. Kids at school talked about diaphragms and condoms, but none of them had any real experience, though Caprice bragged about "finger fucking" in the back seat of her boyfriend's car.

Suzy tried to sound sophisticated. "Better than finding a pregnant student."

"Your mother better come across with the modeling jobs." CeeCee was sweetly menacing. "Or you'll both be sorry."

They returned to the house for what was an astonishingly casual reunion. Suzy expected Pat was scared to yell at CeeCee. She was afraid of what CeeCee might pull off next. CeeCee was weird.

Early in May Pat returned from a charity tea to learn that the headmistress of CeeCee's school had called on "a matter of urgency." Cold with alarm, she hurried upstairs to the privacy of her bedroom and returned the call. The head-mistress was grim and reproachful.

"Cecile is being expelled," she reported coldly. "We cannot cope with a student of her inclinations. She'll

544

be put on a train in approximately forty minutes. I suggest you meet the train. It will arrive at Union Station in Washington at 8:14 P.M."

"Why is she being expelled?" Pat forced herself to ask. God, Paul would be outraged.

"One of our instructors went to the stables this morning. She found Cecile and a stable hand in the barn." The headmistress cleared her throat self-consciously. "I don't think I need to say anything more."

"I think you should screen your employees more carefully." Pat's voice was shrill. "CeeCee is an impressionable young girl!"

"She paid him one hundred dollars," the headmistress told her. "Her exact words in my office were: 'It's absurd to be a virgin at sixteen.' That's not the attitude of this school, Mrs. Roberts."

Pat met the train. CeeCee was characteristically taciturn.

"Daddy's going to be terribly upset," Pat warned when they were in the car. She'd take CeeCee to her gynecologist tomorrow. Please, God, don't let her be pregnant.

"So Daddy'll be upset," CeeCee drawled and stared out the window into the night.

When they arrived at the Georgetown house Paul was pacing in the library.

"Hello, Daddy." CeeCee said sweetly.

He swung around to face her. "What the hell's the matter with you, CeeCee?" he yelled.

"Daddy, it's all a lie." Her eyes were wide and reproachful when they met his. "I went to the stable to take out one of the horses. I know I shouldn't cut class, but I hate math and it was such a gorgeous day. I tripped and fell, and then this boy who works in the stable came over to help me — and that awful teacher

walked in. She—she said we were . . ." her voice faltered. "And she told the headmistress I'd given Jeb a
hundred dollars to do it to me. She's sick, Daddy."

"Is that true?" Paul turned to Pat.

"All I know is what the headmistress told me," Pat
said. Of course it was true.

Paul deliberated a moment. He could never stay
angry with CeeCee.

"I ought to go up there and sue that bloody school.
But I can't afford that kind of publicity when I plan to
announce my candidacy for the Senate in another
month. CeeCee, you're going to school in Switzerland," he said in a burst of exuberance. "It'll be a fine
experience for you."

"Daddy, I don't want to go to Switzerland! I went to
camp there—it was awful!"

"You'll go to Switzerland to school; and when you
graduate two years from now I'll buy you your very
own Mercedes," he promised.

CeeCee stopped in mid-tantrum, her eyes glittering
in anticipation.

"A 190-SL?"

"A Mercedes 190-SL," he agreed. "Provided you
stay out of trouble over there."

"Two years in Switzerland." CeeCee vascillated between dubiousness and triumph.

"And on graduation day you'll have your own
Mercedes," he said. "But for God's sake, CeeCee, stay
out of trouble."

Forty

In August Vanessa was ambivalent when Suzy begged to go with Phyllis and Arnie to the civil rights demonstration Dr. Martin Luther King, Jr., was leading in Washington.

"She'll be with us, Vanessa," Phyllis offered. "She'll be fine."

"I'm scared to death it might turn violent," Vanessa confessed. Part of her longed to push aside her work and go with Phyllis and Arnie herself. Her whole life revolved around the business; there wasn't time anymore to be Vanessa. "I believe it's a wonderful thing, of course—" She felt guilty at her own self-involvement when so many Americans were committing themselves to social causes.

"I'll be with Phyllis and Arnie," Suzy said again. "Mother, it's making a statement. It's very important."

"All right, darling," Vanessa capitulated. Suzy's earnest commitment to a better world touched her. Eddie would have been so proud. It was the Montino way of life—and Suzy was a Montino. Suzy knew only that her father was a war hero and had died when she was a very little girl. "But you must do exactly what Phyllis and Arnie tell you."

"Oh, I will!" Suzy flung her arms about her mother happily. "I'll remember this for the rest of my life."

547

Frank was angry when he found out.

"What the hell's the matter with you, Vanessa? Letting her go down to Washington with all that riffraff!"

"Phyllis and Arnie are not riffraff!" she flared. "They're responsible, loving friends."

"I'm not talking about them. I mean the creeps she'll meet down there. But you don't care as long as the kids are out of your hair. All you care about is your designing."

"I care about a lot of things, Frank." She fought to stay calm. "I care about people. Thank God Suzy feels the same way."

Could this be the same man who only eight years ago had spoken with such respect about the bus boycott in Montgomery, Alabama? Now he had only contempt for John Kennedy's "New Frontier," the fight for integration that was spreading with such fervor.

Over the weekend Vanessa stayed glued to the TV set, mesmerized by the events in Washington. Almost 200,000 people marched for civil rights. When they assembled to hear Martin Luther King, Jr., call out "I have a dream that one day this nation will rise up and live out the true meaning of its creed," the crowd stretched from the Lincoln Memorial to the Washington Memorial.

She was glad that Suzy had gone to share in the demonstration. She remembered Eddie's fight—and that of his parents and his brother—against Fascism and Nazism. Suzy was truly Eddie's child.

Though Suzy would not be sixteen until February, Vanessa began to plan an elaborate birthday party for her at the Colony. She knew that Suzy would have adored to have her party at someplace hip like Serendipity, with its espresso machine and cinnamon-stick-stirred cappuccino and miles of beaded curtains, or at one of the new discos like Arthur's or the Scene or

Ondine, but Vanessa didn't think she was quite ready for that yet. At eighteen, Vanessa promised Suzy, she could have her birthday party at a swinging discothèque.

The custom salon was Vanessa's joy, but these days she was always exhausted. She had to keep abreast of the demands of the three labels bearing her name. And the fashion world was in turmoil. Mary Quant and her designs — skirts climbing to, startling heights — were the epitome of "swinging London." In Paris André Courrèges, the first Paris couturier to lift hemlines, was putting wealthy women into equally short geometrical shifts and coats in windowpane checks and broad stripes. Haute couture at last began to take its theme from the streets.

Vanessa was ever conscious of Anatole France's remark that, shown the clothes of a people, he could tell their history. The new clothes were feminist, liberating. They echoed the new mood of women, as given voice in Betty Friedan's blast against women's domestic bondage, *The Feminine Mystique*.

On November 22, 1963, America was shaken by the assassination of President Kennedy. The nation stood at a standstill until the dead president was buried at Arlington National Cemetery on November 25. Vanessa spoke to Pat frequently during those black days. Pat confided that Paul, while professing to grieve, was in high spirits because a Texan would now move into the White House.

Pat was grateful that CeeCee seemed to be doing well at the school in Switzerland. She was planning to visit her briefly in early February, after viewing the spring/summer collection in Paris.

"Vanessa, it's wonderful to receive letters from the headmistress about CeeCee's progress. Everybody seems to adore her. The teachers, the students. And she's earning top grades. Paul was right in insisting we send her to Switzerland."

The final few days before Suzy's sixteenth birthday, Vanessa devoted herself to the last details of the party. Suzy was enthralled by Phyllis and Arnie's early gift of a pair of Pucci slacks. The slacks, along with an exquisitely tailored navy pea jacket from Vanessa's custom salon, were her prize possessions. With her mother's eye for fabric, Suzy had been happy to trade her army-surplus pea jacket for one of soft, elegant wool.

Shortly before eight o'clock on the morning before Suzy's birthday, Vanessa received a phone call from the hospital in Pinewood. Trembling and anxious, Vanessa listened as the hospital administrator explained that Mrs. Conrad's landlady had given Vanessa's name as next of kin. He advised her that her mother had suffered a massive stroke and was in the intensive care unit.

"Mrs. Conrad apparently has no hospitalization insurance," the administrator reported. "Not even Medicare."

"I'll take care of all the bills," Vanessa said. "If private nursing is indicated, please make arrangements. I'll be driving up within a few hours."

She put the phone down and sat at the edge of the bed. She had not seen her mother in almost twenty-two years. Only her mother's signature on the back of the weekly checks, whose amount had increased dramatically over the years, or on delivery receipts that assured her her gifts had been received, told her that her mother was alive.

Her first instinct was to run to Frank. She remembered how he had rallied to her side during that awful period when Suzy had polio. But that Frank was long gone from her life. She reached for the phone to call

Phyllis.

"Have Don drive you up to Pinewood and stay on call," Phyllis advised after a somber exchange. "I'll make arrangements for you." She hesitated. "You may be gone for a few days. Suzy will understand."

"Oh, Phyllis, Suzy's birthday party!" Vanessa gasped.

"Suzy will understand," Phyllis insisted. "Frank will take over. He always enjoys playing the host."

"Suzy doesn't even know she had a living grandmother." Vanessa felt a tightening in her throat. "Under the circumstances it always seemed unnecessary to tell her."

"Tell her now," Phyllis said. "She's old enough to cope with it. She'll have to know why you're missing her birthday party."

Suzy was bewildered at the sudden existence of a grandmother.

"Darling, she has always been a troubled woman," Vanessa said slowly. "In another era, in a family where there was money, she might have benefited from psychiatric help. But by the time I could have offered it, she had banished me from her life. There was nothing I could do."

"Oh, Mother, I love you." Suzy threw her arms around Vanessa. "I wish you could be at my party, but I know you have to go up there."

"Happy sixteenth birthday, my love." She fought against tears. How grown up her daughter seemed suddenly.

One hand resting on the Russian sable that was her winter uniform, Vanessa stared out the window without seeing while she was driven up the thruway, the day grim and forbidding under cloudy skies.

551

Vanessa's nails dug into the soft fur of her coat and her throat constricted. She had left Pinewood a frightened seventeen-year-old. Even her mother must know that she had carved a name for herself in the fashion world. Did her mother know she had two children?

Surely Pinewood knew about Vanessa Conrad. She remembered Tina's father, who had secretly kept a scrapbook full of stories about his daughter. But Vanessa knew her mother would harbor no such sentimentality.

She remembered Tina's homecoming for her father's funeral. Tina had clung to the discovery that her father loved her — was proud of her — even though he had refused to see or talk to her. How did her mother feel? Even after all these years, Vanessa felt a stab of pain, of rejection.

"Let's stop at the motel first," she instructed the chauffeur, all at once terrified at the encounter ahead of her. "We'll check in, and then I can just walk across the road."

She leaned back with her eyes tightly closed, caught in a rush of painful memories. The terrified five-year-old Vanessa, alone in John G. Meyers in Albany. Those numbing days when she and her mother had stood by her father's hospital bed. Her mother's words the night she graduated high school: "Your father never should have saddled me with a child." That final morning in Pinewood, when she had left without a word from her mother.

She waited in the car while the chauffeur went into the motel to confirm their reservations. Her eyes strayed to the hospital that sat across the road. When the chauffeur returned to the limousine with their keys, she had decided that she must see her mother right away. It would be wrong to delay.

In the hospital administrator's office, Vanessa realized that even in Pinewood she was recognized. The administrator called for a nurse right away. She saw the furtive admiration in the eyes of the student nurse who accompanied her to the ICU. She could be the daughter of a classmate at Pinewood High.

"Thank you." Vanessa managed a smile as the pretty young nurse opened the door to the ICU. She geared herself to face her mother. She had been warned that her mother was in a coma, she wouldn't know Vanessa was there.

There were two patients in the ICU. A man of her own age was attached to a variety of machines and at the other side of the room lay her mother. Vanessa walked to her mother's bedside and forced herself to gaze down at her mother. This woman's face was drawn and colorless, heavily wrinkled. The years had not been kind to her. Even in a coma she seemed to wear the perpetual frown that Vanessa remembered.

She stood by the bed, a little girl again, aching for approval and love. Not one word in answer to all the letters she had written in that first year away from Pinewood. No response to the gifts she had sent. But it was her mother who had lost more, Vanessa thought sadly. She had cheated herself of two precious grand-children.

Tears filled Vanessa's eyes when she thought again of her father. He had been such a warm, good human being. How sad that he had not lived to see her success, to see his two granddaughters. Vanessa fumbled in her purse for a tissue. She stayed by the bed, unaware of the passing of time until two doctors arrived and asked her gently to leave the room. She walked out into the hall, not sure whether she should stay at the hospital any longer.

"Vanessa—" She turned with a start to see Phyllis and Arnie hurrying down the hall. "We couldn't let you go through this alone," Phyllis said tenderly.

"Bless you for coming." Vanessa embraced each of them.

"We'll go to the motel coffee shop across the road and have lunch," Arnie said, knowing she would not have stopped to eat. "Send Don back to New York. We'll stay with you."

By nightfall Mrs. Conrad was dead. She had never regained consciousness. Vanessa insisted on remaining beside her mother's body until it was removed from the ICU.

"I'll go to the office and take care of things," Arnie said quietly while Phyllis held her hand in sympathy as they watched Della Conrad's body being taken from the ICU.

"Let me give you a check to take care of the hospital bill." Vanessa emerged from the fog of unreality that had gripped her since the phone call early this morning. She fumbled for her checkbook. "You know, I don't even remember where my father's buried," she said in anguish. "My mother never went to the cemetery after the funeral — she said it would be too painful."

"I'll handle everything, Vanessa," Arnie comforted. "You'll want a Jewish funeral?"

"Please." Her mother might not care, but her father would have.

The next afternoon, flanked by Phyllis and Arnie, Vanessa stood before the hastily purchased gravesite and listened to the brief ceremony. It seemed so cold and false. The rabbi, who had never known her mother, embellished on what little Vanessa had told him. "Della Conrad was a devoted wife to her late husband and a devoted mother to her only daughter . . ."

She and Frank paid only token respect to their

faith, Vanessa thought. He used to say they would have joined a temple if Wendy had been a boy — a son would have to have a bar mitzvah. She owed the children a closer tie to their religious faith. She and Frank would join a temple when she returned to New York.

Last night's snowfall had disappeared and the sky was a clear, cool blue. She remembered the dank drizzle the morning her father was buried. She remembered how her mother had gone to the cemetery devoid of makeup and that the first thing she did when they arrived home was pull out her lipstick. In her own way her mother had been a survivor.

"I'll have to go to the boardinghouse where my mother lived," Vanessa said tensely when they drove away from the cemetery. "I'll go alone. It's all right," she insisted before Phyllis could protest. "I'd like to do this myself."

Arnie parked in front of Mrs. Johnson's boardinghouse. Phyllis and he waited in the car while Vanessa crossed the sidewalk and approached the porch. The house seemed more modest than she remembered. A row of rockers lined the porch as in the past, but in today's cold nobody sat on the porch. She walked to the door and rang the bell. A few moments later an elderly woman wearing a bulky man's cardigan over the austere black dress opened the door. Despite the passage of years Vanessa recognized her.

"Mrs. Johnson?" Vanessa asked, her mouth dry.

"That's right." Mrs. Johnson's eyes swept over Vanessa's sable coat, settled on her face with disconcerting hostility. "You're Mrs. Conrad's daughter."

"Yes. May I come in?"

"She was paid up," Mrs. Johnson said brusquely, pulling the door wide for Vanessa to enter. No small talk about her return to Pinewood after so many years. "I suppose you want to see her room."

"Yes, please."

"I know she never liked it, but I always kept a spare key." Mrs. Johnson fumbled in a drawer of the hall console table. "With elderly boarders I have to do that."

"How did it happen?" Vanessa forced herself to ask.

"Hiram Talbot, one of my boarders, went to call her to lunch." With a start Vanessa remembered Hiram Talbot: he'd been her chemistry teacher in high school. He must have retired not long after she left Pinewood. "She was slumped over in what everybody knew was *her* rocker. No matter what the weather was like, she sat out there every morning. Wrapped up in that mink coat she got several years ago." Mrs. Johnson stared accusingly. "That was all she had of her daughter."

Vanessa was white and trembling, stung into defensive response.

"Mrs. Johnson, my mother rejected me when I was seventeen. She wouldn't answer my letters, she refused to come to the phone." Vanessa's hurt and humiliation rose within her. "I've never stopped supporting her — she lacked for nothing."

"She lacked a daughter's love," Mrs. Johnson lashed back. "You shouldn't have left her alone all these years."

"I'd like to see her room, please." Vanessa said icily, conscious of the stares of the other boarders.

"Fine," Mrs. Johnson snapped. "She moved into my best room some years back, but she never invited any of the other boarders to come inside. She always kept to herself."

"Thank you, Mrs. Johnson." Vanessa extended one gloved hand for the key. The dismissal was obvious.

At first glance Della Conrad's large corner room

556

resembled a crowded gift shop. The mantel over the old-fashioned fireplace, the myriad small tables about the room were covered with knickknacks. Vanessa's mother, who had kept her house empty of anything that required dusting, owned a vast collection of crystal, silverware, fine china tea sets. The English gilt-bronze musical clock Vanessa had sent from London several years ago held a place of honor above the fireplace.

Staring around her, Vanessa thought of the ugly oilcloth that had covered their kitchen table, the motley supply of dishes and flatware that graced their table, the drab furniture.

Her mother had harbored dreams and watched them die. The pretty young girl from the Bronx stopped being content to sing to her husband in a swing on their front porch. The young wife who had tied ribbons about a puppy had retreated into a world that held no place for people.

Vanessa crossed the lushly thick Oriental rug to pick up an exquisite porcelain cup. Lenox china. The crystal was Baccarat. A box from Tiffany housed a sterling place setting for one.

As she had suspected, her mother was a survivor. She had surrounded herself with all that had been denied her in the past. Vanessa picked up a catalogue from a neat pile that sat at one edge of the mantel. From Neiman-Marcus. She opened it. Her mother had made penciled notations beside the offerings that had pleased her.

Vanessa saw her mother spending hours poring over the mail-order catalogues. She had had the choice shops of the world at her command.

The guilt that Mrs. Johnson had instilled in her evaporated. She had supplied her mother with exactly what she wanted—a world where she could enjoy beautiful objects apart from the demands of others.

It gave Vanessa a deep satisfaction to know she had made it possible for her mother to find pleasure in her last years. The realization freed her of the hurt that had dogged her most of her life. She wasn't responsible for her mother's rejection. Her mother had been marred by life.

Taking nothing from her mother's room, Vanessa went out into the hall. Mrs. Johnson — like how many others in this town? — considered her a bad daughter. Let them think what they liked; she knew the truth. Her father would have been pleased.

"Mrs. Johnson, I understand there's a charity home for the elderly here in Pinewood. Would you please tell the director that everything in my mother's room is to go there?"

Vanessa walked out of the boardinghouse into the early dusk. A part of her life had been put to rest.

Forty-one

The brilliant blue of the early September sky was mirrored in the ocean below. The sun lent summer warmth to the morning. Tina and Vanessa lingered over breakfast on the ocean-front deck of the Southampton house, enjoying their time together.

Tina had arrived from Hollywood early yesterday evening at the recently renamed John F. Kennedy International Airport; and shortly after the limousine brought her to the house, Maria and the girls had left for New York.

The kids had been so sweet, Tina thought with a rush of affection. Suzy was all excited about starting her senior year at high school. Already she was full of plans for college. Adam would go to college, Tina promised herself. His father had taught in a Vienna university before World War II, she recalled with satisfaction. Just let the war be over before Adam was old enough for the draft. Felix had proclaimed at a dinner party weeks ago—never suspecting he had a son who might be involved—that nobody would win in the Vietnam War. That if President Johnson persisted in sending over American troops and planes, there'd be a lot of American lives lost.

"I wish we could stay here the rest of the week," Vanessa said impulsively, drawing Tina back to the present.

"That would be great," Tina agreed. But Vanessa had to rush back to business, and she was heading upstate in an hour. "I can't believe tomorrow is Adam's sixteenth birthday." Tina shook her head, bemused. "Sixteen years ago tomorrow morning I was cursing every man alive for putting women through labor."

"Adam doesn't know you're driving up?" Vanessa asked.

"No, it'll be a surprise. That way," Tina smiled sardonically, "Sal and Eva can't pull anything funny. Sal pisses me off with that bit about how it's not good for Adam to get too close to me because of 'the way I conduct my life.' But Adam is my kid, and I mean to be there on his sixteenth birthday." Her smile lost some of its brightness. "I don't know when I'll see him again."

"Are you sure you want to settle in Rome?" Vanessa asked, suddenly somber.

"Darling, I can hop a jet and be here in no time. I don't like the Hollywood scene anymore. There's nothing for me in New York. In Rome I feel alive."

"You'll be rushing back to do another film soon," Vanessa predicted.

"I'm getting too old to be a sex symbol." Tina was candid. "And I'm too young for character parts. Besides, I've never pretended to be an actress."

"You've learned a lot," Vanessa said vigorously. "It's time Hollywood realized that. Even the critics said as much."

"When I do work, the money's sensational." Tina smiled. "I'm guaranteed a piece of the profits now.

560

The salaries have never been higher. But it's getting harder by the minute to find a really good role. I warned Marty not to send me shitty scripts—I'd rather not work."

"Bring me more snapshots of Adam when you return to the city," Vanessa ordered. "My adopted nephew."

"I promise." Tina smiled. "I can't get over the way Adam and Suzy have grown up. And Wendy is a precious little doll." Her eyes grew serious. "What's with Frank and you?"

Vanessa sighed. "Frank is in love with his business image and his race horses. I don't know him anymore. His older sister died in May, and he phoned Pittsburgh to talk to his family—but he didn't even go out for the funeral."

"Did you ever meet Frank's family?"

"A couple of times for dinner in New York. Once when his sisters were going down to Florida for two weeks, and once when the oldest one and her husband were going to London for a week to celebrate their thirtieth wedding anniversary. Every now and then he talks about having them at the Croton house or at Southampton for a weekend, but he's never followed through. It would have been nice for the kids to know Frank's family," Vanessa added wistfully.

"Did he ever change his mind about joining a temple?" Vanessa had returned from her mother's funeral determined to bring the children closer to their faith.

"He couldn't be bothered. I joined for all of us. Wendy will start Sunday school when she's six, but I haven't been able to involve Suzy. I should have started when she was Wendy's age. I didn't have time then. And I have no time now," she confessed. "I salve my guilt with contributions."

561

"But Frank loves the kids," Tina said with conviction.

"Oh, sure, he loves Suzy and Wendy. But he doesn't know how to handle them. Now and then he makes a sentimental fuss over them. Most of the time he antagonizes both of them. He thinks I'm far too liberal a mother; but when he tries the heavy father routine with Suzy, she fights like mad."

"He got what he wanted, and it isn't enough," Tina surmised.

"I'm not sure Frank got what he wanted. I think he'd be happier if I were a quiet little housewife without a career. But he loves the rich life, and he knows he needs me for that. And he resents it," she summed up.

They sat in silence for a moment, staring out at the ocean. Then Tina roused herself. "I suppose I ought to pack up and be ready when the limo gets here. Remember when I could never be on time for an appointment?" Tina chuckled. "I learned better in Hollywood."

"Are you going to change before we leave?" Vanessa asked, her smile tentative.

"Darling, don't bother being diplomatic with me," Tina teased. Under Vanessa's tutelage she had gradually changed her approach to clothes from the flamboyant to a quiet elegance that dramatized her lush beauty. Though she dismissed such rankings, the press frequently referred to her — along with Liz Taylor and Ava Gardner — as "the most beautiful woman in the world." "You're afraid this number will shock the shit out of my brothers and their little wives."

The dress she wore was from Courrèges's revolutionary spring collection, which had won him worldwide fame overnight. It was of white gaberdine trimmed in caramel with a startling cutaway area at the midriff. The lines were very structured, the skirt length the shortest shown in Paris. With it she wore the low white kid boots Courrèges had decreed should accompany the dress.

"That outfit is . . . strong for a small upstate New York town," Vanessa said laughingly.

"Maybe I like shocking them," Tina said with relish. "If the weather wasn't so hot, I'd wear that luscious trouser suit I bought from his collection. The one I wore on the plane," she reminded Vanessa.

"It's sensational," Vanessa agreed. "Clever the way he cut the legs so the line falls over the back of the heel and curves up over the instep. And I love the wide-set collar that's cut like something from Balenciaga. I'm sure trouser suits have a big future. I'm putting two in my next salon collection."

Tina rose to her feet. "Come inside and talk to me while I pack."

"Did I tell you I ran into Tracy in Rome and then again on the Riviera?" Tina asked Vanessa on the drive into New York. "I hardly recognized her. She works like mad to stay as thin as Twiggy. I didn't dare ask about her husband. Pat told me she's been through four divorces." She paused. "Well, look who's talking. My divorce from Clark was number three."

"Once in a while I run into Tracy at something in New York." Vanessa frowned. "Once at a charity ball at Southampton. I always feel eerie when I see her. We shared such a crucial time in our lives, and now it's as though we're strangers."

The chauffeur dropped Vanessa off at the salon and then cut across town to head north. Tina flipped through the current issues of *Vogue* and *Town & Country*. When she returned to New York, she'd stay a few days to choose a wardrobe from Vanessa's custom salon.

Halfway to the first Saratoga exit on the thruway, she instructed the chauffeur to watch for a restaurant. From what Nick told her, Eva served the kind of fattening meal she had to avoid. At forty it was time to watch her weight. She'd have lunch on the road, with one less heavy Italian meal to work off at the gym.

"You know, you look just like Tina Gregory," the waitress said as she handed over a menu.

"A lot of people tell me that," Tina smiled. "I wish I had her money."

In the car again Tina listened to the radio and thought about her son. In her luggage was the new Beatles album she'd picked up for him. He'd been absolutely awed when she'd told him she'd met the Beatles and the Rolling Stones in London.

She never should have given Adam to Sal and Eva. But what other choice did she have? She would have been dead in Hollywood on two counts — the scandal of having a kid out of wedlock, and the loss of her image as a young sex symbol.

She assumed Sal and Eva would insist she stay with them for the two days she planned on being in town. Despite their distaste for what they liked to call her "immoral life-style," they were proud of their relation to a movie star. There would probably be a rush reunion dinner with Vinnie and Gus and their wives, and Nick. They all lived within fifty miles of one another, though she knew that Nick didn't see much of the others these days. He had never forgiven them for fighting over Pop's will.

Shortly after noon the chauffeur deposited her before the white, two-story frame house that had been home to Sal and Eva since right after the war. He brought out the oversize Vuitton valise she had brought up from New York.

"Pick me up here on Wednesday morning around ten," Tina reminded. "If there's any change, I'll call."

She stood for a few moments inspecting the neat square of well-tended lawn, dissected by a dahlia-lined walk. Not very different from the other houses along the street. A vintage Ford sat in the driveway. Sal would nurse that car until it fell apart. They'd never forgiven her for giving Nick that red Ferrari.

Tina glanced at her watch. Adam ought to be home from school soon. God, she couldn't wait to see him! She moved to the steps, heard the sound of a vacuum cleaner from somewhere inside the house. Sal always bragged about what a wonderful housekeeper Eva was. She knew Eva and he were good parents, though she thought they were both on the strict side.

She walked up the steps, crossed the porch to the door, and rang the bell. She could just see Eva's face when she opened the door and found her here. Did Eva expect her to miss Adam's sixteenth birthday? In her family the sixteenth had always been special. It meant that, from that day on, Pop expected the boys to work in the butcher shop every Saturday and on school holidays. Would Sal have Adam working in his automobile repair shop on Saturdays and holidays once he was sixteen?

The vacuum cleaner switched off. She heard footsteps in the hallway. The door opened. Eva, grown heavier with the passing years, graying, stared at her in shock. Her eyes skimmed the ultra-short Courrèges shift, and she frowned in distaste.

"Hi, Eva," Tina said, her voice dripping sweetness. "I know I shouldn't barge in without notice. If you can't put me up, I can stay with Nick."

"Of course we can put you up," Eva protested and pecked her on one cheek. "Why didn't you write and tell us you were coming?" Eva was trying to hide her irritation.

"I wasn't sure I could come until the last minute, but I couldn't bear to miss Adam's sixteenth birthday." Tina walked inside the dark hallway.

"We're not having a party," Eva said quickly. "People only do that for girls." A faint note of superiority in her tone implied that Tina was not *au courant* about motherhood.

"Adam still at school?" Tina put down her valise.

"He ought to be home in about twenty minutes. Come out into the kitchen and have some coffee. The house is a mess," she apologized, her voice strident despite her efforts to appear poised. "I'll settle you in the guest room later. We have four bedrooms," she added with a touch of pride. "Sal uses one of them for his home office. He works hard all day at the shop; he don't have time for paperwork there."

"How's Adam doing in school?" Tina asked, settling herself at the comfortable colonial maple table while Eva brought out cups and saucers.

"He's smart," Eva said proudly. "All A's, and he goes out for sports too. Sal and I told him right off, mess up on the schoolwork and there'll be no sports." She put up coffee, went to the refrigerator to bring out an apple pie. "I baked this this morning. Sal won't mind if we dig into it without waiting for him."

In the midst of Eva's long report on how well Sal was doing with the shop, Tina heard the front door slam.

"That's Adam!" She rose to her feet in anticipation. *Her baby.*

566

"Adam, we got company," Eva called out, her voice a high falsetto. "You'll never guess who's here!"

"Adam!" Tina rushed forward to embrace her son. God, he was a good-looking boy Felix must have looked a lot like Adam at this age. Even now Felix had that same mop of dark, curly hair, the same quizzical eyes. "You look marvelous," she exclaimed. "Every time I visit you've grown some more."

"You've grown, too," Adam laughed, kissing her warmly. "You've grown more beautiful."

Tina and Adam sat together at the table and chattered in the teasing vein that always seemed to baffle Eva. When Eva excused herself to make a phone call, Tina guessed she was calling Sal. To warn him that she was here. When Eva finally returned to the kitchen, she announced that she had called the brothers to tell them Tina was here.

"They'll all be over for dinner tomorrow night," Eva added. "They were coming anyway, for Adam's birthday."

"Tonight I'm taking the four of us out to dinner," Tina said. "What's the greatest place around here?"

"Dino's," Eva said. "But I don't know if Sal will want to go out. Unless we eat early. On Monday night he bowls."

"We'll eat early," Tina agreed. "Of course Sal shouldn't miss his bowling night," she said with exaggerated politeness. "And Adam, I brought something for you I think you'll like. The new Beatle album. Bring in my valise from the hall." Tomorrow, his birthday, she would give him the marvelous watch she had found at Van Cleef and Arpels in Paris.

"Oh, wow!" Adam's face radiated pleasure. "Mom, can I play it down here?" He was already striding into the hall. "The living room record player is much better than mine." Tina made a mental note to drop by Liberty Music when she was in New York and order the best record player available shipped up to Adam. An indulgent "aunt" could do that, she told herself defensively.

"All right, play that stupid Beatle music down here." Eva sighed. "I hate the crazy music the kids play. The Beatles are worse than that Elvis Presley."

Eva led Tina down the hall to the living room, which, like the kitchen, was furnished in Sears-Roebuck's colonial maple. Adam brought Tina's valise and rested it across the coffee table. Tina snapped the locks open, fished out the Beatles LP, and handed it to him. He inspected the jacket closely, a wide grin on his face.

"Why don't they cut their hair and dress like human beings?" Eva grumbled.

Adam was busy at the record player. When the sound of the Beatles leapt into the room, Tina pulled off her low white boots and jumped to her feet.

"Come on, Adam, let's dance!"

Caught up in the music and the joy of being with her son, Tina moved with playful abandon, gesturing to Adam to follow suit. She felt as though she were eighteen again and a whole wonderful world lay ahead of her.

"Hey, you're cool," Adam said breathlessly when they finally collapsed, exhausted, on the sofa.

"You're pretty good yourself," Tina laughed. She turned to her cold and disapproving sister-in-law. "How about another chunk of that apple pie and some more coffee?"

Sal arrived home and agreed to go to Dino's as long as he could leave by 7:30. He did look smug, after some initial reluctance, about having dinner in the most expensive restaurant in the country with his movie star sister. As long as he didn't have to miss his bowling. Or pick up the check.

"Adam, you go upstairs and wash up and change," Eva ordered. "Put on your suit." She ignored his grimace. "And get out of those sneakers."

"I'll change, too," Tina said demurely and reached for her valise. Adam grabbed it and with a courtly gesture accompanied her to the stairs.

In the tiny guest bedroom Tina discarded the Courrèges shift and replaced it with Vanessa's exquisitely simple long-sleeved emerald satin tunic over a matching short, narrow skirt. She hesitated for a moment, then added the emerald-and-diamond necklace that had been Harvey's second anniversary gift. Her sisters-in-law would probably think it was costume-jewelry, she thought wryly.

At Dino's, Tina's entrance created a stir, and Adam glowed with pride. He looked handsome but uncomfortable in his suit, the jacket sleeves already slightly too short. Sal wore a brown plaid seersucker jacket with beige slacks; Eva wore a semifitted beige cotton suit, the skirt ending decorously at the knee, and a tiny beige straw pillbox, the look Jackie Kennedy had popularized years ago—and that had long since been discarded by the fashionable set.

Tina ordered a bottle of the restaurant's best wine to accompany their dinner. Sal preened when the waiter asked if Tina would autograph a menu for his teen-age daughters.

Over antipasto, delicious frutti di mare, and a green salad, Sal complained about the activities of the young in the sixties. He had nothing but scathing contempt for integration, "flower children," and the surging drug culture.

"I ever catch Adam messin' around with marijuana or LSD or any of that junk, I'll beat the hell out of him," Sal proclaimed grimly.

"Sal, you *know* kids around here don't bother with drugs," Eva said virtuously.

Maybe they didn't, Tina considered, or maybe they just managed to hide it. Pinewood was a quiet town, far removed from civil rights demonstrations and women's lib and the youth rebellion. Yet there was a quiet rebellion in Adam's eyes, a rebellion he didn't dare voice, that hinted at restlessness, dissatisfaction.

While they debated about dessert, Tina asked Adam if he had given any thought to college.

"You're a junior, aren't you?"

"Yeah." He was oddly guarded. "The principal at school said I ought to apply next year for a scholarship at some really jazzy school. He says my grades are high enough—" He sent a defensive glance in Sal's direction.

"Adam, you're my favorite nephew," Tina said flippantly. "I'm ready to pay all your costs to any college you choose to attend. Anywhere in the country."

"Aunt Tina!" Adam's face was incandescent.

"When Adam graduates from high school, he's coming into the shop with me," Sal said flatly. "It's a good business. One day, when I retire, it'll be his."

"But Sal, if Adam goes to college—" Eva was awed by the thought of her son away at a prestigious school.

"He don't need college." Sal gestured in dismissal. "He'll make a good living in the shop. He'll have a trade."

Adam stared down at his plate, but not before Tina saw the mutinous look that crossed his face. He meant to go to college. And she meant to see that he did. Adam would have the best of everything. She would

570

not let him be stuck in this one-horse town in some dead-end occupation.

Early in the school year, Suzy confided that she would rather attend Barnard than any other college. "If I'm accepted," she said conscientiously. "And I'll want to live on campus." She waited for her mother's reaction.

"Of course, darling," Vanessa agreed. She had expected this. Suzy was so young to be leaving home, but at least she would be here in New York. "And I'm sure you'll be accepted."

In November, Lyndon Johnson and Hubert Humphrey were elected president and vice-president in a resounding victory. Paul won a seat in the Senate, and Pat insisted that Vanessa and Frank come to Washington in January to attend the Inaugural Ball with them. Frank was pleased.

Suzy was caught up in agonizing over senior anxieties. SAT's, college applications, last-minute debates over the advantages of one school or another. Vanessa was glad she didn't waver from her first choice. Barnard was the sister college to Columbia, where Eddie had earned his degree in engineering. It gave Vanessa a warm feeling to know that, provided she was accepted at Barnard, Suzy would be following in her father's footsteps.

When replies from college boards arrived and Suzy was accepted at Barnard, Vanessa agreed that she could spend six weeks in Europe with three other friends as a pre-college holiday. Frank was indignant that the decision was made without consulting him.

"Four kids floating around Europe alone for six weeks is asking for trouble. This generation is going berserk!"

"It's her high school graduation present." Vanessa hated these squabbles with Frank. Perhaps she should have discussed it first with him, but she saw so little of him these days. He sat down to dinner with them once or twice a week. On Sundays, if the weather was good, he's take Wendy off to the park for an hour or two. "Suzy's a very responsible teen-ager," she said firmly. But deep down she, too, was a little uneasy about the trip.

Shortly before Suzy's graduation, Pat arrived in New York, en route to Switzerland for CeeCee's graduation. CeeCee had refused to consider college, and Pat was concerned.

"She's back on the modeling kick," Pat explained over lunch at the Colony. She picked nervously at the cast on her wrist, the result of another fall. "I can't bear the thought of her living alone in New York and chasing around in that Mercedes Paul has promised her."

"I don't suppose she'd consider staying with us?" Vanessa smiled doubtfully, knowing CeeCee would want to be independent.

"I'd hoped she'd settle for a girls' residence club," Pat said. "But once they're out of high school, they're all grown up. They've got to get out there and taste the world," Pat sighed.

"What about a modeling school?"

"Not CeeCee. She's going straight out to make modeling rounds. She's dying to see her face in all the top magazines."

"Paul goes along with this?" Vanessa asked.

"Oh, Paul can be absolutely blind where CeeCee is concerned. Of course, she drives him crazy on occasion," Pat admitted. "He's always so terrified of bad publicity. Especially right now. He's a nervous wreck under that self-assured exterior. He knows how much his future depends on how he handles himself in the Senate." A future that included the presidency of the United States, Vanessa recalled. "And Daddy drives him so hard all the time. Mother and I keep trying to slow Daddy down, but he misses being in the House. He's living vicariously through Paul now." Pat glanced at her watch. "I wish we could dawdle all afternoon, but I have to meet Mother at three at the apartment. She wants me to help her shop for a graduation gift for CeeCee at Cartier's."

Vanessa and Pat lingered briefly over raspberry soufflés and coffee. Vanessa dropped Pat off at her parents' *pied-à-terre* and asked Don to drive back down to Seventh Avenue.

On impulse Vanessa left the elevator at the office floor rather than going directly up to the design studio. She'd stop off to talk with Phyllis about possible modeling contacts for CeeCee. She could at least help CeeCee get started.

On the way to Phyllis's office Vanessa stopped at the women's washroom to freshen up. While she powdered her nose, she overheard two women talking animatedly in the next room.

"Did I tell you Irma saw El Stinko with Edie again last Friday night?" one asked. "At some ginmill out on Long Island. That must still be on."

"Somebody told me she's living on Sutton Place in some jazzy apartment." Envy tinged the woman's voice. "She met Ginny for lunch one day at Dubrow's and showed up wearing an autumn haze mink coat. It's not that she's so crazy about Ginny, but she just had to show off that mink coat."

"Bernstein can afford to keep her in style. Why

should she work in his showroom when she can sleep till noon and wear mink?"

Vanessa froze in disbelief.

"It took her long enough to get him into her bed, but she's got what it takes to keep him there."

Vanessa stumbled out into the hall, not wanting to hear any more. "Edie" must be Edie Russell, the model who used to work in the showroom. She had been gone almost three years, Vanessa thought. Frank was keeping Edie Russell. He had been keeping her for almost three years.

Forty-two

"Why didn't you tell me Frank was having an affair with Edie Russell?" Vanessa stared accusingly at Phyllis.

"Vanessa, we didn't know for sure. I don't have to tell you how people gossip around Seventh Avenue." She hesitated. "And Frank's made a lot of enemies."

"He's keeping Edie Russell in an apartment on Sutton Place. They've been seen together in bars. Frank's always off somewhere. I thought it was business or those damned race horses."

"What are you going to do about it?" Phyllis asked, her face lined with concern.

"I'm outraged—and I'm hurt—and I'm not sure what to do." Vanessa managed a rueful smile. "You and Arnie are among the very few who know our marriage has been dead for years. I just never allowed myself to face that. Now even the sewing machine operators know Frank's been cheating on me. I suppose that if he wasn't finding what he wanted at home with me, then I should have suspected he was looking somewhere else."

"With you at home, Arnie said, why should Frank go looking anywhere else?" Phyllis smiled wryly in sympathy. "I don't think Arnie wanted to believe it."

"I'm a threat to Frank," Vanessa said slowly. "He resents my success. I've known that a long time. We need each other in the business, Phyl. I guess that's what it comes down to. And if Frank is happy running off to Edie Russell, then perhaps I can close my eyes to it." She couldn't face a confrontation, a total upheaval in her life. "And the children need a father. So many of Suzy's friends—even Wendy's—live with a divorced parent. I'd like my girls to know they have a live-in father. Even if he isn't living with their mother."

"Vanessa, you're still a young woman," Phyllis protested.

"My life revolves around my daughters and my business. That's all I want," Vanessa said, painful memories of Eddie rising to haunt her. Their marriage would never have come to this. "You and Arnie have something special. Something precious. I love watching the two of you together. Most marriages are not like yours." Her eyes were tender.

"Frank's a bastard," Phyllis said in a burst of frustration. "He doesn't deserve you."

"Frank is a very essential part of my life," Vanessa pointed out. "Together we're Creations by Vanessa Conrad. That'll have to be enough."

But she was shattered to realize that other people gossiped about Frank's infidelity. Not uncommon, she admitted. And the higher the financial status of the man, the more frequently it occurred. She had to hold her head high, work hard to make sure the children never found out.

Suzy's graduation—the exercises at the Waldorf and the series of private parties—brought back bitter memories for Vanessa of her own graduation. She wished again that her father had lived long enough to see her success, to see Suzy and Wendy.

Hiding her anxiety, Vanessa saw Suzy and her friends off for their tour of Europe. They looked so young and sweet and vulnerable as they boarded their plane at JFK. She prayed that they would be all right. On the drive back to the city she fought back tears.

At Suzy's age she had been living alone in New York. And she hadn't been much older when she met Eddie. But that had been during the war — when nobody knew what lay ahead.

Was it that much different for today's kids, growing up in the midst of the cold war? They had lived through the horror of John Kennedy's assassination. They lived with the threat of a nuclear holocaust. In an era when the United States was putting men into space, they weren't sure they'd live to be old.

This generation grew up with a financial security that many of her own generation never knew. They took for granted things that the last generation considered luxuries. Frank called them the spoiled-brat generation. But they were compassionate, Vanessa reminded herself. They flocked to the Peace Corps, to the fight for integration, the fight against poverty.

The familiar night skyline of the city — a myriad of vertical diamond bracelets against dark velvet — came into view. All at once Vanessa recoiled from going directly home. Wendy, and even Maria, would be asleep. Frank would be off somewhere or closeted in his private apartment. Tonight, with Suzy over the Atlantic, the house seemed an intolerably lonely place.

"Take me to the Hirsches' apartment, please," Vanessa told Don. Sweet, understanding Phyllis had suggested she drop by their place on her way home. Phyl knew she would feel a sense of loss with Suzy on her way to Europe. Six weeks in London, Paris, Rome, and Venice.

Suzy had been born in Venice, but she didn't remember anything about it. Suzy might walk right

577

past Eddie's sisters in Venice, never knowing they were her aunts. Suzy knew that her father had died in a car crash in Venice. She thought her grandparents had died before she was born.

When she arrived at the Hirsch apartment, Phyllis and Arnie were watching a TV documentary about the fighting in Vietnam. Vanessa sat down to watch with them.

In Rome, Tina wrote about her concern over the escalation of American participation in the Vietnam War. Adam would be seventeen in September. He was talking about joining the navy when he graduated next June.

In a rumpled pantsuit and no makeup, the one valise she had brought with her from Rome at her feet, Tina waited impatiently for her airport car rental to be processed. On impulse, she had flown to New York for a private talk with Adam.

She had flown to Lausanne for CeeCee's graduation, and Pat had told her that Paul predicted the draft would be escalated soon. As a college student Adam could get a deferral. Tina wanted Adam safe from the draft. She drove away from JFK—no limo his time. This wasn't Tina Gregory, movie star, driving upstate. It was Tina Gregory, mother. After forty minutes on the road she found a motel. Back in Rome it was only early afternoon; in New York it was late evening. At a motel she'd watch TV for a while, then try to fall asleep despite the time difference.

By five o'clock the next morning she was behind the wheel of the car again. With her hair pulled back, wearing no makeup and in sunglasses, nobody would recognize her. Adam's school was finishing up the term. She wanted to talk to him alone, without Sal and Eva around.

Ten minutes before students would begin to arrive for classes, Tina parked before the modern red-brick school. Adam didn't know he was adopted; and she wasn't about to tell him now. But she couldn't stand by and do nothing. She had to make sure he wouldn't do something crazy like enlist. It wasn't just that college would provide him with draft deferment. His whole future depended on his education.

The day was early-June hot. She rolled down the car window and peered at the school entrance, searching for Adam among the crowd of students. Her face lighted. There he was.

She leaned out the window.

"Adam!"

He looked up, startled. He frowned, trying to see who was calling him, then broke into a wide grin of recognition. He trotted to the car.

"Aunt Tina, when did you arrive in town?" He leaned forward to kiss her before she could reply.

"Get in the car, Adam. I drove up from New York to talk to you this morning." Her seriousness sobered him. He circled around the front of the car and opened the door.

"Aren't you staying for a couple of days?"

"I flew in from Rome yesterday expressly to come up here and talk to you," she emphasized. "I'm flying back tomorrow. Now what's this nonsense Sal writes about you wanting to join the navy?"

"We've been having a lot of awful fights lately." Adam was somber. "Dad keeps telling me I *have* to come into the shop when I graduate next June. He doesn't want me to go to college. I figure if I join the navy, at least I'll get away from home."

"You finish high school, and go to college," Tina said grimly. "That's your high school graduation present from me. Nobody knows how long this war is going to last. I don't want you in it."

"I think this whole business of us in Vietnam is crazy." Adam's face tightened. "That's another reason Dad and I fight so much. He says it's our country; and if the president decides we have to fight, then we do."

"Sal spent five months in an army camp in North Carolina. What the hell does he know about war?" Tina scoffed. "I'm writing Eva"—she couldn't bring herself to say "your mother"—"to tell her I'm picking up the tab for all your expenses at college. It's the three of us against your father. He has to agree."

"Aunt Tina, you're the greatest!"

"You promise me you'll forget about the navy?"

"You bet."

"Okay." She leaned forward to kiss him. "Now get your butt into class. And don't tell anybody about our talk."

"I want to go to college," he said with disarming intensity. "I want it more than anything I've ever wanted in the world."

While dusk settled over Manhattan, Vanessa and Tina lounged on floral cushioned chaises on Vanessa's screened-in terrace. The first heat wave of the summer had receded, leaving behind it a burst of fragrant roses, lilies, beds of bright petunias. Vanessa enjoyed this quiet time alone with Tina. Wendy was out at Southampton with Maria, Frank was out of town on business, and Suzy was still in Europe.

"You must be bushed," Vanessa said sympathetically. "The flight from Rome and then the dash upstate and back. I'd be exhausted."

"No, not you," Tina contradicted. "You're a dynamo. How you manage to keep the collections coming the way you do is amazing."

"We're both driven women," Vanessa acknowledged. "I think it's the work that holds me together."

"Vanessa, do you think it's wrong for me to meddle in Adam's life this way?" Tina's eyes pleaded for approval.

"No." Vanessa replied emphatically. "You're doing what's right for him."

"Sal could afford to send Adam to college. Eva told me as much," Tina said defensively. "Maybe not an Ivy League school, but a state college. He's just so damn narrow-minded. The butcher shop was good enough for Pop. The repair shop is good enough for him. 'Why isn't it good enough for Adam?'" she mimicked Sal.

"Tina, you're doing the best thing. Pat's very unhappy that CeeCee won't go to college." Maybe college wasn't right for every teen-ager, but both Adam and CeeCee were bright.

"Pat and I spent an evening together after CeeCee's graduation. CeeCee was off with friends from school. She looks gorgeous and awfully sexy. She has that special something that draws people to her. I thought she might want some introductions to movie people. But she thanked me politely and said, no, she just wanted to model."

"I'm seeing Pat and CeeCee next week. Pat's coming to New York with her to help her find an apartment."

"It won't be like our old studio in the West Seventies," Tina said nostalgically. "That one has expensive tastes—and she has Daddy Darling and Grandpa wrapped around her little pinkie." Tina's eyes grew quizzical. "Doesn't Pat know how Paul chases after other women?"

"Maybe she doesn't want to know." Vanessa's face was taut. "I would rather not know about Frank."

"Vanessa, why don't you dump him? Divorce is not a disgrace."

"I don't want to rock the boat." She had spent endless sleepless nights—furious, humiliated, philosophical—analyzing the situation. "Frank and I are a business team. We've been extremely successful. If I divorce him . . ."

"You know you could run the business without Frank."

"I don't know that." Though she disagreed with his brusque handling of the employees and the stores, everybody on Seventh Avenue considered him a miracle man. "I'd be afraid to try it, even with Arnie. It's Frank who's handled the business details all these years." Vanessa paused while the maid came out onto the terrace with espresso. She changed the subject deliberately. "Tina, I wish you could stay until Pat arrives in town. We'd have a real reunion."

"I have to talk to a man in Rome about a possible film. I don't know if I'll do it, but he's one of these intense young Italians that make me feel young—and passionate. Thank God for all the nearsighted men who think I'm still young and gorgeous."

"Tina, you are young and gorgeous," Vanessa insisted. "Forty isn't the end of the road. It's kind of a midway point," she said whimsically, trying to hide her own anxiety.

"Don't worry, darling," Tina chuckled. "I'm not getting married again. I'm just looking for amusement and a terrific film." Her eyes were restless. Tina had run away to Rome, Vanessa thought, but she still hadn't found peace.

* * *

Vanessa sat at her favorite table at the Colony with Pat and CeeCee and pretended to be interested in her chicken Marengo. Without understanding why, she felt uneasy around CeeCee.

CeeCee's face was Pat's except for the heavily made up dark eyes that were angelically wistful one moment and sultry the next. She had lightened her blond hair until it was a pale silver, and had it styled in London by Vidal Sassoon in his geometric cut. She wore a mid-thigh-length Rudi Gernreich jersey dress that lent a little-girl look to her adolescent figure.

"As soon as I have an apartment," CeeCee was saying, "I'll start making the modeling rounds. I know I'll never be a fashion model." She laughed disarmingly. "Not even with my highest heels would I be tall enough. But I'd adore doing magazine modeling and maybe TV commercials. That would be exciting."

"Come up to the office and talk to Phyllis when you're ready," Vanessa invited. "She's a great publicist. She knows everybody."

While Vanessa and Pat debated about dessert, Cee-Cee excused herself.

"I have to go over to see about picking up my car," she said offhandedly. "I'm driving out to the Hamptons on Friday with some kids from school. They'll just die if the car isn't ready in time."

"We have an appointment to see that apartment at five," Pat reminded her. "Pick me up at four-thirty."

"I'll be there," CeeCee promised.

"The Mercedes?" Vanessa asked softly after CeeCee had departed in a flurry of farewell kisses.

"A red Mercedes." Pat nodded unhappily. "I couldn't stop Paul from giving it to her when he'd promised it." She concentrated on smoothing the tablecloth with the palm of her hand. "CeeCee doesn't know it yet, but her grandfather's buying her a co-op.

A broker is showing us what she thinks are rentals. They're co-ops." Pat looked up earnestly. "Daddy's health is very precarious. He doesn't rest the way he should. He just ignores everything the doctors tell him."

"Come with me to the salon," Vanessa said softly. "I want you to see my sketches for the fall/winter collection."

"When Suzy is back in New York, will you make sure she and CeeCee see something of each other? Maybe Suzy can persuade her to go back to school. Vanessa, I'm scared to death of her living here alone in New York."

Vanessa resolved to try to get to know CeeCee better. Pat had said nothing about CeeCee's therapy in Switzerland, but this child-woman seemed a different person from the one she remembered. She deserved a second chance.

Pat called Vanessa on Friday before she returned to the Virginia plantation to report that CeeCee liked a one-bedroom on East Sixty-eighth, and would move in the first of September. She was sharing a house at the Hamptons with friends until then.

"Suzy will be up at Barnard for orientation week the first week of September, but I'll make sure she comes home for dinner over the weekend," Vanessa replied. "Tell CeeCee to call me so I can set up a night when both of them are free."

"Wonderful, Vanessa." Pat seemed relieved.

Vanessa hung up the phone thoughtfully. CeeCee was spending the rest of the summer at the Hamptons, and Pat wasn't happy about it, but she was afraid to argue with her. This generation demanded such freedom, Vanessa thought to herself, and parents were afraid to put up a fight, held back by fears of crazy communes or heavy drugs.

Was Frank right, was she too easy with Suzy? But Suzy had her feet on the ground. CeeCee had been trouble almost from the day she was born. Had Suzy ever tried marijuana or LSD?

Vanessa agreed that Wendy was old enough, now that she was in the first grade, to have dinner with the family. Tonight, with CeeCee coming to dinner, would be Wendy's first dinner party.

"Mother, do I look all right?" Wendy asked anxiously when she came downstairs, Maria right behind her.

"You look beautiful, darling," Vanessa assured her with a surge of affection. Only in the last weeks had Wendy abandoned "Mommy" for "Mother."

"Awful grown up for six," Maria grumbled good-naturedly, inspecting the white empire jumper, short white boots, and tights. "Exactly like one of Suzy's outfits."

Wendy glowed. For Wendy, that was the highest possible praise.

Suzy and CeeCee arrived within a few minutes of each other, and for a moment Vanessa was startled by the contrast between the two. Suzy, dark-haired with blue-green eyes and milk-white skin, CeeCee with bleached-to-silver hair, huge dark eyes, and golden tan. Suzy wore a London-bought turquoise jersey knit with one shoulder bared. CeeCee wore what appeared an elongated black sweater over black tights and extremely high-heeled silver pumps.

For a while Vanessa was afraid the two girls wouldn't find anything to talk about. In Europe, Suzy had been one of the myriad American students traveling with backpacks and staying at youth hostels. CeeCee had visited the important cities of Europe with the daughters of diplomats and royalty, and she had stayed at centuries-old palazzos, castles, or luxury hotels. In New York, CeeCee had already discovered Arthur's, Steve Paul's, the Scene, and Andy Warhol. Suzy was involved in integration, peace marches, and student rights. They sat in awkward silence. Then Suzy mentioned the "young" fashions, and they were caught up in a heated discussion. CeeCee adored the clothes designed by Rudi Gernreich, whose topless bathing suits last summer had delighted some and shocked others. Suzy loved the dresses and sweaters at a new boutique called Paraphernalia.

"There's this girl there named Betsey Johnson." Suzy glowed with enthusiasm. "She makes clothes that are such fun!"

Boutiques had existed in Europe for a long time, but suddenly they were springing up all over America, catering to the exploding Youth Culture. Vanessa studied their windows — on Madison Avenue, in Greenwich Village, on St. Mark's Place — regularly, ever conscious that fashion was being designed on the streets.

By the end of the evening it appeared that Pat's dream of CeeCee and Suzy becoming friends might become reality. Suzy agreed to meet CeeCee on Saturday to go gallery hopping — both girls were fascinated by pop art. Later Vanessa confessed to Maria that she was mystified by the growing interest in such art subjects as a can of Campbell's soup.

Wearing blue jeans and a psychedelic T-shirt, Suzy hurried across the Columbia campus to Broadway and 114th Street. There was CeeCee, behind the wheel of her red Mercedes on the other side of Broadway. She had been teed off when Mother insisted she come to dinner and meet CeeCee. Before Switzerland CeeCee had been obnoxious. Now she was weird, Suzy decided, but fun.

"You picked Barnard because of all the boys at Columbia," CeeCee said slyly as Suzy joined her on the front seat. "After classes without girls they must be so hungry."

Suzy laughed. "I chose it because it's here in New York and it's a great school."

Mother had told her that her father had gotten an engineering degree at Columbia. Only lately had she started talking about him. Not before, Suzy reasoned, because Mother wanted her to feel that Frank was her real father.

Why did they stay married when they didn't live together at all? Because of Wendy and her? To pretend they were a whole family? She used to feel they were, but not anymore. Maybe it would be more honest if they got a divorce.

"We're going to a twist party tonight," CeeCee told Suzy. "Somebody I met at the Hamptons has a loft downtown. Every Saturday night he has a kind of open house."

"I'm not exactly dressed for it." Suzy inspected Cee-Cee's black leotards and boat-necked white sweater. "Neither are you," she laughed.

"Anything goes at Emil's parties. His name isn't really Emil. It's Robert, but he thinks Emil sounds more glamorous."

"Is he an artist?"

"Sort of." CeeCee gestured vaguely, reaching for the ignition key. "Part of the loft is his studio, and the rest is for living. He came here from Arizona two years ago. He's queer so you don't have to worry about him chasing you into a dark corner, but he's got the wildest ideas. He's talking now about maybe making underground movies. He's taking a course in film-making at NYU or the New School—I forget which."

"I've never seen an underground movie," Suzy admitted. "Just stills of the people in them. You know, you could look like an underground movie star real easy," she speculated. She liked to pretend she was designing clothes for famous people—like Brigitte Bardot or Barbra Streisand.

"What would I have to do?" CeeCee demanded avidly.

"The black tights are sensational," Suzy approved, her eyes moving over CeeCee, "but that sweater has to go. You'd need something campy. And lots of bangle bracelets and earrings down to here—" She held a hand just above her shoulder. "High heels to make your legs stand out."

"My legs are too fat," CeeCee murmured. "I hate them."

"They're great," Suzy contradicted.

"I've signed up for a series of treatments with this masseuse who pounds your legs and thighs till they're terrific. I'm going every day for six weeks." CeeCee stopped for a light. "To hell with the galleries. Let's go down to St. Mark's and look for clothes. When we show up at Emil's party tonight, I want everybody to ask, 'Who's that marvelous girl!' Me!" she said triumphantly.

They headed downtown and east. At the first boutique on St. Mark's CeeCee bought a collection of bracelets. Suzy had to approve each one. They moved on, choosing dangling rhinestone earrings, an ostrich-trimmed black poncho. When Suzy mentioned high-heeled silver sandals, CeeCee revealed she already had a pair at home.

"Let's go back to my pad and put this look together," CeeCee ordered. "And what about you?"

"I'll stay like this," Suzy shrugged. "I'm not the underground movie type."

"No," CeeCee agreed, inspecting the perfect oval of Suzy's face, the delicate features, the unexpectedly full mouth. "You're like a young, dark-haired Grace Kelly. The kind of girl everybody automatically trusts," she jeered in high spirits. "Wow, do we make an eye-catching team!"

"Grace Kelly did all right," Suzy reminded. Not that she wanted to be a movie star. She wasn't sure what she wanted to do with her life. Mother would love to see her come into the business. She had hinted at it all through high school. But if she ever did become a designer, she'd do it on her own.

"Hollywood turns me off, but it might be fun to be an underground movie star." CeeCee's eyes were dreamy. "Like Baby Jane Holzer or Viva. It might be lots more fun than modeling."

"It could be kind of weird." Suzy said doubtfully. Alice Harmon said she'd seen one where everybody took off all their clothes. "A lot of those people are into heavy drugs, everybody says. That's scary."

"Don't you ever do drugs?" CeeCee was faintly patronizing.

"Pot," Suzy admitted. "Once. Everybody does that once." She wasn't comfortable with drugs.

"Suzy, I bet I can talk Emil into making an underground movie. He's got all this money his father left him two years ago. He'll be as famous as Andy Warhol, and I'll be bigger than Baby Jane Holzer or Viva. And you'll design all my kooky outfits. Suzy, I'm so glad I came to New York!"

Forty-three

Suzy was caught in two totally different worlds. From Monday to Friday she was a study-oriented Barnard student sharing a dorm room on campus with Elaine Mason, a friend from high school.

Elaine, and occasionally Suzy, wore the favored "rich" college wardrobe designed by Villager and Pappagallo. All-cotton shirts with little rounded collars — in every possible color and guaranteed to wrinkle — cable-stitch heather sweaters, heavy woolen miniskirts, Bermudas, and pants. Or textured pantyhose with Carnaby-look minidresses.

But mostly Suzy wore outfits from Paraphernalia and the Ninth Street Emporium and other boutiques that surfaced on Madison Avenue and in Greenwich Village. She cherished her mother's beat collection alligator bomber jacket, acquired after much cajoling, and the pea jacket that was the Vanessa Conrad version of the army surplus coats popular on King's Road in London and in New York's East Village.

Elaine had prayed to get into Barnard because Jerry Williams was a sophomore at Columbia. Elaine's and Jerry's parents figured they'd get married someday — once Jerry was through med school and his residency. Their parents never guessed they'd been sleeping together since the summer before their senior year in high school. The pill had made it possible.

Every Friday afternoon Elaine and Jerry drove out to their family homes on Long Island for the weekend. Many of the Barnard girls commuted, so the campus seemed half deserted on the weekends. But on weekends Suzy swung into the bizarre partying that had become CeeCee's career, a career bankrolled by her grandfather.

"You become famous just by being different!" Cee-Cee said with mounting assurance. "Everybody wants to be different. I'll start making modeling rounds soon." Emil was stalling on the underground film. "As soon as I walk into Arthur's or the Scene or Harlow's or Ondine and people stare and say, 'Hey, that's Cee-Cee Roberts.' "

People were beginning to notice CeeCee, Suzy acknowledged. She had a natural magnetism and her way-out clothes added excitement. Maybe she would be a superstar. It would be fantastic to be part of making it happen.

Along with the rest of CeeCee's entourage, and since CeeCee paid the bills this was growing fast, Suzy went to parties at Emil's loft, at Andy Warhol's Factory, uptown to the Ginger Man and downtown to Max's Kansas City.

Suzy protested faintly about partying during midterms, but she was intrigued by the claque CeeCee was gathering about her. Every midweek moment not involved in cramming was devoted to developing more far-out outfits for CeeCee to wear.

Just after Thanksgiving CeeCee's grandfather died, and she disappeared from New York for two weeks. She returned with the triumphant news that her grandfather had left her a million-dollar trust fund.

"I'm putting up part of the money for Emil's first underground film," CeeCee confided to Suzy over a hamburger at the West End Bar. "I know if I'm seen in something really sensational, I'll have it made."

"Do you have control over the money?" Suzy was dubious. CeeCee was only eighteen.

"I control the income that comes in from the trust. And Emil says it'll be no sweat to borrow on our trust funds if we need more."

"Does Emil know enough about underground movies to shoot one?" Up till now they'd been playing. But now CeeCee could lose all the money she put into the film.

"He's taking this course at NYU," CeeCee shrugged. "But that's not important. Emil's genius is that he can dig all kinds of craziness out of people. He finds people to write and act and handle the cameras and lighting. He's been shooting some one-reelers— just for kicks—at the loft. No rehearsals, none of that shit. He has everything in his head, and he just tells everybody what to do. He'll be as big as Andy Warhol. But first he has to have his superstar." Her face was rapturous. "And that's me."

During the winter intercession, Suzy dedicated herself to studying for finals. She was scared now she wouldn't come in with top grades. She'd been giving too much of herself to designing CeeCee's look. Cee-Cee had landed her first modeling assignment with that look—that and the fact that she was a senator's daughter and her grandparents were Old Texas society. It was an irresistible combination.

Early in February Emil began to shoot his first film, with CeeCee as his "superstar." Suzy listened to a minute-by-minute replay of the shooting as CeeCee drove her to the East Village on a shopping spree.

"But CeeCee, what's the film about?" Suzy struggled to maked sense of CeeCee's chatter.

"It's not *about* something, it's a feeling. Emil told the

scriptwriter no plot, *feeling*. But it makes a point. About racial prejudice, I think." CeeCee sounded defiant and Suzy looked at her sharply. That was kooky—why should CeeCee be defensive? Working against racial prejudice was important.

CeeCee continued. "Everybody says Emil is fantastic and that I'm fantastic. I wear my tiny red leather miniskirt and my black tights, of course"—CeeCee's signature—"and a black T-shirt. There's just me and these two guys—one young, one old. Before come on there's this little sadomasochistic scene with razor blades and candles and leather."

"That sounds crazy." Suzy's mouth dropped in astonishment. She had only a hazy conception of what an underground movie was like. Nudity, of course. Rebellion against the phony Hollywood stuff. Presenting subjects—like integration—that Hollywood wouldn't dare tackle.

"Suzy, grow up," CeeCee chided. "I'm not part of the s-m scene. That just sets the mood." She giggled. "I take off my T-shirt and then my tights, and I lie on the bed in a black lace bra that's practically nothing and black lace panties that are like a g-string. And this gorgeous stud who's really gay touches me and says all kinds of profound things. Emil says people will go out of their minds when they see the film."

In the next four months CeeCee made ten films with Emil. Almost overnight, it seemed to Suzy, CeeCee Roberts was an underground film superstar. Suzy was seeing less of her because of schoolwork and her own involvement with student protests. Still, every weekend she and CeeCee made time to go shopping and put together new mad outfits.

Suzy was troubled by CeeCee's intoxication with her new status, her determination to be the most sensational superstar the underground movie world had ever encountered. She appeared on Johnny Carson. She and Emil and chosen few from their inner circle went on a chartered plane to attend a Kennedy party at Hyannisport. When she walked into a disco, Cee-Cee boasted, everybody stopped to stare. And she was scheduled to do a fashion layout for *Life*.

The Carson show and the layout for *Life* and Cee-Cee's name in the gossip columns didn't bother Suzy. It was what went on in the inner circle. "*Suzy, it's so wild. And decadent. I mean, all those gorgeous boys around me, and they just want to fuck one another. Except one night Emil was real high—and we had this marvelous sex. And then when we were on location out at Southampton, Emil put LSD in all the scrambled eggs one morning. God, we were so high! The shooting was fabulous. . . .*"

Suzy knew that CeeCee's mother was upset by what the family referred to as "CeeCee's notoriety." Only her father approved. He saw only the photographs in *Life*, CeeCee's name in all the newspaper columns and on the most exclusive guest lists.

Early in September Vanessa summoned Suzy home for a special dinner. Tina's nephew Adam was a freshman at Columbia and was coming for dinner. Suzy was philosophical about this command performance. She knew how close Tina and her mother were. But the minute she walked into the living room and her mother introduced her to Adam Vigliano, she knew he was special.

"Suzy's a sophomore at Barnard," Vanessa told Adam. "You're practically on the same campus."

"How did you survive orientation week?" Suzy asked, liking Adam's air of puppy-dog friendliness.

"Barely," he laughed. "And this city. Wow!"

"You've never been in New York before?" Wendy was wide-eyed with astonishment.

"Darling, not everybody comes to New York,"

594

Vanessa laughed.

"I've been in California. Does that count?" he teased Wendy with a gentleness that Suzy found appealing.

Over dinner Suzy discovered that Adam, too, was against the war in Vietnam—and was only days away from getting his draft card. We was wary—like herself—of experimenting with drugs. And he shared her admiration for Dr. Martin Luther King, Jr.

"Back home," Adam said thoughtfully, "I wouldn't dare talk this way. We have one black family in town and two Jewish families. Not more than a handful of Italians—"

"Your aunt and I grew up right near there," Vanessa told him. "No blacks in town then. And the Viglianos were the only Italians. The Conrads the only Jews."

"I think one of the reasons I wanted to come to Columbia was because it's in New York, where all kinds of people live together," Adam said, almost embarrassed by his admission. "I'm not sure yet what I want to do with my life, but I'd like to feel I was contributing something."

"We want to see you here for dinner regularly," Vanessa said lightly. "Nothing formal. Just whenever you're in the mood and have the time. Your Aunt Tina is very close to us."

Vanessa reveled in the Russian look—born of the *Dr. Zhivago* movie—that had been embraced by all couture. But she was wary of the trend toward nudity that even Saint Laurent had presented this year, with his transparent dresses beaded only at strategic areas. Business continued to be excellent for Creations by Vanessa Conrad; even the custom salon was showing a respectable profit, despite dire cries in the fashion world that haute couture was dying.

In Paris Saint Laurent had opened his Rive Gauche shop on the rue de Tournon. His ready-to-wear debut, catering to the young market, had been a glittering success. Frank was already plotting to establish their own boutiques in fine department stores in key cities. It might just be, she confided to Arnie and Phyllis at a conference about her next trunk show, that some of the stores would prefer the concession deal, just to be free of Frank.

"Frank's abrasive," Arnie conceded. "But I don't think this is the time to set up Creations on concession."

"You don't like the idea either?" Vanessa probed.

"I don't think we need to worry about it," Arnie said in his low-key manner. "Frank's not making much headway."

"If this doesn't work out, he'll latch onto something else," Phyllis warned. "Frank's spoiling for new worlds to conquer."

"To show off to his darling Edie?" Vanessa asked acidly. "Is that still on?"

"From what I hear," Arnie admitted.

"Warn him to be a little more discreet, will you, Arnie?" Vanessa's face was taut. "I saw them getting into Frank's Ferrari when I went to the Ginger Man for lunch yesterday."

There was an awkward pause. "He probably figured the Ginger Man was off your circuit," Phyllis offered.

"I was at the Ginger Man for lunch with Pat. Paul sent her up to New York to talk to CeeCee. All of a sudden he's upset about his daughter's celebrity."

"I suppose you could call it that," Phyllis said with a touch of distaste.

"He was impressed by her modeling for *Vogue* and *Life*. And he approved of the items in the newspapers. '*Silver-haired, gorgeous-legged underground movie superstar CeeCee Roberts is the daughter of handsome Senator Roberts,*'" Vanessa quoted. "It added to his own publicity buildup. Then he realized what really goes on in underground movies. He wants her to quit doing them."

"Will she?" Phyllis was dubious.

"What do you think?" Vanessa shrugged. "Suzy says she's having a ball. She's the Queen Bee — and she's not giving that up for anybody."

"Vanessa, I know you're exhausted, but Susskind's office is asking for you to do his show," Phyllis cajoled, returning to business.

"Of course I'll do it," Vanessa agreed. "Let's check my schedule."

On a late Friday afternoon just before spring break, Suzy was halted at her door by a ringing phone. She dropped her new maxi coat across the bed and picked up the phone.

"Hi—" Expecting it to be Adam, who was meeting her for a hamburger before they went on to the light show in the Village. He was leaving for home in the morning. He didn't want to go, but his parents were expecting him. Suzy was already a little wistful; she knew she would miss him even over the short time of spring break.

"Suzy, we have to shop tomorrow! I'll pick you up at nine sharp." CeeCee's voice was high-pitched with excitement.

"CeeCee, you'll never be up at nine sharp."

"I will tomorrow. I have this sensational party tomorrow night, and I have to wear something wildly outrageous. Emil says they're expecting Mick Jagger to show up! God, isn't that super?"

"Okay, the usual corner at nine," Suzy capitulated. CeeCee's enthusiasm was contagious.

They talked about the party for a few minutes, until Suzy heard Emil yell in the background that CeeCee was needed for the next scene. Emil was out to break records; he had vowed to turn out a movie a week for the next ten weeks. Off the phone, Suzy pulled on her maxi coat still indecisive about this look, and hurried from the dorm to the West End to meet Adam.

"See me off on the train tomorrow morning," he coaxed while they ate their hamburgers in a cozy booth at the rear of the West End.

"I can't." Her eyes widened in apology. "I promised to help CeeCee shop in the morning. She needs some kooky outfit for a party."

"CeeCee Roberts?" Adam sat up straight.

"Yeah. I told you about her. Her mother and my mother have been friends since they were our age."

"You didn't say she was CeeCee *Roberts*, the one who makes those underground movies."

"I didn't think it mattered." When she and Adam went to the movies, they saw things like *Repulsion* with Catherine Deneuve and *A Man for All Seasons* with Paul Scofield and Wendy Hiller, or *Alfie* with Michael Caine. "I mean, I've never seen any of them."

"My roommate—you know, Tim—is mad about her. Ever since he first saw her."

"Adam, it's not like she's a Hollywood star. Not like your aunt. Underground movies are kind of a cult deal. Not a lot of people go to see them."

"They're what's happening now." Adam's face glowed. "Don't you see, Suzy? They reflect our times. The rebellion, the fight to talk about *anything*, to cre- ate art, make statements without worrying 'is it commercial?" I'd like to see them do an anti-Vietnam movie, or one about the fight in the South for integration."

"I think they're after a different message," Suzy said bluntly. "At least, that's what everybody says. You know, sex and nudity and perversion." CeeCee said all she did was strip down the way she might on the beaches in the south of France and let it all happen around her. "Would you like to meet CeeCee?" she asked because he seemed so awed.

"Wow, could I?"

"When you come back to campus," she promised.

"She'll be mobbed." Adam grinned. "Half the kids on my floor at John Jay will flip when they find out I've met CeeCee Roberts."

CeeCee pulled up at the curb promptly at nine the next morning. Suzy scrambled into the warmth of the Mercedes.

"I love maxis on days like this," Suzy admitted. "Thank God you weren't late."

"I hate that maxi look. I mean, I've got great legs, so why hide them? Why hide yours—they're great, too." CeeCee cast a fleeting, complacent glance at the length of leg on display between her micro-mini red suede skirt and her black vinyl boots. "Oh, we've got to make one stop before we hit St. Mark's. I'll die if I don't get a vitamin shot. I'm so *down*. But at this hour the office won't be busy," she promised. "We'll be out in five minutes."

They parked half a block down from the East Seventies town house where Dr. Tyler had his office. CeeCee was exploding with anticipation—and apprehension—about the night's party and what meeting Mick Jagger would do for her career.

"Emil will have the PR man there with a photographer. Can't you see all the newspaper photos? Mick and CeeCee — it'll be a real happening."

"CeeCee, he might not show," Suzy warned.

"Don't even say it," CeeCee scolded. "But I need a vitamin shot to get me up."

Dr. Tyler's offices occupied the first floor of a beautiful brownstone. Though it was barely nine-thirty when Suzy and CeeCee walked inside, the reception room was occupied by seven patients.

"Hi, CeeCee," a tall blonde in thigh-high boots and miniskirt called out while a Wall Street type ogled the two of them. The others sat staring at the floor or at the wall, tense in the waiting.

"Hi," CeeCee said vaguely and pushed Suzy to one side. "He'll take me first," she whispered. "Old Tyler's got his favorites."

A few moments later a white-uniformed nurse emerged from one of the doors leading off to the rear, surveyed those waiting, then gestured briskly to CeeCee. The others stared resentfully after CeeCee as she hurried behind the nurse.

"I need a shot! I need a shot!" a grim-faced young man muttered to himself. "I come every day. Why in hell does he keep me waiting like this?"

Suzy was uncomfortable in the pressure-cooker atmosphere of the waiting room. She mentally kicked herself for being so naive. CeeCee's "vitamin shot" wasn't just vitamins; it was drugs. She could understand kids messing around with pot, but the hard stuff frightened her. People on speed did crazy things.

In five minutes CeeCee was dancing out of the office, her face wreathed in smiles.

"I love those earrings," she told the long-haired blonde, who had curled up dejectedly on the floor. "They're just beautiful!"

"CeeCee, let's get out of here," Suzy prodded.

"Baby, take it easy," CeeCee giggled. "You're so up-tight."

"CeeCee, what's in that vitamin shot?" Suzy demanded when they were out in the biting cold morning.

"It's vitamins and niacin and speed," CeeCee said in the slow, gentle tones she might have used in talking to a toddler.

"Hard drugs," Suzy emphasized.

"God, are you a baby." CeeCee regarded her indulgently. "Speed isn't hard drugs. Heroin and cocaine are hard drugs. Speed is the wonder drug that makes you fly." She spread her arms and giggled.

"Dr. Tyler shoots you up with vitamins and speed?" Suzy tried to hide her disgust. He wasn't a doctor; he was a pusher.

"Some speed is mixed in with the vitamins," CeeCee acknowledged. "It's wonderful!" Her eyes were bright, her skin luminous. "Yesterday we shot this terrific scene—everybody was on poppers. Stoned out of their minds. I mean, I can't imagine being able to do those things—the camera running and all—without poppers. It was a real orgy. Everybody in love with me and wanting to do it with me. And we did," she said while Suzy gasped in shock. "Emil says everybody will go out of their minds when they see it."

Suzy climbed into CeeCee's red Mercedes.

"I think you're crazy to let that doctor shoot you up with that stuff," she said bluntly when they were seated. "You do things you know you shouldn't."

"You've got it all wrong," CeeCee objected. "Speed frees you—it takes away all those kooky inhibitions."

"So you'll take off your clothes and be part of an orgy?" Suzy scoffed.

"That's being really free. What's wrong with our

bodies that we have to hide them? What's wrong with making love? Anyway, every way. We had a kind of joy when we were doing that scene that was fabulous. Perfect sex. You know—" CeeCee squinted in thought. "I'll bet you would come up with the most sensational outfit if you went back with me and let Dr. Tyler give you just one tiny little shot."

"No!" Suzy stiffened. "I like to know what I'm doing."

"Are you going to tell my mother?" With chameleonlike swiftness CeeCee was hostile and accusing.

"No." She knew that she should. But what difference would it make? CeeCee wouldn't listen to her. She had her grandfather's inheritance; she didn't need her parents. "No, I won't tell her."

CeeCee's smile was brilliant as she reached for the ignition.

"What do you want to bet I can make it all the way down to St. Mark's without stopping for a light?"

Forty-four

Suzy sat across from Adam in their favorite pastry shop on Amsterdam Avenue with a cup of hot cider in her hand, midway between table and mouth.

"Adam, we can't go to the Studio party tonight," she protested. Emil's loft was now known to the public at large — to those who read the daily newspaper reports of the larger-than-life activities of Emil, CeeCee, and their camp followers — as the Studio, where Emperor Emil shot his movies and held court after hours with CeeCee as his reigning empress. "We have to help paint signs for the protest march tomorrow."

Tomorrow — April 15, 1967 — 400,000 protesters against the Vietnam War were scheduled to march from Central Park to UN headquarters. It was a protest organized by the Spring Mobilization to End the War in Vietnam, a coalition of antiwar groups. At the end of the march Dr. Martin Luther King, Jr., and Stokely Carmichael would speak at the UN.

"We'll just stay an hour," Adam coaxed. "Then we'll go help paint signs. We haven't been to the Studio since Sunday night."

"All right," Suzy capitulated after a moment of hesitation. She was excited about the march tomorrow. They were making a statement, and she would be part of it. Phyllis and Arnie would be there, too, and students from all over the country would be arriving by bus. But she knew Adam was mesmerized by Cee-

Cee. It was his first year in New York—he'd never seen anything like the way-out crowd at the Studio. He'd never seen anybody like CeeCee, and he wasn't alone, Suzy acknowledged; CeeCee had that kooky effect on most men—even older men. And on women.

They finished their pastry and cider and headed downtown. When they arrived at the Studio, filming was over for the day. People were milling about or dancing to music on the jukebox.

"There's CeeCee." Adam's face lit up at the sight of her off in a corner, in fishnet tights and no shoes, black leotard and a wide silver belt about her tiny waist. She was just standing there weaving to the music, a mysterious smile on her face as she listened to the talk of the three men flanking her.

"Adam . . ." Suzy wished she had never introduced Adam to CeeCee. She hadn't expected CeeCee would make him part of her court.

"Suzy!" CeeCee called out. "Come over here."

Suzy reached for Adam's hand as they started across the floor. The party was just beginning, gearing up for the celebrities and, Suzy knew, lots of drugs and wide-open sex. She and Adam had to get out of here before it got crazy.

"It's been a fabulous day," CeeCee cooed, an oddly triumphant glint in her eyes as she leaned forward to kiss Suzy on the cheek and then Adam.

Suzy stared in disbelief as CeeCee's mouth met Adam's and they exchanged more than just a friendly kiss. She saw color flood Adam's face. CeeCee was soul-kissing him. She was doing it deliberately to hurt her, Suzy realized with a jolt. She'd seen CeeCee play around before, trying to hurt somebody, but she'd always found some excuse for her. CeeCee was just CeeCee—she did whatever came into her mind.

An hour later, when Suzy insisted it was time they

joined the sign-painting contingent, Adam rebelled.

"Suzy, we're at a party," he reproached, his eyes finding CeeCee across the room. "Let somebody else paint signs."

Suzy left the Studio alone. Angry and frustrated, she walked in the cold dreary night without thinking about where she was, or where she was going. Adam wouldn't be with the Columbia-Barnard protesters tomorrow, she prophesied. He'd defected.

Vanessa sat at the edge of Suzy's bed while Suzy packed for a month down in Alabama, where she would join a group of students working for voter registration among the blacks. From Suzy's never-silent stereo came the sounds of the Mamas and Papas wailing "Monday, Monday." Today Suzy wore her Villager shirtdress and Bass loafers. She knew it was essential to dress conservatively when invading enemy territory.

Vanessa tried to sound excited about this latest project. She agreed completely with the drive to bring southern blacks to the voting machines. But she was worried about Suzy's obvious unhappiness. Vanessa's cautious questioning hadn't brought forth any explanations.

She suspected that Adam and Suzy had had a fight before he'd gone home for the summer. Suzy hadn't brought him home for dinner once during the last six weeks of the semester. She'd mentioned that Adam was upset at the prospect of working in his father's repair shop for the summer, but that was hardly the reason he hadn't come to dinner. Summer would pass fast enough, Vanessa thought, and he'd be back at Columbia.

Pat was out of her mind over CeeCee's so-called career. Hollywood would have been acceptable; underground films were not. Paul was carrying on like crazy about it. His constant refrain: we can't afford a scandal.

Paul was running scared without his father-in-law to manage his career. Jim Owens had been dead for five months, but Paul was determined to follow the shrewd old politician's plans to put Senator Paul Roberts in the White House in 1976.

Tina remained holed up in Rome, waiting for Marty to come up with a really great script. While she waited, she was creating headlines on the night-club circuit with her tempestuous behavior.

Adam was unhappy. Suzy was miserable, though she couldn't figure out why, Vanessa fretted. Only darling little Wendy, already out at Southampton with Maria, seemed normal.

"Suzy, remember to call," Vanessa pleaded as she saw Suzy off. "I'll worry about you."

"Mother, there's nothing to worry about," Suzy insisted. "There's not going to be any trouble."

As always, Vanessa was the first to arrive at the design studio. But this morning it was difficult to focus on work. She worried about Suzy and didn't know how to help. She had failed as a wife. Was she failing as a mother?

Rhoda, Doris's replacement, brought her a cup of strong black coffee. She looked sharply at Vanessa's drawn face. "You're worrying about Suzy running off to Alabama," she concluded sympathetically.

One of the three phones on Vanessa's desk rang, and Rhoda reached for it.

"Design studio, Vanessa's line," she said briskly. Vanessa waited inquiringly. "Frank, Rhoda told her and handed over the phone.

"Yes, Frank." She was finding it increasingly difficult to be civil to Frank. He was being indiscreet about Edie—they'd been seen together too often.

"I have to talk to you," he said. "Let's have lunch at the cafeteria around eleven-thirty, before the mob descends."

"All right. I'll pick you up at the office." What was so urgent that they had to talk at the cafeteria? That was where they went when they wanted to be sure they'd be alone and uninterrupted.

By twenty to noon she and Frank were seated at a corner table. Frank took a bite of his inch-thick pastrami on rye, swigged at his iced coffee, and launched into his subject.

"We're standing still, Vanessa," he complained, a glint in his eye. "It's time to expand into new areas." He paused, and Vanessa prepared to fight the same tired battle. "I've done intensive market research. We have to move into menswear."

Vanessa stared at him in disbelief. Years ago Bill Bartlett had tried to steer them into menswear, and Frank had been soundly opposed to the idea.

"Frank, that would be insane." She tried to sound matter-of-fact. "We know nothing about menswear. I can't design for men."

"Look what Bill Blass has done with menswear," Frank shot back. "He's creating a sensation."

"I can't design for men," Vanessa repeated. "Blass can."

"You don't have to do the designing," Frank said impatiently. "We'll hire designers. I can just see the advertising layouts. You in some spectacular gown, standing between a pair of male models wearing Vanessa Conrad Menswear."

"Frank, that is out of the question. I won't pretend to design what I can't do."

"God, Vanessa, you never change. The same stubborn mind you've always had. If you don't think of it, it's a lousy idea."

"Frank, we're doing well. Our grosses are the best ever. We're — "

"We're standing still," he broke in, glaring at her. "In this business that's like going backward. I've had enough lunch." He pushed back his chair and reached for his punched-out cafeteria check. "You'll never get smart, Vanessa. You'll always think small."

Vanessa sat alone at the table, pretending to finish her lunch. When they were alone the hostility between her and Frank was almost unbearable. Did Suzy suspect? She had to realize there was no real marriage between them anymore — when they'd moved into the house, Frank had made that clear by setting up his own apartment.

Why couldn't she bring herself to divorce him? Did Frank want a divorce? She turned this over in her mind. If Frank wanted one, he'd ask. He must prefer it this way. This way he could avoid any commitment with Edie, Vanessa thought cynically. He would never marry Edie. He was too much of a social snob.

She would hardly be depriving the girls of a father if she divorced Frank. Instead of his presence he gave them absurdly expensive gifts. He'd abandoned his Sunday hours with Wendy. But if she and Frank divorced, what would happen to the business? Together they were Creations by Vanessa Conrad.

Suzy returned to New York from Alabama in late August, with the new school year breathing down her neck. Despite the torrid heat, uncomfortable accommodations, bad food, and loud and ugly resentment from certain whites, she looked back on the summer with satisfaction and pride. But she couldn't get Adam out of her head. They'd exchanged a few vague postcards, but she had seen little of him the last five weeks of school. He had become part of CeeCee's inner circle.

She didn't see much of Elaine because Elaine was mostly with Jerry. This year Jerry was moving off campus, so Elaine would be over there all the time. What would the new school year be like for her and Adam?

On Suzy's second day back, CeeCee phoned to reproach her for losing touch over the summer. They hadn't seen each other since the party at the Studio the night before the protest march to the UN, the night Adam had stayed to dance with CeeCee while she left to paint signs for the march. The next time CeeCee had called, she'd begged off because she was cramming for finals. And right after finals she had left for Alabama.

"I don't have a mad, mad outfit that people haven't seen at least three times," CeeCee wailed. "Let's go somewhere for lunch and then go shopping."

"I'm trying to get packed up to move back to the dorm," Suzy hedged.

"I'll help you." CeeCee was wistful and cajoling. "We'll throw everything into the Mercedes and take it up to campus. Suzy, I *need* you. Mother bought me some super Gernreichs and Balenciagas." CeeCee was overcome with giggles. "She had this weird idea she might reform me if she could get me into some straight clothes. But *you* make me CeeCee Roberts."

"All right," Suzy agreed after a moment of hesitation. Foraging through Greenwich Village and East Village boutiques to create the CeeCee Roberts look gave her a real high. But she hadn't forgiven CeeCee for taking Adam away, just to prove that she could. She'd create CeeCee's costumes, but she'd never trust her again. She'd finally seen through the adorable

CeeCee Roberts to the devious and malicious CeeCee Roberts.

"We'll go to Max's Kansas City," CeeCee decreed. "My treat."

"No," Suzy said firmly. At Max's Kansas City everybody would make a fuss over CeeCee. "We'll never get out of there. Let's go to Ratner's on Second Avenue."

At Ratner's they ran into a bunch of actors on lunch break from a TV rehearsal upstairs at Central Plaza. CeeCee exchanged breezy gossip, then prodded Suzy off to a table.

"Mother keeps telling me I ought to try to make it into Hollywood pictures. She says Tina Gregory would help." CeeCee's eyes betrayed her fascination with the idea. Then she frowned. "No . . . I don't want to be part of that scene. I mean, here I'm CeeCee Roberts—everybody loves me. And I love them. In Hollywood they're all creeps. Not like at the Studio." Her face was aglow with smug contentment—or was it from Dr. Tyler's vitamin shot-cum-drugs? She reached for the menu.

Suzy declined CeeCee's invitation to go with her to the Studio when they'd finished their shopping spree.

"Come with me," CeeCee pleaded. "I have to meet this scriptwriter Emil's come up with. He says he has to pin down my aura before he can write for me. The new film's costing almost fifty thousand. It's going to be fantastic. You should come." She smiled shyly. "Adam'll be there. The three of us could go somewhere for dinner. Just the three of us," she emphasized.

Suzy tried to pretend her heart was racing.

"When did Adam get back?"

"Just yesterday. He said he tried you at the dorm and at home, but you weren't there."

"He didn't leave a message." But Maria had said

610

somebody had called.

"It'll be fun." CeeCee was at her most beguiling, charismatic as only CeeCee could be. "We won't hang around the Studio long. We'll go somewhere quiet for dinner and then up to the apartment and listen to records."

When Suzy saw Adam through the crowd at the Studio, and his eyes met hers, she felt as though they were completely alone. He pushed his way across the room and reached out with an eager, hungry look to enfold her in his arms.

"I missed you like crazy," he told her. "It was a bitch of a summer back home."

It was going to be Suzy and Adam again, she thought rashly.

Not until midterms did Suzy realize Adam was involved again with CeeCee and the Studio. Over a hamburger at the West End he confided to her that he had unofficially dropped two classes because he was terrified of flunking another course. All because of the late nights he'd spent partying with CeeCee's crowd, he admitted. All those nights Suzy had thought he was studying in his room at John Jay.

"I'll get back on the straight and narrow first thing next term," he said with a show of shaky confidence. "How could I be dumb enough to sign up for a 9:00 A.M. class? Only freshmen do that."

"You'll have to write a letter to a dean or somebody." Suzy tried to think of the best approach. "I think you have to file a petition to make it official about dropping the classes. Adam, CeeCee's crowd is a bad scene."

"They're okay; it just doesn't mix with school. I know now I can't stay up all night and then go to classes. CeeCee's fantastic. She's so gorgeous and crazy and electrifying. She'll do anything. And Emil let me hang around and help with the lights on the new film. It was really great—like everybody around was having some kind of mysterious sex with CeeCee without anybody even touching her."

"It sounds sick," Suzy said bluntly.

"It's *now*, Suzy." His face was troubled. "I don't know how to say it, but I have to be part of it all for as long as it lasts. And I know it won't last. It's just one sensational LSD dream."

Suzy went cold with fear. "Adam, are you doing drugs?"

"Just the usual kid's stuff," he shrugged. "I stay away from heroin and coke."

"Speed?" she challenged. "Is CeeCee taking you to Dr. Tyler for those damn vitamin shots?"

"It helps me get through class," he said defensively. "Though it's so goddamn expensive, I can't do it every day, like CeeCee does."

"Adam, I think you're in over your head." Suzy struggled to stay calm.

Adam looked frightened. "It's just for a little while. It's a phase."

"Get out, Adam. While you can. You've got to stay away from the Studio and from Dr. Tyler. Find somebody to tutor you. Work your butt off during winter intercession and come back prepared for finals."

"You think I can do it?" His eyes searched her, pleading for reassurance. "I can't mess up on school. I can't go back to work in my old man's repair shop."

"You can do it," Suzy insisted.

"Will you help me, Suzy?" His forlorn expression brought tears to her eyes.

"Adam, you know I will." She had never felt so close to him.

Though Suzy was right up on the Barnard campus during the school year, Vanessa was pleased to have her home for winter break. She felt warm at night, walking into the house, knowing Suzy was sleeping at home. She was also relieved that Suzy seemed to be seeing little of CeeCee.

A week ago, returning from a hectic designing session with a temperamental stage star, the limo had gotten stuck in traffic on West Forty-fourth Street. For what seemed forever they sat in front of a grimy movie house showing CeeCee's latest film. Vanessa watched the men in line for tickets eye the blowup of a nearly nude CeeCee. She hoped Pat would never walk past one of these movie houses.

At home, after another charity ball, Vanessa remembered she owed Tina a letter. Frank was always her escort to important functions; but, of course, after a curt good night at the elevator he had gone to his own apartment. She'd sit down and write Tina now.

Tina expected regular reports on Adam. From what Suzy had let slip, Adam was having trouble academically. Not because of a lack of intelligence, Suzy had hastened to assure her, just too many distractions. Was Suzy serious about Adam? To her, Suzy was still her little girl. But her daughter was almost twenty.

She started at the sound of a faint tap on her door.

"Yes?" Late-hour interruptions always alarmed her. Was Wendy's cold worse? "Maria?" She headed for the door.

"Suzy, darling, is something wrong?"

"I heard you come in," Suzy said with an apologetic smile. "I thought we could talk a couple of minutes."

"Of course. Let me throw another log on the fire."

613

"Adam called earlier. He's had a bad fight with his father. They just heard that one of his high school buddies has been killed in Vietnam. Adam is terribly upset. He said America had no business *being* in Vietnam. His father is one of those 'my country right or wrong' guys—he flew into a rage."

"It's awful to think of anybody dying in a war," Vanessa said quietly.

"We don't belong in Vietnam." Suzy took a deep breath. "Anyhow, Adam wants to come back to New York now instead of waiting till next week, but he can't get into the dorm until then. I told him you wouldn't mind if he stayed here for a few days. Would you?"

"Adam is always welcome here, darling."

"He'll tell his parents he needs to come back early to do research," Suzy said. "He'll flip his lid if he has to stay and listen to his father carry on about the glory of the American army. And he's so uptight about his high school buddy being killed. If his friend had been in school, he wouldn't have been drafted. That doesn't seem right, does it?"

"I know . . ." Vanessa's mind was on another war, another death. "We manage the best we can."

Long after Suzy returned to her own room, Vanessa sat sleepless before the ash-edged logs in the grate. Suzy was in love with Adam. But she was so young. No younger than she had been when she met Eddie, Vanessa admitted reluctantly.

How could she protect Suzy from the pain that lay ahead? How could she make it easier for her?

Forty-five

Vanessa identified strongly with the young mood of the country. Like Saint Laurent in Paris, she ignored the inconsistency of expressing the feelings of anti-Vietnam demonstrators, student rebels, and mutinous American Indians in terms of couture. And again, she was battling Frank about the look of the collections.

"Damn it, Vanessa, have you forgotten what the critics said about your beat collection in 1960?" he taunted. "It was a disaster."

"Frank, the world has changed since then." She tried not to scream at him. Why was he so blind? "This is the time of the young. They're the voices being heard."

Ignoring Frank's warnings she kept the repetition of black in the collection, the striking number of pantsuits and jumpsuits, headbands, her version of duffle coats — all to be presented in expensive couture fabrics and trim. Frank groaned as each new design took form, but Phyllis and Arnie — and this time, Doris as well — were ardent in their support.

In February former Vice-President Nixon announced his candidacy for the Republication nomination for the presidency. Former Governor Wallace of Alabama prepared to run as a third-party candidate, and Governor Rockefeller leaked to the press that he might be available for a draft. In March, when Senator Eugene McCarthy won a dramatic 42 percent of the vote in the New Hampshire Democratic primary, Suzy and Adam were among the dedicated student volunteers working for him. On the last day of March, in a dramatic TV appearance, President Johnson announced that he would not run for re-election.

Suzy, Adam, and CeeCee maintained tentative ties. CeeCee was battling constantly with Emil. She rejected scripts, complained about casts. Scenes that should have been shot in two hours were taking two days. The atmosphere at the Studio was tense and hostile, with Emil constantly yelling that they were running overbudget and were almost out of funds. CeeCee loved every minute of it.

Though no one knew she was responsible for Cee-Cee's wild clothes, Suzy enjoyed keeping CeeCee in outrageous outfits. But most of her energy, that part not devoted to school, revolved around the McCarthy campaign. She and Adam worked for McCarthy and attended heated meetings about the university's efforts to build a new gym in Morningside Park — a gym that would deprive Harlem blacks of badly needed recreation space. When a dozen students were arrested at a student protest on the site, Adam was shaken.

"My old man would kill me if I got arrested," he told Suzy afterward when they went to the coffee shop. "God, would he be pissed."

"Your Aunt Tina's picking up the tab for college," Suzy reminded him, her eyes sparks of defiance. "You don't need him."

"How would your mother feel if you got busted?" he challenged.

"She'd be upset," Suzy said. "But she'd consider the circumstances and understand." She grinned. "Dad would flip his lid."

"My folks are pissed because I'm not coming home for spring break." Adam was somber. "They don't understand it's more important to ring doorbells for Gene McCarthy."

On the evening of April 4 Suzy was studying in her dorm room, the TV on with the sound muted. All at once a newsflash broke the monotonous background noise. Curious, Suzy leaned forward to turn up the volume. She listened in cold shock to the report that Martin Luther King, Jr., had just been shot.

Trembling, she rushed to phone Adam.

"Adam, have you heard the news?" she said, her voice small over the phone.

"No, Suzy, what—"

"Adam, it's awful!" she interrupted. "Martin Luther King has just been shot—"

"Is it bad?" he asked after an instant of stunned silence.

"They didn't say—just that a sniper had shot him."

"I'll meet you at the West End in ten minutes."

At the West End Suzy found Adam and several other grim-faced students in a rear booth, huddled over a transistor radio. Without a word Suzy joined them.

Within hours after the shooting, Dr. Martin Luther King, Jr., was dead. Rioting erupted in the ghettos following the second assassination of the decade, though New York City was quiet.

Pat frantically telephoned Vanessa when CeeCee refused to accept her phone calls or answer her letters. She reported that Washington was seriously disrupted by the rioting, that Paul was upset Johnson wasn't running for reelection. It was important to him that a

Texan occupy the White House.

"Vanessa," Pat said urgently, "does Suzy see Cee-Cee, is she all right? I worry about her being alone in New York and those people she hangs around with . . ."

"I'll talk to Suzy," Vanessa promised.

Adam guiltily cut his 2:00 o'clock class and headed for the East Seventies to met CeeCee. He usually wouldn't have thought about going with her for a shot, but she'd caught him in a rotten mood. He couldn't wipe out of his mind the sight of Martin Luther King walking out on his balcony in Memphis and being shot by a sniper.

CeeCee had called him several times in the past four weeks, running on about how crazy it was at the Studios and how much she needed somebody normal like him to talk to. He was afraid to see CeeCee again. It was too easy to fall back into the drug scene. It had been a bitch last summer to come out of it and stay clean.

But he felt so rotten. He'd go with CeeCee for just one shot, and that would be the end of it.

He wasn't in love with CeeCee. He was in love with Suzy—he could go out of his mind just holding her in his arms and kissing her. They weren't ready to sleep together—that would be a total commitment, and they weren't ready for that. Sometimes he was dying to sleep with her, but they'd wait for the right time.

CeeCee was waiting for him in front of Dr. Tyler's town house.

"I missed you," she sulked. "Was it fun on campus?"

"No," he acknowledged. "It was crazy and scary and frustrating—but it wasn't fun."

"Come on." She reached for his hand. "Let's go buy

ourselves some fun."

He hated the madness in Tyler's offices. Always a load of people waiting around. But CeeCee would get them in right away — she always did.

"I can't wait for that needle." CeeCee's face glowed. "I don't care that it hurts — I know what it'll be like afterward." She leaned against Adam, her thigh rubbing against his. "Sex with speed is so damn beautiful!"

In less than ten minutes he was pulling up his pants after getting the needle. He had the familiar taste in his mouth; he knew he was getting high. He wasn't thinking about Dr. King anymore or about the shit on campus. He was thinking what it would be like to screw CeeCee until they were both out of their minds.

CeeCee was in the waiting room. Her eyes had that special look that told him she was already high.

"Let's go to my place." She nuzzled against Adam until he felt himself growing hard. "I'm the greatest fuck in town."

On Tuesday afternoon, April 23, the newspapers broke the news that Columbia and Barnard students had taken over Hamilton Hall and later in the day moved into Low Library. On Wednesday night students from the School of Architecture took over Avery Hall. After midnight on Thursday the police were called on campus.

Frank caught the reports on TV and left his apartment to join Vanessa in the library of the town house.

"Where's Suzy?" he demanded.

"I can't reach her," Vanessa admitted.

"What the hell's the matter with those bastards?" Frank yelled. "No respect for authority! The cops ought to throw them all in jail!"

"They're fighting for what they think is right!" Vanessa shot back.

"They're acting like a bunch of fucking commies! They've had it too good all these years!"

It was late in May before the Columbia strike ended. Most of the students took off for home. Adam left reluctantly, knowing he was facing a battle at home. He meant to spend the summer working for voter registration instead of in his father's auto repair shop.

"Look, they can't stop you," Suzy rationalized, waiting with him for the train at Grand Central.

"I feel awful. I mean, doing everything they don't want me to do. But they're wrong," he said in frustration.

"You go up and tell them — you owe them that," Suzy agreed. "Then come back, and we'll start to work for voter registration."

"I'll stay just a few days," he promised. "I'll be back before we're set to leave for Alabama."

Adam was restless on the train, dreading the confrontation ahead. He had deliberately taken a train that would arrive in Saratoga in the early afternoon. That way his mother would pick him up at the station. Mom would look hurt and reproachful; Dad would yell and curse. But Suzy was right. He was an adult now; he had to make his own decisions.

As the train slowed to a crawl coming into the station, Adam spied his mother standing beside their station wagon. He had to tell her on the drive home that he'd be leaving in three or four days. How had they come to be so far apart in their thinking, he asked himself in exasperation. His parents would vote for Richard Nixon if he was nominated — they didn't think much of Governor Reagan, and Governor Rockefeller was too liberal for them.

"Adam, you didn't write much these last few weeks," his mother chided once they were settled in the station wagon. "Your father was worried you might be mixed up with those awful students who caused all that trouble."

"I was part of it," he said tersely.

"Don't tell your father," she warned.

Her face grew taut with disapproval when he told her his plans for the summer. He would have no support from his mother, but then, he hadn't expected any.

His father had a more vocal reaction.

"Are you nuts?" Sal yelled in disbelief. "This whole civil rights thing is a crock of shit. Why don't those hot-shot college kids of yours go over and fight in Vietnam instead of hiding behind their college exemptions?"

"Sal, let's not talk about Vietnam," Eva said warily. Too many local boys were dead or missing for her to share her husband's brand of patriotism.

"We don't belong in Vietnam," Adam said.

"You'd be better off there than chasing down South to make sure more blacks go to the polls! I expect a son of mine to act like a man!"

"I'd go to Canada before I'd go to Vietnam," Adam shot back.

"You're too chicken to fight for your own country," Sal's face flushed an ugly red. "My son's a goddamn coward!"

"I would have fought in World War II," Adam said. "But I'll never fight in Vietnam!"

Sal leaned forward and slapped him hard across the face.

"I'm ashamed to call you my son!"

"Then don't," Adam said softly after a stunned moment. "I'll pack and call a taxi to take me to Saratoga.

I can't stay here, Mom. I'm sorry."

"You'll stay here until we leave for Alabama," Suzy said firmly when Adam called her the next day from a friend's apartment.

"You'd better ask your mother," Adam cautioned.

"I'll ask, but I know it's all right. Hop on the subway and come on down here."

Later that evening Suzy received a phone call advising her that they wouldn't be able to leave for Alabama until June 8. Something to do with accommodations in the towns they were to cover. They had expected to leave within forty-eight hours.

"Now we'll be stuck here for more than a week," Adam said uncomfortably, worrying about staying on with the Conrads.

"It's been a rough year. We can stand a few days of loafing. Let's go out to Southampton for a long weekend," Suzy cajoled. "Maria's going out Friday afternoon with Wendy to open up the beach house. It'll be fun."

"I don't know—"

"Let's go," Suzy insisted and frowned as the phone rang again. "Now who's calling?" She picked up the phone. "Hello."

"Suzy?" CeeCee's voice was a thin, high wail. "Oh, God, you've got to come over here! Something crazy's happening to me! I'm shaking like I have the DT's."

"What have you taken?" Suzy demanded.

"I ran out of barbiturates . . . and then I think I overshot speed."

"Stay there." Suzy struggled to sound calm. "I'm coming right over. Leave the apartment door unlocked."

"CeeCee's having a bad trip?" Adam asked when

she hung up the phone.

Suzy nodded. "We should call Bellevue, but CeeCee would kill me afterward."

"Let's get over there fast—then we can decide what to do."

At CeeCee's building they waited impatiently for an elevator. Finally the doors slid open on the eighteenth floor, and they charged inside. As CeeCee had promised, the apartment door was unlocked.

"CeeCee?" Suzy ran across the foyer and into the living room. "CeeCee?"

"She's out on the terrace. Oh, God!" Adam's voice shook.

CeeCee straddled the railing of the terrace, completely nude. She was shaking convulsively, screaming obscenities.

"Adam, how do we get her in?" Suzy felt the color drain from her face.

"Stay here," Adam whispered. "Don't say a word."

Slowly he began to inch toward the door that led to the terrace. At the door he paused and braced himself. CeeCee was still unaware of their presence. He lunged forward in one desperate move, grabbed her around the waist, and pulled her back onto the terrace.

"You stopped me from flying! You bastard!" she sobbed hysterically. "You stopped me from flying!"

Adam carried her to the sofa and fought to hold her down while Suzy called Bellevue. Haltingly she repeated what CeeCee had told her about the barbiturates and speed. In a few minutes the apartment was bustling with police, ambulance attendants, and a distraught doorman.

Trembling and pale, Suzy supplied what information she knew, and then CeeCee was carried out of the apartment, down the elevator, and into the waiting ambulance.

"You saved her life," Suzy whispered while Adam held her in his arms. "Oh, God, it was so awful." She fought to think clearly. "I'll have to call her mother down in Georgetown."

"Call your mother first," Adam said. "She'll know how to handle it."

Suzy sighed in relief when her mother answered the phone, her voice sharp with anxiety at the late call. Suzy explained what had happened.

"I'll phone Pat right now. I'm sure she'll have Cee-Cee transferred to a private sanitarium, Thank God CeeCee had the good sense to call you. And bless Adam for saving her from going down eighteen floors."

By the time Suzy and Adam arrived at the house, Vanessa had broken the news to Pat, and a New York psychiatrist was talking to the hospital. Pat was leaving for New York early in the morning.

"CeeCee will stay at the Birch Hill Sanitarium in Dutchess County until the doctors are convinced she's off drugs," Vanessa told Suzy and Adam with a show of confidence; but she was shaken by CeeCee's state.

Had Pat known CeeCee was into drugs? The gossip columns almost came right out and said it. Maybe she didn't want to know.

On Friday morning Suzy and Adam drove out to Southampton with Maria and Wendy. Suzy hoped Adam would unwind at the beach. He was so uptight about CeeCee's being committed. But he wasn't in love with CeeCee. She was sure of that now. He was uptight because of the whole drug scene. The drug scene scared him. She was grateful that Maria and Wendy chattered nonstop on the drive to the beach house. She was exhausted from the trauma of these past months.

Maria was busy setting up the summer staff at the house. Wendy was forlorn because her friends had not yet come out for the season. Suzy and Adam included her in their leisurely beach walks every morning and afternoon. It pleased Suzy that Adam was so sweet to her small sister. Wendy was adopting him as a cherished older brother. On Saturday afternoon Vanessa—as usual, bringing work along—joined them for the balance of the weekend.

"Why don't you kids stay here until you're ready to head for Alabama," Vanessa encouraged Suzy and Adam over dinner on Sunday evening. "This is the best time of all out here."

On Monday morning at six Vanessa left for the city. With Wendy, Suzy and Adam spent their days driving about the Hamptons, enjoying the villages that dotted the area, lunching in Bridgehampton one day and in Montauk the next. They spent a warm, relaxing few days, and Suzy was glad to be sharing them with Adam.

On Tuesday night Suzy and Adam sat lounging before the TV set long after Maria and Wendy had retired. In the early hours of Wednesday they listened to rehashed reports of Robert Kennedy's victory over Gene McCarthy in the California primary. They had hoped that McCarthy would follow his Oregon victory with another in California; and they listened somberly as Robert Kennedy made his victory speech in the Embassy Room of the Ambassador Hotel in Los Angeles. He left the ballroom in jubilant spirits, his wife, Ethel, at his side. Minutes later the commentator's mumblings were interrupted by a heart-stopping news flash: Robert Kennedy, along with five others, had been shot.

Suzy and Adam remained at the Southampton house, rarely leaving the TV set for the next twenty-five hours. Shortly before 5:00 A.M. EST on June 6 Frank Mankiewicz appeared at the press building across from L.A.'s Good Samaritan Hospital to inform waiting reporters that Senator Robert F. Kennedy was dead. Assassination had struck down American leaders three times within the decade.

Early Friday morning Suzy woke with the realization that this afternoon she and Adam had to return to the city. They were scheduled to leave for Alabama tomorrow. Neither she nor Adam had slept much since the horror of the second Kennedy assassination. That, combined with CeeCee's overdose, had unnerved Adam. She had never seen him so distraught.

When Suzy arrived downstairs for breakfast, Maria told her that Adam had gone down to the beach.

"He said he'd have breakfast later." Maria seemed concerned.

"We both will. I'll go on down and bring him back." Suzy forced a smile.

She found Adam standing at the water's edge, shoulders hunched in tension, his face twisted in pain.

"Adam," she said softly, and he started.

"Suzy, I can't go to Alabama," he told her. "I'd just mess up."

"Why would you mess up?"

"I'm scared. I saw what happened to CeeCee, and I know it can happen to me. I keep swearing I won't go near drugs, and then something awful happens and I forget. Suzy, I need help."

"All right," she said softly. "Then you'll get it."

"I can't go to my parents. You know how they feel about drugs. I've got the money in my account for the next semester; but even if I take that, it won't go far. Somebody at the Studio said it costs a thousand a week at some of the hospitals. You have to be freaking out already to get any help at a city hospital."

"You won't go to a city hospital!" Suzy reached for his hand. "We'll talk to my mother."

"No!" He pulled his hand away. "She'd tell Aunt Tina!"

"Adam, you listen to me." Suzy spoke quietly, as though he were a small boy. "Your aunt loves you. She'll understand. She'll help."

"Oh, Suzy, I feel like such a shit," he whispered and reached to pull her close. "How did I get so screwed up?"

Tina pulled into the driveway of her villa at the edge of Rome with a sense of relief. She was exhausted from the day's shooting on the sound stage at Cinecittà Studios. On days like today she chastised herself for accepting the role in Felix's new film. Felix was such a demanding perfectionist; everyone alternately worshiped and hated him.

"Signorina, a telephone call from the States." Her maid appeared at the entrance to the Palladian villa as Tina strode up the low, wide stairs.

"Thank you, Nina."

Tina swore under her breath. She wanted only to soak in a hot tub for an hour and then settle down to a solitary dinner. The call was probably Marty, hot on the trail of another big commission, another shitty script.

She picked up the phone in the small sitting room off the entrance foyer and dropped into a chair.

"Hi—"

"Tina, how are you?"

Her face brightened at the sound of Vanessa's voice. They exchanged warm greetings and then Tina listened in shock while Vanessa told her about Adam.

"What the hell's the matter with that stupid kid?" she yelled in a mixture of anger and alarm.

"Tina, he needs help. This is a terrible time for him."

They discussed how best to handle the situation. Tina had weeks of shooting ahead—it was impossible for her to fly to New York even for a few days. Vanessa assured her this was not necessary. She was prepared with the names of prospective psychiatrists and sanitariums.

"Jesus, I'm one of the few in Hollywood who manage to stay away from the shrinks, so Adam does it for me. But no country club deal," Tina insisted. "And he has to promise to stay there until the shrink is sure he's not going back into that mess."

"Tina, Adam's a sweet, warm, fine young man," Vanessa said. "He'll straighten out. A lot of kids are finding it hard to cope in this crazy era. So much is happening so fast."

"He'll have to write and tell Sal and Eva what's happening. They'll blame it on me for taking him away from home and the repair shop. But Adam has to go back to school, Vanessa."

"He wants to go back," Vanessa said. "He'll ask the school for permission to take a semester off."

"When the picture's finished, I'll come to New York to see him. Tell him for me." She sighed. "When the hell does life calm down?"

"When we're dead," Vanessa laughed compassionately.

"Darling, thanks for looking after my baby. He's the most important thing in the world to me. Isn't that a hoot?" She paused. "Tina Gregory, aging sex symbol, devoted closet mother."

"Adam will be fine," Vanessa comforted. "He's just scared to death you won't want to see him after this."

"You tell Adam to do whatever the doctors tell him. And I plan to be there when he graduates from Columbia." She paused, fighting down panic. "Vanessa, he *will* be all right, won't he?"

Forty-six

Alone in the darkened studio, Vanessa nursed the final mug of hot coffee. The staff was long gone on this early August Friday evening. In a few minutes, she reminded herself, she must phone Wendy out at the beach house. She always called Wendy at 8:00 P.M. sharp the nights during the summer when she wasn't out at Southampton.

Frank had stormed out of the studio almost an hour ago, but the air was still tinged with his hostility. He was out of his mind to think they should go into menswear. He couldn't bear it that Blass was doing so well. Still, they continued to show a remarkable gross.

He kept crying that the business was in the throes of a tremendous turn-around—and she agreed with this. Labor costs were soaring because of union demands. Economists warned about a possible slump late next year. Couture, Frank warned, was in serious trouble. Vanessa was convinced that "ready-to-wear" couture would survive as long as its designers were original and innovative. At the custom salon the prices were, of necessity, escalating, but society women and celebrities showed no signs of thrift.

Vanessa made a point these days of not going out to Southampton until Saturday morning because on Friday nights, Frank usually drove out to have dinner with Wendy. She would go home, have dinner, and settle down to work for the evening. She reached for her attaché case, thrust in a handful of sketches and swatches of fabrics, snapped it close. The phone rang, the sound harsh in the nighttime emptiness.

"Hello."

"Mother, don't be upset," Suzy pleaded, "but four of our group were arrested this afternoon. Including me," she added in an apologetic little voice.

"Are you all right?" Vanessa's mind immediately conjured up visions of a small-town southern police force angered by the invasion of their town by northern civil rights activists. "What about bail?"

"We can't do anything about that until morning. It'll be high, more than our group can handle. We wouldn't exactly win a popularity contest with the local administration," she laughed.

"I'll fly down immediately." Vanessa's throat tightened as she thought of the three civil rights workers murdered in Mississippi. *Dear God, let Suzy be all right.*

"You don't have to do that. It's just a question of bail money. Arnie can contact a lawyer down here to handle it. And Danny's father is coming down—he's a lawyer."

Danny would be Danny Fraser, Vanessa remembered. Suzy had talked about how dedicated Danny was to the movement. He was just her age and heading for his senior year at Harvard.

"I'll fly down first in the morning," Vanessa insisted. "I want to be with you."

"There's no commercial airport," Suzy pointed out. "This is a little jerkwater town."

"I'll get there," Vanessa promised. "They can't deny you bail."

"Mother, I have to get off the phone. Just write down the name of the town and the police chief's name."

Vanessa jotted down the vital statistics, put down the phone, then dialed the Hirsch apartment. Phyllis

631

and Arnie would know how to handle this.

"Arnie says he'll go down with you," Phyllis reported after a brief exchange at the other end of the line.

"No, you're going to his sister's party tomorrow." For weeks Phyllis and Arnie had talked about his sister's silver wedding anniversary party. "Just tell me whom to contact about a charter flight down there." Phyllis always made arrangement for her charter flights with the trunk shows.

"I'll take care of everything," Phyllis said. "Go home and pack a valise. I'll call you there."

By 5:00 A.M. Vanessa was en route to La Guardia to board a chartered flight that would take her to Montgomery. There a chauffeured car would be waiting to drive her the sixty miles to her destination. Phyllis had tracked down a small local hotel that would have a room for her upon arrival.

Vanessa arrived at the jail with a clear mind, open checkbook, and an impressive amount of cash—only to be stymied at every turn. She knew it would be futile to scream, so she confined herself to reiterating her right to see her daughter. The clerk insisted she would have to wait until noon to post bail. She would not be able to see Suzy until then.

"Protocol, ma'am," he said with a southern politeness that didn't quite conceal his distaste for the invaders. It was clear he had never heard of Vanessa Conrad. "You be here at noon, pay the bail, and she'll be out until her trial comes up."

"You're Vanessa Conrad—" A mellow male voice, definitely not southern, halted Vanessa as she was about to leave.

"Yes." She turned and smiled inquiringly at the clean-cut, prematurely graying man who stood before her. His blue eyes were warm and intelligent.

"I'm Larry Fraser." He extended a suntanned hand.

"Danny's father."

"Of course." Without understanding why, she was relieved that Danny's father — a lawyer, she recalled — was here.

"I saw the kids earlier," he said softly, taking her valise. "Danny, Suzy, Ron, and George."

"They wouldn't let me see Suzy," she said, her anger rising again in the hot morning sun. "It's outrageous."

"I know. I had to put up a fight to get in to see them. Used some legal hocus-pocus they couldn't handle," he confided with a chuckle. "The kids are all fine — just indignant at spending the night in a crummy jail." His smile was easy, relaxed. "Let's go over to the coffee shop and talk. It's air-conditioned, and the coffee's decent."

The immaculate brick-fronted coffee shop — its small-paned windows adorned with crisscross sheer white curtains — wasn't crowded. Vanessa wondered if they served blacks. Larry Fraser led her to a corner booth, persuaded her to order freshly squeezed orange juice, hot cakes, and coffee.

"We'll post bail at noon," he told her. "Suzy told me you were coming down. The other two boys are afraid to phone their families. I'll post bail for them. We'll all be out of this town before nightfall," he promised.

Over breakfast Vanessa learned that Larry Fraser was a partner in a corporate law firm whose name she recognized as one of the most successful and prestigious in the country. Quietly he told her that his older son had died in Vietnam two years earlier. He had trouble accepting this loss, and like millions of parents he was fighting to understand where this generation of the young was headed.

"My daughter is totally establishment," he confessed. "Like her mother. To both of them I'm a traitor to my class. They're more concerned about their hair spray and whether it's true that Jackie Kennedy will marry Aristotle Onassis than they are about what's happening in ghettos across America and on the campuses."

"We'll have no trouble in posting bail and just leaving?" Vanessa probed, "No repercussions?"

Larry's smile was unexpectedly cynical. "The local authorities and I understand one another. We pay the tab and leave. That's it."

Shortly before noon Vanessa and Larry handed over the required bail money. The four young people—sheepish, rumpled, and angry—were ushered from their jail cells.

"They had no right to arrest us!" Suzy said with whispered rage while Vanessa pulled her into her arms. "They tried to say we were instigating a riot."

Larry embraced Danny, then turned to shake the hands of the other three.

"I have a car rental. We'll drive up to Atlanta for a direct flight to New York. Are you guys hungry?"

"Let's eat on the road," Danny said tersely. "We just want to get out of this creepy town."

Vanessa and Suzy agreed it would be best not to mention the Alabama incident to Frank. Vanessa and Suzy slept most of the way on the drive out to Southampton. At the outskirts of town, Suzy began to talk hesitantly about the summer. She was worried about Danny. They had become close friends over the course of the summer.

"He's having emotional problems—you know, his brother died in Vietnam—but he refuses to get counseling. I guess his parents are scared to push him too hard. Maybe going out to Chicago as a McCarthy volunteer will be good for him. Though McCarthy is

634

telling us all to stay home."

"The Democratic Convention?" Vanessa asked and Suzy nodded.

"We're done with voter registration in the South," Suzy conceded, and hesitated. "I want to take a semester off from Barnard to work for McCarthy in the fall. Danny's taking a year off from Harvard."

"Suzy, suppose McCarthy doesn't win the nomination?" Suzy's intensity worried her.

"Don't say that, Mother," Suzy scolded. "This country needs him."

Reluctantly Vanessa agreed to Suzy taking a semester off. She sensed it would be futile to object to her going to Chicago for the Democratic Convention, though the prospect disturbed her. Suzy would be twenty-one in February—she considered herself an adult.

On Sunday morning before the convention, Vanessa accompanied Suzy to the airport for her flight to the Windy City. They knew from news reports that young people from all over the country had been pouring into Chicago since early yesterday morning. O'Hare and Midway were swamped, the terminals of Greyhound and Trailways jammed with passengers.

Vanessa was pleased that she had been able to use her contacts to secure hotel accommodations for Suzy for the convention week. There wasn't a hotel room in the city that was not reserved. Two girls from Suzy's group would share the room with her. Suzy met with Danny and her two Chicago roommates at the airport. Vanessa smiled in welcome when she saw Larry Fraser at Danny's side.

Vanessa invited Larry to drive back to the city with her, then accepted his invitation to lunch. Like her, he was anxious about possible violence at the convention.

Both parents remembered Mayor Daley's statement back in April that he wanted his police to "shoot to kill" in cases of rioting. But rioting could mean anything.

After a leisurely lunch, Vanessa asked Larry if he'd like to return to the house with her to watch the TV reports from Chicago. Each found comfort in the other's presence.

That Sunday afternoon Lincoln Park, Chicago, played host to what newscasters estimated to be about three thousand young people. About two thousand sprawled on the grass to listen to folk-rock music while another thousand milled about the perimeter. By the time Larry left for his own apartment late in the afternoon, both he and Vanessa felt the gathering in Lincoln Park had been a beautiful happening.

Then evening arrived. The young people were unwilling to leave the park, relishing the closeness of the day. The evening became a nightmare when, after an announced 11:00 P.M. curfew, Mayor Daley's cops arrived with tear gas. Yippies, students, reporters and photographers were beaten in plain view of TV cameras.

On Monday convention activities began in the Chicago Amphitheater. The streets of the city were almost deserted except for patrol cars. Barricaedes had been erected overnight. Residents in nearby suburban areas remained in their homes.

In Lincoln Park police cars plowed. Foot policemen in platoons were stationed every few hundred feet. The young congregated in the meadow. Late in the evening, with the headlights of police cars revolving ominously in the dark, word came through that Allan Ginsberg had arrived. Also Terry Southern, Richard Seaver, William Burroughs, Jean Genet — magic names to those waiting in Lincoln Park.

Suddenly a police car smashed through a flimsy barricade. Infuriated young people threw rocks and bottles, screamed invective. Clubs swung in the darkness. Tear gas exploded.

At Suzy's side Danny cried out and swayed. Suzy saw blood oozing from a cut across his forehead.

"Let's get out of here, Danny." She reached for his hand, knowing he was dazed with the pain. "Come on!"

"The bastards!" he screamed. "The goddamn fucking bastards!"

They darted through the woods and across the wide sweep of lawn. Somebody called to them to go to Clark Street and ask for directions to Henrotin Hospital. Suzy stayed with Danny at the emergency room, where he was treated by a grim-faced, sympathetic resident and dismissed. Afterward, Danny insisted, he wanted only to get stoned. Suzy knew she would never feel like a kid again.

Suzy returned to New York stunned and dejected. She talked endlessly with her mother and with Arnie and Phyllis about the insanity in Chicago. Reluctantly she agreed it would be wiser to get behind Humphrey than to sit back and allow Richard Nixon to walk off with the election. And she continued to rant about the stupidity of a government that sent eighteen-year-olds to die in Vietnam but would not allow them to vote.

She sometimes regretted taking time off from school. The rules, she discovered belatedly — as had Adam — required a year's absence rather than the single semester they had requested.

To Suzy and her clique of students election eve was depressing. She wished Adam could be here to share it with her. She was allowed to see him once a week for an hour. He was growing impatient, alternating between despair at the wasted months of his life and growing optimism about the future. In late December, probably by Christmas, he would be released.

Occasionally, mainly because she knew it would please Pat, Suzy dropped brief letters to CeeCee, along with sketches for future "CeeCee Roberts" outfits. CeeCee wrote that she had had it with underground films and meant to have a try at Hollywood "once these creeps let me out of here."

After the election Suzy persuaded her mother to allow her to rent a small apartment close to campus. She felt isolated away from school. The following semester, she promised, she would take a couple of design courses.

"It'll be something to do until I get my act together," she said.

She knew that, beneath her mother's determinedly casual facade, she was happy to see her daughter show an interest in design. Yet she knew, too, that she could never fulfill her mother's wish that she join the business. If she did, she would be forever in her mother's shadow, fenced in by her mother's will.

Early in December Suzy stopped by Danny's apartment to take him to a meeting of a new anti-Vietnam protest group. He was very depressed, and had agreed to go only if she would pick him up. She worried about Danny. She knew he was taking LSD and any new pills that made the rounds. She had tried, futilely, to persuade him to go with her on her visits with Adam. She'd hoped that Adam might make him understand he was in trouble.

When Danny didn't respond to his doorbell, Suzy made his landlady unlock the door. They found him sprawled unconscious on the floor. While the landlady screamed hysterically, Suzy called for an ambulance.

She rode with him to the hospital and telephoned his father. Standing beside Danny's ashen father, Suzy heard the doctor's prognosis that Danny would never be anything more than a vegetable.

She was anxious for Adam's release. She had to see for herself that he would be all right in the outside world. CeeCee was scheduled for release soon after the first of the year. But for Danny there would be no new year.

A week before Christmas she came home to find a smiling Adam sprawled on the floor before her apartment door.

"Adam!" Her face was joyous. He had said nothing on her last visit about a definite release date.

"Surprise, surprise!" He rose to his feet and reached to kiss her, a long, hungry kiss that told her how much he had missed her. The way she had missed him.

"You look sensational," she decided when they parted, searching his face. "How do you feel?"

"Never better," he boasted.

"Have you been waiting long?" She fumbled in her purse for her keys.

"About forty minutes," he said, grinning. "I wanted you to be the first person — the first person close to me — that I saw."

"You'll have to call your parents," she reminded him, pushing open the door.

"Yeah." He gazed about her apartment, taking in her casual furniture, discards from the family house. "Great pad," he approved.

"Are you hungry?"

"I'm always hungry these days. Let's go over to the West End in a little while for a Special Cut 100 percent U.S. Inspected Beef hamburger. Meanwhile, I just want to hold you."

639

"I'm so glad 1968 is almost over," Suzy told him. "It's been such a rotten year."

Adam sighed. "I guess I'd better get the phone call over with. They'll expect me home for Christmas."

Suzy curled up on a corner of the sofa while Adam dialed the phone. The apartment seemed complete with Adam here. It was home. If he didn't have to go upstate tonight, he would stay here.

"Hi, Mom. It's me!" he said ebulliently. "Adam."

Suzy watched while Adam listened in slack-jawed dismay to what his mother was saying. His face drained of color. Then with an awkward gesture he slammed the phone on the receiver.

"They don't want me to come home." His voice was a stunned monotone. "She said, 'We don't want no part of a drug addict son.'" He shook his head slowly. "It doesn't mean anything that I've spend six months kicking the habit. They don't want me."

"You don't need them," Suzy said defiantly. What kind of people turned away their son? Mr. Fraser was at the hospital to visit with Danny every night, even though Danny couldn't recognize him, couldn't speak a coherent sentence. "We'll go home together. I'm suppose to go home for dinner tonight. I forgot about it when I saw you sitting in front of the door." Her mother and Wendy and Maria would welcome him.

Suzy glowed at the warmth of her mother's welcome when they arrived at the house for dinner. While Adam stared at the floor, she told Vanessa about Adam's conversation with his mother. Her mother recoiled at the story.

"It's their loss, Adam," Vanessa told him. "You know your Aunt Tina feels differently."

"She's the greatest," Adam said softly. "Every week a package arrived from her."

"Call her later," Vanessa said. "It's three hours earlier in California — she's still at the studio." He lifted an eyebrow in surprise. "She flew in from Rome last week to start a new film. She was a sudden replacement. She was in town only long enough to change planes."

"Phone her after dinner," Suzy said.

"Adam, do you have a place to stay?" Vanessa asked. "You know you're always welcome here."

Adam hesitated an instant, his eyes making contact with Suzy's.

"Thanks. I'll be staying off campus with a friend."

"Maria, do you think I should interfere?" Vanessa needed Maria's support. Outside of Adam's adoptive parents, only she and Maria knew that Tina was his mother.

"Of course," Maria approved. "What a terrible thing to do to Adam!"

"When he spoke to Tina earlier, he said nothing to her about the conversation with Eva."

"He was loyal," Maria said softly. "Call Tina, tell her they've rejected her son. He's hers now."

Vanessa checked her watch. Tina must be home studying lines for tomorrow's filming. Yes, she would tell Tina.

Tina listened with a mixture of anguish and rage and excitement while Vanessa told her what had happened. Anguish for Adam's pain, rage that her brother and sister-in-law could hurt Adam this way — and simmering excitement that now perhaps she was free to claim Adam as her son.

"Vanessa, I'm scared," Tina confessed. "I hadn't planned on this."

"Tina, it's time to be honest with Adam. Let him know his mother loves him."

"I don't know how he'll feel when he finds out the truth. Maybe he'll feel I deserted him," Tina hedged.

"Adam needs to know the truth. It's important, particularly now, that he not feel rejected."

"I'll fly out Saturday morning. I'll be there for lunch, then I'll have to fly back on Sunday. Tell Adam I'll see him at your house for lunch," she said with sudden exhilaration. "Oh, God, Vanessa, I can't believe this is happening!"

Tina told no one that she was flying East for the weekend. Instead she put out the story that she would be closeted in her rented house in Malibu to learn lines and unwind from the week's filming. Her thoughts were monopolized by the coming confrontation—a scene as traumatic as any part in any film she'd ever made. But this would be real, she and Adam facing reality.

She was churning with impatience on the flight to New York. Was she dressed properly? Adam might accept a flamboyant movie star as an aunt. How would he feel about her as a mother? She wore one of Vanessa's elegant wool suits. Vanessa had long ago taught her to dress with taste rather than for drama. Her own looks, her jewelry, provided the excitement.

Vanessa was waiting at JFK with the limousine. They embraced warmly and settled themselves in the car.

"Vanessa, I've never been so scared in my life," Tina said, but her face was radiant in anticipation.

"It's the right thing to do," Vanessa insisted. "Adam adores you."

"Will he be at the house?"

"He and Suzy are probably there by now. They were taking Wendy iceskating at Rockefeller Center this morning."

At the house Adam welcomed her with reassuring

642

affection. Vanessa quickly spirited off Suzy and Wendy so that Tina could be alone with Adam.

"Adam, you look marvelous," Tina said. "I'm proud of the way you beat the drugs."

"It was awfully expensive," he faltered, but he was pleased by her acceptance.

"Adam, nothing's too expensive for you." She paused, took a deep breath, exhaled. "Look, Vanessa told me what happened with Eva. I've tried to think up the right words to say what I have to tell you, but I'm not a Hollywood scriptwriter." Her smile was wry. She suppressed an urge to pull Adam into her arms. "Adam, Eva and Sal are not your parents." She saw the startled disbelief in his eyes. "No, Adam. You were adopted. I'm your mother."

Tina told him the circumstances of his birth, her belief that her brother and sister-in-law would give him the real home she could not provide, her battles with Sal and Eva to be part of his life.

"I thought they'd be wonderful parents for you," Tina said. "They loved you."

"As long as I did what they wanted me to do." Adam's bitterness seeped through. "And I loved them," he said with painful honesty. "Even now I can't believe they pushed me out of their lives this way."

"You have your mother," Tina said exultantly, reaching for him. "Oh, baby, you don't know how I've longed for this moment."

Forty-seven

Suzy felt a sense of warm satisfaction when Adam settled into a job at an off-campus bookstore and said he'd work there until they returned to school in September. He insisted on sharing the apartment rent despite her protests. They hadn't told her mother that Adam was living here, though sometimes Suzy suspected her mother knew.

They would have been happy except for Adam's frustration at not knowing who his father was. Tina refused to identify him. All she'd told Adam was that his father had been a university professor in Vienna before World War II and had had to run from the Nazis.

"She told me, too," Adam said one cold January night over a pasta dinner in the Village, "that in the spring my father will be celebrating Passover rather than Easter." He grinned. "That makes me half Jewish."

"If we ever have kids," Suzy said seriously, "we'll raise them Jewish. We'll send them to Sunday school so that they know who they are, and they'll have bar mitzvahs or bat mitzvahs."

"Hey, how many are you planning on?" he teased.

"Oh, no more than two," she assured him. "We don't want to contribute to overpopulation. But meanwhile" — her knee nudged his beneath the table — "let's go home and practice."

Adam was struggling with the lock on the apartment door when the phone began to ring inside.

"Adam, hurry," Suzy said. "You know I can't bear it when somebody hangs up just as I pick up the phone."

The caller was CeeCee. In the background Suzy heard a Janis Joplin record.

"Darling, where the hell have you been?" CeeCee scolded. "I'm a free woman!"

"Adam and I went down to the Village for dinner," Suzy told her. "When were you sprung?"

"This morning. I'm back at my apartment. Come over and celebrate."

"It's kind of late," Suzy demurred, exchanging a wistful look with Adam.

"You and Adam are my two closest friends in the world," CeeCee declared. Were they? Suzy wondered. Probably the most available. "I've got this fabulous bottle of Dom Perignon chilling. Emil's down in Palm Beach — we talked hours over the phone — and there's nobody else around that means a damn to me."

"Just for a little while," Suzy capitulated, ignoring Adam's pantomimed protest. In a funny kind of way she felt protective toward Cee Cee. "We'll be right over."

When they arrived at CeeCee's, she had ordered a lavish spread sent up from Reuben's. She kissed Suzy, then Adam.

"You saved my life," she said softly to Adam. "At the sanitarium I heard about it. But that part of my life is over." She gestured dramatically. "I told Emil I'll do one more film with him, then I'm taking a crack at Hollywood. Who knows?" she said. "I might become the new Brigitte Bardot."

* * *

Vanessa returned in late February from an exhausting trip to the Orient to buy fabrics. She was convinced that the young mood in lush, exotic fabrics and trim was what their customers wanted. Now she sat alone in the office of the design studio and waited for Frank to appear so they could discuss purchases. A dank chill invaded the room, but she felt a comfortable mellowness. Her mind was already at work on new designs.

She straightened up in her chair at the sound of Frank's footsteps in the hall. He would carry on about her being extravagant in her buying; she expected that. He'd boast about his recent run-ins with heads of some of their most important stores, in which he always emerged the victor. Then he'd glance at his watch and mutter something about an appointment with his horse trainer.

They'd seen little of each other since her plane had landed last night at JFK. Arnie and Phyllis had come out with the limousine to accompany her to the house and to brief her on the important developments that had occurred during her absence. Maria had insisted that Wendy remain at the house to study for a test rather than drive out to the airport. Suzy and Adam had been at the house to welcome her back, a gesture she found endearing.

"Vanessa, I've been doing a lot of thinking while you were away," Frank said brusquely as he stalked into the room. His psychedelic tie was incongruous with his finely tailored, conservative Brooks Brothers suit. A tie chosen, Vanessa suspected, by Edie, and worn to make Frank feel young. "We have to talk."

"We usually do when I return from a trip." Why did she always get so tense when Frank was around?

Frank dropped into the chair across from hers, a

faint paunch visible now despite the fine tailoring and his sporadic attendance at the gym.

"We can't stay stagnant this way. You won't agree to a takeover by a conglomerate. You—"

"Frank, you see what happens when a conglomerate moves in," she reminded him sharply. It was unnerving to see how many firms were selling out to the conglomerate monsters. It was an alarming trend that had started slowly ten years ago and was building to alarming proportions. "The original owners become lackeys!"

"The wave of the future is to go public," Frank said grimly. "We gross around $10 million a year. Jonathan Logan grosses around $265 million in an off-year. We can't survive the old way. We're living in a world where everything is *big*. We've got to become part of a giant to stay in the swim." He paused. "Or expand into a giant ourselves. Move into new areas. Look at the sensation Blass is creating with his menswear. He's—"

"Frank, we are not Bill Blass," Vanessa interrupted.

"Blass is doing for menswear what woman designers have done for ready-to-wear couture. He's making men conscious of the *designer*. I want to get in there right behind Blass. We can clean up. 'Frank Bernstein for Creations by Vanessa Conrad,'" he said with relish.

"Frank, you're not a designer." Vanessa stared at him in amazement.

"So what?" he lifted his chin in defiance. "I'll hire a team to do the designing; it wouldn't be the first time. The important thing is to build a designer name in menswear."

"No," Vanessa rejected flatly. She had not expected him to bring up this menswear deal again.

"Yes!" Frank shouted, his face flushed. "I'm tired of

taking all this shit from you. We're equal partners. You keep forgetting that." She flinched before the naked hatred in his eyes. *What had happened to them?* "Enough of this already." He had come in here knowing she would refuse to go along with the menswear line. She braced herself for trouble. "I want out, Vanessa. Either you buy out my 50 percent or I'll sell to an outsider. That won't be hard to set up," he said with savage satisfaction. "And don't go running to check out our partnership agreement." She hadn't looked at that agreement in years. She'd always trusted Frank. "The agreement provides for a buyout by either partner."

"Frank, this is insane," she said unsteadily. Could she run the business alone?

"It's what I want. That—and a divorce."

Vanessa sat frozen. Her whole world was in chaos. Frank had been part of her life for almost nineteen years, her husband for sixteen years. And now he wanted a divorce. To marry Edie?

"The divorce is long past due." She forced herself to respond. "We've had no marriage for years, Frank." Yet visions of the old Frank assaulted her, and she felt a painful sense of loss. That Frank was long gone.

"We won't spread it around right away," he said self-consciously. He wasn't marrying Edie, she guessed with a touch of cynicism. He wanted to keep the divorce quiet as long as possible. "Eventually it'll come out, of course," he shrugged. "One of us can go down to Mexico for a fast one. Of course, I'll expect the right to see Wendy as often as I like."

"Of course." She suppressed a bitter smile. Even living in the same house, he saw Wendy no more than once a week. The hostility between him and Suzy had soared over the past three years. He hated Suzy's idealism.

"Now, about the buyout. I'll have my lawyer contact you tomorrow. It won't be cheap," he warned maliciously. "Launching a new menswear line in the right way is an expensive proposition."

Feeling adrift, unable to concentrate, Vanessa sat alone in her office and tried to deal with this violent upheaval in her life. She would have to carry on Creations by Vanessa Conrad on her own. Thank God for Arnie. But even together, could they swing it? Everything she had fought to build for nineteen years—a Seventh Avenue empire—was in jeopardy.

Needing to share Frank's ultimatum with someone, she reached for the phone. In moments Arnie was on one line and Phyllis was on the extension.

She told them about the divorce, something they had all expected for a long time. And then she rocked them with Frank's insistence that she buy him out.

"He's branching out into menswear," Phyllis guessed immediately. "That goddamn ego of his."

"Vanessa, we're going out to dinner in ten minutes. Join us." Arnie urged. "We can talk this out."

"Come over to the house for dinner instead." Vanessa said. "Wendy will be expecting me. We'll talk after dinner."

At the house Vanessa explained briefly to Maria what was happening.

"Good," Maria said vigorously. "He's not a good man anymore. Get him out of your life."

"Do you think the girls will be upset?"

"No," Maria was frank. "It won't surprise Suzy, not with him stuck away in his own apartment all the time. And Wendy? How much does she see of him?"

"I'm afraid for the business," Vanessa confessed.

"Most of what was good in the business came from you," Maria said bluntly. "You're a strong woman. You'll survive this."

After dinner Vanessa settled down in the library with Arnie and Phyllis while Wendy went to her room to study.

"Frank's going to make horrible demands," she warned them. "And then he's going to take whatever he can dig out of the business and throw it down the drain on that menswear deal."

"You'll need a smart corporate lawyer," Arnie said quietly. "Not me. I'm strictly real estate. I'll make some inquiries and —"

"I know somebody," Vanessa interrupted with a sense of relief. "Larry Fraser. Remember, I told you about meeting him down in Alabama."

"Fraser's good." Arnie turned to Phyllis. "He's handled some major mergers."

"Then I'll call him first thing in the morning. I hope he has time to handle it." Vanessa hesitated. "Frank can fly down to Mexico for one of these quickie divorces. I won't fight it."

Vanessa referred Frank's attorney to Larry Fraser to discuss the terms of the buyout. The evening of his meeting with the other attorney, Larry came to the house to report to her. When she inquired about Danny, his eyes reflected his pain. There was little improvement in Danny's condition.

Larry was indignant about the terms Frank's attorney had presented to him.

"Frank's out of his mind, Vanessa. He's asking for three million for his 50 percent." He took a deep breath. "And he's demanding it within six months."

Vanessa gasped in disbelief.

"He knows I can't put my hands on that kind of money! We have a fortune tied up in inventory! I've just bought heavily in the Orient. I know that on paper we're a wealthy company, but I can't pull out that kind of cash. Does our partnership agreement allow him to make that kind of demand?"

"It does," Larry acknowledged.

Vanessa sat still, reeling in shock.

"Then somehow I'll have to manage it. I'll talk to the bank about a loan. I can mortgage the houses." She frowned in distaste. "I'll have to factor."

"Frank's lawyer pointed out that the houses are owned jointly," Larry told her. "Frank is willing to give up his ownership of the town house. He wants the house in Southampton and the Croton house."

"He has me over a barrel, hasn't he?"

"I'm afraid so." Larry was somber. "That's a lot of capital to pull out of the business."

"I have no choice but to raise the funds. I won't let a stranger come into my business, Larry. An outsider could destroy it."

"I'll be in touch with Frank's lawyer. We'll fight for time," he promised. "Six months is an outrageous period." He eyed her solicitously. "I suspect his pulling out means some major restructuring in management?"

"I've always handled the designing. Frank handled the business. In all these years naturally I've learned a lot. And I've shared in the major business decisions."

"You'll swing it, Vanessa," Larry asserted.

"Thank God Arnie will be at my side. We have to keep the company running. I've worked too hard to let him cut me down."

Suzy hurried from her apartment and over to Broadway to look for a taxi. She resented CeeCee's emergencies—CeeCee always assumed she'd drop everything and run, and she always did. CeeCee had sounded hysterical on the phone. *"You're my friend, Suzy — you've got to help me."*

Suzy spied a cab, lifted a hand. The cab pulled to a noisy stop at the curb. Suzy climbed in and gave the driver CeeCee's address. She'd seen CeeCee only that one time, with Adam, since she'd left the sanitarium. CeeCee was on a Rudi Gernreich kick now, impatient to make a Hollywood contract. She was railing that she should have made this move when she was still on top.

As Suzy emerged from the elevator, CeeCee confronted her in the hall.

"Suzy, I feel so awful," she wailed from the doorway. "You have to help me!" She wore jeans and a wrinkled T-shirt. Her hair was disheveled, her face devoid of makeup.

"CeeCee, are you on something?" Suzy demanded when they were inside the apartment.

"No," she denied. "I'm pregnant!"

"Maybe you're just late," Suzy said.

"Eleven weeks?" she jeered, her voice shrill. "I didn't realize it was so long because I never stay on a real schedule. But my clothes are all tight around the waist! And I feel so rotten every morning. Suzy, help me find somebody good to give me an abortion. I don't want one of those butchers."

"You don't know for sure yet that you're pregnant," Suzy pointed out. "First you have to take a test. Then we worry."

"I'm pregnant, Suzy. I've got all the symptoms. I don't need a test to tell me."

"Who's the father, CeeCee?" Maybe the best way out was for CeeCee to marry and have the baby.

"God, how would I know?" CeeCee squinted in thought, shrugged. "I was so bored at the sanitarium, and some of the male attendants were young and well hung." Unexpectedly she giggled. "I got bored regularly."

"I think you ought to tell your mother." Suzy was somber.

"You're out of your mind!"

"No. Your mother will help. She'll find some quiet sanitarium where you can go for an abortion. Cee-Cee, she'll do it because of your father," Suzy reasoned. "You know how he's always terrified of some scandal that'll ruin his congressional career. Call her, CeeCee."

"I just want an abortion," CeeCee wailed. "I don't want to drag my mother into this."

"Your mother will make sure you go to a sanitarium where there are decent doctors. CeeCee, you don't want to die from a bungled abortion," Suzy said harshly, knowing that was the only way to get through to CeeCee.

CeeCee went white with alarm, her colorful imagination envisioning a tragic catastrophe.

"I'll call my mother. But you talk to her, Suzy. She'll take it better from you."

Suzy stayed overnight with CeeCee until Pat arrived from Washington. She was afraid to leave her alone, worried that in her present state of mind she might head for Dr. Tyler again. And she stayed at CeeCee's request, thoroughly uncomfortable, while Pat fought against CeeCee's having an abortion.

"It's my body!" CeeCee shrieked. "Nobody has a right to tell me what to do! You're just scared because the priests keep saying it's wrong!"

"CeeCee, girls die from abortions," Pat said with calculated calm.

"They also die from having babies," CeeCee shot back.

"Childbirth is a normal event," Pat dismissed this. "You could die having an abortion. Like that girl here in New York who died last week. A lovely twenty-three-year-old secretary. It was in all the newspapers, CeeCee."

Suzy watched CeeCee falter, overcome by indecision. She knew an abortion under decent conditions was no more dangerous that childbirth, but Pat's religious faith rejected abortion.

"I couldn't stand everybody knowing," CeeCee whispered. "They'd think I was a kook not to have an abortion."

"We'll find a quiet little house up in Putnam County where you can stay till the baby's born." Pat spoke with reassuring calm. "It'll be put up for adoption. Nobody'll know who you are. Everything will be kept secret. You'll tell everybody you're going away to a retreat for six months. You want to think about your career. And afterward," Pat promised, "Tina will introduce you to important people in Hollywood. It'll be a whole new start for you, darling."

"I'll go crazy staying up at house alone," CeeCee reproached, but Suzy knew she would have the baby. Her mother had frightened her into submission.

"You won't be alone. I'll hire a housekeeper-companion. And I'll come up often. You'll have your records and television and a car for driving around the countryside. You'll have the baby in a little hospital where nobody will know you." Pat spoke as though to a small child.

"I don't want to see the baby," CeeCee insisted and dropped a hand to her stomach. "Yuch! I'll hate popping out like a balloon. I'll hate the baby for doing this to me."

"Then you won't ever see the baby," Pat promised, staring at her daughter as though she were a stranger.

"I'll arrange for an adoption."

"Are you sure Tina will help me in Hollywood?"

"Tina will do it for me," Pat assured her.

Pat seemed so sad, Suzy thought. She was beautiful, rich, and a celebrity in her own right. But she seemed so sad.

Forty-eight

Edie sat hunched over a copy of the *New York Post*, in her new red bikini, glued to the item in Earl Wilson's column. *The rotten bastard*. He hadn't said one word to her about his divorce. She had to read about it in a newspaper!

Seething with anger, she left her chair to go into the bedroom to change back into hip-hugger jeans and tie-dye T-shirt. She matter-of-factly admired her reflection in the mirror. Tonight she ought to wear a midi when Frank showed up to take her to dinner. He said every man he knew hated midis.

On impulse she dropped to the edge of the queen-size bed and reached for the telephone. She wasn't sure how to handle the new of Frank's divorce. If he wanted her to know, he would have told her. He was afraid she'd start thinking in terms of a wedding dress. But she wasn't prepared for a confrontation.

Her mother listened silently while Edie swore at men in general and Frank in particular.

"Baby, you gotta use your head now," Mrs. Russell said softly. "This could be your big chance."

"Should I threaten to leave?" But suppose he let her

go? Give up this pad? Give up her gorgeous clothes, the summer at Fire Island?

"No," her mother said sharply. "Edie, use your head. Tie him up for good. Get yourself pregnant."

"Ma, he'd be mad as hell."

"At first. But then he'd start to think about it. A guy his age, close to fifty, giving his wife a baby? Tellin' the world he's still got what it takes. He'll marry you, Edie. You'll have everything you ever wanted."

With Larry at her side, Vanessa held long conferences with the bankers. She talked to some about loans on the business, to others about a large mortgage on the town house, which she owned free and clear as part of the divorce settlement. She was still trying to adjust to the fast divorce. In private life as well as in business she was Vanessa Conrad now.

Everybody on Seventh Avenue was buzzing about the divorce. Nobody knew about the imminent buyout. Frank remained for now at the helm of the business. Phyllis and Arnie made sure Vanessa and Frank didn't have to see each other any more than was absolutely essential. They were strangers now. He had vacated his apartment in the town house the day after his return from Mexico. Maria had closed it up.

She met with Larry at least twice a week to work out the myriad details of the buyout. Frank was adamant about the financial arrangements. He wanted the $3 million by September 1, 1969. Otherwise he would turn over his 50 percent stock to a conglomerate. He was impatient to launch Frank Bernstein for Men.

For Vanessa, it was agonizing to saddle the business with these huge loans, but she couldn't allow Frank to sell to an outsider. The business must be hers. She prayed that she would be able to cope with the hurdles that lay ahead: meeting her loans and running the business end of Creations by Vanessa Conrad without Frank. She tried to block from her mind all the talk of a recession within the next few months. The firm must earn its top grosses if she was to meet her obligations.

She heard via the grapevine that Frank was renting out the Southampton house for the summer. Larry urged her to rent a beach house despite her monumental expenses so that Maria could take Wendy out there as usual and she would have a place to run to on weekends, away from the staggering schedule she had assumed.

In quaint and charming Bridgehampton—where briefly she had been Mrs. Eduardo Montino, wife of a young lieutenant—she rented a small house that Maria could handle with only a woman coming in for day work. This summer she would have no time to entertain at weekend dinners for twenty. She was fighting for survival.

Suzy and Adam were planning to spend a week at the Bridgehampton house in July. Both were working until the fall session at school started. Adam at the bookstore, Suzy in a Greenwich Village boutique. Suzy talked vaguely about a job in publishing when she graduated next June, or in sales. Both she and Adam were involved with an active anti-Veitnam group.

Vanessa worried about Suzy and Adam's relationship, but she didn't dare ask questions. She was convinced they were in love and relieved that Adam showed no signs of being drawn back into the drug scene. Perhaps they were waiting for him to prove this to himself as well as Suzy before they made any commitments.

Tina wrote enthusiastically about Adam's plans to switch to pre-law. Early in August she flew into New York from Rome on one of her whirlwind trips and took them all out to dinner at La Cote Basque to celebrate his decision to go on to law school. Later, in the privacy of Vanessa's bedroom, Tina asked if Suzy and Adam harbored marriage plans. Vanessa admitted they were silent on the subject.

"Can you imagine me as a grandmother?" Tina sighed extravagantly. "I'll even baby-sit for them!"

"Don't ask questions," Vanessa warned with a laugh. "Let's just stay on the sidelines and watch."

"Is there some new man in your life?" Tina asked archly.

"Don't be absurd." Vanessa had not meant to sound so sharp.

"What's absurd?" Tina lifted an eyebrow in reproach. "You're forty-four and beautiful."

"Almost menopausal," Vanessa reminded her.

"For Christ sake, that doesn't affect your sex drive," Tina scolded and laughed. "Who's this Mr. Fraser that Suzy keeps talking about?"

"Larry Fraser. He's the father of her friend Danny, the one who had that devastating drug experience. Danny was such a warm, sweet, bright kid, Tina. It's tragic."

"I'd *die* if that happened to Adam."

"Larry has brought in specialists from all over the country. He's grateful for even the tiniest improvement." Vanessa paused. "And he's my attorney."

"How's the situation with the business?" Tina's face grew somber.

"I'll be able to buy out Frank," Vanessa told her. "Everybody on Seventh Avenue is watching to see if I can make it without him. Nobody likes Frank, but they think he's a kind of miracle man when it comes to business."

Edie, one of Frank's Saint Laurent shirts over her bikini, was waiting at the ferry when Frank arrived early Friday afternoon. He had this crazy habit of making sure he came out when the ferry was least crowded. Which infuriated Edie because he didn't have to worry anymore about somebody seeing him and running to tell Vanessa. He was a divorced man; he could screw anybody he wanted.

"Hi," she drawled as he approached with his valise. She had brought along their own little wagon for transport, as did everyone in Fire Island tradition. "Hot as hell in the city?"

"Baby, it's a bitch." He dropped an arm about her waist as they headed toward their rented house. "Got something cool and tall waiting for me?"

"Me," she flipped.

"You're hot and tall. That's for after I've had my drink."

Edie waited until he was stretched out on the bed, a Tom Collins in one hand, before she sprang her big surprise.

He sat up, set down the tall, frosted glass, and glared at her, momentarily speechless.

"I said I'm pregnant," she repeated sweetly. "We're having a baby." A faint emphasis on the "we."

"What the hell's the matter with you? Too lazy to take care of yourself?"

"Frank, nothing is 100 percent sure," she parroted her mother. She pretended to be hurt. "I thought you'd be excited. Our baby, honey."

Frank stared at her, moistened his lower lip with his tongue. His eyes roamed over every seductive inch of

660

her.

"I suppose we'll have to get married," he drawled. "Can't let our kid come into the world a little bastard."

Mom was smart, Edie told herself as Frank left the bed and crossed to pull her in against him. He was hot enough to give her another kid right now. So damn proud of himself. Just like Mom said.

She was going to be Mrs. Frank Bernstein. With a house in Southampton and her own car and a diamond solitaire big enough to blind.

Late in July Vanessa read in *Women's Wear Daily* that Frank had married Edie Russell. For one brief instant she felt as though Frank had smacked her hard across the face. Her ex-husband had married a girl almost half her age. But she had no time to explore her emotions. With Frank away from the business she was carrying tremendous responsibilities.

Several evenings a week Arnie and Phyllis came over to the town house for after-dinner conferences. There were not enough hours during the business day to cope with everything. Sometimes Larry joined them. It pleased Vanessa that Arnie and Phyllis had taken instantly to Larry, and he to them. Both men had been born in the same neighborhood in the Bronx, had gone on from City College, with time out to fight in Europe with the American armed forces, to NYU Law School.

Vanessa was cutting down on her usual business-motivated socializing, though it seemed to her that this fall there were fewer parties than usual. Every Friday, before driving out to Bridgehampton for the weekend, she had dinner with Larry. She knew that his wife and his daughter—with one marriage behind her at twenty-four—were part of the international jet

661

set and were rarely at home. For Larry, the apartment on Fifth Avenue was full of ghosts.

Ostensibly she and Larry were meeting for dinner to discuss various details of the buyout. In truth, they found strength in each other's companionship.

Vanessa tried to tell herself, with the September 1 buyout meeting fast approaching, that she wasn't upset by the rumors that Edie was pregnant. Edie Russell, now Edie Bernstein, was carrying Wendy's half-brother or half-sister. She was anxious about how Wendy would react to this.

On September 1 at 10:00 A.M. Vanessa and Larry sat down with Frank and his trio of expensive attorneys to sign the takeover papers. Glamorous and beautiful in her favorite gray linen suit, Vanessa appeared posed and faintly aloof. The lawyers talked, argued, compromised. At Larry's signal she signed the papers that had to be signed. With an air of triumph — and checks for $3 million tucked in his wallet — Frank strode for the last time from his office at Creations by Vanessa Conrad. The business, hocked to the hilt, was all hers.

Larry came to dinner on a Friday evening in mid-October in rare high spirits. He teased Wendy affectionately when she effervesced about the slumber party at a classmate's house. But not until they settled down for after-dinner coffee before the library fireplace did he confide in Vanessa.

"I'm taking a major step in my life," he said with quiet pleasure. "Yesterday was my fiftieth birthday. I sat down and took a long look at where I've been and where I'm headed. You're the first to know, Vanessa. I'm retiring from my law firm."

She gazed at him in disbelief. "Larry, you're too

young to retire."

"I'll continue to handle your affairs," he promised. "But I'm pulling out of the rat race."

"But you've been so successful," she protested.

"I've been successful financially beyond my wildest dreams," Larry agreed. "But I haven't done what I want to do with my life. I came out of law school with no intention of becoming involved in corporate law. I saw myself in the public service area. I shouldn't have allowed my wife and father-in-law to push me into corporate law, but Muriel was pregnant with my older son and it seemed the way to go."

"What will you do?" Vanessa asked.

"I want to work where and when I please," he said quietly. "As counsel to whatever groups I feel are making a contribution. I don't mean to climb on a soapbox," he said apologetically, "but after what's happened to my two boys, I've become aware of the value of each day. I've promised myself to squander no more days on activities that offer me no real satisfaction."

"I think your sons would have been very proud of that kind of commitment." She felt a sting of tears. Eddie would have understood Larry.

"Next Wednesday the first Vietnam Moratorium Day will be celebrated. With prayer vigils, candlelight processions, mass meetings, and black armbands. Will you take time out of your schedule to observe it with me?"

"I'd like that," Vanessa accepted.

Vanessa was preparing for bed when the private line in her bedroom, known only to a handful of people, rang. Suzy, she surmised. Ever since the divorce Suzy had become touchingly solicitous; she often phoned around this hour, as though to assure her mother that she was loved.

"Hello—" Her voice was warm.

"Vanessa, I'm up at the hospital in Dutchess County." Pat, always in command of her emotions, was distraught.

"Is CeeCee in labor?" She wasn't due for several weeks.

"No. I found her in her room in a coma an hour ago. I'm spending a few days at the cottage with her. Vanessa, the doctors say she's been into drugs again." She paused, struggling for control. "It could be bad."

"I'll drive right up," Vanessa said quickly. "Give me the name of the hospital and the town."

She scribbled down the information, managed a few words of comfort.

"She's registered here as Cecile Reynolds," Pat cautioned. "I'm Mrs. Reynolds."

"I should be there in less than two hours."

If Don was asleep, she'd have to drive herself, Vanessa thought. She hated night driving, but Pat mustn't be alone. She assumed Paul wasn't with her though he had known about CeeCee's pregnancy for the past three months. He'd be terrified of being recognized.

When she called Don, he responded sympathetically. He would bring the car around in ten minutes. Vanessa changed into slacks and a warm sweater. How, she wondered, had CeeCee got hold of the drugs with the housekeeper constantly at her side?

By midnight the limousine was charging up the highway. Did this mean CeeCee would lose the baby? Vanessa asked herself. Didn't she know enough to stay off drugs when she was pregnant? For the baby's sake if not for her own.

At the small hospital, Don parked the car and took Vanessa into the lobby. A nurse at the desk directed Vanessa to the second floor while Don settled down in the waiting room with a magazine. He knew this would be a long night.

"Pat," she called softly and Pat turned from gazing out the window with a look of gratitude. She wore her hair pulled severely from her face, no makeup, her contacts replaced by heavy-framed glasses. No one would ever guess this was the much-photographed wife of Senator Paul Roberts.

"She's in surgery," Pat struggled to keep her voice even. She pointed to a pair of swinging doors far down the hall. "She hasn't responded to treatment. They've decided on a cesarean section. Vanessa, *why?* Why did she go back to drugs?"

"Pat, you did everything possible." She reached for Pat's hand. "Nobody could watch her twenty-four hours a day."

"I should have had nurses around the clock," Pat reproached herself. "A housekeeper was not enough. Somehow, she managed to get cocaine and amphetamines. The doctors found it all in her bloodstream. The housekeeper said she woke up one morning last week; and when she went to the car she found the gas tank nearly empty. She thinks CeeCee may have driven into New York—at almost eight months pregnant—and back."

"To Dr. Tyler's office," Vanessa surmised. "That man ought to be jailed."

She drew Pat down to a sofa and told her about Dr. Tyler. Suzy had been most graphic.

"How much longer are they going to be in there?" Pat's eyes stared at the swinging doors that led to the operating room. "It's been almost an hour."

"Soon," Vanessa promised in the age-old manner.

Only moments later a physician in operating room garb, serious and faintly grim, came toward them. Pat stumbled to her feet, and Vanessa rose beside her, feeling Pat's pain.

"I'm sorry, Mrs. Reynolds. There was nothing we could do for Cecile. We did save the baby."

"Thank you." Pat's face was devoid of color.

"It's a little girl. Just under six pounds. She was at least a month early." His face tightened. "A beautiful little girl, who's suffering from drug withdrawal."

"Oh, my God." Pat closed her eyes in anguish.

"Would you like to see her?"

"Please."

"A nurse will call you in a few moments," the doctor said and left them alone.

"Cocaine and amphetamines," Pat whispered bitterly. "Where did we go wrong with CeeCee?"

A nurse took them to the special care nursery and showed them CeeCee's daughter. Tiny, scrawny, twitching, moving with the stiff-limbed motions associated with drug withdrawal. Her tiny face was beautiful and unmarred by labor. And distorted in pain.

"I'll be her mother," Pat vowed, unaware of the tears that filled her eyes and spilled over. "I'll make it up to her for this awful beginning. Somehow I'll make it up to her."

Vanessa and Tina flanked Pat while CeeCee was buried beside Biff. The funeral was attended by top members of Congress, a Supreme Court judge, and Democratic leaders. The newspapers carried front-page stories about the tragic death of the beautiful young actress-daughter of Congressman and Mrs. Paul Roberts, which followed an attack of peritonitis." Later the country would learn that the congressman and his wife were adopting an infant in memory of their daughter.

While CeeCee was being eulogized at the cemetery

in Virginia, a memorial party was held at the Studio. The sofa and chairs were filled with friends and acquaintances, and people sprawled on the floor and exchanged special stories about CeeCee. Others danced while Janis Joplin on the stereo belted out CeeCee's favorite songs. Suzy and Adam were there, too, to say a final farewell to CeeCee.

"This is the way she would have wanted it," Adam said softly while Emil prepared to show CeeCee's last film. "Everybody talking about her, feeling sentimental and sad. CeeCee Roberts, the star attraction."

Forty-nine

Only a few days after CeeCee's daughter, Cecile Joyce, was born, Edie gave birth to a son. Frank phoned Vanessa shortly past 6:00 A.M. to report the event.

"Tell Wendy she has a new brother! Eight pounds two ounces, with my shoulders," he boasted. "Gave Edie a helluva time—"

"Congratulations." Vanessa struggled to sound fully awake. She hadn't spoken to Frank since their September 1 meeting. But she had mentally screamed at him on endless occasions when the business threatened to collapse under the weight of its debts. She was plagued by insomnia night after night while Frank and Edie were running through what gossips said was almost a million on a showplace at Fire Island and a co-op on Fifth Avenue. He'd rented space for his new firm and hired a prestigious press agent—all on money drained from Creations by Vanessa Conrad.

"He's just three hours and twenty-two minutes old," Frank reported jubilantly. "Wendy will want to see him. Suppose I pick her up in a couple of hours and bring her over to the hospital?"

"This is a school day, Frank," she admonished, her heart pounding. She had known Edie was pregnant. Twice she had hastily left charity affairs when she spied Edie, gowned in caftans by Lanvin, across the room hanging possessively on to Frank. Why was she upset this way? Wendy's life wouldn't change because Frank had another child. She was a bright, down-to-earth little girl; she wouldn't be upset that she had a new half-brother who lived somewhere else. "Wendy can see the baby this afternoon."

"We're not bothering with a *briss*," he said self-consciously. "Every boy baby gets circumcized in the hospital anyway."

"I hope you both will be very happy." Was she supposed to be ecstatic because her ex-husband, whose personal greed was putting her company through hell, was a father again? "Call back around eight. Wendy will be awake by then. You can tell her yourself. But hospital rules don't allow a child her age on the maternity floor."

"Why not?" Frank was indignant.

"It's something to do with children carrying in germs," Vanessa said vaguely. She stifled a yawn. "Call Wendy later, Frank."

Once off the phone Vanessa lay back against the pillows and tried to accept the news. She'd tell Wendy herself, she decided. Wendy must understand that her father's new son was no threat to her. She smiled wryly. Sometimes Wendy must feel that she didn't have a father. How often did she see him?

As 1970 rolled along Vanessa worried, like all of Seventh Avenue, about the flagging economy. She was constantly aware that she needed top grosses to be able to meet her monthly obligations to the banks — at a time when sales were off. Even the custom salon, catering to wealthy socialites and high-earning entertainment luminaries who rarely bothered to inquire about prices, felt the recession. The rich were not entertaining as much as they used to.

Of necessity — a lack of designing time made it mandatory — Vanessa had slashed the custom spring/summer collection to half the usual number of models. Some fashion critics admonished her for neglecting the collection. They didn't know how desperately she wanted to increase the collection to the two hundred of the Dior tradition.

Larry had become an unofficial member of the firm. Both she and Arnie respected his advice. Larry expressed frustration that he was not in a position to help financially. When he withdrew from his law firm, accepting a modest yearly retainer for the ensuing ten years, his wife had sued for divorce. He had set up a trust fund that would care for Danny's needs as long as he lived. And most of his assets had gone to his wife in the divorce settlement.

Vanessa told herself that she and Larry were close friends, brought together by their children. But she was all too aware of heart-stopping moments when their eyes met and held. No, she warned herself. Twice she had been in love. That was enough for one lifetime. She had her business and her children. She needed nothing more.

Suzy's graduation from Barnard was the one pleasurable event in Vanessa's harried existence. Knowing her mother's financial problems, Suzy insisted on only a very small dinner party at home to celebrate. For Vanessa it was a joyous occasion, a brief respite from the tribulation of business. Tina flew in from Rome. Still in mourning for CeeCee, Pat sent flowers and a magnificent gift.

Vanessa and Tina lingered in the library long after the guests had gone. Suzy had succumbed to Wendy's pleas and was staying over for the night. The two girls had gone up to Wendy's bedroom so Wendy could show Suzy her new swimsuits.

Both Vanessa and Tina were in a sentimental mood as they discussed the graduation exercises.

"Eddie would have been so happy to see her graduate from his sister college," Vanessa said nostalgically. "And she looked so beautiful."

"Remember our high school graduation?" Tina reminisced. "I swore to go back to Pinewood one day and throw a wild, extravagant party because Agnes Lowell didn't invite us to her champagne party." She paused, her eyes speculative. "Vanessa, you must know Larry Fraser's in love with you."

"Larry and I are very close friends, Tina." That was true. It shocked her sometimes to realize how much Larry had become part of her life. "But that's as far as it can go. I thought I would die when I lost Eddie. And I hurt a lot when Frank began to change. I couldn't go through another loss like those two. Besides"—she managed a shaky laugh—"I have no time for a man in my life. Except as a dear and cherished friend."

Larry had changed since his divorce, she thought tenderly. She felt a quiet satisfaction in him now because he was involved in a cause, and the anti-Vietnam cause was foremost in his life. He had given two sons to the war. He was convinced Danny's condition was an offshoot of his grief for his brother. But Larry had learned to live with his losses. He was warm and witty; he made a point of coaxing her into laughter. Eddie, too, had made her laugh—a precious trait in a man.

671

Maria brought in a coffee tray, and the other two insisted she stay. Tina and Maria reminisced about the months they'd spent together in Venice when Tina had been carrying Adam.

Had she come full circle? Vanessa asked herself. She had started with nothing. Was she to lose the business and the house to the banks? To return to nothing? At forty-five it would be difficult to start over.

She was prepared for bed but too restless to sleep when she heard a faint knock at the door of her room.

"Mother?" Suzy called tentatively.

"Come in, darling."

Suzy opened the door and walked into Vanessa's sitting room.

"I saw the light under the door. I figured you hadn't gone to sleep."

"Too big a day for me to go right to sleep," Vanessa smiled. "You, too?"

"Yeah." Suzy dropped into one of the chintz-covered chairs that flanked the marble-faced fireplace. "It seems pretty definite that I have a job. At a new boutique that's opening up on Madison Avenue."

"You'll enjoy it," Vanessa said. She relished Suzy's newly displayed obsession for clothes.

"I think it'll be a fun place to work. I hate fashion," she said with an eloquent wrinkle of her nose, "but I love clothes."

"Whose clothes do you like these days?" Vanessa asked. She refused to be hurt that her daughter had moved away from her own designs.

"Betsey Johnson," Suzy said slowly. "And Carol Horn and Liz Claiborne. And have you been watching the sportswear by Calvin Klein? It's great."

They talked a while about the new young designers until Suzy began to yawn. Vanessa suppressed the questions that floated about in her mind. Would Suzy ever be seriously interested in designing?

Adam began his senior year at Columbia in September and vowed to graduate with top grades. He was hoping to be accepted at Columbia Law the following semester. Vanessa was pleased that he often accompanied Suzy to the house for dinner. Despite her long hours Vanessa made a point of having dinner with Wendy as often as she could.

One blustery late October evening Suzy arrived at the house without Adam.

"He's studying for midterms," Suzy explained, collapsing beside her mother on a sofa in the library. "Where's Wendy?"

"She'll be here soon. She's at a friend's house." Vanessa put aside her sketchbook. "How are things at the boutique?"

"Exciting sometimes, frustrating other times." Her smile was wry. "The backers are breathing down the girls' necks to go public." The boutique had been founded by the three young designers as a showcase for their own line of designs. "It won't be any fun then." She paused, frowning in thought. "Mother, it's a secret, so don't tell anybody yet. I'm telling you, and Adam will tell Tina—but nobody else," she emphasized. "Next summer Adam and I are getting married."

"Darling, I'm so happy." Vanessa reached to pull Suzy close. "I already think of Adam as my son."

"We don't want a big wedding," Suzy insisted, her face radiant. "Just family and a few friends. Maybe on the beach at Bridgehampton if you take the house again for the summer." She frowned. "I suppose we'll have to have Dad and Edie."

673

"I don't see how we can *not* have them." Frank was the only father Suzy remembered. They'd been on warm terms until Suzy became a teen-ager and Frank decided to play the heavy. But neither Suzy nor Wendy liked Edie, whom they saw rarely. Suzy had dutifully gone once to their new apartment on Fifth Avenue to see the baby. Wendy was torn between resentment of her father's new marriage and delight in her half-brother. "Actually, he should walk with you to the *chupah*." The chupah was the canopy under which the bride and groom took their vows in the Jewish ceremony.

Suzy groaned in dismay. "Maybe he'll be too busy," she said hopefully. "Don't tell him until you have to."

"I won't tell anybody," Vanessa promised. "And I'll take the house again this summer at Bridgehampton. Such a beautiful place for a wedding." Tears stung her eyes. Suzy and Adam would be married in the town where Eddie and she had been so happy.

"Mother, you're very close to Tina. Can't you persuade her to tell Adam about his father? He'll never be truly at peace with himself until he knows."

"I'll try," Vanessa promised. "But don't expect miracles."

Several times within the next few days Vanessa tried, without success, to convince Tina that she should tell Adam who his father was. She made another attempt on the way to JFK with Tina, headed for California and another film with Felix.

"Vanessa, don't ask me to do that!" Tina reproached. "You know I adore Adam. I'll do anything for him—except tell him about Felix."

"From what you've told me about Felix, he'd be happy to know he has a son." Felix's only child, a little girl, had died in a concentration camp.

"Forget it, Vanessa." Tina said brusquely. "I can't

tell him."

With the arrival of 1971, Vanessa hoped for an improvement in business conditions. But sales continued to be sluggish. The customers were resisting the soaring prices. The manufacturers complained they were being pushed out of business because of labor costs. The union refused concessions. Competition, always fierce, became maniacal.

Vanessa had learned through the grapevine that Frank was having difficulties with his new line, which had received poor reviews. Fashions in the men's field were changing drastically, and Frank's designers seemed to be trailing behind.

At an evening conference with Arnie, Phyllis, and Larry, Vanessa brought up the predictions of the economists. The recession showed no indication of abating.

"It's not good," Arnie acknowledged. "Look at the firms that have gone out in the past year. Some of the best in the business. Hannah Troy, Samuel Winston, Patullo-Jo Copeland."

"Too many people are being priced out of the market," Larry remarked. It was fantastic, Vanessa thought, the way he had grasped the field with his sharp legal mind. "I assume you've cut all possible corners?" His eyes swung from Vanessa to Arnie.

"Every one." Arnie was grim. "Despite the recession our labor costs have soared. And for the same reason our contractors have been forced to raise their prices."

"We need a minor miracle to make it through this year," Vanessa said bluntly. She had not slept more than four hours a night for the past ten days. Each night she awoke with a start and was unable to go back to sleep. In those early, sleepless hours of the

675

morning, she had delved into every aspect of their situation. "I think there's only one way to save the business." She took a deep breath. "Licensing. Provided we handle it well. Licensing means income with no output. The European couture has done it for years. Dior, Chanel, Cardin." Ironically Frank had tried to push her into licensing years ago. Some children's wear deal. But that had been the wrong deal and the wrong time. Now licensing could be their salvation.

"Licensing is taking a foothold in this country," Phyllis agreed, the atmosphere suddenly charged with possibility. "Everybody's playing the name game. Vanessa, it could work!"

"Only if we pursue it at just the right moment," Vanessa warned. "Everybody in the field knows we're in tough straits." Nothing was secret in the Seventh Avenue jungle. "We must come up with a sensational collection before you circulate the word," Vanessa turned to Phyllis, "that Vanessa Conrad might be interested in the right kind of licensing." The licensing value of her name depended upon the current collection.

"The fall collection in May," Arnie said, his face lighting up.

"The fall ready-to-wear couture collection," Vanessa stipulated, her mind running in high gear. She remembered the collection that had had to be scrapped because Linda Odell had stolen all their designs. Frank had been furious at their losing the profits on a whole collection because she had used unusually expensive fabrics and trim on the replacement collection. But the gamble, which had resulted in extravagant praise from the press, had paid off. "It'll be taking a wild chance, one that could throw us right out of business, but I want to bring out the most

676

gorgeous ready-to-wear couture that has been seen in years. We'll be lucky to break even, but if the press likes the collection, we'll be in a command position with the licensing."

"With the right licensing deal, you can pick up more than the business earns in a year right now," Larry said softly. "Go for it, Vanessa."

Vanessa spent long hours in the museums before she settled on the right mood for the collection, a feeling that would trickle "up" into the custom salon as well. She bought materials and trim that normally would have ben rejected as beyond the range of anything except haute couture, and she held her breath lest suppliers deny her credit.

Together she and Phyllis planned a spectacular setting for the fashion show in early May. Robbie and Phil came in to help, providing a background that could have graced a major Broadway production. No commentary, Vanessa decreed. Let the drama of the clothes carry the occasion.

After the usual crises that precede most fashion shows, Vanessa geared herself to show the collection. As always, she hovered behind the scenes, inspecting each model to make sure the right accessories were used, calling for the makeup man to correct some tiny imperfection, showing only confidence to the world while inside she churned with doubts and fears. Her entire future depended on the reception of this collection by the unpredictable press.

Gritting her teeth, she waited in the wings for the showing to begin. Larry hovered at her side as the first model appeared on the runway. By the time the fifth model swirled about in her lush burgundy velvet daytime dress Vanessa knew the collection was a success. The buyers were "writing"—making copious notes on their programs, which meant they would be at the showroom to buy. And most important, the critics showed a lively interest.

Two weeks after the showing, with Phyllis adroitly planting rumors that Vanessa was being approached by hopeful licensees, Arnie came in with an offer for Vanessa's name on a line of fine blouses and sweaters for day and evening wear. A hasty conference was called for that night at the house. With another month's bank loans coming due and suppliers already issuing veiled threats about unpaid bills, Vanessa was being wooed with an offer of a $500,000 guarantee over a period of two years.

"It's too low," Larry decided, rejecting the offer by Waterman Industries. The others stared at him in shock. "Vanessa, I'd like to go in and handle this for you." he turned to Arnie in apology. "I've had experience with Waterman. The guarantee is too low, the royalty is too low."

Vanessa knew that Arnie was ambivalent, but her instinct told her that Larry was not grandstanding.

"Represent us in this offer, Larry," she said firmly. "Let's try holding out."

Larry set up an immediate appointment with the top echelon at Waterman Industries. The first meeting came to nothing. Arnie was a nervous wreck. Phyllis sided with Vanessa, and they waited to see whether Waterman would pursue the offer or if another manufacturer would show interest.

Four days later Larry was called in for further negotiations over lunch in the Waterman executive dining room. Vanessa and Arnie waited anxiously in her office for some word from him. Late in the afternoon, as the employees were already beginning to leave for the day, Larry strode into the office. His face was impassive, and Vanessa's heart began to pound.

"What happened?" Arnie asked, voicing the question that Vanessa couldn't bring herself to ask.

"It was the longest lunch on record," Larry said with a faint smile. "We argued a lot before they came up with final offer, but I told them I was confident you would accept it. One million a year for three years," he told them in quiet satisfaction. "The royalty pushed up to five percent. They grumbled like hell, but they've agreed to total control. Nothing goes into the line without your approval, Vanessa. You make whatever changes you deem necessary. Your gamble has paid off."

Fifty

Ironically, now that Vanessa didn't need it, other prospective licensees came to negotiate. Again Larry represented her. He was a deceptively soft-spoken, gentle negotiator but tough in his demands. In return for glittering royalties, Vanessa would lend her name to a line of women's shoes, a perfume, loungewear. At this point Vanessa decreed no more licensing. Unlike some designers, who lent their names without being personally involved, Vanessa insisted on approving every item that bore her name.

Exhilarated by the knowledge that at the end of the year she would be among the top ten wage earners in the nation, Vanessa bought an ocean-front estate at Bridgehampton that would serve as the setting for Suzy and Adam's wedding in late June. She summoned her long-time decorators, Phil and Robbie, to redo the beach house. They would also redo, to Suzy and Adam's specifications, the private apartment in the town house that was to be their home after they married. Suzy walked around these days with a relieved air: Frank had announced that Edie would be upset if he joined Vanessa in escorting her to the altar.

All through April Vanessa watched the TV reports of the antiwar protests in Washington. On April 23 Suzy phoned to make sure she watched the late news; a group of young Vietnam veterans had earlier that day deposited their war decorations on the steps of the Capitol. The following day a huge parade was scheduled.

"I'll watch," Vanessa promised.

"It's so insane," Suzy lashed out. "Nixon keeps saying he'll get us out of Vietnam, but nothing's happening."

At the beginning of May Suzy and Adam resolved to take time off to go down to Washington. Vanessa was secretly relieved when Larry announced he would go with them. For all his intense convictions, Larry was not one to make hasty moves, and she knew both Suzy and Adam harbored much respect for him.

Watching the TV reports after the three had arrived in Washington, Vanessa was beset by anxiety. In the course of forty-eight hours more than 12,000 protesters were arrested. Bystanders as well as the most militant protesters were swept up by the police. When the three arrived at the town house late that evening, Vanessa welcomed them with warm relief.

"They won't hold all those protesters in jail," Larry predicted. "They don't have room," he chuckled. And reports from Washington soon confirmed this.

Vanessa still fought with Tina about her refusal to tell Adam who his father was. Adam was upset, too, that his father was unaware of his existence. And Tina was furious that Sal and Eva had ignored the invitation to the wedding. Nor had his other uncles responded.

Vanessa strongly approved Tina's decision to say a final adieu to Rome and take up residence in California again. Vanessa suspected Tina was mellowing. It had been many months since New York gossip columns had carried reports of her flamboyant escapades with handsome young Italians. Tina had declared she would work in films only when a good role came along and then only if Felix directed.

"God, Vanessa, after all these years I'm learning to act," Tina said on the phone a few days before she was to arrive for the wedding. "It was the only way out," she laughed. "How much longer could I go on just wiggling my ass and showing off my tits?"

"Tina, why don't you tell Adam about his father?" Vanessa tried yet again. "And Felix about his son."

"Felix is fifty-six years old. It's too late to announce to him that he's a father again. Did I tell you?" Tina was somber. "His wife died a few weeks ago. All those years just sitting in a chair and staring at the walls. When he was in California, Felix went to see her every week. It was a kind of grim punishment he meted out to himself because he escaped the Nazis and she hadn't."

"Give him the joy of knowing he has a son."

"Vanessa, get off my back! I'll see you in New York next week."

Despite her schedule—which had had to be extended to accommodate the TV talk shows and magazine and newspaper interviews that Phyllis had set up to tie in with the introduction of Vanessa Conrad blouses, shoes, perfume, and loungewear—Vanessa could be cajoled to join Larry for outings. A Sunday morning walk in Central Park after an unexpected late snowfall, a last-minute trip to an off-Broadway revival of Shaw, a drive downtown to Ratner's for dinner and reminiscences about his mother's love of the Yiddish theater.

Vanessa was touched that Suzy had asked her to design her wedding dress. Suzy specified only that it be white, long, and that no veil would accompany it.

Vanessa designed a white organza Edwardian gown, a hint of future high fashion that blended with Suzy's current love for the new "granny dresses." Tears filled Vanessa's eyes at the final fitting. She wanted so much for this precious child of hers.

Vanessa was disappointed when Tina called on the Monday before the wedding to say that she would not arrive until Saturday. She'd looked forward to long evenings alone with Tina at the town house. Suzy and Wendy, the joyous maid of honor, had left that morning for Bridgehampton, along with Maria, who refused to allow the wedding dinner to be catered. Adam would arrive on Friday, brushing aside Maria's exhortation that the groom should not see his bride on the wedding day until they met at the altar. Pat would not be able to come; her mother was gravely ill in Houston.

Around 9:00 P.M. on Friday evening Vanessa settled herself in the limousine for the drive out to the beach house. Larry had insisted on an early dinner before she left.

She knew the wedding on Sunday would be a bittersweet occasion for Larry. The shadows of his two sons would be at his side. Though he found solace in tiny improvements in Danny's condition, he knew that Danny would always require custodial care. His daughter, he told Vanessa over dinner, had been married at a splashy affair that had cost him $50,000, and two years later she was suing for divorce in Reno. *"She'll never make me a grandfather."* He seldom saw her.

For a frightening instant, before Larry took her to the house, she had thought he was going to abandon the role of trusted friend for something else. Her smile had grown strained while her heart pounded. Larry, bless him, had understood. They needed each other—but just the way they were.

On the drive out Vanessa slowly began to unwind. It had been so sweet of Suzy and Adam to insist on handling all the arrangements with the Reform rabbi. Phyllis was taking care of the flowers, the music, and the photographer. She felt guilty that she had done little more than design Suzy and Wendy's gowns. But the children and Adam knew the demands on her time since she had undertaken the licensing deals.

When she arrived at the Bridgehampton house, she found Maria alone in the kitchen while strains from Maria's favorite opera filled the house. The servants were gone for the night, and Suzy and Adam were walking on the beach.

"I can't believe our baby is getting married." Maria's face was radiant with love. "I've been cooking since we got out here," she said proudly. "For Suzy's wedding dinner nobody cooks except Maria."

"Maria, did you ever think we'd come this far?" Vanessa asked. She was still amazed by the income—$4 million a year for the next three years—generated by her licensing deals. Now officially her business manager, Larry was diverting substantial sums into trust funds for the girls and Maria and setting up a charitable foundation. "Did you ever expect to see me interviewed as the woman earning the most money in the nation?"

"Yes." Maria smiled brilliantly. "I knew you wouldn't let anyone stop you. Eddie knew it, too."

Sometimes it seemed there had never been another man in her life except Eddie. There had been such a gradual disintegration of her marriage to Frank. In the end it seemed simply not to exist.

Standing with Maria in the kitchen, she remembered that day—twenty-two years ago last month—

when she had come into the kitchen of their apartment in Venice and thrust the newspaper with its tragic headline into Maria's hands. At this moment it seemed yesterday.

Saturday Vanessa awoke to a gloriously sunny morning. The air was fragrant with the scent of roses. She made a mental note while she dressed to remind Don he was to be at the airport at 3:00 P.M. She was impatient to see Tina. She wished that Pat could be here, but she knew how ill Pat's mother was.

Vanessa joined Suzy and Adam on the deck for breakfast and a lively discussion about their honeymoon trip. Because of their jobs and commitments to their anti-Vietnam protest group, they were allowing themselves only one week, to be spent in beautiful solitude in Canada's picturesque Gaspé.

Vanessa caught the hurt and anger in Adam's eyes when he thought no one was looking. While he was ecstatic at the discovery that Tina was his mother, he was especially conscious today of Sal and Eva's rejection. For most of his life he had believed they were his parents, and all those years could not be washed away.

After breakfast Vanessa, Suzy, and Adam lingered on the deck over final plans for the wedding. When Tina arrived, they would have a rehearsal, Vanessa decreed. By then Wendy, euphoric about her role as maid of honor, would be back from the local beauty salon.

When Wendy called from the beauty salon, Vanessa drove into town to pick her up and to shop for last-minute spices Maria required for the banquet she was preparing. Vanessa loved the quaint village, with its graceful windmills from past centuries. The town had grown since she and Eddie had come out after his return from military service. Now it was a well-known resort.

Vanessa vowed that today she would not even think about business. She and Wendy dawdled about town, gazing at shop windows, pausing to buy the local paper, stopping at Wendy's beloved old-fashioned ice cream parlor for luscious scoops of her favorite chocolate ice cream.

Back at the house Vanessa found a congratulatory cable from Frank. He was in Scotland on business and unable to return in time for the wedding.

"Suzy won't mind," Maria commented. "She wouldn't mind him alone so much, but she and Wendy won't *ever* think of that Edie as their stepmother."

Vanessa was in the kitchen admiring Maria's sumptuous three-tiered wedding cake when she heard the car roll into the driveway.

"It's Mother!" Adam called exuberantly as he charged down the hall with Suzy. It was astonishing how easily Adam had switched from "Aunt Tina" to "Mother," Vanessa thought affectionately.

Vanessa left the kitchen to join Adam and Suzy on the wide front terrace. Strikingly beautiful in a lemon yellow linen from Vanessa's custom collection, Tina emerged from the car. The three on the terrace hurried forward in welcome.

Vanessa stared in astonishment as a distinguished, trim man in his late fifties followed behind Tina. His face furrowed, dark eyes intense, his smile compassionate.

"Adam—" Tina rushed to kiss her son. "I've brought you a very special wedding present," she told him as she stepped back to inspect him. Her voice was triumphant. She reached for her companion's hand. "Adam, this is your father."

At sunset, just as the blazing ball of red approached the horizon, the guests assembled on the beach before the *chupah*. The fragrance of the potted flowers lining the improvised aisle from deck to *chupah* blended with the scent of the sea. The string ensemble played softly.

Adam, flanked by his mother and father, emerged from the house to walk across the deck, down the stairs, and to the *chupah*. Wendy followed, her small face glowing and lovely, and took her place beside the *chupah*. Suzy and her mother appeared, both radiating happiness as they walked slowly down the aisle.

At the conclusion of the ceremony, as the rabbi pronounced Adam and Suzy husband and wife, Vanessa's eyes involuntarily turned to find Larry. His gaze met hers. Today she could not bring herself to deny the truth. She loved him. And she was terrified.

After the bride and groom and wedding guests had departed, Vanessa walked along the deserted beach with Larry.

"Vanessa, why are you fighting this?" Larry scolded gently. "It's not a criminal offense for us to be in love. And you do love me," he insisted as she raised her face to his with a frown of protest. "Watching you during the ceremony I was sure. I'd hoped before. I *know* now."

"Larry, I can't make a commitment again," she whispered. But she didn't deny her love. "I've been so badly hurt twice."

"Didn't you hear when you were a little girl?" he teased. "Third time is charmed."

"I want you as my dear and cherished friend," she

687

stammered. "I can't lose that. I need you in my life, Larry."

"All right," he said, accepting defeat gracefully. "I'll be the stalwart family friend. And escort," he insisted. "I'll squire you to charity events and the theater and dinner parties. Vanessa, you have to get off this treadmill and learn to relax."

"I will," she promised, relieved that Larry was accepting her limits. "Let's make a point of going to the theater more often. And the ballet."

"Vanessa, why are you denying yourself what we could have together?" asked in a burst of frustration. "You're still a young woman, with half your life ahead of you. Provided you live to ninety-two," he conceded teasingly. "Remember Browning? 'Grow old along with me! / The best is yet to be,/ The last of life, for which the first was made.'" He chuckled and took her face between his hands. "But it'll be a long road before you grow old." He kissed her. Gently at first, then with growing passion. Her arms tightened around his shoulders while, for a few moments, she abandoned herself to him.

"Larry, no more than this," she insisted unsteadily. "I have this terrible fear of losing again."

"Just this much," he accepted.

The months were passing quickly. The demands on Vanessa's time were unrelenting. She was grateful, though at times impatient, that Larry insisted on pulling her away from the long hours of business. She was perennially tired, running on nervous energy. Labeled a "beautiful, elegantly dressed dynamo" by *Women's Wear Daily,* she was aware of a nagging fear that if she slowed her pace she might come face to face with reality. And the truth was that Vanessa

Conrad—despite her fabulous success, her enormous income, her pleasure in Suzy's marriage—was not a happy woman. But she told herself that happiness on earth was a fleeting thing.

Early in 1972—with President Nixon adroitly commanding international attention in this presidential election year with his visit to China—Suzy and Adam declared themselves behind Senator George McGovern in his race for the Democratic nomination. Larry, uneasy about a possible split in the Democratic party, joined their support of McGovern once it became clear that Muskie, for whom he had a great deal of respect, had little chance of victory. Larry sensed a growing apathy and resignation among American voters, who this year would include eighteen-year-olds voting for the first time in a presidential election. As Adam commented wryly, "Even the Beatles have split up."

In the spring Vanessa rejoiced in Tina's quiet marriage to Felix. They were married before a judge in the library of Vanessa's town house. They both insisted that they be married in Adam's presence.

"I don't feel any different," Adam grinned and reached to embrace his mother and then his father after the ceremony. But he had adopted his father's name. Now he was Adam Koestler.

Despite a fractured wrist, Pat had flown into New York for the wedding. She gave a dinner at the Pierre for the bride and groom and the handful of guests who had been present at the marriage, though she was still in mourning for her mother.

"Tomorrow," she told Vanessa and Tina with warm anticipation, "you're to have lunch at the apartment and see Joyce." She was reluctant to leave her granddaughter—officially her adopted daughter—for even a day, so she had brought Joyce and her nurse to

New York with her. "She's the joy of my life. A sweet, loving, delightful child."

Vanessa depended on Larry in her personal life as much as in the business. It was Larry who forced her to spend long weekends at the Bridgehampton house as soon as the first breath of summer made its appearance — even though she persisted in carrying work along with her. At the shop Larry had an office adjoining hers. He represented her in dealings with their licensees, handled her investments, managed the foundation.

She was upset to learn early in May that Frank's business was close to bankruptcy. Gossip in the trade hinted of a breakup in his marriage as well. She sat rereading the newspaper item on the failure of Frank Bernstein for Men for the dozenth time as the employees left for the day.

"Do you want to look at the sketches for the new blouse collection?" Rhoda interrupted her introspection.

"I'll take them home with me," she said abstractly. "Go, Rhoda," she said affectionately. "It's been a long day."

In a corner of her mind she approved of the new atmosphere in the shop since Frank's departure. Arnie handled people well. He was strong when it was necessary, but every employee knew Arnie was fair. Employee loyalty had improved tremendously.

Vanessa remained at her desk, troubled by Frank's situation. The "miracle man of Seventh Avenue" was in serious difficulties. She remembered his youthful enthusiasm in those early years, his towering ambition. His belief in her talents, even when she had faltered. How could she stand by and not try to help him?

Vanessa rushed from her office to knock on Larry's

door.

"Come in." Larry looked up from the contracts he had been studying. "Ready to go?"

Vanessa nodded.

"Come over for dinner tonight?" she asked hopefully. Two or three nights each week he was busy with the local McGovern campaign group.

"Sure." Larry accepted the invitation with a sympathetic smile. It was uncanny the way Larry knew when she needed him.

At the house they settled themselves in the library for a pre-dinner glass of wine. Wendy was upstairs studying. Maria reported that Suzy would be down from her apartment for dinner but that "a tray's going up to the law student."

"Vanessa," Larry said gently when they were alone, "what is your ultimate dream as a designer? What would give you the most happiness in this crazy business?"

"The custom salon." Her face glowed with an inner light at the thought. "I'd love to be able to do a collection of two hundred, perhaps three hundred, perfect models in the most exquisite of fabrics. To design without an eye to cost. To show America— Europe—that American clothes can be as elegant as anything from Paris or Milan." She laughed and reached for her wineglass again. "But I'm a realist. I know I can't take time out to play games." Nor had she brought Larry here for casual conversation. "Larry, I've been thinking all day about something I read in *Men's Wear* magazine—"

"About Frank going into Chapter XI," Larry guessed. "I gather he's gone through that $3 million."

"I've given this a lot of thought." She paused, took a deep breath. "I want Frank to receive a small percentage of my licensing deals." She managed a wisp of a smile. "In my tax bracket I'll hardly feel it."

"Why are you worrying about him?" Larry looked baffled.

Vanessa frowned. Did he think she was still in love with Frank?

"I'm selfish, really. I don't want his marriage to come apart at the seams. Wendy would be upset." That, too, was a strong reason to help. "Frank's son is her half-brother. She'd be hurt if her father and Edie separated. She'd feel out of touch with the baby. Wendy adores him. And yes," she forced herself to be candid with Larry, "I do feel an odd kind of obligation toward Frank."

"New backing won't guarantee Frank's marriage will last," Larry cautioned, but he appeared relieved by her explanation for her concern for Frank's welfare.

"Edie will stay with Frank as long as money is coming in," Vanessa predicted confidently. "And he's Wendy's father. I have to remember that." She was sorting out all that had crossed her mind in the past few hours. "I wouldn't be where I am without Frank. We built the business together. I haven't forgotten what he did *to* me, but at the same time I must remember what he did *for* me. Larry, what do you think would be a fair arrangement?"

"Five percent of the licensing fees?" he suggested after a moment's thought. "That should put him back on his feet."

"Draw up the papers," Vanessa said. "You work it out with him, please. I don't want to have to deal with Frank myself," she stipulated.

"Vanessa, you're a very special lady," Larry said softly.

"Hi." Swinging a tote bag, Suzy burst into the library. Vanessa started. She had not heard Suzy come into the house.

"Darling, how are you?" Vanessa's smile was rich with love.

"I have sensational news!" Suzy lowered herself into a chair. "The boutique is going to show a blouse I've designed." She was proud and self-conscious at the same time. This was her first admission that she was interested in designing, Vanessa realized suddenly. She had waited so long for this. "And if this one takes off, then they'll let me do more."

"Suzy, that's so exciting. You have the blouse in there," Vanessa pounced, pointing to the tote. "Let's see it."

Lovingly Suzy brought out the blouse, held it up against herself for her mother to inspect, her dark eyes anxious.

"Suzy, it's terrific." Vanessa's trained gaze took in every detail. "It's young and fresh and flattering — and it'll appeal to the mature woman as well as to your own age group." The atmosphere was suddenly electric. Oh, yes, she exulted, Suzy had talent. "But instead of showing it at the boutique, let me present it as part of the next Vanessa II collection. 'For Vanessa II, by Suzy,' " she quoted. She was already envisioning a whole line by Suzy.

"No," Suzy rejected. "I don't think so, Mother." She was faintly apologetic. "I'd like to do it at the boutique."

"But, Suzy, it's so good." Vanessa was astonished. "It'll be knocked off so fast it'll take your breath away."

"I'm not worried about selling a million," Suzy said uneasily. "It'll be more fun to sell it at the boutique. And it'll be expensive. Kathy says I can use the best materials."

"Ten days after it shows up in your boutique window, it'll be appearing all over town at half the price, or less," Vanessa warned. But Suzy continued to shake her head. Her stubborn daughter, Vanessa thought in exasperation.

"Suzy!" Wendy called from the doorway. "They're going to show your blouse?"

"Right!"

"Hey, that's great!" Wendy hugged her sister. "But come up to my room and help me with my crazy math assignment."

Vanessa watched in frustration while Suzy and Wendy hurried from the room. She brushed away the hurt that came from realizing Wendy had known about the blouse before she.

"Larry, she'll be heartbroken when she discovers how fast her blouse is knocked off! She grew up in the business — she ought to know!"

"The young have to learn for themselves," he consoled.

"Suzy doesn't want to come into the business." Vanessa was shaken by this realization. In her deepest heart, ever since she and Frank introduced their first collection, she had cherished dreams of Creations by Vanessa Conrad becoming a family business, with title adjustments to include her daughters in time. *Creations by Suzy, for Vanessa Conrad. Creations by Wendy, for Vanessa Conrad.*

"She'd rather go it alone." Vanessa shook her head in disbelief. "Larry, doesn't she realize how much I could help her?"

694

Fifty-one

Vanessa made a furtive, eager, late evening trip to the Madison Avenue boutique where Suzy worked so that she might stand before the window and admire her daughter's blouse on display. She stood there on the thinly populated sidewalk while Don waited behind the wheel of the limo and remembered her own excitement all those years ago in Venice when Signora Torino had placed the gray velvet dress that was her first design for the shop in the window. It was one of the high points in her life: public recognition of her talent.

She was sympathetic when, two weeks later, Suzy called to report that her blouse had already been knocked off and was selling all over town at half the price.

"And you can be sure some factory in Hong Kong or Uruguay is rushing like mad to make and ship them at even lower prices," Vanessa said.

"Well, it's flattering to know they like it enough to knock it off." Suzy struggled to sound cheerful. "Kathy says they'll show my next design at the boutique if it's as good as this one."

"Suzy, would you like to open your own boutique?" Vanessa asked on impulse. She longed to nurture this newly revealed talent in her daughter.

"Not just yet," Suzy said after a startled moment. She was excited by the prospect, and pleased that her mother respected her ability. "I don't think I'm ready for it."

"Whenever you feel the time has come," Vanessa said, "tell me, and we'll talk about it."

They spoke for a few minutes longer. Suzy told her mother that she and Adam planned to go down to Miami in July for the Democratic convention. They were convinced that McGovern would win the nomination.

"Do you suppose Arnie and Phyl are going down, too?" Suzy asked.

"July's a hectic month in the business. I doubt if they can manage it."

"Larry will go down," Suzy predicted. Just recently he had encouraged her to abandon the formal "Mr. Fraser." To Wendy he was already "Uncle Larry." "He feels the way we do about the need for change in this country."

"Darling, I feel the same way," Vanessa said defensively. When she and Frank used to fight, he'd scream, "You don't give a damn about anything except the business." That wasn't true.

After she hung up the phone, Vanessa sat motionless, lost in thought. Larry had left his law firm because he was disenchanted with his life and wanted to fight for important issues. Now he was spending much of his time handling her business affairs. Was she being unfair to involve him this way?

Larry arrived at the house shortly before nine. He had gone from the office to have another of his heart-rending dinners with Danny, who was now living in a small apartment with a team of male nurses.

"Maria will bring us coffee," she said and lifted her face to his. How desolate he seemed tonight. Today was Danny's twenty-fourth birthday. He had been remembering other, happier birthdays.

Arm in arm they walked into the library. Vanessa listened sympathetically to his quiet report of his evening with his son.

"Larry, sometimes I feel guilty about keeping you so busy with my affairs. You left your law office so you'd have time to do what pleased you."

"It pleases me to be helpful to you." Vanessa lowered her eyes before the naked love in his. "The business is a challenge. I enjoy it." He strived to sound matter-of-fact. "And I schedule hours every week for the protest group. I see Danny almost every day. My life is better than it has ever been."

Vanessa gazed up in relief when Maria arrived with their coffee tray. She felt the hunger she saw in Larry's eyes in herself. She loved Larry with an intensity she had never expected to feel again. But that part of her life should be over.

"Arnie and Phyllis will be here any moment now," Vanessa told Larry. "Arnie says we've earned out this year's million-dollar advance from Waterman Industries and will be receiving close to half a million in additional royalties." Her eyes crinkled in amusement. "And I was willing to accept a half a million advance over a two-year contract."

"You were selling yourself short. You have a tremendous following, Vanessa. I don't have to tell you that."

"It's still nice to hear it."

"You haven't heard anything from Frank about your allowing him to share in your licensing deals?" A hint of contempt tinged Larry's voice.

"No." Vanessa smiled faintly. "And I'm glad I

haven't."

"I can't understand his not even dropping you a note of thanks." Larry shook his head in bewilderment. "In the first year of the arrangement he's picking up roughly $200,000."

"Frank considers it his due. I didn't expect gratitude."

In July Suzy, Adam, and Larry went down to Miami for the Democratic Convention. They were all elated when McGovern won at a tradition-shattering convention that Suzy declared she would never forget. But Larry warned it would be difficult to defeat Nixon despite the uproar over the burglarizing of Democratic headquarters at the Watergate complex in Washington. Too many Democrats would refuse to rally to McGovern's cause. They looked upon him as a radical, were opposed to his proposals to cut the defense budget and institute increased welfare benefits. Some Democrats were indignant that he promised amnesty for those who went to jail or into exile instead of fighting in Vietnam.

Suzy and Adam were crushed by the results of the November election, with Nixon defeating McGovern in forty-nine states—despite the burgeoning outcry about the Watergate scandal and the indictment of the Watergate burglars and former White House aides E. Howard Hunt and G. Gordon Liddy. Larry encouraged Suzy and Adam to continue to work with the anti-Vietnam protest group, as he himself was doing, because despite Nixon's promises to end the war, the heaviest bombing to date was resumed when peace talks broke off.

Vanessa was concerned about the effect of the spiraling inflation of business. Her one joy was Wendy's decision to study at the Fashion Institute of Technology after high school graduation. She knew this was more than a youthful whim — she had watched with elation Wendy's growing fascination with clothes and designing.

On New Year's Day, as had become her habit, Vanessa gathered together those close to her for a late afternoon dinner. As always in this household, the conversation eventually turned to Seventh Avenue. Vanessa was caught up in the lunatic race to launch her summer collections late in the month. Suzy was euphoric because several of her designs were in the works at the boutique, though she confided that there was tension between the three young designers who ran the boutique and their backers.

"The backers are still carrying on about going public. All they want is to make tons of money," Suzy sighed.

"Typical of investors," Larry teased.

"We have to keep raising prices," Suzy said and Vanessa nodded in understanding. "This crazy inflation is closing up boutiques."

"Our bills on fabrics are going haywire," Arnie added. "Still, we don't have to worry. The licenses are making us top earners in the business." He exchanged a complacent smile with Larry. With respect for her soaring income — reported in major financial journals in awesome detail — the two men had brushed aside her reluctance to buy a company jet. She must make her sweeps about the country with more speed and in the greater comfort, they insisted. She traveled now with her personal maid and hairdresser.

"How long do you think the girls will be able to hold out against the backers?" Adam asked Suzy. Vanessa saw Larry lean forward with a sudden glint of interest while Suzy squinted in thought.

"I don't know." Suzy was somber. "They're meddling a lot now." Vanessa's mind shot back to Bill Bartlett and his meddling. She and Frank had climbed the walls with Bill. "They're even telling us what kind of fabrics to use. We *know* what they want to use. The new synthetics are fascinating." Suzy was endearingly earnest. "There's so much we can do with them — and we can sell clothes at affordable prices. I know, Mother, you feel the way Calvin Klein does about fabrics. Everything has to be the best available, natural materials." It was good-humored, affectionate jesting. "But exciting new fabrics are constantly coming into the market. They're fun to work with," she said enthusiastically and Wendy, starry-eyed at this trade talk, nodded in approval.

"Boutiques like yours are really underground Seventh Avenue." Larry's smile was whimsical. But he had an ulterior motive. "Did you ever think how much fun it could be to sell those same designs, in your less expensive new synthetics, in mass market?"

"We'd lose control," Suzy said candidly. "That's when the fun goes out."

"Ah-hah," Larry said with an air of discovery.

All conversation ceased in admiration as Maria brought in her latest dessert creation: Grand Marnier cake with a chocolate mousse filling and covered with Grand Marnier-flavored whipped cream, topped with mandarin oranges. Dessert was always carried in by Maria herself rather than by one of the servants. It was a household tradition.

"Oh, God, the calories," Phyllis mourned. "And I know I won't be able to resist seconds. But I won't eat for the next three days," she laughed. "Okay, for one of Maria's desserts it'll be worth it."

Phyllis and Arnie left around six to attend a New

700

Year's Day party. An hour later Suzy and Adam took off for an off-Broadway opening. Wendy was going to a school friend's house. Vanessa and Larry settled themselves before the library fireplace, where the birch logs crackled in welcome.

"I can't believe it's 1973," Vanessa marveled. Her smile grew nostalgic. "I remember a New Year's back home, when my father ignored my mother — she thought even a glass of wine was sinful — and bought a split of domestic champagne to open at the stroke of midnight. He couldn't have envisioned this house, the business, Dom Perignon for New Year's Eve. He'd have been so proud and happy."

"I'm glad we could spend New Year's Eve together," Larry said pensively. "Though I hated going back to my solitary apartment after we'd seen the new year in." It was a wistful rebuke. For a moment last night, when Larry kissed her, she had wavered. He had known that.

"Larry, do you think I've spoiled Suzy?" Vanessa self-consciously rechanneled the conversation. "She sees designing as fun, not as a way to earn a living."

"Suzy doesn't *have* to earn a living," he reminded her. "She grew up in a different world from ours. At fourteen we knew we'd have to earn our own way. But no, Suzy isn't spoiled," he reassured her. "She's there at the boutique five days a week, despite her income from the trust fund. But I think that more and more, young people are anxious for jobs that provide greater satisfaction than just pulling in a paycheck for survival."

"I think I'm losing my girls to other design markets," Vanessa said softly. "Wendy is following right in Suzy's footsteps. Do you see the way her face lights up every time Suzy talks about the boutique?" She gazed into the orange-red blaze in the fireplace

701

grate. "I offered to set Suzy up in her own boutique. She turned me down."

"Suzy's determined to be independent," Larry comforted. "I know she's stubborn," he laughed affectionately. "And that can be helpful in getting ahead. But you just *might* bring her into the fold." His face wore a zealous glow that told Vanessa he had a plan.

"How?" Vanessa challenged.

"First, let's talk about you. You're working too hard. I can't bear seeing you drained this way. Step back from Vanessa II," he continued. "Talk to Suzy about coming in to take it over along with her three associates—with full autonomy. Each with a label credit in one area. But this can happen only if you've thoroughly studied their work and feel they can handle Vanessa II," he cautioned.

"I've driven by at night when the boutique was closed," Vanessa confessed. "Several times. After all, Suzy is so involved with them. And they're good," she said. "Fresh, original, *young.*"

"Vanessa II caters to the young career girl. Can they design for her?"

"They'll have to pare down on some designs," Vanessa said thoughtfully. "But I suspect they're bright enough to understand that." She paused a moment to consider the situation. They could compromise. "Do you think they'll buy it?" The prospect of Suzy becoming part of the business was electrifying. *Suzy, for Vanessa II.*

"If they know they have total control after you've come to terms about what is right for Vanessa II. It'll be a tremendous challenge for the four of them. But go back again," Larry ordered. "Be sure. Then talk to them."

* * *

Cannily Vanessa insisted that Larry be present at dinner when Suzy brought the three girls to discuss her offer. She suspected that Suzy was ambivalent, excited but fearful of losing her precious independence. Larry would stress the control the four girls would have with Vanessa II. She would explain their market, the flexibility they would have in setting up each collection. They would understand this wasn't simply an eager mother trying to bring her daughter into her business. They would each have a three-year contract, with options.

Larry came home with her from the shop. They settled in the library for a glass of wine before she went upstairs to change for dinner.

"If this goes through, you'll have far more time for the custom salon," Larry reminded her, pouring Chablis into a pair of Galway glasses. "You said that was what would make you happy."

"You remember my saying that?" Her smile was whimsical. "I've never said that to another living soul."

"I remember what's important to your happiness," he said, his eyes making unabashed love to her.

"I'd love to be able to devote more time to designs for the salon." Her face grew luminous as she envisioned this. "To be able to design totally as I wish, without limitations. With the other collections I have to limit expensive, time-consuming work. I know that handwork can't be duplicated on machines. Larry, there's so much that's magnificent that can be created in haute couture." She laughed at herself. "I sound so utterly self-centered, so wrapped up in 'my art,'" she mocked.

"You sound like the warm, dedicated artist you are." He paused. "And while we're talking about your happiness, why don't we consider not continuing with the licenses?" She gazed at him in shock. "You don't need the money. It drains time away from the things that are important to you. Renew with Waterman Industries but drop the others. After Frank's percentage is taken off, divide the royalties from Waterman between the trusts and the foundation."

"Do you think I should pamper myself that way?" She hesitated, aware of the enormous size of her income from the licenses.

"You don't have to strive to be the richest woman in America," he chuckled. "Only the most fulfilled."

"We'll renew with Waterman and drop the others," Vanessa agreed. Larry was so wise, so clear-thinking. The trusts provided her and the children and Maria with financial security for the rest of their lives. The Eduardo Montino Foundation, administered by Larry, gave her much personal satisfaction, as it did Larry. She rose to her feet. "You'll handle it when the time comes. I'll go change for dinner now."

Over wine, before they sat down to dinner, Larry explained to the four expectant young women the offer being extended to them. Though at first they were self-conscious about asking questions, the other three soon joined Suzy in exploring the situation. Before they were summoned to the dining table, Vanessa knew that Vanessa II had just acquired four new designers. And yet, fleetingly, she felt a sense of loss.

"It's madly exciting," Kathy effervesced while they settled themselves at the table. The faces of the others, including Suzy, reflected the same excitement. "We've been so uptight with the backers."

"We were ready to throw in the towel," Caroline conceded. "They don't understand Seventh Avenue. All they understand is a profit-and-loss sheet."

"We're so grateful for this opportunity," Laura said softly. "To have a chance to prove ourselves without interference."

"You girls wind up your business with your backers," Larry told them. "I'll have the contracts drawn up within a few days."

Vanessa forced herself to stay in the background while the four girls began to prepare for the Vanessa II fall collection, to be shown in May. Phyllis moved in to publicize the new line, shrewd as always in her approach. Vanessa enjoyed Suzy's enthusiasm, cherished her moments of confidence, her occasional requests to "let me use you for a sounding board, Mother." Vanessa realized it was natural that she felt uneasy qualms about the reception of the coming Vanessa II fashion show.

Freed from the demands of Vanessa II, and with the ready-to-wear couture fall line in comfortable control, Vanessa abandoned herself to designing her largest ever fall/winter custom collection. Once the terms of the licenses — other than Waterman Industries — expired, she dreamt of presenting a custom collection to match that of the House of Dior in size. Perhaps one day she would surpass that number.

Early in May the Vanessa II fall line was shown. Critics and buyers alike were enthusiastic. The day after the showing, though now the four girls would be swept up in the frenzy of the production schedule, Pat gave a small cocktail party at the Pierre in their honor.

Pat was staying at her late parents' Manhattan co-op for a few days with Joyce and the nurse. Paul was due in sometime during the evening for a political conference. Pat confided he was already pushing for the Democratic presidential nomination in 1976, and he was unhappy that her father was not alive to support him. Vanessa gathered he was in a foul mood. Was he still a womanizer, or was he afraid to tarnish his image now that he considered himself in the running for the 1976 presidential election?

After the party the euphoric young designers left for an earnest discussion with buyers. Pat hurried back to the apartment in anticipation of Paul's arrival. Tired but exhilarated, Vanessa instructed Don to drive her home. Larry would be over at eight for dinner. He had been as pleased as she was with the showing, Vanessa told herself.

At the house Vanessa settled down in the library with Maria to discuss the afternoon's event.

"Maria, these girls are good," she reported in satisfaction. "And Suzy"—her smile was brilliant—"Suzy is superb."

"And why shouldn't she be?" Maria shrugged. "With you for her mother and Eddie for her father." Maria glanced at her watch. "Let me go check on dinner. I suppose Larry will be here tonight?" She was teasing. Larry was here most nights.

"He'll be here," Vanessa confirmed. "Wendy home yet?"

"She's upstairs holed up for an exam," Maria said. "But I told her she's to come down for dinner. She can't study without decent food in her stomach."

Maria left for the kitchen. Vanessa was on her way to her own room when the doorbell rang.

"I'll get it," she called to the maid, who appeared at the end of the hall. Probably Larry arriving early.

Vanessa pulled the door open and stared in shock at Frank.

"I have to talk to you, Vanessa." His face was taut

with anger.

"Come inside, Frank."

"What's this shit in today's *Women's Wear Daily* about you dropping the licenses?" he demanded.

"I didn't read today's *Women's Wear Daily*." Why should she feel defensive with Frank?"

"Is it true?"

"I don't know how *WWD* got wind of it." She forced herself to remain calm. "But yes, it's true to some extent. I'll continue with Waterman Industries."

"Are you out of your mind?" Frank yelled. "You're throwing away a fortune!"

"I don't have time for it," she shot back.

"Make time!" he ordered grimly. "You don't have to look at every fucking piece. They just want to use your name. *The name I made.*" A vein throbbed in his forehead.

"I'm sorry, Frank." She was pale and shaking now. "I won't continue with any license other than Waterman. That brings in over a million and a half a year. It's—"

"Shit compared to what can come in," he interrupted. "Chicken feed!" His 5 percent of a million and a half—$75,000—was chicken feed? His menswear business—with hardworking designers in need of money building up the image of Frank Bernstein, designer—was out of the woods, according to all reports. Not Hart, Schaffner & Marx, but surviving. But of course, that would never be enough for Frank. "You can't do this to me! I made the company!"

"That's it." Vanessa lost all patience. "I will lend my name to Waterman Industries. Nobody else."

"You're cutting my throat!" His face flushed with color. "But what else should I expect from you?"

"Don't you talk to my mother like that!" Wendy

707

hovered a few steps above the landing. Vanessa had not heard her footsteps on the lushly carpeted stairs. Wendy's eyes were ablaze, one hand gripped the banister in fury. "You can't tell her what to do. You walked out on her. You walked out on me. You're not a real father!"

Frank stared grimly at the small avenging angel who was his daughter, then whirled about to the door, opened it, and left the house.

"Wendy, I didn't mean for you to hear that," Vanessa apologized.

"Why shouldn't I know what my father's really like?" A hint of a break in her voice. "But I don't need him. I have you." Wendy lifted her head defiantly, and Vanessa remembered all the times when Frank had promised to be there for Wendy and had not appeared. "I have you and Suzy and Maria and Adam. And Tina and Pat and Uncle Larry." How important Larry had become to all of them, Vanessa thought. "We're a family. We don't need Daddy."

Her daddy had a new young son and a new young wife, Vanessa remembered with rage. He thought that gave him the right to cut his daughter out of his life. Wendy would not lack for love, Vanessa promised herself. But she knew the hurt would be a long time leaving.

Fifty-two

Pat sat beside Joyce's custom-designed youth bed with its frilly white canopy and read from the latest addition to her granddaughter's Dr. Seuss collection, while Joyce lay back against the pillow in rapt attention. It was a nightly ritual Pat enjoyed.

The servants had left for the day. Paul had phoned to say he would not be at the apartment for dinner.

"Mrs. Roberts." Miss Ryan, the nurse who had been with them since Joyce was a few weeks old, hovered in the doorway. "Are you sure you wouldn't like me to come back tonight?"

"You go on to your sister's in Brooklyn and stay over," Pat insisted. "And there's no need to rush back in the morning. I can manage to give my daughter breakfast," she chuckled. Paul and she maintained the fabrication that Joyce was their adopted daughter.

"I left my sister's phone number taped to the refrigerator," Miss Ryan said, clearly looking forward to the visit with her sister. "Good night, Joyce," she said softly and lifted an eyebrow in inquiry. During their exchange Joyce's eyelids had closed.

"She's sleeping," Pat whispered.

"Good night, Mrs. Roberts."

"Good night, Miss Ryan. Enjoy your visit."

Pat drew the flower-sprigged sheet and matching coverlet over Joyce's tiny shoulders, switched on the carousel night light, and tiptoed from the nursery, leaving the door ajar so that she would hear if Joyce awakened.

She was relieved that Miss Ryan had asked to visit with her sister tonight. At the Georgetown house Joyce and Miss Ryan shared the small jewel of a cottage that had been CeeCee's as a child. At the house in Houston and at the plantation she had contrived to have them in a separate wing. In the Manhattan apartment this was not possible. She dreaded these trips to New York with Paul for this reason.

When she had spoken with him earlier in the day, he had seemed upset. *We'll talk about it later. This can't be discussed over the phone.* If there was to be an ugly scene, they didn't need Miss Ryan around. As soon as Paul arrived, she would close the door to the nursery.

Pat settled herself in the living room to read the new novel she'd brought along from Washington. She'd have dinner later. But tonight her mind refused to focus on the novel. The cocktail party had evoked memories of CeeCee. She had never ceased to reproach herself for fighting against CeeCee having an abortion. She might be alive today.

Pat put aside her book at the sound of the doorbell. Impatient as always, Paul was jabbing repeatedly at the bell. She darted hurriedly down the hall to close the nursery door, then rushed to the entrance foyer.

"You took long enough," Paul complained and

710

strode into the foyer.

"I'm sorry," she said automatically.

"I need a drink." He headed into the living room and toward the bar. "What a bastard of a day!"

"Paul, what couldn't you talk about over the phone?" She braced herself for a tirade.

"We're being blackmailed! I had a long meeting with the woman and her husband." He paused, a vein pounding in his forehead. "She knows about CeeCee. She's threatening to sell the story to one of those rotten scandal sheets if I don't agree to pay off."

Pat's face paled.

"How does she know?"

"She was a nurse at that hospital. She moved to New York recently and she saw one of CeeCee's old movies. She recognized her, and then she remembered you. I thought you said nobody would know who you were, the way you looked!" His voice soared menacingly. "You stupid bitch!"

"Paul, you'll wake Joyce—" But Joyce was already awake and crying.

"Go shut her up, damn it!" Paul pulled off his jacket, loosened his tie. "Do you know what this means?" he called after Pat. "We'll be paying off that rotten bitch forever!"

Pat hurried into the nursery and lifted Joyce into her arms.

"It's all right, darling," she soothed. "Everything's all right, my love."

"Come back in here and let's talk about this," Paul yelled from down the hall. "Her husband says they'll give us forty-eight hours to come up with the hundred thousand in cash—"

"Then give it to them," Pat said quietly, walking

toward him with Joyce in her arms.

"We'll give them the hundred thousand," Paul predicted, "and then they'll be back in six months demanding another hundred thousand."

"You can't go to the police," Pat reminded, recoiling from the image of CeeCee's face staring from the front pages of a scandal sheet on newsstands and at supermarket checkout counters across the country.

"Don't you think I know that?" Paul stalked to the bar again, poured himself another shot of bourbon. "They're crucifying me! They know what that story would do to my chances for the White House!" Already his name appeared regularly as a Democratic candidate for 1976. He scowled at Pat while she struggled to calm Joyce. Though Joyce could not understand what was being said, she was terrified by the rage in her grandfather's voice. "For Christ sake, put her down!"

"Paul, before you do anything, I think you ought to talk to the lawyers." Gently she deposited Joyce on her feet. "Let them advise you."

"What the hell can they do?" he bellowed, and Joyce began to cry again. "Shut up, Joyce!" He slapped her hard across the face, and she screamed in terror.

"Paul, no!" Pat clutched at his arm to pull him away. He pushed her off with such force that she fell to the fireplace hearth. "No!" He was turning back to Joyce, his face contorted in rage.

Pat reached for an andiron and with lightning swiftness stumbled to her feet and smashed it across his head as he bent to grab his tiny granddaughter. He grunted. Staggered. Fell to the floor. Cold with disbelief that she had acted with such violence, she dropped to her knees beside his inert body.

"Oh, my God!"

After dinner Vanessa and Larry went into the library for a second cup of coffee, and Wendy went up to her room to study. Vanessa was relieved that Wendy seemed to have brushed aside the ugly encounter with her father earlier in the day. The moment Larry arrived at the house, Wendy had told him in outrage about Frank's appearance earlier. Bless Larry for handling it so well.

While Vanessa poured coffee for Larry and herself, the phone rang. Vanessa put down the sterling coffeepot and crossed to the desk to pick up the phone.

"Hello."

"Vanessa, I killed him!" Pat's voice, edged with hysteria. "I killed Paul! I didn't mean to do it! I just wanted to stop him from hitting Joyce!"

"Pat, you're going to be all right." Vanessa said with deliberate calm, but she was ice-cold. "Are you alone at the apartment?"

"Yes." Her voice was racked with anguish. "Just me and Joyce. Miss Ryan went to her sister's. The servants are off for the night. Paul's lying on the floor by the living room fireplace. I hit him with an andiron. I had to do it."

"He may just be stunned. I'm calling an ambulance, and then Larry and I will be right over. In five minutes, Pat. Sit down in the entrance foyer with Joyce and wait for us there." Away from the sight of Paul's body. "We'll be right there," she repeated. How dare Paul lift his hand against that precious little girl?"

"All right, Vanessa," Pat whispered.

Larry was at the phone and directing an ambulance to Pat's apartment. Her heart thumping, Vanessa waited for Larry to put down the phone.

"Let's take your car — it'll be quicker," Vanessa said.

While they drove to Pat's apartment, Vanessa repeated what Pat had told her.

"He must have done something awful to provoke her that way," Vanessa said. "It wasn't just a grandfather slapping his granddaughter. Much as I detest Paul, I'm praying he's all right. For Pat's sake."

With Joyce cowering in her arms, Pat opened the door at their ring. Her face was devoid of color. She was fighting to hold herself together.

"He's in there —" Not allowing herself to look beyond the foyer, Pat pointed to the living room. Larry hurried inside.

"Do you want me to take Joyce?" Vanessa asked gently.

"No." Pat's arms tightened protectively around the little girl.

"Stay here, Pat," Vanessa ordered and crossed to the living room entrance. Larry rose from Paul's side.

"He's dead," Larry told her softly.

Moments later, as Larry phoned for the police, the ambulance arrived. Paul's body was taken away.

"He tried to hit Joyce again," Pat said in a monotone, numb with shock. "She was terrified. I was afraid he'd kill her. He was furious at her because some nurse from the hospital knew about CeeCee and is trying to blackmail him. He said it could cost him the nomination. He hit her across the face and then he bent down to hit her again. I reached for an andiron and . . . Wasn't it enough that he beat me?" Pat's voice rose almost out of control. "Did he believe I would let him hurt my precious baby?"

The tabloids spread across their headlines the whole ugly story of CeeCee's pregnancy, of the endless beatings Pat had endured through the years, of the blackmail threats that had enraged Paul to the point where he was ready to maim or kill his tiny granddaughter. Tina called from California to tell Larry, who had assembled a formidable team of attorneys to defend Pat, that she, too, had experienced Paul's violence.

Taking time out in the midst of a film Tina made a hasty appearance on the witness stand, along with three high-priced call girls whom the attorneys had persuaded to testify to their own beatings at Paul's hands.

"He was an important senator. I was afraid to go to the police," one call girl admitted. "He said he'd have me thrown in jail."

Doctors who had treated Pat for a series of suspicious injuries testified. They had recognized the situation but respected her insistence on secrecy. Early in the trial it became clear that Senator Paul Roberts had been respected by some, feared by others, and liked by few.

"The jury won't be out long," Larry predicted when the twelve jurors filed out of the courtroom. "No rational human would condemn Pat for doing what she did."

When the jury returned in less than an hour, Vanessa and Larry sat in the first row of seats. Pat was beautiful and composed. Vanessa reached for Larry's hand when the foreman of the jury rose to report their verdict.

"We find the defendant not guilty."

The attorneys hastily guided Pat from the courtroom through a side entrance.

"It's over," Vanessa whispered in relief while Larry and she followed Pat out the side entrance. "Thank God it's over."

Larry led Vanessa and Pat to Vanessa's waiting limousine and instructed Don to drive them to "21" for lunch, where Suzy joined them. Pat needed to know that she was not alone. Pat's sister, Maureen, and her husband had been conspicuously absent from the courtroom. Her society and political friends, too, had made no effort to rally to her side. It was the three of them again: Pat, Tina, and Vanessa.

Today Pat's appearance at lunch, signaling her acquittal, prompted a parade of belated well-wishing table hoppers.

"I'm no longer a pariah," Pat said with bitter humor over Beluga Malossol caviar. But her eyes were troubled. "I pray that none of this will color Joyce's life. I hope she won't remember that awful night."

"She won't," Vanessa said tenderly. "She's such a little girl. Her whole life is ahead of her."

"I'm almost forty-nine years old," Pat said with an air of wonder, "but I feel as though my life is truly just beginning. You know, Vanessa"—her eyes rested with deep affection on her close and cherished friend—"I used to envy you and Tina so much. You were both so talented. I felt so insignificant beside you two. I felt as though I had nothing to give to the world. But now I know that I can contribute." Her face glowed with a new tranquility. "Joyce, of course, will always be the center of my life. But I want to establish a foundation to help battered children and battered wives. I know about these things. At last I've found a purpose in my life."

"We'll always be here to help you," Larry told her. "Pat, you know that."

Exhausted from the drama of the day, Vanessa retired to bed early. But she was unable to sleep. Pat's words over lunch haunted her. *"I'm almost forty-nine years old, but my life is truly just beginning."* Did she have the courage to begin her life anew? So many nights she had lain alone, knowing that a phone call would bring Larry to her side. But she had been afraid to begin to live again because that could lead to pain.

She lay back against the pillows in the darkness and tried to analyze her situation. In every crisis since their first days together she had turned to Larry. It was Larry who had freed her from the velvet bondage of the licensing, who had showed her how to bring Suzy into the business. He had plotted to giver her the time to fulfill her most precious dream: to create the finest custom collection of which her talents were capable.

Larry gave so much of himself to bring her happiness, but she was too involved in herself to understand *his* needs. Their needs. Not only was she cheating herself of a new life — she was cheating Larry as well. Pat was right. Her life was truly just beginning. And for Larry and herself there could be a new beginning.

In joyous resolve she reached for the phone and dialed. How strange that a few words spoken over lunch could change her life. A new door had opened. She and Larry could cross that threshold together.

"Hello." Larry's voice was warm in greeting.

"Larry, something Pat said at lunch rang a bell in my head. She said, 'I'm almost forty-nine years old, but my life is truly just beginning.' I'd like that to happen for us. Remember the poem by Browning? 'Grow old along with me! / The best is yet to be'? Larry, may we grow old together?"

"In time," Larry said humorously, and Vanessa heard the elation in his voice. "For starters, what would you say to a honeymoon at St. John?"

"I'd say yes!"

A whole new life ahead for Vanessa and Larry. *"The last of life, for which the first was made."*